LUCKY RUBY

Ruth Flynn

LUCKY RUBY

Vanguard Press

VANGUARD PAPERBACK

© Copyright 2017
Ruth Flynn

ISBN   978 178 465 212 8

Vanguard Press is an imprint of
Pegasus Elliot MacKenzie Publishers Ltd.
www.pegasuspublishers.com

First Published in 2017

Vanguard Press
Sheraton House Castle Park
Cambridge England

Printed and bound in Great Britain

This book in its entirety is written as a tribute to my grandmother Nellie Campbell. While researching the family tree I gained such respect for this grand lady and only wish I had been able to tell her so.

So Granny this is for you!

Helen (Nellie) Campbell
25/12/1893—14/10/1977

Acknowledgements

This book could not have been written without the help of various people, prime amongst these my husband, Edward, who spent many patient hours in museums and libraries while I researched my material.

I would like to pay tribute to my grandparents, Wull and Nellie, aunts, Nink and Mabel, and my mother-in-law, Sarah, who was actually held at gunpoint during the War, as Nellie was in my story, for taking the time to tell me about their wartime experiences.

I am grateful for the help I received from the local libraries of Ayrshire and Dumfriesshire, particularly that in Lockerbie where I fear I tried their patience sorely.

Most importantly my sister, Jean and my daughter Sarah, who waded through my grammar and spelling mistakes, encouraging me to keep going; but for them this would still be an idea in my head.

Finally, I have to acknowledge the teaching of Peter Sydserf (Big Dan, to those who attended Dumfries High School) for giving me my love of reading and writing.

Preface

As the tumultuous applause died down the host stood smiling benignly out over the audience who had appreciated the last two guests. Each so vastly different but both so essentially Scottish. It had been his idea to have a totally Scottish guest list and he was relieved it had worked so well.

His first interviewee tonight had been Billy Connelly a well-loved comedian who hailed from the shipyards of Glasgow. He made no bones of his less than salubrious background from which it could be argued his humour had emerged. "The Big Yin" as he was commonly called in no derogatory a manner, had become a worldwide success.

Then came the eternally popular Sean Connery, that most famous of James Bonds. Some argued he was the most compelling of the Bond actors, epitomising as he did the quintessentially English gentleman. This of course only underlined his brilliance as an actor as he still frequently described himself as "a milkman from Edinburgh". Sir Sean, now well established in his career, often thought of by his adoring fans as the most charismatic man on the planet, was another Scottish celebrity who despite living amongst the beautiful people had no intention of forgetting his roots.

Yes, the show was going well. The audience had laughed until they cried at the humour of Billy, but they were now relaxed and smiling after listening to relaxed reminiscences from the life of Sir Sean. Would the next guest be an anticlimax? Should he perhaps have scheduled the interviews in a different order? In his opinion he had saved the best till last, but would the audience agree?

Politicians were not normally the most entertaining of guests, always having an eye for the most politically correct statement to make. But Lord John was no longer an active politician and there was every evidence that he had said exactly what he thought throughout his long and successful career. That was what had put him in power and had kept him there, loved by his constituents and the country as a whole. He was thought of by all the major parties as an honest man. No paparazzi ferreted out scurrilous stories or took compromising pictures of him doing anything he shouldn't. He was affectionately known on all sides of the parliamentary divide as "Big Jock". Yes, he had got the running order right!

"Now, ladies and gentlemen, my final guest tonight is no stranger to television studios. Indeed, he has appeared on this show on many previous occasions championing education for the disadvantaged or telling us why we should vote his party into power at the next election. Throughout his political career he has stood by his values and fought for the policies he believed in to make Scotland a better place no matter who or what stood in his way.

"His foresighted policy in education has been influential in the reduction in unemployment to a level not seen in this country since the nineteenth century. An increase in technical education within our schools and colleges has raised the reputation of the Scottish tradesman to a level envied by even the most technically minded of the continental countries. The Great British Tradesman is again sought all over the world as the best trained and most proficient at his job. A fitting legacy for our retiring Prime Minister to bequeath to the nation.

"Am I building him up too much? Do they even know who I'm talking about?" he thought as he scanned the audience for reaction. Mark Henderson had been doing this job for so many years he rarely, if ever, misjudged an audience response. His reputation as the King of the Chat Shows was based on this ability to gauge an audience reaction, but, for some unknown reason, he was apprehensive about the audience's response to his final guest. Casting a surreptitious glance over the rapt faces of the crowd, he let out a sigh of relief. Everyone was paying attention. The atmosphere was crackling with a frisson of anticipation.

With his confidence restored, he continued his introduction: "Ladies and gentlemen. Not from the Palace of Holyrood, by way of the Palace of Balmoral, please welcome onto the show Lord John Campbell."

The audience erupted into cheers and clapping as Jock appeared at the back of the set. He paused as he had been directed and raised his hand in acknowledgement of his rapturous greeting.

A tall man, Jock was able to carry off the few extra pounds that had found their way around his waist in the last few years. He had dark hair and thick workmanlike hands on the right of which he always wore a large signet ring set with an obviously sham ruby. It was an incongruous affectation in such a humble man. Perhaps his nose was too long or not straight enough for him to be called handsome, but Jock had always been able to charm all he met with his twinkling hazel eyes and the crooked smile which changed his rather dour face beyond recognition. It was a face that inspired all those who met him to like and trust him. His patient nature and cheeky sense of humour had stood him in good stead in the early years of his political life.

Jock approached the host with his hand outstretched, greeting him with a firm handshake and the now famous smile as he sat down on the sofa, leaned towards him and joked, "We won't need to talk if they keep on clapping like that. Shall we slip across the road to the pub?"

The audience's level of laughter increased but almost immediately they settled down in their seats eager to hear what the guest had to say.

"John Campbell, former Prime Minister, now, Lord Campbell of Lockerbie in the county of Dumfries. Does it feel any different?" Mark enquired.

Jock rubbed the side of his nose, sat back uncomfortably in the chair, crossed his legs, uncrossed them again and sat up straight. He shrugged his shoulders and then answered, "It's a bit surreal to be honest. I woke up one morning plain old Jock, nobody paying any attention to me as I went out for the morning paper, chatted to a few people on the way there and the way back just as usual. Next morning every passer-by on the street was greeting me as 'My Lord'. Now that's a mite weird. I only use that phrase when I'm saying my prayers and I will categorically state that I have no designs on His job." Again the characteristic charismatic smile lifted one corner of his mouth, enhancing his joke and amusing those watching in the studio.

"You are famed for your support of the working man and especially the education of the unemployed. Do you think accepting this peerage is turning your back on your own kind as has been suggested by the opposition?" came the next question.

"I've accepted the peerage for purely personal family reasons. I'm a private person again. I've retired from politics. As a serving Prime Minister I had to set the policies that were in the best interest of the country highest on my agenda. I think I have carried out my ideas and led the party to the best of my ability. Without sounding conceited, I believe Scotland to be a better country because of these policies carried out by my party. Not by me. By my party. I don't take credit for all the ideas, you understand, but if I heard one I liked, I always wanted to back it and see it come to fruition."

He looked pensively across the sofa to his interviewer as if deciding whether or not he should continue.

"When I became leader of the party, the country was in a very depressed state. People couldn't get training, without skills they were unable to get mortgages for homes, often ending up in expensive rented accommodation, meaning there was less likelihood of employment for the working man in our depressed economy. This, in turn, deprived their children of a decent education or prospects of work. People had lost hope and were reconciled to perpetuating the cycle of state dependence generation on generation. The aim of the Scottish Working Party has always been to promote the well-being of both the individual and of the country as a whole. The thinking behind that is, if the man in the street has a pride in himself, he will take pride in his work and his work ethic will be respected by others in other countries. When foreign countries respect our reliable and capable workforce, and our industry becomes more productive, it makes folks feel pleased to belong to a country to be proud of; and even more to belong to a country that is proud of its workers." He once more smiled his enigmatic grin and apologised.

"I'm not here to preach or to give a political address but I've been on this soapbox of mine for so long I fear I may never be able to get down from it. I'm sorry."

"Don't apologize, that is, in essence, what has made your leadership so long and trouble free. The voting public were never fickle when voting for you. Your majority has always been assured. That being said, why did you decide to resign as Prime Minister? Even your political opponents believe you would have won another election."

"I hope the party under Ross Adam will win another term. He is a fine politician and a strong man. I have no qualms about handing over to him. I will vote for him!" he laughed, looking out over the audience.

"There is a time for everyone to go and I believe it is my time to go. I have been Prime Minister for twenty-two years. I have done my damnedest to keep the House, with all its various factions, working towards the same objectives. I'm not a young man any more. When I entered politics it was with a vision of what I could do to enhance my generation. It is time for the new generation so I believe it to be in the best interest of the country to retire now before I become so megalomanic I have to be prized out of Holyrood. It happens, you know!

Mark waited for the ripple of appreciative laughter in the audience to die down before continuing.

"Your early political career has been well documented and you've always maintained, indeed emphasised, that your upbringing in rural Scotland was instrumental in forming your beliefs. Like my other guests this evening, was the deprivation in your youth the root of your desire to enter politics, and do you think you would be the same person if you had been born into a more privileged family without the struggle to gain an education?"

"Would I have crossed the floor and been a Conservative do you mean?" he laughed. "No, my politics have never been about staying in the same place." He held his hands up in submission and grinned at the audience.

"OK! No political debate! I think we always have to move towards tomorrow but my upbringing was not deprived to my way of thinking. My parents were forward thinking. Small farmers; almost gardeners by today's standards. My father moved about from estate to estate working all the hours of the day and night for other people while my mother farmed the home acres and kept food on the table and clothes on our backs. They were more like a modern couple, both working and contributing to a better life for us children. A close knit nuclear family as we hear so much about today. My brother still lives in the house in which we were born and my sisters and their families visit regularly.

"Pa was the one with the vision. He saw us 'getting on in life' and was driven by that goal. Having a better standard of living with each generation had almost become his religion. His greatest wish for my brother, Bill and myself was a good enough education to provide us with employment less thankless and labour intensive than his own. I think he would be proud of our achievements."

His crooked smile was evident again as he said thoughtfully,

"I'll tell you a story I've not told before that will show how much Bill and I thought of our father's efforts to push us up a ladder we had, as yet, no desire to climb, and yes, it formed my political ethos."

"An STV exclusive?" smiled his host.

Big Jock grinned and nodded his agreement.

"Early in our lives and with seven children to clothe, feed and school; we paid for schooling in those days," he interpolated with a wry chuckle, "the days before Big Jock Campbell! Pa had been away harvesting on various estates for weeks trying to build up a fund for the less productive winter. He came home exhausted but with a very satisfied look on his face as he threw a pair of boots each at Bill and me. They were what our other national treasure, Oor Wullie would have called 'Tackitty bits'.

"'They'll keep your feet fine and warm and dry going over the moor to school,' he said, grinning happily at Ma. She was ecstatic. She had been bemoaning our lack of boots and her inability to make those particular ends meet for some weeks. As Ma and Pa sat bathing in their mutual delight at achieving this not insubstantial dream, Bill and I exchanged horrified glances. We would be bullied. Softies. Mummy's pets. We could already hear the jeering of our contemporaries' scorn at the wearing of boots.

"We had a few weeks' respite as that autumn was warm and there was no use wasting shoe leather until the weather turned cold. Each morning Bill or I jumped out of bed and raced to the window to heave a sigh of relief, for the continued good weather meant the boots resided in the cupboard, safe from the mocking gaze of Johnstone school scholars.

"Inevitably, the morning came when I had to scrape the frost from the inside of the window in order to see out onto the frozen ground surrounding the house. Pa was already out with steaming buckets of swill for the pigs huddling and jostling together behind the dyke in an effort to generate some heat, but we had no thoughts for pigs that morning or for Pa either for that matter. The dreaded day had come. We would be the laughing stock of the school! Sure enough, when we reluctantly wandered through to the kitchen, there were the boots in all their polished glory, warming at the fire.

"You asked if deprivation was my inspiration into politics. Well those boots were the reason for my first attempt at seeing every side of an argument, then making a policy to keep everybody happy.

"Ma and Pa were delighted to have found the money to buy the boots and were satisfied they had done their best for us. We had to wear the boots. The boys at school would make our lives a misery. We must not wear the boots. Deadlock!

"Diplomacy came into play. We left the house with the boots on, we went as far as the home wood near the school with toasted toes. The boots were then removed and tenderly rammed down a conveniently placed rabbit hole. We went to school on bare feet, just like everyone else. We arrived home beautifully shod to a smiling Ma. The plan worked and continued to do so for some weeks.

"I had learned a lesson in diplomacy but fate was not finished with my education. This salutary lesson is perhaps the one that has borne me in good stead throughout my political career.

"One afternoon after school – just as the dark was falling, if I remember correctly, in late November – we came out of school as usual, over the dyke into the home wood and dived into the rabbit hole. No boots! At first we could not believe it and thought we must have made a mistake, but, after a considerably protracted and increasingly anxious search, there were still no boots! They were gone. We were done for. Ma would be mad. *How* to explain it? *Who* would explain it? *Who* to blame? These were the questions we put to ourselves as we trailed unwillingly home. Cold feet were the least of our worries. We had other cold feet to contend with. We reached home and slunk into the kitchen. Ma had her back to us and appeared not to notice our blue toes hanging down from the kitchen chairs. We looked at each other guiltily. Time to confess."

"Ma, we've not been wearing our boots to school we stuffed them down a rabbit hole in home wood somebody has pinched them. Sorry." The words tumbled over one another as I tried to get the confession over as quickly as possible and in one breath.

Ma turned a sad face towards us. "Your father worked himself to a frazzle in order to get you boots. Did without sleep to make things better for you, and you thank him by throwing away the fruits of his labour. I'm so disappointed you didn't tell me how you felt. Think about it boys. Was it worth it?"

"Ma was before her time. We had expected a leathering. We got soft words of disappointment and, believe me, they did more good. Our guilt and repentance were far greater than they would have been had we been resentful of a hot behind. We deserved it, mind!" Jock laughed reminiscently.

"From then until Christmas, we were perfect angels. We helped without being asked; fed chickens; gathered eggs; milked cows; washed dishes; chopped logs and jumped to help whenever we saw a need, all in an effort to make up for saddening our parents. On Christmas morning our boots were sitting in the hearth beside our sister's stuffed stockings. The boots were stuffed too. With cold ashes!

"Pa, who had not mentioned the loss of the boots, took his pipe from his mouth and said, "There is no sackcloth in this house but ashes might serve to remind you that honesty is the best policy." Bill and I wore those boots till they fell off our feet after that. A lesson learned. While your destiny is in your own hands one can perhaps get away with being less than honest, but there is always someone waiting in the wings whose only desire is to queer your pitch, so all in all, it's better to be honest.

"So, to answer your question. My upbringing has been instrumental in my political career. I would not be where I am today if not for those boots. I think I am a product of my parents' parental skills and also that strange creature, an honest politician."

The studio was silent. Big Jock was well known as an orator able to play on the emotions of his listeners. His speeches in the parliamentary chamber on issues he felt strongly about were legend, but this had been so obviously off the cuff and straight from the heart that the audience were stunned. He had them in the palm of his hand. Big Jock Campbell would be sorely missed.

There was a moment of silence while Mark gave himself a shake to get back in control and continued the interview.

"You were ennobled yesterday by King Charles. Can you tell us how you feel about becoming a lord?" he stuttered as something of an anticlimax.

"I said earlier that I had accepted the peerage for purely personal reasons and that is the case. I have been married to Marion for the best part of fifty years. She has put up with me and my ambition; made late night suppers when the house sat late; got up early when visiting dignitaries had to be met and almost single handedly brought up the girls." Again the twisted smile was in evidence as he joked. "They are all Daddy's girls because I only saw them for the pleasant times. She didn't do it without complaint and we've had our share of arguments. And what arguments! There is no reasoned debate when Marion gets her dander up, but throughout our marriage we have been one unit, a strong pair with each other's back, and we've made it through together. We have five gorgeous girls and that is my reason for accepting the peerage."

"Your girls won't inherit that, though, will they, and you have no son?"

"No, it will end when I die, but I will have fulfilled the wishes of my ancestors."

"What do you mean by that?"

Jock held up his right hand on which the absurdly large ring gleamed under the studio lighting.

"You see this ruby ring on my finger? Throughout my life and my career everyone I have come in contact with has thought this an affectation, wearing such an elaborate bit of tat. Yes, I know it is a standing joke; Jock and his ruby. It is in fact the real McCoy. A ruby the size of a pigeon's egg, set in gold so pure it looks man made."

He grinned out into the audience, inviting them to remember how, in an attempt to discredit his opponent, a rival had smirked as he gave his opinion on how the ring had come to be in Jock's possession – as a novelty from a long forgotten Christmas dinner.

"From a cracker, in fact!" twinkled Lord John, showing that he had always known, and ignored, the defamatory remarks made by his political opponents. He silently contemplated the jewel that looked so incongruous on his thick finger, then held it up to allow the audience a better look. He leaned back in his chair, staring thoughtfully into the middle distance, before he brought himself back to the moment and continued.

"This ring has been handed down from father to son from generation to generation in order that we might not forget what the Stuart king did to our family four hundred years ago. I have no son to pass it onto. Friends, and even some members of my family, think it strange that at this time of my life I should change the habits of a lifetime and accept a peerage. When it was suggested that I should become a lord I chose the town of Lockerbie. This was the town in which my ancestor Geordie Campbell settled after his father had his head cut off by the order of Charlie Stuart."

Again there was a stunned silence in the audience. Even Mark, a consummate interviewer, could think of nothing to say. Jock continued as if unaware of the reaction in the studio.

"I found it amusing that, as I knelt before King Charles Ш yesterday, so my ancestor Archibald Campbell, the CaimBeuil, had knelt (metaphorically speaking) before *his* sovereign. Only Charles Ш tapped me on the shoulder with his sword and called me Lord, while Charles Ц cut off Archibald's head and called him 'Traitor'. A full circle."

"That sounds like another exclusive. Would you like to tell us about it?" Mark suggested.

Jock thought for a minute, directing his gaze into the middle distance as if seeing the events that he had been asked to describe. He sat up, leaned forward in his chair and said, "It all started with the Bishop's War in the mid seventeenth century…"

Chapter One

The Oath

As the last rays of the winter sun radiated through the deep window slits, they formed ever-changing rosy patterns on the grey stone walls, giving the impression that the stones were embedded with pink sparkling jewels. The dappled light fell on the contents of the hall both animate and inert, helping to produce an air of festivity about the room.

Soon the great torches set high around the walls would be lit and dispel the shadows, but, in the meantime, the only light came from the narrow windows and the blazing boughs on the fires burning in the enormous fireplaces at both ends of the room. They created both heat and atmosphere as the flickering flames added to the effect of the diminishing rays of sun. The walls of the hall were dressed with great swathes of Campbell plaid interspersed with deep green boughs of holly and evergreen which gave the air the heavy atmosphere redolent of the fragrance which hung on the hillsides above the castle.

Soon these fresh aromas would be contaminated by the combined smells of woodsmoke from the huge fireplaces overshadowing each end of the great stone hall and the harsh unwashed smell of the gathering clansmen, who wandered around the high vaulted chamber in trepidation as they waited to hear what their chief had to say.

Most of the men, although related to the chief, were poor farmers, clerks or lawyers attending the gathering in their best work clothes of breeches and homespun shirts, but the majority of these men wore their bits of the more muted grey and brown with pride, whether it be a bonnet, a plaid or a kilt to indicate their connection, however tenuous, to the great CaimBeuil.

Geordie and his brothers were a dazzling sight in their full clan regalia as befitted the sons of such an important lord. Their kilts, plaids and bonnets in the deep blues and soft greens of the dress of the Campbells denoted their position amongst the undulating throng of clansmen.

Geordie was perhaps marginally taller than his brothers, definitely no runt of the litter despite being several years junior to them. His long, well-muscled legs supported his massive torso, which in turn supported the great expanse of his shoulders. The dark hair that could be seen escaping from the boundaries of every article of clothing he wore gave him the look of an untamed black bear dressed up to frighten children at the fair. This shock of hair extended to his head and face where it had been restrained by shears and comb into something resembling the mode of the day. On this occasion his hair had been tied back into a long queue giving him a neat facade. Shaggy eyebrows overlooked his deep-set, almost black eyes which gave him a fierce warrior appearance to any who did not know him.

Despite his looks and great dimensions Geordie had a gentle and amusing nature. Against the fashion of the day Geordie adored his children and never tired of playing with them when he was at home in the castle. He took on the role of steed for his daughter, Helen, a small replica of himself both in looks and daring, and was often to be seen with that damsel riding on his shoulders around the grounds of the castle demesne, both returning to the nursery dirty and dishevelled but happy and contented. To see him cradle his newborn son, Neal, in the palm of his great paw of a hand and witness the look of wonder emanate from those deep eyes, which softened the rather hard plains of his face. was a great contradiction to the man his kinsmen knew from the battlefield.

Veteran soldiers of hard campaigns had been known to turn tail and run at the sight of the 'Black Campbell' bearing down on them with his sword. Although he was not an advocate of war, preferring peace to turmoil, he had an unbeaten record in hand-to-hand combat.

Apart from his height and build Geordie resembled his French mother while Jamie, next in age by two years, and Alexander the eldest by some four years, were carbon copies of their father. None of the boys were less than six feet tall and had physiques to gladden the heart of any warlord, but the two elder boys had inherited the Celtic red hair and fair skin more predominant in their countrymen.

Together the Campbell sons gave an awe-inspiring impression and they realised that they were making their kinsmen uneasy by standing together, so, in an attempt to bring some relaxation to the gathering, the boys separated and prepared to act as hosts to their father's guests. They wandered around the Great Hall offering refreshments and enquiring for the families of the men present. From the workers on the estate to the more affluent kinsmen everyone knew and respected the sons of the CaimBeul. Like their father they were extremely personable men with brains geared to see every side of a situation, which made them very able lawyers but also enabled them to be excellent hosts. As they made a circuit of the Hall they encouraged their kinsmen to approach the many dishes laid out on the heavy oak tables that lined the walls. The brothers were aware that many of the poorer clansmen who worked endlessly to feed their families felt guilty about eating such victuals when their family were eking out their oats to make thin porridge. Each man from their own estate would receive a portion of the feast to take home on the morrow as a reward for pledging his support to the CaimBeul.

To this end the kitchens had been busy for several days preparing this feast for the clan. Merlaine, Geordie's wife had flitted about the castle giving the impression she was capable of being in several places at once. If she was not in sight her melodious tones could be heard ringing from some distant region of the castle giving orders for decoration of the Hall or instructing the French cook on the meats more suitable for the Highland palate than the French delicacies that he was in the habit of preparing. Great haunches of venison from the estate were roasting in the enormous ovens while wild boar was spitted over the huge open fire, being turned by a red-faced urchin who periodically thrust a crust of bread under the spit to catch the juice as it oozed from the joint to spit in the flames, creating a mouth-watering scent.

There was great bustle in the scorching kitchen with maids running hither and thither collecting the makings for pastry or chopping vegetables for soup while the scullery maid had not seen her bed for two days, so many dirty pots and platters were there to be scoured and washed. One and all the servants of the castle accepted Geordie's wife as mistress and would have gone to any lengths to please her. A sweet smile or a soft word of thanks was all they needed to spur them on in the thankless conditions of the kitchen.

As the only female of the Campbell household she took her duties seriously. The maids and footmen had been scolded and chivvied about their business of cleaning and preparing chambers for the more important clan members who would need to remain overnight after the allegiance had been taken to talk tactics with the Caimbeul. Not that many of the clansmen would go home tonight but the majority of them would sleep in the Great Hall, wrapping themselves in their plaids just where they were after imbibing vast quantities of the ale and whisky provided for the occasion.

There was an expectant air of excitement among the circulating men as they quaffed tankards of ale and chatted to distant relatives, unseen since the last gathering at Inverary. For they were all here for the same reason. They had been commanded to attend Archibald today, by polite invitation, but there was not a doubt in their minds that they had been called together to take an oath of allegiance to CaimBeul in order that he may raise an army against the King and his disreputable cat's paw Montrose. Despite being a predominantly peace-loving family, well cared for by the chief, there had always been a desire to get the better of the MacDonalds, so although some would rather not have waged a war, they would not ignore a chance to get one over on their old enemy.

As the piper fingered his chanter, hunching his pipes at a more comfortable angle on his shoulder, a pregnant hush fell over the hall as the creak of the great studded door was heard. The door opened. There stood the CaimBeuil. Archibald stood well over six feet tall with broad shoulders, slim waist and a youthful physiognomy for a man with three grown-up sons. He appeared to fill the giant space made by the opening door as he stood astride looking into the hall with his sharp navy-blue eyes. At his peak Archibald's hair was as long and fine as that of his sons standing in front of him.

As Geordie stood admiring the proud stance of his father he noticed the twitch of his lips change the shape of his mouth into the wry shape from which the first CaimBeuil got his name. Like most of his kind he had been named by some physical idiosyncrasy that was apparent to onlookers. That first-named Campbell had possessed a crooked smile and so had been given the name CaimBeuil (meaning 'crooked mouth') and, as none of his decedents had been slow to take advantage of political fashions to promote the family's interests over the centuries, it was sometimes said that the Campbells could twist words from their crooked mouths to turn any argument their own way. The present incumbent was predominantly referred to as "the CaimBeuil".

Many of the CaimBeuil's enemies would have sworn that his great success as a leader and lawyer was dependant on the oratory that flowed from that 'crooked mouth.' Until this day, Archibald had been a major political power, as well as a friend and mentor, to royalty. Today's gathering would irrevocably move him to the opposite side from King Charles, who wanted to return the country to Catholicism.

The CaimBeuil had searched his soul in an effort to reconcile his ambition with his devotion to the doctrine of John Knox. Even such a shrewd lawyer as the CaimBeuil could not find an argument to reconcile both Catholicism and Calvinism.

Each and every member of the clan knew what was expected of them and was willing to lay down their lives to follow this charismatic leader into battle. It would be a short war. There was only the threat of Montrose's army. They would be back and settled before the spring.

Archibald strode through the hall. Men moved to give him passage. He nodded greetings to familiar faces as he carved his way to the dais. Unconsciously he noticed that the members of his family had all accepted his invitation, not that he had ever doubted they would respond to his call to arms. Even the few members whom he knew were against him had put in an appearance and waited now to hear what he had to say.

He turned to face the gathering. The piper removed the instrument from his shoulder.

"Na Obliviscaris."

"Na Obliviscaris!" came the great roar in reply.

Archibald, not a lawyer for nought, spoke to the assembly in his soft native tongue, at once praising them for answering the call and threatening dire repercussions for those who failed to meet the challenge. With every word and phrase he stressed the reason for the need to thwart those who dared deny them the right to worship as they wished. He played with them as a maestro on a violin until, when asked who would take the oath, the resultant thunder had no dissenters.

Geordie and his brothers recognised this as their cue. Alexander signalled to his brothers to follow him as he made his way to stand below his father and took the oath. Jamie followed suit. Then it was Geordie's turn.

He drew his small sword, turned it blade toward his heart and knelt before his father.

"I promise by my Faith and by this weapon that I hold to give thee fealty, and hereby pledge thee my loyalty. I promise to observe my homage completely to the good of Clan Campbell and against all who would cause harm to those who bear our name. If ever I raise my hand against thee may I be struck dead."

Clasping the hilt of his sword in both hands he prostrated himself on the ground before rising to his feet, resheathing his sword and offering his hands to be grasped appreciatively by his sire. The CaimBeuil took his son's hands in his own and accepted his fealty. A hard man, Archibald did however recognise the more moderate nature of his youngest son and realised what it cost him to pledge to fight a war he did not believe in. He was proud of this son today. He had put family loyalty at the top of his agenda.

Each warrior in turn knelt and offered the same vow. The clan was prepared to go to war.

Cruachan! Cruachan! Cruachan! A Holy War!

The Aftermath

After the feasting and drinking Geordie sat alone in the hall deep in thought. All around him sleeping bodies were scattered. Those who had settled first were close to the great fireplaces at either end of the hall, but there was scarcely a foot of floor that did not do service as a bed for a Campbell this night. Geordie sat in a sea of tartan as each had wrapped himself in his plaid to sleep off his potations.

He felt the waft of air passing him as his wife Merlaine dropped softly at his side. She sat for a few moments neither touching him nor speaking. She seemed to sense his need for she glanced up quickly, edged a fraction nearer, and slid her hand onto his knee. For several minutes she remained silent but she rubbed her finger along the length of his thigh.

"Oh, what have you done, my Geordie?" she whispered in her silky voice that barely moved the air.

Geordie's jaw tightened and he straightened his hunched shoulders.

"I have sworn fealty to my father. What else did you expect me to do? It would have been gey disrespectful for his son to withhold his loyalty with every Campbell from Inverness to Ayr here to honour our name. Have sense, woman! "

"You did what you thought best. Do not plague yourself about a thing you canna change. As the son of the chief you would have been dishonouring yourself as well as him by your disobedience."

"Where will it end, though?" he sighed. "All those men today have families to support, children to rear, land to husband. I cannot believe that war is the only option and the cost to our family will be very unsettling."

Merlaine knew the confusion that her husband was feeling. She understood his passionate dislike of war and the waste of human life, but equally she knew he felt it was inevitable and right to stand up for their beliefs.

She had been married to Geordie for seven years since they were both little more than children. It had been love at first sight. Geordie and his brothers had accompanied their father to Oban to visit an old counsellor of the CaimBeuil. As they sat down to dinner that night Merlaine had taken her place at table opposite Geordie and he was immediately enamoured of her. As he ate his way through the meal he tasted nothing, for he was so engrossed in taking surreptitious glances at the beauty sitting across the groaning board.

Merlaine was very tall for a woman, standing almost up to Geordie's chin and as dark as he was himself. Since she was still very young her abundant black hair hung down her back, almost reaching the rising swelling of her buttocks. Her figure was only just blossoming from a child to a woman, but to Geordie it epitomised perfection. She held her head proudly with such a turn of her neck as to make her seem unobtainable and when he looked into the dancing, sparkling blue eyes beneath her well-shaped eyebrows he was lost. He gazed into her face with such intensity that the colour rose in her cheeks to match the already dark rose hue of her pouting lips.

They were married within the month and were both still very much in love.

Taking his hand between both of her own, Merlaine stroked it.

"You can change nothing now, my Lord. Come to your couch, where I will endeavour to make you forget your woes for a few hours. Look, dawn is almost here and your strength will be wilting." She laughed up through her curtain of hair into his face in a very provocative way.

"We'll see how much of my strength has waned, shall we?"

Geordie hauled himself up from his seat, returning her seductive smile with a twitch of his mouth into the crooked shape that gave him his name. He swung his wife up into his arms and made for the stairway to their chamber. He ran up the great staircase and round the gallery carrying her as easily as if Merlaine had been no heavier than her small daughter, reaching the door of their chamber without loss of breath. As the door closed behind them Geordie tightened his hold on Merlaine as she would have slipped to the floor.

"Nay, nay, my wee temptress, you just stay in my arms where ye are. You need to be taught a lesson for making mock of me." He laughed down into her eyes before he buried his face in the dark tresses of her hair, then turned his attention to nibbling her ear and trailing his lips across her cheek until he came to her mouth. Merlaine lifted her hand to trace the crooked line of his mouth but, as his lips were descending on hers as a fitting castigation for her cheek, she wriggled into a more comfortable position within his arms, parted her lips and submitted to her chastisement, as a good wife should. They kissed for several long lingering moments each enjoying the touch and smell of the other before Geordie deposited his wife on the bed and began to make love to her in his own special way.

Much later, satiated by each other's bodies, they lay entwined on the dishevelled bed, Merlaine's long, silky black hair splayed out over his broad chest where she lay listening to her husband's heartbeat as it returned to normal after their frantic lovemaking, Geordie's thoughts once more returned to the forthcoming battle and the possible repercussions.

"No matter what the outcome, you will never be far from my thoughts as I fight with my fellow clansmen. Everything I do is to gain a quiet peaceful life for you and

Neal and Helen. One day we will live in a country where men may worship as they please. Father is right in that, you know? It is wrong to dictate how a man may praise his God and force him to submit for political reasons.

"I despise the need for us to fight, the damage it will do to our family and the inevitable waste of the lives of talented men. So many are needed to work the estates and the farms, but it is every man's duty to defend his beliefs."

"And every wife's to stay at home and entreat our Lord God for the safe return of her husband. We will pray for you every day while we are apart."

"Well, as to that, I'm not sure I want you living in the castle when the clan is fighting, perhaps far distant. The family seat will be a target and the garrison left to defend it will be mostly old men and young boys. I would have you go to your father's keep at Oban where you and the children will not be at risk of becoming hostages. Ye are all very precious to me," he whispered as he bent his head to kiss the top of hers where it still rested on his chest. "Mmm, the smell of the hills is always in your hair. It is what I dream about when I am not with you. Go to your father, Merlaine. Take all the women and children to keep them safe and I will come for you as soon as this blasted war is over and the country is at peace again. But don't forget me, my heart."

"As soon as the army marches off I will gather the womenfolk together and have the garrison send its most prestigious soldiers with us to protect us on the way. We will be safe with father; my Lord, never fear. Come back safe to me."

The Battle

In the quiet of the February morning, the towering white-capped mountains surrounding the castle looked invincible. The weak winter sun was just rising in the sky, adding a sparkle to the silver frosted ground around the moat and the river to the rear of the castle. The skeleton branches of the trees made a picture of an abandoned landscape making Alexander, from his vantage point at the top of Comyn's Tower, feel as if he was the only human being left alive. He slowly did a full turn, ever watchful for movement near at hand or in the distance, but despite his attention to duty, he breathed in the sharp clean air. It was a beautiful morning. Not a morning when one could envisage a bloody battle.

He was glad his father had decided to leave him to watch for the approaching army. The job was a sinecure really. The road the opposing army must follow came almost in a straight line to the entrance of the castle. All he had to do was watch for signs of movement on the road indicating that the English army, with the traitorous MacDonalds marching along, was on the move, then raise the alarm, hence giving the Campbell men the advantage.

In the castle below him, spirits were high in the ranks, for the men were convinced this coming encounter would end the war and they could get back to their real lives. Inverlochy would be the nemesis of the English.

The fighting had been going on now for some months. First the Campbells had been routed at Aberdeen in October, then when the army had retreated to Inverary in the hope of recruiting its strength Montrose was joined by Alisdair MacColla and his band from the clan Donald, whose most important weapon was their absolute detestation of the Campbells. MacColla was therefore able to command many Highlanders of the MacLean and Cameron families to plunder and burn the Campbell lands around Inverary. The fighting had been fierce and had now been brought to this place, which would be known in future as the Battle of Inverlochy, where MacColla intended to live up to his nickname of "the Devastater"

There was no doubt about it, MacColla thought himself a brilliant soldier. He had invented the tactic known as the Highland Charge where his men would swoop down from the hills straight into the enemy's tight ranks, firing a volley of musket shots which unsettled the infantry men, often causing such a surprise that they were unable to defend themselves before the rampaging opponents were upon them with their swords. His men were well trained with the broadsword and targe and this approach was his attack of choice in the hilly areas of the Campbell country. He had little doubt he would win this battle.

The lines were set. Each side was confident. Who would take the honours tonight?

Jamie and Geordie had accompanied their father before the battle, so had not been present in the thick of the combat. The CaimBeuil, a wily old tactician, had sent Alexander, the eldest son, to view the battle from one angle while he, with his two younger sons, prepared for any outcome in the middle of Loch Linnhe.

The CaimBeuil, always with one eye to the future and a plan for every eventuality, had packed up any legal papers or political speeches that he thought could be used to advantage in the future and would entrust his two younger sons with their safe bestowal in a cave, known only to his closest kinsmen, if the outcome of the upcoming clash did not go in favour his clan. This was to be their insurance policy. To ensure that if he lost power to the dreaded Graham of Montrose he could use blackmail to restore his family's position. Whatever the cost it was imperative that the future of clan Campbell be assured.

CaimBeuil had watched the battle from his yacht moored in the middle of the loch. He had been injured in a mild skirmish the previous day and was forced to watch in frustration as his liegemen, led by Duncan Campbell of Auchinbreck, misdirected his men. Auchinbreck drew up his forces in front of Inverlochy Castle in the early morning with the intention of reviewing their position when he saw where the attack would be greatest. Alisdair MacColla divided his men so as to attack the Campbells on all sides with his infamous Highland Charge.

No one was prepared for this charge since the Campbell army had been watching for an attack along the military road, not from the snow-covered hills. By the time Alex, alone in his eerie, had realized where the attack was coming from, the battle was all but lost. The invincible Inverlochy Castle had been no protection and a bloodbath followed.

When Montrose, pre-empting Duncan Campbell, gave the order to attack at dawn, Auchinbreck was taken by surprise and, with his retreat blocked, was forced to stand and fight surrounded by the enemy forces as they poured down from the hills, motivated by the very name of their enemy. The result was a complete rout. Although the Campbell army fought fiercely, it had been all but destroyed. Montrose's men, egged on by the Devastator, were making the most of what they interpreted as their legal rights to plunder the enemy and were intent on destroying as many Campbells as possible; to this end, they took no prisoners but awarded any injured Campbell soldiers left alive on the battlefield a swift end with their daggers before relieving them of their belongings. They rejoiced in the amount of enemy blood that darkened the honed edges of their weapons

Geordie could see tears in his father's eyes as he witnessed his brave lieutenant, Auchinbreck, beheaded on the battlefield by MacColla. Even at that distance it was possible to see the delight on the face of the Irish leader as he confronted his enemy. He had a personal grudge against Duncan Campbell ever since Auchinbreck had been in command of the force of Scottish soldiers who had savaged the Irishman's cousins and had been responsible for putting a price on the head of 'the Devastator' himself. MacColla had sought out Auchinbreck after his army's defeat to gloat over the demise of his old enemy. He offered him two options.

"I can make you shorter or longer, your choice," he smirked

Understanding this to mean he would either be hanged or decapitated the unrepentant Campbell shrugged, as if it was no concern of his.

"You can't shame me whatever your choice. I am a Campbell. You may murder me at will but you will never slay the pride of my name."

Infuriated by Auchinbreck's reply, MacColla raised his sword, swinging it at his enemy's head, missed his target but took off the top of Duncan Campbell's head above his ears, thus proving himself the lesser man.

"That damned MacDonald! Montrose would never have come down from the hills in the winter if it hadn't been for MacColla!" thundered the CaimBeuil as the yacht glided silently towards the loch shore. On seeing the tide of the fighting swing in the favour of the MacDonald clansmen, the CaimBeuil had slipped his mooring and quietly made for the opposite shore of the loch in order to send his sons on their mission. The loss of the battle was a setback, but the ignominious demise of his friend and comrade Duncan Campbell was a severe impediment to his plans.

"Geordie, you must make sure you get these parchments into the caves to safety. Gather as many men as you can find and hide them in the hills so that we have the leaders for the next attack. I am depending on you and Jamie for the future of the family." He drew a large signet ring from his little finger and placed it on Geordie's. It had the crest of the clan engraved into the ruby at its centre and was obviously the property of the CaimBeuil. "If you have trouble or are in need of protection, show this ring to any of our clansmen and they will grant you aid in whatever manner they can.

"Go with God, my sons."

So saying he kissed each of his sons on both cheeks. He watched from the rails as Jamie and Geordie manhandled the heavy leather satchels, holding the very future of their family, onto the shore before pausing to take a last look at their sire and chieftain who had trusted them to do their duty. He raised his hand to his mouth as if to blow them a sentimental kiss before his active brain began to plan for that future. He turned his back on his personal sorrow, applying his mind to the next phase of this war to allow men the freedom to worship their God as their conscious dictated. His yacht sailed silently out of the loch, carrying the CaimBeuil away from the devastation being exercised upon his clan..

Jamie and Geordie knew their father was looking to the future and was retreating in order to regroup his army for retaliation, but it appeared to them that it was more important to gain revenge on the MacDonald enemy than to fight the Holy War at this point. Was this the outcome Geordie had stifled his own beliefs for?

The two lads stood with their men in silence as the boat slipped out of the loch, carrying away their father whom they would never see again.

The pitiful, tattered remains of the once proud army were attempting to make their way from the battlefield into the hills above the scene of inhuman decimation where once a pretty meadow had existed. They were trying to avoid being seen by the opposing soldiers. The smell of blood was so strong you could taste the sweet metallic tang at the back of the throat. Each breath was heavy with the warm suffocating miasma of death that floated on the air thick enough to choke the life from their bodies.

The men had been involved in fierce battles against 'the Devastator' before but that Irish MacDonald had fuelled such hatred in his clansmen that the winning force was determined to leave no Campbell left alive to take revenge. The men of the clan Donald were mad with bloodlust; not content with rampaging over the battleground killing every wounded soldier they could find, they had vowed to hunt down every Campbell left alive whether he had fought with the army or not. They would take no prisoners. The earth ran with rivers of blood. Severed heads lay in heaps on the churned earth, sometimes still with the lifeblood pulsing out of them. Horses' legs were entangled with human where a cavalryman had had his horse killed below him. Men, who had escaped the battlefield only to be too weak to continue their flight, lay begging for aid from their horrendous wounds, only to be granted callous relief by the pursuing army with the severing of a head or a sword thrust in the heart.

The noise of the marauding victors could be heard in the hamlets miles away where the inhabitants crossed themselves, gathered their moveable possessions in a plaid and slunk silently into the thick undergrowth of the towering hills. This proved to be a good move as the victorious MacDonalds were so bent on keeping their vow to leave no Campbell living that they slaughtered any Campbell they came across, whatever their age or sex.

Geordie and Jamie crept quietly to a vantage point to assess how bad the devastation was. It was vital that they were not captured with the papers in their possession but some attempt must be made to save their kinsmen.

As the boys carefully made their way along the side of the river toward the back of the castle they became aware of the heavy price their fellow men had paid for their faith.

"My God, I've never seen so many bodies in one place before. It makes my blood boil to think my kinsmen are lying there helpless, not knowing when the fatal blow will fall," whispered Geordie breathlessly.

"For some it might be a blessing. There are some pretty gruesome injuries out in that field. I'm not sure we will find anyone left alive to spirit away to safety."

Jamie's sad gaze played over the field of destruction before he replied.

"No point in waiting here to salvage lives. We will be better making for the hills in order to find those who escaped. There may be precious few."

Reluctantly the brothers had retraced their steps to the side of the loch and, as carefully as possible with the leather, document-containing satchels heavy on their shoulders, they made their way up into the hills. There was a good covering of gorse and heather, which hid them from view by any stray enemy soldier, but having witnessed the euphoria patent among the victors, they surmised there would be a period of safety while the conquerors revelled in a killing spree.

They moved with trepidation round the side of the hill always on the lookout for movement around them. As the sights and sounds of the battlefield diminished they began to breathe more easily. Just as they were beginning to think they were out of danger, Jamie spotted a movement above them to the right. He nudged his brother and nodded to the area.

Geordie quietly acknowledged the signal and, hiding the satchels as well as possible under some heather and old leaves, they drew their swords, split up and made for the place where the movement had been noticed.

Used to tracking animals over these hills as boys, Jamie and Geordie were as silent as any trapper. Keeping their eye on their target they approached a clearing surrounded by dense undergrowth where they could hear the sound of whispered voices.

Geordie could feel the blood bounding in his veins as he anticipated meeting members of the opposing army. Charily, he eased his way to the edge of the scrub and cautiously peered into the clearing. Suddenly he saw his brother's grinning face through the brushwood on the other side of the clearing and, following his eyeline, was delighted to recognise about twenty of his kinsmen, who were clustered together as they tended to their wounds.

The little band of exhausted men were overjoyed to see Jamie and Geordie who immediately helped with the binding of wounds. As the small contingent tended to their hurts, Geordie was surprised at the stoicism of many of the soldiers. When he realised the severity of some of the wounds, he speculated on how his kinsmen had been able to escape the battlefield with such horrendous injuries. He knew that what was needed was a secure place to rest the shattered troop, but to burden themselves with these weakened men would slow the progress of their vital business. He quietly consulted Jamie about his dilemma but the two of them were of the same mind; little discussion was needed for the brothers to agree to take the risk of being caught in charge of the papers rather than desert those who had fought so well at the instigation of their chieftain. Jamie, more suited to the position of leader than Geordie, took command of the men telling them he knew where they would be safe.

"It's a fair bit of a trek, but it will be safer to get as far away from today's victors as possible and we must get Father's letters to safety. Do you feel fit enough to carry on?" he asked

"Aye," answered one of the older men who was no stranger to battle. "You lads collect your gear and then we will be ready to follow you." He looked to his fellow survivors for support, and he was quick to realise that the presence of the CaimBeuil's sons had breathed new life into the disconsolate group as they immediately nodded their agreement..

Meeting Jamie and Geordie had given the men new heart so they prepared to help one another on the trudge up the mountain to the caves. By the time the papers had been collected the valiant band were rallied and ready to march. The men were tired from the battle and progress was slow, with the less wounded helping the more seriously injured to painstakingly climb the side of the steep crag. Swords, which had been swung in defence, were now doing service as crutches whilst powder horns were doubling up as drinking vessels for the men unable to use their arms to tip the water bottle. Hard though the climb may be, the once stalwart men followed their chieftains as best they could.

Incident of the Barn of Bones

"The men are tired and hungry, Jamie. We need to make camp for the night and allow them a space to breathe," Geordie said as he caught up with his brother at the head of his rank of bedraggled and silent highlanders, all that remained of the once valiant Campbell army.

"Aye, yer right Geordie, man. We'll need to find a bit of shelter for the night and maybe make a fire to warm the men up and make a hot meal. The constant fighting and the losses they have seen this day has disheartened the men, to say nothing of the pain of their wounds, but a wee heat and a drink round a fire will put new vigour in their step." His brother agreed.

"We can't be far from the Crook of Eriska where there is a hay barn belonging to Angus Buchanan. We could shelter there tonight and maybe even for a few days until the hue and cry dies down. It will give us a chance to tend to the wounds and get the men in a better state. Jake and his brother Malcolm have worked this hill with their flocks for years and should be able to lead us there even if the moon wasn't so bright."

Fleeting memories of lazy spring days flitted through Jamie's consciousness. Happy days spent on the craggy, grey faces of the mountains. Happy days spent barefoot, chasing after a stray ram or hog. Happy evenings at lambing time, when he had shared the shepherd's simple supper of bread and the piquant, hard sheep's milk cheese, which had been cut by the evil, horn-handled, worn-bladed knife that had served the shepherd both at home in his hovel and out on the hill amongst his flock. Happy nights. Wakeful nights, when Jamie had bedded down on the floor of the creaking wooden hut, dreading that he might fall asleep and miss the waking of the shepherd, thereby missing the opportunity to assist at the miracle that was the birth of a new life. Happy mornings, after the night-time toils, when he had been allowed to sit quietly by the crackling fire and feed an orphaned lamb. Times when he had not been required to follow the CaimBeuil into battle.

There were other memories crammed into his weary brain. Times when he had imagined that he was the son of one of his father's tenants. He had fond memories of romping over the hills. He had eaten bread and cheese and quenched his thirst at the many cold, clear waterfalls that carved their route through the rock of the crag down the mountainside, lazy and tinkling in the summer months but torrential and deadly when the winter snow was melting and swelling the burns as they tumbled downhill into the fast, dark Highland rivers and lochs. Then he had sat cracking jokes and playing games with Malcolm and Jake, now he was dependant on their knowledge to lead them all to safety. This was a poignant reminder to Jamie that times had indeed changed and perhaps not for the better, but at least he had confidence that they would not be lost on the hillside in the deepening gloom.

"Let's get going then. Come on lads. We have only a short distance to go then we can eat and sleep. Jake, you and Malcolm take the lead so we don't end up over a crag," Jamie said in a half-hearted attempt to raise the spirits.

Jake stood still for a minute getting his bearings. He seemed to sniff the air like a dog before deciding on a line slightly more west than the direction in which they had been marching and made off with a loping gait over the thick undergrowth.

The men, restored with the thought of hot food and a fire, had a renewed spring in their step. They set off behind their kinsmen safe in their belief that the shepherds would lead them well.

They made good progress over the next half-hour and were growing close to Buchanan land when Jake, his likeness to his own collie dog becoming even more noticeable, sniffed the air again and signalled the following convoy to stop and be quiet.

"I can smell wood burning and meat cooking, perhaps a mile away. It is not likely to be the Buchanans at this time of year. Anyway, it is a strange smell. Meat, yes, but I've not smelt anything like it before."

"Stop off and take a few minutes' rest while Geordie goes with Jake to reconnoitre the trail," whispered Jamie. "No sense in walking into an ambush or worse."

Geordie and Jake took off at a smart pace and quickly gained the brow of the hill which gave them a panoramic view of the land below. Before them the sky, black with thick smoke, was mottled with the orange flames and red sparks flying upwards into the black sky from a fierce, gigantic fire. The barn that had been their target was an inferno.

Geordie, who had been straining his eyes to see what was happening in the immediate vicinity of the barn, began to make out figures in a large circle round it. It was impossible to decipher the colour of the plaids from this distance but Geordie's heart sank as he surmised they were the dreaded enemy. The McDonalds.

The area around the barn was obviously serving as a camp for a group of men. Swords, claymores and targes lay abandoned on the ground in no particular order. Plaids and bonnets had been discarded as the men danced around the burning barn quaffing from stone jars of whisky. A few injured men were having their wounds attended to in a rough and ready way. Small groups stood around the blazing pyre laughing and joking while others unpacked rations from the nearby saddlebags. It was apparent that these soldiers were settling down to celebrate the victory, confirming that they were the enemy!

"My God!" exclaimed Jake. "They have burnt the barn. Why on earth would they have burnt the only bit of solid shelter for miles around? It would have served them as a barracks while they rested after the battle."

Just as Geordie was about to offer some explanation the silence of the night air was broken by a piercing scream. Geordie and Jake stood frozen to the spot. The hairs on the back of their arms prickled and cold terror entered their hearts. This unearthly sound, like a soul in torment, echoing over the silent crags could have been made by a demon from Hades on the hunt for new spirits to torment. It made their blood run cold as, simultaneously, they realised that the barn was not empty.

"We are too far away to be of any use. We won't get there before whoever is in there is burnt to a crisp." Jake voiced both of their thoughts.

Then those in the barn must be members of their own Campbell family.

"There's nothing to be done by ourselves, but let's get back to the others and make a plan of attack. We will revenge those deaths," Geordie growled, looking very black and angry.

When they joined the others and explained what they had seen the men were immediately up in arms. All tiredness was forgotten in the desire for revenge. They gathered their weapons and would have made off without delay if Jamie, a sounder tactician, had not stopped them in order to formulate a plan of attack.

"We will only get ourselves slain if we go off at sixes and sevens. We need to catch the marauders when they least expect it, with no warning."

He marshalled his forces and led them to the edge of a clump of trees about a hundred yards away from the still burning barn. The men who had set the fire had given up patrolling the fire since none could possibly have survived the conflagration. They were singing and drinking from flagons of ale in celebration of their victory and the destruction of a barn full of Campbells.

"They are pretty well drunk and certainly not protecting themselves. Even the guards on the outskirts of the clearing are swaying in a very inebriated fashion. Jake, Malcolm, Graeme, you go that way, Peter, Malc, Alex over there. Geordie, you and I will charge from here. Everyone else follow on as best you can." Jamie indicated what he wanted by a wave of his arm, instructing the able-bodied to lead the attack. He would have preferred to leave the injured behind but they were so incensed by the treatment meted out to their clansmen that no order to hang back would have been attended to.

All the men drew their swords and followed Jamie's directions to the letter. Each had visions of the slaughter they had witnessed earlier that day and, of course, the idea that their kinsmen had been roasted alive did nothing to alleviate the anger they felt.

Within a few minutes, pandemonium prevailed. The MacDonald soldiers were too drunk to defend themselves in any organised way and were soon overcome by the irate Campbells.

The skirmish was short-lived. MacDonald soldiers had, for the most part, discarded their swords and targes to join in the revelry that had followed the euphoria of the day. They had been drinking for some hours and had enjoyed the cruel destruction of the barn full of Campbells as a fitting end to a glorious day. They were tired and befuddled and would have easily been taken prisoner, but so great was the need for revenge among their attackers that such an option was considered by none. Each and every last man was put to the sword, and their bodies were left to feed the scavengers.

Jamie and Geordie along with their most trusted clansmen had a hurried discussion as to how they would proceed.

"It could be dangerous to stay in this vicinity for too long with the flames from this fire announcing to the whole district that something cataclysmic has been taking place, but there is plenty of food and drink here and the men could certainly benefit from it," said Jamie.

"Aye, It would be a shame to waste what has been prepared. But man, could you eat here with the thought of your kinsmen dead behind you?" asked one of the lieutenants dubiously.

"This is war. In war, the normal niceties have to be set aside as need dictates," Geordie answered him in a clipped voice.

The majority of the men agreed to this. Although in normal circumstances they would not have considered sitting to eat the food of the men they had just killed, their own bodily requirements had to be met. They had injured, tired and disheartened men to fend for and the destruction of supplies desperately needed would be no less than a criminal act. Weak men could not fight.

The brothers looked around the group, some of whom were dropping from exhaustion and loss of blood. They noticed that already the worst of the new wounds were being attended to and those men being revived with sips of fiery whisky left by the enemy. The decision was made. The men were in no fit state to carry on.

"The best we can do is post lookouts around the camp so we are not caught in the way the MacDonalds were. Gather what weapons and supplies we can easily carry and secrete them in several caches away from the barn at the edge of the copse. Make sure to pack some food with each stash in case we have to make a run in one direction," ordered Jamie.

"We will eat around the fire but rest amongst the heather as inconspicuously as possible. Then, when the men have slept and recovered from the shock, we will make for the caves. We will have to be extremely vigilant with MacColla and Montrose's men combing the hills for the survivors," he continued, thinking out loud.

"First we need to bury the dead. It is what we would have wished our enemy to do for us if we had been defeated," said Geordie in a quiet voice.

"Damn, man, there's not a man here who's fit to dig a grave. Even if we put them all in one it will need to be deep to save the bodies from the ravening wolves," swore Jamie through gritted teeth. "No! I'll not ask that of the men. What dignity did they show to our brothers today on the field? None. No, Geordie. Enough."

Jake, who had been listening to the brothers argue the point, interrupted at this moment with a suggestion.

"Why not use the fire to dispose of the bodies? I'm in agreement with ye both. Enemy or not they were men fighting for what they felt was right. They deserve the same dignity we would expect if the tables had been turned. To deny them that is to contradict our own beliefs. A few of us could easily fling the corpses onto the flames and all consciences will be settled."

"Aye, well, let's get to it then, Jake. Leave the injured to rest and ask only for volunteers," agreed a disgruntled Jamie

However, there were no dissenters and very soon the bodies had been arranged on their funeral pyre and were blazing their way to the next life.

The men stood round the fire with bowed heads as they commended the souls of their enemy to their God, whichever He may be. That was the whole purpose of this war. To worship God in the manner of your conscience. Be you Catholic or Dissident.

As the moon shone through the smoke from the smouldering barn that hung on the frosty air, each of the men felt the ghostly presence of a kinsman hovering over the scene of devastation. It was done. They had revenged their family, given dignity to the dead and now the need was to find comfort for themselves.

Jamie noticed that Geordie was standing to the side of the clearing stroking one of the anxious horses tied up there. Something in his stance alerted Jamie that something was amiss with his brother.

He strode over and, putting a hand on his shoulder, asked, "What's the matter?"

"It's Merlaine's pony. Remember Father made such a fuss about her bringing it when we married? My God! She was in that inferno."

"Surely they wouldn't have harmed the women and children? Perhaps we'll find them tied up in the wood on the other side of the clearing," said Jamie but Geordie could tell by the timbre of his voice that he did not really believe his words.

Nevertheless, the stunned brothers searched every inch of the wood, but to no avail. They knew in their hearts that there had been no mercy for the women and children; they had been burnt alive in the barn with the menfolk. Geordie recognised this was not the time to mourn for his family; he and his brother were responsible for the surviving men and they must not forget that it was imperative they get the papers, entrusted to their care, to their destination and safety or the survival of the whole clan could be at risk. Yet he was unable to keep the images of his wife and children from settling in his mind.

The men were unnaturally quiet as they quickly ate the food already prepared and quenched their thirst from the abandoned stock. Talk was at a minimum. No one wanted to discuss the happenings of the day, so, fed and watered, the men went about their allotted tasks and dispersed to the edge of the copse to spread their plaids amongst the heather to make a sleeping place.

As the men settled down to get what rest they could Geordie sat on a tree root, staring into the glowing embers of the dying fire. His thoughts flew away to avoid the hurt of his loss but he looked at his sleeping kinsmen with compassion and pride. Here were men who had fought for the honour of the clan in a deadly battle, barely escaping with their lives but still determined to recover as soon as possible in order to get back to fight the enemy again. He was proud to belong to such a loyal family.

Slowly, shifting his eyes from the sleeping men to the pile of ash and bones where the barn had once been, he felt a pain pierce his heart. He must be as strong as his men. They had suffered more today than most, had accepted their wounds and the loss of their friends and continued to fight for what they believed to be right. He could do no less. There would be a time to mourn Merlaine and the children when they had prevailed over the enemy. For now, he must put his men and his allegiance first. He began to plan for the trek up the mountain to the caves. He wanted no more sacrifice from his family.

The Caves

It had taken the best part of two days to make their way up the treacherous terrain of the mountainside to the dubious shelter of the caves. In the early hours of the day after the battle the men had been roused from sleep looking far from rested. The uncompromising cold dawn offered no promise of good marching weather with the ground being hard beneath their feet, the sky heavy with threatening snow and the keening wind freezing their aching bones. As they slowly gathered themselves together and dressed once more in their plaids many thoughts winged their way to the tiny cottages where a warm fireside might see a buxom wife tending the porridge pot, with children huddled round the fire, hale and hearty, but these idle dreams were soon overshadowed by the coarse reality of their present circumstances. Those with painful and suppurating wounds wondered if returning to their families was at all likely and even the uninjured awoke with little belief in a happy outcome from their current venture. Each and every one of those who had previously believed they were following a path designated by their God, questioned their decision to follow the lead of the CaimBeuil.

Despite the thickness of their plaids they were a cold dishevelled bunch who scrambled over the heather to collect the strategically placed bundles of supplies from the previous evening's struggle. It was too dangerous to light a fire so breakfast had to be a cold collation.

"Hand round the whisky jars to get a bit of warm blood circulating through the men," Jamie ordered one of his lieutenants. "But no too much, we dinnae want drunkanrds tae haud us back this day," he warned

"By, it'll tak mair than whisky tae warm some o them this morning," Jake replied as he nodded towards the still bundle that had been Gavin Campbell. His had been some of the more serious injuries yesterday and what the MacDonalds had started the harsh Highland climate had completed, leaving the band depleted by one. Gavin Campbell had succumbed to his wounds during the short, chill night.

While the main body of men tried to flex their muscles ready for the trek ahead, Geordie and Jamie aided by Malcolm and Jake carried the body of the illustrious warrior away from the camp to discuss the best way to tend to the burial of his corpse.

"We have no way of digging a hole in this ground. It is like granite, but we cannot leave him for the wolves to feast on. We did as much for our enemy and Gavin has given his life as he pledged." Geordie grimaced as he slammed the point of an enemy sword towards the impenetrable earth. Oh, how he deplored this senseless waste of life!

"Let's find a hollow and wrap him in his plaid. The men will happily set about finding stones to fashion a cairn over him to mark his resting place, and we will be able to tell his family he was buried with the honours of the clan," came the decisive words of Jamie after a moment's thought.

As expected those not suffering injury took themselves off into the trees with a few scrambling further up the barren grey hillside to gather the necessary rocks to cover their kinsman, each of them silently thanking the Lord that it was not he who was to be buried so far away from hearth and home, but also pleased to show this last vestige of respect to their comrade in arms. Each knew that if it had been him he too would have been treated to this respectful end.

It was a sorry little band who started off round the mountain aiming for the caves high in the mist and snow-clad towers above them. Those who were able to walk helped those with leg wounds, clumsily bound with any available piece of cloth; even plaids of enemy tartan had been pressed into service as dressings, or used to insulate those suffering the bitter chill most through loss of blood. Those who had trunk and arm injuries rendering them unable to pull themselves over the many overhanging ledges were pushed from behind and pulled from above by their companions. No one considered the possibility of leaving the injured behind, even although a journey so very difficult for healthy men should not be undertaken by those who were unlikely to survive the harsh march up the uncompromising scree of the Ben. It was unthinkable to abandon an injured clansman.

Towards the end of the first day they had covered a pitifully insignificant distance. The men had found it necessary to turn their plaids into stretchers in order to carry the most seriously wounded, but at least their exertion kept the blood pumping in their veins, negating the frosty bite of the uncompromising wind. Swords had been fashioned into splints in an attempt to alleviate the suffering of those with open wounds on their legs. The MacDonalds had slashed their way through the rank and file of the opposing army with much ease, maiming where they had not killed outright.

"At least in this cold the wounds will not suppurate and fester so quickly but there is very little chance of getting all those injured to our destination," thought a worried Jamie, who felt his responsibility to his followers extremely deeply. Not as much of a pacifist as his brother, he still resented the useless loss of life that was taking place. "Another night in these conditions will finish off most of those we are carrying. Even if we could get them into the warmth and get a leech, I doubt if he could save them," he continued.

"Jamie, man, you cannae change anything at this late stage. Let's make the lads as comfortable as we can and leave the rest to the Lord."

"Is it that easy, Geordie? Can God really be on our side? When you look at Christopher there, red wi' fever and his leg only attached to his body by the bandages and they hard wi' his own life blood. Has God forsaken us?"

"Who is to say what God's plan is for any of us? When we took the oath, it was in His name. To fight for what we believe in. Ye know I'm no lover of war, even as the son of a warlord I would have gladly tried a more reasonable method of settling the affair, but would you revert to the idolatry and corruption of the Romish Church?"

Geordie sighed before continuing. "I don't think it would have mattered what the cause. King Charles and Montrose were intent on breaking the power of the CaimBeuil and a Holy War was just as good an excuse as any to get us to fight. I foresee this unrest with religion becoming more widespread and Charlie might have to take his fighting men nearer to home."

"Aye, Geordie, I think you may be right about that, but what a price to pay. By morning we will likely have lost all but a few stalwarts. Who will feed their wives and train their sons?"

Geordie answered automatically. "The family will look after its own." He indicated the heavy leather bags slung over their shoulders. "If we save these precious documents in order that the CaimBeuil may come back to prominence, we will have done our bit just as much as those who have fought and died in the battle." Geordie was trying to convince himself to have faith in his father's belief that they were fighting with right on their side. Even giving voice to his trust in the family's integrity Jamie noticed there was a questioning note apparent in his younger brother's voice; he did not really believe his words. He paid lip service to the creed but it was clear he was wrestling with his own conscience.

Despite the care the wounded men had received from their kinsmen since the battle, the next morning Jamie's prophecy had come to pass. Without exception, the wounded, having exhausted their small resources in the climb of the previous day, had gone to a better place.

As the tiny band looked down on the now peaceful faces of their clansmen, they became even more determined that the clan would win this war in order that those honest countrymen might not have died in vain. These were not trained soldiers who had taken the decision to belong to the army but shepherds, weavers and cottars who had accepted the responsibility of affiliation with the Campbells and given their lives by following the command of their liege lord.

This time with a number of bodies to inter and on barren rock the problem of burial became more difficult to solve. The men scouted round the mountainside looking for a suitably safe repository for the earthly remains, but the best they could find was a shallow cave with a narrow entrance.

The six remaining men heaved the bodies up the incline and placed them as reverently as possible in the confined space. Again they gathered the grey stones scattered over the hillside to block off the entrance, thus entombing the dead, plaid-wrapped corpses of the brave men. With bowed heads, the pitifully few remaining men prayed for the souls of those who had made the ultimate sacrifice.

With no injured men to contend with the more robust team made good progress and by mid afternoon they had reached their goal.

On the approach to the secret cave they again smelt the distinctive smell of woodsmoke and approached with extreme caution. Luckily this was not a stray band of soldiers from Montrose's army but a dispirited little group of women and children who had been led up the mountain to the safety of the caves by an elderly relative, too old for the battle.

"I saw the way the MacDonalds were slaughtering anyone left alive on the battlefield, and vowing to rout every Campbell – man, woman and child – from the area and put them to the sword," the ancient kinsman explained. "So I spread the word around the villages and advised them to take to the hills. The hamlets are not safe!"

"As we climbed through the foothills, we have seen some heartbreaking sights where the enemy had been before us," one woman sobbed.

"My sister was married to a shepherd and they lived quietly with their sheep at the base of the hill. We found her body lying spreadeagled with her clothes torn off. The soldiers had obviously raped her repeatedly then killed her when they had taken their pleasure. The product of their maleness was everywhere, clinging to her hair, running down her poor thighs, lying in puddles on her belly."

She broke into a cataclysmic bout of keening and, cuddling herself and rocking back and forward in her anguish, mumbled, more to herself than to those listening, "She was such a modest lass."

Jamie and Geordie had a quick conference, the outcome of which was to offer what little protection they could to the pathetic group. However, the older man thought their chances of survival to be better without a fighting contingent, so, after sharing their supplies and each glorying in a reviving hot whisky toddy, they warned them of the danger of smoke alerting the enemy to their presence and then they again climbed off en route for the secret caves.

"I hope we remember how to find the entrance," Geordie worried.

"Father's instructions are emblazoned on my mind, as I'm sure they are on yours, Geordie lad," said Jamie, laying a reassuring hand on his younger brother's shoulder. "The CaimBeuil depends on us to save the future of the family while he goes to raise another contingent of the army to follow on where these men have left off. We will need all the persuasion we can find to regain the position father had before his conversion to Presbyterianism."

Minutely following the instructions, the intrepid brothers found the almost invisible entrance to the catacombs where they were instructed to hide the papers for retrieval by their father or older brother in the future.

The brothers sent off the five remaining men to find water and wood, primarily, so that they may build a fire deep in the caves and warm themselves, dry off their clothing and revive and recuperate from the horrors of the last few months, especially the tribulations of their recent defeat, but also to protect the location of the secret cave.

While the men were off about their tasks Jamie and Geordie, following the precise instructions from their father, proceeded to enter a dark cave where they investigated what appeared to be a hair crack in the wall which no one would notice if they had not known it to be there.

"Here's the entrance to the further caves, Jamie," Geordie whispered. Then they both jumped as Geordie's voice echoed back in a ghostly whisper. "Caves, the caves, -aves, -aves."

"Man, my heart almost stopped beating there." He laughed and was immediately answered by an echoing, ghoulish-sounding laugh.

The brothers decided not to speak any more in this area so they silently slid through the slit in the cave wall, which immediately became a low narrow passage. Both boys had to bend almost double to walk along the path in the eerie light. Neither could see where the light came from, but it was filtered along the passage like the first streaks of dawn on a foggy morning.

The floor beneath their feet was strewn with boulders and pebbles, both large and small. Despite progress being slow, the boys pushed on, aware that the job must be completed before the return of their compatriots. They came to a steep decline where it appeared that steps had been hewn out of the rock.

"Be careful going down these steps Jamie, I don't fancy hauling you back up into the first cave. Hang onto the wall and feel your way down," Geordie whispered. In this space there were no echoes and Geordie immediately felt his spirit rise.

"We might be better to go down these steps as if they were a ladder, then we could feel with both hands and feet," suggested Jamie as he turned himself around.

"Always the smart brother," grinned Geordie. "Let's get on with it."

"I'll go down first leaving both satchels with you. You throw them down to me and come on down yourself. That will be safest," Jamie explained, removing the satchel from around his shoulders.

He climbed down the steps, giving Geordie a running commentary of his doings, hoping to aid him as he followed him. When he reached the bottom, he called to

Geordie to throw down the satchels, which he caught before looking around to take stock of the position in which he found himself.

The cave he now stood in was illuminated with soft evening sunlight from a great hole high in the hillside which filtered around the walls, making the dull, grey rocks dappled with pinks and mauves and sparkle like diamonds where crystals were embedded in the walls. The overall effect was to appear to be standing in a bejewelled room with the atmosphere of a cathedral. Jamie stood looking around himself, awed by the grandeur that nature had shaped once left to itself in the dark silence of the mountain. Never fanatically religious, Jamie realised the power of the God, for whom he was fighting to be allowed to worship in his own way, and reconfirmed in his own mind that he was fighting a just war.

Geordie descended the last stair and landed beside him. He also took a minute to look around himself in wonder at the awesome height and majesty of the cave, but they were not boys on a sightseeing trip but trusted advocates entrusted with the very future of Clan Campbell.

"Where now? We have to look for a low entrance in the rear of this cave. Shall we try opposite the staircase?" whispered the overawed Geordie.

"Aye, that seems the best plan," answered Jamie.

There was plenty of daylight left but both men were aware that they would not like to find their way out of the caves in the dark, so they crossed the great expanse of floor, taking care as before not to trip or slip on loose stones that covered the uneven area.

They searched for some minutes before Jamie gave a shout of delight.

"I've found the hole! I don't think it leads anywhere else, but I'll crawl in just to be sure."

"Be careful there is nothing living in there. Dark caves are favourite homes for snakes to bring up their families," Geordie warned, but too late.

A blood-chilling scream emanated from the hole from which Jamie's rear portion stuck out and a long, dark shadow slithered towards Geordie from between the great thighs of his brother.

Without thought Geordie stamped on the head of the snake and with a single movement removed his *skihn dhui* from his belt and with one fast downward stroke beheaded the escaping snake.

Jamie had in the meantime extricated himself from the rocky hole. Blood poured from a wound on his head where he had collided with the solid rock of the cave roof when the adder had struck, but the most frightening sight for Geordie was the twin punctures, already becoming red, that now adorned his brother's arm.

Jamie was chalk white as he indicated the bite to his speechless brother.

"I, I, I'll suck out the poison, Jamie," stammered Geordie. "I know how to do it. You must rest still and quiet though until it's done."

Placing his hand on Jamie's shoulder he pressed it in compassion as he prepared to try to salvage the life of his brother. "It will be all right, lad," he said. Despite his brave words Geordie was shaking almost as much as his brother as he prepared to extract the poison from the now terrified Jamie.

He spoke softly as if to himself.

"Cut into the site of the bite, until it bleeds, then suck the blood and venom out and spit it out."

Clasping the dagger with which he had killed the snake he proceeded to make the cuts in his brother's arm. His great hand was shaking as he sliced the razor-sharp blade through Jamie's now puffed-up flesh, then repeated the cut until the blood flowed freely. Lowering his head, he sucked the putrid blood from the man-made wound and spat it into a corner of the cave. He repeated the treatment time and again until he felt he must have drawn the life's blood from the inert man. Time stood still for both men as they prayed together for Jamie's salvation.

"We'll get you back up those stairs, man and into the sunshine. The others will have water and with the fire going we will soon have you back to normal." Geordie tried to rally his now shivering, pallid invalid.

Jamie placed his hand on Geordie's arm to stay his next repetition as the younger man bent his head again to the self-imposed task.

"I fear it is too late, Geordie. I can feel my whole body becoming stiff from the poison. At least my end will be quick and clean."

"Nay, don't lose hope. I've sucked out the venom and once I've tied up your head you'll be right as rain," was the answer barely audible through Geordie's tear-choked throat. He knew he had been unsuccessful. His brother would not leave the caves with him.

"Make sure the papers are safe and go back to the men. Father or one of the elders will find me when they come to retrieve the documents." His last earthly words for the good of the clan were urgent.

Geordie looked into his sibling's eyes and realised that despite all his efforts they were becoming glazed and his stare was far away. He cradled his elder's head in his lap, wiping away the blood that now trickled down his beloved face.

Jamie raised his hand to clasp Geordie's as the two sat in the glittering cave in the fading light until Jamie's body became limp and his fingers loosened their grip on Geordie's for the last time. After twenty years of arguing, wrestling and fighting, both with each other and side by side as soldiers, Jamie was no more.

Geordie sat still for a very long time as the shadows grew deeper and the light faded in the room around him. He tousled the hair of his dead brother, not quite believing that their adventure together was over. Then, realising that it was almost dark, he pulled himself together to complete the task that had led them to this place.

He stowed the heavy satchels into the cave, being excessively careful there were no stray members of the snake family still loitering in the hole.

He gently lifted his brother's shoulders and, with tears running unchecked down his face, moved him from the entrance to the inner cave.

"He is right. Father or Alexander will find him when they arrive. The best I can do for him is wrap him up in his plaid and leave him at the foot of the steps where he won't pinpoint the entrance," he thought.

Fitting the actions to the thoughts he completed his final duties and made his way back to the steep incline. As he climbed onto the second step in the now almost black stairway he turned and was just able to make out the plaid-shrouded shape that had so recently been his big brother. He said a silent prayer for his soul, reluctant to leave him in the deep, dark hole in the ground.

"God rest your soul, Jamie," he intoned in a reverential voice. As he turned to face the next challenge, a ray of dying light caught the one of the facets of the ruby adorning his finger and, in that moment, he realised that they had all been fighting for the glory of the CaimBeuil, not that of their maker. Was the sacrifice of his beloved Jamie too high a price to pay for such glory? Was this God's way of telling those fighting in his name to stop and live in peace? Had the fact that he was still alive have anything to do with his being in possession of the trinket now sparkling on his finger? God's will or witchcraft? Whatever. He was done with war. The price was too high!

Chapter Three

The Lamb Fair

"Rosie, will you stand still?" cried an exasperated Maggie, as she tried to fasten the laces dangling from her charge's stays. "Every time I get my fingers on the ends, you jump off in another direction!

"How can I make you presentable when you wiggle about like a worm on the end of a trout pole? Your father will certainly leave you behind if you're not dressed and ready when he gets in from the byre," threatened Maggie as she gave one last sharp exasperated yank on the stay laces and tied them into place.

"Not that you need stays," she sighed, taking in the neat figure of the slim girl in front of her, who glowed with excitement. "You're not a fat old heifer like me," she said laughingly as she gave the stay laces a final pat over Rosie's pert derriere.

Rosina, face flushed, eyes shining and with tendrils of damp, jet-black hair curling onto her brow, turned towards her old nursemaid and friend with the dimples showing in her rosy cheeks and answered indignantly, "You're not fat, Maggie, just cuddly." She laughed as she suited the action to the word. She peeped out from beneath her long lashes and half turned away before continuing to tease, "I've heard Jake Graham say you would make him a good armful if you could be made to look in his direction, but I don't suppose you would be interested?"

Maggie flushed to the roots of her tightly scraped-back hair but nevertheless aimed a playful clout at her nurseling, saying good-humouredly, "You are getting too old to be hanging about in the byres listening to talk that is not fit for a lady, young madam. Jake Graham says a lot of nonsensical things when he thinks he can get away with it. It's time the Maister found you a husband to give you something else to think about." Although her reply seemed to be stern, there was the glimmer of a smile, which tugged at her lips, at the image of Jake Graham.

If it hadn't been for her love for Rosina and her father she would not have been averse to taking a walk through the fields with Jake. He had a nice wee cottage just the other side of the stack yard that would have done very well for him and her. She sighed at the though of how things might have been, then pushed it out of her mind. Today was not the time to think about the lack of romance in her life, and besides, the

Herminstones could not do without her and she had such a lot to repay. Aye, she owed the Maister and his wife a great deal.

"Stop dreaming o Jake." Rosie interrupted her reverie, bringing her back into the room and into the present.

"I'll say again, 'tis time that faither o' yours got you a man to take up your attention, there's nothing like a couple o' bairns to prevent ye sticking that snib o' yours into other folk's business," answered Maggie, trying not to show her mirth.

"Oh Maggie! I'll be good! I'm just that excited faither is taking me to the fair," Rosie said, attempting to be contrite but failing miserably.

Rosina rushed to catch Maggie round her ample waist and gave her a crushing hug.

"I'm sorry, Maggie but I'm just so excited I could burst. I know it's leaving you with a pile of extra work but I promise to buy you a present with the money I make from my bread. Father said since it was my idea I could keep what I made and there will be plenty of time to visit the stalls when mine is empty. People always buy the best stuff early and my bread *is* the best."

"Such conceit! As if I hadn't taught you how to make that very bread," growled Maggie, narrowly missing Rosina's ear with the swipe she directed at her. But it was all in fun and Maggie was secretly touched that her nursling was thinking of her despite the excitement of the promised jaunt.

"Never you heed spending your pennies on me lass, buy yourself a few ribbons to tie back that mop of yours, or a fancy bit of lace to make a collar on your new dress for Christmas." Maggie smiled, turning her back just in case Rosie should see the tears in her eyes.

While Rosie donned her petticoats Maggie thought how like her mother she had grown. She remembered back to her first day at the farm and how frightened she had been when she had been told at the Poorhouse that she was to be a farm servant. Who would have thought then that she would be the one here to take pleasure from the almost grown-up Rosina? For a minute, looking at the glowing girl, Maggie almost believed she was again seeing Lizzie, which brought a tear to her eye. Not normally given to sentimentality, she held out her hand and stroked Rosie's highly coloured cheek with her workworn hand.

"Oh Rosie, Rosie, your mother would have been so proud of you this day. She used to talk about the time when you would be grown up and how you would look. Ye are very like yer mother, ma pet," she ended gently.

"Am I really?" Rosie was taken aback by the sudden softness in Maggie's tone, for Maggie always tried to pretend she was a strict harridan and Rosina and her father pretended to believe that was the case. They both knew that Maggie's life revolved around them and their home. They were grateful for the care they received from the devoted servant, indeed neither thought of Maggie as anything other than part of their family.

"Your mother was such a beauty as yourself, both on the outside and the inside. Her curls hung in a tangle – just like yours do – over eyes of deep brown with sparkling light reflecting her happy nature; with those dark eyebrows giving her a cheeky look. Her face was a bit fatter than yours; you've more the shape of your faither but that long, white neck... and skinny arms and pert tongue." Maggie finished with a shake of her shoulders to bring her back to reality.

"And not dressed! Get moving, girl!" she said, pretending to be cross as she bustled about the room, picking up a slop jug and making for the door.

"Aye, she's a grand lass, and kind to think of me, despite the Maister spoiling her since the Mistress went," thought Maggie as she clumped down the stairs.

"I am off to get the porridge dished," Maggie threw over her shoulder as she whisked out of the door, down the rickety stairs and through the dark passage into bread-soaked ambient atmosphere of the kitchen. "No dawdling now or the Maister will be away and you still up here dreaming."

Rosina was too excited to dwell long on the matter of her mother. Indeed, she barely remembered her and this was a very important day. This was to be the first time her father had allowed her to go with him to the Lamb Fair in Lockerby and, at seventeen, she was itching to see all the wonders of the stalls, the plays and the fairings. They were to meet up with Will Halliday and his three daughters from the nearby Rigghead Farm and travel together to the fair.

While the men dealt with the serious business of hiring for the winter and perhaps socialising in the Blue Bell over a few jugs of ale, the girls had made wild plans to see and do *everything* that the fair had to offer. Belle, the eldest of Will's pretty daughters had been regaling Rosina and her sisters with tales from previous fairs she had attended with her father, ever since the two men had been persuaded that the girls were old enough and sensible enough to merit this indulgence.

Outside in the stack yard Rosie could hear the rattle of harness as the horses, having a day off from the fields, were harnessed into the cart which held the excess cabbages, turnips and potatoes not needed to feed them over the winter. The noises of the farmyard did not normally intrude on Rosina's daydreams but, today, the cacophony in the yard gave her such a rush of pleasure as she imagined the squealing pigs, the senseless lambs and even the cow and calves to be as excited about their trip to the fair as she was herself. She giggled as she imagined the conversation going on in the farmyard if only she was able to understand the language of the animals.

Despite this flight into fantasy Rosina was an immensely practical and capable girl, having been well trained by Maggie in all housewifely and farmhouse duties as befitted a good farmer's wife, so she had prepared for the fair in a businesslike manner.

Earlier, Rosina had carefully packed up all the eggs, cheese and butter that she had made, as well as a batches of her own bread and pies and several flagons of her own home-made ale. There were always people needing to buy a bit of food at the fair, so despite her own excitement, and being a shrewd businesswoman, Rosina had been up before cock crow to bake the bread she had left proving by the hearth overnight. As she slipped on her petticoats she sniffed the gloriously measly aroma of freshly baked bread filling the house.

Maggie entered the kitchen still smiling about the interlude in the bedroom above. The porridge pot and the kettle were competing for her attention. As she wielded the spurtle in the big black pot she wondered if the Maister was right to take Rosina to the Fair. She was young to take charge of the stall in the town where there was always a lot of toing and froing from the alehouse as the deals were settled with a drink. "Farmers are a rough lot," she thought, "and Rosie is such a pretty maid."

She had the plates of steaming porridge on the much-scrubbed table and was just about to mask the tea when the back door opened and in came the Maister, rubbing his hands, for there was a nip in the early morning air of this Autumn day.

Peter Hermistone was dressed for market in tweed knee breeches and coat over his lawn shirt and leather waistcoat, woollen stockings and buckled shoes. He looked what he was, a prosperous peasant farmer. His rotund figure was not over tall, standing just about five feet seven, but he had the look of a much taller man as he held himself erect. The years of heavy farm work had broadened his chest and put muscle on his legs, which looked well in breeches, while leaving his stomach flat. His weather-beaten countenance had crinkle lines from the laughing and smiling that he was noted for and this face was topped by a crop of dark brown curly hair which showed just a touch of grey at the temples. He had been much sought after by the local women after the death of his wife ten years ago, but he had not had a fancy to replace the one woman he had loved. He would not have described himself as a sensitive man, perhaps thinking that a characteristic not to be looked for in a working man, but he had been devoutly in love with Lizzie since he first met her at the Michaelmas Lamb Fair twenty years before. He had walked the eight miles to Bankshill regularly on a Sunday after church to court her before finally bringing her home as his wife, expecting to live out the rest of his life with her at his side.

But fate had been fickle. When Rosina was just seven a tinker had come to the farm looking to make cloggis and Lizzie had invited him in to take a can of tea while he whittled the wood for the soles. Three weeks later she died from the typhoid he had carried with him, himself being immune and going on his way leaving devastation in his wake. It was thought in Lockerby that he was responsible for more then fifty deaths in the area. The death of Lizzie was nearly the end of Peter. Maggie despaired for his life, but slowly and surely the presence of Rosina brought him back to life. It was only rarely now that the shadow fell over his face. Rosina was the light of his life but she was also the living image of her mother, recalling at odd moments his grievous loss.

"Well, Maggie, timing perfect as always. Is that young madam not finished primping herself yet and Ben here to give you a hand?" he laughed as he strode across the kitchen to the ladder like stair into the loft where Rosina and Maggie slept. Tilting his head up, he held Maggie back with one arm as he made the call up to Rosina.

"Wheest, woman, I'll get her moving," he chuckled.

"Rose, I'm that sorry, pet, but there is so many extra pigs to go the day that there will not be room enough for you, perhaps you can come at Whitsuntide." He turned with a grin on his face that turned him from a hard working farmer of forty-five into a cheeky lad of fifteen, making Maggie sigh, thinking of all the heartbreak he had had in his life that had changed his normal expression.

"Just see how quickly she gets down those stairs now," he whispered. Then he held one hand to the back of his ear and his thumb in the direction of the ceiling as the unmistakable scamper of angry feet was heard overhead. The steps got faster as they descended the stairs, then a positive termagant flew around the kitchen door in a flurry of skirts and shawl with her day cap dangling from her balled fist by its strings.

"Oh Father, you can't mean it. I'll sit with the pigs! I've been so looking forward to today and you know we agreed to meet up with Mr Halliday and the girls."

She had opened her mouth to continue her harangue when she caught sight of the twinkle in her father's eyes and she flew towards him, arms akimbo to cuddle this dear man. She looked up lovingly and laughed into his eyes.

"You horrid old man. I believed you. Why do I always fall into your traps? Will I be a credit to you?" she said as she whirled away from him and postured about the kitchen.

Peter Hermistone was a broad, burly, hard-looking man, a man not to be meddled with or cheated in business, but as he looked at his daughter tears sprang to his eyes for he saw in her the lovely hair and eyes of the wife he had fallen in love with twenty years before. As she looked up at him, her sparkling eyes and the curve of her elegant neck could have been those of her mother and Peter felt the lump in his throat as he remembered a Michaelmas fair, twenty years earlier.

"Put on your cap, maid, or folk will think you a disreputable woman. Try to tuck some of that morass of hair under it or it's the sheep shears I'll be taking out."

Rosina made a face behind her father's back as she tied the strings of her cap in a neat bow under her chin, put a demure face on, danced over to the table, curtsied low and, with a devilish glint in her eye and in a soft voice, asked, "Am I presentable Maister, to go jaunting with you?"

"Aye, lass, but you're a bonny wee thing. I'm thinking you could be breaking the hearts of the young lads at the fair this day."

"Come on, you pair of idiots, the porridge will be cold, then who will get the blame, I ask you?" said Maggie in a rough voice which hid the emotion she was feeling at seeing this expression of emotion between father and daughter. As she turned away from the table to lift the teapot from the whirlie on the fire, she was glad to be part of this family.

By the time the porridge was eaten the sky was becoming lighter so father and daughter donned their outdoor clothes and, armed with a rug to cover her legs, Rosina jumped up onto the cart beside her father, prepared to suffer any hardship in order to enjoy the promised pleasures of the trip.

Maggie stood at the door of the farmhouse watching the cart and the two dear people in her life disappearing from sight before turning back into the kitchen to get on with her daily grind. As the cart rolled ponderously down the dry rutted lane, away from the farmhouse, Maggie stood staring after it, remembering all the years she had been at the farm and the love she held in her heart for Rosina, who was like the child she never had. As the years went on and Maggie grew nearer to thirty the prospect of a child of her own had begun to fade from her dreams.

Maggie had been at Capelfoot since leaving the Poorhouse in Dumfries at the age of eleven. She had no idea who her parents were and was of the opinion that she could not have had a better life if she had. A young Peter had collected her just after his marriage to Lizzie to help his new wife in the house as well as to work in the fields. She remembered now her first sight of the farm as she rode on the cart up the rough track to the house. There was no way of deciphering which of the low buildings was the farmhouse and which the byre and stables. The grey stone walls were build in a very haphazard fashion, the cracks and spaces between the stones filled in with mud and dried grass. The roof beam allowed for a slanted roof of turf through which a curl of smoke rose in a welcome from the hole cut crudely above the fireplace.

As the cart came closer a woman burst out from the door, threw her plaid over her shoulder and danced on thin legs and bare feet between the ruts towards them. The grin that lit up her face showing her healthy teeth was enough to remove the last vestiges of fear from Maggie's heart. Without waiting for the horse to respond to Peter's instructions, Lizzie drew up her skirts and bounded up beside her husband where she at once disappeared into the embrace of his long arms.

That had been Maggie's first sighting of Lizzie, who was from that moment on to treat her as if she was a daughter or a sister. She remembered what a relief it had been to see Lizzie after the fear she had that she would have a harsh, cruel mistress and vowed she would work her fingers to the bone so as not to give them cause to wish they had picked another inmate.

Even at eleven Maggie had been a tall, healthy girl despite being raised in the workhouse on not enough food and absolutely no love. Lizzie had taken to the girl as soon as she saw her in the meagre, ill-fitting clothing doled out by the workhouse. The contents of Maggie's box, the petticoats of flannel and dugget, cotton to make shifts and a rough linen pair of stays had seemed a poor start for a girl to the kind-hearted Lizzie, who very soon supplemented them with a thick wool plaid and woollen skirt and stockings so that for the first time in her life Maggie was warm. Lizzie welcomed another female in the kitchen to talk to while they worked together rather as companions than mistress and maid.

For her part Maggie had never since that day felt hunger or cold and was totally devoted to the needs of Peter and Rosina. She grew into a statuesque, plain girl with stringy fair hair that she kept in a bun and severely scraped back from her high brow, pushing her small pale blue eyes deep into her cheeks, making her face appear sheep-like from some angles. But Maggie was no sheep! When her mistress died, Maggie, despite her own distress at the loss of the only mother figure she had encountered, set to to bring up Rosina and hold the household together when Peter was nearly out of his mind with grief. When he forgot to milk the cow, Maggie milked it; when the hay lay wasting in the field, Maggie stooked it; when the sheep needed brought down from the hill, Maggie brought them. She kept the farm going until, slowly, Peter recovered, thanked God for Maggie and again took over the reins of the farm. Although Peter entrusted Maggie to continue to nurture and care for the motherless Rosina, he doted on his daughter. Maggie was an indispensable part of the farm, neither thought of nor treated as a servant. Maggie was abruptly brought back to the present as a deep voice just to her right startled her.

"Aye, when the cat's away the mice will play," it said quietly. "Maister's no even out of sight an there ye are day dreamin' about yer lad when a working man's standing here near droppin' for want o' a drop to drink."

Maggie flushed and looked into the laughing face of Jake Graham, cowman, shepherd and right-hand man of Peter.

"I'll sin skite the thirst of ye, Jake, ye didna half gie me a flie. My heart's thumping, ye big galloot. Come on in an I'll see if there's a wee bite o a bannock left to go with yer ale or maybe a plate o' porridge."

Jake put his arm round Maggie's shoulders and gave her a squeeze. "Well, Peg, you're wasted in that kitchen; you'd make a grand armful for some lucky man. If you ever decide you've had enough o lookin oot for that pair there'll aye be a corner fur ye in ma cot."

"Get away wi yea, Jake Graham, ye'd huv a hert attack if a took ye up on that offer," said Maggie, nonetheless looking flushed and pleased. "Ye've been a bachelor so long you wouldn't know what to do if ye had a woman in yer bothy tae keep ye in line. You men are all the same. Talk, talk, talk, but nae action," she joked.

"Feed me, woman and have less of your cheek. Women! Huh, think the world revolves roon them," he answered cheekily as he pulled out a stool and prepared to address the bowl of porridge Maggie placed in front of him. As her hand left the bowl, Jake grabbed it and looked into her face.

"Joking aside, I'm askin ye to think about walking oot wi me. That braw wee lass will be getting a lad o' her ain soon and it would make me happy to care for you as mine."

She smiled at him, patting his shoulder before turning back to the fire to hide the emotion she was feeling. She felt her face and neck becoming redder as she remembered the conversation she had had with Rosie earlier that morning.

She smiled to herself.

"Bide yer time, Jake, there's still work for me here. Bide yer time."

****

Geordie sat halfway up the Lamb Hill, watching the preparations for the Fair taking place around the lochs below him. The tiny hamlet with its few scattered cottages had been gobbled up by the vast numbers of drovers, cattle and sheep men who came to this fair because of its proximity to the border of England and Scotland. All along the banks of Loch Flosh and Loch Quaas a veritable city had appeared overnight. Drovers erected makeshift pens for their cattle and tents for themselves and the guards they had brought with them, for the areas they had travelled through were notorious for the rustling and disappearance of migrating herds and flocks. Even last night while the drovers from all over socialised in the makeshift taverns among the pens before the main business today, the flocks, especially, were a temptation to the rogues who flooded the village in an attempt to find easy pickings.

Geordie himself had arrived the previous night with a band of sheep drovers who were depending on a better price in Lockerby with its proximity to the English border than they would have been able to command in Glasgow, or Edinburgh even. Hoping his size would be a deterrent he had been allocated the night watch over the sturdy sheep pens build in a sheltered spot on the side of Loch Flosh. For this reason, he had climbed the side of the hill this morning to rest an hour in the heather before joining those hopeful of being hired for the next season. He had been unable to fall asleep, since the turmoil below was building up as refreshments were taken with seldom-met friends and badinage was exchanged among the groups, but with half-closed eyes he viewed the sights lazily and dreamily.

He had been to fairs before as a lad in the Highlands but had not been aware of the work that went on to establish the order of sales, where each lot of animals was stalled or penned, how they were fed and watered, how they were kept safe or any of the myriad duties delegated to a drover. The last few months had been hard on Geordie. He had not been brought up for manual labour and, although he was as capable as any of his grooms to tend his horses, his contribution to the running of the estate and the care of the livestock had been restricted to the giving of instructions rather than carrying out the orders of masters. Since his decision to leave the fighting to others, Geordie had become a drover, but the life on the move was not for him and he was determined that at this fair he would hire himself out as a shepherd or groom if he could find a willing employer.

The noise of animals was immense. Drovers continued to arrive, look for fodder and water for their animals, knock up pens, argue with the burghers about fees, meet old friends and generally have a good time at the end of the long drive.

Geordie watched all the activity taking place at the foot of the hill as the outlying farmers brought their stock to the sale with high hopes of a good profit from their husbandry. It was essential to get a good price to stave off the deprivations of the hard winter months on the hill farms.

With each cart that arrived the atmosphere became more jovial as neighbour met neighbour and gossip was exchanged. Each man paid grave attention to his rival's prize beast and looked over every herd and flock. The price paid for the cows and sheep in the auctions depended on the quality of the animals and to what degree they matched with the best animals on offer. If you had the best animals, you had the best price with everyone vying to buy your animals.

More than a few carts held the wives and families from the farms, children shouted and jumped up and down with the excitement of the day while their harassed mothers were trying to cope with them as well as the demands of finding a good spot and setting up a stall to display their wares. Most farmers' wives were able to make a bit of extra money from their culinary skill or the fruits of the orchard or dairy.

One cart in particular caught Geordie's eye from his viewpoint above the fair. It was unusual as it contained only what appeared to a father and his young daughter who were laughing back in a relaxed manner at a similar cart behind, again holding a father figure and three ravishing blonde women. His daughters, Geordie guessed, as none looked old enough to be his wife. In the midst of all the turmoil of the fair the older men seemed to be enjoying the obvious delight of their young companions. Geordie could almost feel the excitement rising from the young woman in the front cart as she twisted and turned to look around herself and take in everything at once.

The maid might have been any age from her diminutive height but her air of being in charge was unmistakeable. She ordered the driver of the cart to a spot she had chosen by the simple expedient of standing up, looking over the ground to establish where best met her needs and pointing.

The older man touched his cap in deference to the maid but Geordie still thought he was her father and that he was hugely enjoying obeying her commands. The look on his face told of his pride in the lovely self-confident creature.

As Geordie's idle gaze passed over the bustling scene below, his eyes were continually drawn back to the young woman who sprang down from her perch on the cart and, taking stock of the goods on the other stalls, directed her companion on where exactly to place her trestle table to best effect. Her antics tickled Geordie's imagination as, happy now with the positioning of her table, she began to heave the heavy bags and bundles from the back of the cart, so that, in no time at all, she had an appealing array of fresh farm fare spread out for sale.

He had not felt interest in a woman since the demise of his wife, yet he acknowledged that the sight of the maid awoke an unexpected tingle in his body. Although she was pretty, it was more the way that she carried herself and the air of suppressed excitement that caught his attention. With her flushed cheeks and lush lips framing her wide smile, she appeared to be savouring the thought of an anticipated treat rather than setting up to work her stall.

Geordie smiled to himself as he continued to follow her antics and thought, "She will be a right handful for some man to manage but it might be a rewarding task to undertake."

The sounds and activities began to blur as Geordie's eyes started to close and, before he knew it, he had become oblivious to the clamour around the hill and had fallen asleep. It was not a restful sleep however, as his recurring nightmare again raised its ugly head and he once more found himself following Merlaine's final path, watching her drive with her women and children along that fateful path. In his dream he saw the woefully inadequate protection the small group had driven away from the castle with. How could he ever have thought it would be safe to leave her to the protection of infirm old men and untried boys? Why had he not kept her safe from the marauding McDonalds?

She had been caught and murdered in the barn. His children had been slaughtered and it was all his fault! He had sent Merlaine out from the safety of the castle walls to meet her horrific end at the hands of the dreaded McColla.

As he dreamt of Merlaine's beautiful placid face that he had loved since first he had set eyes on her, the flames began to claim her body, the tongues of fire licking her face without changing her expression. He heard the voices of his children crying for him to save them as they, too, choked on the thick black smoke that eventually hid

Merlaine's ghost from his pained eyes. Suddenly the curtain of smoke lightened and he once more saw that much loved visage of his wife but, unlike the other times he had dreamed this dream, she did not look at him accusingly but smiled her sweet smile, appearing to gaze directly into his eyes. It was as if after all this time their two worlds had collided and they were in contact with each other. As he continued to feel the pull of her presence in his dream her lips parted and he could hear her words. "My Geordie, my Lord, my Love. Go to your destiny. It is no longer with me."

As the flames again began to conceal her image, the features he had loved so well changed and the image that emerged from the flames was that of the young girl he had watched setting up her stall. Geordie groaned as he awoke from the restless sleep and looking down the hill he espied that very same vision laughing and talking to one of the young girls from the other cart that had followed them in, as they worked side by side to sell their wares to the considerable queue of folk who had gathered around her stall.

****

"Only two pies left," crowed Rosie as she grasped her companion, Mary. "I knew we would sell out before everyone else and have plenty of time to look around and enjoy the fair. Thank you for staying with me and not going off to gad about with Belle and Jenny. You are a good friend."

"I have enjoyed it. I only wish Ma had allowed me to have a stall, then I'd have some pennies to spend on ribbons," Mary replied, gazing longingly at the multicoloured ribbons dangling from a stick held by a nearby pedlar.

"You have helped me so much when I was busy that you have earned these to spend on yourself," said Rosie, pressing some coins into her friend's hand. She hurried on before Mary could protest. "And if we don't sell these last two pies soon, we will eat them and close the stall!" She laughed, looking every inch the haughty lady with her little nose turned up and stretching to her full height.

"Aw, Rosie, you don't half make me laugh with your posturing and carrying on. Do you take anything seriously?"

"No, life is too short not to have fun while we can, Faither taught me that because he stopped having fun when Ma died. But today is for fun, pleasure, music and entertainment and we are going to enjoy every minute of it. We have worked hard, so now let's play hard."

Mary joined in her friend's infectious laughter. They were very much the same age but there any resemblance ended. Mary was a good six inches taller than Rosie, with thick straight blonde hair, blue-green eyes shaped like almonds, either side of a small straight nose, and her pale complexion glowed like the inside of a river oyster's shell. Rosie was a complete contrast with her dark hair and eyes and rosy cheeks. Rosie did not grudge her friend her good looks. While accepting easily that Mary was unarguably the most beautiful girl in the area, the only pang of jealousy she ever felt was in connection with Mary's straight nose, Rosie's own being tiny and stubby. She always felt it made her ugly. No amount of reassurance by her friends could convince her that her nose, instead of detracting from her beauty, enhanced it and made her just a little bit out of the usual pattern.

"The lads always look twice at you, Rosie," was their common argument when she bemoaned her imperfection.

Not only were Rosie and Mary complete opposites in colouring but also in build, with Rosie's boyishly slim figure emphasising the difference between them. Mary had a much more mature and well-developed figure that went in and out in all the right places. Occasionally Rosie would yearn for a bosom like her friend's but this little seed of jealousy did not affect their friendship. They acknowledged the differences while each accepted that the other had traits they would have liked and Mary stood as a surrogate sister to Rosie.

The girls were bent over the accumulated wealth Rosie's foresight had made possible when a dark shadow cut out the winter sun and they heard a man clearing his throat.

"Are these pies for sale young lady? They look very fresh and tempting to a hungry man."

Rosie looked up with a startled expression for she had not noticed this black giant approaching the stall. As she raised her eyes she met the twinkle in the dark orbs perusing her, for despite his imposing height and build she instinctively knew this stranger was a gentle giant.

"To be sure they are, m'lord," she mockingly replied, a glint in her eye as she sketched a subservient curtsey in his direction.

"The finest pies you'll find in all the fair today. And baked this very morning with these very hands." She held up her small but rough hands for his inspection.

"So I'll guarantee their quality." She smiled across at him. 'But will two pies be enough to assuage the appetite of such a man as yourself?"

Despite months on the droving roads Geordie had maintained an aura brought about by his upbringing that was apparent even through the straggly beard and unkempt hair. He was still obviously a Highlander wearing his plaid like a skirt rather than the rough trews favoured by the Lowlanders, but Rosie immediately recognised he was not an ordinary drover.

"Och, aye, fine lass, I'm just getting a bite to eat before I go looking for the hiring square. You never know how long you might have to stand waiting until someone takes a liking to what you are offering, and, if you move off, you might miss the very chance ye have been waiting for." He smiled his crooked smile, which lit up his face.

As Rosie took the money for the pies she asked, "What kind of position are you looking for? It's a bit late in the day for a ploughman or yardman. They are usually settled first thing to allow the men time to move their bits of furniture to their new cottage before they start work tomorrow. Folks are pretty settled in this area and there is not a lot of moving about, anyway."

"Ye know a bit about the hiring then?" Geordie enquired.

"Well, my faither is a local farmer, as is Mary's, and if you listen to the men talk you can't help but know what's happening where and who's moving when. Everybody nearly always knows who needs a ploughman or a byre man."

"And does anyone need a groom or a shepherd around about?" Geordie asked, amused but obviously interested in what the answer might be.

"Not that I've heard, but there is not much need for grooms on the farms, the ploughmen tend to the shires and each farmer will groom his own riding horse."

She drew her brows together in thought as she turned to Mary to ask, "Have you heard of anything going at the Bruce's of Lochmaben Castle or with the Johnstones at Netherplace or Lochwood Tower?"

"I've heard no word of any of the grooms leaving. They don't generally for the lairds are generous and fair maisters. You'd be better looking for a herd's cot if you've a mind to bide local," Mary answered shyly, squinting up at this man mountain smiling down on her from his great height. He then amazed the girls by executing an elegant bow which set them giggling.

Rising from his posturing, he continued, "Thank you, ladies, both for your intelligence and your sustenance. I'll bid you good day." He took his pies and strolled off in the direction of the hiring square, leaving Rosie and Mary to discuss this pleasant interlude.

"Have you ever seen such a big man? Father is tall, well above most around here but even he would seem like a midget compared to that haystack," giggled Mary.

"Aye, but there is something very gentle about him despite his great height and rough appearance," Rosie answered abstractedly as her eyes followed the giant making his way through the thronging crowds. "That bow he made us would not have disgraced him had he been addressing royalty and he has a tender look in his eye. Not your common drover, I think," said Rosie meditatively.

Mary eyed her friend speculatively. "I think you have fallen in love with a frog and dreamt him into a prince." She laughed.

Rosie blushed but hurried to reassure her friend that she was not smitten by any man, frog or prince but then the laughter left her eyes as she looked seriously at her companion.

"Mary, something Maggie said to me this morning has been prickling at the back of my mind all morning even while we have been busy on the stall and having a laugh. She said it is high time Faither found a husband for me to keep me in line. You don't think he will make a match for me without consulting me, do you?"

"Your faither? Don't be daft. He thinks you're so perfect no man will ever be good enough to wed you, besides he still thinks of you as a wee lassie."

"Well, I think she was joking, but although I've been fair distracted with the fair and the stall and all that excitement I have been mulling over a few things. I'll be seventeen in November. Jane Henderson and Maisie Pollock are my age and have bairns by now. There is no doubt Faither would like to marry me to a farmer's lad so as to keep the farm in the family when he gets older. He often asks me what I think of such and such a lad or tells me some farmer's son would be a good catch. Until Maggie mentioned getting me married this morning I just didn't put the facts all together." Rosie stared off into the distance and through half-closed eyes spied on her friend to watch her reaction to her next words.

"Oh but Mary, I don't want to be carried off to be married to a farm lad."

She clasped her hands to her breast and went on melodramatically.

"I dream of a handsome young lord to fall at my feet in admiration and plead for my hand. I want him to slay dragons and scale turrets to save me from peril, then carry me off on his charger to his bastion high on a hillside where he will worship me forever. I want to dine off gold plate, wear priceless jewels in my ears and on my fingers, dance to the fiddlers playing on the gallery of my love's castle and have him prostrate himself at my feet professing undying love at all hours of the day and night."

She opened her eyes fully to take in Mary's mesmerised look, chuckled convulsively before continuing prosaically, "At least I don't want to marry any of the lads around here."

Mary, who had been standing with her mouth agape as Rosie had propounded her future dreams, now realised that Rosie had been having another of her romantic flights of fancy. She herself would be happy to follow in the footsteps of her elder sister Belle, who was to marry Peter Kinsmuir from nearby Piersby, come the spring, but Belle was nearly twenty and Mary felt marriage was safely too far in the future for her to be worrying about in the meantime. It had not occurred to her that her playmate might be contemplating marriage either.

"Enough of that for now!" exclaimed Rosie giving herself a shake. "Let's get the baskets back to the cart and find Faither. I've too much money here to carry around the fair with me. I never imagined it would be so profitable to make a few loaves and pies. It is a pity the fair is only twice a year or we could make our fortunes and have silk dresses bought with our immense wealth," she joked.

"You are such a tonic, Rosie. You always find the positive in every situation. Maybe you should not make believe so much. If your dreams don't materialise, you will be disheartened," the more stolid Mary worried.

Rosie lifted the front of her gown between finger and thumb and with her pert little nose stuck up in the air minced off in front of her long-suffering friend, saying, "I have great wealth, woman, follow me and we will purchase satin and silk to adorn our incomparable beauty to dazzle the eyes of swains for miles around."

Mary copied her friend's pose for a few yards before they collapsed into each other laughing and hugging as they made off to find Peter in the Blue Bell where he was settling a deal for pigs.

****

As the girls ran off to the busy yard of the inn they were followed by two extremely disreputable men who had been listening to their banter intently and had pricked up their ears at Rosie's mention of purchasing satins and silks. Lockerby was full of such men at the time of the Lamb Fair, and Jim and Joe had had more than their fair share of ale that morning since they had been paid off from the Drove.

They were an odd couple to be mates. Joe had been a skinny lad when he had entered the workhouse in Ayr and the food he had found there had done nothing to aid his growth to the strapping lad he could have been if properly nourished. He had very few teeth left in his mouth, which had collapsed in on itself, while his eyes were always peering around him warily, hunting for some purse to pilfer or an unsuspecting shopkeeper to rob. His companion on the other hand was built on more robust lines. Coming from a family of clever thieves in the back courts of Edinburgh, Jim had not wanted for food in his youth and now stood straight and tall and, despite his unwashed condition, thought himself a bit of a ladies' man. Although they were physically unalike there was nothing to choose between them when it came to villainy, each willing to kill a man for sixpence. Just now they had their sights firmly fixed on the heavy purse they had seen in Rosie's hand.

"We will keep an eye on those two, eh? Pretty girls and with a bright penny in their pocket." Jim leered at Joe

Joe mimicked his friend's look and nodded. "It won't be difficult in this crowd. We'll have them at our mercy before they realise they are in danger." His expression became even more lecherous than before.

****

As Rosie peeped in at the door of the tavern Peter caught her eye and excused himself from the group of farmers round the table and came out to meet the girls.

"What, sold out already? You'll make some man a grand wife, so you will, my Rosie," he joked as he wrapped her in a great bear hug and looked at her proudly.

This remark, coming so soon after their previous discussion on what her father's plans might be for her future, did nothing to dissolve the fear now festering in the back of her mind. She knew that all her father's hopes for the farm were tied up in her. He had had many opportunities to remarry after Lizzie's death and, by this time, might well have had a sturdy son waiting back at the farmhouse to take over as he aged, but his had been a marriage; so good he had never taken up with any of those young women willing to provide him with an heir. A shiver ran up Rosie's spine as she reviewed in her mind the lads her father was likely to think best suited to marry his daughter. But today was a fun day. Plenty of time to consider the future and Peter's ideas for her after the fair. After all he was her beloved faither; he wouldn't want her to be unhappy. She was being silly letting her imagination run away with her. She laughed up into his face.

"Aye, I've brought my riches for you to take care of since I'm a silly maid and might easily lose it or spend it on fairings." She handed over the bag containing most of her earnings from the morning.

The bag was considerably heavier than Peter had anticipated, but he exaggerated the effect the weight had on his balance as he staggered off to one side, eyeing Rosie with a more thoughtful glance.

"You've done well, lass. I should have made a better deal rather than allow you to keep what you made. Why, I'll warrant there's enough in here to keep us fed till Christmas."

Rosie was extremely pleased at this praise from her father blushing rosily at the compliment. In order not to appear sentimental, she continued her previous flippant tone as she commanded her father.

"Keep it safe, my man. My companion and I are off to investigate the pleasures of the fair." She dimpled at her father as she took Mary by the arm and they turned away from the alehouse yard in the direction of the myriad stalls and pedlars thronging the streets. They had every intention of enjoying all the pleasure there was to be had in the fair.

Peter watched them out of sight with a smile on his face.

"She's a cheeky madam, right enough, and mayhap I've spoiled her a mite, but, between us, Maggie and I have brought her up so her mother would be proud of her.

Perhaps Maggie's right and it is time we looked around for a young man for her; but I really don't want to lose her to another man yet, not even a husband." He sighed at his thoughts and turned back into the tap where he rejoined his compatriots in a second tankard of ale to celebrate the good deal he had completed. Prices had been high and he was well satisfied he had procured the best price he could have hoped for. He lifted his glass in the direction of his friend and neighbour Willie Maxwell and shared with him the pride he had felt as Rosie had handed over her earnings from the morning, while repeating the idea that she would make a good farmer's wife.

Willie agreed and added, "She's not only clever in the kitchen and the dairy but a comely wench too, Peter. You are very lucky to have such a bright lass willing to work alongside you. I am often sorry that Ellen and I didn't have a daughter and when I see the way Rosie loves you and listens to you, I admit to being a bit jealous."

Peter looked at his friend of many years standing and replied, "I was just thinking as she walked away that I will be losing her soon to some bright lad. I know it is a natural progression but I do hope she marries a local man so that I don't lose her altogether."

"Well, Pete, we can fix that right now and then we can have the best of both worlds. Rosina should marry my Liam. You get to keep Rose with you and I get to have her as a daughter. Done?" he questioned, holding out his large calloused hand across the table to his friend.

"Nothing I would like more, Wull, but I'll not arrange a marriage yet a while. Let the lass have a bit of life before she takes on the cares of the adult world. She still dreams of knights and shining armour. Aye, let her dream a while more but don't think I don't like the idea. I do. It would be just the solution to my old age." He drained his tankard and, picking up Wullie's, strolled off to have them refilled. When he returned he leaned back in his seat and relaxed with his legs out in front of him, the conversation was not forgotten but most definitely had been put on a back burner. He too would have a period of relaxation before making his way to the meeting place with Rosie. He lifted the tankard to his mouth, took a mouthful savouring its bitter taste, closed his eyes and let out a contented sigh.

If Peter had tarried a few moments longer, watching the departure of the maids as they skipped their innocent way into the heart of the stalls, he would have been able to observe two very disreputable figures carefully tracking them. Jim and Joe were so sure there was money to be had from their purses that they had decided to trail them until an opportunity arose to relieve them of their wealth. They were puzzled when the girls entered the Blue Bell but, since they did not want to be noticed in their vicinity, they had hung back behind a nearby stall and therefore did not notice the handover of Rosie's full purse. They were unaware that between them the girls had only a few pence and most certainly were not worth robbing.

"Aye, you may laugh wench but before long your wealth will have transferred itself into my pocket." Jim grinned licentiously at Joe. "And anything else they might be hiding under those virginal gowns. That dark-haired temptress has my blood near to boiling with her posturing and preening."

The thought of having his way with either of those clean nubile wenches excited Joe no end. With his looks and lack of money it was rare for him to find even a doxie in the city slums who would lie with him.

"Aye, a grand idea, Jim," he agreed. "But keep well behind until we are sure there is none to interfere on their behalf. They might have husbands or brothers looking out for them. They don't look like sluts out to sell their wares so they are likely here with someone."

Jim, as full of bad ale as his companion, agreed and with exaggerated care they continued to follow the erratic path of the young women as they enjoyed the sights and sounds of the fair.

Rosie and Mary were laden with fairings. They had originally intended to find Belle and Jenny to join them in their wanderings, but a combination of the excitement of the morning and the hordes of people swarming about made them change their minds. They were worried that if they held off inspecting the wares on show until they found the other girls they would be too late to enjoy the spectacle. Of course, as they wandered around they kept an eye open for Mary's sisters, but there were so many sights to see, so many pedlars' packs to investigate that they rapidly forgot to hunt seriously for the sisters. Rosie was still a bit disgruntled with them for choosing to go off without herself and Mary in the morning, and felt that it was now time for the workers to have some fun. They would find them later when it was time to meet up with their parents

The girls had watched a band of wandering players act out a story guaranteed to make your blood freeze, with witches and warlocks and battle scenes full of gore that left them clinging to each other, thrilled and terrified. They clasped each other in petrified delight, alternately screwing their eyes shut and peeping through their fingers to see what would happen next or staring with goggle-eyed amazement at the antics of the actors portraying these ghoulish characters.

They bought ribbons of many colours. Rosie had chosen deep red and emerald green that showed her to her best advantage, while her less vibrant companion preferred more muted light blue and pale green to set of her sparkling blue eyes and fair hair.

They had munched on hot gingerbread while they discussed the merits of Mary's choice in comparison to Rosie's own before being distracted by cheers, which led them to watching a group of young lads wrestling in the new way that had come across the border from Cumberland with the Union of the Crowns and the expansion of the animal fairs. They listened to the minstrels sing songs that told tales of politics and royalty from both sides of the border and the more romantic ones that made the girls long to fall in love and have a handsome swain performing deeds of great valour for their pleasure. Mary nudged Rosie and pointed to a group of happily chattering girls coming towards them heads together as they loudly discussed the fortunes they had been given by the fortune teller.

"Shall we have our futures told by the gypsy?" asked Mary, eyes shining in anticipation.

"I'm a bit frightened of gypsies, to be honest," replied Rosie, "but we won't come to any harm if we go together."

Taking each other's hand and holding tightly, they made their way giggling, self-consciously, towards the gloriously coloured wagon where Romany Anna sat perched on the step.

The girls had never seen anything like this house on wheels. Just the colours made them gasp in delight as they took in the shining red wheels of the wagon and the black iron spokes protruding from the hub of each. The wooden sides of the caravan were painted with all manner of little animals. The details of each left no doubt in the minds of the transfixed girls that the artist who had painted these had an intimate acquaintance with the creatures he had depicted. On the back of the canvas covering of the structure was portrayed all manner of bodies found in the night sky. The moon was the most predominant of these being shown in its many phases from crescent to full.

As the girls approached the caravan, Romany Anna descended the high steps on which she had been perched, waddling her way to her fire where a billycan of delicious-smelling liquid was brewing, the girls were able to peep inside the unusual wagon. They gasped as they looked up at the ceiling, which was made from some form of material that they had never seen before and held tight over bent boughs that made the wagon look like a cave on wheels. On the taut canvas ceiling, puffy white clouds and a bright orange sun dominated the inside of the caravan and the girls felt it must be like lying on your back in the hayfield on a golden summer's day to go to bed in this beautiful home.

The inside of the strange wagon was remarkably spacious and Rosie and Mary were able to see an iron stove with a crooked chimney that vented through a hole in the canvas roof. It was so shiny and gleaming that they were quite taken aback as they had always been told to stay away from the 'dirty gypsies', but this wagon home gave the lie to this idea.

As Rosina's eyes strayed, fascinated, around the room she was able to see beautiful multicoloured blankets covering the bed and, on a table near the stove, lay a plate on which had been placed one of Rosina's own pies. It was apparent that this was just waiting for the addition of the contents of the billycan to complete Anna's repast.

Afraid to disturb the gypsy at her food Mary and Rosina stepped back from the opening and turned to take in the sight of the old gypsy woman.

Anna was grotesquely fat and it appeared to the girls that it would be a Herculean task for her to prise herself through the small opening in the covered wagon to reach the splendour inside. At first glance she appeared to be an old crone but, as they looked more closely, they saw that despite the weather-beaten wrinkled face Anna had masses of long jet-black hair hanging down over her shawl-covered shoulders and her dark eyes were overhung by bushy black brows. Although this made her a bit sinister looking, it could be seen that these eyes were sharp and twinkling. Rosina didn't think they would miss very much of what was happening in her vicinity.

Both girls were enchanted by the clothes worn by the Romany woman. They were like nothing the girls had ever seen before, brightly coloured and flowing. Rosie was astounded to realise that Romany Anna was wearing layer upon layer of clothes. All of different and clashing colours so unlike the plain, dark apparel that she and Mary, along with their contempories wore.

As Mary and Rosina stared open-mouthed at the woman attending the billycan on the fire, she swung round towards them on surprisingly dainty feet, with a jangle of her numerous golden bracelets and earrings that dangled from her ears. It was as if the youngsters had been turned to stone as this shimmering vision of colour and spangles approached them. With each movement of her arms the rolls of flesh hidden in the garish costume trembled and flowed around her body, giving her the appearance of perpetual motion.

"You want Anna to tell the future, my pretties?" She smiled as she beckoned them towards her. "Come closer and let Anna look for your future in your eyes.

"I can see into the mists of time. You want to know who you will marry? How many children you will have? Come, come, Anna knows all," she wheedled enticingly, beckoning the girls towards her.

They exchanged a glance before stepping forward. Romany Anna held out a smooth brown hand.

"Place a coin in my hand and I'll give you a fortune to be happy about in return. The mists of time will move for you."

A trickle of cold fear ran down Rosie's spine but she couldn't back out now, so she dug a penny from her pocket and placed it in the incredibly soft-skinned palm of the gypsy. Romany Anna took her hand and squeezed it until she could feel the hard metal digging into her own palm, as if deciding if the sum was sufficient for her to give her time. Still holding Rosina's hand, she plucked the coin from her palm and quickly dropped it into her pocket. She slackened her grip, turned her hand over and peering into the palm settled a mysterious expression on her face. Rosie was quite taken in by this ploy and craned her neck in an attempt to see what Anna was seeing, only to be disappointed to see a slightly grubby palm where she had envisioned moving images of her future or even the face of her husband to be. She was not prepared for Romany Anna's chilling prophecy.

"There's much blood and terror associated with you," she said quietly, making a frisson of excited fear send tingles jump along the length of Rosie's body. "There is blood and fire in your hand. It is in your hand and will be on your hand, but not in your future. Because of this blood and fire, you will be happy. There is one watching over you and will keep you safe."

"Will I be married and have children?" Rosie asked in a very tentative voice, a bit scared by the words of the gypsy which made no sense to her.

"Soon you will be married. It is in your hand. You have met your husband who will be, it is he who brings the blood and fire into your life, but you will not keep it. He will love you well and give you three blessings. Out of trouble and danger will come much pleasure of the flesh." The gypsy looked hard into Rosie's face and realised that she did not understand the cryptic message from her reading of her palm. "All will become clear as time goes on. Before many moons have passed you will have known heartbreak and have found the man who will protect you from all ills."

Despite Rosie's obvious confusion with the gypsy's prediction she turned from her and towards Mary, gently taking her hand in her own before peering into the much larger hand.

The gypsy recoiled and dropped Mary's hand, exclaiming, "Beware, beware, the sins of the flesh are dangerous for you!" She stretched her hand out to regain Mary's hand and continued to examine the lines on her palm. "You too will meet the man who will be your master before the setting of the sun."

"Oh, I can hardly wait!" exclaimed the gullible Mary. "Will he be handsome, rich and powerful?" she asked breathlessly.

"You will live high above others, with many to wait on you. You will have children to gladden your heart and have a long and happy life,' Romany Anna finished. "That's all I can tell you. Remember my warning and take care. Go now."

As they wandered aimlessly amongst the crowds they discussed what the gypsy fortune teller might have meant by her remarks, congratulated themselves on purchasing a pretty brooch just the right colour to match Maggie's Sunday shawl, but mostly wondering at the money they had taken at the stall and toying with ideas to increase the sum next time by a joint venture. They were so engrossed in this that they did not notice they were becoming separated from the stalls and tents of entertainment as they found themselves amongst the now vacated pens where the animals had been lodged prior to the sales. They wandered on through the hustle and bustle of drovers and farmers as they claimed the animals they had bought and arranged to have them transferred to their own custody. The girls, having been brought up among most of these men, were not worried. In the main they were ignored or the odd farmer who knew their fathers nodded to them or cowmen might touch a forelock to acknowledge the maids as they moved past to deliver their new charges to the nearby hills around the village. The girls wandered on until they reached the end of Loch Quaas.

By this time, they were very pleased with themselves, having had an exciting day and seen all there was to see at the fair. But now they felt the need to sit and rest for a while before making their way back to meet their fathers and Mary's sisters for the return trip.

The sun was warm on their backs despite it being so late in the year and the girls sat down on stones near the edge of the loch, just far enough away from the animal pens to soften the raucous noise and smell of the animals. They found a sheltered spot where a half-circle of trees cut them off from civilisation.

For a few moments they sat eagerly chatting about the sights and sounds of their day, and like most young girls wondering if the predictions of the gypsy had had any truth in them. Mary laughed about the idea that she was to be a lady and live in a big house and have lots of children, while Rosie scoffed that if they were to meet the men of their dreams today they had better hurry up and appear since they only had a very short amount of time left before they departed back to their everyday lives.

"And aren't we here just to fulfil that very prophecy, me darlin'?" whispered a quiet chill-evoking voice very close to Rosie's ear. So intent had she and her friend been on their re-enactment of the pleasures of the day, they had not heard the furtive approach of the men.

Rosie gasped and turned round to be confronted with the leering, drunken face of a cattleman. She opened her mouth to scream but, before she could draw breath, the villain had covered her mouth with his calloused, evil-smelling hand.

Chapter Four

"Now, my pretty, we don't want any more company than we have already, wheest now, Jim and Joe just want to give you another pleasure from today for you to think back on."

Rosie's frightened eyes peered over the horny, stinking fingers that covered the lower part of her face to see that Mary had suffered a similar fate to herself. There would be no help from her. They had been attacked by two ale-soaked men determined to have their fun with them.

Mary, of a much less robust nature than Rosie, was dumbstruck by the sight of the rogue who held her in his grip. There were tears of fright and pain running down Mary's cheeks as the scoundrel, who held her, manhandled her to her feet in an attempt to turn her towards him. Despite being paralysed with fear Mary was forced into a standing position held up by her captor, who smirked and called to his companion.

"I've got the better deal this time, Jim, look at the lovely ripe tits on this one and an arse just right for me to ride to pleasure, eh me, darlin'?"

He planted a wet kiss at the base of her throat before covering her breasts with his square-fingered leathery hands whilst thrusting his groin towards hers.

Jim, who had a penchant for raping unwilling girls and was always on the lookout for unsuspecting females, had automatically made for the darker of the two women. Since he had taken a fancy to Rosie when watching her antics on the stall earlier he had not paid much attention to Mary's more womanly attributes, but now he thought perhaps he had erred in his choice as he compared Mary's ripe bust, made all the larger by the position Joe held her in, and the less well endowed girl in his grasp. He was the leader and felt he should always have the choicer morsel; at least he should have first go at her. His wily, but ale sodden, brain began to work out how he could dupe Joe into taking his leavings. He would not easily give up a ripe peach such as Mary.

"Well, I dare say you will have enough lead in your pencil to manage both. What about taking this one first for a wee bit o practice?" He leered at his friend, showing green-pointed teeth in rotten gums.

The sight and smell of those decaying teeth, mixed with the noxious stench of her assailant, who had slept with the sheep on the long drove over the hills and who had not thought it a priority to bathe at the end of the trek, provoked her to retch against the suffocating grip of Jim's hand clamped over her mouth. She was also aware of the gut-wrenching acrid reek of fear emanating from both herself and Mary. She was forced to draw in quick, shallow breaths whenever she could, as she was terrified that, if the sour contents of her stomach were allowed to rise into her mouth, she would choke.

With one hand still tightly gripped round her mouth, Jim pulled Rosie up until she was trapped against his chest and held in place by his neck, before plunging his other hand deep into her bodice and painfully gripped her budding breast. He fumbled for a few seconds until he found her nipple and squeezed hard on it.

"Not much there to offer me, darlin'," he mumbled as he freed her tiny breast by the simple expedient of ripping her bodice. Her almost flat bosom was totally encompassed by his dirty, gnarled hand which intermittently pinched her flesh and painfully squeezed her nipple. He was obviously disappointed with their lack of maturity.

"Get the paps out o' that wench and let's have a look-see. There's little to excite a man here," he grunted disconsolately.

His fellow attacker duly obliged by gripping the now hysterical Mary around the waist, pushing her face into his putrid shirt front and holding her there while he freed her much more substantial attributes. Mary was nearly fainting. Her legs wobbled as she collapsed in terror against her violator.

"See here, Jim," grinned Joe. "She fancies me so much she has swooned on my chest." He giggled in a maniacal drunken manner as he turned Mary round. She was not unconscious, although perhaps she wished she were. Her big blue eyes were wide with fear and disbelief but she was so shocked by the speed of the attack she was unable to help herself and appeared to have removed her conscious self to another place.

Joe grabbed her plump breast in both hands, kneading and pinching while Jim watched avidly.

A terrified Rosie tried to squirm away from her captor but he held her tightly against himself. As he watched his mate manhandle Mary's bosoms, she could feel him grow hard against her buttocks and a chill of fear ran through her veins for the first time. She could not escape. This awful man was going to take her maidenhood unless she could think of some way to stop him. "Be calm, Rosie," she berated herself. "You have to think of some way to distract their attention so we can escape. You can't do that while you are fighting and panicking."

Meanwhile Joe continued to roll Mary's nipple in his huge horny fingers, murmuring obscenities in her ear, telling her just what he planned for her.

"But it won't be a quick buck, oh no. We are well away from traffic here and I'm going to enjoy all of you for a very long time."

"Then we will swap and you'll pleasure me just like you will for my mate," added Jim who was beginning to think he had indeed made a poor choice when taking first pick.

Joe smirked at him. "I don't think I'll want to hand over this beauty too soon. Just feel the weight of these jugs," he taunted, grasping Mary under her breasts and holding them in the palm of his hands as though offering them up at an altar. "Do you want to watch while I slake my thirst at her fountain?" he mocked as, keeping his eyes on Jim's jealous countenance, he pressed a breast into his open mouth, nuzzling noisily like an overgrown baby at suck.

Rosie could sense that her captor was becoming tense with anger. Although he was holding her in an iron grip his interest was definitely fixed on Mary as his mate manipulated Mary's pliant body.

His eyes were fixed on the white orbs that appeared to glow in the dark-skinned grip of her assailant. Mary's eyes were staring and Rosie worried that her friend had died from fright, but she could just see the rise and fall of her chest giving the lie to this thought. She realised that Mary would not be able to escape of her own volition and that, if they were to be spared this ordeal that threatened, she must watch for her chance and grab it when it came; there was unlikely to be a second one.

Jim idly covered Rosie's tiny breasts with his hand and almost absent-mindedly played with her, while he watched his friend undo the buttons of his breeches and allowed them to slide to the ground, unleashing his already erect manhood. Joe was slobbering over Mary's breast, nipping and biting as he fondled her rear through her skirt. Every so often he would guzzle on her nipple, now hard from the attention of his tongue, gripping it between his teeth, casting sly glances over at his friend while he stretched his neck away from the confined girl, all the time keeping her teat between his teeth so that the pressure stretched it, elongating her nipple.

"See how much she likes me? She is so excited by a real man that she can't tear herself away from me," he taunted his comrade. "Knows that old Joe will give her a good stiff prick." He moved his position until he had the transfixed girl kneeling in front of his naked loins. When he had her in a position that satisfied him he grabbed his erect member in one hand and forced it between Mary's flaccid lips while pressing her head towards his groin, giving her no choice but to accept the horrific organ into her hot, dry opening. Joe became highly excited as his dick rammed in and out of his captive's mouth, bringing him to the point of no return. He held Mary in a vice-like grip as he ejaculated into her mouth and the resultant liquid oozed out from the corners of her swollen lips. This excited Jim beyond endurance and Rosie felt his muscles tense as he watched his friend use the unresponsive maid with envy.

Although having been brought up on a farm and being no stranger to the copulation of animals, Rosie had no idea what a man's penis looked like and was severely shocked by the size and width of the one displayed before her. She was by now seriously worried about Mary's lack of reaction. Her own legs had become weak at the knees but her brain had been cleared by the desperation of the situation. She was able to estimate the best route for escape when the opportunity occurred. She rapidly made a new plan as she realised that Mary was in no condition to help herself and if they were to be saved Rosie would have to be both instigator and deliverer. Her best plan would be to get away and bring help back to Mary as quickly as possible.

Meanwhile, Joe had recovered from his exertions and was treating Mary like a rag doll. He had her inert body draped over one arm, her breasts dangling forward and obviously exciting the man who had Rosie clamped in his grasp. Joe was slowly removing Mary's skirt and underdrawers, noticeably fascinated by the appearance of her milk-white buttocks. He continually glanced up at his co-conspirator, intent on enjoying the covetous expression on his face.

Jim caught his breath as his penis jerked to attention when Joe revealed the rise of Mary's bottom. He leaned back against the trunk of the tree, grudging Joe the use of the near-naked submissive girl within his arms. Although his attention was directed at the scene in front of him, he maintained his vice-like grip on Rosie. His intention was to keep Rosie clamped securely to his side while he watched Joe have his way with Mary, and then, with his desire reaching fever pitch, he would enjoy taking his pleasure and making her pay for not being as well-proportioned as her friend.

Joe's hands roamed over Mary's body at will. He pinched the nipple buds which topped her now swollen breasts. He was pleased to view his hand and nail marks showing livid against the pale skin. His hands glided over a plump buttock and down her thigh to her knee, then made a return journey skimming the dimple of her behind, up her spine to the base of her neck and back down as if magnetically attracted to her swelling buttocks. He functioned like a sleepwalker. He left no part of her exposed body untouched as his excitement mounted for a second time. His hand ventured to his semi-erect member as he manipulated it until it was encaved between her delicious cheeks, where he left it while he pulled her into an upright pose to enable him to have the best of both worlds. Joe had never imagined himself in such a situation before and, with the worst of his passion spent, he was inclined to taunt Jim with the more substantial quality of this wench's assets.

He carefully pulled her skirt and drawers down over her belly until Jim could make out the triangle of hair nestling in the join of her legs. Joe pushed the rough fingers of one hand into this mass of curls while he continued to move the bulky mass of her clothing towards the ground. Mary, silent until now, gave a moan as Joe's fingers slid into her womanhood while he bent her over almost double to allow Jim a view of his antics.

He looked up and gloated at Jim, saying, "I'm going to enjoy riding this sweet tight little virgin. So clean and docile. Hear how she moans for me already? She won't want any other when she has tasted Joe Burns."

Jim couldn't hold his patience any longer. He was so mad with jealousy that his normally subservient partner had got the cream, he loosened his hold on Rosie and made towards the couple just a few feet away.

Rosie was ready for the chance but even she couldn't believe it could be this easy. While her erstwhile captor had his panting attention fixed on Mary, she turned and without a backward glance pelted off in the direction of the cattle pens.

By the time she had reached the main area of animal enclosures, she was weeping hysterically and unable to make herself understood by either of the young men in sight, who themselves were suffering from an overindulgence at the taps in the town. However, even in his inebriated state, one of the boys was able to see how distressed she was as she pulled at his sleeve. He hurriedly dragged his soft, woollen blanket from his pack and, with some embarrassment, threw it over Rosina in order to cover her nakedness.

"Men! Bad! Rape! HELP!" she wheezed, pointing vaguely back in the direction of the scene of her trauma. The lad threw an appealing look over his shoulder at his friend, who shrugged, having no more idea how to deal with the situation than he did. It was at this time that several other men came into the yard, intent upon picking up their new flocks. Geordie, hoping to pick up a new drove, was amongst them and immediately realised that something was very amiss with the maid. He rushed forward, thrusting the nonplussed lads aside just as Rosie tried once more to make herself understood.

She took a deep breath and managed to get out a few words. "Help! Now! Mary!" she screamed before she broke into a paroxysm of weeping and wailing.

Whack! The hand bounced off Rosie's cheek, making her take an involuntary gulp of air. She choked and swallowed, then glared up at the worried black brows that met her gaze. From her disjointed words, Geordie had realised that danger still threatened her friend. He was anxious to be off to her aid.

He grabbed Rosie by the arms, saying tersely, "Where?"

The girl swallowed, took a deep breath and, staring into the giant's face, explained more clearly. "Two men attacked us. They are raping my friend by the side of the loch." This she managed to blurt out before she swooned at the feet of the Black Campbell.By this time, a crowd of men had come out of the many howffs to see what the commotion was about. Many of them were ripe for a fight, picking up cudgels in anticipation of a brawl. To a man, they were ready to follow Geordie's lead: Having handed the fainted girl over to an ancient shepherd, who agreed to stay with her until she was herself again, Geordie led the way towards the loch that Rosie had indicated, hoping to get there in time and prevent the men from having their way with the innocent maid. As they exploded en masse on to the beach, they saw two men rolling about by the edge of the water. Had the situation not been so serious, the advancing band of men would have roared with laughter.

Joe, with his trousers around his ankles to hamper his movements, was warding off blows from his erstwhile friend who was belabouring him with blows from both left and right fists.

Just as the rescue party arrived on the scene, Jim threw himself at Joe, propelling them both into the icy water of the loch, shouting, "It's all your fault, ye glaikit bugger! Ye had to try to get the better o' me [pant, pant] wi' the best bit o' skirt we have seen for many a day. [Gasp] If ye had only been content tae [wheeze] tak my leavins, we would nae have lost that wench." All the while he ranted at his cohort he continued to throw punches, oblivious to the crowd of men descending on them. With a final punch to Joe's jaw, he knocked him unconscious, there to land spreadeagled on his back in the shallows of the loch.

The band of would-be heroes had little to do but to restrain Jim. Two of the party grabbed his arms and held him up so that each of the angry men could use him for target practise. These were men who used their bodies daily in hard labour, therefore the punches rained on Jim lacked nothing in weight and he was soon thrown onto the ground a bloody mess of cuts and bruises. Several of the men finished their punishment with hearty kicks to his genitals as they turned away in disgust.

Meanwhile, abandoned on the ground as the two villains fell out, lay the almost naked figure of Mary. It was obvious that the scoundrels had forgotten all about her in their need to blame each other for the loss of Rosie.

While the grinning drovers watched the pantomime occurring on the loch shore with glee, one man detached himself from the group and gently lifted Mary into a sitting position, wrapped his fur-lined cloak around her bare shoulders and gentled her as though she was one of his thoroughbred horses, unsettled in its stall.

"Sh, sh, my dear, all is well. No one will cause you any more harm. The danger is gone. Hush now, hush."

All the time Mary had been at the mercy of her attacker it was as if she had not heard the threats he offered her, but now the gentle voice of this stranger broke through the barrier and she broke into a torrent of tears. The young man gathered her in his arms and rocked her back and forward as if she was a babe until she ceased to cry; she opened her eyes and looked into the handsome face of her rescuer and immediately fell in love.

Just at that moment Rosie landed beside her friend, throwing her arms about her.

"Did they harm you? Oh, Mary, I'm so sorry. I had to go myself or we would both have been in a worse state. Forgive me Mary, I would not have that have happened to you for the world."

She again hugged the shivering girl to her holding her tight. Mary's arms came around her back as they wept and hugged until they were both calmer.

The young man, who had retreated on the appearance of Rosie, again stepped forward and suggested that the girls be taken to a more secluded and safe place while the farmers could be trusted to deal with their attackers in a way unfit for the maids to witness. Geordie appeared at his shoulder and the two of them gently removed the traumatised girls from the vicinity of their recent ordeal.

"Where can we have the pleasure of escorting you ladies?" enquired Mary's white knight quite as if it was everyday occurrence to rescue damsels in distress.

"Our fathers will be waiting for us beside the milestone at the foot of Lamb Hill," said Rosie. "We must be very late by now and they will be worried, but I think they will have waited rather than send out a search party that might also be lost in the crowds."

The girls clung to each other, Mary shivering despite the warmth of the thick fur cape around her. As they hurried through the fair that was now preparing for the frolicking and jollifications that took place after the more serious business of the day was finished.

As they made their way across the square the figure of Peter Hermistone appeared. He looked anxious and angry when he noticed the girls coming towards him with the young men in tow. As he took in the dishevelled condition of the girls as they drew closer his physiognomy changed from rage to concern.

"Where have you been? What has happened? Are you both all right? Who are these men?" he glared angrily at their escorts.

"What have you done to these girls? If you have hurt them, by you'll answer to me and I'll take no excuses!" he stormed.

"Allow me to introduce myself, sir, James Johnstone of Lochwood Tower at your service. These young ladies have had a distressing and unfortunate experience from which my friend," he indicated in Geordie's direction, "and myself have had the honour of extricating them from some part. Be assured, sir, this was none of their doing and the lads are dealing with their attackers."

Rosie rushed into her father's arms, dragging Mary in her wake since she was still clinging to her arm.

"Faither, we have almost been ravished by a pair of drovers. Mary has had a terrible ordeal, far worse than me. We were both terrified of what might have happened but for these gentlemen who brought us back to you and left the other men to deal with the villains. Oh Faither, I'm that pleased to see you again. I thought we would never escape from those… those beasts."

"Are you all right, girls, they didn't harm you? Are ye sure? Oh, why did I let ye go wandering in the fair by yourselves?" As he spoke he pushed the tangled tresses of his daughter's hair from her face and peered anxiously into her eyes. Satisfied that there was no irrevocable harm done to her, he turned his attention to his daughter's friend, noticing immediately that she was in dire need of an older female and it became his most imperative task to return her to her mother.

"We just want to go home, Faither," whispered Rosie from the safety of his comforting embrace. Mary said nothing but nodded her head in agreement, confirming his urgent desire to be gone from the village.

"Sir James, the necessity to remove my daughter and her friend from the scene of their distress excludes me from thanking you in a more appropriate manner. I have no possession more precious than my daughter and I'm sure I speak for my neighbour, whose daughter Mary is. Be assured there will always be a welcome for you at Capelfoot." He turned to Geordie.

"And you, sir?"

"Geordie Campbell, sometime drover, presently unemployed," smiled Geordie.

"You didn't get a position at the hiring square, then?" questioned Rosie.

"No. but I'll be sure to get something with the drovers again." He smiled at Rosie, surprised that she should remember their chat after such a frightening incident.

"Sir, I would be honoured if you would care to spend the night with us and we can talk employment in the morning," said Peter, "but meantime I must get these girls handed over to the females of the family to tend their hurts."

"I agree, sir, and I am pleased to accept your offer," answered Geordie. "I'll be glad of a barn to sleep in and a bite of breakfast before going on my way.""I will bid you farewell, then," said Sir James, shaking hands with Geordie and Peter and making his bow to the ladies.

His gaze remained on Mary for a few seconds longer and his heart was touched by the anxiety and fear still apparent in her eyes. "I hope you will very soon be able to put this horrible experience out of your mind and not think all us men are cruel violators." He bowed once more to the assembled group and turned away. "Good day."

Sir James took his departure in the direction of the Blue Bell, while Peter, with one arm around each girl and with Geordie following behind, made his way back to the farm cart and the journey home.

Chapter Five

The crowd in the studio sat in enthralled silence. Mark could not believe his luck. To have managed to get Jock Campbell on the day of his investiture had been a feather in his cap but this unprecedented story would make his career. From here on he would be the interviewer who got the biggest scoop of all time. There could be no argument; the cameras would continue to roll even if this recital took all night. Big Jock was well away with his story and showed no inclination to stop.

"Thank God for the politician's garrulous tongue," thought Mark as he continued to show interest in Big Jock's tale. He dragged his attention back to the interview as Big Jock continued.

"…And that is how my ancestor came to Lockerbie and settled at Capelfoot, from laird's son to shepherd in one fell swoop."

"So I expect Geordie married Rosina and they all lived happily ever after?" joked Mark as he desperately tried to regain control of his show.

Jock did not answer for a moment. He appeared to be sitting back at his leisure, with his crooked grin fixed firmly on his face. Although Mark thought that the ex-leader had lost none of the charisma that had made him the people's favourite, he detected a rare moment of doubt in Lord John's expression. Indeed, Big Jock was having a rare moment of regret. The reaction from the audience to his story had hit a nerve, leaving him to wonder if resigning had been the right decision for his beloved party. "Was I right to give up now? Is it the best decision for the country and the party? Can Ross command this kind of attention from his supporters, never mind the dissenters?" He took in the almost stunned silence among the totally spellbound audience, gave a metaphoric shrug and brought himself back to reality. Rightly or wrongly the decision had been made. Ross Adam now carried the burden of maintaining the stability of his beloved Scotland. He turned the full force of his personality on Mark and answered him, confident once more in the path that he had chosen.

"Yes, Geordie married Rosina, but life was not so easy then as now and there were trials to be gone through before that resolution was reached. And that's when my family began to see this bauble," holding out his hand and lovingly caressing the ring on his finger, "as a symbol of good luck. You may recall the circumstances of the ring getting into Geordie's possession. So he did not immediately think fondly of it. It was a constant reminder of all he had lost. He had gone against his own instincts to follow his father, as a good son should," he added, "and led his men to what in fact, with hindsight, was a murderous disaster. To him, this ring meant dishonour. A lesser man may have sold it to set himself up, but Geordie was a Highlander, a patriot and a faithful son so he kept the ring which, every time he looked at it, brought back the sense of failure and disgrace. It became his bête noire!"

"How did he come to see the ring in a different, more friendly light?" was Mark's next question. He was aware that his questions were superfluous. Lord John, a consummate orator, needed no encouragement to continue with his story. It was as if after all the years of speculation and innuendo by his opposite number at Holyrood, when he had smiled at his opponents and turned the tables on their attempts to mock his upbringing, he had finally at the tail end of his career decided to "spill the beans" about his infamous trinket. However, Lord John did not continue from the previous recitation, but diverged along a path that none of his listeners could connect to his previous tale.

"My wife, the Lady Marion," he stopped on a choke of laughter. "Does that make me Little John?" he continued to chuckle to himself for a minute or two but the listeners were enjoying this joke too. "As I was saying, my wife, that long suffering, patient woman was Marion Johnstone. No secret that, you may say. All the romantic nonsense of how we met and married has appeared often in both the legitimate and the less salubrious publications. It has become an initiation for new journalists to find dirt on me and mine, but none of these have dug deeply enough to uncover the connections of the Campbell and Johnstone families over the centuries. Now there *is* dirt!"

"Lord John, I know, none better," laughed Mark, shaking his head in remembrance of the many previous interviews with John Campbell, Prime Minister, where he had come second in a battle of wits, "that you are a bit of a jokester so are you telling us now that Lady Marion's ancestors are connected to this story?"

"Unfair, unfair," laughed Jock holding both hands up in front of his grinning face and ignoring the latter part of the question. "I'll admit Mark, that there has been the odd occasion when I have allowed you to misconstrue my meanings and have left you with egg on your face, but man, I'm giving you the Jock Campbell exclusive now, so maybe you'll forgive me my wee jokes from the past."

The look on Lord John's face had the audience in gales of laughter. Many had witnessed the past attempts of Mark to interview John Campbell while he had been Prime Minister on a subject that he had no intention of discussing. They had a history of fencing around a variety of subjects, from Lord John's opinion of the lady who had become famous by becoming the first woman to be Prime Minister of England to his view on Scotland storing nuclear weapons. Mark had failed dismally to get anything from him other than the official party line. When Jock Campbell didn't want to disclose his personal opinion, no interviewer however persuasive could pierce his armour, in fact they were convinced he had none. He may look like everyone's genial uncle or even grandfather as he undoubtedly was now, but behind the innocent smiling facade was a mind so honed and sharp that he had never publicly revealed his private thoughts but turned each enquiry off with a joke.

Mark Henderson had made his name by gaining exclusives from politicians who entered his studio intending only to use it as an opportunity to eulogize their party policy to the vast numbers who watched the most popular chat show on TV. Mark, a benign presence, always allowed these pretentious members of Parliament to have their say before using his own, not inconsiderable personality, to outmanoeuvre them into revealing much more than they had intended. Former interviewees had been known to say they didn't know what had come over them. One minute they were expounding the merits of their strategy to the camera and the next they were mesmerised like a rat with a snake by Mark's pale-eyed, hypnotic gaze and found themselves truthfully answering questions of their opinion on subjects they had had no intentions of disclosing on their arrival at the studios.

John Campbell, alone saw this as amusing and revelled in the tussles he had experienced with Mark in this studio. They held each other in mutual respect.

"Do Lady Marion's ancestors come into this story or are you just baiting another hook for me to flounder on?" Mark tried hard to maintain his professional demeanour as he made this remark.

"Lady Marion, such a fine title for my wee lass. I just can't get over it. I'll need to watch my Ps and Qs or I'll find myself being dominated by my wife." He twinkled at the audience who roared in appreciation. It was common for Jock to give the impression that he was henpecked and feared the wrath of the tiny sweet woman he had been married to since his youth.

"Mairn comes from a family of outlaws." He shot a speculative look in Mark's direction. "I don't of course mean she's a gangster's moll." He paused as if giving this some thought before continuing, "Well, being married to me might leave her open to being seen in that light, but way back, when Lockerbie was a wee village, William Johnstone was the kingpin. Despite being a warden of the marches, he met his own ends before those of the community. You might call him the Alex Salmond of the seventeenth century!"

"What exactly was a warden of the marches?" interpolated Mark. "I've heard of the border celebrations of 'Riding of the Marches'. Is there a connection there?" Mark was floundering from lack of research but who could have known that this interview would need such extended knowledge of Border traditions? He felt himself blushing for his lack of familiarity with the subject. Usually so erudite and up to the minute on any aspect of the life and times of his interviewee, he was out of his depth in this case. However, he tried gamely to keep control of the situation. It was a fruitless attempt as he would have been the first to admit. Lord John Campbell of Lockerbie was indisputably in charge.

"Aye, my wife's ancestor became Warden of the Middle March on the death of his father, not long after the events I've just related." He stopped and looked keenly around him, aware that this interview was long over its allotted time.

"Do you have time for a wee history lesson?" he asked.

Mark, who had long since signalled to his production team and cameramen that he had no intentions of losing this headline-grabbing television exclusive, indicated with an all-encompassing sweep of his arm around the studio.

"The floor is yours, Lord Campbell and I, for one, am all agog to hear your story." The audience showed their agreement by a standing ovation, resettled themselves more comfortably in their seats and waited for Big Jock to continue his tale.

Long years of political rallies and speech making allowed Jock to gauge the attention of his audience. Every eye was upon him.

He smiled.

"Are you all sitting comfortably?" Without waiting for a reply, he continued, "In order to understand the Borderers, you need to know what made them as they are today or at least how they were in the early years of our country. The political climate between England and Scotland, as you no doubt know, has never been easy. The Scots annexed England and Scotland lost her Stone of Scone to the English invaders. I'm impartial, you'll understand," he smiled in an aside. Both countries had been the victims of invasions by sea, some invaders staying to 'civilise' their conquests, others raping and slaying in order to take possession of the lands they coveted. The most prominent of these invaders were the Romans who built that infamous wall between the two countries; whether Romans built it or local blokes were persuaded to do the dirty work is a matter for scholars. The purpose of the wall is also in dispute, whether it was a protection from the warlike Scots for those south of the border or a corral to fence in the English depends to a large extent on which side of the border you were born. We won't debate that here. Whatever the viewpoint, Hadrian's masterpiece of earthworks and towers formed the border between the two countries and has stayed much the same to this day. Since Flodden, that ignominious defeat by a much smaller English army, until the amalgamation of England by the Scots when James VI of Scotland became James I of England there existed a condition of state terrorism where the kings of both countries encouraged border barons to fight amongst themselves to keep them from thinking about challenging the sovereignty. So three hundred years of Border unrest took place. In an attempt to keep the peace a separate law of the Borders was devised."

He looked over at the spectators with an impish grin, "I'll show off my knowledge of Latin. Once a lawyer, always a lawyer. This set of laws was the *Legis Majeorum* and was overseen by the wardens of the marches. Three marches either side of the border." Again looking out into the audience he conducted them. "Western, Middle and Eastern. James Johnstone became Warden of the Middle March and it was his responsibility to judge cases of lawbreaking specific to the Borders and to ride the borders of his march to see no boundary was broken. Hence the Riding of the Marches as we know it today."

Looking in Mark's direction, he asked, "Do you know about the border reivers?"

Mark showed a blank face and replied, "Vaguely, I have an image of a cattle rustler in my head. Would that be correct?"

"Well, for the most part that is the case and they came to have a reputation for stealing animals over the border, but the original reivers were small armies made up of the baron's liegemen with a remit to cause as much trouble as possible to the neighbours across the border. Both sides were at fault. There were no angels in these bands of men. Each army consisted of between thirty and fifty retainers of a baron and wore the uniform of a soldier, with sword, targ and breastplate under a tweed Jimet, but the defining image that is responsible for their romantic image today was the steel helmet that has led to them being called the Steel Bonnets. All over the world there are descendants of the border reivers: Grahams, Maxwells and, of course, Johnstones.

"James Johnstone was a Warden of the Middle March, but how do you decide which cow belongs to which man when it has changed its field so many times? The reivers were often poor men desperate to feed their families, so it was easy for him to turn his blind eye to evidence if it was in his best interest. He might even have been funding some of the raids and, as the motto of the Johnstone's is *Num Quam Non Paratus*, 'Never Unprepared' or 'Ready, Aye Ready', it could have been he who instigated the reivers' habit of carrying the colours of their opposite number in case they were caught in the act."

Again his gaze swept the listening crowd.

"You might say they hedged their bets. Does that remind you of the politicians of today? We haven't come so very far in five centuries," Jock said sadly.

"Lord John, I don't want to interrupt your so fascinating story but I'm sure I speak for the audience when I say, interesting as it is, what have these reivers to do with your wife, Lady Marion?" Mark asked with some trepidation; the last thing he wanted was for Lord John to stop his narration, but he felt he had allowed him to wander too far from the point.

"Aye, the Steel Bonnets are one of the passions I intend to indulge now that I am no longer called to Holyrood. You are right Mark; they are incidental to the story but touch on it only where it affects our families. By the time my ancestor settled in

Lockerbie, these wild days of baronial infighting were over, but old habits die hard and farmers and cotters were still making the occasional foray across the border to rustle cattle and sheep in an effort to make ends meet, and sometimes it was just too much hassle to bother with the journey over the border and they just went next door. As I said, one sheep looks very like another."

He took in Mark's quizzical look before remarking, "A politician has always to take the long way round to his point." He held up his great paw so that the studio lights caught the sparkling ruby.

"No, Mark, I've arrived. Rosie was betrothed, unhappily it appears, to Liam. A man with an eye to the main chance, Geordie is in love with Rosie and her friend Mary is about to become the wife of James Johnstone and my Marion's many greats grandmother."

Chapter Six

Geordie looked up from his porridge plate with his spoon poised midway between his half-eaten oats and his mouth. His eyes slowly worked their way round the momentarily empty kitchen as he thought about the changes that had taken place in this room since he had first been welcomed into it nine months before.

"It's funny how I never noticed how things were changing," he mused to himself.

The happy convivial atmosphere had become strained, there was discontent where once there had been harmony, each inhabitant of the kitchen sensing the change that had taken place so subtly that no one could quite pinpoint the source of their growing unease.

Three months after Geordie had accepted the job of shepherd and general yardman that had been offered, Peter had fallen off a ladder in the granary and hurt his leg. True to form he had struggled on with his chores, ignoring the pleas of his womenfolk to rest and recover. The injury had become infected but, until it had swollen to a size challenging the girth of the old oak tree in the yard, he continued to accept only Maggie's ineffectual ministrations.

Eventually, after much persuasion the doctor was called and the healing began, but fate had not yet finished with Peter Herminsone. The long hours lying in the chair or bed had caused a clot of blood to form in his vessels and just as recovery had become a certainty, the clot shook loose, travelled to his brain and Peter sustained a stroke which had kept him chained to his bed, totally dependant on Maggie and Rosie for the last six months.

"Peter's incapacity is not the cause, though," Geordie mused. "Things were not so bad; even when Peter was at his worst there was still harmony in this kitchen. We were all pulling in the same direction. It is more radical than that." Geordie just could not put his finger on the feeling of unrest he felt every time he entered the house.

During the initial days of his disability Peter had become extremely fretful, worrying continually what would become of Rosie if he were to die leaving her unprotected.

Much to Rosie's chagrin he had arranged for the Reverend Hugh Ramsay and Doctor McLean to negotiate for a marriage contract with his nearest neighbour's son, Liam Maxwell.

Rosie had argued vehemently against the match, but then the doctor drew her aside, saying, "Lassie, lassie, ye'll kill your guid faither wi your argufying. It is your duty to mind your faither. This is his only way of being at peace. You do what you're told and give him your obedience."

"But Doctor, Liam is a boy I have never been friendly with. He always taunted us girls whenever we met and I don't think he has changed that much since he grew up."

"Nevertheless, he is your father's choice of a husband for you and you have no option but to obey. It is your father's right to give you to any man he sees fit. It is a shame that he has indulged you so much for you'll be a sad burden on young Liam," Doctor Mclean said sternly. His tightly drawn brows made it apparent with whom his sympathies lay.

It was evident then to Rosie that she had to accept this decree or perhaps be responsible for the death of her much loved father. So it was with heavy heart that she had become betrothed to Liam and the marriage arranged for the week after Rosie's nineteenth birthday in November. Never had a girl looked forward less to a birthday. She looked on the bright side though, for Rosie's cup was always half full. She had managed to screw a small concession from her father, convincing him that she could not marry until she was comfortable that he was on the road to recovery. Peter was loath to accept those circumstances since his whole reason for arranging the betrothal was to secure Rosie and the farm, but he had never been able to withstand the pleas of his darling daughter so had given in. Rosie prayed for his recovery, not only because it would stay her wedding day, but because her father held first place in her heart.

"But that rapscallion wasn't pleased," reflected Geordie as he brought his attention back to the cooling porridge in his bowl and quickly consumed the remainder. "Liam is already lording it over Peter's acres. I often have to bite my tongue not to tell him where he is going wrong."

Geordie had initially tried to give advice to the young pretender, who despite being the son of a prosperous farmer, had had very little to do with the day-to-day running of a busy farm. Liam knew very little about ploughing or planting seasons, when to put animals together for breeding to give them the best chance of producing living offspring.

"In fact," thought Geordie as he drew in a deep sigh, "he knows next to nothing about any of the mundane matters that constitute the running of a prosperous hill farm, and this one is slowly sinking into the mediocre."

All might have been saved if only Liam had been prepared to ask for advice from his father or Peter or even from Jake Graham who all knew the land like the back of their well worn hands, but Liam was an arrogant youth, mighty blown up in his own estimation of himself as master of Capelfoot and would listen to no one.

The crease deepened on Geordie's brow as these thoughts passed from his mind and he moved on to the relationship between Liam and Rosie. The quiet giant shook his head as he recalled the many occasions when he had come across Rosie standing, legs akimbo, hands on hips giving Liam a piece of her mind because he had countered her decisions in the dairy or had moved Jake from a priority activity to a less vital undertaking.

He recalled the sly smile on Liam's lips as he stood nonchalantly listening to Rosie while all the while making her angrier since she could see he was taking no notice of her words. When she had completed her reasoned argument he would nod and murmur quietly, "But I'm the farmer here and before long you will have to dance to my tune too, pretty Rosie."

"That poor wee lassie is caught between a rock and a hard place," reflected Geordie as he contemplated his empty bowl. "Can't talk to Peter for fear of making him ill and can't stomach the man her father has picked for her. I'm only the hired help, as Liam is at great pains to make me understand, but it will be a crying shame if that bonnie wee lass is tied to a tyrant whose only care is to gain her father's farm."

Without any conscious thought on Geordie's part the pretty, fiery Rosie had slipped into the place vacated by the cool, aristocratic Merlaine in his unconscious soul. Since the day he had first set eyes on Rosina he had ceased to have the dreadful dreams depicting Merlaine's end. It was as if she had told him to stop grieving and get on with life without her. If anyone should have intimated to him that he was in love with the maid he would have vociferously denied it, yet, secretly, he admitted to himself that he found thoughts of her invading his being when lying in his cot at night, leading him to spend many sleepless hours trying to figure out ways to help her without bringing on the demise of her father, or enraging Liam. It was definitely Geordie's intention to allow Liam to continue to believe him to be a blockish shepherd, as thick as his own sheep. If ever Liam got the notion that Geordie was working against him he would have him off the farm and out of the area quicker than he could blink an eye. And then who would there be to protect Rosina from that arrogant youth now that he had rid the farmhouse of Maggie, who had been there all her life?

Rosie entered the kitchen where Geordie sat at his breakfast almost hidden behind the pile of bed sheets she had just taken from Peter's bed. An acrid eye-watering stench of stale urine emanated from the pile. Her brow was furrowed as she thought about her poor father lying in the cold damp clothes all night. All the time she had been cleaning him she had felt guilty that she could not tend to his needs both day and night.

As she made her way through the kitchen out into the stockyard and across the muddied cobbles to the washhouse, her shoulders slumped.

"If only Maggie were here," she thought for perhaps the hundredth time that morning as she did nearly every morning, but Liam had made her see how selfish she had been in expecting Maggie to remain as housekeeper when she had Jake and her cottage to see to. A rogue thought flashed through her head that it was unlike Maggie to leave her to her own devices, since she had thought neither her father or Rosie could do anything without her managing their lives for them. They had often laughed together about Maggie's bossy ways.

Rosina thought back to the conversation she had had with Liam when she had voiced her concern about her old nursemaid looking sad rather than glad since her marriage to Jake. Liam had looked at her worried face and seized the chance to gain his own ends.

"Maggie is such a good soul, Rosie, ma pet, that she is torn between her own happiness with Graham and what she sees as her duty here with you in the house. She wants to have her own fireside and keep her cottage cosy for her man to come home to, but she thinks she has to stay with you, at least until we are married." He caressed her cheek and smiled sadly into her upturned face.

"I'm afraid you are being a little selfish, what with delaying our nuptials and keeping Maggie away from her man; while she thinks you are in need of her, she will put her own happiness second to yours."

Rosina's first reaction to this remark was anger. How dare he question her behaviour? Liam, who only ever thought of a situation in terms of how he could benefit from it, telling her off for being selfish! The cheek of the man! The words, however, made her think of Maggie and the many extra hours she was kept away from her new husband now that, with the care of the invalided Peter, the work in the house had more than doubled. Since she could not see how Maggie's leaving the kitchen could in any way benefit Liam, she was forced to acknowledge that he was, for once, thinking of someone other than himself. Although she still did not want to be married to Liam, his consideration of the housekeeper gave her a better opinion of her fiancé.

Nevertheless, she was puzzled.

"I've known Maggie all my life. She has been like a mother to me, indeed she is the reason I haven't missed a mother in my life. Surely she would tell me if she wanted to stop keeping house for Faither and me, wouldn't she?"

"Aw Rosie, you are an innocent! If she were to tell you how she feels about all the extra work your father's illness has made and how many hours she has to stay away from her own hearth and husband to tend his needs, you would think her ungrateful for all the years Peter has fed and housed her. She was only a workhouse brat after all, not a member of your family. The truth is that when she married Jake she expected to stop work altogether and become a housewife and that is what Graham wants for himself; a wife who cares for him, but he knows they would not be welcome on the farm if he complained of the hours Maggie spends in the farmhouse. Believe me, Rosie, Maggie just stays with you to safeguard Jake's job. They would have no home or livelihood if she were to displease you. She is protecting her man to her way of thinking."

He glanced up surreptitiously from under his long lashes to see how successfully he had made his point. He never knew with Rosie. Other girls would have gone to any lengths to be in Liam Maxwell's good books but Rosina was of a different stamp. Pity she was the means of him gaining his independence from his father's rule.

Satisfied that Rosie had indeed taken on board his words and was busy mulling over this new and unexpected information he went on, "If you were to make Maggie believe that you were no longer a little girl in need of her constant help and guidance, but a maid desperate to make a home for her husband, she would be out the back door and across the yard to Jake's cott so fast the sparks from her clogs would set the hayricks alight.

"Aye, Rosie, I think it is you who are being hard on Maggie," he said this with a sad, sheepish expression as if he were displeased at the behaviour of his betrothed for not living up to his expectations.

"In any case," he continued, "how hard would it be for you to find a maid, either to take over the care of Peter, or to manage your chores in the dairy? I could find you a dozen willing to live here with a full belly in exchange for the work."

"But Maggie would be offended if I employed a maid. This is more her kitchen than mine: I can't upset my good friend, Liam. Maggie is no ordinary housekeeper," she argued back.

Liam's lips formed a straight line of annoyance. He was not used to his women defying his whims but Rosina was responding exactly as he had anticipated when he had prepared his arguments to swing her to his way of thinking. Getting rid of Maggie, who never failed to show her dislike for him or for the bargain his and Rosina's parents had made for them, had to be Rosina's idea. He knew Rosina was not in love with him but while this state of affairs riled him, he was arrogant enough to expect instant obedience from his wife to be; this charade of being a fond betrothed, which irked him considerably, had to be maintained. After the wedding Rosie would pay dearly for questioning his plans.

"You could tell her you wanted to keep the house yourself to show me what a good wife you will be. And it would please your father to think you were looking forward to being mistress of the house when we are married. You must convince Maggie that to stop working in the house is in your best interest. She needs to believe she is doing what is right in leaving you to it and not that you are thinking about her happiness." He almost purred the last words as he stroked Rosie's cheek, but he was unable to completely hide the look of satisfaction on his face as Rosina nodded an understanding of the delicacy required to wean herself from Maggie without the housekeeper suspecting the real reason for her removal from the kitchen and Rosina's life.

Rosie had noticed this look at the time but she had been so distraught by the notion that she was holding Maggie back that the fleeting thought that Liam was angry had not registered, but slipped, unnoticed, through to the back of her mind where it had lodged, until this moment. Now, months later, when she had followed Liam's plan of action and pretended to Maggie that she neither wanted or needed her in her kitchen or helping to nurse her father, she revisited the thought and wondered why Liam, usually only interested in his own well-being, had been so anxious to plead Maggie's cause.

Did Maggie really not want to come to the house even to visit? She had barely shown face since she had stopped working in the house and, although she occasionally visited Peter, she never stopped in the kitchen for a hot drink or even a chat but hurried out the door with barely a word.

Rosina stopped in the act of dunking the stinking sheets into the wash barrel with the poss stick and spoke her thoughts out loud.

"It's just not like Liam to think about anyone but himself."

She absent-mindedly stirred the tub while her mind worked on the idea before coming to a reluctant conclusion.

"No, Liam must have been right and Maggie wanted to give up work and look after her husband. Isn't that what he was always telling her? That after they were married her first duty would be to care for him."

Rosie made a face at this idea but, for the moment resigned to her fate, returned her attention to the washtub taking out her frustration at the defection of Maggie and the pending nuptials on the malodorous tangle in the scummy water.

She toiled on, getting more and more hot and sticky even in the ice-cold washhouse. Her face and neck flushed and her hair, never easily contained, took a life of its own with loose tendrils adhering to her sticky skin. As she became hotter she opened the neck of her blouse and fanned herself with the loose material in an effort to cool her rosy skin.

Dumping the clothes into an old tin basin she lifted this onto her hip, using her behind to hold open the door of the washhouse, made her way back through the stockyard, past the kitchen door and into the orchard at the rear of the house where there were wire strands attached to the lower branches of the trees, making it an excellent place for the sheets to blow in the gusty cold wind. With the drying of the clothes Rosie hoped they would take on some of the sweet-smelling air blowing down off the hills and give her father a taste of the life he was missing.

"Faither is so sad not to be out in the fields anymore. At least if he gets a whiff of the fresh air it will be some consolation," she thought, sighing sadly at the thought of her once robust father unable to leave his bed unattended.

With this idea in her head and thoughts of how she and Peter had tramped into the hills to look at the sheep, and how they had sat on top of the highest hill and Peter had pointed out landmarks to her while telling her stories both of the farm and her mother. These had been great days out and this vision of Peter was the one she kept in a focus as she dealt with his weakening body. Even although she adored her father and would do anything to make him whole again, she couldn't help a sense of resentment at his insistence on her early marriage to Liam. Never one to dwell on matters she couldn't change, Rosie shrugged her tired shoulders and bent to deal with the sheets.

She struggled to throw the waterlogged sheet over the wire. Each time she attempted to fix it the recalcitrant sheet took on a life of its own and slipped off the wire as she bent to get a peg to secure it. With each playful gust of wind, the sheet billowed out, catching the wind and making a break for freedom away from the line. After several attempts to contain the washing to its drying line Rosie's sense of humour, which had been well buried over the last few months, reasserted itself and she laughed out loud, remonstrating at the sheet she was struggling with.

While she was laughing Geordie passed by the edge of the orchard to be confronted by the sight of Rosie, flushed and dishevelled, wrestling with the wet bed sheet, which was blowing all over the place, slapping her indiscriminately as it thrust itself into her unsteady figure.

Geordie leaned on the gate enjoying the rare sight of Rosina with sparkling eyes and laughing mouth. With the neck of her blouse still loosened Geordie had a good view of her throat and the top of her white breasts as she panted with the exertion. The thought came into Geordie's mind that she looked her age today. For too many weeks now, Rosina had looked as if she had the cares of the world on her shoulders as she struggled to care for Peter and keep house without the help of Maggie.

"Poor wee lass," he thought. "And that so-called lover of hers far more interested in gadding about in the inns with his fancy piece than taking care of wee Rosie. I wouldn't be surprised if it was his idea to turn off Maggie. There's another one that doesn't laugh much these days and Jake as taciturn as can be. Well, at least I can help her to hang out her washing, poor help though that may be."

He swung open the gate and entered the orchard. Rosina was alerted to his presence by the squeaking of the hinge. As she turned towards him the laugh still lighting her face his heart turned over in his chest with the realisation that Rosie had secured a prominent place in his heart. She was no longer just his employer's daughter, engaged to a man who was not fit to tie her bootlaces, she had wormed her way into his very core and replaced the image of Merlaine in his unconscious mind. He was struck by the fact that he loved two women. He didn't love Merlaine any less than he had done since the day he met her, but Rosie was a living, breathing woman, very different from the cool Merlaine but just as loveable and he did love her. He admitted it.

"You're in need of a ladder to get that sheet on the line," he joked, gently taking the offending article from her arms and, in one casual movement, threw it over the line. He secured it with one of the wooden pegs purchased from the itinerant gypsies who frequently stopped at the farm on their way to the Appleby horse fair, just over the border.

"We can't all be the size of an oak tree," she responded indignantly as she stepped back to survey Geordie's handiwork. He was in the throes of pegging the second sheet to the line as he replied, having first removed the pegs from between his teeth.

"You never know when I might need to earn my living as a washerwoman," he grinned. "It is as well to have some practise." He sketched a comical curtsey with such a look on his face that Rosina again went off into peals of laughter, which echoed through the apple and pear trees in the orchard, at the vision of the big man scrubbing clothes in the washhouse.

She caught back the laugh and straightened her features into what she thought would look like a serious expression, but succeeded only in appearing impish. Tilting her head to one side to better observe Geordie's antics she continued slowly, considering the bulk of his bulging biceps as he wrangled with the sheets.

"Mmmm, I'm needing to employ a washerwoman, or a dairymaid, with the extra work I have at the moment. I can see the advantages of having a sturdy man in the position. Hanging the clothes on the line would only be a part of it, mind. Oh, how easily you would wring the water out of the jumpers? And when it comes treading blankets and curtains, those massive feet of yours would make short work of them. Would you not consider the position, Geordie?"

"No, no, not me, ma'am," answered Geordie backing away in the manner of a frightened maidservant from her stern mistress. He had finished hanging out the clothes while they had been playing out their little comedy and the wind was billowing the sheets like sails on the ocean and the nightshirt looked for all the world as if it was inhabited by an invisible being. Loath to leave this interval of fun in their workaday lives, Geordie struck a thoughtful pose.

"Mind you, if my hands were always in water they would become nice and soft and my ewes might appreciate the gentle touch when I'm delivering their lambs, but can you imagine my mates in the Black Bull if I entered an arm-wrestling contest with my washday-reddened forearms? How they would mock me! No, all things considered, I will have to decline your kind offer of employment."

He touched his forelock as he turned away from the heart-wrenching picture of the young maid smiling at him. It was rare to see Rosina in such good spirits.

Rosina halted him as he reached out for the sneck on the orchard gate.

"Geordie?" she started, then came to an abrupt halt as though thinking better of what she had been about to say.

"Aye, lass?" he questioned, waiting for her to continue.

"You work a lot with Jake Graham, don't you? I mean, you are friends, aren't you?"

"Well, most days we pass the time of day. There's not much to do on the hill while the animals are grazing on the lower pastures, and since your father took ill I have been trying to help Jake with the beasts. I'm not much good with a ploughshare but cows are just happy to be milked by any hand, even ones as big as mine." He laughed, holding up the offending members. He wondered where Rosina was going with this line of questioning.

"Does he mention Maggie not coming to the house any more?" she asked, wondering about the wisdom of spearing one workman about another.

Geordie tried to evade a straight answer since he did not want to upset Rosina by telling her of Jake Graham's anger at Rosina for getting rid of Maggie.

"He's mighty made up to have married Maggie at long last. The lad had almost given up hope of her ever making an honest man of him." He laughed. "Jake never tires of telling anyone who will listen how lucky he is to have carried off such a prize. My lugs are fair worn out with the battering they get about his Maggie's cooking, his Maggie's knitting, his Maggie's bread. It's a good job he's a reticent soul or I'd be blushing at his Maggie's night-time antics." He laughed, noticing how Rosina still paled at the thought of any physical contact between a man and woman.

Despite the look of anguish on her face, Rosina continued with her train of thought.

"He's never mentioned how Maggie feels about not working any more? I have a horrid feeling that she is angry with me every time I see her, which is not very often. She hardly ever visits Faither, but when she does come I hear her chattering away to him. Even when he doesn't answer with anything but a grunt, she interprets those noises as if she understands them and either agrees with him or has a laugh as if he were cracking a joke. It's good of her to come and he is always brighter when she has visited, but as soon as she comes out of his room her lips close and it is as quick as she can get out the back door. She never waits for a cup of tea or a chat. I only get one-word answers if I ask her a question.

"Oh, Geordie, I did it for the best. Liam said she was only staying for fear of Jake being sacked and that she wanted to be a housewife in her own cottage and the only way to get her to go was to tell her I didn't need her. But, Geordie, what have I done?"

"Now, lass, is it likely that Maggie would be angry with you? You are like a daughter to her although there is no doubt she wouldn't have married Jake if you had needed her. It is a pity you listened to Liam's advice, but a woman must be guided by her man."

"I really did mean it for the best. I could see Maggie and Jake were in love. I used to tease her about it and she blushed every time his name was mentioned. She even made excuses to take the bait out to the fields just to see him. Faither and I used to laugh at her behaving like a young maid but never to hurt her, you understand, just between ourselves" she said quickly so that Geordie wouldn't think they had been insensitive."

She continued.

"With Faither being so ill, and you know he doesn't have much control of his speech, I haven't been able to discuss anything with him, and Liam sounded so sincere and disappointed in me when he told me Maggie was pining for Jake that I took his advice and made it possible for them to marry, but I never wanted her to stop coming in and giving me her guidance. Indeed, I didn't think it was possible that Maggie wouldn't want to instruct me as she has always done."

Geordie, who had weeks ago made up his mind that there must have been some underhand dealings for Rosie to tell Maggie she had no more need for her. He knew Rosie as a kind, considerate maid who would not have hurt her old nurse for the world, so hurried to console her by his words.

"Look, lass, it will be something and nothing. Both you and Maggie have to get used to the idea that you are a grown woman and the situation between you has changed. I'm as sure as can be that Maggie still has your best interest at heart and that you will become close friends instead of child and nurse as time goes on. Leave it as it is at present. I'm certain time will heal the rift."

The sight of her woebegone face tore at his heartstrings and for one moment he almost took her in his arms in an attempt to smooth the worried frown off her face, but just as he made the initial move forward, he was halted in his tracks by a stentorian voice.

"Hoy, Campbell, what are you doing in here? You are supposed to be digging a ditch in the bottom field. Keep your mind on your work or you'll find yourself back on the drove roads!" shouted Liam as he advanced into the orchard, holding the gate open for Geordie to pass before him into the stockyard before sallying forward to meet his betrothed.

Rosie, never comfortable with this young man her father had chosen for her, unconsciously copied the vacant look that had come over Geordie's face at the arrival of Liam, turned towards the line and straightened a sheet that had tangled itself on her wire.

"It was my fault, Liam," she said. "I was having trouble hanging out the washing in this wind and I asked Geordie to help me." She laughed a bit self-consciously, "You must admit he made much lighter work of it than I would have done."

"His duties are with the animals," he started curtly before softening this voice to one he felt would make Rosie's bones melt with desire for him. "Yours on the other hand, have yet to be defined." He circled her waist with his right arm while using his left to turn her face towards him "I can't wait for your birthday and our marriage, pretty Rosie. I'll teach you not to be coy with your husband."

Although this was said in a light flirtatious manner, Rosina was left in no doubt what part of her education he was interested in. She shrugged away from his embrace, quickly lifting the basket of pegs from the ground as an excuse for breaking the hold. How on earth was she to manage being married to Liam when she was unable to tolerate his touch? The very thought of intimacy with Liam reminded her of the almost rape she had suffered.

"I must get back to the kitchen in case Faither is needing me. You won't be best pleased either if I dally here with you and there is no dinner on the table."

"You should not be too busy to pay me some attention. I'll see about getting you a maid from Lockerby to help with your father. I should have done it before like we talked about when Maggie gave up," was his smiling reply.

"Meantime, I must get back to work and so must you." She excused herself as she, all but ran, out of the orchard and away from her betrothed.

"If only I could ask Maggie's advice," she thought with a sigh as she once more entered the kitchen.

****

Liam lifted yet another brimming tankard to his lips, his normally ruddy visage even more flushed from its predecessors as he took in the interested faces of his cronies crowded round a tables in the Blue Bell tap. He took a swift draught of the foaming liquid, wiped the moustache of foamy head on his shirtsleeve and continued to boast of his good fortune.

"Just a few more weeks and I'll be master in truth instead of Peter Hermistone. He already relies on me to tell him how to do things since he is no longer in control of his own bladder, never mind his farm. He pisses and shits in the bed or the floor, just like the sheep in the field," Liam laughed as he eyed the other occupants of the bar who were privy to his loud bluster.

"And he won't get any better now that I have got that interfering old fuss bag in my power. Little does she know who was responsible for her being relieved of her duties," smirked Liam as he looked to see how much his cohorts were admiring his managerial ability.

"How did you get rid of her then?" asked his neighbour in a sceptical voice. His company were not as gullible as to believe Liam's version of events. They knew him for a braggart but were prepared to humour him for the sake of the ale he bought. "She has been in charge of his kitchen ever since his wife died and some say not only his kitchen but also his farm, he was so reliant on her."

"Aye, she was and he believed every word she told him but her big mistake was to defy me. If she had been content to obey my orders, she would still be ensconced at my kitchen fire. I'm maister at Capelfoot and any who are against me will not last long." He spoke in what he thought was a tone such as a laird would use.

"So how come she has gone?" asked a voice from the next table. "Half a story, man, no good to us." He laughed around the associates at his table.

"I have Maggie Graham by the short hairs," Liam persisted. "I'm master of Capelfoot," he repeated, savouring the sound of the words on his tongue, "and Maggie must do as I wish or that stolid man of hers will lose his place. She can't complain to the old man because, just like the wench, she is frightened for his life and if she ignores my instructions her man will lose his place. I bet there are nights when she lies in her bed beside that wrinkled old goat she married and wishes she had not listened to that nursling of hers and stayed single. Still no matter, I would have found another way to ease my path."

His listeners were taking in this gossip avidly and, as Liam took another swig of his ale in preparation to continue his boast, a confused voice asked, "How come you take credit for her marrying Jake? Surely he's no fan of yours to do your bidding?"

Liam glowered at the lad who dared to question his story.

"No, he's not, but he is a mate of my father's, just like Peter. They used to spend many a night together at our kitchen fire with a bottle between them, and he let fall after a couple of glasses how he wished Maggie would see Rosina had grown up and didn't need her to be with her every hour of the day then she would surely agree to marry him. He was fair besotted with her."

"So?"

"Well, I overheard that conversation and, although I wasn't betrothed to Rosina then, I knew Peter and my old man were planning a marriage between us in order to increase the hill acreage, so romantic a proposition don't you think?" he asked scathingly. "Mind, she *is* a sweet armful," he gloated in an aside.

"I thought how much easier it would be to control Rosie if her old nurse wasn't there to take her part if she complained. This was all before old Hermistone's accident, you understand, so there was I playing the ardent lover visiting Rosie as if she were heiress to the crown of Scotland, keeping her at arm's length and no funny business to frighten her off. I just happened to mention in passing how sad Maggie looked and that Jake Graham often sported a similar phisog and how sad it was that she kept turning him down because she didn't want to leave Rosie alone."

He smirked, glancing around the curious faces of his mates before continuing.

"Rosina is such an unselfish wench, which will make her easy to manage after the wedding, that she was aghast that her beloved Maggie was resisting Jake on her account and immediately started a campaign to bring the two together."

"So she married Graham and they live happily ever after then?" came the sarcastic rejoinder from the other side of the table.

"For the moment, but she still lives a bit too close for my liking and visits Peter and Rosie too often. After the wedding, they will both be collecting their bundles and making off for the fairs." A malicious gleam appeared in his eyes as he continued, "Then the sweet, pliant Rosie will only have her adoring husband to think of!"

Carefully keeping his voice at a level which everyone could hear, he continued, "And that sweet maid Rosie, she can't wait for the wedding, always creeping round for a wee cuddle."

He gave a malevolent chuckle before going on with his unrelenting diatribe.

"Such an armful. I'm undecided whether to let her think she has a choice or to make her bend to my will. There's no doubt but she has a fiery temper and a rasping tongue but, you'll see, I'll tame her on our wedding night!"

"You'll not have time for such dalliances when you are running Capelfoot. There are so many acres of hill it's not likely you will be home much to tame that she-devil. And what a she-devil! I don't know if I would change places with you," commented his bosom buddy Gary who was courting a quiet maid who had no thought in her head but to be everything and anything her swain wanted.

"You don't expect I'm going to be up on the hill do you? Peter hired a bucolic highland moron to tend the sheep. Granted he is huge, but he'll be putty in my hands just as Rosie will. The sheep have more inside their skulls than Mister Geordie Campbell. Besides, Faither has seen to it that I will have the deeds of the farm on the day I marry, so I may not keep Capelfoot or Rosie. I might well sell both to the highest bidder."

Liam's steely cold eyes again surveyed his companions as he quaffed the remains of his ale. He noticed the looks of shock and the expression of disbelief on his friends' faces. He really had only made the statement for effect, having every intention of living off the hard graft of Geordie and Rosie, but he was so piqued by his companion's obvious disgust that there and then he decided that Capelfoot would be on the market no later then the day after his marriage had been celebrated.

"But Rosie will not be transferred intact," he thought sneeringly to himself. "I'll see to that all right."

Another round of drinks was called for and the subject changed, since the real object of the gathering was to sample the ministrations of the ladies of ill repute who hung about the alley next to the inn. Liam had a long-standing agreement with Norah Jeffries just as his cohorts had their own arrangements in place. In fact, the lads were only waiting for their female companions to materialize so that the actual business of the evening could begin.

Just on that thought the door of the tap swung open and four prostitutes bustled their way into the company of the young men. Norah lifted Liam's mug of ale and quenched her thirst, thrusting her hips into his shoulder as she leant over to replace the empty mug on the table. She smiled down into his upturned face saying, "One for the road or perhaps a bottle for the bed?"

Liam grinned back, clutching her round the waist and running his hands over her ample backside. "Bed it is!" he cried, raising his voice over the clamour of his followers. "Landlord, a bottle of whisky, if you please," and, throwing the price on the table, he escorted Norah most disreputably out of the Blue Bell.

****

James Johnstone, sitting with his brother Malcolm in the private parlour next door, had listened to the conversation which had taken place in the tap and now had a frowning look of concentration on his face. He and Malcolm were only present in the establishment to meet the coach from Dumfries, which was bringing their young sisters home from the convent for his own wedding that was due to take place in the following week.

Malcolm had not been present at the fair where Rosie and Mary had been attacked so he had no knowledge of the tall giant or where he was working, but James was now betrothed to Rosie's friend who, like Rosie, was being married on attaining the age of nineteen, but in Mary's case this was truly a love match. She had looked up from her terrifying experience beside the loch into the gentle features of a notorious Johnstone and promptly fell in love. James had reciprocated her feelings and, after his initial visit to Mary's father's holding at Rigghead with the excuse of hearing how she fared after her horrific ordeal, he had been a constant visitor and his horse could be seen heading out of the Tower six days out of seven in the direction of his love's home.

He slowly lifted his glass to his mouth and sipped the fiery brandy it contained while he thought what action would be most beneficial to him. He was the biggest landowner in the county and the addition of the Capelfoot acres would be most advantageous to him, since it marched with those of his soon to be father-in-law. Land was always an advantage. His thoughts were interrupted by Malcolm's petulant voice.

"This coach is more than an hour late. I do not like this revolting, malodorous hovel, James. Just because you have demeaned yourself to marry a peasant doesn't mean the rest of the family has to descend to the bog also."

"Mary is not a peasant and even if she were I would still be making her Lady of Lochwood. She is the sweetest and purest thing that it has ever been this family's fortune to merge with. I love her with all my heart, dear brother, and although I may be a devil in other departments there is no ulterior motive for marrying her. Just keep that in mind when your voracious desires rear their repulsive demands."

Just about to call the landlord to replenish the glasses, the sound of heavy coach wheels could be heard entering the inn yard. With one accord the brothers rose, left the cosy snug to brave the chilled night air, hustled their excited young sisters into the waiting family carriage and made the short drive home.

Ignoring the shrill prattle from his gregarious sisters, James continued to cogitate on the information he had gathered in the Blue Bell. "Who said eavesdroppers never hear aught to their advantage?" he mused.

"Is there any left in the bottle?" Norah queried as she lifted herself up on her elbow to survey the disarray in her room.

"There's nothing left in my bottle at any rate. I'm empty," grinned Liam, lying naked on the tangled bedclothes. Since he knew himself to be a fine physical specimen he felt no need to hide his body from Norah's gaze. Although after their exertions he was feeling pretty lethargic, he anticipated his desire for Norah to return momentarily and he toyed with a scenario where she could be reserved for his enjoyment only.

Liam lay sated on the hard flock of her pallet, enjoying the sight of her long shapely limbs from between which he had just emerged. His survey was minute and critical but in this post-coital miasma he could find no fault.

"Norah, Norah, there never was a woman like you. You are magnificent. I wish you could warm my bed every night."

Despite her calling, Norah was a fine-looking woman. It could be argued that business was not so very brisk in Lockerby on a nightly basis and as such she had not had time to become haggard as those of her profession often did, but nevertheless her dark brown hair shone as it fell over her bare shoulder, mirroring the deep brown eyes that looked out from her heart-shaped face. Her neck appeared twice as long as she tipped her head well back in order to drain the very last of the dregs from an almost empty bottle in an attempt to quell her violent thirst. As she slowly removed the bottle from her plump and kiss-bruised lips, she cast a speculative glance over Liam, harking back to his previous remark.

"I would like that fine, Liam, but I have to put bread on my table and you can't afford to pay for me every night. But wouldn't it be grand? No more cold arse up the alley or freezing in some draughty drovers' hut with the loch lapping at the door. If only you were a fine lord, I could be your personal maid."

Giggling drunkenly, she bounced out of bed and pantomimed across the room, bobbing up and down in exaggerated curtseys. "Yes m'lord, I'm ready, willing and able to service you right now. No milord, I won't scrub the floors of your pigsty but I will scrub your back."

Clutching her arms tightly around her stomach she flew back to the bed where she sat astride the sprawled Liam and rubbed her naked womanhood along the length of his flaccid member while the nipples on her large, rounded mammaries hardened in front of his eyes at the thought of the pleasure they had both enjoyed. She was young and vivacious and, having not been long at the pleasuring game, she had a laviscious craving for the warm arms of her partner that was not feigned. In fact, she was enough to turn any young man's head, however handsome he thought himself.

Liam's interest became re-awakened and as he once more began to slake his thirst at Norah's overflowing well, an idea began to germinate in his fertile imagination. As he came to the height of his excitement, he called out, "Why not? Yes, yes, yes. We'll do it!"

Chapter Seven

"Yes, ma'am, I can cook, clean and make butter with the best of them. My family are cotters on the Castle Estate and are tenants of my Lord Bruce," Norah replied demurely to the latest question asked by Rosie. "My mother has been preparing me for this work since I was young."

She did not add that that was the very reason she had left the confines of her parents' home to haunt the back alley behind the Blue Bell where the services she offered had little to do with the employment for which she had been bred or the subsequent breech between herself and her parents, but a great deal to do with the fact that she had no love for household drudgery.

Her features were schooled to foster the belief that she was a plain simple maid, keen to work hard at any of the menial tasks Rosie had detailed to her, while she was inwardly seething at Liam for leading her to believe the position of housekeeper in *his* house was in *his* gift alone. He had made no mention of Rosie, his intended wife, when he had laughingly encouraged her to become his servant. A slight crinkle at the sides of her lips almost gave her thought away as she remembered the moment, immediately after satisfying Liam, when he laughingly offered her a permanent position "as my body servant".

Norah had not anticipated the need to do any actual physical labour and had no intentions of doing so once she had procured the acceptance of his betrothed. She brought herself back from her thoughts to again listen to the words of Rosie.

"You understand that a large part of your duty will be to attend to my father's bodily needs; to feed, bathe and change him, and some of that work is not very pleasant. It will require you and I to work together and take turns to see to his needs in the night hours as well as to help with the household chores."

Rosie smiled which changed the haggard planes of her face and Norah saw the warm, attractive nature of the girl opposite her blossom for a brief second and she thought to herself, "She is a beauty when she smiles and seems to shrug off her cares," and perhaps a glimmer of respect was born in Norah's cold and selfish nature.

For her part, Rosie looked appraisingly at Norah. "There's something not quite right about her story but I can't put my finger on it," she mused but, taking in the fine physical condition of the girl, decided she would be an asset to the farmhouse and, jumping to her feet with a look of decision on her face, said, "Right then, the position is yours if you want it. Let's have a cup of tea to seal the deal," and she swung the kettle over the kitchen fire to bring the water back to the boil. "Then I'll introduce you to Faither before Liam and Geordie appear. You can set the kitchen clock by their stomachs. Never been known to miss a mealtime, those two!" she laughed as she poured the water into the pot and sat it down to mask.

****

That night Geordie lay in his bothy mulling over the events at the evening meal. While maintaining his bucolic countenance he had endeavoured to watch the new addition to the kitchen as the four able-bodied members of the household sat around the table eating a sustaining stew cooked and served by Rosie. She had bustled around filling plates and tending to the fire while the new domestic sat at the table as if an honoured guest. Norah had made no move to help, either with the serving or clearing of the food or offered to feed Peter his portion. Geordie was hard put not to keep his entire attention on Rosie, for the heat of the fire and the exertion of attending to the table and to her father in the adjacent room had heightened her colour, giving her a glow which went straight to Geordie's heart like an arrow from a longbow. Geordie flicked occasional glances at Liam who showed no signs of discontent with the manners of the new addition, which to Geordie's mind was uncommon, for he liked nothing better than to exercise his assumed position as head of the household. On one of these occasions Geordie intercepted a smirk from Liam in the direction of Norah and this was answered with a very pert wink before she resumed the mask of a shy maid.

His alert brain noticed she was also sending furtive calculating looks in his direction, but, when she succeeded in meeting his eyes, her gaze was full of speculation, holding none of the teasing promise she had directed at Liam.

When the meal was over and the kitchen tidied somewhat, Rosie turned and smiled at Norah, saying, "Come up to the top floor and I will show you where you are to sleep. It is warm and cosy up in the rafters and an ideal place for you to hear Faither if he should need you in the night as it is directly above the book room. Poor Faither, the running of the farm has always been his pleasure as well as his life's work, you know, and to have to make his business room into a bedroom has sorely tried him, for he must depend on Liam to know what is best since he can no longer express his wishes."

She sent a piercing look over the table to Liam before continuing.

"I wish you would spend more time talking to him about the fields and the animals for he greatly misses being involved in the everyday decisions. It might help his recovery to hear what you men are about."

Liam shrugged nonchalantly, saying, "I can make no sense of his mumbles, so I can't answer what he is asking, and besides, I am running the farm now and he need have no more concern with it."

Rosie bit down on the answering arguments that jumped into her mouth, rightly assuming that Liam would not take kindly to being thwarted in front of the 'hired help' as he had taken to calling Geordie and Jake. She sighed as she reflected that every meal was a battlefield these days. "Gone are the days when maister and servants gathered together as one happy family," she thought before continuing aloud, too exhausted to continue her urging, "Come on Norah. Let's get you settled."

Geordie lay wide awake in his bothy staring at the ceiling wishing for the languor to take hold and send him off to rejuvenating sleep. He had another hard day tomorrow – "no, today," he grimaced – as he once more tried to find a comfortable position to help ease his mind over the edge into slumber.

For some unknown reason he had been unable to sleep despite the hard physical labour he had been involved in since dawn. Sometimes in the night watches he laughed to himself as he remembered his early life and wondered what his sire and brothers would make of him sleeping in a draughty bothy at the beck and call of those far beneath his former social position. He knew his proud and arrogant father would be disgusted, but Geordie was surprised, several months after his incursion into the ménage at Capelfoot, that, if not exactly happy (since memories of Merlaine's fate still haunted his conscience), then he was at least contented with the manual work and camaraderie he had encountered from all, save Liam, at Capelfoot.

After several more attempts to make himself comfortable enough to induce sleep, he gave up the ghost and, swinging his long legs out from under the quilt, pulled on his breeches and pushed his feet into his boots, and then quietly left the bothy, crossed the stockyard and entered the orchard. He wandered among the trees taking in the sweet smell of the fruity bark that hung heavy in the crisp, clear air. Everything smelt so fresh and new as if the night had washed away the dirt and grime of the daytime to provide a utopian paradise for the creatures of the night.

Geordie stopped to look up at the heavens where the tiny bright twinkling stars appeared like diamonds sparkling on a velvet cape. "I wonder what is happening at home," he mused. "This country is so different from my birth land but if Jamie had survived the onslaught, he would have been gazing at the same stars in the same ebony sky." He sighed for the loss of his brother with a sadness tinged with what-ifs. What if he had not led the company? What if Jamie had lived? What if Merlaine had not been slaughtered? What if the children had stayed at Inverlochy?

Without taking his gaze from the midnight sky he shrugged himself back to the moment, again enjoying the peace and serenity that the quiet night always instilled in him. Even the snuffling of the small nocturnal animals going about their nightly business did not in any way disturb the peace and tranquillity that the night brought him.

He had been leaning on the trunk of an old apple tree and, with his dark clothing merging into the deep shadows, he had been almost indistinguishable from the trunk itself. Just as he was thinking about returning to his cot he was alerted by noise that was at odds with the peaceful surroundings. Geordie froze in his position as he realised he was no longer alone in the orchard. "Who else is unable to sleep this night?" he wondered as his ears became aware of another being breathing close by.

As he started forward to make his presence known to this fellow night owl a whisper was heard from the direction of the stockyard.

"Liam, Liam, are you there?"

"What a time you have been. There will be no time to enjoy ourselves before the men are up and at work. You'll have to do better in future if you are to remain here," Liam's voice was heard to answer crossly.

Always confident in his own worth, he saw no need to lower his voice. He was maister after all; who would dare to ask questions of *him*?

"Come in here now and give me a cuddle. I have need of your ministrations, mistress housekeeper," Liam laughed as the sight of Norah in her bedgown restored his good humour.

From his discreet position by the apple tree Geordie was able to overhear Norah's earthy laugh as she at once obeyed Liam's commands, entering the orchard and sashaying over to him, turning a petulant face up to be kissed while she explained that she had been unable to get away any earlier as Peter had needed attention and, even though it was Rosie who had attended to his needs, she, Norah, had been unable to get out of the house until Rosie had returned to her room and could be expected to have gone back to sleep. Despite her urgent desire for her handsome employer, Norah had made up her mind that Liam should be made to suffer for not telling her the situation at Capelfoot. She had been taken aback when greeted by his prospective wife, and even more upset to be offered the menial position of maid when she had understood Liam to be making her his housekeeper. This would have been bad enough, but she was undecided whether he could be forgiven for foisting upon her the care of the paralysed and incontinent man now sleeping comfortably in the best room downstairs. When Rosie had taken her in to introduce her to her father Norah had been rendered speechless while Rosie listened to his grunts and mumbles, pretending to understand what he needed.

When they had come out of the room again, Rosie had explained. "I can see you are surprised that Faither and I can communicate" she grinned. "We can't actually, but he is my faither so I can mostly anticipate his needs. When you start caring for him you will be able to work out what he needs for yourself. It's pretty simple. If he wets the bed, you change it and wash him down. If he is slumped down on his pillows, you lift him up." She smiled a reassuring smile at her new maid, laying her hand gently on her arm. "He is not a cretin, you know; he had only lost his speech, not his wits."

As Norah thought about her first day in Capelfoot farmhouse she was minded to take off back to the alley behind the Blue Bell. It was touch and go for a few moments as she stood inanimate before Liam.

"For goodness sake, I left home to avoid mucking out the cows. How much worse is the situation Liam has landed me in?"

But as she looked up at the ardent expression on Liam's face she was lost. She knew he was taking advantage. She knew he was sly. She knew he didn't love her, but she was pretty sure he didn't love Rosie either so she kept her recriminations to herself. "For now, at least, I'll accommodate him. Until it serves me better. Capelfoot is warmer and more comfortable than a drover's hut."

Arrogant as he was Liam had no notion how close he had come to being deserted. His mind was running on how to make Rosie amenable to moving Norah's sleeping quarters to where she would be more accessible to tend to his manly needs. He pondered this while holding Norah in the circle of his arms.

Unconsciously stroking her ample assets, he mused, "We will need to find you a better place to sleep so that you are available for your duties." Looking down on her pretty face, he quickly caught her lips under his and soundly kissed her, leaving them both breathless. "These are the duties I want you for, not cleaning up Peter's shit and stuffing his face with food to keep him alive longer. As soon as the wedding is over and Capelfoot is mine it will not be long before he meets his maker and that saintly prude of a daughter of his finds herself begging for my favours."

Geordie felt a hot and cold shiver run up and down his spine as the penny dropped and he realised that Liam had succeeded in admitting his mistress into his betrothed wife's home. He would need to find a way of protecting her. This he vowed to do, whatever the cost.

Chapter Eight

The Wedding

Rosina awoke to the sun forcing its rays through the deep window embrasure and a gust of soft, warm air caressing her cheek. For a minute, she was confused, then she remembered that today was Mary's wedding and that, as a bridesmaid, she had spent the night with her best friends in preparation for the wedding feast that would be taking place today here at Lochwood Tower, the castle and keep of the Johnstone clan.

Rosie's sunny mood soon evaporated as the thoughts of her own impending wedding entered her head, casting a black shadow over this happy day. For a few moments she lay contemplating how she could get out of the betrothal for she was far from contented with the current state of her matrimonial prospects. No matter how often she applied her brain to schemes to avoid the marriage, she always came up with the same stumbling block. This was a plan her father had set his heart on and she loved him far too much to endanger his health. What if he had another shock and died? How could she ever be happy knowing she had caused the death of her beloved father?

"I will not think about it today," she decided as she swung her legs out from under the rich fur coverlet under which she had snuggled the previous night, wallowing in the luxury that was soon to be Mary's after her marriage today.

She cast her eyes once more around the sumptuous appointments of the room; from the rich wall hangings, sewn by the women of the clan Mary was about to join, to the luxurious skins that covered the floor. She was jealous of none of this but the one thing she envied her friend was the huge fireplace that took up most of one wall, where, even at this early hour, the remains of last evening's fire still gave off heat into the stone-built room. She stopped in her tracks for a moment to contemplate the extravagance of rising in the farmhouse bedroom in the dead of winter to an atmosphere such as this.

"Ach well!" she shrugged her shoulders, "I've survived thus far," and she continued to start her day.

"This is Mary's day and she is so in love with James. Who would have thought such a horrendous experience could have brought about this joyful prospect?" she mused as she poured cold water from the jug into the basin. She shivered as the icy splash shocked her system but she continued her ablutions, far too excited to wait until the many servants of the Johnstone family brought hot water up to the chambers. Deciding against getting dressed so early, she tiptoed across the palatial room still marvelling at the many rugs covering the cold stone floor keeping her bare feet from getting chilled. No matter what the time of year little heat penetrated the austere stones of the building. Despite being the family home, the tower had been built firstly as a defence from raiders crossing the border between England and the Lowlands of Scotland. From the outside, the tower looked very drear and imposing, a threat to any who thought to breach its walls, but the Johnstone family over the years, whilst maintaining their reputation as hard fighting men, were extremely shrewd in matters of marriage and had been fortunate over the centuries to have married sensible women who had turned the interior of the tower into a comfortable home for their menfolk.

As Rosie left the room she had been allocated and wandered along the corridor towards that which Mary had temporarily been allotted while still a guest, she let her gaze meander along the walls and marvelled once more at the opulence of the house.

The walls of the square gallery that surrounded the grand staircase were lined with a fair representation of the life of the Johnstone men. There were portraits of ancestors that clearly intimated the connection through the ages; each of the men showed the traits of his progenitors, the bright blue eyes and straight thin nose being most noticeably descended from generation to generation. There were trophies that showed the prowess of the men in both the hunting and fighting fields. The horns of deer and weapons and banners covering most of the grey stone expanse paid tribute to the men of the family but, as Rosie continued her perusal of the walls, she was struck by the notion that women were not highly esteemed in this area.

"Fighting men who hold women cheap," was Rosie's thought as she unconsciously lifted her chin in vexation at the lot of the female of the species.

"I hope Mary knows what she is getting herself into, marrying herself to this family," she mused. A grin appeared on her pretty face as she realised she was worrying about nothing. Mary and James were so much in love and he treated her like a piece of precious porcelain when near her and despite his outward brash manner it was obvious that nothing was too good for his beloved Mary.

"Yes, this will be a good marriage." For a fleeting moment her thoughts left Mary and James and focused once more on the relationship between herself and Liam, and the future they might have together, before she pulled herself back to the present moment and continued into Mary's chamber, where the bride to be was propped up on her pillows, drinking a cup of chocolate.

The look on Mary's face was enough to send any thoughts of the tough Johnstone men out of Rosie's mind. She had never seen her friend look so radiant.

"Well, if this is what the thought of a wedding does to you, maybe I should consider following you to the altar," she joked.

Mary smiled up at her friend. "James' mother brought an army of servants in early this morning to make up the fire and feed me breakfast and chocolate, for she says I must be feeling and looking my best all day and you can't do that on an empty stomach." She laughed over the rim of her cup.

"Oh Rosie, she looks so stern when she is dressed and presiding over the dinner table but she is so kind and motherly. She came specially to tell me that she was delighted with James' choice of bride and looked forward to having me in the Tower as a friend and daughter." Mary's eyes were brimming with tears at the kindness of this great lady.

"No tears today, young lady," said Rosie with hands on hips. "This is a day of pure pleasure and she is right: James has made an excellent choice for his wife."

Mary patted the cover over her legs as she said, "Sit a minute before the melee starts and my sisters steal the quiet. I am so excited but a bit frightened of the night. I love James, but after that time at the fair I'm scared what I will do when the time comes to go to bed with him. I want to be a good wife." She blushed prettily and with her fair hair spread behind her and her eyes still wet from the earlier tears she looked just like a china doll, fragile and delicate.

"He is a vigorous man and I expect he has much experience with women, so he will know perfectly how to deal with the situation. He knows all about your ordeal," Rosie answered with a thoughtful look on her face. She continued, "When Maggie was telling me about growing up and marriage," she screwed up her face at the memory of Maggie's no nonsense disclosures, "she said that there was nothing to fear if a man and woman were in love; that it would all come as naturally as night follows day." She laughed. "You know Maggie!"

Giving herself a shake to scatter her fearful thoughts Mary bounced out of bed and hugged her childhood friend. "I am so grateful to James and you and Maggie and everyone," she ended as she whirled away round the room before stopping short as the door opened and her sisters entered with minds set on dressing the bride for the ceremony ahead.

"It will be a good marriage," Rosie thought to herself again as she joined the sisters as they prepared Mary for the day to come.

****

"Guid luck tae ye, Maister Johnstone."

"Gran lass ye've got yer haunds on, m'lord."

With each greeting from neighbour and worker the grin on James' face grew wider. The wedding, held in the great hall of the tower which had previously served as a barracks for the personal army of the Johnstones, had gone well and Mary was now his wife. His eyes followed her as she circulated amongst their guests. She made a good hostess, talking to each and every person in the room, whether they hailed from castle or cottage. She was not in the least bit shy even of the rough men "and who could have blamed her after her horrendous experience at the Lamb Fair if it had frightened her off all men forever?" he mused, thinking back to how he had dealt with those men. They won't bother any more young lasses," he grimaced.

He looked forward to the night hours aware that he had to use his bride with care. He smiled to himself as he thought of his salad days when he and his brother had frequented the 'ladies of the night', who had their stomping ground in the alley behind the Blue Bell.

As his eyes continued to watch Mary he saw that she was talking to her best friend Rosie. He frowned as it occurred to him that she was no longer the cheerful, smiling girl she had been. She looked pale and washed out, and, although she had a smile pinned to her lips as she laughed with her companion, there was no reciprocal gleam in her eyes and her body had an odd tension about it.

"You'd think she was the one who had a near escape from ravishment on the banks of the Quaas," he reflected.

Just as this was passing through his mind her betrothed, Liam Maxwell arrived at her side placing a proprietorial hand on her arm and attempting to draw her away from the conversation.

Rosie jerked convulsively, trying to evade his grip, but Liam was not to be spurned. As James took in the scene playing out in front of him he was struck by the change in both of their faces. Rosie's lost what little animation James had been able to discern while talking to Mary, while Liam's eyes burned with an anger that was apparent even from the other side of the room. He was whispering something in Rosie's ear. If it hadn't been for the white-knuckled fingers with which he held her, any onlooker would think he was spooning with his bride to be.

"Now that lass is not in love with that lad," James considered from his position as ardent husband. He kept his eyes upon the pair as he quaffed more ale from his tankard. He was keeping well away from the strong spirits that were being pressed on him, with the knowledge of his forthcoming first night with Mary, so it could be argued that he was the soberest person in the great hall.

Removing the tankard from his lips, he caught a movement out of the corner of his eye.

"It appears I'm not the only one who has noticed this less than lover-like Maxwell and he's none too pleased about it either by the face on him," thought James.

He laid his tankard down on a handy shelf and wandered over in the direction of the glowering shepherd who stood against the grey stone wall, looking for all the world as if he was trying to blend in with the masonry.

Geordie Campbell and he could not be said to be great friends, but they had formed a loose bond by the side of Loch Quaas as they had striven together to save the virtue of Rosie and his wife. If James had thought about him at all, it was to wonder how a shepherd and drover was so well versed in the gentlemanly arts and courtesies. There was something just not quite right about Campbell but James had given this instinct very little consideration.

"How goes it, Campbell?" James greeted the big man with an outstretched hand and a smile.

"It's a fine day you are having and I must congratulate you on the looks of your fair bride, my Lord," answered Geordie as the two men clasped hands.

"Aye, I'm a lucky man, right enough." Something triggered in his brain as he took in the lop-sided grin of his companion. He had a feeling of déjà vu, but the image that entered his brain was not of a shepherd in Hoddam Grey but of a tall, sumptuously dressed older man at court in Stirling.

"Are you not toasting my beautiful lady wife? Let me get you a dram."

"No thank you, my Lord. My maister yonder," he nodded in the direction of Liam where he still held Rosie captive, "desired that I keep myself away from strong spirits and capable of driving him and the lass home. And mind I've an idea that sobriety might well be needed to protect the maid." This last was almost inaudible but James caught the words and also the implication.

"It's like that, is it?" questioned James as he looked consideringly at Geordie.

"Aye, I don't know what got into Peter's head after he had that stroke, but I cannot believe that he has chosen that braggart for his lass. He idolises her but on that subject he is firm. She will marry Liam rather than harm her father and there is little doubt he is only after the farm, so the poor wee lass is between a rock and a hard place for you can see she does not relish his attentions." He nodded to where his eye rested on Rosie.

James squinted again at the pair before continuing slowly, "You know my brother and I were in the Blue Bell, keeping the chill out, you understand," he grinned, "while waiting for my sisters' return from the convent in Dumfries for the wedding, and he was boasting to the farmer lads he was with that he would be Maister of Capelfoot on his wedding day and the very next he would be selling to the highest bidder."

"The bastard!" exclaimed Geordie clenching his fist even tighter. "It's bad enough that he has inveigled Rosie into taking in his fancy piece," he snorted. "As a nurse for Peter and help for Rosie, you understand, but Rosie does all the work and Norah swans about like the lady of the manor. Mind, give her her due, though she's not grand at dealing with the shitty sheets she does keep Peter's spirits up. I don't know what they talk about or how she understands what he says, but I've heard her prattling away and him making noises like laughter and he always seems more cheerful when Norah's with him. If only…" Geordie stopped his speech abruptly and drove his hand deep into his sporran, drawing James' attention to the movement.

"What? If only what?" his companion questioned the obviously angry man. Then his eyes widened as he caught a glimpse of what was in Geordie's hand. He was so surprised that he was momentarily struck dumb. Within seconds, his numbed brained had reasserted itself and his vague recollections had fallen into place.

"You have some care for Mistress Rosie, I think?" he enquired after this moment's pause in the conversation. Neither man had noticed the silence between them since they had both been deep in their own thoughts.

"Aye, she's a fine lass and deserves better than that wastrel. The Lord knows what will become of her when she marries him; and marry him she will if Peter doesn't die before her next birthday." He sighed.

"Need it be Peter who dies?" quietly asks James with a raised eyebrow.

"Oh, Peter will go to his rest in the end, but despite his incapacity he's not an old man and that lass looks after him like he was the King of Scotland. She'd not wish her father to die to save her from the marriage bed, no matter how much the connection would distress her."

James looked at Geordie and stared down at the fist still tightly gripped inside his sporran. It was a very tentative glance from which he raised his head and looking Geordie fixedly in the eye said, "I am privileged to be Lord of the Middle March, as you know, and there are times when my sovereign King has requested that I meet with his close advisors and lawyers at Stirling or Perth to discuss the *Legis Majeorum* and how to deal with the infernal reivers." He cast a quick speculative glance in his companion's direction and noticed a tick at the corner of his lips as he listened to his cohort despite his obvious effort to maintain a deadpan expression. As he continued Geordie's shoulders stiffened and he assumed the mien of a simple shepherd listening to his master's instructions.

"The CaimBeuil, his greatest advocate, has recently mislaid his sons. It is said they were all slain at Inverlochy and that he lies a broken man in the Tower of London, awaiting the pleasure of King Charles."

Not by a flicker of an eyelid did Geordie reveal his emotions on hearing of his father's predicament, and knowing full well that the CaimBeuil's eldest son and heir was hiding somewhere in the Highlands he momentarily wondered how much truth there was in this statement.

"Aye, it's surely a sad thing for a father to grieve for his sons and his clan," he replied in a nonchalant tone.

James made a lunge, catching Geordie's wrist and holding his hand prisoner in his sporran, and he carried on.

"It would be an honour and a privilege to aid the son of such a man. A man who showed his faith in his son to such a degree that he entrusted him with the Campbell Ruby," he almost whispered as he held Geordie's blank gaze.

"But, man, this is my wedding night and my bonny bride awaits me," he laughed, breaking the spell that had kept both men in thrall.

Noticing that several of the guests were approaching the groom they simultaneously laughed as if sharing some lewd joke and included the boisterous group into their conversation. As the group broke up each man went his separate way wondering what the other might be making of the recent conversation.

Geordie came to rest near the great fireplace as he contemplated the recent events. Anyone looking in his direction would see only the dour Highland shepherd he portrayed, who had no original thought in his head but was content to follow the orders of his betters, but the stoic face he showed to those in the banqueting hall hid the ruminations of his active brain. Question after question flitted through the conscious mind of the massive Highlander.

"Was there a danger from James Johnstone?"

"Had he read the implications correctly?"

"Could there be a way to help Rosie out of her current predicament?"

"What price would he, Geordie, have to pay for the silence of James Johnstone?"

"Was there a price he would be unwilling to pay to relieve Rosie of her intolerable burden?"

No matter what the cost, Geordie realised he would sell his soul to the Devil to deliver his beloved. Even if she never cast her eyes in his direction, and what did he have to offer such a grand lass? He quickly realised that if James Johnstone came up with a resolution to the problem he, Geordie, would embrace it with open arms.

"Hoi! Campbell! Get yourself out of here and get ready to drive us back to Capelfoot. Get a move on man!" he shouted as he raised his foot and kicked Geordie in the rear end. He grinned round at the crowd of revellers, who were observing him, and, taking their silence for respect and awe at his position, he made to shove Geordie towards the door. However, Liam had not been as abstemious as Geordie, who quickly moved out of Liam's reach, occasioning the man to lose his balance and measure his length at the feet of the sniggering wedding guests.

Keeping his face deadpan, Geordie pulled his forelock and muttered, "Aye, Maister," as if he had had nothing to do with Liam's embarrassing faux pas. He straightened his broad shoulders and left the hall.

Chapter Nine

The Raid

"Must ye go out tonight?" asked Maggie of Jake as she watched him pack his saddlebag with the requirements for the forthcoming raid. You know I don't approve of the reiving and I canny rest while you are out lest you be caught and hanged." A tiny crinkle at the edge of her mouth indicated to Jake that his wife was not so against the raids as she made herself out to be. She knew that since the raid was sponsored by James Johnstone, Warden of the March, there was really little danger to her man, as if Jake was caught he would be sentenced by the very man who put him in the position in the first place. Her man was safe!

Along with many other wives in the Border country she understood that following the family traditions of rustling was a badge of honour which she would not like to take away from her husband.

The Steel Bonnets was in the blood of the men on both sides of the Borders and as she had married a Graham she had to accept that along with the love and affection of this man went his total loyalty to the Johnstone brothers.

Despite Jake and Maggie having carried on a flirtation almost since Maggie's arrival as a wee lass from the poorhouse, it was only after her marriage to him she had become aware of his fealty to the Lord of the Middle March as great as any lord to his sovereign king.

As she watched his preparations it dawned on her that that there was a difference tonight from any previous night she had watched as he prepared to fulfil his obligations to the Graham name. She frowned as she saw him remove a flask of black powder and ball from the kist in the kitchen. As a general rule the reivers, did not carry weapons these days. In past centuries, yes, but she had never witnessed Jake leave armed with so much as a knife. She cast her eyes over his body and observed a bulge around the waist of his breeches.

"Jake!" she asked sharply. "Why are you taking your pistol?"

"Now, Maggie, never ye heed about the pistol. There have been a lot of set-tos recently and a wee crack will send the militia's horses off if we run into trouble," he answered, putting his arms around her and allowing her to feel the hard metal of the concealed weapon. She opened her mouth to continue with her questioning but Jake stemmed her flow by covering it with his own, kissing her soundly.

"Wheest, woman, have I ever come back deid?" he queried, trying to turn her concern off with a joke. "Since ye stopped working in the farmhouse ye have nothing to worry yerself about but yer auld husband."

He drew her into his arms and gently bussed her cheek with his bristly chin. He still couldn't quite believe that he had won his bonny lass. Never mind that she believed that Rosie had replaced her with Norah because she wanted rid of her. Jake thought he knew why Rosie had made Maggie believe she was superfluous. For a moment, his rugged face held a look of astonishment, for he was almost certain that Liam had been the instigator of the plot to remove Maggie from Capelfoot's kitchen and into marriage with himself. He would be the first to admit he was not gifted with brains, but for the life of him he could not work out why Liam had become such a partisan for his, Jake's, cause. Liam was so surely a selfish bugger.

The result of her ousting from the house had led to Maggie and her nursling falling out disastrously. He couldn't work it out.

"For that lass loves Maggie like a mother and she would have been as like to take it into her head to alienate herself from her father as to push Maggie away. Aye, there's deep workings there nae doubt."

His thoughts abruptly changed course and he grinned to himself as he remembered that, sharp though Maggie's tongue could be and how adamant she was that her way was the only way, he had never been so comfortable and happy as he was now that he had achieved his heart's desire and had his darling Maggie residing in his cott and making him feel like a young Lothario.

"Well, whatever the reason, I am certainly the victor, and to the victor the spoils." He gave her another quick squeeze and was about to peck her cheek when she pushed slightly away from him to look up into his face with a quizzical expression on her homely face.

"There's something going on tonight that you're not telling me about. Something different." She held up her hand to stop his response

"Don't try to bamboozle me, Jake Graham. I may have come from the workhouse with no education but I know when something smells fishy and this smells of rotten fish."

A worried expression ousted the normal loving look in her eyes as she took in her husband's hodden grey jacket and breeches covering the metal breastplate he had inherited from his father and grandfather before him. A sudden cold feeling of dread washed over her.

"Aw, lass, I promise you I won't get into trouble but I'm bound like any Highlander to his clan. You'll have heard many times, in Lockerby, the wifie's making mock. I've heard them myself." He drew himself into the perfect imitation of a gossiping wife on a street corner, saying bitterly, "There are nae Christians here. Only Johnstones and Grahams!" Jake, looking at Maggie's worried face, gave her a mischievous grin and added, "The De'il looks after his ain!"

"And don't forget," he continued, "with all the taxes on salt and tea and coffee there are very few men in Lockerby who can afford to look askance at the reivers."

He pulled himself to attention and saluted like a soldier.

"I am a Graham, harsh and true and I mun follow James Johnstone and stand by my family."

With a final kiss and an admonishment not to wait up for his return Jake blew out the candle on the dresser and slipped silently out of the door.

Waiting impatiently in the stackyard was a similarly clad young man. Jake had been surprised to be told of Liam's invite to tonight's proceedings, but he was pretty sure it had not been Sir James' intention for Liam to be in charge of the venture, but until they met up with the main contingent he could see no harm in letting him think he was in command.

"You took your time. We need to meet up with the others before it's too light to get going," Liam immediately accosted Jake

"Well, lad, it's barely dark, there's plenty of time yet to get to the meeting place and get our orders," said Jake calmly as he packed some baccy into his pipe, irritating his companion.

"Don't you lad me, you moron. You work for me and will take your orders from me. James Johnstone does not intimidate me. And whatever happens tonight if the cattle we seize are not grazing peacefully in my fields come morning you and your precious Maggie will be out of a job and a home, so listen well."

Jake adopted a cowed expression and agreed that he understood what was required of him.

The arrogant young man swung himself onto his horse and headed out of the stackyard and onto the country lane that led towards the meeting place at the bend of the river Annan. Even although he was made up by the invitation to join the raiding party, he was extremely nervous. No amount of bravado could take the place of experience and that was something he did not have.

Neither his father or any of the Maxwells hereabouts had been part of the reiver community in recent years which meant that, despite bearing the name of a notorious reiving family, he had not been raised in the expectation of belonging to the band he was about to join.

Some, much younger than Liam, who had grown up with the knowledge of reiving raids since their babyhood, would be looking for him to fail in his enterprise and would no doubt mock him if he did. Part of him was ecstatic to be invited, and by none other than James Johnstone himself, but a part of him was terrified that he would meet with violence if they happened upon an opposing gang. For all his strutting and bravado in front of Jake, Liam was a coward!

They rode in silence down the heavily heathered hills that deadened the sound of the horses' hooves. Liam could feel his heart thumping in his throat as the moonlight disguised the landscape making it appear ghostly and surreal. How he wished that Jake would speak and take his thoughts away from the upcoming adventure, but he made an attempt to drown his fear in pride; he straightened his shoulders and sat more firmly in his saddle.

"I will be fine. Johnstone didn't ask any of my friends from reiving families to join this expedition so he obviously recognises that I am as good as him. He probably wants me to take charge while he sits back and reaps the rewards. Well, Jake will do the dangerous stuff and see the sturks get back to my fields. I'll be rich soon enough!"

Accurately assessing the thoughts floating around in the younger man's head, Jake rode quietly behind him. He had no love for the conceited youngster, but, ever a man to give credit where it was due, he had to admit that Liam was hiding his fear well. Liam might have felt better about himself if he could have read Jake's thoughts

"Ye have to give the sprog credit for stoicism. Ye'd never guess the lad was shitting himself," he chuckled to himself before continuing his thought process.

He had no idea why James Johnstone had instructed him to make himself responsible for ensuring Liam took a dominant part in the raid, but his remit was to follow orders. He thought back to the conversation he had had earlier that week when, just as normal, Sir James had slipped into the byre just at the darkening and there, surrounded by the sweet smell of the dairy cows, he had given his orders. There was nothing particularly strange about the orders in themselves; only that Jake was to carry a loaded pistol and, if Liam were to show any inclination to renege on his promise to support Sir James, he was to threaten to, but not actually, shoot him.

"You will take him to meet the rest of the lads at Kirklands, then allow him to put on his airs and graces. It doesn't matter how much noise he makes but if there is any resistance, you fade away and leave Maxwell to take his medicine. Understand?" he barked.

Jake was quiet for a moment, then peered up through the gloom of the lantern-lit byre at his liege lord, wondering if he had understood him correctly. The soft breathing of the docile cows and the occasional swish of a lazy tail accompanied his slow mental perambulations. Sir James stood quietly allowing his henchman to come to his own conclusion.

As he saw the truth dawn on Jake's mobile features he grasped him by the shoulder and repeated, "Understand?"

"Yes, sir," saluted Jake with a wary smile. "Never unprepared, ready, aye ready!"

114

"I'll warrant young Maxwell will not be so apt to tolerate your cheek as I am," he chortled, slapping Jake on the shoulder and disappearing back through the byre door like a shadow.

While Liam and Jake silently covered the ground, each immersed in their own thoughts, James Johnstone and his other new recruit were on a collision course with the pair.

****

In common with Jake and Liam, Sir James and Geordie rode in silence but their thoughts were taking a very different route.

As they covered the ground in single file, weaving through the clumps of trees that could later provide cover if they were to be pursued by militia, neither gave a great deal of thought to the upcoming raid. James allowed Geordie to ride ahead of him at one point to allow him to take stock of the huge Highlander.

"A shepherd who rides a horse like he was born in its saddle, I think not," his thoughts ran. "A colonel leading his troops to battle, more like. That lop-sided grin could have been on the face of the cunning old fox himself and he's built tall and straight. No, I don't think I am mistaken in concluding he is a son of the CaimBeuil. Only... Well, no red hair. Surely all the Campbells have the deepest red locks? But I'm as sure as I can be that there was a mighty Ruby in his sporran at the wedding."

Geordie was aware that his companion was assessing him but he shrugged off the implications. He had made the decision to accept help from James Johnstone and no matter the price, he was prepared to pay it.

"I have wrestled with my conscience before and lost my darling Merlaine because of it. I don't want to take the chance of harm coming to Rosie. Even if she does not return my love I will have saved her and her farm from the advent of Liam Maxwell." He choked on a wry laugh as he considered the change in himself from the pacifist before Inverlochy to the would-be murderer. "Even if I don't fire the fatal shot I will have slain him by agreeing to be party to this raid."

James brought his horse alongside Geordie and the pair went on their way through the evening gloom. The countryside took on a very different complexion with the setting of the sun and, with very little imagination, the men could believe themselves to be riding through a foreign landscape. The Border country was an amalgam of hills and fertile valleys kept green by the many small rivers that surrounded their area. The near darkness served to enhance the rolling hills making them appear as tall as the mountains in his homeland and Geordie felt a nostalgic pull to his past. The lush grass gave a whispering swoosh beneath the silent hooves of the horses, releasing an aroma that epitomised warm summer days. On leaving yet another stand of trees a movement in the shade of a black-silhouetted hedge alerted them to the possibility of a militia patrol but this turned out to be a family of roe deer, normally too shy to leave the sanctuary of their leafy home tempted out by the verdant pastures though which they were riding. The men stopped for a moment to take in the beauty of the leggy animals before them. The doe lifted her head and sniffed the air but, not sensing danger from the intruders, urged her offspring to continue feeding whilst she herself stood guard.

The spell was broken when a large hare came bounding along the edge of the field, startling the deer that made off with a white flash of its rear to the safety of the copse and bringing the travellers back to the urgency of the moment.

They continued their ride until they came to the arranged meeting place where they met with a good dozen men, all similarly attired in the type of armour synonymous with their kind.

This consisted of a tweed or plain-woven jacket covering a metal breastplate topped off by the round steel helmet which had given their predecessors their alternative name of the steel bonnets. Each man had a horse or pony to ride. There was a mixture of all classes of men, each bound to the other by name and history. Geordie recognised the landlord of the Blue Bell, a lawyer's clerk from nearby Lochmaben and a few agricultural workers from the adjoining Bruce Estate. On a reiving raid, there was no class. All answered to and obeyed James Johnstone implicitly.

"We are just waiting for another couple of men to arrive, then we will be off on our jaunt," smiled James as he released his charismatic personality on the men who followed him. James was not known for his pleasant nature, indeed, as a magistrate he was felt to deal out harsh punishment to lawbreakers, but, here among the men who owed him loyalty, he could turn on his magnetic charm on the instant.

"While we wait, though," he glanced around, "you, Will Jardine, can choose a few men and take the scouting party up along the River Ae as far as the Moat. Just make sure there are no hidden ambushes; lay low and wait for the next contingent."

Just as Will moved to choose his troop, they heard a scuffle of hooves, followed by an over-loud voice. "Is this the spot then? If you had spent less time with your cursed woman, we would have been here on time," chided Liam as he brought his horse to a halt on the bridge above the meeting place.

Jake's deferential answer of, "Aye, Maister, ye mun be right," brought a hoot of laughter, quickly stifled, from the listening horde.

Alec Wilson nudged his neighbour, showing a huge toothy grin in the dim light, and commented, "It does my heart good to hear Jake sound penitent. A less remorseful man you're unlikely to come across. He could go off with the travelling players since he portrays so well sentiments he is a stranger to."

His fellow raider and brother-in-law smothered a chuckle. "Maybe he could play the spurned lady or mayhap a shy virgin?" he quipped in reply.

"Enough, men!" came the order out of the gloom, but it could be heard in the tone of his voice that James Johnstone was also amused by the apparent submissive reply made by Jake.

The incident had put the men in a good humour so when Liam arrived on the scene they greeted him kind-heartedly, though many had grave reservations about James' decision to include him in this raid.

"I am here as I said I would be and I've brought Graham along too," postured Liam for the entire world as if he was master of the situation.

His bombastic manner tickled James's sense of humour but he maintained a businesslike countenance as he replied, "Good, good. Now let's get underway. We have a fair way to drive these cattle tonight and I want no truck with a hot trod come the morning."

Dumbstruck that he had not understood the first words spoken on his new venture Liam pulled Jake's sleeve and whispered to him. "What's a hot trod? Will I need to watch out for it?"

Jake was torn between spinning him a story to frighten him out of his wits or the truth. Not without a feeling of regret did he decide on the truth. He had a notion that his leader would be less than happy if he taunted his recruit.

"The hot trod is a law used in the marches. It assumes that your animals have 'accidentally' wandered out of the grazing of their own volition. If you can trace your herd or flock within six days, you are entitled to take them back without a fight. There are no repercussions allowed against the owner of the land on which they are found, either, but it is very difficult to prove ownership of an unbranded animal. There are certain things a 'trodder' must do. He must carry a sod of his own field and come prepared to herd his animals home," he explained, before hurriedly continuing, "If you are found with rustled cattle you will lose the cattle and be up before the magistrate or the Warden of the March. What's more, you'll never be admitted to a reiver raid again. Rustling can be forgiven. We all have to eat. But being caught? A whole other kettle of fish," he finished.

Thinking about his own thieving intentions for the stirks he had planned for Peter's acres, Liam paled at the explanation.

"Does it happen often? Will Johnstone protect a reiver at the assizes?"

Jake shrugged "Mebbe, mebbe not; depends who gives the best bribe," came his nonchalant reply. "Best to make sure there are no witnesses, if you know what I mean."

Taking on board this information from Jake, Liam began to consider if he was wise to get involved with the reiving band and its dangers. Up until this moment Liam had not really thought about the danger of sheltering rustled animals, just of the benefit of animals someone else had paid for. Should he slope off home and rescind this chance to impress the Lord of the Manor?

"I'll hang to the rear and at the first sign of trouble I will be able to ride off." He was still decidedly uncomfortable with the possible repercussions of this, his first raid.

All of a sudden the mood of the gathering became serious as leaders were announced and told to pick their followers. Liam was aghast as he realised he was to lead the final team of men. So much for his plan to ride off in case of trouble! Despite his misgivings, he felt a surge of pride that the Warden had felt able to trust him in this role. A coward he may be, but this show of faith in his abilities pandered to his vanity, and prompted him to make a vow to be worthy of the trust shown, and incidentally reinvigorated his plan of thieving a few cattle for his own benefit.

Liam, had he but known it, had been allocated a strange task for a first timer and, if he had been paying attention to some of his cohorts, their faces might have given him a clue to their thoughts on this odd choice of leader. Liam had no time to worry about the thoughts of these inferior beings or to worry about the whys and wherefores of the situation. In any case he was too full of himself, even if he had asked the question he would have preened himself, taking James Johnstone's faith in him as his just deserts.

The men he had been put in charge of were all seasoned reivers from families who had reared their boys from babyhood to understand the Reiver's Code, so, if the Warden wanted them to follow the instructions of a greenhorn, theirs was but to do his bidding. Each man had been hand-picked by James himself. He had issued precise directions; to follow Liam's orders, unless told otherwise by Jake Graham.

Liam grew in confidence as the party approached the marches of Kirklands Estate where they were to remain hidden along the dark reaches of the holly hedges until the main group had completed their work of gathering the best stirks from the herd. From that moment, Liam's faction was to take over a number of the rustled beasts and guide them into the valley locally known as the Beef Tub for obvious reasons. They were to make the cattle safe until the hue and cry had passed. Breaking up the herd made it easier to move the animals quickly and if one drove was found it meant that all was not lost. Each hiding place was known to only the elders of the reiving community and, unlike the Beef Tub, most were well kept secrets. James Johnstone had assigned the most dangerous location to Liam!

The Warden of the March, due to his elevated position as magistrate, took no part in the actual stealing of the cattle. That wasn't to say that he had never taken part in a raid. Indeed, as young men he and his brothers had revelled in the lawlessness of the Borders and relished being involved in the planning and execution of the raids. Today, although he missed the adrenaline rush of the cross-border dash, he masterminded the plan and left his able lieutenants to carry out the legwork. When he had been invested into the local band, raids had almost always been over the border but these days it was much easier to take animals from fields closer to home. As he was often heard to say to his intimates over a bottle of port, "A bullock doesn't have any accent so who is to know if it's Scottish or English?"

The main group had lifted the cattle so expertly that barely a low was heard on the still night air. It was obvious that these men were at home with livestock husbandry as they selected the very best of the herd and moved them towards the waiting teams for their next leg of the journey to their ultimate safe havens.

"Remember well, Graham," Liam hissed in Jake's ear, "the very best of these animals are to be grazing in my fields in the morning. You can take off home as we leave this place. I will vouch for the safe passage of the creatures and manage the other men." His voice rose as he puffed out his chest with great pride in himself.

Jake, knowing he had other orders to follow, bit his lip while he tried frantically to think of a way to distract Liam from his plot. Then, suddenly, he grinned into the darkness. "I'm not saying you're wrong to take your share of the beasts," he said, "but every man jack here will know who took them if I go immediately and I don't reckon it would be long before the news filtered back to the Warden. Sooo…" He took a deep breath before continuing. "If you want to outsmart James Johnstone it might be as well to make the cattle safe in the valley and return after you have dismissed the rest of the men."

Liam gave this suggestion some thought. "Probably not wise to get on the wrong side of Johnstone," he said. Loath though he was to give Jake credit for his plan, it was one that made sense. "Mmm, maybe I've changed my mind" he whispered nonchalantly. "It would be better for us to go back later when we can take our time selecting the very best of the bullocks. We will know where they are because we will be the ones putting them there," he finished before raising his voice and giving an order that none of the men needed. "Keep those beasts moving! We will be meeting the milkmaids in the morning at this rate." He scolded for all the world like a little boy mimicking his father.

Although well fed up with the posturings of the arrogant youth these hardened men kept quiet as they sped the coffle along the banks of the river towards their destination. No word was spoken between the men but each used a type of telepathy when droving cattle. An inherent sense of where each was in relation to the other. That's not to say they had no thoughts of their own. They knew that there was something extraordinary afoot tonight. They had no idea what plans Lord James had made but they had no intention of putting a spoke in his wheel.

Like the others, Jake did not know what was planned for Liam. A plan he knew there was, but one thing was for sure; Lord James had read the workings of the lad's mind accurately, since he had predicted the boy's greed.

"Maybe it takes a bad lad to know how a bad lad thinks," he chuckled irreverently.

****

"I tell you there is to be a raid tonight and the animals are to be quartered in the dip in the hills north of Moffat," Geordie repeated, trying not to show just how exasperated he was becoming. It was remarkably difficult for him to maintain his surly, gormless expression while confronted by the captain of militia.

"How do you come to know about it though?" questioned the captain, who had little desire to go chasing ghosts in the dark hills around the barracks. "And why would you tell me? Surely it would be more profitable to offer your services to the rustlers?" he continued suspiciously.

Captain Bruce McEwan, a well-built, handsome, dark-haired specimen of manhood turned his startlingly bright blue eyes on the shepherd and assessed the likelihood of his story. He could read nothing in Geordie's carefully moronic expression to lead him to believe he was being hoaxed.

"But you just never know with these rustics," he considered.

This was Bruce's first posting and he was green where the workings of the neighbourhood residents were concerned, but even he had gained enough knowledge of the district to be surprised that information was being volunteered to him about the activities of the reivers. He cast a scrutinising look once more in Geordie's direction, assessing his well-built physique and estimating the possibility that this huge specimen of manhood was trying to bamboozle him.

He quickly reviewed his options.

"If I don't listen to his tale and it's true, my post will be history," he thought. If I take a brigade out on a wild goose chase, I'll lose the respect of the men. Can I afford not to take action on the information?"

He lifted his eyes once more to meet Geordie's unblinking stare and shrewdly demanded. "What's in it for you?"

"I'm just a drover working the stretch from Edinburgh town to Carlisle," Geordie explained, keeping his features severely in check. "Those reivers," he continued on a grunt, "as they call themselves, are no less than thieves. They give drovers a bad name, blaming us for the loss of sheep and cows. Droving might not be great work but if you lose a few sturks or a flock of sheep on the way, it's hard to get a farmer to give you work again. And," he continued, well away with his story, "it's often the same farmers who are thieving the cattle themselves," Geordie finished, somewhat red in the face.

"And you heard this while you were in the Black Bull?" McEwan was still sceptical.

"Not exactly. I was in the Black Bull having a jug of ale. The robbers were whispering quietly on a bench outside the open casement."

Geordie gave a great sigh and made to depart.

"I've given you the information. I can do no more."

As the door closed behind Geordie, Bruce remained in a brown study staring at the place where Geordie had stood a moment before. Suddenly he bounded out of his seat and made out through the back door to the barrack room where his patrolmen were taking their ease.

"Attention men!" he commanded bringing the comradely banter to an end. "Mount up and make your way to the tracks leading out of town to the hills. I have information that there will be a coffle passing through from a reiver raid."

The silence that followed this announcement could have been cut with a knife as the men took a few seconds to take in the implication of their commander's words. But in a short space of time swords were being buckled on, pistols were primed and holstered and a procession made its way to the stables where the men collected their mounts. Within minutes, the corps was in motion, automatically dividing into smaller contingents as they passed the Market Cross and headed into the wild countryside.

Geordie stood concealed behind a hedge on the main route out of the town to ensure that his plot had succeeded and, as the unit passed by, he smirked, pleased that he had managed his part of the bargain without a hitch. The plot did not sit easily with him. Indeed, his emotions were very mixed up. On the one hand he saw the giving of information as a vile act of betrayal, while on the other he recalled how Liam had so far treated Rosie and, if he were allowed to wed her, there would be no end to trauma he would cause the lass. On consideration, he decided that Liam deserved everything that was coming to him, so, hardening his heart, he remounted his pony and headed off to report the success of his ploy in the military barracks.

****

Over the miles between Kirkland and the secret hiding place for the reivers' booty, Liam had gained confidence in his own ability. Up until this moment the raid had gone like clockwork, the main raiding party had not been detected, the cattle had been divided up and the quota he had been responsible for were safely stowed in the former sheep pen hidden in the valley of the Moffat hills.

He could not prevent himself from bragging to the men about his part in the night's activities. For the most part they ignored him, letting him vent to his heart's content, occasionally smiling to each other without comment when he, drunk with his own opinion of himself, described how he would execute a further raid for his sole benefit.

"Why let Johnstone have the lion's share when he takes none of the risk but hides his precious backside in some warm inn?" he enquired of Jake who was at that moment riding tandem with him. The threat of being caught in possession of the animals was nearly over, but adrenaline continued to pulse through his veins and contributed to his cocksure attitude.

"Lord James mun get his share of the prize, Maister. Nae raid can be guaranteed to go off under the eyes of the militia or even another gang of reivers if he doesn't get his cut," Jake warned the arrogant youth.

"What he doesn't know can't hurt him. He would have to have knowledge of where a band were striking and then he could do nothing about it without revealing himself as a leader of the bandits." Liam was sure he had found a way to bypass James Johnstone's stranglehold.

"Ye dinna ken whit ye're blethering about, ye daft lad," interrupted Alec Wilson as he had overheard this last speech echoed on the still night air. "Lord James be the overlord and ye'll find yersel hinging by the neck if he should hear ye voice such intentions." Alec laughed uproariously and turned to pass on this joke to the others who had been out of earshot.

"I'd like to hear him explain to the Warden why he is a better reiver than him after one raid." A disembodied voice came from the darkness, falling on Liam's reddening ears.

"The lad is desirous of giving up the ladies, it seems," another unknown voice commented and was answered by an equally amused companion.

"Aye, his bollocks will be hanging in the Merkat Square for all to see."

"Naw, the new lady up at Lochwood will have her fancy chef bread them and served up at his Lordship's breakfast table. He's mighty fond of the sweetbreads," sniggered another.

"No sic a fine delicacy, if what I hear from the ladies at the Blue Bell is only half true," a snickering voice echoed from the rear of the single file riders.

This last comment infuriated the somewhat cowed young man. He turned to Jake and commanded, "Let that rabble take themselves off to their byres. We will make our own arrangements."

And without waiting for a response he dug his heels into his horse's flank and took off at a canter.

In no way put out by the orders flung at him, Jake hung back to give instructions to the other members of the riding party.

"Get yersels hame lads. I'll deal wi' that wee rascal." The others could hear the amusement in Jake's voice as he spoke.

"Ye ken fine well what the loss of his matrimonials means tae a young buck. Can ye remember that far back?" teased Alec. "Yon lad will be checking to see they are still intact every day for the rest of his life if the Warden hears his bragging."

With sounds of hilarity, mostly at Liam's expense, the men rode off in the direction of their beds, for, reiver raid or no reiver raid, the morning would still bring an early start in the fields.

Jake caught up with Liam just as they entered an avenue of beech trees.

"Hold hard. Ye have nae need to pay heed to those lads. They are jubilant that the raid went so well. Mark my words, they are impressed by the way you did your part," he blatantly lied. "Are we for home now then, Maister?" he continued innocently, hoping he would not have to 'persuade' Liam back to his original plan after the warning from the other band members.

"No indeed, moron," came the arrogant reply "I'm of the same mind. We will return to the Beef Tub just as soon as the coast is clear and serve them right if their share is smaller!" He pouted like the boy he obviously was.

"We can bide a while here then and rest the horses for it's a fair wee trot back to Capelfoot driving cattle and you're unused to it." Jake had been busy removing his pipe from his pocket that he had forgotten to maintain his cowed demeanour.

"Mind your tongue!" snapped Liam still bristling from the recent humiliation. "Remember who is Maister and if you want to keep a roof over the head of that harpy of yours you had better watch how you speak to me." He repeated his threat for the umpteenth time since leaving the farm.

Jake was an even-tempered man for the most part but this night had tried his patience sorely. Until this moment he had had a feeling of remorse for his part in the lad's fate. He knew James Johnstone had something planned for Liam and he didn't think it would be a pleasant surprise.

"Whatever is coming to the conceited peacock it's no more than he deserves when he threatens my Maggie. I'm sore tried not to teach him a lesson myself," he thought. "He is so set up in his own importance he even believes that I, at my age, would turn my coat and be disloyal to the Warden." He shook his head in disbelief at the stupidity of the other man before taking the pipe from his mouth, knocking out the wattle and extinguishing it underfoot.

While this contretemps had taken place the sounds of the riders had diminished and the only noises to disturb the silent night was the rustle of a nocturnal creature in the undergrowth as it hunted for sustenance or the occasional waft of owl wings as it accurately located its prey along the borders of the fields where the corn stalks drooped heavily with their unharvested grain.

Liam had several times tried to move Jake along with their plan, but not until he had had his smoke and safely stowed his empty pipe in his waistcoat pocket did he indicate it was time to get on with the deed. Despite his bravado in the company of hardened reivers, he was loath now to take any action without the sanction of his more experienced companion. Liam was anxious to get it over with now and get back home to creep under the covers with the luscious Norah, whom he planned to regale with the story of his brave endeavours.

Jake had accurately assessed that now that the thrill of the chase was over Liam was feeling the after effects of the previous excitement. It pleased him that the younger man was quieter, since it allowed him to follow the orders of his lord without any need for violence toward Liam.

Glancing up through the canopy and noticing the slight lightening of the sky he nudged his horse forward saying, "Let's be off on this fools' errand then. Are you sure ye want to go through with it? James Johnstone is not a man to cross."

"How will he even know anything about it? A bullock more or less is nothing to him."

"Lord James believes in fair shares for all. Every cotter on his estate knows the taste of beef, be it English or Scottish, and taking these cattle is stealing the food from the estate bairns."

"What do I care for the bairns on the estate? Oatmeal is all that is needed for them. I intend this to be the first step in putting me where James Johnstone thinks he is by right. When I'm in charge of the reivers, and mark my words, it won't be long until I'm Lord of the March, all cattle will be sold to fill my coffers."

Deciding that he had done all he could to clear his conscience for aiding the lesson Liam was about to be taught, Jake followed his lead as they retraced their steps to the captive beasts nestled quietly in the dip between the hills.

Geordie met James as arranged near the top of the highest prominence where a handy copse served to conceal them from any stray glance from below. As the conspirators clasped hands to the jingling of their horses' harnesses, James peered into the other's face, keen to detect how his part had gone.

"All go according to plan?" he asked anxiously

"Indeed but what a trial to get that militiaman to get off his rump," he laughed in reply. "I suspect he had just settled himself down to a strong hot toddy and had no desire to lead his men out after reivers."

"It is lucky McEwan is only just consigned to the area. If the previous commander were still active you've have had your arse flung in gaol and up before me in the morning for attempting to dupe an officer of the law away from his duty." James executed a perfect imitation of the now retired commander of the militia.

The pair dismounted and tied their horses to one of the myriad young saplings that had sprouted from the fruit of the tall straight birch trees before settling themselves, well concealed, to watch the antics below. The nature of the land at this point, a remnant from the long gone ice age, gave the area the feel of an ancient Roman amphitheatre and indeed both men felt the anticipation of a crowd about to relish in the uneven battle between man and beast.

The men sat on the bank in silence. It was a companionable silence and James was surprised at how comfortable he felt in Geordie's presence. A small man, he almost always felt the need to impress with his considerable personality when dealing with more robust men but, here on the quiet hillside, he felt no urge to posture or try to impose his will upon the taller, stronger man.

While these unusual thoughts passed through his brain James felt Geordie stiffen beside him as his sharp ears had caught the ringing sound of a horse's hoof as it struck a stray stone. Both men focused their attention on the dark bowl beneath them gradually making out dark shadows appearing at the open end of the valley. These shadows moved cautiously towards the penned animals confirming to the watchers that this was indeed their prey.

"Got you, you blaggard," mouthed James so quietly his breath barely moved the warm night air.

"I knew you would try to double cross me. Any sorrow I might have harboured at what I have in store for you has disappeared," he thought with eyes firmly fixed on the action below.

****

Jake dismounted and allowed his horse to roam free while Liam, as expected, gave orders from atop his steed.

The watchers were able to discern that Jake's instructions were to select the best of the bullocks and remove them from the pen and, closing up the gate behind himself, drive them off in the direction from which they had arrived.

From their post high up on the hillside, James and Geordie were now able to discern the shadowy horses and riders as they silently closed in on the pair below. Liam began to feel uneasy as he cast glances around himself. It was the first time since leaving the farmhouse that he had felt alone and exposed. Maybe the reputation of the Beef Tub had spooked him, for he was looking around for ghosties and ghoulies, sure that they were hiding just out of his sight. Maybe it was the fear of repercussions from James Johnstone if he ever heard of his deeds tonight. Maybe he had a premonition of things to come. Whatever the reason for his uneasiness, Liam now sorely wished for reassurance from Jake and to that end peered into the pen trying to untangle the shadowy form of his henchman from the other sinister shapes, but Jake had now completed the task allotted him by his lord and had made himself invisible between the legs of the beasts as he made his way into the shelter of the stone dyke, preparing to let the rest of the action unfold without his assistance.

"Graham, Graham, where the hell are you, man?" squeaked Liam, all his bombast gone in the fear of the moment.

No answer.

"Graham, get here this instant!" demanded the now terrified man.

The silent couple on the hill turned to grin at each other.

"Not such a big shot now, eh?" whispered Geordie. "Give him a minute and he'll be crying for his mammy."

With Jake now out of the picture it took only a minute for his erstwhile cohorts, who had crept back to the scene while Jake was enjoying his pipe, to surround Liam, enjoying the fear they heard in his voice as he turned this way and that in an attempt to elicit where his danger lay.

"Try to renege on your word, would ye?" croaked one voice, the mask over his features making his voice as indistinguishable as his face as it's owner darted forward and landed a punch on Liam's chin.

A hard blow landed on his shoulder with harder words spoken by another: "We ken fine how to deal wi those who would cheat their own kind."

In the same instant he was attacked from the front as a stout stick was thrust with such force into his belly that, as well as taking away his breath, it made him wobble in his saddle.

His jerked his head from voice to voice as the blows and taunts came thick and fast. There was no escape. He had been found out and the reivers were not known for their leniency.

"Please, it was all a mistake. I'll not take any of the cattle," he pleaded to no avail. In a last ditch attempt to bring Jake to his rescue, he threatened, "You'll pay for this, Jake Graham. Don't think you'll spend another night at Capelfoot if you don't get these men off me." Jake, however, had by this time been reunited with his horse, by the simple expedient of giving a sharp whistle, and was riding away from the scene.

The anonymous horsemen continued to take it in turn to lambaste Liam with blows, being careful now not to unseat him. He tried valiantly to induce his mount to take off, but found his reins were being held by one of his attackers.

For some minutes his senses remained confused as he tried various methods to escape, the blows raining down on him. As he swung his body this way and that it eventually occurred to him that he had a loaded pistol in his waistband, but how to reach it without unseating himself was more difficult. Just as his fumbling bore fruit and he grasped the cold steel in his hand, he heard the noisy approach of galloping horses.

"Thank goodness!" thought the relieved victim as the blows suddenly stopped. "I'm saved!"

"Militia! Scatter!" yelled the commanding voice from within the scuffle and like the ghosts Liam had originally thought them the raiders vanished into the night before the lead militiaman had even entered the valley. Liam's relief was short lived as the final reiver to leave the skirmish gave his horse a hefty slap on the flank, urging it to bolt in the direction of the oncoming militiamen. Still holding his pistol, he grasped the reins of the fleeing horse in an effort to lessen its pace. This unexpected action unbalanced him and in his disoriented state his finger tightened on the trigger. The firing of the weapon frightened the already upset animal, taking Liam along as it flew pell-mell towards the oncoming infantrymen.

Bruce McEwan, way out of his depth in this situation, never expecting the reivers to attack, spoke the order: "Shoot to kill!"

Realising his imminent danger too late Liam tried to turn the speeding horse, but all the noise and kerfuffle was too much for the beast and it continued its progress towards the rifles pointing straight at Liam's heart.

The cacophony of pistol shots could be heard from their position high on the hill where it could be seen that Liam had ridden directly into the line of fire. He stood no chance of surviving a bombardment of men trained to be cool under fire.

His body jerked as he released the reins and toppled onto the ground where he lay, bleeding from his fatal wounds.

Bruce McEwan dismounted, approaching the erstwhile reiver with pistol drawn, but he had no more need for firearms. Liam lay dead at his feet.

The watchers on the hill stood silently looking down on the scene playing out beneath their vantage point before turning as one, making for their horses, mounting and riding off in the direction of Lochwood Towers.

"I will never become used to the sight of death," Geordie commented.

"It is always as well to be rid of the rogue bull before it upsets the whole herd," answered James. "We live in wild times. Think how many lives he would have harmed if he had been allowed to continue his selfish path."

It came into his mind that hard fighting men though they were, able to make difficult decisions, still they both had a measure of compassion for the dead man.

Noticing the frown that had replaced the sad look on Geordie's face and sensing all was not well with the shepherd, James continued, "What's amiss Campbell? You're not regretting the end of that bastard are you?"

"No, no, not that," came the slow answer as Geordie looked speculatively into Johnston's eyes. "I'm grateful for your help in relieving Peter and Rosina from their predicament, but I've wracked my brains to think what you want in return."

James's sly look further disconcerted Geordie but his look belied his words.

"Nothing but your friendship," he thrust his small hand out for Geordie to grasp. "I admired your father." He held up his hand to stem Geordie's protest. "Let us agree he was not your father if that is how you want it, but I admired CaimBeul. He held his army loyal without force. A fair and good chieftain but not afraid to take difficult decisions, just like yourself," he put in the aside with a grin. "I would be honoured to call his son 'friend'. I admit at the start I aimed to gain a hold over you, but after tonight's ructions I give you my word no hint will leave my lips about your part in this furore."

He scanned the face above him, thinking to himself that, for all the fealty and obsequious attention at his command in this wild county, there was no one who drew his respect as this tall virtual stranger before him.

Johnstone compared their relative statures. He was naturally an arrogant man, having been from the hour of his birth doted on by his parents and lionised by those who owed their living to the Johnstone clan. He realised that until this moment he had failed to wonder how he might compare to other men.

Short even by Border standards James' was not a commanding figure. His slight build tended to exaggerate his lack of height and standing next to this near giant he felt overwhelmed. He continued to cogitate on his physical features and decided that his hair was arguably his best feature. It was of a deep, burnished copper colour which he wore tonight with no wig or powder. He grimaced as he remembered how he always felt these flowing locks gave him a very feminine aspect. This unusually frank account of his attributes strangely did not make him feel inferior to Geordie but, looking up into the ruggedly good-looking face of the tall Highlander, he realised that he had spoken the truth. He *did* want only friendship from Geordie and would not use blackmail over tonight's doings.

Chapter Ten

"So, from that time on, the ruby became an omen of good luck. It bound the Campbells and the Johnstones for ever and if you remember I am married to Marion Johnstone, so you can see the luck of the ruby carries on to this day," ended Big Jock.

"Is there more to the story, Lord John?" enquired Mark, too deeply immersed in the romance of the tale to worry about his audience reaction.

"Like all good fairy stories the hero won fair maid. Yes, Geordie married Rosina and just as the gypsy predicted they had three children. They remained at Capelfoot caring for each other and for Peter and Maggie and Jake. Their children grew up and the saga of the ruby continued."

"So that is the tale of the ruby is it?" Mark queried.

"Well, that is the start of the story and how the Ruby came to be a symbol of good fortune for each generation." He squinted down at the massive ring as it sparkled in the studio lights.

Big Jock shifted position on the couch and looked off into the middle distance before continuing, as if plucking his words from a different dimension.

"You see, Geordie was in a dilemma." His crooked grin became apparent once more as he recalled his ancestor was an accessory to murder. "My, what a field day the gutter press would have had if they could have ferreted out that story when I was leader. Mind you, King Charles's ancestors have a few skeletons in their cupboard too, what with missing heirs and beheading their wives so, maybe the Campbells were not so bad."

Lord John again shifted his position obviously uncomfortable with the antics of his predecessors. He clasped his hands together and, leaning his forearms on his knees, bowed his head to look at the floor as he continued with his account.

"Geordie and Rosie had three children as I said before. There was James, the eldest, then came John just a year later, followed by the delight of Geordie's life, his little daughter Margaret. No more terrible events took place. The family grew up in a tight little community where Maggie and Jake's children played with the farmhouse children and visits between the farm and Lochwood Towers were a frequent occurrence."

He continued:

"But that is only beginning of the ruby's story and its influence on the Campbell family. At that time no one, especially not Geordie, recognised what might happen if the ruby ever left the custody of the Campbells."

"You must remember the times they were living in. The violent borders are one part, but, as a whole, the population of Great Britain, both English and Scottish, were a superstitious lot."

"You don't mean to tell me that Lord John Campbell, arguably the greatest statesman ever seen in our country, is governed by superstition?" Mark asked, unable to believe Lord John was not reeling him in as he had in the past.

Big Jock glanced at Mark from under his heavy brows before asking, seemingly irrelevantly, "Do you have children, Mark?" asked Big Jock in a total change of subject.

"No, Lord John, I am not so fortunate," was the answer.

"Well, when you have children, you must remember to relish the time, for, in the blink of an eye, that sweet smelling, smiling baby becomes an adult person with views and ideas of their own, and you have missed your chance to influence the adult," he reflected sadly. "I missed a great deal of the early life of my girls and I can never get those years back. However, the reason I bring it up is that the children grew up and, before they knew it, the boys were bringing home wives and the family expanded.

"John married Jemima and they moved into the farmhouse but, when James was courting his Jenny, she wanted to have her own kitchen. Rosie to some extent wanted to have her daughter-in-law and her grandchildren to live at Capelfoot but, being a wise woman, she made no attempt to influence James's decision and allowed them to move into a tied cottage on the Annanwater estate without argument. They became a happy family there as first Mary and Janet were born while their father worked as a ploughman."

The audience still sat spellbound as they listened to the tale unfolding before them. Men hushed wives who tried to speak to them, many being forcibly held in their seat when they wanted simply to be excused to pay a visit. No one could have anticipated that this evening would turn into such an incredible event. Even Mark Henderson, with all his experience in interviewing techniques, was loath to interrupt his guest's flow to ask a question.

"Now it has been said by some of my opponents that I am an arrogant man. I would dispute that." His grin once more surfaced cheekily as he continued, "Well, if I am arrogant, and I confirm or deny nothing, perhaps it is an inherited trait." Big Jock thought for a moment before changing his mind.

"No, not arrogant. Proud. Aye, that's the word. A proud man and that is what Geordie was. He couldn't settle to his son being a working labourer dependant on a master for his wages. Soo... with true entrepreneurial spirit he again visited his friend

James Johnstone and the two of them set about hashing out a plan to make James independent.

"As in the past Geordie wondered if he was wise to tie himself to the Johnstone clan and he did much soul searching before he committed himself to the idea. But from my experience it is a smart move to be connected to the Johnstones." He gave a sly glance at Mark Henderson before shifting his gaze to the audience.

It had appeared to Mark that Jock was looking out through the studio lights into the dark space inhabited by the spectators, not to a specific place, but, as his eyes followed Lord John's stare, he realised that his rarely seen and very private wife had found herself a space near the front of the audience, where she was sitting as much entranced by his recollections as everyone else in the studio. He had been quick enough to catch the glance that they exchanged and found himself wishing that his girlfriend would look at him as Marion Campbell looked at her husband. There could be no doubt in anyone's mind that the diminutive little lady gazing at her spouse while he held court was still infatuated by the big man.

Mark was distracted for an instant as he took in the love of Big Jock Campbell's life. In no way could he see this petite woman scaring her large husband as he always claimed. Lady or not, she was still sporting the same hairstyle as she had when John Campbell had become MP for Lockerbie. Her translucent skin owed nothing to cosmetics and she dressed smartly but not ostentatiously. If you met her in the street, you would not look twice at her, but to observe her watching her husband as he held court in the studio was to see the beauty shine out of her hazel eyes and a glow emanate from her smooth cheeks.

"If only I knew her secret. Would that some woman would shine like that in my presence," he thought to himself.

Sighing he tuned back into the story unfolding in the studio.

Big Jock continued, "A deal was agreed in which Geordie would put up the ruby as collateral for a sum of money to buy James Hill End Farm near Powfoot and that the ruby would be returned when James had refunded the purchase price."

"So did the ruby stay with the Johnstone family then?" asked Mark but caught himself up as he recalled that the ring was twinkling in the studio lights right there on Lord John Campbell's workmanlike fingers.

"No, Geordie was right in his instinct to trust James Johnstone and he never had reason to regret that trust either in his friend or in his son. James worked hard to make Hill End pay and, since he had married a smart woman who could make a shilling do the work of two, it didn't take long for the ruby to be returned to Geordie and for the most part, squabbling children aside, the family remained happy and peaceful for the rest of Geordie's life."

A mischievous look came over Big Jock's face as he continued, "But fate had more in store for the Campbell family and the ruby."

"You mentioned, Lord John, that superstition played a part in the story and implied, did you not, that the ruby left the family?"

"You never miss a word, eh? And I thought you were bored." Big Jock laughed at Mark's expression.

"I asked you if you had children, and it doesn't matter that you haven't, but I'm sure it won't be news to you that many families are larger than the parents intended in an effort to beget a son."

He held up his left hand splaying his four fingers and thumb as he named each in turn. "Jane, Nell, Mary, Margaret, Janet and I've run out of fingers and no lad. I'm no better than any man when it comes to the desire for my name to carry on," he hastily added,

"I use this only as an example of what brought about the behaviour of my ancestors. I wouldn't swap my beauties for a mere son; and I have grandsons now to spoil, but not too much. I've learned from the errors of my ancestors."

He looked up at Mark, smiling.

"After six daughters the miracle happened for James and Jenny. A son was born and called Walter."

"And?" urged Mark.

"Well, great excitement was experienced by the proud parents and nothing was too good for this precious son. And therein lay the clue to the next chapter of the ruby's journey towards my finger."

Chapter Eleven

The atmosphere in the kitchen was strained as each person present struggled to be heard. A sullen Watt stood with his back to the sink, to all intents and purposes removed from the discussion even though he had been the cause of it. He was confident that in the end he would have his own way. Didn't he always? Jenny and James would refuse him nothing.

If Watt had been able to read James' thoughts at that precise moment, he would not have been so confident. As the maelstrom of voices circled the kitchen James was chastising himself.

"What did I do wrong?" But it was a rhetorical question because he knew well that, after all their hopes and prayers had eventually produced a male child, he and Jenny had spoiled him and allowed him to believe that his was the most important, and indeed the only, desire that should be fulfilled. He sighed.

"If only his nature was as sweet as his countenance."

He looked across at his handsome son and admitted that he was a son to be proud of, at least in looks. He stood above six feet tall and had inherited the dark eyes and straight nose of the Campbell family. Jamie's eyes roved over the sturdy lad, taking in his strong legs and arms, his burgeoning chest, the broad shoulders and neck that supported the handsome head topped by the flowing deep russet locks that had been a surprise to his father when he was a mischievous infant, but his grandfather swore he was the living image of *his* father, the CaimBeuil.

The peculiar character of his mouth, that on Jamie indicated a pleasant nature, was more likely to sneer than to laugh and the cocksure way he held himself left Jamie wishing he had the upbringing of his son over again.

"For he stands there as if he is Lord of the March," Jamie thought. "Och, well, he is what he is, and he's but a boy." Immediately the reason for the meeting in the kitchen belied his thoughts, for Watt was determined to marry Jean Graham, the fifteen-year-old daughter of his own playmate and granddaughter of his grandparents' lifelong friends.

For a moment or two Jamie let his mind wander back over the years of his childhood when Maggie and Jake's cottage had been a second home to him. He recalled the many autumn days when Maggie had formed a squad of the children from both families to raid the hedgerows for fruit for his mother and herself to turn into preserve. He could almost taste the bramble jelly on the pancakes, hot off his mother's girdle. And Jake? Despite his children being of an age with Jamie and his siblings, he filled to perfection the role of Grampa. Jamie knew he had Jake and Geordie to thank for his knowledge of the seasons and in no small measure, his success with farming Hill End Farm.

As the crescendo of voices rose in the kitchen precincts, Jamie was forced to bring his thoughts back from his happy childhood and bend them towards finding a solution to the current family crisis.

"I'll not have my lass wed sae young," repeated George Graham for perhaps the twentieth time since entering the kitchen with his timid little wife, Jane who gazed up at him with a wry look.

"But if they don't wed maybe there will be worse happen," she whispered to her angry husband. "We can't lock her up till she's twenty!"

"I can! And I bloody will!"

Turning to Jamie he pleaded, "Ye see how I'm fixed, Jamie? Jeanie's but a bairn. I know they think they are the first couple to be in love but don't we all? Will ye not forbid yer lad to see my lassie?"

Jamie took in the turmoil in his friend's face and was sorry for it, but he gave a huge sigh before answering, "Man, I wish it hadn't happened but Jane is right, if we forbid them to see each other, before we know it there will be a wee lad or a lass calling us Granpa."

He caught the smirk on his son's face. While staying back from the group as if nonchalantly watching a mildly amusing play. Watt had been waiting for what – to him – was the inevitable outcome.

He now pushed himself forward towards Jeanie, catching her in his arms and cuddling her back against his broad chest, saying, "There, didn't I tell you they were all bluster? Once they knew we had been handfasted on the beach there was nothing they could do about it. In the eyes of the law…" He paused to ensure that the adults were taking in his statement; he was the great grandson of the greatest lawyer of them all, wasn't he? "We don't need a minister of the church to live as a married couple."

As soon as he had realised how he felt about Jeanie he had listened to all the old stories told of handfasting and its connotations. He knew that was the stick to beat their respective parents with for they would do anything rather than have their children opt for the 'irregular' marriage allowed by the simple exchange of promises to marry.

On the beach overlooking the Solway the young lovers had clasped hands.

"I promise to be your husband from today on."

Watt had said this proudly, gazing into the eyes of his childhood friend, who had answered in a tremulous voice, "I promise to marry you and love you until one of us dies."

They had sealed the promise with a chaste kiss and hurried off to inform their relatives of the deed. That was what had instigated the gathering in Hill End kitchen.

As his thoughts ran along the past happenings he noticed that Jeanie's father had become purple in the face with rage on hearing him crow about how clever he had been, and he thought it might be time to end the animosity. After all, he and Jeanie would need help in establishing themselves and who better to foot the bill than their parents?

"We will be wed as soon as the banns can be read." He scanned the adults standing open-mouthed like effigies. He had a smile on his face which quite changed his character as he turned to his soon to be father-in-law, exerting all his charm now that he was assured of getting his own way. Beaming at him, he said, "Thank you, sir, for agreeing to let me marry your daughter. I will take great care of her."

Somewhat mollified by the boy's good manners but nevertheless disgruntled by the outcome, George held out his hand to be shaken, still wondering that his lovely young lass could not see what kind of man it was that she was marrying.

"For I'll not believe he will ever give a damn for your comfort, the spoilt brat that he is." His thoughts were echoed by everyone in the room, apart from the young couple themselves.

The deed was done. Jean Graham had become Jean Campbell. Both families were standing in the graveyard of Ruthwell Church where just moments ago the Reverent Paul Higgins had bound the couple together as man and wife.

Jenny took in the beaming smile on her now daughter in law's face and, in a moment of reflection, thought, "I couldn't have picked a more ravishing wife for him if I'd had all the girls in Annandale to choose from." Her thoughts flew back to the previous evening when the kitchen of Hill End had been full of giggling young girls, for the task of preparing the bride for her wedding had been undertaken by Jenny and her daughters, but overseen by the shy Jane and her domineering mother-in--law Maggie.

Left to Jane and Jenny there would have been a quiet night spent at the table reminiscing about the couple's childhoods, but Maggie and Rosie were made of sterner stuff and there was nothing they liked more than to plan a party on the least excuse. They had been firm friends who knew everything about each other's families and were determined to give Jean a good send-off. Although penny bridals had for the most part died out, the spirit of the community paying to attend the wedding had not and, instead of the pennies previously donated to the festivities, neighbours and friends came calling on the eve of the wedding carrying all manner of food and drink to celebrate the occasion.

"Leave that door open," ordered Rosie from her seat near the fire. "You must be exhausted jumping up and down to let folks in."

Even though Jean was the bride, she was included in the ordering by the oldest of the women, who were most definitely in charge of proceedings and enjoying themselves mightily; a glass of dark ale was sitting next to each of them, from which they took surreptitious sustenance while sending the others scurrying to obey their instructions.

The younger members of the family were sent off to the barn with each new consignment of food or drink to set up the tables for the feasting to follow the wedding itself.

Jenny noticed the two women had their heads together with some of the girls present and were giggling as if they themselves were fifteen rather than sixty and seventy. As she drew closer intent on finding out what the women were finding so amusing she heard her mother-in-law draw in her breath.

"Shssh. Not a word now!" she exclaimed, indicating with a wave of her hand that the girls should be off about their business.

The chuckling girls giggled themselves out of the room, obviously following some objective just given to them by Maggie. With the departure of the younger girls the women began a more serious discussion about the weather, how the bride was to get to the church in her finery, how they would all return to Hill End for the bridal and other such important matters.

In a short time, the whole of the neighbourhood's womenfolk were ensconced in Jenny's kitchen with the bride blushing at the remarks made to her by the married women each time she returned from an errand.

"Make the most of tonight, Jeanie lass, fur efter the morn ye will be shackled an' no have a mennit tae caw yer ain," laughed one of the cowmen's wives from nearby.

She was nudged by a pretty rosy cheeked neighbour who reminded her, "Don't let on you canna mind yer first night wi' Jeemie an' how many meenits you and him would 'hae a wee lie doon' afore the bairns came."

"I mind fine well what it's like to be new wed. It's not as long for me as it is for you." She paused. "But then I'm marrit tae yin as thinks he's still a lad; no like your auld man," she finished cheekily.

"Ye hussy…" began her tormentor, only to be hushed by Rosie as Jean entered through the back door. By the colour in her cheeks it was not difficult to surmise Watt had been in her near vicinity.

"Jean, my wee pet, will you go ben the hoose and get me my bag? It's lying on the bench with my coat," asked Maggie with an innocent smile and a wink in Rosie's direction.

"Sure Nana," she smiled as she kissed her on the brow before leaving the room.

Seconds later she was heard to squeal, then individual voices could not be deciphered as all the young girls spoke at once and in highly excitable voices.

"I know who put you up to this. And to think I trusted those two auld harpies!" Her chuckles could be heard over the sound of splashing and chattering as each young woman took her turn at washing Jean's feet in the bath of water they had previously prepared at the older women's directions.

All but Maggie and Rosie followed the noise, wishing just for the one evening to be reminded what it was like to be carefree and on the brink of life.

At the exodus, Watt popped his head round the door, asking, "What's ado, Nana? It's like as you've brought the hen coop in and set the fox amongst them."

"You young rapscallion, you!" exclaimed Rosie, unable to stop herself from smiling at this naughty grandson of hers. "Come in and see for yourself. You can come and tell us what is happening, for Maggie and me are too old to be running back and forward."

Taken in by his grandmother's innocent reply, Watt made his way through the house guided by the cacophony of voices to be heard coming from his mother's parlour. As he walked into the room, he was set upon by four sturdy females, one of whom shrieked in his ear as she cavorted around him.

"Caught in the trap, brother. You're not smart enough to outfox Nana. *She's* the smartest in the family. Papa always said so!"

Coming to rest behind her brother she assisted the others in manhandling Watt to the side of the tub where, being already unbalanced by the force of his surprise attack, it took only a swift push to land him in the now tepid water where he was wantonly soaked at the hands of the attending horde. Not in the least pleased by this assault on his person he made to get up with a scowl marring his features, but his fortune was not to improve as his mother – "my own mother, damn her!" – bore down on him with a bucket of ashes and proceeded to rub the black, smoky-smelling mess into any inch of skin visible.

The young women, some with long-held grudges against the lad now at their mercy, were not as gentle as his mother and soon there were few part of Watt's body that had not been anointed with the sticky morass.

Jenny, seeing the good-natured smile leave her son's face, shooed the girls out of the parlour and returned to help her son out of the bath. She handed him a rough towel, one she used in the dairy, and laughing at his outraged expression ushered him out through the front porch and into the front garden instructing him to go find his father and grandfather. She stood watching her 'drookit' son making off and spent a moment wondering what would become of him. She had made excuses for his behaviour almost since the hour of his birth but, seeing him unable to accept a joke against himself, she worried how he would cope with married life and bairns of his own. She sighed as she turned and re-entered the kitchen where she was just in time to see her daughter Mary, flushed with pleasure, handing Rosie her wedding ring. She smiled, thinking of the superstition that if you found the wedding band of a happily married woman in the tub while washing the bride's feet, you would have a happy marriage soon.

"Well there's no doubt Rosie's has been a happy marriage and although Mary didn't say anything, I think she was a bit peeved that her wee brother would be married before her."

Taking in her daughter's soft cheeks framed by her dark unruly hair, all lit up by her pretty smile Jenny, was sure it wouldn't be long before she was attending the washing of her daughter's feet.

Meanwhile Watt was in the warm byre with his father and grandfather sharing a nip of whisky to warm him up after his ordeal.

"You need to get up early in the morning to get one over on yer nana and Maggie. Well, if you can tell me anyone alive who has got one over on her, you'll be telling me news." Geordie laughed, although noticing Watt was not taking the joke light-heartedly.

"I can't get over Ma doing that to me," Watt remarked for the third time. "I mean, Ma, who loves her parlour and her cushions and never a word of rebuke at them for splashing water everywhere. And look at me, will you? I'm wet to the skin and black and sore and smelly," he continued to moan.

Geordie put a hand on his shoulder and gave it a squeeze as he said, "Here's a bit of advice for you. You will be wed tomorrow and never again will you be master in your own house." Taking in the incredulous mien of his companion, he joked with Jamie, "The lad thinks he'll be able to call his soul his own. Can you? Can any of us men?"

"I will," said Watt determinedly. "No woman will tell me what to do and when to do it. I don't see either of you being henpecked either."

"That's all bluff. Your granny and your mother have always been in charge and made the decisions; they just let us think we make them. They like us to be manly and strong as long as we don't go against them." Geordie smiled at the two others.

"Mind you it's all in the picking," continued Jamie. "Rosie picked Papa when no one else would have seen what a good man he would be to her, and my Jenny, your mother, she had the whole county to pick from and she took me on, so remember, your wife needs to be cherished for she's the best thing that will ever happen to you."

Watt looked at the two men as if they were madmen. Then, deciding they were just teasing, he drank off his dram and made off into the house to change his clothes.

As it transpired he was so excited by the first part of his chat with his grandfather that he forgot about his wet, smelly clothing in his hurry to light a candle in his room in order to give himself the chance to scrutinise the present he had received from his Papa. In the flickering light of the tallow dip he pulled out the purse Geordie had given him and once more examined the contents. He was much struck by the sparkle of the ruby ring when he placed it on his middle finger. As he watched the flames reflected in the stone he recalled what his grandfather had said about it being the good luck piece of the family, how he had come by it and how it was responsible for him finding contentment with Rosie. James had told how it had been the reason he had been able to buy Hill End and that now it was handed down to him it was his charge to keep it safe for the next generation.

The next morning, while Jenny chivvied her son into his wedding finery, Jamie harnessed up the grey mare to the cart and made off to Newbie where his sister Margaret lived with her husband. They had been housing George and Jane Graham and, of course, the bride for her last night as a maid.

When he arrived in their kitchen the women were still engrossed in adorning the girl, so he took himself off to find his brother-in-law and indulge in a pre-marriage dram.

During his absence on this manly pursuit the women had been busy and Jamie was struck by the pretty girl as he never had before.

"I've known you since you were a babe but by, you're a fair young lady. I'm shy of you, my dear," he smiled down into her face.

"That young rogue of mine is a lucky lad." He finished taking in all her finery, for Jane was determined she would start her married life on the right foot.

She assessed her daughter carefully. She looked lovely in her new style dress with its open coat and underdress. Jane felt a smidge guilty that she had traded some of their vegetables for a piece of smuggled lace to add a finish to the dress and give it an air of gentility, but, when she looked at her daughter's smocked brown and cream tartan bodice, which clung to her figure without need for a corset, she forgave herself.

"That French lace around the cuffs make her wrists and hands look so frail and pretty and the ribbons in her hair match the tartan so well," she congratulated herself. Remembering Jeanie was marrying into a farming family, she thought, "I hope that Watt Campbell doesn't have her working so hard this is the last time she will have a chance to wear such a dress for in that wide skirt and petticoat she'll not be much use in the turnip field." But she knew Jamie and Jenny and trusted them to see no harm came to their lovely daughter.

Jeanie was flushed with excitement. Her skin looked soft and delicate with a subtle pink hue enhancing her beauty. Her little chin shaped the bottom half of her face and neck, which rose from the blushing swell of her bosom where it modestly peeked out of the lace neckline on the bodice of her dress.

When all was ready and the horse had been prevented from eating the garland of flowers round its neck, the wedding party set out for the church with only one setback when a neighbour had forgotten to shut the door of the pigsty, allowing Jeanie to catch sight of the pig and, as custom dictated, she returned to her overnight accommodation and started out again. There were no other hitches and the wedding party soon arrived at the little brown church nestled in a fold in the hills.

As Jean was helped down from the cart by her father, she caught sight of her betrothed where he stood, just under the overhang of the church porch. The reverend came to meet her and escorted her to her place beside Watt, where they rapidly made their vows and became man and wife. The reverend kissed the bride, giving her a shy peck on the cheek before conducting the couple into the Church and inviting the spectators to follow.

Jamie gave Jenny a shake to bring her out of her reverie and they all followed the newlyweds into the Church for a lengthy service, where it took Jenny and Jane all their time to control the children who were ripe for the upcoming feast.

At the end of the service Jeanie and Watt led the many family and friends and neighbours in a procession back to Hill End Farm where the wedding feast had been made ready by the women the previous evening.

On nearing the farmstead Jenny bustled off to the kitchen ahead of the procession to collect her cakes of shortbread, so that when Jeanie entered the barn as the new Mistress Campbell she was able to break a cake of the sweetmeat over her head to welcome her to the family. Jenny, realising just how many young girls would be scrambling for a fragment of the shortbread, had made a few extra cakes which she broke and threw into the crowd, in the hope that each young maid would go home with a tiny piece to lay below her pillow so that she may dream of a husband to come.

"Some traditions need to be kept up. Life is pretty drab if you have no dream to sweeten the hours of hard toil," she thought, remembering her own young days when she supposed the handsome, funny James Campbell would not look at her for his wife but, as he had told her after their marriage, "You need not have worried. You were always for me from the first day I saw you."

Whether true or not, it was a sentiment that warmed her whenever she thought of it and wished the girls today to have a wee dream to hold onto.

The festivities lasted well into the night. The women were tired, the men a bit drunk, and Jeanie? Well, at the first opportunity, Watt had swept his wife off to his room to initiate her into the duties of being a wife.

****

"Jeanie, Jeanie, where are you lass?" Jenny called up the stairwell. "Hush, hush, my bonny lad. Your ma'll be here directly. Jeanie!" she called again in exasperation. "This bairn is hungry and I can't quieten him."

She took a deep breath and turned with the infant in her arms. She threw a plaid over her shoulder and, snuggling the baby into its warm folds, opened the back door and made her way across the stackyard into the byre where she found the object of her search. Gently, she disentangled her errant son from a hay feeder, where he had hidden himself some time before. As this delicate task was underway George was giving his mother chapter and verse as to why he should be left where he was until his grandfather were to come in for the milking.

"I want to give him a hand with the *cows*. He *said* when I was a big boy. And *you* said I was your big boy. So…"

Jenny turned her head away, for who could match the logic of a three-year-old? She hid her face in the folds of the plaid that had taken on the sweet smell of the baby and chuckled at the antics of her sturdy grandson.

"I like being a granny more than a mammy," she thought, still smiling, "for I can hand this one over to his mother to do the dirty work while I have all the fun. Here, Jeanie, you take this hungry boy and I will see to the new cowhand," she suggested holding the screaming baby in the direction of his mother while grinning at George.

"Right, Ma, I'll sort this monster out while you smack that bad lad's bum." She flung a last look at George before taking the baby in her arms, plaid and all, and, quieting him by pushing her pinkie into his mouth, rushed out the byre door before he could detect there was no result from his loud sucking.

"Come down, Georgie."

George looked up at his Nana from under his over long fringe. "It's time you had a haircut," she thought, "or we'll be thinking we have a granddaughter," but pushing aside this idea for later she held her hand out to George, who was still perched on top of the hay trough with a scowl on his face.

On seeing Jenny's hand stretch out towards him he quickly hid both his hands behind his back and replied, still with a mutinous look on his face, "Are you going to smack my bum, Nana? I doesn't like it."

Making a dive at the unstable youngster Jenny swung him up into her arms and whirled him round as fast as she could.

"No, but if you run away from Ma again, I will take Papa's belt to you and you won't sit down for a week. Now promise Nana that you will be a good boy."

"I tries to be good but it takes a long time to be growed up and I want to help Papa *now*," he whined, screwing up his features in an effort to express his longing.

"I think you are a big enough boy to help, so I will set you your chores. Let me think," said Jenny, making her face very serious. She knelt down so that she could look George in the eyes before continuing. "Before Papa and Da will believe you are strong enough to help them… You see what strong arms and legs they have, don't you?" She paused for his answer.

"Yes." he replied, not quite sure about this, but his grandmother continued, pleased with his response.

"Before you start with the mummy cows you will have to help with the baby cows, so that will be your first job. Then you have to be fearless in case you get set on by the pig or Johnny Bull so your second job will be to feed the hens and the piglets. Now, do you think you are responsible enough to deal with your chores? You don't need to do them, but, if you start, you must continue."

George pulled himself up, proud that his Nana was going to trust him with jobs of his very own. "Yes, Nana, I'm a big boy."

"That's sorted then. You will start tonight. You must always come with Nana so that I can tell your Papa how you are doing. If I can't tell him how good you are you won't get any pay." She held out her hand and, taking hold of his, walked off with him to feed the calves.

"However, will Jeanie manage when the new wee one comes? I just don't know, but, for now, hopefully this one will stop running off to be a farmer." She sighed, considering what else she might take off Jeanie's shoulders. "For that wastrel son of mine is neither use nor ornament."

Jenny and George were feeding the calves, giggling at the greedy way they guzzled the milk, then laughing as George wiped the foamy bubbles from their velvety lips, while Watt was off meeting his friends at a secret Jacobite rendezvous in the woods.

The young men had each arrived at the clandestine meeting by sloping off unseen from some chores necessary to the farms from which they came. They were for the most part young men, boys almost, who were excited by the romance of the secrecy of the meeting to hear about the army required to put the handsome young Prince Charles Edward Stuart on the throne on which his grandfather had been so precariously perched. Having heard the story of the Campbell Ruby, Watt was full of desire to avenge his own grandfather and, if truth be known, ripe for an excuse to escape his own family and the tedious life on the farm. His face shone as he listened to the tall Highlander who was so eloquently addressing them.

"I wonder if Papa looked like him when he went off with his brothers to fight against the English?" he mused, his eyes devouring every aspect of the speaker's mien and dress.

The commander of the Jacobite force currently recruiting in the area knew exactly how to appeal to the fighting spirit of raw young men and had chosen Sandy MacAlister because of his striking appearance. Who would not want to feel themselves an equal of such a fine specimen as Big Sandy? Like many Highlanders he had inherited his stature from the Northern invaders, so he was a tall man, built to generous proportions; the ox-like shoulders combined with legs like tree trunks gave him the appearance of a giant to these much shorter Lowlanders. He was wearing the red dress MacAllister tartan kilt and plaid and, with his unfettered, unkempt dark hair blowing out behind him, he presented a picture these youngsters had rarely seen and stood in awe of.

However, the thing that was most impressive to his audience were his weapons. Each of the young men present could imagine themselves in battle waving that huge broadsword that glinted in the sun where it stood, point first in the undergrowth in front of the giant soldier. On entering the glade, he had unsheathed his sword, knowing well the impression it would make, and swung it warrior-like around his head before planting it where it now stood. On his back those close to him could see the metal-studded targ strapped over his shoulder with a leather belt, the pistol and powder horn attached to his waist by a leather strap. It appeared to the onlookers that every part of the man housed a weapon capable of destroying the enemy; even in his sock he carried a *sgian dubh* for use in hand-to-hand combat.

"The Prince is lying at Dumfries preparing to march his army off to meet Cumberland. The men are massing in a field nearby not only celebrating the defeat of Johnnie Cope, and that was a great victory, but to march once more on the English intent on putting the Royal Backside back on the throne of Great Britain." He was a great orator and brought the fervour of his audience to fever pitch with his rousing speech and, if they had been allowed, at that point every man listening would have followed him into battle but, although his remit was to recruit men to replace those lost at Prestonpans, he had orders also to have men bring money and food for the almost destitute army they were to join. Indeed, the Prince himself was currently inveigling the burghers of Dumfries to provide him with provender, money and most importantly heavy shoes for his force.

"Any of you who want to do your patriotic duty to our true King should meet over there," he indicated the road running out of the village with one sweep of his massive arm, "Tomorrow evening with as much food, money and weapons as you can beg, steal or borrow. Let's not blab about what has taken place here; if you decide you are a coward and afraid to fight for your King, stay at home and let your wives and mothers shield you under their aprons, but, breathe no word of the Prince's whereabouts, for there are any number of English spies in this blasted country." So saying, he dismissed his audience with an intimidating glower under which every man trembled, but, as they turned to go, he called after them, "Remember your King will be grateful to those that follow him!"

As the men trudged off back to their everyday lives, a man appeared at the elbow of the tall soldier, ready to guide him off to his next rallying point.

"You make a grand speech," Leslie Rome commented. "You've got those lads so excited there can be no doubt they will be marching into England in the Prince's train."

Sandy, who had been surreptitiously landed in the area from Leslie's boat, agreed but tempered this by saying, "Men are good, but, if we can't feed them, we will not keep them long. In a normal rally to arms, I would have marched these boys off while their blood was hot for the fight and many would have stayed; but when they get home and realise what they are leaving behind, how many will be on the road when their valour has cooled?" He sighed, wondering how his fellow recruiters, also officers of the 'Young Pretender' (so called by the English because his father had already raised an army thirty years ago in an attempt to prise the German usurper off his throne), were faring.

"We were specifically sent to the Borders and Lowlands because, of all the places in this country, there is an abundant crop and the cows and sheep are not so scrawny as their Highland cousins. We can train any raw young lad to wield a sword or fire a musket, but the hope is they will bring flour and meat with them."

Sandy was a bit sceptical about the outcome of this foray for, although he had been treated well by the landowners he had been sent to approach, being wined and dined as befitted his position of Prince's ambassador, the promised money and supplies had yet to make their appearance. Sandy had the idea that the great and the good of the Borders were only paying lip service to the cause and that the promised bounty may never find its way to the forsaken army.

"Are you gan tae go Watt? What about your Jeanie and her about to have another bairn? Ye'll no leave her surely?"

His friend Bobby was envious of the stories Watt told about having a wife on tap. Bobby was the sixth son and ninth child of the family living at Carselea farm and thought Watt didn't realise how lucky he was with his family. His parents, while hard working and always contriving to ensure their large family had enough to eat, would not have been able to find a corner for a wife and bairns of his. He knew in order to share in the pleasures Watt endlessly bragged of he would need to find a place of his own. "And by that time," he grimaced, "I'll be too old to enjoy a roll in the hay. But, just maybe, if I get lucky and share in the spoils of the war I'd be able to rent a few acres of my own."

With these thoughts running through his head, he had missed Watt's answer but came out of his reverie in time to hear him moan, "It's not much fun being married when she's with child all the time or even feeding the wee brats. No sooner had one stopped hanging from her tittie than another has taken its place." He conjured up an image of Jeanie's milk-swollen, blue-veined breasts with disgust. "And she has no time to pretty herself up for her husband like she should," he finished gloomily.

"I've a good mind to follow the Prince. Maybe he'll make us rich plundering the English lords. Will you go Bob? We could have an adventure and," he continued slyly, "when you return a hero, all the maids will be desperate to walk out with you."

Bobby thought about their conversation as they wended their way back along the tree-lined lane toward the coastal farms they both inhabited. He weighed up the possibilities for his future and, finding them depressing, spoke to his friend.

"I think I might go with the army, Watt. I'm not likely to get such a chance to make my fortune again. I've nothing to lose. If there are no riches to be garnered, I can still come back and work on the farm. The only thing bothering me is I don't like to take food out of my family's mouths and that soldier said we had to take food or money." He gave a half laugh. "And well you know we have no money."

"You're daft. Your ma will never let you go gallivanting off after the army. Talk sense."

"Wasn't planning on asking her, or Faither either for that matter. Might be days before they miss me and then it will be because the cows are unmilked or a fence hasn't been repaired. That's what I'm doing at this moment, you understand? No, it will be my hands they miss and not my handsome physiog!"

Watt cast a glance in his direction, recognising the seriousness of his intent, and, as they continued their walk, contemplated the opportunities offered by the characterful Highlander.

Surprisingly the thought of Jeanie was more of a spur than a hindrance to the plan. Loath though he was to admit it, his father, and Jeanie's too in actual fact, had been right and they had wed too young. He could hardly remember the pretty, slim girl he had fallen in love with so much had she changed with the difficulties of the children and, he admitted, his own more selfish demands. In the few minutes it took for him to make his decision he had turned the adventure he wanted to embark on into a gracious favour to his wife to allow her time to get the 'baby thing' sorted. When he came back with his splendid prizes, and who knows, a title from the new King Charles, she would again be his darling and welcome him as a hero.

"You know, sheep can't tell which field they came out of." His eyes sparked with mischief as he considered his friend's woeful look. "We could help ourselves to a few of someone else's on the way to meet the sergeant. I won't have any trouble getting a sack of flour out of the granary. There might even be a boar or two roaming the woods. And…" He stopped to make sure Bobby was listening. "I have my grandfather's ruby ring which will buy swords and pistols. I shouldn't be surprised if the Prince makes us lords immediately."

Bobby was very dubious about the ruby Watt was bragging of. He, like everyone else in the boy's circle, had heard the story of Watt's grandfather's ring but it had been so exaggerated that it had taken on the mantle of a fairy story. He made up his mind to say nothing either for or against its existence, but not to depend on its appearance. Plans were made and the young men parted with promises to meet again the next afternoon, ready to plunder their neighbours stock and make their way to join the gathering army.

Chapter Twelve

As the tired group of men first saw the mustered army at rest in the field outside Dumfries, they were astounded by what appeared to them to be a carpet of brightly coloured tartan spread out as far as the eye could see. Each of these Border men were dressed in the breeches and jabot of the area. En masse their colour was grey since they wore grey shirts, grey socks, grey bonnets and carried grey blankets or plaids. Although as the army had made its way south it had picked up Lowlanders willing to fight for the rightful King, the army was predominately made up of Highlanders of the various clans affiliated to the Stuarts.

There was a sea of blue, green and red moving over the space with the many MacDonald, Clan Ranald and McDuff standards blending with the Stuart's royal banners, but there was a good representation of the more delicate hues in the blues and greens of the MacBeth and the MacBean. Tents were erected at irregular intervals and various fires were billowing smoke over the plaid-covered women, who tended the huge black pots which were held over the flames by tripods of branches lashed together to form a hook. Men sat about in groups, some smoking clay pipes, some attending to their weapons, some just sitting looking off into space, but, at the sight of the newcomers, they all stood to attention. It was not the advent of the raggle-taggle band bearing down on them but the livestock which they drove in front of them that caught the attention of the men. It was a long time since they had seen so much meat on the hoof and their immediate instinct was to kill the animals and have a feast. They rose almost as one man to approach the oncoming horde only to be ordered back by Lord George Murray, who happened to be wandering among his troops to establish their needs. He welcomed the recruits, telling them he was glad to see that the Border country was behind their sovereign, before ordering the animals and food parcels to be taken to the tent at the extreme end of the field where there was a small contingent of the army responsible for the feeding and clothing of the men under the command of the quartermaster sergeant.

Once the animals had been settled into their new pens, Watt and the other men who had followed MacAlister were led towards another much smaller tent where a kilted soldier met them and asked them individually what experience they had, what weapons they had brought, and if they had any money to throw in the pot.

Watt sidled up to the table, puffed up with his own importance to be bringing such a valuable piece, and threw the ring into the wooden bowl.

Not having expected anything of this order to have come from the ill-dressed, ill-shod men MacAlister had found, Alan Stuart removed it from the table, held it up allowing the light to hit its surfaces while he scrutinised the quality of both the stone and its heavy gold mount. He glanced suspiciously at Watt.

"How came you by this jewel? Speak up! Did you steal it? Tell the truth now. This is no fairing but a very famous jewel. It does not belong with a farm lad."

Watt was enraged by being spoken to in this manner and was determined to make the other eat his words. He pulled himself up straight and looked the older man in the eye; had his grandfather been there he would have recognised the stance and demeanour of his own father in the cold, angry stare of his grandson.

"It belonged to my grandfather and he had it from his father, the CaimBeuil, leader of the clan Campbell and it is rightly mine, passed into my hands the night before I married," he said with pride apparent in his tone.

"Married?" scoffed the Highlander. "You're nought but a bairn still wet behind the ears. Not even a mad Campbell would confer such a distinguished jewel on a ploughboy."

"Don't you dare speak to me in that manner. I do not lie. I have offered up this ring to furnish myself and my friend with weapons so we may follow Prince Charles."

Alan Stuart ignored this remark and began to look bored. He threw the jewel at Sandy, MacAlister saying, "Take this yokel off and his friends with him. Settle them with the Lowlanders or wherever you think they will be most useful and make sure they get some training with swords and pistols. You never know when your life might depend upon them." By the expression on his face the men were left in no doubt how unlikely he found that idea.

MacAlliser, never the most ardent of Alan Stuart's followers, beckoned the twenty or so men he had brought in with him and took them off across the field to meet a group of his own clansmen. On his approach he was greeted with good-natured camaraderie and jokes were made about him cavorting all over the countryside to avoid his share of the work. He introduced the men, laying stress on how they were a much needed addition to their forces since he knew that, after their encounter with the commander, they would more than likely be wondering why they had bothered to volunteer if they were to be thought so little of.

"What is the point in sending me out to recruit if, within five minutes of being in the army, they are being belittled?" he thought before continuing out loud, "These fine men I've brought today have walked many a mile to join us in our fight, but, if you cannot welcome them for that reason, maybe the livestock they brought with them might make you more friendly." He smiled at his cronies.

"Fat chance there is of us getting any meat, what with Clan Ranald being in charge of rations," moaned one of the rough men in a thoroughly disreputable-looking group. "Our pot has oats and onions and not even Aggie's herbs can make that taste good."

Sandy MacAlister, used to the remonstrances of his clansmen, bent his massive head and, putting his hand into the folds of his plaid, fumbled for a few seconds before pulling out several bloody joints that, to any countryman, were still recognisable as a deer and threw them in the direction of the moaning man.

"Takes these to Aggie with my compliments." He bowed from the waist as a courtier to his King. "Tell her I 'found' them this morning and, since they were not provided by these recruits, can be kept only for our stewpot."

With a totally changed appearance the MacAlister clansman loped off towards a smouldering fire where a pot was being attended to by a very aged woman who greeted her visitor with a toothless grin, patting him on the arm as he produced his contribution. MacAlister looked at the others under his command and realised they had been idle while he had been off about his recruitment duties. He decided it was time for them to earn the supper he had provided.

"Iain, get a few of the men together and try to instil some idea of warfare into these men. Make sure they can all load, fire, and clean, a pistol and a musket." After surveying the motley crew in front of him he continued, "If any of them show any likelihood of handling a broadsword, give them a few tips," he laughed. "I lost a good number of my best swordsmen at Prestonpans and need my ranks filled." With a wave of his gauntlet-covered hand, he turned and walked off, greeting other officers as he went but stopping to speak to no one.

"Come on then, you lot, you heard the orders. Let's see what you are made of," Iain Stuart said as he led the men over to where a group of his compatriots were oiling and priming firing pieces and cleaning and sharpening their swords till they sparkled in the afternoon sunlight.

For some hours the recruits were schooled in the way of fighting both with pistols and muskets by the Highlanders. Watt and his crew were excited to learn about the weapons and were soon able to prime the pistols. Watt desperately wanted to have a swing at the broadsword, but, when he was presented with one by his instructor, he was unable to lift it with one hand, never mind swing it round his head in the manner of these giant Highlanders.

"Ye'll be needing to eat a bit mair porridge in the morning afore ye can go into battle wi' yin o' these blades," laughed Iain as he saw Watt made a third and fourth attempt to raise the sword that was almost as long as he was tall.

"Stick to pistols is my advice, but tomorrow I'll teach you to fight with a dagger in case you get close up to the enemy."

As dusk began to fall the field took on a surreal atmosphere. The figures moving about appeared like huge grey shadows flitting here and there as the men moved in and out of the light cast by the flickering flames. A slow drumbeat could be heard floating on the air and the shadows merged into one another as the men hurried to see what was cooking in their own battalion's particular pot.

Watt walked along beside Bobby taking in all the smells and sounds that were new to them, passing the odd remark to the other men they had met on the long trek to Dumfries. They stood self-consciously at the back of the circle around the fire, where Aggie had used her time with the venison to good effect, and a very mouth-watering aroma accosted their senses.

"What do you think, Watt?" Bobby asked

"I think we have become part of the Scottish army about to eat a hearty supper provided by our leader and I, for one, will be glad to eat it."

For the group of men Watt and Bobby mixed with around the campfire the stew tasted like nectar from the gods and they gobbled it up with gusto. Some came from the best Highland estates, some from the poorest hovels of the central plains, some like themselves from the Lowlands, but, one and all, they were treated alike round this fire. Each man accepted his portion as his due. Some may have embarked on this hazardous affair more from fealty to their liege lord rather than a firm idea of following the Young Prince, but each man had given up what comfort there was in their homes, high or low, to eat a poor meal in a cold field in the name of Prince Charles Edward Stuart.

As the dark night encroached and the cooking fires died, the field took on yet another cloak of disguise as the men unhooked their plaids, wrapped them around themselves and lay down where they were to sleep.

Watt was too excited to sleep. Nevertheless, he wound himself up in his hodden grey blanket and stared up at the clear night sky, watching as the stars began to come out making it appear he was encased in a deep purple velvet cloak sprinkled with sparkling gems. As he lay there his thoughts focussed on the future campaign and how on the morrow he would be having lessons in fighting. Not for one second did his thoughts stray to the family he had left behind, neither for his parents or for his wife and children whom he had not even kissed goodbye as he had slunk off two days ago.

He awoke with a start as the men around began to rouse to face the new day. Watt lifted himself up onto his elbow and took in the activity around him. Men were in various stages of undress, some were making off into the wood to relieve themselves, some were aiding each other to dress their wild hair and tie it back with thin strips of leather, others were advancing on the site of the campfires with kindling and wood, for no hot food could be had until the fires were alight and fuelled.

As one of the tutors from yesterday passed by with a massive armful of twigs, he caught sight of Watt, saying, "If you get your arse up and help with the firewood, I will see about teaching you to use a small sword. You don't have the build for a broadsword but I reckon you could handle the wee boy."

"Thank you, thank you," stammered Watt, immediately jumping to his feet in delight. Unlike many of the other men Watt had not undressed or even removed his boots as he settled for sleep the previous night so with a bound and a laugh he was off in the direction of a nearby copse. It was not so easy to find material for the fires now since they had been bivouacked here for a few days, and each clan or sept had their own fire. It took much ingenuity to find enough fuel, but each seasoned soldier knew that when there was a chance of a hot meal they should take it, for who knew when they might get another?

After a breakfast of porridge Watt and a few other men were selected to be taught swordplay. He was proud that he had been chosen, but his natural bombastic nature led the others to shun him when he made his grandiose statements.

"I will be the best swordsman of you all. My grandfather is the son of a very famous lord. It's in my blood."

"It's your lordly blood we'll be letting if you don't stow it!" growled the man nearest him.

"Leave the bairn alone," laughed another. "All weans like to boast. Let him put his sword where his mouth is."

"I'll show you how good I am and make you eat your words," barked Watt, making towards the man with his sword pointed at his heart.

"Enough!" came a sharp command as MacAlister approached. "Never point your weapon at your own men. The first rule of battle is to keep your eye on each other's back and fight as one and never against each other."

He turned to the soldiers instructing his new swordsmen and asked, "How are they doing? Can they be trusted not to kill each other?"

Iain Stuart laughed and pointed at two or three men in the rank in front of him. "These men have got the hang of it. They cut and thrust at the legs and arms and I'd be happy to have them in my troop."

"What of the braggart lad?" Sandy queried.

"There's no doubt he has an aptitude for the fight, but he's erratic and thinks of glory for himself and I'd not like my life to depend on his actions," came the reply.

"I'll watch him. Match him with one of our better swordsmen."

"Here, you!" shouted Iain Stuart at one of the rank. "Take a small sword and put that recruit through his paces. Don't go easy on him, but don't injure him either," he commanded.

Watt was delighted to be singled out. He had expected to be chosen to swell the ranks of Iain Stuart's band and was taken aback that the senior man did not think him worthy enough.

He fought with very little skill, but, if swordplay could be bred in the bone, it certainly had been bred in his, for he had an instinct where the next strike was coming from and nearly always managed to block the more experienced swordsman.

After watching for a short time Sandy MacAlister made a decision. It was almost as big a surprise to him as it was to those who heard him say, "Well done, young Campbell. You can join my rank and fight with the Highlanders. I expect total obedience or you will be back where you started. Understood?"

Watt tried hard to conceal his delight but his crooked grin lit up his face as he replied immediately. "Yes, sir."

"Collect your gear and bring yourself to my tent yonder," MacAlister ordered as he turned to walk away from the training ground.

Watt hurried to obey and in a short space of time was settling his pack into a miniscule space amongst the others in MacAlister's rank. Sandy called him over and brought him back to earth with his next command.

"You will tend the horses; it is most important that they are fed and watered. More important than if you or I are fed, for these animals have to take us into battle and must be fast as the wind if we need to outrun the enemy. Pick a lad from the ones you know to care for the other animals while you are at it. While we are marching and not actually fighting we will keep the beasts alive, so that by the time we reach London town we will still be able to have fresh Scottish meat."

"Sir, Bobby, my friend from home has been brought up on the farm, just as I have, and he will know exactly what to do, but, well, we have no fodder."

"There is plenty of grass and you and Bobby can take turns to keep the water butts full, but, when we are on the march, you need to stop wherever there is a stream so they can drink their fill."

That day was busy, running hither and thither setting up hurdles to keep the animals corralled, tending to and grooming the horses; another round of musket practise and some wrestling with sticks to simulate daggers and, of course learning all there was to know about battle.

As the daylight receded, Bobby and Watt were companionably walking back to the clan fire when Bobby complained, "Tending the animals, that's what I was doing at home. There's not much chance of becoming rich unless the sheep shite gold."

Watt, never one to take any notice of another's predicament unless it directly affected him, laughed joyously at his comments.

"At least we are set for adventure and the sheep and pigs will all be eaten soon. What we brought is little enough to feed these men." He took in Bobby's disenchanted face and added, "You've learned to fire a musket and to prime it and how to fight the enemy both in close combat and at a distance, so you are ready to go to war."

"With my luck, I'll be so far back in the ranks I won't even see the English army," said Bobby, not willing to be consoled.

"You'll see them all right, for they are so thick they have red coats to make them an easy target," he laughed, throwing his arm over his friend's shoulder. "Don't forget we are to return heroes," he ended.

That night after they had all been fed at their own specific fire the boys noticed a massive fire lighting up the field and the sky above. It crackled and spat as the wood being fed onto it was a bit green, but it gave off a cheery flame. Standing up to get a closer look, Bobby and Watt noticed that men were converging on this fire from all angles so they decided they too should see what was happening. When they were a few hundred yards away they heard the beat of a drum and the drone of the bagpipes being filled with air. In a very few minutes a pleasant sound was heard floating on the evening air. A man began to sing in a deep voice and was shortly joined by others until, gradually, all that could be heard was the army singing as one man.

"Wow, I've never heard anything so good," whispered an awestruck Bobby.

"Me neither," agreed Watt. They stood a short distance away and revelled at the scene in front of their eyes. The song went on for a very long time. At times it sounded like a lament, at others a rousing battle cry or even as gentle as a lullaby or a love song, but to the Lowlanders it made no sense as the words were foreign to them; despite being Scottish the men of the Borders for the most part spoke the hard vowels of the English language rather than the softer, more poetic Gaelic of their northern countrymen. Suddenly the drum beat to a different rhythm and the piper's fingers moved faster on the chanter, and sets of wild-looking kilted soldiers began to dance a reel.

Not having been educated in the ways of dancing Watt had not before seen men dancing with other men and he suddenly realised what, in the barn at home, was a breathtaking gambol, when danced by these tall broad barbaric-looking men was indeed a sight to make your heart swell with pride.

"I wish I could join in but I've no idea how, and look how no one gets in the way of anyone else even at the speed they are going," said Watt.

"They are whirling like devils, kilted devils," laughed Bobby as he took in the sight of the many coloured whirling kilts and plaids as the men cavorted and spun each other by the arm. The music stopped and laughing, breathless men threw themselves down to rest while the piper screwed his pipes and a melancholy tune dictated by the placing of the piper's limber fingers on the chanter floated over the field. A slow hand clap started and the army of soldiers all looked in one direction until a solitary young soldier stood up, which gave the cue to the audience to become silent and all that could be heard was the tune of the bagpipes while the young soldier was lit up by the flames from the fire. He was neither tall nor well built, a slim waist defining a narrow chest and hips, but he stood straight and proud. He raised his arms above his head in an imitation of stag horns and began hopping up and down on one leg in time to the music and danced a most beautiful dance with very intricate footwork that neither Bobby or Watt had ever seen. They had heard about the Highlanders' love of dance, but felt very privileged to witness it in the flesh. In the flickering flames you could almost imagine him to be the stag he represented. There was an awed silence among the men, but, when the final bow had been made, the men clapped and clapped for more.

"Gie us the swords," came a voice from the crowd. "Let's see if we are to be victorious in our battle."

"Naw, naw! Let the lad be," spoke another.

"Make him dance. We want to know our fate."

A general argument began among the men but neither Watt or Bobby could understand what it had to do with the dancer, who, while the subject of the sword dance was being discussed, slunk off into the black shadows.

"What's the commotion?" asked Bobby of a bystander wearing a red kilt and black jacket of an officer.

"The sword dance is reputed to foretell the outcome of a battle. All the dances tell a story but the sword is the one revered above all others."

"How does it do that?" Bobby looked puzzled.

"To dance this dance you dance over the crossed swords and place your feet in the squares made by the cross. As the music speeds up through the progression of the dance the footwork speeds up to match it and, if you are clumsy or mistime a step, you can be cut by the honed blade of the sword." He stopped to look at the spellbound men. "If the dancer completes the dance with no cut, the army will be successful in its campaign. In order to cut the odds of the dancer having a toe severed the sword dance is always danced by a young soldier who is not prone to taking a dram. If he is cut…"

"So the lad didn't want to dance in case he made the army lose and the cause be lost?" Watt stated the obvious.

"Smart lad, you'll go far. I wonder…" He broke off as a horseman galloped up to the main body of men, threw himself off and pushing through the restless men approached Alan Stuart, saluted and delivered a letter.

Stuart read it then read it again.

"This is a letter from my cousin the Prince," he said, flourishing the paper for all to see. "We are ordered to march south to meet the Duke of Cumberland who is marching north to meet us.

"Nobliseat ira Leonis"

"The wrath of the lion is noble," intoned those surrounding Stuart.

So saying, the standards were moved to indicate the rallying points for each clan and Watt, who was close by, heard Iain Stuart murmur, "Maybe it was fate there was no sword dance tonight."

****

The Army on the March

The pouring rain that had been hindering their advance for the past several hours was soaking not only into their heavy woollen clothes but into their very souls. The Highlanders with their kilts and plaids fared little better for all their dress was designed to withstand the inclement weather. The heavy grey sky made it appear dusk even though it wanted only a few minutes to midday. Hindered as they were by their weapons, they made a sorry sight as they wended their way along the country roads towards the Border with England.

There were no bystanders or supporters lining their route today to wish them well and spur them on to victory. The truth was that the men of the Borders cared very little who was on the throne of the country, for they were so far away from that seat of power that they continued on and held to the traditions of the Borderers ruling themselves.

Of course the leaders, the colonels and chieftains and captains of the battalions rode their great warhorses and were more successful in repelling the unseasonally cold winds and rains that slewed in from the sea than were the foot soldiers, but even they were faring ill on this tedious march south.

Since the horses, which were primarily the concern of Watt when the army was camped, were now in use by their owners, he had elected to assist Bobby with the transportation of the animals at the rear of the column.He was a bit disappointed that he had not been given leave to ride one of the horses. They heard the jingle of harness and the clash of metal on metal, and, when they craned their necks round, they were just in time to witness the Prince and his retinue gallop past at speed. The Prince looked very fine, though definitely foreign to the Lowlanders' eyes. He had been raised in Paris and was dressed in the fashion of the French court. To see him would not have led you to have faith in his competence as a leader of soldiers. Watt had no experience of such finery of velvet and lace over which he wore an ornate breastplate. The pseudo-monarch wore his own hair free from powder, and loose, and waving over his shoulders, atop which was placed a velvet hat decorated with a white cockade, the emblem of the Jacobites for almost fifty years.

"Doesn't look much like a soldier does he?" remarked Bobby as the small troop rushed by.

"He's certainly well looking and fair of face. A handsome Stuart king to fight for but the fleeting glimpse of him I caught there doesn't make me think he's off to fight a battle, more like to hunt the deer in the forest," replied Watt, much disappointed in his first sighting of the Prince he had pledged to serve. In no way did he match the image he had in his head of the wronged king determined to win back his kingdom because God had decreed he was the rightful ruler. Yet Watt had started out on this adventure determined to fight for a real cause and was loath to let Bobby see his disappointment.

"It might have been better if I had not seen him in the flesh but was able to hold the image of the strong ruler at the front of my mind," mused Watt.

"Indeed, had the Prince been more of the stature of Sandy MacAlister, or even Alan Stuart, I would have been clamouring to be brought to his attention." Bobby broke into these contemplations in quiet voice. "I don't think I want adventure anymore. You know what? I walked all this way from my home to Dumfries husbanding these animals to join the Prince's army and here I am, acting the part of a drover driving them all the way back. Feels like I'm going down in rank rather than seeking my fortune."

"It will be different when we start to fight with the English army. *Then* we will see some action and excitement. It's only a matter of time."

"It's all right for you," came the quick rejoinder, "you have been promised a place with MacAlister's swordsmen while I'm just an ordinary makeweight, running errands for all and sundry. And I'm wet, cold and hungry. However bad it was at home, I never was wet, cold and hungry!" he expostulated.

"Bobby, Bobby. Think of the glory when you go back home after the battle as a hero. Think how proud your parents will be then."

Bobby did not look convinced, but shut his mouth tight and continued his weary walk behind the baggage train, "Even behind the old hags who tend to the cooking pots," he finished, feeling very woebegone.

The army continued on its way. The pace was not fast, for, as well as the animals, there were the heavy cannon to be moved ponderously on their gun carriages, drawn by the slow carthorses, and, as the horses were a prime commodity, those who had the tending of them had to ensure that they did not become overstrained. A halt was called and the men were issued with large chunks of bread and meat with tankards of ale to wash the food down. It was not a pleasant picnic as might have been enjoyed on a hot summer day, for everything was dripping wet and the men, knowing the stop would be a short one, felt it better to stuff the food in as quickly as possible and carry on their progress.

While the men were refuelling Watt was called upon to attend to his duties and quickly settled bags of oats over the horses' noses before leading them off to drink from a nearby burn. As he returned with several of these giant chargers to their owners, Sandy was standing talking tactics with Alan Stuart and one of Watt's sword-fighting teachers from yesterday, who immediately beckoned for him to come forward.

"I've been looking up and down the ranks for you. You are to attach yourself to the guard of the baggage train and keep an eye out for trouble. One of the scouts has just reported a sighting of a party of Cumberland's men and we might get into a little spat with them." So saying he handed Watt a pistol, a powder horn and a small sword and indicted where he was to position himself, riding just behind the lead horse of the baggage wagons.

"Here, take a drop of this," commanded MacAlister, handing him his whisky flask. "You look frozen to the marrow. Find yourself a tarp in amongst the baggage."

"Thank you, that has warmed me," said a grateful Watt as he handed the flagon back to his commanding officer, and, munching on a crust of bread, made his way almost gaily to what he saw as a position of great importance.

"I know it won't take me long to climb to a higher station," he smiled to himself, well pleased at being singled out by MacAlister.

The order was to continue the march until they were on the English side of the Border and no camps would be set up until they had achieved that goal, so despite the day darkening, both from the heavy persistent rain and the short winter days, the soldiers moved quietly along the route south. Morale was low but each man was instilled with the determination to carry out their duty until the cause was won. The officers and chieftains rode up and down the columns of struggling men giving encouragement and praise here, chivvying and ordering there, detecting what means would be most likely to keep their men at their designated tasks.

It was about nine o'clock in the evening, the horses hitched to the wagons were very tired and ready to lose their burdens, when a glimmer of light off to the left alerted the guards to the presence of others in the area.

Watt had just seen the flash of light, as if a lantern had been lit and immediately shuttered, when he felt a tug at his sleeve and a quiet voice say, "Prime your pistol and draw your sword. We have been sighted by the enemy and if I'm not mistaken we will be set upon by the villains any minute. Good luck, lad." came the disembodied voice.

As soon as he had warned Watt, he was off to do likewise to the others in the train. They rode on for perhaps another mile on high alert. Watt frequently jumped as the movement of a branch nearby spooked him or a shadow moved on the edges of his vision. It was black dark and when the raiding party eventually struck they did so without being detected.

Peering off to his left where he had previously seen the flicker of flame Watt was startled to be unseated by a quick yank on his leg from the right-hand side. The marauder had managed to come right up to him without his being aware of his creeping approach. Despite being green in the use of the sword, Watt defended himself as he had been shown. His heart beat a tattoo in his throat but, as parry after parry was successful, the dread of being killed that he had experienced in the beginning began to dissolve and he fought off his assailant. One lucky swipe, aimed at the legs of his opponent, struck home and he heard a cry of agony as the attacker fell away. With no time to preen himself on his prowess he was immediately beset by another of the band.

"God damn you, you blaggard!" he shouted.

"Hold hard!" came the reply from one of the Highlanders. "In this damned inky blackness you can't see if you are fighting the enemy or ourselves. Are you for the Prince?"

"Aye," answered Watt, still ripe for the fight. He gave a half laugh that was stifled at birth by the advent of a posse of English soldiers bent on skewering the Jacobites.

Watt raised his sword with difficulty for he was unused to long bouts of sword fighting, but where his comrade led, Watt followed, taking on another of the attackers. He was surprised that the fight took so long for he knew they were outnumbered at least three to one, but he held his ground and the two managed to keep the attackers at bay. The Highlander, with a great shriek of a war cry unintelligible to Watt's untrained ear, fell about the redcoat and slashed him across the throat; he fell back with a gurgle which led Watt to believe him to be dying. He tried hard to emulate the warlike clansman, but he was not a strong enough swordsman to hold back his more battle-seasoned attacker and soon found himself with a disabled sword arm. He had been pressed back into a corner by the aggressor until there was nowhere for him to turn, and he was not surprised to feel a trickle of blood run down inside the sleeve of his jacket as he prepared himself to meet his maker at the hands of an English swordsman.

His last conscious thought was, "Some soldier I am, killed on the first sortie."

Then blackness descended.

****

He opened his eyes not knowing where he was or how he had got there.

"Is this Heaven?" he asked, only to be answered by a cackle as a round, white orb floated into his vision.

"Aye, lad, and I'm an angel," chortled the old woman who was busying herself binding up the gash on his arm. The lantern nearby gave off only a glimmer of light, but he was close enough to it to realise that he was bare-chested and being washed down, not by an angel as he had supposed but by an ancient crone, one of the women whom he had seen attending to the cooking pots when the army had been garrisoned in Dumfries.

"You're lucky," she smiled her toothless grin at him. "You've only got a wee scratch, no very serious at all. You'll not can use your sword arm for a wee whiley but you'll live to fight another day. I thought at first you were one of those English scum." She stopped to hack and spit on the ground, leaving Watt with no difficulty in deciphering her opinion of the enemy army. "I've sent MacAlister to find you some dry clothes but maybe you had best put this back on meantime." She held up the sword-damaged, rain- and blood-soaked jacket, then changed her mind and threw her shawl over his shivering shoulders.

Cuddling into the shawl, warm from the heat of the old woman's body, Watt tried to rationalise his situation.

"How did I get here? I don't remember much but drawing a sword and being beaten back by a redcoat."

"You fought well. MacAlister brought you to me to be patched up, for you were looking dead and white as a ghost, but don't complain; that's likely what saved your life. Maybe the bugger thought he had killed you, for he made off and MacAlister found you lying beside a redcoat with his thrapple cut open."

Just at that moment a shadow appeared out of the dark and Watt made for his belt to retrieve his pistol when he heard a familiar voice.

"Hold on, don't shoot me, for I'm bringing you dry clothes. You'll have to make do with a kilt and a shirt, but, once your breeks are dry, you can put them back on again if you're afeared for your modesty." He had noticed Watt casting glances at Maggie and rightly suspected that he did not want to take off his wet trousers in her presence. Choosing to ignore his discomfort he threw the pile of clothes at him and brought him up to date on proceedings.

"We have decided to camp here for the night. Since you are the wounded hero," he cast a sly look in Watt's direction, "you can sleep here tonight with Maggie, but I warn you not to try to steal her virtue for she's a dab hand with a dagger."

He smiled in the old woman's direction and she answered him, highly delighted with his joke. "He's no man enough for me. I'd soon tire him out and then what good would he be to you as a soldier? I'll thank you to leave me to deal with my honour."

Although the words were stern, it was obvious that she had a high opinion of Sandy MacAlister and had taken the joke in good part.

MacAlister turned to Watt. "Maggie will bring you some hot food when the wifies have it ready, but I can't promise what it might be for we lost about half of our supply wagons to that raiding party."

"I'm really sorry I failed to stop them. If I had been more alert maybe they wouldn't have got near," said Watt in a sheepish tone his mother and father would not have recognised.

"You could not have helped it. They were lying in wait and the rain and the dark were in their favour," consoled Sandy. He laid a hand on Watt's uninjured shoulder and went on, "You fought well. I know this because you were alongside my kinsman who told me you reacted quickly and what you lack in skill you made up for with will. You'll make good soldier. Sleep now, you'll need your strength for we still have a day's march to Carlisle." So saying, he made his way out of the tent, leaving Watt to Maggie's ministrations.

The advent of the English raiding party had changed the plan of the Prince's army. Their already minimal stores had been much depleted by the raid. Of more worry to the quartermaster was the loss of the animals that had in the middle of all the kerfuffle been scattered. There was no time to look for them, no money to buy more food, so rations would be pretty slim in the meantime. Although there had been no lives lost in the raid, other than a few English ones that that had fallen to the barbarous Scotsmen, many had minor injuries, so it was decided to rest for one day to allow the army to resettle itself into a fighting force. After a day's rest Watt was deemed, by Maggie, to be healed enough to go back to his post. If his opinion of himself had been high before the turn-up with the English, it had now soared to previously unthinkable heights. He strutted back and forth around the compound, proud of his war wound and exaggerating his story of how he came by it with each telling.

He was anxious to tell his friends from home about his experience but as he walked round the perimeter of the camp he found many fewer than he had expected. The Highlanders showed no respect for his prowess and he felt the need to be praised, so, of course, his thoughts turned to Bobby whom he knew would listen avidly to his tale. At last he spied someone he had known slightly since his childhood and he rushed off to accost him and question him about Bobby's whereabouts.

"I'm told there was no one killed so it can't be that and he wasn't with me and the others who were wounded. Maybe he's off looking for the lost animals." Unknown to them, as the two men stood chatting in the frost-rimed field, Bobby was now making his way in quite another direction. He had been terrified by the onslaught of the English patrol. To begin with, he had tried to stay with his animals in an attempt to keep them together and safe, but, as the noise of the enemy force increased, the animals ran hither and thither and were soon lost to Bobby. He pushed his way into a hedgerow and prayed for his life. As the sounds of the altercation faded, he felt he had been sitting in his hiding place for days, but he was still afraid to stick his nose out from his safe haven in case he was caught by one of the raiding party.

"What on earth am I doing here stuck like a fox in his den hiding from the hounds?" he thought as he sat frozen stiff in the depths of the hedge. He dozed and woke in fright, wetting his already drenched breeches with the pungent contents of his bladder just as the sky began to lighten indicting that a new day was arriving. He smelled the reek of his own bodily fluids, even tasting the acrid scent at the back of his throat, felt the warm pat stuck to his rear where he had shit himself at the height of his distress, and repented that he had ever heard of the Jacobite army or listened to the nonsense spoken by his friend.

"How could I be so stupid?" he chided himself. Peering out from the shelter of the prickly bush he recognised where he was. That was all the motivation he needed. This was not a faraway battlefield but a sheep pasture only a few miles from his home, which at that moment had lost all its disadvantages of shared beds and hard work, appearing to him to be like the Holy Grail.

Taking another peek from his hidey-hole he checked that the spire he could see not far distant was indeed that of the Ecclefechan Church. With no further thought of becoming a hero or winning prize money or gaining a title from Prince Charles, he decided that his adventure was over. He did spare one thought for Watt but before he could talk himself into going back and persuading him to abandon the scheme too, he recalled that Watt always got his own way and, far from accompanying him home, would be much more likely to convince Bobby to continue with the escapade.

"Boys dreams," he scoffed at himself as he quickly disentangled himself from the clinging branches of the bush and took himself off in the direction of home, where he hoped he would receive a warm welcome, from his mother at least, and if he had a hiding from his father, well, it was better than dying in a cold field.

So when Watt spoke to his acquaintance about where he might be Bobby was had almost reached home.

Watt missed his friend, more for someone to talk to and lionise with, but, within hours of Bobby's departure, Prince Charles had conferred with his generals and the plan had been formed to attack and capture Carlisle and thereby give the Prince a toehold in his country. The plan was to set up the machinery of war under cover of darkness for if the black dark had been so effective for the English, it stood to reason that it could also be used against them. So the army was once more on the march.

It took another day of marching for the Jacobite army to reach the walled town of Carlisle, but when they had the town in their sights in the early afternoon they were ordered to spread out and lay low out of sight of the sentries on the castle battlements.

Once night fell, the soldiers were split up into squads, each squad being in charge of one of the precious cannon that they had hauled from one end of the country to the other. Quietly and under cover of darkness they set up the artillery and surrounded the town. Occasionally, spooked by strange noises of the night, a volley of musket fire could be heard coming from the ramparts of the town, but they made no impact on the Jacobites toiling below.

Watt was part of a contingent who would initially be required to man the cannon but be ready to advance, sword drawn when the walls were breached. He was as excited as any schoolboy and anxious to play his part. He worked companionably with several, tall, fearsome Highlanders whom he had at first stood greatly in awe of because of their strength and experience, but gradually they developed a camaraderie that increased as they prepared the cannon, digging a pit for it to ensure its stability when fired. The work was hard and the men sweated and strained as one. The leader of the group handed Watt a jug, nudging him to show he meant him to take a swig from it.

"Thanks," said Watt after taking a long, cool drink that washed the sand and soil out of his throat. He handed the jug back.

"How do you come to be fighting with us? I thought all the Lowlanders with us were doing the field work and not tending the cannon."

"Don't know," shrugged Watt shortly. "I'm just following orders. And they were to take my orders from you. So here I am."

"You're wearing a MacAlister kilt but you don't sound like any clansman I've heard, but if Big Sandy thinks you're good enough for this jaunt, then that's good enough for me."

Few words were spoken after this interlude but the work continued until the leader was happy that the cannon was sited properly and would not move from its position when the explosion occurred.

"When we start firing you need to make sure we have a steady stream of cannonballs. If we run out, then you can gather big stones and rocks but keep a musket handy because you will be a target for the sharpshooters above."

Just as they had finished getting their equipment into order another volley of musket fire could be heard. The sky had lightened and the lookouts had caught sight of the army surrounding their town. The musket balls fell short and, after a second burst of fire, the Scots realised that they were out of range of the musket balls.

"Look at them wasting their shot just to make a noise! Give us your bonnets and we will make them some targets to shoot at." Watt had no idea what the men meant but was willing enough to hand over his bonnet as directed. There was much glee among the men as the planted their spades just behind the line where the musket balls had landed propping a bonnet of various hues on top. In the early morning light these dummies looked like soldiers and the ranks on the fortress walkways fired continuously at them. The Jacobites stood back, well out of range and shouted obscenities at their opposite number.

"Hae a wee shottie with your wee musket. See if you can hit the target. No? No? It's too far away!"

"Come a wee bittie closer. Out from behind your wall."

"Are you not allowed proper guns? No! For you're all bairns and dafties!"

"Come on, red coat. Hie a shottie!"

The guards on the ramparts were infuriated and continued sending volleys of musket balls over the intervening space, becoming more and more frustrated as they continued to miss and the Highlanders' taunting, hooting and laughing made matters worse. The joke spread around all the cannon entrenchments as the Scottish army found they could cause the maximum of havoc without using any of their precious ammunition. As the mocking soldiers continued to exchange insults with the town's defence force the thrump, thrump of the cannon could be heard as, one by one, they loosed off their first shots. In the smoke-laden silence that followed the third of these explosions a white flag was seen emerging over the castle battlements. Great jollification among the Scotsmen followed as they yelled and cheered at the surrender of the town.

"Well, that's what happens when God in His Glory is on the side of the righteous," cackled a jubilant supporter of the Prince.

"Aye," quoth another. "The rightful King and his followers are immune from defeat because God is on the King's side."

Watt had not until now realised that the army he had joined believed themselves to be a religious army. In the short time he had been with them he had seen no signs that they believed themselves to be fighting a Holy War they could not lose. Many of the Highlanders were indeed fighting to bring back the Catholic Church by restoring the Catholic King, but many more had it ingrained in their soul that as Prince Charles Edward Stuart was the grandson of an anointed King and, as such, was God's representative on Earth.

Watt, who attended church more from a desire to keep the peace in his household rather than from any devout feelings, felt unmanned as he took in the rapture on the faces around him.

A drumbeat notified the army that they must fall in rank as a procession was being formed to enter Carlisle and take the surrender formally. The army marched behind their officers, weapons drawn as they rode into the town, where the burghers and townsmen lined the streets looking very woebegone. There was no cheering for the invading troops, but neither was there any noticeable antagonism towards the men as they passed by. They continued up to the heavy door of the Castle where they were met by a group of English soldiers under the command of Colonel Durrant, who formally surrendered the town and the castle to Prince Charles. In a day or so there would be a ritual humiliation of the keeper of the castle and the mayor and councillors of the town when they would be forced to swear an oath to do no harm to the army of the Scottish King for a year, but, in the meantime, Lord George Murray accepted everything material and living within the town as the property of Prince Charles, while the former keeper and his minions were marched off to enjoy the luxuries of their own dungeons.

Alan and Iain Stuart, together with Sandy MacAlister, approached their troops and selected some of their most reliable men to post as watches on the ramparts, then dismissed the army to the pleasures to be found in the town.

Watt was caught by the arm by one of the officers he had been sharing the night watches with.

"Come along with me and we will find a glass to drink and a wench to bed with, for we deserve the spoils of war as much as our masters."

"No, no, you don't want to get drunk, not yet a while at any rate; there are plenty of houses and shops for us to plunder first. Come with us. We'll need some coin in your pocket if you are to find a woman to lie with us willingly," argued another of his comrades from the cannon siting squad.

"Away with you. We are Highland gentlemen. *We* will not rob, pillage or rape," came the sharp reprimand from the first man.

"Go your own way, McPike. I am off to see what treasures lie within the silversmith's or the blacksmith's. Either money or weapons will suit me fine. Then I plan to visit an alehouse and even later a bordello. Now admit, that sounds like a better outing than that offered by old sober sides there." He nodded in the direction of McPike.

Watt was thrilled at the prospect offered by his unknown friend and answered, "I think I'd like to look around the town for a bit with these men, sir."

"Well, the choice is yours. You can suit yourself what you do but, as soon as the drum beats to call you back to arms in the morning, you must respond, for, if you don't appear, I will have you charged as a deserter, hunted down and shot." He finished speaking, turned round and marched off towards the castle.

Watt stood watching him go wondering if he had made the right decision to throw in his lot with these companions but the picture conjured up by the man's words was decidedly more to his taste. "After all, that is what I joined the army for. To make my fortune and experience life."

"Are you throwing in your lot with us then? Equal shares?" queried the man next to him. He held out his hand and introduced himself. "I'm Euan MacAlister and these scamps are my brothers David and Donald. Are you with us?"

"Aye, I'm Watt, Watt Campbell and new with the army so you'll need to lead so I can follow." He laughed showing his crooked grin. When Watt chose to exert his personality there were few who could resist his charm and these boys, stunned that a Campbell Lowlander was fighting with the predominately MacDonald army, were taken in by his personality.

"Let's be off," said Donald. "The longer we stand here gawking, the less time there will be left for us to have some fun." As they headed off towards the main street of the town, he went on to explain, "We have today and tonight to take what we find without any redress from the chieftains; it is what is called the spoils of war, all armies live by the rule. If you fancy a drink you can take what you want from a wine merchant, food from a bakery or a grocery and if you fancy a maid there is only her to stop you."

"I really could do to wet my whistle. Ale would be my preference," replied Watt with eyes goggling at the prospect of riches to come in their many differing forms. He would never have imagined he would be in a position to pluck treasure from the street as he would pluck apples from a tree in the orchard back home.

"Stick with me. I know my way around," bragged Donald who was much the same age as Watt, although it would be another year before either reached their majority. The two boys linked arms, then joined up with the elder MacAlister brothers and proceeded running and laughing down a hill to a posting inn by the roadside. On entering the tap, they could see that the inn had already been taken over by soldiers. A Highlander of middle years with his kilt drawn up over his knees and his russet locks flying wild and loose was sitting astride a barrel of ale filling tankards that were handed to him one at a time and passing them on to anyone who came within reach. He appeared to be enjoying himself immensely, occasionally taking a long draught from one of the tankards as they were filled but, before starting on this enterprise, he had provided himself with a flagon of whisky which he had tied to his waist with a leather strap.

Watt felt a tankard being pushed into his hand and he accepted it gratefully, enjoying the feel of the cold liquid as it ran down his throat. So great was his thirst that he drank the tankard full of ale in a few gulps and handed it back to the new tap master to be refilled. With a cheery grin the man once more pushed the tankard into his hand and this time Watt savoured the cool beer as he let his eyes travel round the Inn. By this time the tap and the parlour were overflowing and Euan signalled to Watt that it was time to go. They shoved their way out onto the streets of the town where the shopkeepers had put up their shutters in the hope of keeping their possessions safe from the invaders. It would be useless of course, for, to the conquering horde, nothing was more attractive than a shuttered shop.

Donald, with the use of his dagger, levered the shutter off the window of a wine merchant's and wrapping his plaid round his arm broke the glass to afford the revellers access to the premises. The other three men followed him and found themselves in a dark space, but it was light enough for them to see that the walls of the room were lined with barrels and bottles of spirit and wine. Having heard the glass shattering the owner of the shop came running down the staircase at the back of the shop brandishing a large club in one hand and a sword in his other. He stopped abruptly near the bottom taken aback by the size and substance of the men who appeared to fill his shop. Watt had a moment's sympathy for him as he himself, the tallest man in his parish, felt cowed and dwarfed by these giant Highlanders and most certainly would not have voluntarily got himself into a fight with one of them, never mind three of similar girth and height.

Believing his best bet might be to try to reason with the men, he started, "Please don't take all my wine." His voice came out as a whine despite his efforts to sound bold. "I've a wife and family to feed. I don't wish you ill but leave my stock."

"Where's your wife?" asked David, a spark glinting in his eye.

The wine merchant said nothing but his surreptitious glances to the staircase from where he had descended gave away her location. Realising what was on David's mind, he began to plead. "No, no leave my wares. Take my wife, but leave my wine alone." He got down on his knees at the foot of the stair but his supplication had awakened the beast in David McPike and he made to pass him to reach a cask behind him.

In a frenzy of anxiety, the wine merchant struck him across the legs with his club, meaning to bring him down so that he could finish him off with his sword but before he had raised his sword as much as an inch he found himself lying in a pool of blood with David nonchalantly pulling his sword out of his breast. He wiped his blade on his late opponent's jacket and ran up the stairs two at a time, calling behind him, "What manner of animal is that who values his goods over the virtue of his wife?"

Watt was struck dumb but excited at the same time. The total absence of feeling shown by the McPike brothers was something he envied.

"And something I could not have contemplated before joining the army." He was lost in thought for several minutes but brought back to the present by Euan's voice.

"Give us a hand to move this lump and we will be off upstairs to see what glories we can find."

The men heaved the gory body of the still-breathing man away from the stairwell and followed David to the living quarters overhead. They had no trouble in finding David, since they could hear him, and without seeing him were left in no doubt that he was ravishing the injured man's wife while he lay dying downstairs. His soft word came from a room at the back.

"You like it like that, don't you, my beauty? Better than your old man, eh?"

"Just take what you want and go," came the harsh words from the woman. Perhaps living in a garrison town meant that this was not the first time she had been so used by an invading army, for she did not struggle but allowed David to make use of her body.

"Now that's no way to speak to a man who is giving you the best fuck you have ever had," said David, grinning at his brothers and Watt, "or are likely to get tonight. Now don't tire yourself out, for there are three others needing serviced when I'm done with you."

The three others entered the room where the sight of David's bare arse above his thick socks and heavy brogues made Watt choke on a laugh. He did not know why he found it funny to watch the big man holding the woman over the table with one arm while he manoeuvred himself into her, He had thrown up her skirt and pushed her thighs wide to allow him entry to her most secret places. He rode her hard and fast giving no thought to her discomfort but she said not another word appearing to be resigned to her ordeal. She did not respond to him but neither did she fight him. He entered and withdrew from her time and time again, and, as Watt watched, he felt his own manhood stand to attention beneath his borrowed kilt, where he itched to experience the thrill his friend was obviously enjoying.

David's buttocks shivered as his thrusts gained momentum until he finally exploded and sent his seed hurtling into the woman with a yell of joy. He stilled for a moment to catch his breath, then, rising and wiping his member on the woman's skirt, he gave her a gentle slap on the leg and said, "Tell me that was better than your old goat can do." He grinned, happy with his prowess, and said, "My, that was good. Do you want to have a go?"

He winked at the woman, still stretched face up on the table legs akimbo but half covered by her skirt. He indicted the other men and spoke softly to the woman, pinching her on the cheek as if she had been willing partner. "Now don't be expecting anything as good from them. They lack the experience."

Watt was just about to accept the offer of taking the woman but Euan gave voice before he had time. "I have another need for her for the present." He walked over and helped the woman to her feet, saying, "What we really are in need of, Mistress, is some hot food and a few bottles of wine. I'm sure you can accommodate us to save us messing your kitchen."

Still very shocked from her recent ordeal she walked shakily over to the fire where a pot had been simmering over the fire and, removing it, she brought it to the table along with plates and spoons and a breadboard with a bread and a gully. Euan jumped for the knife quickly, thinking she might attack with it, but it seemed as though she was doing their bidding without thought, for she seemed surprised when he lunged for the knife. The four soldiers set about feeding themselves, telling the silent woman how good the food was and that they had not tasted anything like it before. She did not respond but backed away from the men to the furthest corner of the kitchen, keeping her fearful eyes on the men every second of the time.

After they had satisfied their baser needs, Euan and David left the room with a nod to the two younger men. They were off for a scavenge round the house, leaving Watt and Donald to watch over the woman. Watt had been extremely excited watching another man rut and he was in dire need of a woman.

"Euan said she was the spoils of war," he whispered to Donald. "Shall we?"

"We can take turns," agreed Donald, who was just as anxious as Watt to venture between the woman's legs. She was quite a pretty woman and the fact that she would not be giving her favour freely added spice to the occasion. "I'll hold her first, then you can do the same for me." He spoke quietly, hoping the woman would not realise this would be the first time he had taken a woman without her consent and, if truth be known, he didn't think he would be able to hold her down and ravish her all on his own.

As they looked over to where she was still cowering in the far corner, she became aware of the desire in the men's faces and tried to escape through the door, but Watt was too quick for her and hung on tightly as she scratched and bit him. A smile came across Watt's face at her frenzied attack and quickly upended her, making her teeth and nails redundant. She continued to twist and kick for a moment or two, but, seeming to realise that by fighting him she was only increasing Watt's fervour, she stilled, allowing Watt to hoist up her skirt, exposing her white buttocks. Donald stared in amazement, wondering what Watt was about, but he was intent on stroking the woman's plump cheeks.

"This kilt is certainly the easiest thing to deal with when you want to get your old man out," he joked as he spread the front of his kilt up the woman's back. "You might have to hold her up if she doesn't do it herself," he said to Donald, then, lowering his voice, he spoke softly to his captive. "I won't harm you or hurt you." Then he got down to business.

Within seconds he had impaled her on his hard cock and was plunging in and out of her for all he was worth. Desperate to get as much of himself inside the warm haven as he could, he raised her up and repositioned her over the kitchen table as she had been with his predecessor, but this time face down. He lifted her until she was almost standing on her head and he pushed further and further inside her body. Faster and faster he went until he heard her gasp. Realising she was enjoying his presence he rested for a minute to let her get her breath back before racing to his own conclusion. He clung to her with sweat dripping off his brow and making tiny rivulets down her now rosy behind before pulling away from her and gently lowering her to the floor.

He sat down on a chair at the table and downed a mug of wine, as his friend made to position the exhausted woman as he wanted he realised Donald would have no need for his help and his thoughts flew back to the early months of his marriage, when lovemaking was all he and Jeanie wanted. Images of his sweet wife whispering words of love in his ear as she held him in her warm arms and urged him to come inside her, but in all the times they had lain together it had never felt so good as it did with this strange woman.

"Is it because she was doing what she was told and not willing to have me enter her secret place? But *she* enjoyed *me*, I swear." He passed these notions through his mind while he followed the movements of his friend as he sped towards his climax in the dark cavern where he and his brother had also been. Again, the woman lay still with her eyes shut, making no movement or sound, and it took very little time for Donald to ejaculate into her, thinking himself a fine fellow.

Donald joined him at the table where they helped themselves to some more wine and decided that they now had everything they desired for the evening; a full belly, good wine and sexual satisfaction. They were shortly joined by Donald's brothers who had been successful in their endeavours and threw their booty on the table. It was clear to the men that the wine merchant had been successful in his business as they had found many coins and silver and gold jewellery about the house. They set about dividing up the goods. There was no dissent about most things but David had taken a fancy to a pair of silver shoe buckles and wanted to keep these for himself. With good-natured banter, the brothers taunted him about looking fine to go courting but, when Watt had indicated that he was fine with relinquishing his share of the price of the buckles, he tucked them into his pocket with a contented smile.

Paying no attention to the corpse-like woman lying just as the men had left her, they picked up the wine bottles they were using and, packing a few more into an empty flour sack for later, they clattered down the stairs and left the shop by the same method as they had entered it.

As they left the kitchen Watt looked back just for a last quizzical look at the exhausted woman, to be surprised at what he later decided was a satisfied expression on her pale features. He gave a shout of pure joy as he bounded after the long-legged Highlanders.

"She *did* enjoy it." No matter how she felt about the other two men who had ravished her, she had enjoyed being shafted by him, he just knew it. This inflated his ego so much that, no matter what the rest of the night brought, he would never forget those few hours spent in the wine merchant's shop.

The men met many more of the invading army carousing in the street. No shop on the main thoroughfare had been missed and shutters hung loose and doors stood open as the rampaging army made its way to the lesser streets of the town. The four men joined up with the crowd and entered a good many alehouses until they were well and truly drunk. For a short time, Euan left their company but returned after his liaison with a serving wench had reached its inevitable conclusion. He was received back into the company with ribald cheers from his brothers and a few of his fellow clansmen.

"Needs a bit of privacy does our Euan."

"Can't get it up if he's got company."

"Euan McAllister, master seducer."

Donald explained quietly that there was a queer kick in Euan's gait that led to the men's teasing. "Euan will never take a woman who is not willing. There can be all sorts of virgins and wives ripe for the taking but Euan will always seduce his woman. With all the rape and debasement that follows an army he will stand in the middle and make no demur when his fellow men humiliate the women of the conquered town. It is brave of him and I think I want to follow his example, then I see David and you enjoying the spoils and I can't stop myself from joining in." He sighed.

He felt a slap on his back and the grinning face of David leered over his shoulder.

"That's it little brother. A standing cock has no conscience. But our Euan has achieved his goal and I think we have had enough fun for one night and should find a place to sleep, for I've a notion we will soon be on the march again."

The small group left the inn and wandered companionably along to the edges of the town near the protecting walls where they spied what they thought to be a barn and a perfect place for a night of undisturbed slumber. As they entered through an unlocked door hard against the wall they were surprised to realise they were in a blacksmith's forge, with the fire still glowing and giving an inviting ambiance to the small workshop. Above the fire and hung by chains from the wooden rafters was a circular iron ring from which depended swords in every stage of their making. The smith had obviously left off work and abandoned his stock, probably correctly assuming that his forge would be a target for men desperate for arms. Indeed, it was surprising that these four were the first to find it, but now they were here and with such a choice of weapons they were ecstatic. Sword after sword was removed from the rank above as each swung and lunged with the weapons, judging which was best for each.

Reaching up to remove one very ornately chased weapon Euan let out a gasp of pleasure.

"I think I have just found the Holy Grail," he mouthed reverently as he stroked the razor-sharp blade and stared at the edge, taking in every aspect of its perfection.

"Oh my God, Euan is in love!" chorused his brothers as they took in his delighted gaze. "He's always trying to get the perfect sword. Perfect balance, perfect weight, perfect length, oh perfect everything," Donald informed Watt as he cast his hands up and shrugged his massive shoulders.

"That looks very fine Euan, but I don't have your knowledge and would be indebted to you if you could pick one for me," Watt asked.

Euan, never leaving go of his own prize, weighed up a few of the swords before eventually choosing two and showing them to Watt.

"Try these. They are both well balanced and should be about the right weight and length for you. Match up with David and see how you handle it," he said, throwing a fine steel sword hilt first towards him.

Watt caught it, and there followed much hilarity as neither of the men were exactly sober and were so unevenly matched that David was hard pushed to stay out of the way of the inept swipes that Watt made with the sword.

"Enough, for any sake, stop before you cut someone's head off and though I often think there is nothing in David's head I would quite like it to remain on his shoulders!" laughed Euan, realising his mistake in inducing the boys to sword fight when in their cups.

"You can practise tomorrow. You need to use your sword until it becomes an extension of your arm. Now let us get some rest before we have to be back on duty."

Watt placed the sword carefully in a scabbard he found and, placing it at his side, wrapped himself up and settled down to watch the glowing embers of the forge fire.

"It has been a strange and exciting day," he thought as his mind replayed the events of the last twenty-four hours, but, as a procession of images flitted through his brain, they kept stopping at the encounter with the unnamed wine merchant's wife. As he drifted off to sleep, the picture of her was imprinted on his eyelids, that last look when he had been sure she was revelling in the actions they had taken together, albeit with her as an unwilling partner.

Just on the verge of sleep a statement jumped into his head and remained there:

"Victors in the enemy's castle."

****

The Siege of Carlisle

They were awake and alert in reasonable time the next morning and Watt's first though was for his sword. He found it lying on the ground at his side, but, before he had time to do more than look at it, his attention was taken by Euan who was chivvying them on to get up and on their way before the drumbeat started.

"That was a grand night," Watt started to reminisce as he gathered himself together and straightened his jacket. "I wouldn't have missed it for anything." He took a breath to continue, but was sharply shut down by Euan.

"Never speak with pride of the harm you have done to another human. When an army runs riot in the enemy town, it is no more than relief that they are not dead and can be forgiven for their crimes by their senior officers, but we, like everyone else, overstepped our own standards and that makes us the barbarians we are portrayed to be."

"But, but…"

"Quiet!" Euan barked. "I am and you should be ashamed of our behaviour. We are gentlemen." He waved his arm to encompass them all. "We acted as savages and that is nothing to brag of."

Having had his say he shut his mouth tight and continued to make his way in the direction of the castle keep which overlooked the town.

Puzzled by the reaction to his words Watt walked along in silence, unable to decipher by what trick the men who had urged him on to greater and greater acts of defilement could just a few hours later condemn him for his part in it.

Defiantly, he thought, "But I did enjoy every minute of the robbing and drinking free ale, and especially the taking of the woman. And now my pockets are full of silver, I have some good weapons and my lovely sword. So yes, I don't regret it." But as the words passed through his head so did the picture of the badly used woman the men had used and tossed away as so much rubbish. As this image intensified, he understood what Euan had been saying.

"These were the vile instincts of a beast and the beast in every man on the rampage yesterday had taken over, but as the cold light of day has brought a different image to our brains, we despise ourselves for not having been strong enough to have resisted the beast."

As the four men strolled along, each with their own thoughts and occasionally taking a sip of the contraband liquor, the drum began its plaintive beat and the companions increased their pace, entering under the castle arch to join their fellow campaigners. The men looked dishevelled and very few had made any attempt to groom or wash themselves after their night's slog in the taverns, but all stood to attention when their commander Lord George Murray could be seen standing at the foot of the steps, waiting for Prince Charles to come beside him.

They both turned to face the army and a great cheer spontaneously rose from the collective clans. Prince Charles again opulently dressed in a coat of figured satin, heavy with gold braid and buttons, snow-white breeches and fine golden buckles on his shoes that sparkled and dazzled in the watery winter sun, stepped forward and addressed his audience.

"I thank you…" he started but those were the only words that Watt could understand. He stood transfixed in amazement.

"This man is my king but he does not speak our tongue."

In reality Prince Charles Edward Stuart, nicknamed 'Bonnie Prince Charlie', was speaking in English, but since he had not spent much of his life in his native country he spoke English with an accent that many present could not recognise. After his words raised only a desultory cheer, Lord Murray leaned forward and whispered to him, after which he smiled his charismatic smile and began to speak again. Watt still did not understand a word of what was being said, but he could see that those around him were listening attentively.

"What is he saying?" cried Watt in frustration as he turned to a neighbour. "I can't make out a word."

"You don't understand him because he is speaking in his father and grandfather's native tongue. He has the Gaelic, the language of the Highlands."

"Oh," was all Watt could find to say and, for the first time since joining up in Dumfries, he realised that he had pledged to fight for a cause and a people that, living so close to the border with England, he felt neither a fealty nor a sympathy with. Remembering the depravation of his time, be it ever so short, in the army, it was clear to him that the gallant Prince had suffered none. While he let those thoughts percolate through his brain there was a shift in the crowd and men began to form different groups. He quickly followed Euan MacAlister, but, as he came up with him, he was rebuffed.

"My brothers and I are to form part of the force to march to Newcastle and chase Wade and his redcoats back where they came from."

"But what of me? Am I not to come with you?"

"Stay here with the garrison and practise with your sword and I'm sure you will be in the next battle." Euan tried to temper Watt's dejection but was too keen to be off towards the coming conflict to spend any time consoling him. He gave Watt his hand and made his adieu. "I hope, God willing, we will meet again."

Thinking of the departure of his friends he began to feel sorry for himself.

"Even Bobby deserted me," he thought morosely, for he was finding that, all things considered, being in the Prince's army was not at all as he had expected it to be.

"Campbell, hurry along," snapped MacAlister, also readying himself for departure in the hunt for redcoats. "You will be under the orders of Alan Stuart and will remain with the garrison troop here in the castle while we put old Geordie Wade through his paces." He laughed at Watt's deflated features and went on, "It will be no sinecure, for we are only leaving three hundred men to hold the town for the Prince, so see that you are worthy of my trust."

Watt was sure MacAlister had chosen him because he was a good soldier and felt a little less down in the mouth and MacAlister, a good manager of raw recruits, was careful not to say anything to reverse his belief. Watt gave a half bow, feeling a bit silly but nevertheless glad to show his obeisance to the older man, before hurrying off to the rallying point for those left to man the ramparts of the town.

"Maybe there is a soldier in there after all," mused MacAlister as he watched the youth run away, then turned and put all thoughts of Watt Campbell out of his head as he mounted his warhorse and rode off to do his duty.

A few hours later, with many more horses, more food and most importantly money, to buy stores as the army progressed south, safely stashed in their saddlebags, Watt was able to watch the refurbished army set off from his vantage point on the bulwark of the castle. As the army snaked along the bank of the River Eden, the Prince rode at the head of the procession, still dressed as if ready to attend a ball but with the addition of a breastplate that caught in the rays of the midwinter sun; he did indeed look as if God was smiling on his endeavour and Watt once more changed his mind and wanted to do his best for his cause. He watched until the last cloud of dust had settled and then stared at the place where it had been until he was disturbed by the muster drum and ran off to answer to his master's voice.

For the next several days he carried out sentry duty when he was rostered to do so, caroused in the alehouses, although now that Martial Law had been established the soldiers were not allowed to steal food and drink but had to pay for it. This did not bother Watt for his pockets were full from his first evening in the town and, since he was a handsome lad, could have found any number of maids to lie with him for a groat, but he did not avail himself of their offers for always in the back of his mind was the woman he had raped on that same first evening.

"I just can't get that woman and her reaction out of my head," he thought one evening as he was lying on a hard cot after his duty period was over. Being in the garrison was not like being on the march and often the hours between his shifts on lookout on the battlements hung heavy. He had made no close friends here as he had with the MacAlister brothers and he only occasionally found anyone to practice sword skills with. Most of the soldiers left to hold the town were older men or youngsters like himself. The older men had no time to be bothered with a callow youth and the younger men all seemed to band together and vanish from the barrack room when their presence was not required. Watt was bored. It was a new experience for him. He did not know how to entertain himself. Once more the image of the woman was displayed in front of him and, flinging himself off the bed, decided he would go and see if she still lived in the wine merchant's house. He had moved so quickly that did not think about how he might be received until he was outside the house where he had denigrated the woman such a short time ago.

As he approached the shop he could see that the shutters had been repaired but remained closed and not open for business. He stared up at the windows of the living quarters but could see no sign of life there either. Now that he was standing here in the street, he did not know what to do next. Perhaps if the shop had been open, he might have entered unrecognised by the wine merchant, but surely the woman would have recognised him?

"Even if I was not a welcome partner she would not forget the face of a man who had ravished her only days before." As he stood there wondering how to proceed, the door of the wine shop opened a fraction. Watt stared at it, unable to decide if he should enter or not.

"Is it a trap?" he wondered, making no move to take advantage of the incipient invitation. After what might have been an hour, but was in fact barely five minutes, the door opened a little further and, by shifting his position, Watt was able to establish that, standing in the shadows, was a woman. Watt could not be sure it was the woman who was in the house the night he was there, but it was decidedly a woman.

"Well, if it is a trap and her husband is standing behind her, ready to attack me, I am forewarned," and drawing his sword from his scabbard at his hip he used the tip to gently open the door a bit wider to give him a better view of the interior of the dark shop.

"Come in quickly and don't open the door any wider," came a small voice hardly audible but Watt caught the words and gingerly advanced into the room, looking this way and that to ensure there was no danger waiting for him. Before he had a chance to speak the woman darted behind him and closed the door with a click.

"My husband is not here. Your friend injured him to such an extent he has been smuggled out of the town to stay with his mother, for he is not fit to protect his wine while he is so weak." She gave a wry grin, "I am to stay here and protect the wine in his place. It is a wife's duty." She shrugged but Watt, despite his first encounter with her, was angry that her husband had chosen to save his own skin. To leave his wife to the mercy of the enemy was a dreadful act.

The woman smiled and nodded, "Yes, his wine is more sacred than I am, I'm afraid. He even said I must offer myself to any looters and make them take me in exchange for his wine. It broke his heart that there was no room on the cart to take more than two barrels of the best brandy." She smiled and the smile lit up her face.

"So in lieu of the best brandy sir, will you take his less than best wife?"

Watt stood stock still. He was a rapscallion and had always been a bit of a lad, but for a husband to ask his wife to sell herself for a few barrels of wine was not how he thought a man should behave. He hurriedly reassured her.

"You are safe enough now, for Martial Law has been declared and any of our forces who steals will be court martialled."

"So Christopher's wine is safe and I have no need to offer myself to you for its protection?"

She sent him a sceptical look but he replied firmly. "No. You need do nothing you do not want to. I admit I can't get you out of my head and I would be happy to re-enact the pleasure I took of your body, but I will not force you to comply. It's just..."

"Just what? You don't find me attractive on second viewing?" she asked with an edge to her voice.

Watt looked sheepish, realising he was not making a good job of explaining himself but ploughed manfully on.

"It's just that when I left the other night and you were sprawled on the floor I imagined I saw a look of pleasure on your face." He glanced down at her before averting his eyes and continuing, "It was such a fleeting look, but I can't get it out of my head. It excited me, for that was the best experience of my life."

"And I suppose you have had lots of experience of loving women, you being such a greybeard?" she mocked.

Watt tuned to walk away and out the door, but he turned and looked at the woman. "At least tell me your name so that I can imagine you as I recall that evening. I am not proud of my actions and I have been made to see that they were ungentlemanly, but they haunt the night watches."

She slowly approached him, touched his arm and said quietly, "My name is Alice and I would very much like to repeat our actions, but not to save my husband's wine. Never that! You said you would not harm me and none of you hurt me apart from forcing me to accommodate you, and as Christopher's wife I have been hurt far more than I was by three big Highland lads." She caught hold of his arm and pulled him in the direction of the stairs.

For the rest of Watt's sojourn as part of the garrison militia he spent every hour he had free drinking the brandy and wine of the cuckolded husband while his wife entertained him in his bed. They were well matched and drove each other to greater heights of ecstasy at every meeting. Watt was at peace. It was a small window of harmony in the battle for the Crown of Scotland, England, Ireland and Wales.

****

Capture of the Castle

Watt continued to visit Alice and spend all his free time with her. They both knew this was just a brief interlude and that when life was more settled her husband would return to his beloved wine shop and her assignations with Watt would end. Watt's initial desire to fight for the cause of Prince Charles had waned, indeed it had not survived the army's departure by many days, but he did his share of the watches and patrols and strolled about the town in a MacAlister kilt for all the world as if he had been raised in the Highlands.

The peace in the town was not to last, however. The Prince's army, whether from wrong information or from a change in the enemy's tactics, had not been met where they had expected them to be, and, although the colonels sent out scouts, they totally missed the advancing force. As they headed south looking for Wade, Cumberland was bringing a contingent of redcoats to relieve Carlisle.

One morning, about three weeks into his sojourn at the castle, Watt was once more on sentry duty high above the town and overlooking the River Calder. He was bored. Being a soldier in Prince Charles's army held none of the romance it had promised as he had listened to MacAlister, what felt like years ago, in the woods of home with the security of his family so close by. That's not to say that he had not enjoyed some of the experiences he had passed through and the camaraderie he had found among some of the most hardened of Highland clansmen, but surprisingly he missed the physical work that had been his lot on the farm; the early morning to sundown graft that was necessary to husband a farm so close to the sea. He smiled wryly as he thought of the many chores he had been able to wangle his way out of with a smile and a totally selfish attitude.

With the advent of Alice and her stories of how her husband misused her, he realised he had not been a good husband to Jeanie. He had bragged to all his friends about the pleasures of married life but he had taken on none of the responsibilities of a man. He was embarrassed as he remembered how he had brought Jeanie into his parent's home and left them to feed and clothe her, and the bairns, as they had come along. He had expected them to treat her as they did him while he continued with the life he had enjoyed before the wedding.

"I'm lucky they are such good parents for others would have thrown us out to fend for ourselves." He smiled, bringing the picture of Jamie and Jenny to his mind. "Not them. They accepted Jeanie as if she were their own and Ma is far more help to her than I ever was. Da was more help than me," he admitted to himself as the picture of his father nursing his older son while his mother helped Jeanie with the baby crossed his mind.

Thinking of Jeanie again brought his thoughts back to Alice and her situation. "How to stop the bastard beating her, that is the question," he mused. He had been horrified when seeing Alice that second time to notice her body was covered in bruises and he had apologised for using her harshly, assuming the multi-coloured bruises were the work of himself and his cohorts when they had raped her, but she had quickly explained that none of the three men she had been taken by in quick succession had been in any way responsible for them.

"Christopher just loves to beat me with a stick, or anything he happens to have to hand. He is very fond of telling me it is his right to beat his wife. He says it is the law and I must submit to his chastisement, for it is up to him to turn me into a good wife."

Watt, furious with himself for adding to her pain, stroked one of the fading bruises and asked, "Can you not leave him? Run away?"

"Where would I go? I asked my mother what I should do to stop him and she shrugged and said I would need to do as I'm told, for a wife who disobeys her husband would be shunned by the townsfolk," she explained.

"But need you stay in Carlisle? You could go elsewhere couldn't you, somewhere where he wouldn't find you?"

"No, for the only way I get to see my children is if I do as I'm told. I told you he had gone to stay with his mother to keep him safe from the big bad Highlanders, didn't I? Well, he has sent my children to stay with her too; as soon as they were weaned she arrived and without a word to me took them off, one by one, to be reared 'properly'. I get to visit and it breaks my heart for they are such beautiful little scraps. The only pleasure in my life is to see them occasionally. I can't leave him."

He remembered how, when they were both lying naked and sweating after their exertions, that they had discussed ways of changing her position. Some were serious and others had them doubled up with laughter by their ridiculousness. Perhaps knowing that Watt sincerely, if only superficially, cared for her future added a piquancy of their meetings for she revelled in the ministrations of the young man.

In the solitary hours he spent on watch he had considered several scenarios where he disposed of her husband, but would that make any difference to her? He wished with all his heart that David MacAlister's sword arm had been truer and that the violent beast was resting in his grave, but then there was the mother to think about. Was Alice strong enough to withstand her? Would she exchange a hard master for a cruel mistress? His thoughts ran round and round in his head without him reaching any conclusion. Despite all his soul-searching, he knew deep within himself that, when her husband returned, Watt's interlude would be over and although he might retain fond memories of his times with Alice, it was indeed Jeanie he loved. He had come to realise he had been a spoiled brat; feeling himself a fine fellow, not a farm boy like his contemporaries, and now, while he kicked his heels in Carlisle he had found plenty of time to ponder on how he had failed Jeanie as a husband, albeit not the beast that Alice was married to, he had given no thought to her comfort. Marching with, then living among the determined men following Prince Charlie he had been brought to the realisation that there was nothing special about him. The daydreams of being named a hero were in fact only likely in his imagination. He would not desert this army he had joined as a thoughtless boy, but he was anxious for the rising to be over. Leaving him free to return to the farm, not as a conquering hero to be feted, but as a man, ready and willing to care for his family as he now saw they needed to be cared for.

"I will be a good husband, father and son," he vowed.

Watt Campbell had grown up!

While his thoughts had been idling in this way he had caught a flash of red far off to the left. At first he had thought it something reflected by the sun but, as he saw more and more of them, it finally occurred to him that what he was seeing was the redcoats of English soldiers. He screwed up his eyes the better to focus and confirmed his first impression that this was a red coat, a whole army of red coats winding their way down the river bank towards the point where the River Calder met the River Eden, and the town of Carlisle was their target. Just for a moment he stood dumbfounded, but he quickly ran over to his opposite number on the other side of the ramparts and demanded he come and confirm what he was seeing. They were both seeing the same thing and immediately raised the alarm to alert the men on the gates to close them and make the town safe.

Watt had never been detailed to mind the gates of the town as it was deemed too important to be in the hands of a raw recruit. The task had always been given to the older men of the garrison. Food was still in pretty limited supply as Prince Charles' army had requisitioned much of the food and other provisions in the storerooms to provide for the southward-pushing troops, so every morsel of food that entered the town was held in a central store and portioned out as required. Likewise with the livestock, although it was mainly hens and a few pigs that were kept within the town walls by individual inhabitants, for despite Carlisle being a market town the farmers were taking their wares to another market, wishing to get the best price they could for them.

All the soldiers of the garrison were summoned by the drummer and lookouts were posted at various places in the town and on the walls. Three hundred men were not an adequate force to hold back what appeared to be a large contingent of the English army. All the Highlanders were aware of how vital it was to hold the castle so that their own army would have somewhere to retreat to if they fared badly on the march south.

The cannon which had been the means of them capturing the castle had been taken off with the main force and would have been virtually useless anyway, as they could not have fired them on the enemy and kept the gates intact. There was much dithering and flustering among the commanders but eventually the garrison got itself organised and prepared to repel the army. There would be no sleep for the soldiers, since there were too few of them to man the ramparts properly, so an hour here and there in their position was all that could be expected. Watt was ordered to take a musket and ammunition to his post on the walls and to shoot at anyone trying to scale the fortifications. The amount of ball and powder issued to the men was pitiful, for again most of the ammunition had departed along with the Prince. The best the old and the young of the Prince's army could hope for was to hold out until either they were relieved, which seemed an unlikely event, or the English ran out of supplies, which seemed an even more unlikely event as they had the benefit of being outside the town walls with access to the fruits of the agricultural landscape.

As the castle was surrounded by the attacking force Watt thought back to how easy it had been for them to commandeer the castle just a few weeks ago and with less men and equipment than he could see from his vantage point above the town. The English appeared to be well organised and happy to starve them into submission rather than waste good ammunition. As he stayed at his post he worried what would be the fate of Alice. She had been attacked in her own home by the previous invaders and there was no reason to believe that she would be any luckier with the English contingent. A wine merchant's shop would be a target for any victorious army. He wondered if he would be able to sneak off and warn her, perhaps bring her to the castle for safekeeping, but when he brought this suggestion up with one of the older men he vetoed it saying she would be safer in her own house, where she might have her virtue violated but would almost certainly retain her life, so Watt resigned himself to leaving her to her own devices.

As day followed day and the food rations dwindled the men became most disheartened. Many of the townspeople took the chance every time they could to cause as much trouble as possible and the hungry men, with such divided duties, were no match for the attacks they often met from bands of men and sometimes women as they patrolled the walls of the town. Food was so scarce and ammunition, although being used sparingly, was running out. The army camped outside the walls made only half-hearted attempts to scale the walls, knowing that it was only a matter of time until their ammunition ran out.

"How much longer can we hold out?" asked Watt as he accompanied his partner round the walls, muskets at the ready.

"Not more than a day or so, I think. Today's ration of shot is very small and there was no dinner at midday, so that means we have had the food ration cut again. Unless our army comes soon we will be enjoying the hospitality of this castle from its dungeons. How long will we live might be a better question," came the gloomy answer.

As it happened the English army decided to attack the very next morning. They had allowed their soldiers a good hot meal, hoping the aroma of freshly cooked meat wafting over their earthworks would further depress the sieged town, and stood down all but a few sentries to sleep in order to be fresh for the coming attack. They had the undoubted advantage and when they advanced over their fascines with their ladders and set them up against the castle walls, there was little the tired, hungry and depressed garrison could do to repel them. In a remarkably short space of time, and under a month from the time the town had surrendered to him, the commander raised the white flag over the ramparts and ceded Carlisle once more into the hands of the English.

It did not take long for the Highlanders to be rounded up and soon the captive soldiers were, as prophesised by Watt's fellow sentry, entombed in the dungeons of the castle. As soon as the thick wooden doors were closed and the trap over the fretwork grill fastened, their captors promptly forgot about them.

Watt was terrified. He had, as had most of the Highlanders, spent most of their time before joining the ill-fated force out of doors breathing the fresh air of the countryside, be it Highland or Lowland air. The room in which they were being held had thick walls, covered in moss and fungus and running with water; a cold uneven flagstone floor with deep crevices where the water from the walls gathered in puddles, freezing over in the icy temperature permeating the cell. There were no windows and the only light that filtered into the room came from the grill above and that was very minimal, since it opened into a room of the castle already denied light by the low ceilings and narrow windows of the keep.

The men huddled together to keep warm, those who had them sharing out the thick hand woven material of their kilts and plaids, but they were no defence against the bone-chilling cold that infiltrated their very souls.

"They will bring us some food soon," said one to another, after what felt like a week but was in fact only three days, but his optimism was soon shattered by the curses of the other man.

"Do you think they will waste what little food there was in the town on their prisoners and do without themselves?" he scoffed. The effort of talking had started him coughing and as his hacking cough echoed round the cell others coughed as well. They were becoming ill living in the vile conditions. There were no sanitary facilities, not even a hole in the wall where they could relief themselves, so they were living in their own filth along with the rats and other vermin who habitually called the dungeons their home. The air was fetid and hung like a pall only several inches above the heads of the slumped men.

By now every stitch the men had been wearing was dripping wet and, with no means of drying the material, they had given it up to the four-legged inhabitants of their cell. As it became clear to the men that they were neither going to be freed or fed, the spirit left them and the older men turned their faces to the wall and let nature take over.

One day, Watt, who had been dozing and dreaming of Jeanie and him walking by the shore in their courting days, was awakened by a persistent gnawing noise and, before his senses were properly alert, put out his hand to try to feel what was happening when he was attacked by a fierce set of teeth that clung onto his finger. In the dark he could see a pair of red eyes malevolently staring at him. He squealed and shook off the rat, which immediately attacked him again, this time on the leg. Jumping to his feet he stamped and stamped his feet until it appeared the rat had taken fright.

Much discomfited by the attack, he turned to speak to his neighbour. "My, that bugger fair gave me the willies." He attempted a laugh he was far from feeling, but there was no answer.

"Hey, John." He bent down to give the man a shake and his hand landed upon a warm, furry body. He quickly pulled his hand back and made to attract the man's attention by kicking him gently with his foot, but there was still no response. He tried to peer through the murk in an effort to discern what had become to his companion but all he could see was a heaving mass of moving bodies. While he had been asleep the man had died and the rats were feasting on the corpse. Even although there was no food in his stomach, nor had there been for many weeks now, Watt turned and retched and retched.

The noise disturbed others in the cell and they tried to be philosophical about it.

"If the rats hadn't got there first, maybe we would have been tempted to have done what they are doing. It's survival of the fittest in here and who knows if we will ever be free from this hellhole?"

"No!" exclaimed Watt. "I could never eat a man. The very thought makes me sick."

"If there was any chance of getting out of here before I died I might well take to cannibalism. It can't be worse than eating a cow or a sheep, can it?" he said in a weak voice. "I wish you hadn't told me because now I know what will happen to me after I'm gone and it can't be long now."

Another chimed in. "I always dreamed of being buried in the heather on the side of the Ben. I fancied I would be able to smell the heather and feel the soft rain from my seat up in Heaven."

"We'll get out of it," said Watt, trying to buoy up the obviously low spirits of his comrades. "The Prince's army will be back and free us."

"Do you think Prince Charlie will buy us back? You were here when they offered us release if we had aught to buy our freedom with. Naw, naw, that Bonnie Prince that sweet-talked us into following him will keep well away from Carlisle until our bones are white and dry."

In his heart Watt knew the man was right. After their captors had been to ask for payment for their release he had regretted the donation of his family's greatest procession to a false cause but, when he had voiced this to his fellow prisoners, they had felt it made no odds where the ruby was now.

"For mark my words, lad, it wouldn't have mattered if you had it upon your person. Those English scoundrels would have taken it, and taunted you in your belief you had bought your freedom and left you do die here anyway while they toasted your stupidity with ale bought from the sale of your gem."

"Aye, better to go to the upkeep of a Scottish king than to fill the bellies of Englishmen."

Watt gave a sigh at this recollection. Very little conversation was undertaken in the cell. To talk meant to take in the stale, putrid air and the taste in their mouth was grim. It was fortunate – or perhaps unfortunate, depending on how you looked at it – that the walls were running with water for without the licking of this nectar the men would not have lasted as long. Some had tried not to take in the liquid, reckoning if they were to die it were best to die quickly, but the raging thirst that plagued them all had been too much. Many, Watt included, had developed fever and were often out of their minds as they slowly starved to death.

"It would have been better to have been Alan Stuart or one of the other commanders," thought Watt to himself in a rare moment of sanity. Although to a man of twenty dying didn't seem real, he knew that, although the leaders of the garrison force had had a horrendous death by being hung, drawn and quartered, he envied them the quicker release.

With not enough strength now to move about the cell, he sat himself down where a trickle of water seeped through the wall to ease his thirst and settled himself to meet his fate.

Chapter Thirteen

How the ruby returns

The audience was struck dumb and to be honest so was Mark. No matter what question he phrased in his head it died before it ever reached his tongue. There were so many things he wanted to ask Lord Campbell that he simply did not know where to begin.

Big Jock, so long used to avoiding talking about his private life, was finding the telling of the Campbell story quite cathartic, but could not keep an expression of sympathy off his face. He had long known of the barbarous Borders and their inhabitants and was enjoying every minute of this off-the-cuff interview. He looked across at Mark and noticed he was floundering and decided to help him out.

"It took more than four years for the ruby to come back to the Campbells and it is a story to make you proud to be bred from the genes of the Highlands."

Mark, trying hard to grasp where Big Jock was going, asked, "So you are claiming Highland blood. After all these years of proclaiming yourself a working man of the Borders, and after receiving your knighthood so recently, are you claiming affiliation with the chief of the Clan Campbell?"

"Well man, I can hardly disassociate myself with Clan Campbell when my name is Campbell, now can I, Mark, really?"

Mark blushed realising this had been a stupid question given what the story had been so far. He gave himself a mental shake and, taking a deep breath, continued, "Are you going to enlighten us to the fate of Watt? How does that ring sit on your finger when it was given to Bonnie Prince Charlie's supporters? How did it get back? Lord Campbell, you are playing with us." Mark tried to cover his frustration with humour.

"I'm afraid it is another history lesson, but not such a long one since we all know or have at least heard of the plight of the Old and Young Pretenders. Neither were successful with their attempts to take the throne from the Hanoverians and when the final battle in the campaign was lost at Culloden." He paused. "Even you will have heard of the battle of Culloden, Mark?"

"Yes and the escape of the Prince by boat aided and abetted by Flora MacDonald," Mark answered a bit sulkily, fearing Lord John was making mock of him again.

"Now that is the whole crux of the matter and why the ruby was brought back to Geordie's descendants. The main supporters of the Jacobites in Scotland were indeed the Clan MacDonald in its many branches. I'm not a clan specialist, so I don't know who is affiliated to who, but suffice to say for my story that Campbells and MacDonalds have not been good bedfellows since the time of the massacre of Glencoe, long before Watt joined the Pretender's army."

"Round the houses and round the houses!" exclaimed an exasperated Mark Henderson.

"Patience, I have arrived. Four years have passed since we left Watt wallowing in the dungeon at Carlisle Castle, where he died, as did all the other men in his cell. Some of the prisoners were transported, and I have no idea how they chose who to starve to death and who to sell as slaves in the Americas, but that is what happened," said Big Jock.

"Jeanie, can you take this calf out to the field to its mother? I'm fair wabbit today. I don't know if it's the heat or I'm getting old." Jenny smiled at her daughter-in-law, not for the first time noticing how tired and drawn she was looking.

"None of us have an hour to call our own at this time of year, but, if you don't mind, when I've dropped this little sweetheart off to her mother," she bent down to put her arms round the calf's neck, "I might go and sit with my feet in the burn for a few minutes before the boys come in from the fields clamouring for food. I've never seen lads that can eat like our two, and you too, madam." She smiled down at her sturdy daughter.

"Off you go and don't hurry back. If Georgie and Jockie get back before you, Jannet and I will see to them, won't we, my pet?" smiled Jenny as she tousled the unruly crop of fair curls on her granddaughter's head.

"Aye, Nana, we can deal wi' they rogues," she answered in such a good imitation of her grandmother's voice that both the women laughed out loud.

"There's not enough laughter in this house since my rogue went off, with never a word mind; if Bobby Baxter hadn't deserted and come and told us we never would have known where he was. I wish he had bloody deserted! But then, the daft bugger never did have any sense!" thought Jenny. "If we knew if he was living or dead Jeanie could get on with things and not sit fretting about him."

She took Jannet's hand and, before walking back into the dairy, watched her daughter-in-law guide the calf off to the bottom field.

After depositing the calf and making sure its mother was happy with it, she strolled off towards the burn, lifting her heavy hair off the back of her neck in an attempt to cool down. She steered clear of the shore even though it would be more likely to find a cooling breeze there because she could not bear to remember how she and Watt had plighted their troth.

"Oh, how I miss him," she thought. "If he was to come home, I'd skelp his ear for causing me so much worry, but I'd hug him till he begged for mercy."

She sat down and took off her shoes and stockings and lowered her hot feet into the gently tumbling water, giving off little squeaks as the cold clear water tickled the soles of her feet. She shut her eyes, savouring the quiet. Jenny was good to let her have a bit of time to herself but she knew that the boys would come in hungry and ready for a meal and she liked to take as much work off Jenny as she could. It was peaceful, like another world sitting under the green canopy on the edge of the wood, listening to the call of the peewee and the cuckoo and the gurgle of the water as the burn hurried off to join the sea. With her feet dangling over the bank she threw herself back on the grass, savouring the heat of the sun as it dappled on her eyelids.

She became aware of the sudden silence. There was no sound of small animals scuffling in the grass, the birds were quiet and the air seemed to have a heavy quality. She stayed stock still for a moment, then opened her eyes just a slit to see an unknown man coming towards her from the stand of trees. He looked gaunt, dishevelled and unkempt. He had long tousled hair with a straggly grey beard and wore a strange assortment of clothes. As he came closer she could smell that it was a long time since he had used soap and water. She took him for a tinker and resolved to be on her guard. Despite this immediate impression, Jeanie was surprised to realise that she felt no threat from the strange individual and held her position on the riverbank.

"Are you Jean Campbell?" the man asked and Jeanie realised that he spoke in the way that Watt's grandfather did. For this reason, she answered instead of calling for help.

"I am, yes."

"Wife of Watt Campbell and mother of his children?"

"I am, yes."

"I am Sandy MacAlister, late of the army of Prince Charles Edward Stuart." He gave her a courtly bow exactly as he would have if he had been at a clan gathering and requesting the pleasure of a dance with her at the ceilidh.

"Oh, you're a Jacobite?"

"I was a supporter of Bonnie Prince Charlie for my sins but now I am an outlaw hiding from justice. I beg you will not give me up to the magistrate." He smiled a tight little smile. "I am making off to the Continent by a circuitous route, but I had first to come to return some property to you."

Jeanie jumped to her feet and looked excitedly all around her. "Watt? Is he here with you?" Sandy was able to see how the thought of her long missing husband had taken years off her features and was loath to be the cause of removing that hope.

"I'm sorry, my dear, but I have bad news for you. Watt was with the garrison at Carlisle when it was overrun by the English army and I'm afraid he is dead. He has been dead these four years. I would have been here before, but for a Jacobite to travel about the country is still not safe and when I got home to tell my wife I was alive, I had to stay hidden until the hue and cry died down a bit."

The delight washed from her face. Jeanie took in the news Sandy had brought and sat back in her place on the bank, much deflated.

"I think I have known for a long time that he was dead. We heard the news of the siege at Carlisle and the fate of those imprisoned there. There is no chance that he was transported?" She lifted her head in a vain hope that there might have been a mistake.

"No, he died of a fever in Carlisle. I'm sorry, lass."

Jeanie could see that, even though Sandy appeared to be on his last legs, he was trying to comfort her, so she caught herself up thinking, "There will be time enough to mourn later," then continued out loud. "How long is it since you ate or slept in a safe place? Come down to the farm with me and we will see about finding you clean clothes and a meal."

"Thank you, Mrs Campbell, but I came only to return this to you." So saying he drew the pouch from his pocket and handed it to Jeanie. "When this was given to me to buy stores I recognised it from stories I'd heard at home and knew that it is said to be a cursed stone if it is out of the hands of the Campbells and as most of the Jacobite army were MacDonalds I did not think it right to use it to arm the Campbells' greatest enemy. I did not add it to the Prince's war fund, always intending to give it back to Watt, but, as the war progressed and we were split up, I vowed to return it to Watt and if not to him to his son."

Jeanie took the ring and gazed at it. "It holds the luck of the Campbells and without it in his possession, my Watt lost his life. I swear no son of the Campbells will ever let it out of their possession again. I thank you with all my heart, Mr MacAlister."

"Sandy," he said as he bowed and made to go back the way he had come.

"Mr MacAlister, you will dishonour us and break our luck if you do not accept our hospitality. It's little enough thanks for risking your life to bring this back."

****

"Did Jeanie keep her word?" asked Mark.

"She did indeed. The ruby was kept to give to her son Georgie, but was forgotten about as it lay quietly in its pouch and the family continued to grow, so Georgie was never in possession of the ruby ring."

"Why do you think that was?" was Mark's next question.

"I think Jeanie was so traumatised by what had happened to Watt that she was afraid to give the ring to her son in case it carried bad luck with it. Sadly, when the family talk of the ruby you will not hear the story I have just told you. Watt has been well and truly demonised."

"Would you then describe Watt as the black sheep of the family or a skeleton in the cupboard that should never see the light of day? Do you think that, given that he had had the best of everything in his life, he wasted his potential?" asked Mark.

"Do you know, Mark, I have a bit of a sneaking liking for Watt. In fact, I often think he and I had a lot in common," answered a thoughtful Lord Campbell.

"You're not going to tell me, are you, that you see yourself in Watt? Now that is laughable Lord John. You have been the epitome of all that is just and honourable in this country. I mean, there is no politician or indeed, voter in this country who does not respect the straight talking and honesty you have brought to the office of Prime Minister. You cannot surely expect us now to believe that you are the black sheep," ejaculated Mark, now very sure that he was being made mock of.

Big Jock held up his paw-like hand to quieten the tirade. Whither by design or coincidence, the facets of the ruby ring were caught in the studio lights, bathing both the men in the centre of the stage in iridescent light.

But, seemingly unaware of the depths of Mark's frustration, Lord John continued, "We both were blessed, or cursed, with a desire to have our own way. We both fell in love at a ridiculously young age, he with his Jeanie and me with my Marion; a love that proved to be the love of our lives, his short and mine long. We both had an urge to see Scotland as a power in its own right; he to give his life, literally, for what he believed to be right even though he came to see his error; me to fight in Parliament for what is right for Scotland. So he may be called the Black Sheep but we have learnt lessons from him and I like to think, because of these lessons, I am a better person. I often wonder if what was seen as a bad man was just a boy who, like Peter Pan, never grew up. Or maybe, just maybe our talisman makes us the men we are and giving it to aid the Jacobites did indeed relieve Watt of luck."

"But the lucky ruby stayed with the Campbells? They continued to prosper?"

"Until today the ring has not been out of the possession of one Campbell or another. Since the time of Jeanie and Watt it has rarely been passed from father to son. It is more often a grandson, as what happened to Watt was taken as a warning that the ruby should not be passed on too soon. Watt was blinded by the monetary value of the ruby and held it in low regard, giving it away almost as soon as it came into his possession. So, after a conclave after its return, it was decided that missing a generation was the best plan."

"Is that still how the ring is transferred today? And if that is the case Lord John, who will be the next recipient of the ruby given that you have no sons," Mark wondered

Ignoring Mark's question with consummate ease, Big Jock again took inspiration from the audience before continuing as if Mark had not spoken.

"From grandfather to grandson has been the way of it for four hundred years, except for one notable exception. There was a queer set of circumstances and they led to the ruby becoming the property of Watt's great-grandson."

"So life did not run smoothly for the family even with its mascot safely back in its rightful home? What happened to Watt's grandson? You can't torment us with innuendo and then not satisfy our curiosity," said Mark, keen for the story to continue and glancing at his audience, knowing that there would be a riot if Lord John stopped his story halfway. "He's a sly old fox, right enough," thought Mark. "But still a man of honour. He'll tell us the rest of the story."

"Lord John?"

"Yes, yes, I'm just gathering my thoughts. I'm a politician, Mark, we never speak without thinking," he guffawed.

"It was nearing the end of the century when the world was rearranging itself. The French had had a revolution and the dictator Napoleon Bonaparte was rampaging about Europe and the Caribbean and Britain was at war with the French and Spanish, and the Borders were getting on with living life as they always had, by their own rules. It was at this time that Watt's great-grandson became owner of the Lucky ruby."

Chapter Fourteen

Bill Campbell sat gazing out over the rough sea, revelling in the strong salty smelling wind that ruffled the curly black locks that hung unruly over his brow, making him look as if he was peering at the world through the leaves of a bush at midnight. These dark tresses only emphasised the whiteness of the visage over which they presided. His pale skin had always been the bane of his life for it belied his nature and made him appear extremely feminine. His sister, Margaret, more often called Peggy, envied him the smooth cheeks but in the schoolroom he had taken much abuse, some good natured, some more malicious, from both master and pupil alike. His mother, Sarah Campbell, maintained that he was an amalgam of his paternal grandparents, often dwelling pleasurably on how he had inherited the dark hair and lop-sided mouth of George and the soft features of Sarah that had combined to make him her darling. The firstborn of her sons, Sarah could see no imperfection with her tall, muscular lad.

At this moment, although he distractedly raised a hand to brush the flying mane out of his eyes, he was not thinking either of his schooldays or of his looks. He had survived the former and had no fault to find with the attention the young ladies of the village paid him. He stared contemplatively at the sea. He could feel the excitement growing in his belly while his heart raced at the sight of the peaceful waves crashing onto the rocky shore.

"Oh, how I wish I could take ship and be off to see the world." He pondered how exhilarating it would be to stand before the mast of a brig as it sailed over the ocean to the warm, blue waters he had heard so much about during his clandestine visits to the alehouse.

"I don't care for the drink so much but to hear the tales from those salty old tars makes me itch to be out on the waves."

He sighed because he realised that there was no way on this earth that his parents, especially his mother, would sanction him joining the crew of a ship. He was a farmer's son like it or not: he was bound to the land. He had been prompted to take a quick walk to the shore by the scorching heat of the day. No matter how hot it might be inland, there was mostly a cooling breeze along the banks of the Annan estuary.

This last thought made him realise he had tarried too long by the shore and should be getting home to deal with the evening chores and settle the animals. He arose from his comfortable rock, where a hollow that just fitted his behind appeared to have been moulded for him. Sticking his hands deep into the pockets of his breeches and with sagging shoulders, he strode off along the beach towards the farm lane, kicking up a sand storm as he went. As he walked he wondered if other young men of previous generations had sat where he sat with the thoughts that he thought. The idea amused him as he imagined a previous occupant spending his lifetime sitting disconsolately wearing the rock into a smooth comfortable seat, growing older year by year as he gazed out over the estuary, dreaming of what might have been.

"But I'll not spend my lifetime craving for adventure and exploration. I'll be off to make my fortune before I'm much older," Bill vowed to himself. "I'm my own man!"

With this decision and the plans for achieving it running though his busy brain, he gave a little skip, threw back his massive shoulders and jogged back to the farm buildings where he was due to complete the day's tasks.

Despite his yearning for the sea Bill was not unhappy attending to the mundane matters of farm life. He was content when communing with the cows in the byre or walking the hill during lambing, as there was nothing he enjoyed more than spending time on the hillier reaches of his grandmother's acres.

"I should be grateful to have a roof over my head and a full stomach," he continued his meditations. "Most lads my age are working long hours at thankless toil for little reward and without benefit of Gramp's stories and Granny's scones." He finished the thought with a smile as he remembered that, not only was he his mother's darling, but also the pride and joy of his grandmother.

He smiled reminiscently, his head leaning against the rounded belly of the milch cow as he gently drew the milk from her udders. He recalled his grandparents saying, "We love you all the same" but with such a doting glimmer in their eye that no one was deceived about who was the favourite.

"Hey, Daisybell!" He smacked the placid cow's rump gently to move her from her stall as he took the bucket of frothy white liquid out from under her. "Away you go, lass, and eat your fill. We need cream for the porridge and butter for the market."

Before moving to the next stall Bill took the bucket of milk out of the byre, crossed the yard and entered the dairy from where the sweet sounds of song emitted into the evening air.

As he opened the door a lithe young woman with her sleeves rolled up over strong forearms met his eyes. She was oblivious to his interruptions and continued to sing a ballad to the accompanying beat of the butter churn, where the butter was almost ready to turn out.

He stood for a minute, taking in all aspects of his sister, not wanting to disturb her at a crucial point in the butter making. They were not paupers its true, but no careful housewife could afford to waste a churn of the precious commodity and Bill did not wish to anger his sister. As the churn stopped, Margaret opened up the hatch and turned the slick, golden material onto the pristine board on the scrubbed pine table where she was working. As she turned to collect the butter paddles from the shelf, she realised that Bill had entered the cold room.

"Hi, Billy," she beamed out at him, showing off her perfect teeth as she stretched her lips into a huge grin. "I wondered if there would be time for a sup of tea before you brought me the next lot. Even this cool dairy isn't protected from this tremendous hot weather we're having." She picked up a cheesecloth and wiped down her face to remove the most of the beads of sweat shining on her upper lip. Her damp hair fell in ringlets over her rosy cheeks and she presented an image of a beautiful, healthy girl ripening into womanhood.

"Why don't you go into the house and make a pot of tea, Peg? I could fancy a cup and I only have Amy left to milk. By the time you have that on the table I'll be finished, then in exchange for you being my sweet adorable sister, I'll churn your next lot of butter while you rest under the trees."

"Deal!" Peg answered almost before the words had left Bill's mouth. She rushed towards him throwing her arms round his neck and allowing him to swing her up off her feet and deposit her laughing form on the other side of the room. She moved back towards the table saying, "I'll just pop this butter into the water barrel before I go." Suiting the actions to the words she then made off towards the farmhouse kitchen, calling over her shoulder, "Don't let the tea get cold, Bill!"

Leaving the dairy and on his way back to the byre Bill spied his father entering through the far gate carrying his scythe, having just returned from testing the ripeness of the barley in the field furthest from the farmyard. He waved to the stocky man who returned his salute as he continued his approach. Knowing that his father would come to find him, Bill went back to the byre. He was just untying Amy and encouraging her out from her stall when George Campbell entered. His bare torso was dripping, as was his hair, for he had ducked himself in the water barrel after cleaning and sharpening his scythe ready for the morning.

The resemblance between father and son was not at once apparent but on second look, although George was of shorter stature, they shared the same hair and eyes. Without a shirt, George's muscular chest and arms glistening in the sunshine would have made a prize fighter proud.

"My, it's hot." He held up his hand as if to stop Bill's next words. "I know; I'm not complaining but it makes it harder work in this heat." He looked round, noticing that the byre was empty and carried on, "You've done the milking, lad. Thanks."

"Well," laughed Bill, "I'm not such an old man as to have forgotten how long it took me to get home from Cummertrees school in this weather when I was a lad, so I thought I would give Peter a break, just this once."

His father clasped him by the shoulder noticing how he had to stretch up these days to reach his eldest son who topped him by a good six inches. "You're a good man, Billy. Leave the mucking out to Peter."

"Well, I will," replied Bill, "for Peggy has a drink on the table and I promised her I'd turn a churn for her. Come on, Father, let's go while we can."

Later that same evening, after the working day was over, Sarah and Peg were seated under a tree in the garden where they had taken some darning to get away from the heat of the kitchen fire. No matter the weather, the kitchen fire had to remain stoked and alight for all food was cooked on the fire or in the oven built into the side of the fireplace, so it was a relief to Sarah to get a bit of respite. They sat companionably listening to the screams and squeals of excitement from the younger girls as they played hide and seek in the orchard.

With this evidence of the proximity of her younger children Sarah wondered idly where the boys might be.

"Mam, I don't believe you need to ask," laughed Peggy, looking up at the still blue sky and estimating just how long it would be before the wondrous sunset might be seen.

"Like me you know fine the boys, and likely Pa as well, will be down in the water."

She screwed up her face in an attempt to imitate her father being serious and intoned, "I had to go with them, Sal, just to make sure they didn't drown in the sea. You can't trust the sea. She's a fickle lady." She resumed her everyday voice, noticing that her mother was trying hard not to laugh at her antics.

"Now Peg, that's enough cheek. Let your father think we are taken in by his posturing. He deserves a bit of a rest before the reaping starts."

She caught the open neck of her blouse and wafted it around in an attempt to cool her neck but to little avail, then continued, "Neither of us gets much sleep these nights with the heat but the work gets no less," she sighed. "It's lucky for us that we have such good children," she finished. The two sat in companionable silence as the evening advanced into night.

As the women suspected, George and his sons were frolicking in the shallows of the sea. After a time, he left his sons to their play and retired to sit on a clump of grass and peruse the horizon. As he looked out over the sea, relishing the breeze coming in from the Irish coast, he scanned the coastline of England where it was visible across the sound.

He wondered at how close it seemed today and how he knew this coast in all weathers, despite having grown up much further inland on Capelfoot where his stepfather and mother still reigned as King and Queen, notwithstanding the machinations of their daughter-in-law Janet.

"Poor Janet," he thought. "You can't help but feel sorry for her. She most definitely didn't get what she bargained for!" His brother Peter, younger by some eighteen months, lived and worked with their mother's second husband, which was fine since he and John Graham had always got on well, but, on marrying Peter, Janet had thought to take over as mistress of Capelfoot and had fancied herself as a lady of leisure. Jeanie, however, had no intentions of giving another woman sway in her kitchen, so, for the meantime, Janet had to bow, with bad grace, to her dictates.

"Not that Ma dictates," he grinned, remembering how when he had married Sarah his mother had been full of suggestions but gave no indication of what her preference might be and, after weighing up her options Sarah had decided not to take Jeanie up on her offer to move in to Capelfoot with the rest of the family, but to take over the care of the aging James and Jenny at Hill End.

"I love Jeanie and she loves us. She adores for us to visit her and for them to visit their grandchildren, but she's far from giving up control to one daughter-in-law, far less two," she had stated after making her decision to live with George's grandparents.

"And she was right. There is not a day goes by but I give thanks for my luck. Every time I went into the kitchen Granny was laughing with Sarah. I don't think I ever heard a cross word between those two from the day we married." This thought brought him sadness as he considered the happy times they had shared as a family while his grandparents had been alive.

That kind and gentle couple had shared their home with George and his family and in the end left Hill End Farm to them, as they had brought delight to their old age.

****

The Ruby Moves On

"I'm off for a bit of a dander," said Bill nonchalantly, as he rose from the table where he had stuffed his food down his gullet with barely a chew, as if fuelling a fire.

Sarah and George caught each other's eye before immediately adopting a deadpan expression, ignoring the newly shaved face and clean shirt that adorned their firstborn. If this was not enough to give the lie to the statement, the deep red colour climbing the strong column exposed by the open-necked shirt was a clear indication to Sarah, at least, that her normally open son was taking himself courting.

She carefully aligned her features, hiding her delight in his obvious discomfort and said, "It's a grand night for a walk over the fields or a wee sit down on the shore."

"Aye, off you go and blow away your worries," agreed George, who despite his apparent ignorance of his son's aspirations, knew just how unhappy Bill was living and working with his family when his heart cried out for the adventure of a different lifestyle. He sighed as he thought, "Maybe a wee lass and a dalliance will cure him of the wanderlust and he'll settle down to be a grand farmer in the end."

Bill cast one last glance into the mirror hanging on the wall next to the sink and, feeling happy that he could not improve the features reflected there, he hurried out the back door and with swinging gait hurried away from the farm buildings in the direction of the village.

He smiled to himself, comfortable in the belief that if his parents had not totally believed his excuse of a lonely stroll in the evening sunshine, they were not aware of his actual destination. Like all young men both past and future he thought love had been invented by his own generation.

Excited though he was to be meeting Ellen Irvine he was confused by his feelings. One day he was excitedly planning a future of adventure on the high seas, the next contemplating a marriage and a family connection that would undoubtedly be frowned on by his mother. A wry smile, never far from his lips, now sprang into being. "The notorious Irvines! Mam would have a fit if she knew I was meeting up with Ellen. She has no love for the smugglers and they none for her." But as he loped along the side of the field he allowed his features to relax into a mischievous smile while his heart beat faster at the thought of Ellen waiting at their meeting place.

"No matter what Ma says Ellen is the girl for me." Bill realised, when he came to think about it, that his opinions, more often than not, did not conform to the ambitious plans he knew his mother had devised for him. He fell to contemplating the reaction when he should announce his intentions towards Ellen. It had always been a sore point between his parents that, despite the farm's proximity to the beach and its quiet location, Sarah would not hear of her husband being in cahoots with the smugglers. Sarah was convinced she was the brains of the family and her husband allowed her to believe she made all the decisions. He listened, quiescent, while she ranted at him as she had since they had moved to Hill End Farm.

"Think with your brain, George, and not your heart," was her constant cry whenever she realised George had again been approached to shelter a consignment free from tax. She knew George had sympathy with the 'Free Traders' as they liked to call themselves, and left to his own instincts would have been happy to accept the odd barrel of wine or a bit of baccy as a thank you for allowing his barn to be used when a run was in progress, but Sarah was relentless.

"The very reason the booters want to use your barn is the very reason the excisemen will be watching for the load to be cached in your barn," she had repeated frequently with increasing exasperation at her spouse's indolent shrug. He had heard it many times over the years he had been married and his response was always the same, for he grudged Sarah nothing, not even the right to nag him if it pleased her.

"Aye, lass, you're right," he sighed, anxious to change the subject because he always felt a little bit guilty that he gave assistance to his neighbours, the Romes and the Irvines, without his wife's knowledge. "Let her think she is the one doing the thinking. God bless us, does she think we don't know our barn is a target for the Watch while we laugh up our sleeves at them?"

Normally George and Sarah discussed and argued over every aspect of their shared life, making joint decisions, rationalising each problem to its conclusion, but the smuggling issue was one where a man had to stand up for himself and live with his own conscience. Shortly after taking up residence at Hill End George had come to an amicable agreement with Andy Irvine which had lasted all through the intervening years.

"And you being so vocal in the village and markets about your dislike of smugglers has aided and abetted us." George smiled to himself before continuing with his thoughts. "And no matter what your opinion, Sarah, we would never have been able to build up the farm or increase the herd if I hadn't thrown in my lot with the booters." As he looked around his cosy kitchen, taking in all the luxuries most farmers were unable to provide for their families he, yet again, convinced himself that he had made the right decision in keeping his underhand dealings to himself.

"Let her continue to think she is the one keeping her poor stupid husband out of trouble by preventing him lending his barn to the smugglers. I've seen the troopers myself cooried up in their greatcoats watching the countryside from the shore to the barn on a cold night." His smile turned into a broad grin. "And while they're freezing their balls off watching the sea and my barn, the ponies are wending their way round the coast to my hayricks." He chuckled as he remembered the many instances when he had been happy to open his barn doors as his wife belaboured the poor souls who had been sent on this thankless mission, with indignant protests and the wrath of the innocent.

However, as Bill went on his way to meet his paramour he was unaware of his father's involvement and was more than a little dubious about the reaction of his parents to his association with the eldest daughter of a known brigand. What he felt in himself was that this was no mere dalliance. The very thought of holding Ellen's slim form in his embrace made his blood flow faster. When had this reaction to his childhood classmate started? Bill could not have said when it was that Ellen, the woman, had caught his attention. It was true that the pair had been part of a noisy group who gathered to walk together to the school at Cummertrees.

"But she had no effect on me then," he remembered and, as he continued to try to recall when Ellen's face had begun to force itself into his consciousness, he began to list her more special attributes.

"Those long eyelashes that tipped her smiling eyelids that in turn covered her sparkling blue eyes, that one minute were smiling loving and compliant, the next flashing daggers as her temper flared. No shrinking violet, my Ellen!" he thought. He continued to pass each point of her appearance through his head, trying to be critical in the hope that one element or feature of her personality would detach itself from the whole and explain why he was so attracted to her.

As if by magic his thoughts became reality as he looked up and saw the product of his mental picture moving in his direction, framed by the soft branches of the lime trees, through the leaves of which the setting sun was casting her in a fairytale light.

Not tall, Ellen was just the right height to fit into Bill's shoulder and she had a slight, willowy physique. "Like a fairy princess," thought Bill, very much in love, before he recalled the many tussles they had taken part in as children and the soft female image melted before recollections of her effective fists.

"Built like a fairy princess, but with muscles and sinews like a prize fighter." He grimaced as he considered the number of times a well-placed punch from his erstwhile schoolmate had landed him flat on his back as a consequence of teasing the hot-tempered young miss.

As the vision approached Bill stopped and watched, her dark curly hair raised by a slight evening breeze, her cheeks flushed and her lips curved in an expression of pleasure, showing good strong teeth. Bill could almost feel her curves in his grasp before she arrived in front of him.

"Out for a quiet stroll before bedtime?" she enquired demurely before laughing up into his face; a face she saw nightly in her dreams.

The sight of her took his breath away for an instant but, regaining his muddled senses, he took her into his arms and kissed her soundly.

Holding her at arm's length the better to see her face, he grinned at her.

"I've been looking forward to that all day. It feels such an age since we were together," he hissed in her ear. "You smell so good and wholesome." His words were muffled as he buried his face in her soft curls. She stood within the circle of his arms enjoying their reunion for a minute or so before lifting her face in order to get a look at his as she speculated.

"Miss me, did you? No little damsel from the Toll House Inn been enticing you with her promises?" She spoke lightly but she was achingly aware that Bill was a catch and that many of the local lasses had a long eye for her sweetheart and any one of them would better please his mother. She lived in fear that some night when he was awash with ale, he might wander into the arms of another.

"You know I only have eyes for you…" he began. He caught at the sentence, not wanting to commit to her while he was unsure of his future and where she fitted in it. "… at least tonight," he finished, letting his crooked smile peek up at her.

She pulled away from him, flouncing back towards the copse from which she had so recently emerged. A few yards on she turned her head to look at him over her shoulder and studied him for a few seconds with her piercing glare, before shrugging and continuing to walk away from him, shoulders straight and hips swaying in a very provocative manner.

"Plenty more fish in the sea."

Ellen knew exactly how to deal with him. She had no intention of replacing him, but equally it was not part of her plan to let him know just what an important part he played in her dreams of the future.

Bill stood watching her departure, enchanted by the swinging movement of her skirt and the sting in her words but, despite being almost out sight, she showed no signs of slowing or repenting of her decision to retreat; he worried that she may have meant her heated words he sprinted after her. He caught her up but by this time Ellen was in a temper and not to be easily placated. Since she was peeved and her feelings were bruised by his words, she had no intentions of allowing him off the hook too easily. She ignored him, turning in the opposite direction and continuing to march away from him.

"All right, Ellen, all right. You're right. There are plenty more fish in the sea and for me too."

With one last glance to see how Ellen was responding to having him call her bluff, he secreted his bulk as well as he could behind the massive trunk of a nearby tree hoping this tactic would be more effective than running after her.

Ellen swung round, discombobulated by Bill's ploy. One second earlier and she would have scuppered his plan to hide from her.

"Oh my goodness, what have I done now? The stupid man! That's not what's supposed to happen!" she cried in alarm. No matter where she looked there was no trace to be found of her paramour.

From his position concealed behind the tree Bill heard her bemoaning the failure of her scheme and breathed a huge sigh of relief. She had only been making mock of him. He admired her spunky attitude, realising that a girl with less fire in her blood would be too tame a partner for him. He enjoyed the thrill of a battle with Ellen.

"You just never know where you are with her, but that is what attracts me. A bit of spice!"

Deciding it was time to put her out of her misery and perhaps to calm her temper, he pinned a sad expression on his face before peering around the massive tree trunk and whispering, "Oh, Ellen, what kind of fish was it you were hoping to catch?"

Ellen spun round in the direction of the voice and, catching sight of his woebegone face, launched herself at him, pummelling her fists at his broad chest.

"It's too bad of you to hide from me, you monster," she rebuked him but unable to stop the laugh of relief escaping her tight lips.

Catching her wrists in his hands to arrest the attack on him Bill smirked at her. "Caught in your own trap, Nellie." Then, shifting position in order to fit her comfortably into the space in his arms, he held her tight against his chest and hushed her as he was wont to gentle a young animal on the farm.

Cuddled up in his embrace as she was she could hear his heart beating. In that heightened state of emotion, she imagined she could hear their two hearts beating as one and suddenly a very strange feeling engulfed her. Her cheeks flushed and her head was spinning. It was as if she was listening to the world from a great distance.

At the same time Bill was experiencing emotions he had never imagined he could feel for a woman. He had a weird and wonderful tingling feeling running down his limbs. At the same time his sense of smell was so acute that the fresh smell of Ellen's hair was intermingling with the sharp tang from the green undergrowth around them. He could hear his own heart beating a tattoo in his ear and, as he bent his head to kiss Ellen's plump lips, they felt like the velvety petals of his mother's rambling rose. Keen to prolong this exquisite feeling Bill kept his lips attached to Ellen's as he let go one of her wrists and manoeuvred her into his arms where he could enfold her. Never had he felt the way he was feeling now. His skin was on fire and his fingers quivered as they touched Ellen's bare shoulder.

They clung together, bonded by their mouths, each entranced by the other to a state neither had before experienced. While Bill's lips were moved to kiss Ellen's eyelids and neck, she was moving as if in a dream, in turn caressing his neck where she could see and feel the pulse racing and stretching out her fingers to feel the crispness of his hair and the shape of his ears.

With no words spoken between them they sank with one accord on the undergrowth where they looked into each other's eyes in wonder as they absorbed the new and wonderful sensations cascading over their disrupted senses. As they pulled their bodies together they realised that their clothing was hindering them and, as Ellen lifted her fingers to run them along the V of Bill's shirt, she had to fight the urge to rip off the buttons, the better to feel the flushed skin still hidden. She delicately opened one more button, then another until his shirt was only anchored by the belt of his britches. She looked greedily at the dark curly mat that covered the substantial expanse dwindling down over his flat belly to disappear where it tapered into a line, disappearing below the material of his waistband like a river running into a cavern in the ground where the treasures to be found were unimaginable. As her hand softly caressed the broad chest she looked up into Bill's face to see him, head thrown back, eyes shut, enjoying the exploration of her touch. Amazed at the sensitivity of Bill's skin, Ellen ran her palm across his breast, surprised as his nipples hardened at her touch. Eager to probe if it was her touch that was instigating the tightening of his chest muscles, she repeated her movements on his other side, eliciting an identical reaction. The sight of Bill's naked chest was not new to a girl brought up in the country where young men spent long summer days shirtless. Men and boys were involved in hard physical labour both in the fields and on the fishing boats and, in the summer months, gave no thought to modesty while going about their daily business, but Ellen had not been within touching distance of these hot sweaty muscles so the feeling of Bill's hard muscles, overlaid as they were by warm skin and soft hair, had a very erotic effect on her own senses. She continued to revel in the sight of his bare torso as she played lightly with the hairs on his chest, sometimes touching them with a delicate touch, at others pulling almost roughly. As her hand persisted with its examination her eyes were drawn up to the agonised expression on Bill's face.

"Am I hurting you?" she asked anxiously, stilling her hands over his breast.

"No, it is absolute pleasure to feel your touch." He half opened his eyes to look at her wondering if he could explain what was the problem she was creating in his healthy young body. Indeed, she had excited him to such an extent that he was having difficulty controlling his rampant manhood which was pressing to be released from his trousers. He brought his head down and snuffled into her neck before pursing his lips and gently blowing in her ear.

"Oh Billy, that does give me a queer feeling. My legs are like jelly and I'm shaking all over."

"I think it's love you are feeling," whispered Bill. "I feel it too. Every part of me wants to be part of you and keep this feeling for ever and ever."

Ellen glanced shyly up into Bill's eyes.

"Do you think I could get the same feeling if you touched my chest as I touched yours?" she queried in an almost indiscernible whisper.

Bill could not quite believe he was being permission to venture where he would never have dared of his own volition.

"Yes, I think you might. Is it all right? I won't hurt you," whispered Bill, his emotions almost rendering him breathless.

Ellen nodded, still not really understanding what she had agreed to, but at the same time anxious to share Bill's euphoria.

Bill manoeuvred into position with his back leaning against the rough tree bark and settled Ellen on his strong legs stretched out in front of him. He used a work-roughened finger to turn her face towards him as he gently kissed her lips. This tender feeling, he felt towards Ellen was unlike the few times he had dallied with the doxies near the docks. He wasn't experienced at loving but he knew how to go about the business. He realised that, although Ellen was curious as to what feelings he was experiencing, she had no idea where this might end. Continuing to kiss her lips and stroke her hair his excitement became so heightened that all thought of guilt about the act he was about to perform vanished like snow in the sun. He let his hands wander from Ellen's hair to her neck and caressed her tiny ears, his lips following the in the wake of his hands. He could feel Ellen's excitement building as he unlaced her bodice and touched the delicate skin of her breast with a feather-light strokes. For several minutes he enjoyed the touch and feel of her virgin skin, wallowing in the thought no man had ever touched her so. His head ducked down to her bosom. Her eyes flew open in surprise as she realised he was kissing her nipple, and just as she was revelling in this experience it was further enhanced when Bill took her taught nipple between his teeth and gently nibbled on it. This was shocking to a gentle young maid such as Ellen was, but it engendered such a glorious feeling in her body that she soon began to embrace the novel experience. She felt weak. She felt excited. She felt naughty. But oh, oh yes; she felt good. As Bill's hands continued to move southwards, taking her clothing with him, he alternated his hand and his mouth to each of her tiny hard nipples, sucking one moment, gently rubbing the next. Ellen was almost demented with the elation she was experiencing. She had shut her eyes, a little embarrassed as he had laid her bosom bare, but when Bill stopped manipulating her breasts in order to lay them in a more comfortable position she felt the loss of the exquisite touch most powerfully.

Bill struggled to remove her underclothes and lay her beautifully voluptuous body out before him. He was quite taken aback with the difference between the clothed, almost boyish body and the beauteous apparition before him.

"I want to worship your body, my beautiful Ellen. I want to make you mine for all time," he mouthed when he tore his gaze away from her more obvious features.

Ellen could not have stopped the experience now if her life depended on it. She lay shivering and aching for the return of his touch to her hot, sensitive skin. In her wildest imagination she had never expected she could be made to feel like she did at this moment.

"It can't be wrong to feel this good," she thought as, clasping Bill's hand, she indicated she wanted his stroking to recommence. Bill duly obliged, all conscience burned up in the flame of their twin desires. There was only one thought in his head right now and that was to possess this wonderful body.

As if made of fairy dust their clothes seemed to disintegrate at touch and in the blink of an eye they were both naked, wallowing in the sensations that the other's touch was eliciting.

Ellen became aware of a tightness gathering in her belly as Bill measured his length beside her, touching every inch of her body that by this time was glowing in the rays of the evening sun where it struck them within their leafy bower. As she slid her hand along Bill's body, slick with sweat, she felt the resistance along his bare flank and became hypnotized by the muscles that were honed and toned by the daily burdens of farm work. Her random survey brought her hand in contact with yet another muscle and, without stopping to think what she was doing, she began to gently stroke its length just as she had his rump and flanks. Already engaged in some exploration of his own between Ellen's legs, Bill gave a groan as her touch excited him into almost explosive ejaculation: he gently moved her fingers from his danger area and placed them on his backside before spreading her legs and tenderly placing himself in position between them. He knew there would be some resistance and that he might cause her some pain, so he tried valiantly to control his own urgent need by taking a couple of deep breaths. Positioned as he was at the entrance to her female core he could feel the soft, wet tissues ready to receive him. Their joining was delicious. Bill, having had some experience of coupling, was gentle to begin with but as Ellen became more used to the sensations he was creating she encouraged him to gain greater and more pleasurable heights. When the encounter had reached its inevitable climax they were both spent but euphoric. As their blood cooled and their senses returned to normal neither could quite believe how they had come to be lying naked and satisfied among the roots of the tree. They lay in each other's arms until the last heat from the sun had disappeared, but they both knew that no matter what the future held they were bonded forever by their love.

Before leaving the copse Bill drew Ellen towards him for a final kiss; then, holding her at arm's length, he said seriously, "This is not just a roll in the hay for me, Ellen, I truly love you and to show how sincere I am I want you to take my papa's ruby ring." While he was voicing the words he fumbled in his pocket and took out a soft leather purse from which he removed the CiamBeuill's ruby ring.

Ellen's eyes opened wide at the sight of the stone. "I can't take that from you," she said, placing her arms behind her back as if to stop her fingers clutching the ring of their own accord. "It's too precious for me to wear."

Bill looked a little taken aback since in his muddled thoughts he had not envisaged Ellen actually wearing the ring. No one in his family since his grandfather's grandfather had ever worn the ring. The family saw it more as a talisman. However, he had produced it so now he had to explain its significance.

"It's a pledge of my love. Not for you to wear but to keep safe until we hand it on to our son or grandson. I had it from Granny on my last birthday and she told me the story of how the ring came to be lucky for the Campbell man who owns it and how it must always stay in the possession of a Campbell to keep the luck intact. Please take it so you know how important you are to me."

She smiled up at him, unable to speak because his words and the sentiment they implied brought all her emotions into her throat, cutting off her ability to form her words. She realised that more than the act of love they had just completed this was

Bill's way of declaring his noble intentions; that she should be in no doubt that she was no casual encounter but that his heart belonged to her.

"I want you to have it now so that when you lie in your bed tonight, you know beyond any shadow of a doubt that although we let the heat of our bodies take over our senses tonight I will love you tomorrow and tomorrow and tomorrow."

To Ellen, who had just begun to realise that Bill may think less of her now she had allowed him the freedom of her body and was wondering if he would still want to meet her after she had been 'easy', this speech was a great relief.

"I will take it and thank you for understanding how sleepless my night would be worrying. Now I can dream of our future." She reached up on tiptoe to give him a feathery kiss on the cheek while her tears trickled a salty tang over his lips.

****

"Where are you off to? Slipping off to visit Ellen, are you?" Peggy grinned at the nonplussed expression on her brother's face. "Did you think I didn't know? Me, who has known you all my life and most of yours?"

Realising his reaction to her words had well and truly given himself away, Bill pulled himself together to grin back at his sister.

"And would you, sister dear, like to tell me how you know I am courting Ellen, if you didn't hear it from her cousin Alec?"

Peggy blushed prettily before answering, "We are a right pair, aren't we? All it takes is for us to be told we can't do something then it is the exact thing we will do. Alec wants to speak to Pa about us getting married, but I told him not to because I'm feared Ma will stop us meeting and I just can't and I won't live my life without Alec."

Bill, recognising the stubborn expression on Peggy's face of old, realised that they were in the same boat. It was a dilemma from which there appeared to be no satisfactory outcome. Admittedly it could be argued to be easier for him since he would have little difficulty gaining permission from Andy Irvine to marry his daughter, but how could he bring her to live at Hill End with his mother not to be depended on to welcome her, such was her inherent fear of the smuggling families infecting her own kin?

He gave his sister a rough hug to show his sympathy for her situation, then noticing she was wearing her Sunday best dress and shoes asked, "Where are you off to anyway? You'll never be telling Ma you are off courting," he laughed.

"No, I'm going into Annan with Eliza and the Paterson girls to a talk at the Church by a missionary. I'm pretty sure Mary Paterson is thinking of going to save souls in Africa." She choked on her laugh at the grimace that crossed her brother's face.

Bill laughed with her before commenting, "Well, she won't need her soul saving that's for sure. Every time any of the lads see her approaching they remember an urgent need to attend to an errand in the opposite direction."

"That's really unkind Billy, for you know she is the kindest soul," Peggy remonstrated trying to conceal her amusement for, despite being cruel, it was true that Mary was nicknamed 'Virgin' not for her piety but because no self-respecting boy had ever as much as passed the time of day with her. "All she wants is a good man to look after," finished Peggy.

"Even a good man wants a pleasant smile and a laugh occasionally, and little less piety and a bit of sugar on her tongue would do more to get her a man than visiting the Kirk three times on a Sunday with her face as sour as a goosegog. Maybe if she has hundreds of heathen souls in her mission she might lose her need to preach, so I'll wish her well."

Bill made to walk on as Peggy turned in the farm road to the Paterson steading, but stopped to say, "I'm heading into Annan too as it happens, not off to meet Ellen. There is a frigate in the estuary and I'm hoping to hear some tales of derring-do. Do you want me to wait and walk in with you?"

Although she was fond of her brother and they shared the same sense of humour, she did not encourage him to wait despite them all heading in the same direction. If truth be told she would be on tenterhooks all the way in case he made jokes in bad taste and embarrassed her in front of her friends and their family.

"No. I might have to wait for Liza to get ready; you know what a fidget she is, so off you go to your tavern and tales of piracy and treasure on the Spanish ships. Little boys never grow up. They just grow into big boys and get bigger toys." She waved her hand at him in dismissal.

As it happened, Bill had not corrected his family when they assumed he was off courting, as he did several nights each week, since the evening in the copse when Ellen and he had let their passion take control of them. Neither parent asked questions about who the lucky lass might be, allowing him to take his own time in deciding to introduce a sweetheart into their family. Listening to the younger children taunting Bill as he preened himself Sarah speculated on the identity of his inamorata and turned to her husband where he sat quietly by the fireside, watching the steam rise from the kettle on the whirlie over the dying fire. This was his favourite hour of the day when he and Sarah could relax together, just as they had before the children started to come along.

"I'm sure he's courting and seriously too," she started the conversation as the door closed on the children as they each set off to indulge in their own special pastimes now that the chores were completed. "He fair has me flummoxed. No one I've met has mentioned him calling for their daughters or seen him out walking with any of the local lasses."

"Stop fretting, Sal." George laid a calming hand on her arm. "When the lad has a serious lass in his eye, he will tell us. He might not be meeting the same girl every time he goes out, you know. He's a handsome enough lad and will have his choice for he is pleasant natured into the bargain."

Sarah looked shocked at her husband's remark. "You don't think he's playing fast and loose with their affections, do you? I don't like to think that of my son."

"No, I don't; he's a good lad but you would want him to be sure he had gotten it right, wouldn't you?" He paused before continuing thoughtfully, "I don't want you to get upset or even talk to him about his doings, but he doesn't go courting every time he's out. He likes to talk to the sailors that are wetting their whistle at the Sailors Rest and listen to the stories the old tars tell for a tankard of ale. He's but a lad yet, Sal. Don't make him grow up too soon and don't try to force him down a path he thinks he doesn't want or we might lose him to the sea and she's a cruel mistress."

"I know he has a love of the sea but he will settle down to the farm when he meets the right lass. The sea is just a passing phase. Once he has a wife and bairns he'll forget all about it," Sarah replied, shrugging off her husband's warning.

"Just don't push him to grow up too soon, that's all," George kept any further thoughts he had to himself. "I've given her a hint," he consoled himself. "No need to worry her unless I need to."

George was right in that Bill was not off courting. He planned to spend some time in the harbour bar. Perhaps he would hear some news about the frigate that had been hanging about in the sound on the English side of the estuary. The sighting of a naval vessel off the coast always brought tales from the old timers who were excited by the proximity of a ship. The younger lads often bought these old salts ale and encouraged their reminiscences of their glory days as they vied with one another to tell the most blood-curdling tales of their past exploits.

On entering the Sailors Rest Bill found several of his mates already seated round a table encouraging the older men in their romancing. Bill joined a group that included his sister's sweetheart and settled in for a pleasant hour or so in manly pursuits.

****

"Peggy! Will you hush? We have heard every word said by the missionary, twice!" her mother held up two fingers. Although laughing, Sarah was just a bit annoyed by the chattering of her daughter and the effect it was having on her younger siblings as they listened agog to Peggy's excited words. It wasn't so much the talk about the missionary that had unnerved Sarah but the story Peggy had related about the contingent of the press gang they had come across on the way home. The men had flirted with the young women, as is the way with sailors who know themselves to be the answer to a maiden's prayer. Even Mary had been seen to blush at the complements paid to her by these arrogant young men.

Sarah had seen how young Peter's eyes had shone as he listened to her account of the episode. "He's just at an age to think it romantic to be off on a ship and finding girls in every port. I don't need another son to be fascinated by the sea."

She slanted a look at the children and breathed a sigh of relief that Peter had lost interest in his sister's tale. "Not so grown up, then." She smiled her relief as she watched her son stuffing his mouth full of bread and butter while chivvying his reluctant younger brother to hurry off to school.

She sighed as calm descended on the kitchen. This was a moment every day when Sarah felt bereft as her noisy family left for their day. She found the loosening of her apron strings difficult. Her children were her life and, for a few moments, when the silence was exaggerated by the previous noisy bustle, she felt deserted and out of control. This was her five minutes' peace in the day. After the children had left she filled a cup of tea, added a drop of milk and sat down at the messy table to plan out her day. They always ate breakfast in two sittings. The men were out early to deal with the animals, milking and cleaning down the byre, leaving the milk to cool in the dairy for the womenfolk to deal with later, before they had their first meal of the day. The children had to leave early to walk to school so they ate first, allowing the grown-ups time to have a leisurely meal. Sarah benefitted from these few minutes to herself when she could plan the lives of those she was responsible for. At present she was mildly worried that Amy did not enjoy lessons and caused trouble in the schoolroom. She found reading difficult to master and her mother worried that unless she could be made to pay attention, she would never know how many beans made five. Maybe her girls were destined to be farmer's wives and work on the farm, but they still needed to know how to count and deal with money. Peggy, however, was a more imminent worry as she was just at the age to get involved with the wrong kind of man; just listen to how excited she had been by the mild flirtation of the sailors they had met last night. Sarah knew her daughter's sunny nature and that she was happy working in the dairy, but she would need to keep an eye out. Sarah had no intention of letting Peggy marry the wrong man and a sailor, no matter how handsome and strong, would be a wrong man.

"Then there's Bill," she thought. "He's the biggest worry. Is he courting? Is he thinking of marriage?" Sarah was not ready to lose any of her chicks to marriage but she had decided it would be better all round if Bill married a local girl and settled down, here at Hill End, than for him to follow his instinct and go to sea.

"Maybe if I hadn't been so set on not sharing a kitchen with Janet we would all be happily settled at Capelfoot, far away from the sight and smell of the sea, and the lad would love the land best."

While she was still contemplating the might-have-beens and imagining herself and Janet agreeing in the kitchen, a thought that brought a stray smile to her lips and a sparkle to her eyes as she visualised them being polite to each other constantly, the back door opened to reveal George ready to eat the breakfast she had not yet started to cook.

Leaning her hands on the table to help her hoist herself to her feet, she froze midway as George's remark made her blood turn to ice.

"Is that lad still lying in bed, the lazy sod? No more nights out for him if he can't get out of his pit in the morning," he laughed, leaning over to drop a kiss on Sarah's cheek. He took in her shocked expression, and pulling out a chair from the table, sat down, asking, "What's ado, lass?" As he straightened up after removing his boots, he noticed his wife was not responding. He gave her arm a gentle shake. "Sarah?"

"He's not in bed, George. I was up to get Peter a clean vest and the bed was empty."

"Well, he didn't appear in the byre this morning and I had to go and bring in the kid myself. They were all gathered at the gate waiting to be collected. Now Sarah, don't get yourself in a fankle. He won't be the first lad who forgot to come home when he discovered the joys of sleeping in a woman's bed. He'll be home shortly with his tail between his legs. Or if he's not with a woman he maybe drank too much ale with his pals."

"He's not used to strong drink, certainly," agreed Sarah with pursed lips, but, in her heart that had dropped when George had told her of her missing son, she could find no belief that her son had not come to some harm. Putting both hands up to her mouth Sarah moaned, "Oh, my darling boy." Coming to her senses almost immediately, she jumped up saying, "Oh, your breakfast, George; I'll not be a moment."

"Never mind about the food just for now, lass. I'll away over to the Rome's place, for Alec Irvine works there and he and Bill are mates. He'll likely know where the rascal's hiding himself."

Giving Sarah a reassuring pat on the shoulder, he put his boots back on and left the kitchen.

Sarah sat back down at the table where only minutes before she had been reflecting on her family's problems and thanking God they had escaped major conflict with her children. She automatically raised the cup of cold tea to her lips and drank it off in an effort to moisten her mouth, suddenly dried up by her fear that some catastrophe had overtaken Bill.

"For he would not have stayed away all night, whatever his father says," thought Sarah.

The thoughts flew around inside her head. One minute she was convinced he had been shot on the banks of the river by poachers mistaking him for a bailiff; the next she was angry at him since she believed he had drunk himself into oblivion and visualised him waking heavy headed and nauseous on the taproom floor. Each scenario that flitted through her busy mind was discarded until she recalled this morning's breakfast conversation and how Peg had related her meeting with the press gang thugs on their way into Annan.

Opening the door, she called across the yard, "Peggy, Peggy, come in a minute!"

Peg appeared at the door alerted by the strange quality of her mother's voice.

"Come in, lass, and tell me that story you were telling the bairns this morning about the press gang. Did they tell you that's what they were?"

"No, Ma, but you could tell. They were fit and strong. Big muscles on their arms and legs and bragging to us girls that they were the best recruiters in the King's Navy."

Sarah slid into the chair now convinced that the group who had been spooning with his little sister had abducted Bill.

Peg tried to distract her mother's thoughts by begging her to wait until her father returned, but long before this event took place Sarah had convinced herself that she would never see her beloved eldest son again.

"He's just the sort of man they are looking for their bloody navy. He's straight and strong and well fed. The kind of young man who would never be conscripted in a normal way."

Covering her face with her hands Sarah moaned her pain out loud, then ranted at the stupidity of herself and George for allowing their children so much freedom as to allow them to be put in danger.

No matter what arguments Peg put forward, Sarah was convinced that Bill was now on board the frigate that had been loitering in the river mouth this past week.

By the time George returned to the kitchen with a heavy heart, there was no need for him to impart his fears as to the fate of their oldest offspring. He opened his arms for her and they silently clung together, each blaming themselves for the loss of their lad.

Chapter Fifteen

Ellen's Story

Grace Irvine looked at her daughter across the cold slab where they had been working companionably for some time. The fruits of their labour were lined up along the shelf, bearing testimony to their skill in the dairy. Golden butter pats, indented with the thistle pattern that identified them as being from Meadow Farm, lay ready for market beside rounds of creamy cheese wrapped in cheesecloth to hold their shape. There really was no need for the Irvine women to work on the land or in the dairy, for their menfolk earned the bulk of their income by running tax-free goods from the Isle of Man over to the quiet Scottish coast from where they could be clandestinely transported over the countryside. The most profitable runs were those that defied the heavy tax levied in England so that the surreptitiously conveyed luxury goods found a ready market close to home. The Solway coast was a smugglers' dream, however the women of the family not only provided a cover for the frequent absence of their men but they enjoyed the thrill of producing food by their own efforts.

Grace had been casting glances at her daughter all morning but up until now had managed to keep quiet about her worry for her daughter.

"Are you feeling ill, Ellen? You've barely said a word in three days. Are you sickening for something?" her mother now asked, no longer able to hide her concern.

"Just feeling a bit off colour this morning. Nothing to worry about," Ellen shrugged off her mother's questions.

"You would tell me if there was anything upsetting you, wouldn't you?" she persisted, for she had noticed Ellen's swollen eyes above the incriminating dark circles.

Ellen had been unable to sleep since Bill had been absent from their trysting place four nights ago and, despite her wandering as close to Hill End as she could, she had not been able to find him at work in the fields. His father and younger brother were often to be spied in the distance as she kept vigil at their spot under the lime tree, but she had had no word from or sight of Bill himself since she had broken her news to him.

She ignored her mother's attempts to get her to share her problems. She had vowed to herself that if Bill did not appear tonight she would approach his mother at market in the morning.

"I will not languish about the farm feeling sorry for myself, either he accepts me and the babe or he tells me to my face he is finished with me." She bit her lip on the decision for deep down inside Ellen believed that Bill would not have failed her unless something dreadful had happened to him. He had vowed she was his dear love and swore he thought of nothing else but their clandestine meetings in the cool of the evenings.

As she thought about Bill a cold fear sent random ideas in all directions as she became less sure of his sentiments and wondered if perhaps he had changed his mind about marrying her and had deserted her in her hour of need.

"If only I hadn't told him about the baby," she though,t trying to convince herself that this was not the reason Bill had not turned up at their assignation.

"No, he was pleased and excited and promised we would go together to tell our parents we wanted to wed."

But the fact that she hadn't seen hide nor hair of him since she made the announcement preyed on her mind, making her imagine him scorning her and leaving her to carry the shame of unwed motherhood by herself.

"Hey, lass, you're miles away," laughed her mother but quickly changed her tone as she continued. "And it doesn't look like those daydreams are pleasant ones. Come on, out with it. Nothing can be so bad you can't tell your auld mither."

Ellen looked up at her mother with a sorrowful expression marring her normally pretty face and, seeing the other's determined chin, she decided that as her mother's daughter she would face her problem head on. Her mother's favourite saying when the children were squabbling was, 'Tell the truth and shame the De'il'.

"Ma, I'm not feeling so good. Can you spare me to take a short stroll down to the beach? The sea air might help."

"Aye, on you go lass but don't go to the shore. There's been talk of the press gang being in the port. Best stay clear of the sea." Not realising her words were the cause of the sudden pallor that overtook Ellen's face, Grace wondered if it was wise to allow her to wander off on her own, but decided Ellen was probably right and that a bit of fresh air would cure her lethargy. God knew this heat was enough to make anyone ill, and the farm buildings were very humid and sultry. Wiping the sweat of her own neck with a nearby towel Grace continued, "This is the hottest and driest summer I ever remember."

Ellen smiled at her mother's hot, worried face as she removed her dairy apron and hung it on a nail behind the door before making a hasty exit from the dairy.

On leaving the precincts of the farm she straightened her shoulders, stuck out her chin and screwed up her courage before she ran off through the field in the direction of Hill End Farm. She went as fast as she could, making no plans of what to say or do when she arrived, not even thinking of the meeting in case her bravado would leave her and she might slip from her sticking point.

The speed at which she had ran the distance between the two farms had brought colour to her cheeks and disorder to her hair, so, before making her way through the farm orchard, Ellen stopped to tidy herself, then gripping Bill's ring in its leather pouch for added courage she marched right up to the kitchen door and rapped smartly on the wooden panel before she could chicken out.

The door was opened by a Sarah Ellen had never seen. The families were not on visiting terms but passed the time of day if they passed in the local area or met at church. Ellen had always seen Sarah as a happy, healthy soul but the drawn look on the woman's face told a tale of sorrow. She was so taken aback by Sarah's appearance that she stood frozen to the spot in a dumbstruck silence. Her mind darted to an erroneous conclusion that made her heart thump with dismay. Was Sarah mourning the death of her son? Had there been an accident? Surely if he was dead the community would have been humming with the news?

"Well, what brings you to my door?" asked Sarah in an unfriendly tone. "If you have a message from your father, you'll find George and Peter reaping in the top field."

Sarah delivered this speech in a flat voice and barely had the words left her mouth than she made to slam the door.

Ellen was unable to get the words from her seething brain to her dry mouth, but held up her hand to prevent the door closing in her face. Even then she was at a loss how to deal with this obviously mourning woman. They stared unseeingly at each other until Ellen, still using her weight to keep the door open, got herself enough under control to speak.

"Please, Mrs Campbell," she pleaded quietly. "I must talk to Bill. Where is he? Is he well? Has there been an accident? Please tell me he has not been killed."

"Oh my God. No, no, no…" Sarah's voice faded away as she crumbled onto the floor where she lay immobile.

Not knowing what else to do Ellen got down on her knees beside the recumbent woman and cradled her head in her lap. There appeared to be no life left in Sarah and Ellen feared that the sight of her at her door had caused Bill's mother's death.

She sat stroking the woman's hair away from her face, but, when she felt a slight movement of the prone body across her knees, she realised that Sarah had only fainted. Laying her gently down on the ground she entered the kitchen, grabbed a jersey from the pulley overhead and, bundling it up, used it as a pillow under Sarah's head. Having made her as comfortable as possible in the circumstances she then plied the handle of the pump and filled a cup with cold water. Returning to her position beside the unconscious woman and manoeuvring her head once more into the crook of her arm, she noted that Sarah's colour was improving and her eyelids were flickering sporadically, indicating her return to consciousness.

When Sarah opened her eyes the first thing they settled on was the worried face of Ellen, who supported her as she tried to sit up.

"Don't try to stand yet," she begged. "Take your time and sip some of this water," she suggested, offering the cup to Sarah's lips.

Sarah knocked away the hand that held the cup and growled.

"You're with child," she accused. "He ran away to sea to get away from you. My boy, my darling boy. Lost! Not pressed but gone willingly. I'll never forgive you for this as long as I live."

Sarah was so distressed that she gave no thought for the hurt she was causing the young girl. She continued to keen like a spectre on All Hallows' Eve. She garbled her words and no sense could be made of the noises that emanated from her mouth, but, despite the incoherency of the words, her tone left Ellen in no doubt that Sarah was laying the blame for her missing son at her door.

"Was it true? Had Bill run off to sea?" To her horror she realised that it could indeed be true. On the last occasion they had met he had seemed so happy, but he did say they would not meet the next night because he was going to the Sailor's Rest in the port of Annan. "Had he deliberately lied and gone off to sea without telling her?" She could not believe it of the gentle giant who had wooed her all these months.

"His mother obviously knows he has gone to sea but did he really go to get out of being responsible for our child?"

Neither woman appeared to have the strength to rise from the floor. Each looked at the other as if they were trying to inflict their own hurt on the other; both felt that they had been betrayed; each incapable of any empathy with the other since their hurt cut so deep.

They remained sitting together but alone with their differing views, wrapped up in the meandering of their thoughts. Each felt guilty that they had in some part been responsible for Bill's dilemma. The idea of Bill having taken the King's shilling was so new to Ellen that her numbed brain could not begin to process what this might mean in everyday life, while Sarah, by now accustomed to the absence of her beloved boy, clutched at Ellen's condition as a reason for Bill being willing to join the navy. The one thing that they agreed on was that they both blamed Ellen!

It soon dawned on the women that they could not remain sitting like graveyard statues on the kitchen floor. Eventually reality reasserted itself into their sorrow, but it was the smell of burning food that brought Sarah back to her senses and, pulling herself out of the clasp of the catatonic Ellen, she jumped up and rescued the stewpot from the hook over the fire where she had been tending it before the appearance of Ellen. As she grabbed the handle of the iron pan with a rag she again rounded on Ellen, venting all her poison.

"Not content to have me lose my son, making him so desperate as to put himself in danger of his life, you want the rest of my family to starve!" she shouted.

She knew she was being unkind and unrealistic in her accusations, but, just as she was hurt by the disappearance of Bill, she was driven to make Ellen take the worst of the guilt on her insubstantial shoulders.

As Ellen looked up at Sarah's ugly expression she felt the hatred radiating from every pore of the older woman's bristling body and understood that her presence was only making Sarah angrier. If Bill wasn't here, then she needed to take herself away and formulate a survival plan for herself. In the short space of time she had been in Sarah Campbell's kitchen she felt she had aged many years. Her limbs were stiff and did not feel as if they belonged to her body. She was so shocked by the news she had heard from Sarah that her brain appeared to have stopped sending messages to the muscles in her legs. She staggered like an old crone as she got to her feet, swaying to such an extent that she had to make a grab for the door post to keep herself upright before taking herself out across the stockyard as if she had spent the morning in the alehouse. Afterwards she could not recall removing herself from the farm but, when her senses began to reassert themselves, she found herself curled up in the shade of the tree where she and Bill had sealed their love with the passion from their young bodies. She did not know how long she had spent there as she cried her grief into the undergrowth. Her weeping had to some extend cleared her anger at Sarah's treatment and had given her a new sense of confidence in her ability to cope with what everyone else would see as a fall from grace. As she pushed herself into a sitting position she tried to harden her heart against Bill, but no matter how many times she told herself that he had abandoned her, she could not bring herself to believe it of him.

"Surely I'm not so dim that I would believe his promises if he was making them just to break them the very next day?"

She cast her mind back to the evening when she had gone surreptitiously to their meeting point, worried that the news she had to impart would ring the death knell on their romance. "No man wants to wed a fallen woman," had been the thought in her head as she slowly approached her waiting swain. She thought now of how Bill had received the news of her pregnancy. For one dreadful moment his features had frozen before a great grin had stretched his lips and he let out a loud whoop, grasping her round the waist and whirling her in circle making her dizzy with his delight. After setting her back on her feet he had knelt in front of her placing both of his giant hands over her tiny belly. There was barely a swelling yet, but Bill was in enormous awe that his son was residing in this cosy space.

"Take great care of young Master Campbell," he had breathed reverentially. "He is the start of our own little dynasty. Thank you sweet Ellen for this best of news," and he had followed up this statement by taking her tenderly in his embrace and raining gentle kisses all over her neck and face.

Thinking back on this occasion now after her emotional interlude with Bill's mother, Ellen shrugged her shoulders and decided that whatever the reason for Bill's sustained absence from his home, it had nothing to do with her and his child. In the deepening shades of the day Ellen remained in the place where she felt closest to Bill and tried to formulate a plan of action

"It's pretty certain that the Campbells at Hill End will not be any help since Sarah, at least, blames me for her son's disappearance, so…" And here the next dilemma started. Would her parents face the embarrassment and disdain heaped on them by the community and allow her to give birth to Bill's child in her own home? On the whole she thought her dogmatic father would chase her from his roof even if she managed to gain the support of her mother. She sighed. Her father was a proud man and although, like many of his kind, ignored his daily lawlessness on a Sunday while ushering his family to church, she felt sure that his erring daughter would be cut no slack.

Could she bear to be shown up in church as a fallen woman? If she did suffer the indignity of announcing the child's father would Sarah deny Bill was responsible for the child and heap more scorn and derision on her head? She didn't think she could bear to ask the forgiveness of the sanctimonious congregation, for to do so would be to deny her love and repent of her actions.

"Even the thought of being in Bill's arms makes me flush with pleasure. I would not be able to show enough remorse to convince the elders of Ruthwell Church," she thought to herself, immediately relegating this embarrassing option to the back of her mind. But what options were open to her?

She sat lost in thought for some time, letting her wits play over all the facts and likely outcomes. At no time did her certainty that Bill loved her and her unborn child waver, so, whatever the final plan was, it had to take into account her having the baby and rearing it until Bill returned, which she had no doubt he would.

"Despite Sarah's certainty that Bill had chosen to take ship, I don't believe he would have left me to take care of our problem," she sighed.

A plan to hear more of the story of the press gang being seen formed in her mind. So before she made any steps to determine her future well-being she determined to take herself into the port of Annan and listen to the gossip that was bound to be rampant if indeed the pressmen had been at their work. There were many young strong men in any farming community and, with the smugglers and sailors around the area, it was not unreasonable to suppose that the King's Navy had decided the Solway estuary might be a productive hunting ground. Having fixed this idea firmly in her head and thought through the excuses she would make to her mother to allow her to carry out her visit to Annan, she felt happier about herself and her situation.

"I just hope Mrs Campbell doesn't tell my mother about the babe." She blanched at the idea that all her planning might yet be brought to nothing by a stray word in the wrong quarter but, on balance, and taking into account Sarah's anger, she decided that the older woman would be as keen as she was herself to keep the secret while it could still be kept.

Vowing to herself to be mistress of her own fate Ellen picked herself up and dusted the dried earth from her clothes before making her slow progress back to her home.

"For how much longer will Meadow Farm be my home?"

Chapter Sixteen

The Studio

Lord John Campbell paused in his tale, leaned forward and, raising the water glass to his lips, quaffed the contents.

"Dry work this speechifying," he quipped.

"But surely the ruby has now gone from the Campbell family with Bill missing and Ellen not being welcomed by his family?" asked Mark who was having difficulty getting his head round the finer points of the story.

"There are times in every family, more especially the Border families, when it gives us pain to hear the machinations of our ancestors. They were a wild lot. The whole Borders were wild. They had to be to make a living on the Borders of two warring countries and even today, after hundreds of years of peace, our national identity has not been absorbed into British. A Scotsman will always be a Scotsman. But I digress again." He grinned up into Mark's face, "You really need to keep me to my subject and not let me wander off piste." Since this was the direct opposite of what Mark had spent years trying to do to John Campbell when he had him in his interview seat, it tickled Lord John's fancy.

"As I was saying, in the history of every family there are times when our ancestors have done things we are not proud to acknowledge and Sarah Campbell and Andy Irvine between them did the young couple a great disservice. But that was the time they lived in and I have come to accept that likely I would have made the same decision if I had been raised as they were."

"So Ellen was cast out of the fold, in a Biblical sense?" enquired Mark with a worried frown. "But how come the ring is still on your finger after all this time?"

"If I have learned nothing else over my years at Holyrood," laughed Big Jock, "it is to know when to keep your listeners in suspense." He pondered this thought before adding, "A lesson to be learnt by the would-be politicians of today. Never get too fond of the sound of your own voice." His crooked grin again appeared, lighting up his heavy features. "Maybe I'll turn publicist and make the next leader of the party people friendly. It's been done before." His loud laugh rang out and echoed from the corners of the studio.

"Another Jock Campbell?"

Big Jock held up his massive right hand and denied any serious thought of mentoring. "No, one of me is about all a nation can take in a lifetime. Mind, fashions do repeat. Before I continue with the family saga you need another history lesson" he smiled winningly at his audience. "Do you want to hear the rest of the story?"

The reaction of their audience left no doubt in anyone's mind that they would lynch him if he ceased now that they were all hooked on the life and times of the Campbell family mascot. The audience was gagging for more.

"What an orator," thought Mark before turning back to Lord John and saying aloud, "You have already found me lacking in my knowledge of the Borders so carry on and educate me some more. Maybe I should take notes?"

"No, I won't be asking for your catechism, Mark, so breathe easy. As I said just a moment ago there are fashions in politics just as there are in medicine and morality. No, I'm not going to preach morality. You all know my views on the laxity of society. During the most recent wars we have had conscription of our young men into the armed forces and our young women into the jobs previously held by men. It has been argued many times that these conscriptions were unfair, but many of my constituents have voiced to me their belief that if we were to put our young men and women into the army as they did in the days of National Service we would produce a better class of citizen, but forced labour fighting for your country is not an invention of the twentieth century."

"Which takes us back to Bill's being pressed into the Navy and leaving Ellen alone and pregnant," interrupted Mark, keen to prove he was following the gist of Lord John's argument.

"A product of the great Glasgow University, I see," laughed Big Jock. "Debating a point before it has become apparent there is one. Yes, Bill was not alone in being pressed. There was a government ruling to allow His Majesty's frigates to seize crew where they could.

"I know it sounds barbarous to us now midway through the twenty- first century, but two hundred years ago – when we were constantly at war with the French; whilst one day the Prussians were our allies, then the next they were fighting with Johnny Crapaud against the British army and navy – it was necessary to recruit somehow or we would no longer have been the nation we are today. We would have been a mere appendage of Europe." He paused momentarily. " Well, it came to that in the end anyway, but that is more of a peacekeeping plan than being invaded by terrorist forces.

The Borders have always been notoriously warlike, with reivers and smugglers and, later, in the War to End All Wars, an ideal place to make the weapons of war. So, at the time of Bill's abduction, the Navy was recruiting strong, adventurous young men to serve on their warships as they prepared for the great Battle of Trafalgar. The only problem was that few strong young men wanted to have their adventure under the cannon of Napoleon's army. In the Borders particularly they turned rather to smuggling for their kicks."

"But they would be good seamen and therefore ideal for the Navy. Almost a ready-made crew, needing little training to be seaworthy," agreed Mark, pleased to be following the story.

"Now here is the history bit," laughed Lord John. "The government of the day gave the captains power to persuade the right type of young men to enlist for the cause. The wording of the act may have been intended that the payment be offered *before* the recruit was sailing away from his homeland, but it was pretty loosely interpreted by the navy recruiters, or press gang as they came to be known.

"They would land quietly in a likely spot and like most mariners make straight for the pub where they would appear to be just another lot of sailors in port for a good time. They had two methods of entrapment, sorry persuasion. The first and easiest was to drop a shilling in a man's pint pot so that when he knocked back his ale he 'took the King's shilling' and was immediately part of the Navy. He was often on board before he realised he had signed on. However, men were wary, especially in times of war, of the ploys of the King's men and were careful not accept this offer of employment, at least while they were sober."

Big Jock gave one of his guffaws at the delicate phrasing and stopped to savour his own words, but Mark was anxious for him to continue with his tale.

"So what was the second method?"

"That's really how the press gang got their name. They couldn't meet their quotas just by normal methods or by taking the strong from the prisons, they were allowed to free prisoners if they agreed to go to sea for a specific time, so they eventually developed 'persuasion tactics'. They pressed the men, literally, with big clubs."

"Do you fancy joining the Navy and having the time of your life? No. Then wallop, the inattentive victim was clubbed over the head and when he woke up bearing an aching head, he was well off shore and had no option but to work his passage."

A frown appeared on Mark's face. He was decidedly feeling his lack of research on this subject.

"But surely as soon as the ship hit port they would desert and make back home?"

"Aye, well a few did, but it was often many weeks before a frigate came to port, often on mainland Spain or in the English Channel. That made it pointless to desert as they couldn't get home anyway, left as they were penniless on a foreign shore, and, although the men were initially forced to join up, they were not treated as slaves, you know. They were British ships." Big Jock's impish smile shone out over the studio audience. "They were usually better off in the Navy than they had been on land. They were given a suit of clothes, in some cases armour, a hammock, offered a reasonable pay and if the food wasn't as tasty as they had had at home, it was washed down by good strong Jamaican rum. Each man had a daily allowance of an eighth of a pint of almost 100% proof which needed to be watered down to protect the lining of their stomachs and possibly to prevent drunkenness. That's actually how grog came into our language. Old Admiral Vernon, nicknamed, 'Old Grog', ordered his sailor's rum to be diluted, presumably to stop them being too inebriated to climb the rigging.

"Anyway, back to our tale." Lord John again focused his attention on the ruby glinting away in the studio lights as he gathered the strands of his story before continuing, "As Bill awoke to find himself aboard *HMS Phoebe* as it sailed down the west coast of England, making for hostilities, so Ellen was to be left to her own devices. Reviled by both families, she set off to find herself a new home."

Chapter Seventeen

After attempting to lift his head to establish just where he had fallen asleep and deciding it was not a good idea to move a muscle, since even blinking his eyes caused the hammering behind them to recommence. He lay still trying to gather some evidence of where he was and, more importantly, how he had got there. For some minutes his brain could cope with no rational thoughts, but gradually Bill became aware of his surroundings. Still not moving for fear of more explosions in his head he realised he was lying on a wooden floor, he could smell the scent of the wood assailing his nostrils, but he was unable to identify the other more alien smells that accosted his nasal passages.

"Am I in someone's new barn?" he wondered, but almost as soon as he raised the thought he rejected it, as he realised that, wherever he was and in whatever type of vehicle he was being carried, he was moving.

Unable to decipher any more about his current position and due to the drifting of his thoughts, he decided nothing could be done until his head had stopped pounding. Giving a sigh, pleased that he had made this momentous decision he again closed his eyes and drifted off to sleep, lulled by the gentle movement of the floor beneath him.

"Time to wake up, sleeping beauty," came a raucous voice far above him, causing him to open one eye to discover who had so rudely disturbed his slumber. Not recognising the two faces hovering over him with what appeared to be bodiless heads, he realised that one was poised to douse him with a bucket full of water. He quickly opened both eyes to prove he was responding to command.

The smaller of the men, the one with the bucket of water, appeared disappointed not to have been able to administer the water treatment and reluctantly lowered his burden to the floor. Convinced now that his head was not going to burst open, Bill decided that to change position would indeed be desirable. He cautiously brought himself into a sitting position bending his legs up to support his arms which, in turn, supported his still painful head.

"That must have been pretty strong ale I drunk last night," he grimaced at the two men whom he was now sure he had not met before the previous night. He scanned them surreptitiously still trying to remember how it had come about that he had woken up with them. Now that he could see them from a more accurate angle he noticed that they were both thickset individuals, possibly prize fighters, was his initial thought.

The taller of the two was tattooed down both of his brawny arms and as he stood astride, the obvious contours of his powerfully built legs were obvious. The smaller man was just as beefy. They both looked healthy and clean. "So not gypsies or vagabonds," went Bill's thoughts. In his befuddled state he could not recognise the clothes they wore as workmen of any trade he knew. Both men wore baggy blue canvas trews and long shirts over which each had a rough waistcoat. On their feet they wore canvas shoes that more than any other aspect of their attire indicated to Bill they were not men of the land. They were both clean-shaven but sporting extra-long hair tied tidily in a queue and bound with cloth.

As these thoughts slowly pervaded his consciousness, he continued to address the men. "I've not been unconscious with a pot of ale before. I'm obviously not used to strong drink." He gave the man a very sheepish look that made him appear extremely young in the eyes of his companions.

"There may be a lot you don't recall of yestre'en," explained the taller of the men. "You and that lad over there have joined the King's Navy and are currently indentured for five years' service on *HMS Pheobe* under the command of Captain Capel, but you take your orders directly from me." He grinned, pointing to himself with his thumb to his chest as he delivered this information in a grand pompous voice.

"The Navy!" exclaimed Bill. "But.. but... I'm a farming man. I know nothing of the sea. How did I come to join the navy?"

At this point the information he had just received burst upon him as he realised what must have happened. He remembered the frigate they had watched make its way up the estuary and came to a conclusion.

"I've been pressed and am on board a ship!"

Even with the delicate state of his head and the nausea he was beginning to feel in his stomach, Bill's eyes shone and it was hard for him to hide his delight in his current situation.

"Well, it's a relief to know that this head I'm suffering from is not due to too much liquor, for my ma would kill me for touching strong drink. She'll kill me for being stupid enough to be caught by the press gang as well." He laughed up into the faces of the seamen. They, catching the pleasure of the young man's face, relaxed their vigilance, realising that this youngster, at least, was not too unhappy at finding himself aboard His Majesty's Ship *Pheobe*, and grinned back at him before outlining what would be expected of him.

"It's not such a bad life, you know, sailing the sea. The captain is a fair man with many years of experience and likes a happy crew, so we land often to get fresh meat and fruit and, once you get used to the work, it's a companionable life. Give yourself a sluice down in that there bucket, but don't drink it mind; it's salt water and will send you mad," warned the taller man, showing he was the one in command. "We'll get over and see to your pal. I hope he's as sensible as you."

So saying they moved to the shadows of the other side of what Bill now recognised as the hold of a ship, where they meted out similar treatment to his fellow conscript, but he was not so easily roused. Bill could hear from the noise of the rough treatment, although it was too dark to see what lengths the men would go to carry out their orders. Listening to the obvious physical abuse they were meting out, he understood just how lucky he had been to have avoided it. As the sailors dealt with his fellow captive Bill was forced to acknowledge the unease in his stomach, which increased as he made an attempt to follow orders. As he brought his body into an upright position it disgraced him and, before he could stop himself, he had vomited all over the deck. He sank to his knees as his legs gave way beneath him. He could not stop retching even when his stomach had voided the sour-smelling yellow liquid, which now tainted the air in the hold. His head was spinning and he was engulfed in hot and cold sweats.

The smaller of the two tars came to stand over him, as he lay prone on the deck and moaned, "I have spent years yearning to have adventures on the sea and now my dream has been realised without upsetting Ma, I'm a bloody useless sailor."

The other man told him that his name was Mac. "Short for King Macbeth of Scotland," he joked as he helped him to his feet, with what Bill's confused senses acknowledged was empathy, and then continued, "It will be fine oncst ye have been aboard for a wee whiley. I'll take ye up on deck tae get some fresh sea air. That's the best cure in the world for what ails ye. Auld Neptune wants to see if you can handle his kingdom, tha's all it is." He added, "When I first joined I was just as sick as you and I was only on the River Clyde, no the sea." He guffawed. "But oncst ye've cast yer innards ye never will agin, no even in the roughest storm so, gan on lad, up the ladder," he finished in a bracing manner as he followed Bill up to the windblown deck.

Meanwhile his erstwhile partner was dealing with a very confused young man still unable to retrieve his senses. Job, the mate, was beginning to worry that they had given him too hard a 'tap'. The methods they used were not strictly orthodox, nor indeed legal, but many a blind eye was turned by their captain who trusted them with the task of sourcing recruits who were fitter and smarter than the lowlifes and criminals who made up most of the conscripts. Often petty criminals were offered the option of gaol or enlisting, which did not always make them competent sailors since it stood to reason if they had been smart enough to learn a trade they would not have turned to crime, been caught and been summoned before the beak.

When eventually the young man was brought back to his senses, Bill and Mac had returned. Bill's complexion showed the improvement in his condition, the strong sea breeze had blown away the remnants of his illness, though his stomach remained in a delicate condition, and he was ushered back belowdecks to take care of his mess. As he listened to the animadversions happening in the gloom he reflected that the other young man was not being dealt with as sympathetically as he himself had been, but then he was putting up a fight with his captors who were holding him in a tight armlock.

"I'm a bloody smuggler, ye daft git. Why would I be brainless enough to give up my lucrative business to join the bloody navy?" he demanded in frustration, realising there really was no escape from the situation but determined not to give in without a fight.

"I'll ignore that you have admitted to a punishable crime to an officer of the King's Navy for it will be best for both of us if I don't condemn you as a felon to stand your trial the assizes and you accept you are bound body and soul to this ship for five years."

"Unless o cors ye ha drowned by then," came the ominous warning from Mac. "For we are bound for the Spanish coast to watch out for the French and Spanish ships and keep them on their side of the Channel. All in all I reckon ye've changed one hazardous employment for anither of equal uncertainly." He let out a roar of laughter at the rueful expression on the smuggler's face.

Although unable to distinguish the other's features due to the gloom, Bill recognised the familiar voice of his childhood friend.

"Alec? Alec Irvine?" he queried into the darkness. "It's Bill Campbell. It would appear that we are neither of us as smart as we thought ourselves."

"They got you too then?" groaned Alec as he strained to make out his friend in the darkened cabin.

"Now lads, take my advice and accept your portion and make the best of it," said Job. Mac, a bit unhappy at being deprived of the pleasure of dousing Alec by Bill's sickness, agreed.

"Aye, take yersels up on deck and get yersels thegither. Here are yer slops and a hammock each. They will come oot o' yer pay but ye mun need them the noo."

At the bewildered look on their recent captives faces Job realised they had no understanding of Navy language and sighed as he went on to explain.

"You are here to work, and work hard, but you will be paid at the end of the voyage. Since you did not fully agree to enlistment," he eyed the boys with a wry smile, "youse will not likely be allowed on shore leave in case you were to take it into your heads not to return, and since our gracious captain demands that all hands are clean and louse free you are issued with the basics when you come on board. As time goes on you can buy cloth and needles and thread from the purser and make your own."

Again taking in the dumbfounded appearance of the young men he nudged his cohort, doubled over in a bout of mirth.

Mac lifted his head to say, "You'll not only learn to sew and wash clothes in this man's navy. You will find that what you country bumpkins call 'woman's work' will very soon be second nature to you."

So saying the two pressmen about turned and left the amazed boys to come to terms with their changed circumstances.

They took the advice; at least part of it, from the seasoned sailors and Bill helped Alec tentatively climb the ladder onto the deck where they had the remnants of their indisposition blown away out to sea. As the salty sea breeze caressed their cheeks they did indeed become reconciled to their situation as their constitutions righted themselves and they began to feel more human. Alec, used to the movement of the sea, gave Bill advice on keeping his balance and rolling with the motion of the ship.

For some moments they stood taking in the sea as the frigate swathed its course through the Irish Sea on its way southwards, before the noise of the sailors carrying out the everyday duties of the ship came to the forefront of their minds. They turned to take in the sight on deck. Barefooted men and boys ran in all directions, some clambered across the wooden decks, some scaling the rigging, some tending the flapping sails as they strove to make best use of the prevailing wind. Neither man spoke as they each in their own way assimilated the boom as the wind filled the sails. At first Bill thought the frigate was under attack and he felt his stomach churn, but he soon realised the wind hitting the taut sailcloth was the cause rather than the firing of a cannon as he had at first imagined.

The boys looked at each other, reading the same thoughts written clearly on each of their faces.

"Will I be able to live and work on board?" More used to the sea than Bill, who, despite his love of the adventure, was now having his first actual experience of sea travel, Alec wondered if he was surefooted enough not to be thrown overboard when it came time for him to scale the rigging. He held his hand up to shield his eyes as he peered up to the crow's nest where a figure, appearing tiny in the distance, was installed on lookout duty.

Eventually Alec realised that Bill had a huge grin on his face and was holding it up to feel the wind on his hot skin.

"You look mighty pleased with yourself," he grumbled.

"Aye, well, I'd not have chosen to put to sea in this manner but I am mighty glad to be here. It has the advantage of not going against my parents, well, my ma really. She never missed a chance to tell me horror stories of the pirates and harsh life but while she thought she was preventing me from daydreaming about an adventurous life she was all the time whetting my appetite. She can't blame me for being pressed... at least she won't be able to blame me for a very long time if what the mate said is true and we are bound to protect the British Isles from the Frenchies."

"Well, for you, but I had plans that didn't involve leaving your sister Peg to her own devices. I was just waiting my chance to ask her to marry me. What's ado?" He broke off noticing the horrified expression come over Bill's unshaven features. "You look as if you've seen a ghost," he finished.

Bill groaned and clutched his head, not as might be expected with the residual effects of the cudgel or in reaction to the movement of the sea, but because Alec's words had recalled his recent conversation with Ellen.

"Ha, so not so happy now eh?" laughed Alec.

"No, it's no laughing matter. You can say and do as you like to me when you hear what I have done. Your cousin Ellen is with child and I said we would tell both sets of parents together and get the banns sorted. I was well pleased; although we didn't plan it this way, we thought with her having the babe in her belly it would smooth the road for us. Ye must know my mother has no liking for smuggler families and would be against our wedding as much as she would be against you and Peggy."

Alec clutched at Bill's arm and gave him a sympathetic grimace, but said, "I ought to knock you into next week for messing with Ellen, but I know fine that you have made her happy just as Peggy has made me." He gave a deep sigh and, clutching his head in despair just as Bill had done a moment before, he moaned, "We are both in a pickle but we will get through it together. There's no point in wishing we could change it now. These sailors are not going to renege on their deal now. I expect they are paid by the body... well, a live body, at any rate."

"If it wasn't for Ellen I would be glad as I told you before you brought her to mind. What will she think of me? I bet she will think I have run away to escape her and my responsibility and Ma won't help her; she's more likely to chase her off as the cause of me leaving. Oh, my poor Ellen, my love. What have I let you in for? I could have missed going to the Rest last night but oh no, not me; I wanted to hear what the sailors from the port were making of the appearance of the frigate." He punched his fist into the palm of his other hand exclaiming, "Stupid, selfish bastard!"

"Don't take on so; there is nothing you can do about it now for five years. As to Ellen, I can't say. Aunt Grace is a fine woman but there's no saying what Andy Irvine will do to a fallen daughter. He has a mighty high opinion of himself when he enters his pew on a Sunday. Conveniently forgets HE breaks the law on the other six days of the week."

"I know Peggy is champing at the bit to get you to the altar and I'm sure Ma would never desert her if she should be in the same situation as Ellen," Bill said in an effort to be a comfort to Alec.

"No need to worry on that score, at least," returned Alec with a relieved note in his voice. "To think I'd live to be glad Peggy wouldn't lie with me after all the hours I spent trying to persuade her. Yesterday I would have laughed at the thought."

During their soul-searching conversation nature had carried on with its business and the billowing sails overhead were transporting the ship towards the Solent and on to intercept the Franco-Spanish fleet. Both young men, despite their cares for their loved ones, began to enjoy the fresh air and as their senses realigned to become increasingly excited about the adventure they had unwittingly embarked on.

"Hey, you there, Bosun wants ye in the fo'csle. Jump to it!" shouted a scrubby cabin boy, trying his hardest to sound like a rough tough seaman. "Better look sharp!"

The men exchanged grins at the lad's orders and there and then decided they would make the most of their enforced employment.

Realising they had no idea where the fo'csle was, Alec grabbed the lad by the shoulder saying, "Lead on, Nelson; we need an old sea dog like you to show us how to go on at sea. Now, where's that Bosun?"

****

The two friends followed the lad across the well-trodden, polished wooden deck, each a little wary of what would be expected of them. Although Alec was in the habit of going to sea his experience was all on much smaller craft than this. Even this frigate, which was not the largest vessel in the navy, seemed daunting to both young men. To their untutored eyes it appeared that the crew numbered far more than could be accommodated on the vessel. They scurried over the decks in an extremely random way, heedless of the swell of the tide as they tended their duties. As they passed along a sudden swell left Bill clinging on to a rail, which saved him from plunging directly into the turbulent waves. He spent a moment thanking the powers that be that he was not now fresh meat for the creatures of the deep, but the thrill of being on board and afloat soon came flooding back and he righted himself with a laugh and caught up with the cabin boy, who had not waited to see if Bill went overboard.

"I'll need to get my sea legs pretty quick," said Bill, a little embarrassed to have lost his balance when others ran hither and thither without a check.

"You'll be fine in a day or so. You'll not remember land or what it's like to walk on firm ground by the time our service is up," grimaced Alec. "Come on, let's catch up with the lad and see what fate holds in store for us."

They hurried after the running lad and when he pointed to a cabin they knocked smartly on the door and entered when told to do so. A small rotund man confronted them, with the skin on his face so dark and wrinkled Bill fancied he looked like the trunk of a tree. Alert black eyes took in the young men from the top of their heads to the tips of their boots. He appeared to like what he saw for his mouth opened in a toothy grin as he offered his hand in introduction.

"I'm Jim Perks and I own your soul for the next five years." As he shook hands with the men he was alert to their reaction to this information, but as neither young man showed great distress at his statement he concluded that his subordinate had been accurate in believing that these two would cause no trouble and, with the ship bound for war, trouble was not needed on his ship.

A lengthy catechism followed as the bosun worked out how best to use the men. If they were unlikely to be any use as sailors he would hand them onto the gunner to train to service the numerous cannon sighted on the frigate. He was surprisingly impressed with these two lads and immediately decided Alec would be able, with a little instruction, to be an ordinary seaman and swell the compliment of his crew. Bill, however, showed no skill in seamanship and would take some teaching before gaining a position on the crew. It was imperative that each crewman responded instinctively to an order and although Bill was keen to learn and impressed the bosun with his enthusiasm, he was not used to the language used at sea and in all likelihood would stutter in his aim to comply with orders in an attack situation.

"You will be a landsman since you have not been to sea," he said, sizing up Bill with a shrewd look before continuing slowly, "Or... you could be a ship's boy."

Seeing the repugnant look come over Bill's face he held up a hand before continuing to explain, "You look like a smart strong young lad ripe for adventure, but you have not been aboard so much as a rowing boat in your life and you need to learn ship's language, how to stay on your feet in a rough sea, tend the sails, handle a cutlass and a musket, recognise enemy ships on the horizon and many more duties. Your mates need to be able to rely on you in an emergency so for now I want you to be a boy sailor. Understood?"

"Yes, sir," answered Bill reluctantly. He was disappointed that he was found wanting but vowed to learn all there was to know in as short a time as possible and be able to join Alec as a proper sailor.

Perks smiled at the answer. It gave him a good opinion of the man and he made up his mind to keep a special eye on Bill. He began to outline Bill's duties as a boy. He would tend the animals on board. Each mess was allowed to house animals where there was room at their own expense. At present there were pigs, sheep, goats and chickens aplenty since they had recently left Greenock where the ship had provisioned. There was a cow in calf which belonged to the captain and, since his wife and daughter were on board, it would be Bill's duty to ensure that fresh milk reached the captain's table every morning after the calf was born.

"The captain has his own servants with whom you will deal and they must be given first call on what is on board no matter to whom it belongs. Many captains take advantage of this rule of the sea to purloin the rations of those inferior to him, but Captain Capel is an honest man and deals favourably with his crew."

"I'm to be a farm boy then?" asked Bill morosely, for he had entertained delusions of sea battles and swashbuckling adventures and was deflated at the thought of exchanging milking in a byre for milking on a ship.

The bosun gave a half smile. "If you attend to these duties and the others I'm just about to describe to you, you will be given over into the keeping of Macbeth, the best jack tar in the navy, and he will teach you how to be a competent sailor. With Macbeth on your side, the dour Scotchman, you'll soon be climbing the ranks as well as the rigging," he joked.

"The rest of your duties are not likely to be as agreeable as the care of the animals. You will be responsible for cooking the victuals." He choked at the look of disbelief which came over Bill's countenance. "Not something you're familiar with?" he queried in a shaky voice. He was enjoying this encounter. It was very different from the more usual recruits he had to deal with.

"You will stand in rank, that's queue to a landsman, at the ship's copper for beef or burgoo; that's porridge to you, and pease pudding to feed your mess mates. You'll be responsible for washing the pots and plates and keeping your mess tidy. Mess and the mates you will have in it is your family on board this ship. Questions? No? Good!"

Bill had taken a breath as if to ask a question, but he swallowed the impulse feeling he would fare better if he asked his questions of a lesser man.

The bosun continued. "Normally I don't like new recruits to be set in the same mess but on this occasion, and you have MacBeth to thank for this, I am putting you both into his mess and you will be entered as such on the muster book. You are lucky for he has taken a liking to you and will help you to adjust. You have been wise in accepting your service. Dismiss!"

Alec had been finding it hard not to laugh out loud at Bill's obvious dislike of his duties, but, once the cabin door closed behind them, his mirth burst out.

"Your face. Man, it's a picture. You'll have lass's hands before you're done. The cow will fair welcome those washday hands. I wonder if I can get you to wash my kecks as well."

He was so intent on mocking his friend that he didn't see the massive black man standing behind him until he spoke, and Alec swung round to find his face buried in the curly chest hair of the huge man. Dingo, for such was his name, had been on the ship for as long as he could remember; he could have been born on its deck for all he knew. It was his home; he had been waiting for the men to conclude their meeting with the bosun and was to show them how to make a start on their clews. He ushered them over to a deserted part of the main deck where they could sit leaning against the jolly boat which hung on ropes ready in case of emergency. Without saying a word Dingo indicated that they should make themselves comfortable and nodded to a pile of material that neither boy recognised. At their clueless expression he hunkered down and, taking a few lengths of the material, laid them lengthwise beside one another in one of his big hands tying a knot with the other. He began to plait the strands together, showing them how to twine in new strands to make a longer rope. His fingers flew and very soon he had a few feet of rope. He grinned showing perfectly white teeth with a bright red tongue protruding between them as he concentrated to his task.

"You try. Make ropes to hang hammock." He stood up, towering over the lads. Bill was thought to be tall but this mountain of a man stood head and shoulders taller than him.

"I wouldn't want to be on his bad side," whispered Alec, grabbing some of the sisal material and making his first attempt at lashing them together. "Come on. Get started."

Dingo watched for a few moments, then, content that they were managing some semblance of a rope, he smiled once more and loped off towards larboard.

For some minutes the boys concentrated on the task in hand without communicating with each other, but very soon they got into the rhythm of the task and were able to pay less attention without making errors.

"Do you think we need to make these ropes before we can get a sleep?" asked Bill of his more erudite companion.

"I don't know. I've never made rope before. We always bought it from a chandler when our boat needed new rope. I will say though my fingers are not nimble enough to make yards and yards of rope before bedtime. They are beginning to sting already with the rough sisal running through them and I haven't made more than two yards."

Just at that moment they heard the sound of a bell. They counted the peals and found there were eight. As the echo of the last clang died away it appeared to the men watching that the decks became alive as men ran in every direction. Bill paused to watch in confusion.

"How do they know where to go and how do they manage to go at such a pace without knocking into each other?" he wondered.

Alec, a bit more au fait with the habits of the sea, answered, "That will be the end of the watch. Eight bells mean the boys who have been on the rigging or in the crow's nest have been on watch for four hours. The bells ring every half-hour so in half an hour from now we will hear one peal of the bell and that will indicate it's half past midday."

"How do you know what hour it is?"

"The watches are started at midnight and last four hours, so you can tell by the light approximately what time of day it is. Since the sun is high in the sky that tells me it is the middle of the day and the watch is changing and will have their time off now. Our lives will be ruled by the bells from now on."

229

They went back to the painstaking plaiting of their ropes. For beginners they were making a good hand at it. It was not unpleasant sitting on the deck with the breeze in their hair working at their task.

A few young men approached after a while and started a conversation with the boys. Bill was a bit shy to take part because, to his consternation, he was only able to make out about one word in ten; the sailors seemed to have a language of their own but, although he could not quite decipher what was being said by watching the body language of the men, he was sure they were making friendly overtures so he smiled in return and acknowledged the greeting of his shipmates.

Dingo came along with some tankards of small beer which each of the men drank off at one gulp. They were extremely thirsty from their time on watch. Bill and Alec were included in this ritual and they too were glad of the chance to quench their thirst. As Dingo gathered up the empty tankards and departed the young men slumped down on the deck beside Bill and Alec and in a friendly manner each gathered up some lengths of sisal and absentmindedly started to plait these into rope.

"Ye be a mess mate," started one man, but Bill was unable to catch the rest of the sentence, so strong was his accent.

"Mac sez ye maun hay a mite elp fur yez be gwan ta elp us," said another who had, as nearly as Bill could work out, called himself Den.

Bill thought he might have understood him since he sounded like a Geordie from just over the border from his own home. He watched in fascination as the quick fingers of the lads speedily made long lengths of rope. As time went on Bill and Alec were more able to join in the conversation as their ears became more accustomed to the different dialects. Den it turned out was indeed originally from Jarrow, fairly near to the border with Scotland and Bill was quite used to hearing drovers and cattlemen with this Northern English twang. Flynn, a small wiry Irishman with a shock of bright red hair and deep brown eyes, was more difficult to understand but it was easy to see he was a convivial chap since his face was creased with smiles. The boys listened hard to him but still could not pick up his meaning.

Noticing their bewildered expressions, he burst into gales of infectious laughter and slapped Alec on the back, saying, "I. am. a. paddy. I. speak. no. English." He spoke very slowly with an upper class accent and continued with his raucous amusement, totally enjoying his own joke.

"Never mind old Flynn there," came a voice just behind the bank of cheerful men. No one had heard the arrival of Mac on the scene but as he made his presence known the other men jumped to attention, pulling a forelock just as the serfs were used to do to the master of an estate. Realising this was the correct etiquette Bill and Alec also jumped up and stood rigid, making Macbeth glad he had spoken up for the boys and had been allocated them to his mess.

"Quick learners the both of them," he thought, pleased.

"I see you have met the scum of my crew," he continued, glancing over the men standing in front of him. "Laggards every one. Believe nothing they tell you for they are worse than schoolboys with their tricks. And don't come running to me when you lose all your pay to these sharks." Despite the words it was apparent to Bill and Alec that Mac was actually proud of the men and they did not flinch at being called laggards and sharks. Indeed, although they still stood at attention waiting for Mac's orders, they all had amused expressions. They rightly divined that to be in Mac's mess was an honour and each made a vow to themselves that they would endeavour to make Mac as proud of them as he undoubtedly was of these members of his mess.

Mac noticed that the messmates had been giving the young less experienced men a hand with their rope making and this pleased him even more. He would have ordered the lads to get stuck in to help, but it was much better that they had done this off their own bat and it was confirmation, if he indeed needed any, that he had not been mistaken in the character of his men. They lived in such confined quarters that it was imperative that they all got on well together. Feuds and fights only brought trouble to the ship, and, with the battle to come, he wanted the only fighting to be that against the enemy fleet.

"Finish up your ropes and Flynn here will show you where to take them to be dipped in tar so that they don't rot and drop your sorry arse on the hard deck in the middle of the night." He laughed and turned towards his men, "Carry on then." And with a salute took himself off below deck.

A couple of hours later, with their newly tarred ropes hanging up to dry and the promise from Den and Flynn to show them how to hang their hammocks for the night, they were ushered below to their mess room where the cabin boy they had met before was busy collecting the plates and mugs for the forthcoming meal, while Dingo had just materialised in the cramped area with a black iron pot, which he laid down before going automatically to aid the young lad. The smell below decks was not something Bill had ever encountered before and he wrinkled his nose in dislike.

"No point in coming the prima donna here, lad. We have so little room to live in that even although we wash and delouse and the boys keep away the rats, our smell gets into the wood. It combines with the smell of gunpowder from the guns and smell from the animals in the hold wafts up through the timbers. The one consolation is that you won't smell it in a few days. It will become part of you."

Anxious not to upset his new mates Bill quickly denied any delusions of grandeur and blamed his reaction to his aversion of the smell of chicken shit, which to be truthful really had been a quirk of his since his childhood. He glanced around the small area noticing how tight they were for space since they were to eat and sleep amongst the cannon. He could not see where they were to sleep for it appeared to his untutored eyes that every space was accounted for. And where to eat? He looked around and as he caught the aroma from the pot on the floor his gastric juices, which had been in abeyance since his bout of seasickness, once more became rampant and he realised he was hungry.

Den good-naturedly cuffed the cabin boy, saying, "What's up, Jenks? The stew ain't on the platter."

"I've been up top wi' bosun. Not be but a moment," he said with obvious pride in his voice as he began to remove a wooden plank from its mooring on the bulkhead. He deftly arranged it at table height from the ropes hanging from the beams. Thus the table appeared. In their hunger the sailors went to the lad's aid and before you could blink an eye, casks, upended barrels and sea bags were set as seats around the impromptu table and the complaint was now that Jenks was slacking. It was all good-natured banter and no evil intent could be detected in the attitude of the men to the cabin boy. He carelessly balanced a pile of utensils on one arm as he nimbly skipped round the limited space depositing items as he went. Bill and Alec were surprised at the speed and strength of the boy for he was short and skinny and, when he peered up shyly at them from under his over long tow-coloured fringe, he displayed features more fitting for a young girl than a future tar. Soon the table was set ready for the meal with square wooden plates with a raised rim (Bill was to learn later this was called a 'fiddle' and carved into the plate to stop food from slipping off with the roll of the ship), horn and wooden beakers and spoons and a wooden trolley in the shape of a boat that held thick slices of bread.

Jenks grinned at Den and lifted the ladle to dish up the appetising stew while Den took care of filling the horn and wooden tankards, rummaging in a sea chest to unearth a pewter pot and calling on Flynn to lend his spare tankard to the recruits until they could fend for themselves. The men around the makeshift table were like the brothers in any farm kitchen with Mac taking the father role of maintaining order. They came from all walks of life, few, if any, choosing the navy of their own volition but each making the best of the opportunities to better themselves that being on board a warship offered. Prize money from a captured enemy ship was what all the sailors hoped for. Since most of them came from poor backgrounds, the thought of enough gold to set them up for a better life was what spurred them on. However, in the meantime, each man made extra money by plying whatever trade he was best at. Den had been a shoemaker before poverty in his home village had forced him to enlist in the Navy and he supplemented his wage by cobbling together deck shoes for the men but, more lucratively, shoes and boots for the officers. Flynn, like most Irishmen, was a jack of all trades and masterminded many improvements on board ship. He was in great demand to make sea chests when timber was available. A sea chest was a luxury, for on board a ship overrun with vermin it was as near to impregnable as anything could be at denying the rodents' sharp teeth. The men had little money, only being paid when they reached a home port, but the barter system worked well on board and very few disagreements escalated into fights among the messmates.

As Jenks filled one of the strange wooden plates for Bill with a stew like nothing he had been presented with before, and told him to help himself to bread, Flynn chimed in with, "Enjoy that fresh bread while you can for it will be back to hard biscuits with weevils before you know it. We only have fresh bread, and even that not so fresh when we have just been in port so today is your lucky day. Eat up now!"

Despite the look of the food, it smelled good and, helping himself to a slab of the already stale bread, dunked it into the gravy. He could not decide what kind of meat he had been served with but it tasted good and his stomach accepted it without protest.

Nodding round at the other men, he said, "Good, aye, tasty."

Catching Jenks' eye as he looked around the table, the lad smiled shyly at him, saying, "I have to give up my job to you tomorrow so you need to be following me all day. You'll need to learn quick, mind, for I am being promoted." He stuck out his chest feeling very proud of himself. "Bosun says if you're quick I can start to larn from Mr Allen, midshipman, and before we get into battle I'll be an asset," he preened proudly.

It was obvious to both Alec and Bill that the hard, uneducated men in their mess all looked out for the boy and would be sorry to see him leave their protection. One man whom the recruits had not yet spoken to clapped Bill on the arm with a friendly, if painful, punch and a wide grin and said in his strong Liverpudlian accent, "You'd better learn fast then for Mr Jenks here is bound to be captain, eh lad?"

Jenks blushed. He was ambitious to become an officer and had had his sights set on it since he had stowed away on board his first ship more than a year ago. He had, of course, been found hiding in the bottom of a barge after an on-shore expedition, but, because he took the punishment dealt out by his captain without a tear or a complaint and still remained adamant that a life at sea was what he desired above all things, he had become the crew's pet. Now, at almost twelve years old he was being given a chance of a lifetime. There was only Bill standing between him and his dreams and, "Bill does not look stupid" he thought as he assessed him with a critical eye.

As the evening wore on Bill became aware that life in the mess was not so different from life on land; it just all took place in a smaller space. After the meal had been cleared and Bill had taken his first lesson from Jenks in the art of washing up, a talent he had not shown much interest in at home, but despite the implements being less cumbersome, there was not so much difference between washing domestic pots and dairy utensils, so he felt he had made a good start. When he and Jenks returned to the messroom pots of ale were laid on the oak table and the men were settling down to enjoy their free time. Two packs of dog-eared cards had been disembowelled from someone's kit. The camaraderie in the cabin was instantly apparent. On spying Bill had returned Den and Flynn nominated themselves to help the newcomers suspend their hammocks from the newly plaited clews. Much hilarity followed as the boys were not conversant with knots, meaning that after struggling to thread the ropes into the holes of his hammock then jumping onto it, Alec landed with a thump onto the deck with his hammock under him. When Bill attempted the same procedure his ropes held, but, on each occasion he tried to get into the hammock, it swung away from him. On one attempt he actually got into the hammock, but, like an angry stallion unhappy with having an unexpected weight on its back, Bill, just as he let out a crow of satisfaction, was bucked out the other side of the swinging hammock.

More lessons followed as the men took great pride in sharing their knowledge, and soon the men were capable of tying knots that would not unravel in the night and land them on the floor.

"There's not much room to sleep in," Bill noted taking in the proximity of his fellow shipmates' berths.

"There be seven hunner men on this ship and two women. The women have the large space, being they are the captain's lady and her maid, but even they don't have enough space to swing a cat," explained Mac. "You are allowed fourteen inches to sleep in and you are lucky, for if you are a soldier in this ship you sleep between the cannon on the gun deck with hard floors instead of a downie hammock, poor sods. At least in the Navy you mostly know what you're getting, but the soldiers didn't enlist to go to sea. It won't be the first time one has thrown himself overboard because he has gone mad with the confinement and the constant movement of the sea," he reminisced sadly before continuing with Bill's education.

"The watches are designed to make sure that every alternate hammock is empty at any time so you generally have an empty one on either side. Things are a bit different when we are in port because we have less watch duty, but then anyone who is allowed shore leave is on shore. It's not as bad as you first think, but it is why our captain insists on cleanliness."

"Aye," Flynn butted in, "he believes that dirt causes illness and he is fanatic about head lice. We each have to be deloused every week. I've never been sae free o' the wee bitin' devils in aw ma life."

"You bog trotters are all alike. Afeared o' the water," joked Den.

Bill and Alec exchanged a look, fully expecting this statement to cause a fight as it undoubtedly would have had it been uttered in the Sailor's Rest at Annan, but Flynn merely laughed and flung back a rejoinder.

"Where would we be without the bogs to provide the fuel that heats you up and cooks your food when you are in an Irish port, and how do you think the ale in Ireland gets its strength and colour, ye daft Geordie?"

While the men had been good-humouredly initiating the friends into the art of Hammock Hanging no one had noticed the departure of Jenks. Mac looked around the room, gloomy despite its lamp, which lit up only a tiny portion of the mess, and let out an exasperated breath.

"That lad's gone rat fishing again. I've told him repeatedly we will not eat rat!"

"Now Mac, don't get worked up. You know it is only the sport that entices the lads. When you were a lad I'll bet you were out many an evening fishing trout from the stream and if you can get the chance you will still fish in a river when we are in port. All the lads are doing is making a sport to take up their spare time."

"Rat fishing?" Alec whispered, looking quite green as he recalled the unidentifiable meat in the meal he had just eaten. "Do they really cook rats? Have we just eaten rat?"

Flynn paused before answering to debate whether or not to tease the raw men, but eventually thought better of it and replied, "No, no. Not tonight. Not but that on some ships rat is a delicacy; after a long cruise with nothing but salt meat a rat can make a pleasant alternative. You can't stop the blighters getting in. The holds have all the things that rats like best; they are dark and wet and have an abundance of food at the start of a trip, but they cause so much damage with their gnawing teeth. Now the lads on ship are full of vigour and they have invented a way to keep the rat population down that gives them much pleasure. Ye ken whit lads are like?"

"But how do they catch them? I spent my life on the farm and we go ratting but the dogs take care of the business end, all I have to do is bang my stick to make them run. I can't imagine how they fish for rats," asked Bill.

Flynn, with a sly glance at Mac, continued, "The boys have the hatch opened into the hold where the vermin live and breed. They gather round it as if they were on the riverbank, legs hanging down into the dark hold. They each have a stick with a long line of string and a hooked wire at the end. They attach a bit of food, and rats eat anything, they don't mind if it is unfit for humans to eat; then they wrap the hook and bait in sisal from the rope making and dangle it into the hold. When the rats grab for the food they get caught in the fibres and become hooked. The lad pulls up the line and one of his mates whacks the rat into oblivion. On some boats the cook uses them but our captain has a dislike of feeding his men rats, so you can rest easy on that score. On the *Pheobe*, the lads gamble on who will catch the most or the biggest or the fiercest, depending on what their desire is. Mac dislikes Jenks taking part for he thinks it will hinder his chances of becoming an officer."

"I want that lad to get on," growled Mac. "It's few enough that get the opportunity captain has given Jenks. He has no sponsor and although he speaks well he is not so very educated. He needs to keep his nose clean and attend to his letters."

The evening progressed with Bill and Alec being given all sorts of advice from their peers. The men worked at their leisure pastimes. Some passed the time playing cards while Flynn had donned a pair of eyeglasses and employed himself by diligently darning a hole in his thick woollen sock. Den was helping Mac cut out a pair of deck shoes from an oddment of canvas while Dingo, much to Bill's amazement, was carefully sewing ruffles into a garment. Bill could not quite make out just what kind of garment it was. It looked remarkably like a nightdress of his granny's he had seen blowing on her clothesline. He found it very difficult to take his eyes off the big black man who paid no attention to anything other than his task as he plied his needle as assiduously as any young lady.

Just as six bells sounded Jenks slunk back into the mess and commenced to pour the grog rations into beakers which he then handed round. He included Bill and Alec who were not used to strong liquor but on a wink from Flynn accepted their portion and sipped it conservatively.

"Did ye win yer bet, rascal?" he asked Jenks who flashed a look at Mac before grinning his answer.

"No, Hendry had the biggest rat. It was *that* size," he replied, indicating a length that it was surely impossible for any rat to grow to between his outstretched arms, "and Gregg caught fourteen. Good pickings. We hung them from the top rail until Captain gies us permission to throw them overboard."

Mac gave no indication that he had heard this news, keeping his head bowed over his task, but when Jenks handed him his rum ration he looked up at him and smiled, quite restoring Jenks' mood. He didn't like to be at odds with Mac but neither did he want to be made mock of by the other cabin boys.

Peace reigned in the mess and, as Bill looked around in the dim light given off by the two lamps allowed, he thought, "So much for an adventurous life. I will get back to the farm better able to be a maid than a ploughboy!" Yet he was far from dissatisfied with his lot, so far.

The lamp dimmed as the candle neared its end and the messmates prepared to settle down for the night.

After this convivial evening spent listening to the stories of their peers aimed at indoctrinating them into the life aboard ship, Alec and Bill, after a few abortive attempts at mastering their hammocks, settled down with their thoughts. Alec was soon asleep but Bill, less used to the rolling of the ship, lay wondering what trial might be ahead.

"It has been a good start but am I able to learn all the things young Jenks is dying to teach me? How long will it be till I see Ellen again?"

If it hadn't been for the constant nagging worry of Ellen and her predicament, he would be a happy man tonight, but even the thought of Ellen and their child could not keep him awake while the gentle movement of the ship bore him off towards the adventure of his life.

****

Life over the next few months was a trying time for Bill for every time he mastered a skill another, more difficult one was still to be learnt. He had passed out of the hands of Jenks within days of coming aboard and he prided himself that he was now a vital part of the mess. Unlike other messes on board Mac's was a peaceful haven after a day's toil. If Bill had thought, he worked hard on the farm he had now found out his mistake. Never being used to taking orders blindly without rationalizing them himself he took the discipline on board hard at first, but he had learnt not to contradict an order or question a task but simply to say, "Aye aye, bosun," or Mr Allen or whoever had given him the order. His biggest problem was with Mr Allen, the midshipman who had Jenks in training, as he was only a lad of fourteen and so puffed up in his own importance that he frequently gave contradictory orders just for the fun of making the older men obey him when they knew he was in error.

Bill had once questioned an instruction from Mr Allen that even in his limited experience he knew to be wrong. The midshipman, inflamed by the disobedience, jumped up on a cannon and began to belabour Bill about the head and shoulders with his staff. Fortunately for Bill, he did not fight back or he would have been hanged for insubordination, but he would carry the scars of the beating as a reminder not to answer back. This encounter made him an enemy of the young midshipman who made him a butt for his temper, with the result that there were few days when Bill was not sporting some example of the other's malevolent discipline.

Even allowing for the attitude of the young midshipman Bill was revelling in every aspect of life at sea. He had been disappointed not to be allowed shore leave in Southampton where they had a brief sojourn in order to take on fresh water before the long weeks of their cruise, but he was somewhat placated by Den offering to take a letter to the mail office. In his letter Bill apologised to his mother for being caught by the press gang and begged her to take care of Ellen.

He wrote:

Dear Ma,
You will know by now that Alec Irvine and I were prest the night we went to the Rest and I am sorry for I know you will be worried for me. Both Alec and I are well

and, although we are not let off ship in case we run away, to be honest as yet we are
well cared for with plenty of food.

I beg that you let Ellen know what has overtaken me and plead with her to forgive
me for I truly would not have left her in such a case.

Yes, you have guessed, Ma, Ellen is with child and but for my stupidity in going to
the Rest that night would be married as soon as may be. Please take care of her for
my sake as I do not know when I may return. The mate on board the Phoebe tells me
I am indentured for five years but that means nothing if the war with France goes on.

We are about to go on a cruise. That is what they call the ships that guard the
merchant fleet. Phoebe was laid up in Greenock so we will be sailing at full speed to
catch up with the rest of the fleet.

I hope Pa managed the harvest and you can tell him I am still husbanding animals
although this is a much different prospect than on land and all contrivance must be
taken to feed the creatures. They smell mightily in the hold of the ship but in good
weather I am told I may bring them on deck. They are more prized on sea than at
home.

I will write whenever I get a chance, but do not fear for me.
Your Son
Bill.

In truth Bill, now that he was relieved of his anxiety about Ellen, was enjoying his
new life. He was appalled but somehow quite excited by the antics of the men while
they were anchored outside Southampton. Almost as soon as the jolly boat had left
for shore to collect bread, flour and most importantly casks of fresh water, Bill, from
his vantage point at the ship's rail looking longingly at the departing boat full of his
shipmates bound for shore leave, saw a myriad of little boats approaching the larboard
side.

"What are these boats doing?" queried Bill of a man he had previously not come
across on his short time afloat.

The other grinned at him, pleased to initiate the newcomer into ship board
practices.

"These be the bumboats that come out from port to meet any ship that docks here,
and most do because it is a convenient port to stock up before any kind of voyage.
They will bring the wives and families of to the crew." He laughed.

"Is your wife coming out then? Is that why you are waiting? Which one is she?"

"I don't know yet but I'll know when I see her."

Bill looked at him quizzically, not in the least understanding what he meant.

"Surely he must be joking," he thought, laughing uncertainly. "Is it so long since you saw your wife that you have forgotten what she looks like? Fair? Dark? Short? Tall?"

"Well, last time I was in port here she was a sweet little armful, with sparkling, bright eyes but I was lucky then for she was new to the business and didn't value her assets as she might, but it's unlikely I'll afford as good a prospect again. She's likely to have been set up by some gentlemen by now."

Hearing this it dawned on Bill that it was not really wives and families that visited the ship but what were commonly known as 'ladies of the night'. He had never been in a situation where he had to pay for favours; before Ellen and he had been carried away by their desires he had indulged in a few fumblings with the lasses in town, but he had not had either the inclination or the money to indulge in a prostitute. To be truthful, he felt it a bit sleazy to go with a loose woman even if any of the ones he had come across had had any interest in the younger men in the port. They generally courted the more lucrative business that was to be found among the older tars who had been at sea for long months.

His new friend continued his education, breaking into these thoughts.

"There are so many men on board who are here either to escape gaol or because they have been pressed and it is more likely than not they would desert if allowed shore leave. You are pressed yourself. You know you would make for home if once you got your feet on dry land."

"I suppose that's true; though how I could get to the other end of the country with no money in my pocket I don't know," he agreed.

"That's why we are not paid until our time is up and we are back in our home port."

"What's that got to do with the prostitutes coming on board?" asked the puzzled Bill.

"Men are men everywhere and need their comfort and the frustration that builds up worries the officers, for sometimes men resort to bestial habits. To prevent this happening, the captain turns his blind eye to the prostitutes coming aboard as long as they stick to the fantasy of being wives or even daughters of the men. A wife is allowed a 'conjugal visit' while we are in port." He ran his eyes over Bill's sturdy form, considering his build.

"You might find one to lie with you for free since you are a handsome big lad but don't get your hopes up. For the most part they are grasping harpies!"

While this conversation was taking place they had been watching the kerfuffle near the stern as each of the women in the boats tried to lay claim to her 'husband'. Deals were made in loud voices and women began to swagger across the deck from the ladder to be received into the arms of a sailor as they were allowed on board.

Bill could not believe how many couples had appeared in no time at all. Some of the women who were old hands at the game brought with them commodities long desired by the men and did a roaring trade in socks, soap, razors and combs, but their main purpose was to relieve the men's pockets by spending an hour lying with them.

"Where do they…?" began Bill before he realised that his friend had gone. In the twinkling of an eye he had made a deal with a promising young woman and was now handing her off the ladder and greeting her with all the aplomb of a gentleman greeting his lady.

This illusion soon dissolved as the pair walked out of earshot of the officer on duty at the ladder head. Once on board and handed over to one of his crew the officer lost all interest in their respectability.

Bill had no appetite for sex with a strange woman. "And I couldn't afford it even if I wanted to," he thought ruefully as he made his way to the hatch to the lower deck, intent on dealing with his animals. However, as he approached the ladder, he was brought to an abrupt halt by a beefy arm striking him across the chest and momentarily depriving him of breath.

"Not so fast there. It will cost ye a shillin to get down that there ladder. Cough up now! My wife has a lot of men to see to today."

Bill felt the blood rush to his face in embarrassment and stuttered a reply, "I'm only going to get milk for the captain's pudding."

"A likely story. A shillin' or you stay just where you are."

Bill turned away. He didn't know whether he was more embarrassed to be taken for a customer or if he was abnormal not to want to take a woman in an animal pen.

"Let him down, moron. That's the oaf that is too stupid to learn to be a sailor and tends to the hogs," came a sharp command. "He's not man enough to get his cock hard enough to service a woman! A sheep, maybe…" he finished as if dubious if Bill could even manage that.

Mr Allen, flanked by six mean-looking bullies escorting a very raddled looking, toothless woman, sneered at Bill.

"I'll give you a lesson if you like. You can watch me fuck this bitch."

Bill was taken aback to hear such language coming from a lad of such tender years. He reflected that at that age his father would have taken his leather belt to his arse if he had voiced such profanity. He hung his head in order not to be tempted to teach the arrogant youth a lesson and mouthed, "No thanks, Mr Allen, I'll pass if it's all the same to you, sir."

Mr Allen smirked round at his bodyguards and dismissed Bill with disdain.

"Get about your business and be quick, for the captain's steward is waiting for the cream. Captain is entertaining the Admiral of the Fleet to dinner."

Bill let out a sigh of relief as his head disappeared below the level of the entrance hatch into the bowels of the ship but, as he landed at the bottom, he felt a vibration further up the ladder that indicated that another had begun the descent. Anxious not to give Mr Allen any opportunity to punish him he made off into the dark reaches where the animals could be heard moving restlessly around, disturbed by the unusual activity in their domain. He felt himself blushing again as he identified the muffled noises that had upset the animals as the sexual gratification of man and woman.

"Well, if that really is his wife she is spreading her wifely duties pretty thin. I wonder if she gets any of the shillings for she must have some stamina, poor sod."

So thinking he quickly passed out of earshot and attended to his duties, collected a jug of milk and made his way back to the foot of the ladder in readiness to ascend into the daylight. He could hear the panting cries off to his left. He was several rungs up the ladder, precariously balancing his jug in one hand, when he heard an unearthly squeal rent the air. It sounded like a soul in torment; definitely not a cry of pleasure. He paused, wondering if he should interfere, but then had his mind made up for him by a scream followed by a small pleading voice.

"Please, please, no more, sir. Oh, let me be."

Bill, against his better judgement, retraced his steps down the ladder and, placing the milk out of harm's way, took off in the direction of the cry.

As he arrived unnoticed at an empty sty, which only that morning he had cleaned out in preparation for the animals that would arrive on board in the morning, he saw an unholy sight.

The pen was dimly lit by a storm lamp and two women were being held captive by Mr Allen's bullies. It was obvious the men had been responsible for the screams and pleadings Bill had heard. The women were only distinguishable from each other by the colour of their hair, for both were naked and being held in position by two of the bullies while the other four pushed their rampant members into the women's orifices. They were attacking the red-haired woman from both back and front at the same time forcing her body into unnatural positions as each strove to satisfy his lust. The other, dark-haired and perhaps slightly taller, was being skewered on one man's prick while having the other tar's huge organ pushed into her throat. She was gagging with each thrust of the man's loins. Her eyes were frightened and bulging in her head while the lips stretched over the man's penis were a frightening shade of blue. The two rouged cheeks that she had been that morning so pleased to note made her look five years younger accentuated the ashen colour of her face. In fact, the pale skin of her naked body appeared luminous in the dim light.

The men kept darting glances into the darkened corner where Bill noticed Mr Allen. With his face glowing, his eyes shining with a fanatic light, slavering at the mouth like a ravening wolf he held his stick in one hand while his right hand was buried deep in his breeches. From the movements of the material it was apparent he was getting great pleasure from watching the actions of his gang. He was masterminding the action with the men responding to his instructions.

"Fuck her faster, fuck her faster, harder, harder!" he screamed unaware that his directions were having the opposite effect to that which he was encouraging. The men were uneasy. Despite being rough, tough sailors they were not naturally cruel men and when ordered to accompany their superior officer they had envisaged a bit of harmless fun, after all these women came on board for the purpose of having sex with the sailors, but this was not harmless fun!

"Mr. Allen, sir, I've no strength left. I can do no more. I'm shagged out," complained one of the men who had been with the redhead.

Flying at him with his stick raised the officer belaboured him about the buttocks.

"You will fuck her until she dies. I want her dead!" he screamed. "The dirty slut will wish she had stayed on shore. You!" he indicated one of the men currently holding the fainting women in position. "Get your pecker up her arse. Fuck her like the bitch she is."

He pushed the spent man off balance, kicking him hard between his legs as he landed on the floor of the pen.

"Call yourself a man? Can't manage to keep your cock standing." He bent down and took the flaccid phallus in his hand and began to rub it roughly with his fingers. The movement he was indulging in was exciting him so much the bulge between his legs looked likely to burst his trews. As his excitement grew he ordered the men to release the dark-haired prostitute and bring her to where he sat masturbating the massive tar who was so terrified of the young officer, who he had now decided was deranged, that he sat motionless with his manhood cradled in his officer's hands.

He had the girl positioned with her head in the man's hairy, dirty groin and ordered, "Suck his cock till it stands to attention and mind you do it right. You, there," he said turning his attention to another of his group, "beat her arse with a nettle. That will let her know what I expect of her."

The seaman paused only for a moment, worried about the consequences of using the knotted rope on the woman's delicate skin, but fearing even more for his own hide he tentatively laid the weapon of torture about the woman's bony behind.

"What the devil are you tickling her for?" demanded Mr Allen. "You have plenty of brawn. Take the skin off her back."

Kicking out at the woman, who had momentarily stopped her ministrations on the slowly arousing organ, he commanded, "Get on with it, slut, or it will be the worse for you."

The terrified woman could do nothing but obey and began her ministrations with alacrity in case the officer deemed she had not obeyed.

"While she makes a man of you, you can make yourself useful."

He slid his breeches down over his hips to reveal his penis standing to attention. It was threatening to explode so great was his excitement. Grabbing the older man's hand, he indicated that he should manhandle him until he came to his inevitable end.

As Bill watched, trying to decide whether to interrupt the antics or to go to find help and advice from Mac or Job, for he feared the midshipman would indeed have the women fucked to death, all other activity stopped as the crewmen watched in stupefaction the action taking place between the men.

The woman not under direct instruction from Mr Allen pushed herself to a sitting position and surreptitiously moved herself into the darkest corner of the stall from where she crawled, slowly and quietly, out of the pen. Her escape was nearly ruined as she bumped into Bill but before the sound had escaped her lips he had motioned to her to be quiet and follow him. When they were away from the scene he took off his shirt and handed it to her.

"Put that on and follow me. I will take you up on deck but you must hurry because I must get help for your friend for I fear he really does mean to kill her."

"Oh, sir, I'm that frightened. I thought I was done for. I did really. My legs are so shaky I don't know if they will hold me up."

"They will have to for you need to get out of this hold before they realise you have gone or we will both be feeding the fishes tonight," whispered Bill, then added, "By the look of him, it won't be long before he shoots his load and then the others will come out of their trance and send a search party after you. They are not to know I am here to lead you to the ladder. Come on now. Don't let go yet awhile."

Bill had a job getting the semi-naked, trembling woman onto the ladder but by dint of much pushing and encouragement they eventually made it out onto deck.

"Where have you been, you rascal?" came the deep voice of the captain's servant standing at the top of the ladder, "I've been stood here since six bells for you to appear. I need the milk for the captain's chef. You know he's a temperamental bugger when he is kept waiting."

Glancing at the barely clad woman sniffling beside Bill, his voice became ever sterner. "I thought better of you, lad. Wasting your time with the sluts."

"I haven't Mr Bell. They were treating her badly and all I did was bring her back on deck. I must get off to find Mr Perks for he might be able to stop them killing the other one. The milk's at the bottom of the ladder," he called over his shoulder as he sped off in the direction of the forecastle.

By the time Bill had found Mac and explained the situation and his fears for the woman in the hold, and together they had found the first mate, some time had passed.

"Go back to your mess and say not a word about what you witnessed unless the captain sends for you," commanded the mate as he and Mac hurried over the deck to the hatch Bill had indicated and descended the ladder into the hold.

Obeying his senior's order Bill made a slow progress along the deck and down into the space that he was to call home for the next five years. He was more shocked than he liked to admit. He had been enjoying being aboard ship, making friends with the seasoned sailors and spending time with Jenks learning how to be a cabin boy, but now he saw the seedier side of the life and his eyes had been well and truly opened to the barbarity of some of his shipmates. As he walked he unconsciously noted how many men were openly coupling with women out on the deck and in full sight of any who passed. He couldn't help noticing that although the couples were actively engaged there did not appear to be any of the brutality he had witnessed below deck. Much laughter and good-natured banter could be heard among the men and their inamorata but the women and girls all seemed to be treated tenderly, unlike the couplings Bill had so recently witnessed. Being a country boy he was used to animals copulating and just as easily accepted that these 'wives' and husbands were just following the laws of nature, but what he had observed in that dark stall was surely not natural.

"Do men really like to fondle another's prick?" he wondered. "I definitely don't fancy a man doing to me what that lad was doing to Mr Allen." And after further consideration he decided, "And *he* didn't like doing it either. The other men were just as shocked as me."

He did not hear the result of Mr Perks and Mac's visit to the hold. When he tentatively brought up the subject with Mac later that evening, he shrugged and shook his head.

"Better ask no questions and forget that you were ever in that hold, lad." He gave Bill a piercing look from beneath his bushy brows, clutched him on the shoulder in a gesture of sympathy and turned away.

He could only assume that by the time they arrived the party had broken up and moved away. The following day the prostitutes left the ship a good deal richer for their day on board. Bill looked for but did not see either of the women whose ordeal he had witnessed, but Mr Allen did not seem in the least bit changed by his experiments with the crewmen and the whores.

The only other reference to the incident came a few days later when, without any words spoken, Dingo proffered him a soft white linen shirt. Taking in Bill's puzzled look, he merely said, "You be a good man," before he walked away.

Bill had learnt a valuable lesson. Mr Allen was dangerous and it would serve him well to keep out of his way. Although it continued to invade his dreams, the scene in the pen faded from his memory as he strove to learn all he could about being a mariner.

****

He rapidly learned how to care for the animals on board but that was the easy task. Life on board a warship meant that overcrowding was a massive problem. If an illness was brought on board it spread like wildfire so, in an attempt to keep infection at a minimum, everything had to be kept spotless. Bill, alike with all members of the crew, and often the marines, who strictly speaking were not required to take on shipboard tasks other than drilling and attending to their guns, would take a turn at scrubbing the decks and 'holystoning' them. This was backbreaking and dirty work. Before breakfast the detail would scrub the tarry decks, often covered with the excrement of the animals that were allowed free range on deck when the ship was not in action. While the deck was wet Bill and his partner for the morning had to wield the 'Holy Bible', a huge stone with ropes fixed to either end and pulled backwards and forwards to brighten the decks.

When he collected the burgoo or porridge to take to the mess he was often sweating and stinking as badly as his animals, which made him the brunt of teasing by the others in his mess, but he took in all in good part, remembering how the messmates had tormented Flynn on his first night aboard.

His next job was to bring up his mess's hammocks and bedding, tightly rolled to stow on deck until evening. On alternate days he aired all the bedding and once a month he was responsible for washing the bedding. He often thought, ruefully, "If Ma could see me now washing dishes and clothes and airing the beds, she would laugh, for I always told Peggy she had an easy life because she was a girl. Had I been asked before I would have said sailors were dirty and idle but with all this washing there cannot be a cleaner, smarter set of sailors than the British Navy."

It had been a big surprise to Bill that the sailors on board were pernickety in their appearance. Twice each week the sailors washed their clothes and often the ship looked like a laundry as the mast chains and ropes were used as makeshift clotheslines. Apart from the pressed men or those just come from the prison ships on the south coast each man had a variety of 'slops', these being older clothes used on days when there was no inspection. As Bill had soon discovered the decks were covered in tar and any clothes worn during deck scrubbing were soon in a very disreputable state, covered in tar that could not easily be removed with cold water. Sometimes the men would be requested by Mac to piss in a bucket and the tarry clothes would be steeped in this and a mixture of sea water, which was partially successful at cleaning the cloth.

Unlike the soldiers, or marines as they called themselves on board ship, they were not issued with a uniform but had to present themselves for inspection twice a week and woe betide any man who showed up in dirty clothes, so for the main part the men made themselves a 'good set' and worked in veritable rags. Bill had been instructed by Dingo how to cut out and sew a second set of clothes but he was in debt to the purser for the material and sewing kit.

He had that first evening been amazed at Dingo's dexterity and longed to be able to replicate his skill. He was slow to learn to ply the needle and agonised over every stitch. In fact, had it not been for Dingo's constant vigilance Bill, and Alec too, would have presented a sorry sight. On a rare occasion when Alec and Bill were at liberty to share their experiences they laughed at their unhandiness and considered what state they might have been in if the Bosun had not berthed them in Mac's mess. Clothes were either made on board or bought in port, but on occasion the men had a chance to increase their wardrobe if a shipmate died at sea.

They had witnessed a 'sale at the mast' where there was much rivalry to buy the many shirts and waistcoats made by an old tar who had recently succumbed to ship fever after a lifetime at sea. After the man's body had been committed to the sea with prayers and the respect of the whole crew under the guidance of the chaplain, Bill was amazed to see such immaculate garments as had been fashioned by the man. He had bid on several items but was only successful in gaining a knife and a horn tankard. Although he had had no wages he had been able to sell some of his grog allowance to another messmate and was thus able to supplement his equipment, but the price of the old man's shirts went way beyond his pocket.

"Never mind, young 'un," said Den sympathetically. "We will soon see some action and you will be able to buy silk shirts with your booty. That's how auld Pat had so many treasures. He was a veteran of many a skirmish with a Spanish barque."

"Would it not have been fairer to send his belongings to his family? Just one of those silk shirts would feed a family for a week."

"Now don't go getting sentimental on me. Bosun sells his things, and at a better price than his daughter would get from the Jews, and sends the money for her to collect at his home port."

One night when Bill came into the mess after being initiated into the dogwatch by Flynn he was just in time to hear Mr Allen's name, but didn't hear the whole conversation when the men, on noticing his entry, stopped their discussion. Bill realised that there was something happening in the mess that he was not a part of and he determined to find out what the secret was. To this end he kept himself on permanent alert and did in fact pick up snippets of conversation from his mates on watch or when they thought he was not in earshot. He had not quite worked out what it was that was being kept from him when, returning from milking and bedding down the cow and its calf, he heard a sob coming from behind a bulwark and changed direction to see what was taking place. As he rounded the bulkhead, he came upon Jenks curled up in a ball, sobbing.

Forgetting that now Jenks was a senior officer and just seeing him as a heartbroken lad, Bill hunkered down beside him and placing a sympathetic hand on his back asked, "What's amiss, young 'un? Come on. Sit up and tell me what the matter is and we can set about fixing it." He treated Jenks as he would have his younger brother Peter, and this thought brought a pang homesickness with it.

Jenks immediately sat up wiping his eyes and nose with the cuff of his jacket just as any street urchin would and tried to gain control of himself.

"'Tis nothing, I'm just missing home," he tried to convince Bill, but for the few days Bill had been under his tutelage he had heard how Jenks was glad to get away from a home where he had been ill used by his ambitious father in the mistaken belief that he would forget all about the navy and enter the profession his parent had chosen for him.

"Won't wash, sir!" came Bill's reply with a slight smile as he realised that, although Jenks was his senior officer, he was just a wee lad who needed a bit of help to overcome a problem.

"It really is nothing. I am finding it hard to reach Mr Allen's standards. Everything I do is wrong and the punishments get harder and harder. I try to bear it but sometimes it is hard." He rolled down his stocking to show Bill an angry weal suppurating on his leg. "It is very painful so sometimes I have to hide away because I can't hold back the tears."

"Come on and I'll help you to the cockpit and let the surgeon fix it up," said Bill, offering his hand to help the boy to rise, but he was staggered by the awful look of terror on Jenks' face.

"No, Mr Allen expressly commanded that I bear the pain to remind me not to make mistakes. I will be unsuitable for an officer if anyone even suspects I can't suffer the pain."

Bill's expression hardened as he realised how the officer was bullying the younger boy and there and then made up his mind that sooner or later Mr Allen would get his comeuppance. A dreadful thought sent a cold shiver down Bill's spine as he recalled Mr Allen's proclivities he had witnessed at Southampton port.

"Surely he wouldn't sodomise the lad?" he worried, but adopting a light-hearted tone Bill gave Jenks a mocking salute and continued, "Well sir, I've seen it now so it will be our secret. Come down into the hold with me for I have some salve I use on the animals that will take some of the pain away." Collecting a bucket of salt water as he went Bill led the still sniffling boy back into the bowels of the ship where the remaining animals were kept. Sitting Jenks on an upturned water barrel he gently washed the pus off the wound with the salty water. Jenks gave a yelp which he smothered with his hands and Bill pretended not to have heard, allowing the young man to keep his pride as the salt stung the broken flesh.

"How did he do this? Now don't play a martyr to me. I've already noticed you have bruises all over. Does he beat you?"

Jenks nodded as his head drooped onto his chest.

"He says I am stupid and the only way for me to learn seamanship is to have it beaten into me. He beats me with his stick, but not like he beat you, where everyone can see it. He makes me undress and uses the stick on the parts of my body that are normally hidden then he leaves me in the hold all night with no clothes and the rats for company. I only escaped tonight because he was summoned to the captain's cabin and I thought if I hid till he got back he might forget about me. You mustn't tell on me, please," he finished, almost pleading with Bill to keep his secret.

Bill was inflamed by the brutality shown to Jenks but he had learned a bitter lesson when answering the officer back, so, promising to keep his own counsel, he reassured Jenks of his compliance. But Mr Allen's card was well and truly marked and Bill knew that no matter how long he had to wait he would give Mr Allen a taste of his own medicine. Meantime he intended to keep a very close eye on the boy sailor.

Now that the wound on his leg was less uncomfortable Jenks was happy to sit and keep company with Bill. He told him how the mate was teaching him to calculate the course and steer the ship. How he dreamed of becoming a captain and being in charge of his own ship. These imaginings showed to Bill more than anything else that this boy, trainee officer as he was, was still only a child and his heart went out to him in his predicament. An hour or so later after they had talked of all things maritime and Jenks was almost back to his normal jocose self, they parted at the entrance to the hold and Bill took himself thoughtfully to his hammock where he continued to ponder the situation and how to resolve it.

Bill saw no more of Jenks until the following Sunday when they both attended the service. He did not approach the youngster in case it was noticed by the midshipman and caused Jenks to be the recipient of yet another beating. Bill was not really listening to the chaplain since his thoughts were fixed on Jenks, but he was brought back to reality by the stir of excitement in the congregation. The chaplain, when he came to attend, was blessing the ship and its crew and asking God to keep them safe in the battle to come. Bill was stupefied. Yes, he knew he was aboard a warship and heading out to meet the Franco-Spanish fleet, but he had been so focussed on the more mundane ship's matters he had not given a lot of thought to a battle. However, as he looked around him there were smiles on most of the faces. Some of the older tars were less impressed, for they had already seen action and knew it was brutal and the massive sacrifice of life was not worth the benefit gained, but the younger men, especially the soldiers, were ripe for a fight. When the service of dedication completed the men gathered in small clumps to discuss the news, but they had very little time for speculation as the seldom seen captain appeared on the poop deck to set his men to their battle stations.

He was a sight to behold, perfectly turned out in a heavily laced shirt and deep blue coat, which seemed moulded to his figure, over white unmentionables and shining Hessians, the whole topped off by his tricorn hat set upon his wig establishing his status. He gave a rousing speech urging every man to do his duty to the glory of God and King George, then handed the ship's company over to the first mate, who was to be in charge for the duration of the encounter. The mate was all business, explaining that one enemy ship had been sighted on the horizon but it was not yet known if it was a forerunner of a Spanish fleet or a single ship that had been parted from its flotilla. Bill was to be sent to the guns to help with manning the cannon. He was to be accompanied by Jenks and under the orders of Mr Allen.

****

His heart sank for he had little confidence in the ability of Mr Allen to plan a sortie. But orders were orders and if there was one thing Bill had learnt during his short months on board, it was to carry out the orders of a superior officer without question.

Alec, being more used to ships and with experience of tactical manoeuvring while avoiding the Customs' cutters, was in place on the rigging, cutlass in hand in case of one to one combat if by some fluke the enemy boarded their vessel. His cheeks were fired by his excitement as he anticipated a break from the monotony of his daily tasks.

Before Bill made off into the bowels of the ship to be a powder monkey for a gunner, he screwed up his eyes and gazed out at sea trying to see the vessel that was causing all the excitement. However, his eyes were not accustomed to spotting objects so far distant and all he could see was sea and sky. He would have liked to accompany Alec in the rigging and was jealous of the other's position, but he made his way down the ladder grimacing at the thought of spending time with Mr Allen. His mind on the forthcoming ordeal, he forgot to watch where he was putting his feet. The ladders on board were nothing like the ones he had been used to shinning up and down as a lad on the farm, but perfectly upright and narrow and descending into the gloom of the lower decks. This was a skill Bill had yet to master and one that required his full concentration in order not to come a cropper which is what he did, landing at the feet of a sneering Midshipman Allen who barked an order while landing him a vicious kick in the leg.

"Get yourself up and to your position beside the soldiers at the cannon, you ignorant farm boy," he screamed.

Tongue tight between his teeth and arms glued to his sides to prevent him from reacting to the words, Bill pulled himself to his feet and made to descend the next ladder to the gun deck. As he made his careful way down a grinning face appeared out of the gloom above him and he was kicked in the mouth with full force, knocking him backward off the ladder. He landed on his back with a thump, all the breath having been forced out of his lungs. He lay for a minute, quite disorientated, but, once he got his breath back, he jumped up and made off to his post, determined not to allow Mr Allen any chance to put him on a charge for not attending his given post. His mouth and face stung and he felt pain in the muscles of his back and leg where he had been injured, but he was no quitter. He arrived at the cannons and presented himself to the corporal in charge, making a joke of his ineptness when questioned about his injuries.

"Glad to have you in whatever state you appear," said a distracted marine as he tried to get his orders obeyed as soon as possible. "Get over there and start removing the bulkheads so that we have room to move around."

Having given Bill his order he caught sight of another marine and set off at a tangent to give him his orders.

"Here, grab hold, help me move this piece over to the side and lash it safe," smiled a tar Bill knew slightly by the name of Pat. "We need to get a move on while we can still see. Once the guns start firing you won't be able to see your hand in front of your face."

The two men lugged the wall of what had previously been the midshipmen's mess over to the side of the ship, manoeuvring it between cannon that were being rolled into place. To Bill it seemed amazing that everyone managed to get on with their allotted tasks in the dim, human-infested gun deck. As they were returning to repeat their performance with another bulkhead Bill became aware that Midshipman Allen was standing on the barrel of a cannon shouting orders in every direction but was being, for the most part, ignored by the marines. Luckily for Bill he was not in the vicinity of the angered leader for, as a tar passed by him about his duties, the infuriated officer hit him on his head with the blade of his sword, cleaving open his skull. The man dropped to the deck while Mr Allen jumped up and down on the oak frame, lashed by a series of ropes and pulleys to the ship's side that held the gun in place, in an agitated manner.

"Have him put in chains!" called the marine in charge before calmly continuing with his duty to oversee the setting up of the cannon.

Four soldiers converged on Mr Allen where he was jabbering and spewing out orders interspersed with curses to all who would dare to disobey him. Seeing the men approaching he began to swing his sword around him in all directions. It was quite like a pantomime as the men ducked and swayed to avoid being hit by his lethal weapon. These were trained fighting men, however, and tactics had been part of their training; so while the four soldiers in front of the mad midshipman were engaging his attention, two more came at him from behind and, seizing his sword arm, quickly disabled him by the simple expedient to hitting him on the jaw, such a punch as Bill had not seen outside of a prize fight. Mr Allen dropped to the deck unconscious, to be dragged away by the marines and secured out of harm's way.

"Let's get Ames up to the cockpit," Pat nudged Bill, who was standing frozen in disbelief at what had played out in front of his eyes.

Bending to help Pat with his grizzly task he too became covered in blood but Pat hurried him on with, "The blood is still flowing so he is still alive. Maybe he can be saved, poor bugger."

The men hastily half carried, half dragged the injured man away from the melee around them and left him, the first casualty of the battle, to the mercy of the surgeon.

Bill and Pat hurried back to their posts and soon had all the bulkheads removed and lashed to the hull with ropes. They were out of the way of the cannon but also added an extra layer of protection to the hull of the ship.

The next job they were given was to make sure all the gun ports were open and secured and that fire buckets and sponges were in place beside each post.

"Why the buckets of water near the guns, surely there is enough water in this place and they will surely spill around our feet?" asked Bill of Pat.

"You will probably be given the job of keeping the cannon cool and for that you need to sponge it with water, for it would be fatal if the powder exploded in the gun and blew us out of the water."

This image settled in Bill's brain and he just hoped that he had learned enough seamanship to stay upright when the ship was rolling and tend to his post. He sent an arrow of prayer up to his Father in Heaven asking him to give him the strength and the will to do his duty.

Orders were being called from all parts of the ship, but in the noisy gun ranks it was impossible to hear what was being communicated. As he was handed a huge sack of sand and told to scatter it on the decks around where the gun crews were gathering, he obeyed without question. It appeared to him now that some form of organisation had taken place. Jenks and other of the younger boys had primed the gunners with a supply of powder and cannonballs that stood ready piled up at each cannon. Soldiers stood at attention with ramrods ready to push the heavy balls into place and a shaded battle lantern stood at the armourer's elbow to provide the flame to set off the explosion when the command should be heard.

The atmosphere on the deck was strangely quiet all of a sudden as if everyone present were holding their breath and waiting for the battle to begin. Into this eerie silence a lone voice could be heard that galvanised everyone to a state of alertness. Although Bill had not been able to understand the words it was made plain to him that the ship had been identified as of the enemy fleet and they were about to claim it and add it to the British Navy.

"Attend your posts men, and may God keep you," came the command from the gun captain.

The ship began to roll as it changed course to come broadside of the enemy ship and the guns were primed ready to have the fuse lit on instruction. Bill and Pat had both been assigned to the same gun crew and were to be in charge of the fire buckets.

"Ready ..." a long pause from all the gun posts

"Why don't we fire if the ship is in range?" queried Bill, not understanding the tactics.

"It is a matter of deciding where we are going to hit. Some of the gunners will be firing on the downwards roll of the waves to send our shot into the hull of the ship and disable or kill her crew, while others will be firing on the upwards roll in order to target the masts and sails. If we prevent her from filling her sails, it will be easier for us to catch her and board her and as we are not yet sailing with the fleet that is what we will be trying to do." He sounded extremely proud as he carried on with Bill's education.

"The enemy will also be waiting her time to attack for the same reason, but we are the British Navy, the best in the world, and ship against ship they stand no chance."

"Prepare... Fire!" came the command of their gun captain and the explosion deafened the men close to the gun port."

"Sponge, sponge!" screamed Bill's partner, not that he could hear the words but he understood the gesture and immediately began to douse the gun.

Blast after blast was heard in the enclosed space as each cannon was fired when its captain felt it would do the most damage. While the crew were reloading the guns, Pat handed Bill a long length of thick sacking. "Wrap that round your head covering your ears. It won't stop you hearing the blast but it may protect you from the worst of the damage."

"Thanks," said Bill and grinned at what he could see of his mate and went off to refill his bucket at the gunwales.

Before he could get back to his post he was blown off his feet as the ship was struck by an enemy blast. Bill, unable to hold himself erect, slid on his back along the deck and came to rest against one of the gun carriages on the other side of the deck. He was unhurt apart from having been drenched with the contents of his bucket, but could not see where he should go. The gun ports on this side of the ship had not been opened since they were fighting only one ship and were broadside of it. Lying prone with his head against the gun carriage he had struck it on, Bill peered into the gloom. The dark, smoky, choking atmosphere, dimly illuminated by battle lanterns was like nothing Bill had ever experienced and for one minute he wondered if he had landed in Hell.

The groaning of the timbers and the moans of the injured men as well as the echoing explosions of the guns would have led him to believe that Hell was where he was if Pat's disembodied arm had not reached out of the smoky blackness and pulled him up, saying, "We took a hit but I don't think it has breached the hull. We have to check before the next round of fire. Come on."

So saying, the two men, bent almost double with their heads well down, ran as fast as they could to where they thought the cannonball had hit. They had to feel around in the dark as what little light there was on the gun deck was negated by the acrid black smoke that poured out of the guns when they were fired. Bill felt a dribble of water run down his arm and he called to Pat that there was a crack in the hull.

"Better stop it up for the moment until we can get time to fix it properly." They scrambled about the deck, now strewn with debris, until they found some sacking then they packed it up against the trickling struts before jamming a spar of wood against it in the hope of preventing the breech increasing. When they could no longer feel any water dripping in through the crack Pat led the way back to the gun crew. Bill didn't know how he found the right one but, when he saw the grinning teeth of Jenks appearing ghostlike out of his soot-blackened face, he knew they were back in position.

Jenks had been steady at his post and Bill felt like a landlubber beside the thin youth who had been able to keep his feet while he, a bulkier, heavier man, had been unable to stay upright.

"Cease fire, the enemy is defeated. Cease fire, cease fire!" came an ever louder call from deck to deck as a tumult of running feet could be heard on the deck overhead.

"Huzza, huzza!" called the marines as they congratulated one another on the outcome of their firepower.

As they were below decks, they had no way of knowing what was happening above board, so they stood at their posts for what seemed an infernal amount of time. The running footsteps could no longer be heard above and, as the smoke and ash from the cannon cleared and they were able to see their companions, they exchanged quizzical glances, each wishing they could be taking part in the action above.

Alec was taking part in the boarding of the beaten ship. He had been in the rigging, clinging on for dear life while the two ships had been firing upon each other, so he had had a good view of the action. He had often been afraid he was going to be catapulted into the torrid sea below as the ship rolled from side to side with the movement of the ocean as the ships exchanged fire, but the superior maneuverability of the British ship had meant that the heavier, less speedy ship of the French fleet was no match for the *Pheobe* and the *Intrepid* had run down her flag after firing only one shot and surrendered.

There were many sailors on the rigging each armed with dagger and cutlass, and as they swung on their long ropes across the boiling water to land on the deck of the *Intrepid*, they looked more like pirates than sailors of the Great British Navy. In fact, many had been forced into piracy at some stages of their career, but now they were landing on the enemy ship and claiming her for King George and England.

When the sailors arrived on deck there were a few skirmishes and Alec enjoyed a fight with swords, but he swiftly disabled his opponent and sent him to a fishy grave by the expedient to leaning him back against the rail, then catching him by the ankles and tossing him over the side. He turned hoping to take on another opponent, but by this time the crew had acquiesced and were lined up in front of their officers and behind a pile of weapons: pistols, blunderbusses, cutlasses, daggers, swords, side arms, all ceded by the crew of the *Intrepid*.

Alec joined a group of sailors from the *Pheobe* who were to take the officers in charge and have them transported to the *Pheobe* where they would be kept as prisoners of war until the ship made port or was able to transfer the prisoners onto a ship bound for England. As they waited with their prisoners for the jollyboat to be launched Alec was able to observe his own officer giving the captured sailors the option of sailing on the *Intrepid* under the flag and command of the British Navy, being imprisoned below deck or being thrown overboard. Alec was aghast at the lack of emotion the officer showed as he made this last offer.

One of the captured men stepped forward and said in Spanish, "En lugar de la muerte en el mar que servir al Inglés."

"Any more of you feel like that?" the officer asked, nonchalantly.

"Oui, nous ne servons pas de porcs Anglais," sneered another from amid a group of nodding heads.

"Very well. You need not serve on board this ship. Throw them overboard," he commanded.

A group of Alec's shipmates hustled the men to the rails of the ship and casually tossed them into the foaming waves.

"Any more?"

"Monsieur, moi vous prie de ne pas moqué de mes hommes. Ils sont de bons marins," came the cultured voice of the Captain as he tried to break free from his captives, then, turning to his men, said, "Hommes accepter ces vainqueurs comme vos maîtres."

"Well said, Captain. Your care for your crew does you credit, but, even if they are good sailors as you say, they will only sail under my orders if they are willing to fight against their countrymen. Better a quick death in the sea than the treatment they will receive if they disobey me while sailing under my command."

But the remaining crew, after seeing their shipmates' demise, had decided that it would be better to remain on board the ship and sail under the British flag. Officers and crew were designated to take over the running of the ship while a search party was sent below to see what wealth could be gained. Alec was sorry not to be able to stay on board the *Intrepid*, for he imagined that was where the fun was to be had. Since they had been on board the *Pheobe,* there had been little but hard work and he felt that plundering the *Intrepid* sounded like light relief.

The prisoners were escorted to their captain when they arrived aboard the *Pheobe,* and Alec never knew what became of them for he never saw hide nor hair of them again.

As Bill, black as a coalminer and dirty as a sweep, ascended from the lower decks, every part of his body ached. While he had gone about his chores and obeyed the orders of the gun captain he had not felt his injuries but now, that the threat of being captured had vanished, he realized that he had many bangs, cuts and bumps. Even after all the injuries he had sustained below deck, the most painful was his face where he had been kicked by Mr Allen. By this time his eye was closed and he could barely open his mouth, such was the swelling of his lips, so he trotted off with some of the other casualties to be tended by the surgeon.

The mess that evening was very quiet, every man had had a part to play in the capture of the enemy ship but they were far too tired to exult in their victory. There was no hot food for Bill to collect from the galley since, as soon as the ship was called to battle stations, the range had been put out in case a roll of the ship should set free a stray spark and burn the ship down.

The men were even too tired to make a table and seats, many lying on the deck, others tying up their hammocks and tumbling into them caked with soot and smoke, others staring into space. They had spent the last two days fighting not only for their ship but for their own lives. They had been allocated a double measure of grog and each man had drunk their share, even those, like Bill, who normally traded their portion for more basic needs.

"At least we don't have to worry about Mr Allen anymore," commented Bill, then went on to tell Alec of the happenings just before the skirmish had started.

"Couldn't have happened to a better person," laughed Alec, but then noticed how the other men had been alerted by the story.

Mac had raised himself onto his elbow, giving the story his utmost attention but there was no sign of humour visible on his face. He listened until Bill had given Alec a blow-by-blow account of the incident, then asked sharply, "Were you preparing the guns or actually under the command of the gun captain?"

With a puzzled look on his face, Bill tried to remember the exact time of the event. It was difficult because all his senses had been alert and he had been excited about the upcoming experience.

"I think it was as we were setting up, for Pat and I were just moving a bulkhead out of the way, but I'm not sure. Why? What difference does it make so long as he is out of our hair?"

Mac looked around his messmates, who were now sitting up paying attention, all thought of sleep gone for the moment. His eye landed on Dingo, who nodded his vast head in agreement, seeming to understand Mac's unspoken question.

"He was in charge then. Until the deck was set up with the artillery and the guns ready to fire he was in charge of the seamen. He would only cede his command when he handed them over to the gun captain as part of a gun crew."

"But he caught Ames on the head. I don't even know if he is still living. Surely, anyone could see he had gone mad!" exclaimed Bill, touching his painful mouth where the skin on his lips had been broken by Mr Allen's spiteful kick.

"Mad or not, he will be released and on the captain's order. I hope it was marines who chained him up for if it was tars they will be punished for mutiny."

Bill stood with his mouth wide open in amazement as he heard but did not really understand Mac's words. He pictured again the dark bustling gun deck and the men advancing on Mr Allen where he stood, cursing and promising all kinds of retribution to any who disobeyed his orders and was able to say, "I'm pretty sure they were all marines, for they obeyed an order from their commander. What will happen to them?"

Mac shrugged but spoke in a subdued voice. "It's up to the captain. He might just let Mr Allen free to go about his duties; and that is what we must hope for or Ames may be punished for not obeying an order or someone may be court-martialled for mutiny. It all depends, but one thing is for certain; Mr Allen will be about his duties tomorrow."

And so it proved. As Bill struggled on deck with his first consignment of hammocks the next morning, Mr Allen was strutting about the deck like a peacock.

Life at sea went on as usual. There was a bit more room since some of the crew and officers had been transferred to the captured ship and were sailing it under the command of their own captain and with what remained of the Spanish and French crewmen, now, if not happily, at least willingly accepting their lot.

Bill and Alec were excited to receive a 'rated' share of the captured vessel. The promised gold, which would only be delivered when the ship could be handed over to the admiralty and the crew given a portion of its worth, was not of much use to Bill or Alec, but, to Bill, the sharing out of the clothes and other ephemera found on board was a boon. They had both suffered from lack of basic equipment, such as razors and combs and been hard pushed to maintain the level of cleanliness expected by their officers. Since the *Intrepid* had only recently left port she had an abundance of fresh meat, bread and – much to Bill's disgust – live animals. Caring for the animals had become problematic for Bill since, while under fire, the few animals remaining on the *Pheobe* had been tethered in a jolly boat that was pulled behind the ship to keep them out from under the feet of the tars, and *Intrepid* followed this normal pattern also. So, until the ships could make landfall, the animals had to be fed in the boats by the expedient of Bill being hung over the gunwales of the ship on a rope secured by his messmates while he tossed food into the boats. It was a perilous escapade and Bill was constantly to be seen scanning the horizon in the hope of spying a land mass, any land mass would do for him.

Eventually he was delighted to hear a call from the crow's nest:

"Land ahoy, on the starboard bow."

After some to-ing and fro-ing by the captain and the mates, it was decided that they would head for the land, which the officers had decided was uninhabited but would give them a chance to take on fresh water and balance their crews more evenly.

As the *Phoebe*, followed by the *Intrepid*, anchored off the island, and since no human life could be detected, a jolly boat was launched and some of the sailors sent off as scouts. Since Bill and Alec had been pressed they wondered if they would be allowed off the ship, but, when the landing party returned with the news that there was no habitation on the island, that they could see, but they had sighted an abundance of ripe fruits and good grazing for the animals, Bill was delighted to learn that he was to be one of the landing party in charge of the animals.

After so many months at sea Bill found it strange to stand on dry land that did not move about and at first was quite disorientated, but since he had to manufacture some kind of enclosure to keep the sheep, pigs and cows from straying he quickly became used once more to terra firma.

He had been told by the mate that he was to remain on the island overnight to allow the animals as much grazing as possible. The grass was lush and high, there was plenty of fresh water and while he was tending the animals he helped fill the barrels of water that were then transported back to the ships. In between these chores he stripped off his clothes and bathed naked in the sea, as did a few of his shipmates. Bill was astonished that so few of the men entered the sea above their knees and only then when they were getting in or out of the smaller boats that brought them to shore.

While sitting on a grassy knoll languidly keeping watch over the animals and having been joined by Mac, he said, "I feel so good and clean and fresh after bathing in the sea. It is as if I have been reborn."

He stretched back, extending his bare torso the better to catch the heat of the sun. Indeed, he did look like a new man. He was bronzed by the continual exposure to the sun which did not reach below the decks of a warship. The darkening of his skin made his eyes appear sultry and any maid looking into them would have felt her heart beat faster at the sight of him. In contrast Mac was still dressed in his normal clothes, shirt sleeves no higher than his elbows and his straw hat shading his features from the sun's rays. The only concession he had made was to remove his sea boots and now sat, bare-footed, on the ground.

"Don't you want to get in the sea and feel it cleanse your skin after so long in the bowels of the ship?" asked Bill.

"How many of this crew do you see arsing about like fish? The safest place, the *only* safe place for a sailor to be is on *top* of the sea. When you sail the sea you have to remember that she is the mistress and you are alive only at her pleasure. Like all women it is best not to antagonize her."

Bill turned to look at the man who had been responsible for his having an easy time on board and thought that perhaps he was joking, but Mac looked solemn as he went on.

"You need to watch out that a mermaid doesn't take a liking to that strong body of yours, for when you are in the sea and she can see your long legs, they are very jealous of legs, mermaids, you can be breathing the air above the waves one minute and have a mermaid for a bride the next. So thank you I don't wish to take the risk of showing my body to a mermaid, lad." He got up and walked off in the direction of the shoreline and cast his glance longingly at the ship.

Bill, not put off by the thought of being dragged to the sea bed by a lovesick mermaid, enjoyed the days he was ashore. More than anything else he found he was glad to get away from constant company. While aboard the ship it hadn't really occurred to him that he was missing home but, as he sat lazily on the white sandy beach listening to the gentle whoosh of the waves breaking on the rocks, he felt a nostalgic pull to his home shores. His thoughts drifted to Ellen and he wondered if he was the father of a son or a daughter for it had been six months and more since he had left his native shores.

"She'll have my mother and Peggy to help her though and I will go back with enough money to set us up in a farm of our own," he consoled himself.

The idyllic few days were almost over and Bill was sad that this was his last day on the island with his animals. Today he was finishing the plaiting of some ropes and fashioning them into a harness to hoist the beasts onto deck from the much lower boats. The last two days had been extremely busy as he had had to scour the boats free of the excrement of the animals while they had been housed in them, and he was hurrying to complete his tasks in the hope of one last bathe in the warm sea before he too was back aboard the ship.

As the vessels were to sail with the high tide early the next morning there was only a smattering of sailors on the island, but Bill was delighted to see Jenks loping over the sands in his direction. He stopped what he was doing for a moment and raised his hand to wave to the young boy. No matter how many times he told himself that Jenks now warranted the title of Mister, he could not bring himself to think of the youngster as anything other than a lad and treated him like a younger brother. He had become very fond of Jenks since their conversation in the hold amongst the animals. Neither mentioned the incident again but Bill was constantly on alert when the boy was on deck.

Jenks threw himself down on the sea grass beside Bill and grinned up at him from under his wayward fringe, which, no matter how he tried, just refused to stay slicked back from his brow, hanging over his eyes to such an extent that he had to squint to see the other man. The long fair hair, free from its tether, was bleached by the sun and lay loose over his sunburned shoulders, making him look more like an adolescent schoolgirl than an officer of the navy. Freed from his duties on the ship whilst it was at anchor, and despite the scars and mottled bruises on his limbs, he looked the picture of health as he sprawled at his ease beside Bill. He chattered on while Bill listened and smiled indulgently. "It has been like a holiday but we are back under sail tomorrow and coxswain is going to teach me to steer," he grinned exuberantly, showing Bill his obvious excitement.

"You'll soon be master of your own vessel if you progress at this rate, sir," he laughed as he mock saluted the lad, thinking how he would fare if he was so cheeky to Mr Allen, but Jenks paid no heed to how he was addressed. He was too thrilled by the coming treat.

He stood up, dropping his white trousers on the grass, saying, "I'm off for one last dip in the sea before I get back to my duties. Are you coming?"

Bill hesitated only a moment before shucking off his own ragged trews and chasing after the swift-footed lad. As they ran into the sea, they splashed each other and dived and played like porpoises until both were exhausted, and exiting the sea, they looked like a couple of gods. Jenks was a golden God of the Egyptians while Bill's dark hair and bronzed skin made him appear as if he had descended from Valhalla.

Neither of them noticed that they were being watched, and by a very jealous watcher, who rubbed his crotch as he felt himself respond to the sight of the naked men.

****

In no time at all to the men on board, the pleasant interval spent on the island was a distant memory. To Bill, who had never lived away from the temperate weather of the south-west of Scotland it was still exciting to get up and find yet another sunny day, but this feeling lasted only as long as he was on deck and most of his duties were carried out in the dimly lit nether decks. Since the ships were again sailing south in an effort to catch up with the main fleet he was allowed to bring his animals on deck. He did this in the mornings, but was careful to water the animals when as few tars as possible were on deck to witness it.

In the soul-destroying heat, the officer of the watch always delegated some of the marines to guard the water casks as fresh water was precious and the matelots were rationed quite severely but Bill had orders to water the cows as they required. This seemed to the common men on board to be grossly unfair as they felt they were having their water rations cut in order to provide the officers with milk puddings. Tempers flared and, since the men could not take out their angst on either the animals or the officers, Bill came in for a good deal of their animosity.

The ships continued with their cruise south and in the next few months were in port only once, in Gibraltar where they learned they were not far behind the main fleet with the Admiral Lord Nelson aboard his flagship *Victory*. Neither Bill nor Alec were allowed shore leave but since the bumboats brought everything they might need to them it was not such a hardship. Bill, slightly wary after the encounter he had witnessed of Mr Allen's treatment of the prostitutes, and after ensuring that the vile midshipman was ashore, invited his 'wife' aboard and spent a very agreeable afternoon and evening in her company. When he was escorting her back to the boats and waving her off he was surprised to see that Jenks was also shyly bidding farewell to a woman who could easily have been his mother but, by the way she was manhandling him, it was clear they had no family relationship.

Bill could not resist chiding the boy. "Mr Jenks, what have you been up to?" he asked slyly, coming up behind the lad as he followed the bumboat's progress towards the shore.

A blush bloomed rosy on the young man's cheeks giving him the look of an embarrassed girl.

"I have had my first fuck," he answered proudly. "She said I was a fine man and if we docked here again I should look for her in the tavern you can see just over there." He pointed to a building just near the harbor wall where there was much activity. "Jacktars in port gather round an alehouse like flies round a shite." He finished on a laugh.

"I bet that is not something you learned from the coxswain," Bill replied on a laugh.

Jenks' face straightened immediately. "After we leave port, I am to return to Mr Allen's watch. I'm not looking forward to that, I can tell you." Looking up at Bill, he gave himself a shake and carried on. "I will think of that tomorrow. For today I'm a man with a man's appetite." Smirking away he said, "Taking a woman has made me ravenous." He blushed. "For food, I mean."

"Me too," agreed Bill. "Let's get ourselves into the galley and see what is cooking." As he was too liable to do Bill had again forgotten the status of the boy, linking arms companionably with him as they strolled off to the galley.

The ships made only this minor stop and, after being in port, life changed not only for Jenks but also for Bill. Throughout his time on board Jim Perks had been keeping a watchful eye on Bill's progress and had decided that he was now capable of learning to be a seaman, so Bill was ordered to hand his animals over to one of the convicts who had enlisted to avoid transportation, while his duties as cabin boy were allocated to one of the many boys on board.

Life was hard and the everyday jobs Bill had to learn did not play to his natural skills, but when he was climbing the rigging and fearful that he would be washed away with the swell, or when the ship rolled and he was hanging parallel with the rolling waves with only his hands and feet gripping on to the mast to save him from drowning, he remembered the times when, as a lad, he had sat wishing for a life of adventure and exploration on the sea.

The only thing that marred his contentment was the sight of Jenks who, once more in the service of Mr Allen, was becoming more and more withdrawn and anxious-looking. Every time Bill saw the boy he was covered in bruises, but the thing that unsettled Bill more was that Jenks seemed to have lost his enthusiasm for life. He carried out his duties with a solemn expression on his face. When Bill or any of his old messmates joked with him, his mouth moved into the form of a smile, but his eyes remained dull and there was none of his former backchat.

One afternoon just after four bells, Bill was coming off watch and making to the galley when he saw the back of Jenks disappearing round a bulkhead dragging his feet and with his head hanging on his chest.

"That lad looks as if he has the worries of the world on his shoulders and it doesn't need much nous to guess who is causing his sorrows," thought Bill as he carried on walking in the direction of the bow.

There, he sat smoking one of his periques, a habit he had formed since gaining a share of the booty from the *Intrepid*. He had been curious to see Dingo and Flynn buy tobacco leaves from the purser, soak them in their evening's rum ration and roll them up tightly in a strip of canvas and stow them carefully away in their sea bags. Several days later he was in the galley collecting burgoo when the two men came in, each with a tightly rolled tobacco parcel and, setting light to one end, draw the scented smoke into their mouth and down their nose.

"What is that you are doing? It smells wonderful."

"This be my prick," laughed Dingo. "My mama was born on a plantation in the Indies and she learned how to make a smokee from her mama. When she was sold to a slaver on this ship, the old Captin do buy her and set her free cos she was a great cook. She dead now but when I smoke my prick, I always thinks of her."

He had offered Bill a toke of his burning tobacco which Bill had accepted. Although that first perique had made his head swim and his stomach heave, he had become addicted to the pungent smoke and liked nothing better after a watch than to light one of his own in the galley and talk to the other tars about manly matters.

But today Bill could not settle himself to gossip with the other tars for his mind kept coming back to Jenks. He soon knocked out his burning ember and wandered off in search of the boy.

There was no sign of Jenks as he walked around the upper decks so he took himself off to the lower decks to see if he was hiding. As he landed at the foot of the ladder onto the gun deck he could hear a persistent rhythmic sound coming from close by the midshipman's mess. Being careful to remain inconspicuous he crept along the bulkhead until he could see where the noise was coming from and, when he saw Jenks spreadeagled and bare-arsed over one of the cannon, being flogged by Mr Allen, he was hard put not to attack the midshipman.

Jenks was biting on a stick to prevent him from squealing as the older boy flayed his already inflamed and bleeding buttocks with a stick, stopping on occasion to ask, "Are you ready to obey me?"

Jenks answered with a shake of his head and the beating continued.

Bill did not know what to do. His sympathy was with Jenks but he was under the command of Mr Allen and he had every right to chastise Jenks in this manner if he felt he needed to, but surely it was not necessary to beat the boy so badly? As he considered his options, still remaining out of sight, he heard Mr Allen speak again.

"I know you frolic with that Campbell scum. Playing with each other, naked in the sea. If you can do it to him, you can do it to me."

He continued with the flogging until Jenks cried out, "I did not let him stick his cock in me. I didn't touch it. We played in the sea but not with each other. Please, Mr Allen. It's true."

"I have seen you often batting your eyes at him and flirting through that mop of curls you have. You think because you plait it when you are on duty I don't know you play whore when I'm not around?"

Jenks gave a shrug and resigned to his fate, bit once more on his stick and mumbled incoherently. "Go on beating me. I will not be *your* whore."

Mr Allen was so angered that he threw away his stick and, beating on the boy's back with his fists, screamed at him. "I *will* have you. You have to obey me!"

The stricken boy froze in his position over the cannon unable to do more than wiggle his bum since his hands were manacled together under the gun, but the twitching of the pale buttocks inflamed Mr Allen's senses and he tore open the buttons on his breeches and unleashed his hard member, parted the boy's buttocks, making ready to force an entry.

As the angry midshipman placed himself in position, Bill's rage boiled over and he attacked from behind, startling both of the boys. Mr. Allen turned to see who dared hit him and, when seeing it was Bill, a crazed smile came across his face.

"Want to save your little darling, do you? Well, I might overlook your insubordination if you take his place else you will be whipped from here to Portsmouth."

"Let the lad go," growled Bill

Taking this for agreement to his terms, Mr Allen was delighted at the prospect of swapping the skinny, leggy youth for the broad strong man he fumbled with the manacles and freed Jenks' wrists. Bill indicated with a twitch of his head that he should get himself out of harm's way and he did not need telling twice.

"Take off your trews and bend over the cannon just like Jenks was," ordered Mr Allen, unable to hide what the idea of impaling himself in Bill was doing to him.

"If I do as you ask will you leave that boy alone, neither beat him nor try to seduce him?" Bill asked.

Mr Allen smirked, leaving Bill in no doubt that he thought he could have both Bill and Jenks to dance to his filthy tune.

"You want to make a bargain? Too late. You have already put yourself in Jenks's position. Now get your arse over here when I tell you."

"I want you to know, sir," began Bill in a servile voice, "that I am well aware where my actions will take me and am willing to take the penalty." And as the last word left his mouth, he knocked Mr Allen to the deck with one punch from his mighty fist. The stricken midshipman was unable to get himself to his feet since his breeches were around his ankles and, as he tried to jump up, he tripped and landed face down on the deck. By the time he had managed to get himself to his feet and look around he was surrounded by the officers of the watch who instructed him to put himself to rights before marching him off to the brig.

The next morning a cry rang out over the ship.

"All hands on deck. All hands on deck to witness punishment."

As all the tars and the soldiers came out on deck and formed ranks around the grating where a flogging took place, the officers and captain appeared on the poop deck.

A series of whistles came from the bosun's whistle and Bill was brought out on deck by Mr Perks and Mac. He made no attempt to free himself and turned to face the captain.

"You are accused of striking a senior officer. How do you plead?"

"Guilty as charged, Captain," answered Bill loud and clear.

"Since you immediately informed the bosun of your flagrant disobedience, I will sentence you to twelve lashes only. Begin the punishment."

Bill was led over to the grating where he was positioned with his feet and wrists tethered with seizings to the rope rings on the gunwales and the mesh of the gratings.

The bosun appeared with the cat o' nine tails, a vicious instrument of plaited ropes, each of the nine sections with knots along their length, and prepared to administer his punishment.

"Brace yourself against the ropes and let the cat swing around you. You need not worry. Twelve strokes is lenient."

With his bare back facing the flogger and his eyes focused on the horizon, Bill heard the drum begin to beat. At first, he didn't feel the bite of the malicious whip but with each further drumbeat and each stroke his back began to burn. He had never felt pain like it. It felt like there were a hundred fires each burning off the skin on his back and cutting into his muscles. After a few lashes he heard no more, so intent was he in keeping the grinding pain at bay. In an unbelievably short time he was cut down and pulled into position to face the officers.

"Thank the gentlemen for your punishment," whispered Mac.

Bill lifted his spinning head and. hoping he was looking in the right direction. said, "Thank you for my punishment, sir."

The captain indicated that Bill should be let go and he slunk off to the back of the crewmen and waited to be dismissed.

"All hands on deck to witness punishment!" came the call again and Bill froze, thinking his ordeal was not over, but he breathed a sigh of relief when he realized that some other poor bugger was to receive the next instalment. He could not see who was standing between Mr Perks and Mac, but he could hear that he was not being cooperative.

"You are accused of sodomy. How do you plead?"

"Not guilty. It is my right to punish any sailor who does not obey an order," was the answer and Bill recognized Mr Allen's voice.

"Did you ask men on this ship to pleasure you? Yes or no? Be careful how you answer."

"It is my right to punish men under my command," came the defiant answer.

"Corporal Hicks?"

"Yes, sir!" and a marine in full dress uniform including highly polished black boots, which were all Bill could see, addressed the captain.

"Please state how you found this man when you were alerted to his offence."

The marine looked around, uncomfortable about giving evidence in front of so many people, but he took in a breath and told how he had found Mr Allen where he had been told he would find him and in a state of undress not suitable to an officer. He blushed as he described the scene.

"I ask you again, Mr Allen. You are charged with the crime of sodomy on the high seas. How do you plead? Have you asked men aboard this ship to have improper relations with you? I ask you to remember you are an officer of the Kings Navy."

"I maintain it is my right to punish any man who disobeys my order," Mr Allen replied sullenly.

"I will ask you one more time and if you continue to deny your actions I will bring forward witnesses to your depravity. Do you wish to change your plea, Mr Allen?"

"Guilty!" he shouted.

"Then hanging from the yardarm is the punishment for this crime. Take the prisoner back to the brig and prepare the rope. Forbear!" he called and the bosun whistled to tell the men they could go back to work.

Dingo, Mac and Flynn helped carry Bill back to the mess where Dingo bathed the weals on his back and Flynn dug deep in his chest to find some soothing ointment to ease the sting in his back.

"You did good, Bill. Worth a tickle from the cat."

"If this is a tickle, I wouldn't ever want to have full rations from her," grimaced Bill as he tried to put his shirt back on.

As the ships sailed on and met the rest of the fleet they had been chasing, Bill's back improved, leaving only silver scars to show for his flogging, but the dead body of the hanged midshipman swung high on the topmost mast of the rigging until it was lost at sea in a freak storm.

Bill continued his training and, before long, Mr Jenks was promoted to midshipman. Despite their difference in rank, they became firm friends.

Chapter Eighteen

Ellen's Story Continues

Ellen had stopped to cool her burning feet in the gently lapping waves of the castle loch and was enjoying the icy tingle as the water flowed over her hot feet. She had no real destination but was confident that when the right opportunity made itself known to her, she would grab it with both hands.

It had been a hard slog from her seaside home to the little village of Lochmaben where she was idly watching the activity of the workmen from the Bruce estate as they prepared the fields for winter. The last of the potato crop had been lifted and stored in the myriad outhouses of the impregnable Castle demesne. A few spires of smoke swirled up from the centre of the densely wooded area on the far side of the loch, telling her that the travelling Gypsies who had been given leave to camp in these woods were in residence. Ellen remembered hearing the story of the Gypsy fortune teller who had predicted great things for the Bruce family and how their predictions had been proven correct when Sir Robert Bruce had been crowned King of Scotland and, although his reign was well in the past, the Romany Gypsies were still awarded the right to camp on the estate of the once royal Bruce.

At the back end of the year, the Gypsy men were grateful for the work as 'tattie howkers', that backbreaking work not much favoured by the local agricultural labourers. Whole families of Gypsies dug up and collected the big tubers, the men digging and the nimbler women and children filling large hessian sacks with the crop, leaving the sacks ready to be collected on the farm cart at the end of each day. For this work, the Gypsy community were authorised to trap and hunt small animals in the surrounding woods and, with the generous allowance of potatoes and turnips, it meant the families in the vardos were able to keep body and soul together over the winter months.

Ellen sighed as she lazily watched the smoke rise from the Gypsies' fires into the cloudy sky. Her brain formulated pictures suggested by the shapes of the shifting cloudbanks, sometimes a dog begging, which made her smile, sometimes a knight on a warhorse but sometimes, no matter how hard she tried, she could find no image to stimulate her imagination.

"That looks just like a caravan moving through the sky," she thought to herself as her eyes drifted once more over the leaden sky. Taking in the heavy black cloud that followed her 'caravan' she grimaced, realising that summer really had gone and here she was six months along with her child, no home and no destination. Now to crown it all it was going to rain.

"Pity that caravan in the sky can't be a reality for me," she spoke her thoughts aloud as her daydreaming was brought to an abrupt end by the thought of an imminent soaking.

"Are ye on yer own then lass?" came a soft voice out of the silence.

Ellen jumped at the unexpectedness of the intrusion for she had neither seen or heard anyone approaching the lochside. Looking all around her she still could not pinpoint the source of the ethereal voice.

"Is someone there?" she whispered, unsure whether her imagination was playing tricks on her.

"Are ye on yer own?" repeated the voice, but this time Ellen happened to be looking in the right direction and saw a pair of startlingly green eyes staring unblinkingly at her.

"Oh you didn't half give me a fright. I'm afraid I've been wasting time dreaming and gazing at the sky. I only stopped to cool my feet for I've walked a long way," Ellen responded, without taking her eyes of the strange figure who seemed to be trying to read her soul.

"You don't look like you are hurrying towards a destination if you don't mind me saying so." And nodding at Ellen's obvious swollen belly continued, "Mayhap yer folks have caused ye to take yer swollen belly for a walk?"

Ellen may have been tired from her long walk but she was not cowed so, keeping her eyes focused determinedly on the place where she had glimpsed the bright eyes, she said," It's too strange to talk to a pair of eyes. Come and talk to me or I'll think you a wood fairy," she challenged, patting the ground by her side.

The bush parted and a woman stepped onto the hard ground in front of the dense hedge. Ellen took in the appearance of the slight figure and half believed she had conjured up a wood nymph. The woman could have been any age; her skin was weathered to the colour of tanned leather, but, although her hands and bare forearms looked strong and well-muscled, there were no wrinkles to give evidence of her age. The only impression Ellen gained on first sight was that the tiny figure was not very young; she could have been any age from thirty to ninety. Just as her face gave no indication of age, her clothes gave no hint as to her position in society. She was arrayed in a combination of colours and materials that Ellen had never seen before. She wore clogs on her feet but here the resemblance to a working countrywoman ended. She was flamboyant; she wore a bright blue skirt many sizes too large and had tied it round the waist with binder twine, obviously garnered from some stackyard or hayrick where the sheaves were tied with this rough sisal-like material, to keep it anchored to the slim waist. Under a huge plaid shawl which covered her head and shoulders and hung almost to her heels at the back she wore what once must have been a very bright cardigan, even now in its last stages of decay it produced a gay façade, over a man's collarless shirt; the whole effect being striking but extremely strange to Ellen's eyes. She could feel a sensation of panic beginning to attack her body as, after having been watching the smoke from the Gypsy encampment, she took her companion for one of that community, but her fear was dispelled when the woman smiled at her. The broad grin totally changed the personality of the woman before her, making it apparent that she was aged closer to the younger end of Ellen's estimation. She had good teeth too, which very few travelling Romany people possessed. The two girls assessed each other for a few moments, then, deciding they liked what they saw, they both began to question at once.

"Are you from the Gypsy camp?" asked Ellen as her companion spoke over her words to question her with, "When's the baba comin'?"

They laughed at their mistake in speaking together.

"You first."

"When's the baba coming then?" repeated the newcomer. "Have you walked a long way?" She nodded at the down at heel clogs Ellen had kicked off before lowering her feet into the loch. "I'm Maura, by the way, and no, I'm not a Gypsy, although I do have dealings with them and have no fear of them."

"I'm Ellen and I've walked from Powfoot along the coast," she smiled shyly at the older girl. "I'm more than six months gone and I need to find shelter and work until the babe is born. You're right; my pa disowned me and wouldn't listen to anything my ma said in my defence. She pleaded and pleaded with him but once he had his mind made up I had disgraced him, it was, "Out! And never darken my door again!" So now you see me, homeless and almost penniless."

"You got anywheres in mind, for you don't look like a lass who has had much practise at fending for herself. Is there no faither for the baba?"

Ellen lifted her chin in a defiant manner before answering, "We were to be wed. He was happy about the babe but he was pressed into the navy and his mother blames me and won't help." She detected a whimsical look in the other's eyes and her temper rose.

"He *was* pressed, no matter if his mother says he ran away. I made enquiries and he didn't go voluntarily but was seized with a group of men he was with in the Sailor's Rest. My own cousin was taken too. He will be back. I know it.

"I'm hoping to get taken on in one of the smallholdings up along the Ae valley. I've heard they are not so fussed about how you live as long as you can cope with the sheep and the dairy, and I can do that in my sleep. Been doing it since I was a nipper. If I can find somewhere until the babe comes then I'll think again, for I'm sure Bill will be back as soon as he can."

"It's true the farmers up the Ae often employ Romanies, but a Romany woman in your condition would have a family to fall back on," came the dubious words in response to this. Maura eyed her up and down before continuing, assessing the strength of her limbs and the fragility of her blossoming body.

"Lass, they will not take you on. You would be trouble they don't need."

Ellen's face fell at the other's words. It was as she had feared when she had left her family home with her father ranting and raving and calling her names.

"What am I to do?" wailed a dejected Ellen. She was tired and the thought of getting work had buoyed her up on the long trudge she had already made. "I must have work and I will work for very little, not even money which I know is scarce, but for a roof and a bite to eat. Maybe I will need to make for the workhouse in Dumfries, just till the little one arrives."

Maura was quiet as she listened to Ellen tell how she had heard the crofters looked for cheap labour over the winter to tend the sheep they pastured for the upland farms. There, hard weather made it impossible to manage the large numbers of sheep that spent their summers grazing along the heather covered hillsides.

"During the winter and into spring and lambing season the hill farms always farm out their animals to the lower pastures where grazing is not so sparse and I was raised on a farm so caring for animals is not new to me; and I can make butter and cheese with my eyes shut," she listed her skills as if pleading with an employer, but Maura was still sceptical of her ability to find employment on these poor farms.

Hearing the girl's desperation went to Maura's heart, but it would not be kind to let her walk all that way thinking she could gain employment with her belly big with child.

"What you need is a place to rest and care for that child you are carrying, not walking the roads looking for work or giving your soul into the care of the workhouse. We must prevent that at all costs."

"I know, but what else can I do? There is no one who will help me since I've shamed our whole village, but Bill will be back to take care of us," she finished emphatically. Deciding there was nothing to be gained by convincing a stranger of her absolute belief in her lover she remained silent and dejected as she slowly gathered up her bag containing her change of clothes and what little money she had managed to save toward this journey.

With her feet still wet from the loch, she shoved into her clogs and, smiling at Maura, said, "Thank you for your advice, Maura, but I have to at least make an attempt to find work before the weather becomes too harsh to sleep outside. If the worst comes to the worst, I will go to the workhouse. I can earn my keep there and, when the babe is born, I will be strong enough for both of us." Thus saying she turned from the lochside and made for the track that led into the tiny village of Lochmaben.

"Not so fast, lass. I have a proposition for you that is surely better than the workhouse, for I'm sure that will be the outcome of trying for work in your condition. You know your Bill will not be able to have you released from there when he returns because you're not wed to him. Think on that before you make a bad decision."

Ellen stopped in her tracks, taking in this new piece of information. "I hadn't thought beyond having a roof over my head when the time comes. I'm feared to be having a baby without a place to call home."

"Come back to my home with me," invited Maura before continuing, "I may look like a Gypsy but I don't live in a vardo in the woods. I have my own little cottage." She thought for a few moments before explaining further, concerned that her words might frighten rather than reassure.

"I grow herbs and make cures for the good people of Lochmaben. I have been so successful and with the patronage of the Bruce family no one has tainted my name by calling me 'witch'," she laughed.

"My cottage is little more than a sheep pen with a roof but it is warm and cosy with a fire burning on a cold night. You are more than welcome to share it with me."

"But I need to find work to feed myself and the child. I cannot expect you to keep me for nothing."

"I think I might have a solution to that as well. I am too busy to keep up with the number of people who come to me. Mind, I'm no witch, good or bad," she added, perhaps reading Ellen's unease. "I can teach you to make simple remedies that are needed so much during the cold months, then we could make enough to take to the market. Thus you would be helping me increase my business while I will engage to help you deliver the baba. What do you think?" She looked an enquiry at Ellen. "At least come home with me today and we can talk about the details, and if tomorrow you still want to go on your walk to the Ae and look for work, fine. Deal?" She held out her hand to Ellen, who slowly accepted it.

"What harm can it be to spend one more night on the road? At least I will have shelter if this rain that has been threatening settles in," she thought to herself. A cheeky grin appeared on her face under which Maura detected a certain look of relief as she took Maura's proffered hand and declaimed, "Deal!"

The two women barely made it to Maura's house before the gigantic raindrops plopped onto the ground around them heralding an autumn rainstorm. They ran the last few yard at full tilt entering Maura's dark residence out of breath and laughing at their antics. The room was very dark with the only light being the red glow that emanated from the banked-up fire that heated the room to a welcome temperature.

"Stand a moment," suggested Maura. "Your eyes will become accustomed but I will light the dip lamp so you can see where to put your feet," she laughed, making her way across the room without any hesitation and on reaching the hearth selected a spill, held it the fire then touched the flame to the mutton-fat lamp which brought the room to light.

"Let there be light," giggled Maura, pleased to have someone to show off her little house to and delighted to see the surprised look on Ellen's mobile features. "It will be nice to have Ellen to chat to on the long winter nights. That's if I can persuade her to stay," she thought.

Meanwhile Ellen was struck dumb. True, the room was little more than a stone-built sheep pen, but the walls were hung with bunches of all kinds of flowers and plants, some freshly gathered berries, some flowers dried to skeletons of their former selves. Baskets hung from hooks on the ceiling with a cornucopia of the harvest of the woods and fields. Some freshly gathered herbs perfumed the air. The whole surreal appearance of the cottage gave the impression of a warm underground burrow. There was too much for Ellen to take in all at once but the combination of the pleasant aromatic smell and the warmth that pervaded her body did much to reassure her that she had indeed made the right decision in agreeing to accompany Maura. She turned a slow circle in the middle of the small room taking in every detail, noting the pallet bed that lay along the side of the hearthstone, the rough table that bore evidence of its constant use for centuries past with its dipped centre and bowed legs, but still grand enough to have spent its early existence in more exalted circumstances. Indeed, this table had at one time graced the kitchen of the nearby castle; perhaps even King Robert the Bruce's dinner might have been prepared on it. The only other furniture in the room was a sturdy wooden chair, again a relic of the castle kitchen, drawn up to the table, and two three-legged milking stools either side of the stone-built hearth.

"Well, do you think you could bear to sleep in my castle?" asked Maura tentatively. Not for the world would she show how anxious she was for her visitor's opinion. It was obvious to Maura that Ellen was used to much better surroundings and she was afraid that, no matter how reduced her standard of living had become by her current circumstances, she would be horrified at the poverty found in her house and pour scorn on Maura's attempts at homemaking. But she need not have worried. Far from being revolted by the cottage, Maura was delighted with it.

"Oh yes! Oh, Maura. It is just perfect!" exclaimed Ellen still looking this way and that in utter fascination. "I have never dreamed of anything so lovely. I've seen nothing I like better. It is so homely. Oh, you are so lucky, Maura."

Maura reddened with delight. "I made the right decision to invite the poor soul for the night."

If truth be told Maura had never had a female friend, having been brought up by her grandmother who had not been welcomed by the previous minister of Lochmaben Kirk, which had promoted the idea locally that she was a witch. Since her grandmother had been under the protection of the Bruce family she had been able to raise her granddaughter without fear of interference, but the minister's attitude had denied Maura the opportunity to attend the church school and make friends with other girls her age. Since she lived alone now she was wary of the local girls in a way she need not have if she had been able to meet them before they grew to adulthood. As children they had been programmed to shun the shy lonely girl and as they grew to adulthood few had attempted to change the situation.

Ellen, being the daughter of a known smuggler, had suffered at bit of discrimination among the holier-than-thou brigade at Ruthwell so understood how special it was to be invited into Maura's home. So their relationship was off to a good start.

Each girl was a bit shy of the other to begin with. Ellen stood quietly in the shadows while Maura bustled about the little hut, attending to her chores. She pokered up the fire into a more active flame. She lit a spill from a jar on the hearth, using it light the sheep fat dip lamps, which sent shadows flickering around the room, giving it a cosy appearance. Looking at the other woman, Ellen detected a sadness in her companion, which led her to believe that Maura perhaps needed a friend as much as Ellen herself did.

Eventually, their eyes met for a moment before Maura broke the spell by saying, "Let's get a bite to eat, eh?" She turned to the fire and swung the iron pot on its chain over the fire, positioning it carefully to make sure the contents heated evenly. "The best thing about living on this estate is that the gamekeepers have been told to allow the village people to trap rabbits and hares. There is an unwritten law that we do not kill the deer but if one is killed accidentally it usually makes its way into a Gypsy stewpot. Locals adhere pretty much to the rules since we have been granted many privileges for supporting the family when King Robert was on the throne. They are a family that approve of loyalty but do not take it for granted. Generally, my pot has something tasty in it even if it is a woodcock or a pigeon. You won't starve here," she stated proudly.

While the pot heated and began to produce a mouth-watering aroma Maura bent down and lifted the lid from a heavy kist that Ellen in the gloom had not previously been aware of. From its contents Maura selected two bowls and two wooden spoons, a gulley and a loaf of oat bread which she placed on the table, indicating that Ellen should share this feast.

"I can't eat your food," Ellen demurred. "I only have a few pence to my name."

"You can tell me the story of your life in payment. Like a wandering minstrel," joked Maura, but, realising that Ellen had no intention of accepting charity at the hands of her new friend, had to think quickly to come up with a plan to get Ellen to eat.

"Tonight you pay for your bed and board by relating the tale of your sweetheart and tomorrow, if you decide to stay, you can work your fingers to the bone with a pestle and mortar. Believe me, it is a treat for me to spend the dark hours with company at my hearth so you won't be beholden to me."

Ellen gave a shy smile. She felt humbled by the generosity of the other girl, coming as it did so soon after the shock that her erstwhile loving father had thrown her out and disowned her. She, who had been her father's pet, had taken his abandonment more sorely even than the heartbreak at losing Bill. She knew it would be a very long time before she forgave her father his outrageous behaviour, if she ever could.

"At least I'm convinced that Bill had no say in his disappearance and I just know in my heart that he will return," she whispered almost inaudibly but nevertheless Maura heard her and spoke her next words in a comforting tone.

"Come and eat. Remember you have not just yourself to think off and that baba inside you will be wanting its supper."

The evening passed pleasantly. Both young women relished the company of the other. They sat at the fireside long after the meal had been consumed and compared notes on their upbringing. Maura told how she had never known a mother or a father and that her grandmother had always become coy when she asked about her heritage. She was a bit sad that since her grandmother had not told her how it came about that she was living with the old woman, or even if she was her grandmother, she would not now have the chance to find out if she had any living family, with the old lady dead the last two years.

Ellen became less reticent about her situation under the skilful handling of Maura and was soon telling her sad tale to the sympathetic girl. She confided her love for Bill and her determination to have the baby and rear it until her beloved returned from the sea. She also described her work in the dairy and with the animals, letting Maura see she was not afraid of hard work.

Before they settled down for the night by the light of the flickering flames a firm bond had been forged between the girls and each was convinced that fate had taken a hand in their destiny. Ellen felt she had been blessed to have met Maura and Maura was convinced they had developed a lifelong bond as they compared their previous life experiences, sitting together cosily in the soft, luminescent glow that changed the crude lochside shanty into a magnificent haven.

****

As Ellen hurried back into the cottage that had become her home over the last weeks she was conscious that time was passing. If they were to make it in time for the weekly market in the village they would need to scurry about to gather their salves and potions. Today's market was in Lochmaben but the girls attended other markets within walking distance, even sometimes venturing further afield if there was a cart from the estate going to the cattle mart at Gretna or Dumfries, for these opportunities were too lucrative to miss. Maura's reputation as a source of cheap cures for everyday illnesses meant that she had, before the advent of Ellen, often ran out of supplies, but once Ellen had been taught the simpler recipes Maura was happy to leave them in her friend's capable hands. This gave Maura more time to deal with the more complicated requests she received.

In the weeks since the girls had become friends, Ellen had become used to making herself scarce when some of Maura's clients came calling. Maura had explained early on in their acquaintance that, as well as her expertise in simple herbal remedies and ointments to prevent chapped fingers and chilblains, she had other skills she did not advertise in the market place. Occasionally a heavily veiled presence would appear in the clearing and this was Ellen's cue to absent herself while Maura attended in private to their more challenging requirements.

At first Ellen had worried that Maura might have lied about being a witch but Maura, sensing her friend's concern, assured her that far from casting spells or turning people into toads she was consulted by women either desperate to conceive a child or, in some rare cases, those who were ardently trying to reduce their fecundity in an effort not to add to the strain of trying to feed an already overlarge family.

"It's not witchcraft you know, Ellen, it is just knowledge handed down through the centuries. Can you imagine what the first person who realised that rubbing dock leaves on the poisonous bite of a stinging nettle felt? Did he think it was witchcraft that the sting receded or did he feel pride that he had found a cure for a very irritating occurrence? You don't scorn to use a dock leaf when you have walked into a nettle bed, do you?"

"No," Ellen answered slowly as she let this idea penetrate her mind. "I suppose it is all trial and error really. Like..." and here her face lit up as if the thought had just made sense, "... like eating a raw potato, thinking it horrid and throwing it in the fire to learn that cooked it was luscious." She laughed at her analogy as it conjured up a picture in her mind of a man tossing the hot potato from hand to hand as he took bites of its soft white pulp.

Maura laughed with her and agreed, "But you need lots of experiments to make sure you use the right herbs or plants for the right disease or ailment. Raw potato that has gone green is mighty poisonous, so if your man had died because he ate the wrong potato we would not have them in our diet. Foxglove root is another example. It is often used to make the heart beat stronger but if used on the wrong heart condition it slows the heart down and causes death. That's where centuries of knowledge, passed down from mother to daughter, or in my case granddaughter, is so important. Granny told me it must not be used when the heart beats slowly. It's the same thing really with the women who come to me for help to have children. The easiest is women who get with child but keep miscarrying. A potion made of black haw leaves or powdered cramp bark will settle down the baba and let it grow till it is ready to be born. There is not a perfect way to prevent a baba sticking if it has already been started, but rosemary leaves sometimes works or thistle tea will often stop it starting. A woman might come to me the day after she has been with her man and an infusion of smart weed leaves drunk every day mostly brings on her monthlies, so washes any chance of a baba away."

Seeing the surprise on Ellen's face, Maura continued, "Put yourself in the position of a roadman's wife with six children to feed on the pittance he earns as a day labourer. She lives in fear of having another nine months traipsing about her chores with the bairns crying around her, to say nothing of the swollen ankles and swollen belly, only to have the baba die of starvation because she is too weak to make milk to feed it. The minister, of course, would tell her it is her duty to lie with her husband," she growled through gritted teeth. "He would; he's a man. Can you honestly say I should turn my back on her when a few herbs will ease her suffering? She can make her own peace with the Lord when she gets to heaven.

"I don't deal with things I don't know about. There is plenty of hemlock in the woods and Queen Anne's lace is rampant but I don't know how to use them without harm so my potions are always harmless. I follow where Granny led. She was a wise woman and living on the estate of the Bruce's was able to practise her talents openly, unlike many of her kind who were harassed by villagers and blamed for every cow that died or child that threw out a rash. I benefit from Granny's reputation and the fact that she was always sent for when My Lady Margaret was ill. What is good enough for those at the castle is good enough for the village."

Although Ellen, eagerly awaiting the arrival of her baby, was not sure where her conscience sat on this matter, she decided on the route of least resistance and the subject was never raised again.

As Ellen slipped through the cottage door Maura grabbed her hat and her basket of unguents and tonics and, ushering Ellen back out of the door, chastised her. "We don't have time to stop with your gadding about when we've work to do. Come on. We can catch up on the walk to the market." Eying her companion she said cheekily, ignoring Ellen's attempt to explain it was the other girl who had held them back, "Well, waddle in your case. That baba will be here before you are much older, my girl." Becoming serious as she took in the height of Ellen's bump and her tired face she continued, "Why don't you give the market a miss? Spend the day resting on your pallet."

"No, I'm as fit as a flea. In fact, I'm full of energy and raring to go. I can barely keep my legs from running ahead like a bairn," Ellen chuckled in reply.

Recognising this energetic rush as sign that the birthing would not be long away, Maura decided it would be better to have Ellen with her and active. There was no need to worry yet and the exercise would perhaps relieve the first labour pains, so the two women bustled off onto the lochside tract that led to the village. They had to hurry a bit in order to be in the market in time to make the best of their sales before the crowds dispersed.

Later that morning Maura had no time to worry about her companion as she was inundated with farm labourers' wives looking for the ointment to relieve their swollen joints and to treat the painful hacks that manifested themselves on their poor husband's hands as soon as the weather turned colder. Even the farmers' wives did not disdain to benefit from Maura's unguents.

"I have my granny's receipt that she handed down to my mother but it is not as effective as yours," bemoaned a rotund wifie as she looked up at Maura, hopeful of a hint at the secret ingredient. "My Jim says it is a penny well spent when I return with this," she laughed as she indicated the large jar she had just purchased, "and ye ken whit a snatch farthin' he is."

Maura smiled at her customer. She knew that the woman would no doubt be making her own ointment with the dripping from the mutton cooked in most farmhouses that was saved up for the winter months when red, chapped fingers were rife and almost everyone suffered from chilblains on both hands and feet. There was very little difference between their salve and Maura's. She had learned from her grandmother to use the crushed seeds of the yellow daisy that relieved the pain of the tight skin to enhance the mutton tallow or lanolin that she extracted from sheep's fleece. This, when rubbed on to painful swollen joints softened the skin, which in turn made it less taut and with the addition of the roots made it all less painful. There was no way for anyone who worked the land to escape these minor ailments as they constantly used their hands in all weathers. Since she made a good living by not disclosing her secrets she kept her knowledge carefully to herself.

As Maura dealt with her regular customers Ellen was unable to stay put, so she wandered off through the farm stalls, smiling and passing pleasant comments back and forth. Ellen took this walk most weeks since it had increased their simples business as those who had to mind the stalls often missed the chance to buy a physic from Maura's stock and, by carrying their requirements to them, Ellen felt she was making a contribution to the household.

At first she had been shy about bartering her wares but, when she brought this up with Maura, she explained, "A bit of butter or cheese is naught to a farmer's wife, or a couple of eggs. They don't miss them but butter and cheese would never grace my table if I didn't barter what cost me little for what they value little."

Ellen was not so sure. Having been able in the dairy she imagined the making of butter and cheese as using up leftover milk so had little idea what a valuable commodity dairy products were to those who had no means of making their own. The farmer's wives, whom she bartered with, placed little value on their butter and cheese, so, like Ellen, they felt that they were getting the better of the bargain. When Ellen aired this opinion, Maura laughed and explained that it was a very even deal. "It costs me nothing but my time to make these potions and lotions that are so much sought after by the farming community. I could not come to market and buy cheese or butter or eggs or milk; the farmers' wives for the most part don't know enough about herbs to be confident of not poisoning their family, so it's a fair deal. Neither of us has to spend precious groats on what makes us both happy."

"So when I'm offered food for a physic, I look cowed and accept," grinned Ellen.

"Yes, the secret is to always let them think they are shrewd housewives carefully preserving their husband's hard-earned money and, God forbid, if any of their family have a fever or a wound festers they will send for me instead of the doctor, who always needs coin, and farmers don't like to part with their coins. It's just good business."

Ellen proceeded through the market making sales as she went. As the unguents and tonics changed hands so her basket got heavier. She stopped for a moment, passing the basket from one side to the other to relieve a stitch she had become aware of, but the movement of the weight did not alleviate the stabbing pain in her side. Placing the basket on the ground between her feet Ellen stretched her hands backwards placing them in the small of her back and stretched to ease her muscles. The pain disappeared but, deciding she needed to sit and rest for a while before attempting the walk back to the cottage by the loch, she hurried off to find Maura. Just as she had the other woman in her sight she again felt the sharp pain in her side and back. It quite took her breath away and she stopped short, breathing shallow so as not to increase the pain.

Maura, having witnessed the movements of her friend and having been alerted earlier in the day, had no doubt that it was time and more to return to the cottage and prepare for the advent of the baby. Cutting short her transaction with a young woman, where she had been admiring the handsome little boy whose mother always though him ailing, thus was a good customer for tonics for her offspring, she hurried to Ellen's side, took the basket from her whispering, "It's time we returned or the young one will be born in the middle of the market for all to gawk at."

Ellen, who hadn't associated the pains she was experiencing with the coming of the baby, was aghast at the idea and was all for running out of the market square as fast as possible. The fear on her face as she envisioned giving birth here and now made Maura smile. She remained calm, hoping to instil confidence in Ellen.

"You have time and to spare to get home and have some warm ale to buoy you up for the birthing to come. We will dander home just stopping when the pain halts you and you will see how easily you give birth to your baba." Maura made a motion with her hand to indicate that giving birth was an easy matter. Indeed, she had little fear for Ellen. She had attended many births with her grandmother and a good few now by herself. People couldn't afford to have a doctor unless there was a problem and the goodwife who practised both midwifery and the laying out of the dead, was often too drunk to worry about which chore she carried out. It had become the practise, although frowned on by the medical profession, to call on Maura's calm, sensible knowledge since she had gained a reputation for easing the suffering of labour.

The two young women wended their way home along the lochside, stopping when Ellen's pains were at their peak to allow her to breathe through the onset of her labour. Maura kept her calmly talking of what they would eat and drink when they arrived home and how they would set about preparing for the baby. Weeks ago Maura had used her influence with the estate bailiff to beg a broken feed trough they had come across on one of their foraging expeditions that, with minor adjustments undertaken by the master of the hounds, would do duty as a cradle. Ellen's petticoat had to be sacrificed to make a gown for the coming infant and Maura had donated some of her wool stash from which she obtained lanolin for her unguent. With instruction from Maura, Ellen was able to tease the fragments of fleece gathered from the moors and hedgerows into a yarn from which she had knitted a warm jacket and a blanket for the cradle. This exercise had given the girls many nights of laughter as the inept Ellen struggled to spin and knit. The first attempt at a blanket was so full of holes the women were only able to laugh and start again, but finally a soft cosy blanket was the culmination of her effort.

On arrival at the cottage Maura settled Ellen on a chair at the table while she pokered up the fire and thrust the iron rod into the heart of the embers. While it was stuck there heating she measured some ale into a mug, added a pinch of this and a few leaves of that, regretting she had no moonflower dust this early in the year, then taking the glowing poker from the fire plunged it into the ale. A sweet smell arose from the mug which she placed in front of Ellen. She was confident that the ale with its additions would ease the prolonged pains to come.

"Drink it up now while its warm," she urged Ellen who was riding yet another wave of pain. "Soon we will need to get you into position but first I would like just to check all is well."

Grateful for the help of her friend, Ellen swallowed the last of the ale and allowed herself to be lowered onto the bed where Maura drew up her skirt and examined her taut belly, well pleased with the progress being made by the impatient child.

"You'll need to take off your skirt and drawers. You can keep on your stockings for warmth meantime if you like, but as your time gets near you will find them too hot so it might be just as well to take them off at once."

As she was helped to undress Ellen remembered that she had the purse that contained Bill's ring tied to her undergarment, but just as she was about to grab it to hide it in her blouse another pain gripped her, ripping all thoughts other than the sheer agony that engulfed her from her mind. As she rode the wave of pain she allowed Maura to gently remove the rest of her clothing, taking the precious keepsake along with her clothes. Maura quickly tossed the garments from her in order to free her hands to help support the labouring woman. With all modesty gone in the urgency of the moment, Ellen, buoyed up by Maura, walked round and round the table, resting occasionally between the pains. For several hours the pains grew stronger and more frequent with Maura encouraging her friend by talking about the baby to come, how exciting it would be to have a baby in their home; how delighted Bill would be when he came home to find his family; all this in a calming, reassuring voice that kept Ellen's mind off the searing pains. Later, and thanking God for the support and ministrations of her friend, Ellen let out a squeal when she was taken by surprise at the nature of the pain becoming more persistent. Maura held another mug of her concoction to her lips, urging her to drink deep.

"For it won't be long now. Drink as much as you can. It will ease the pain of the baba's passage."

Clutching at the mug Ellen emptied the contents in greedy gulps, hoping it would indeed make the birthing easier.

"If only I had not lain with Bill," she moaned. "I don't want to have a baby. Make it go away!" she screamed; then, caught by another pain, focused her attention on Maura's voice.

"Everyone thinks they cannot do it at this stage but the birth is very near and you must do as I say and we will have that baba here in the cradle before you know it."

So saying Maura took Ellen's weight on her strong brown arms and, turning her towards her, got them both into a squatting position on the floor.

"Shouldn't I lie down?" puzzled Ellen, who had only a very vague idea of how childbirth happened, but anyone she had heard of having a child had done so in bed.

"No," came the answer. "It is much easier for the babe to come straight. It may not be a dignified position but take my word Ellen love, it will be less painful."

Ellen's stomach became very taut and she could no longer hold in the terrific grunt that escaped her as her lungs emptied. Gritting her teeth against the pain she felt the baby move to the entrance of her body.

"You are doing a grand job. Now, every time you feel the urge to shit you have to push as hard as you can to help the little bugger out," laughed Maura, trying to keep a lid on the other woman's emotions.

"Maybe I should have given her the second dose of herbs earlier," she thought to herself, but realising there was no more she could do now to relieve the pain she concentrated on the imminent arrival.

"After all she will forget the pain once she has the little one in her arms. Granny always said the sight of the baba was the best painkiller of all."

The pains were coming thick and fast and Maura had to support herself with her back to the wall in order to keep the labouring woman in the optimal position. Ellen's nails dug into her forearms, causing her to grimace as she struggled to push the baby out of her body. Maura could see that Ellen's legs were unable to support her as they trembled under the strain of maintaining the squatting position, indicating to her that if the baby were not delivered soon she would need to rethink the situation.

From her cramped position on the floor Maura could now see the top of the baby's head and she breathed a sigh of relief. She smiled at Ellen in encouragement, telling her she was close to the end and to bear up.

"One more big push with the next pain and it will be over," she chivvied her. Ellen's face was bright red and running with sweat as she gave one colossal heave and an animal grunt as the baby's head freed itself from her body.

Prising Ellen's clawing hands from her wrists Maura repositioned her so that she was able to support herself while Maura caught the head and manipulated the shoulders out of Ellen's birth passage. Still quietly encouraging, she informed Ellen that with the next push the baby would be in her arms.

Shivering and shaking with the effort of supporting her exhausted body on her frail arms, Ellen nodded her understanding and with the next pain the little body of the babe was delivered into Maura's competent hands. Just as she was reaching for the gulley to cut the umbilical cord, which she had immediately tied with string, a loud wail echoed round the cottage proclaiming the presence of the new baby girl.

Quickly wrapping the baby in an old towel to keep her warm until she could be washed, Maura handed the crying infant to her exhausted mother, whose eyes lit up at the sight as she clamped the tiny creature to her bosom.

"Just let's get rid of the afterbirth, then we will get you settled," said a beaming Maura, but Ellen was in a world of her own, having neither sight nor hearing for anything but the wonder of her new infant. She did however obey Maura's instructions and the afterbirth was soon dealt with and when Maura was happy there would be no haemorrhage she reluctantly allowed her friend to relieve her of her precious bundle and made herself comfortable on the straw pallet, where she immediately held out her arms to encompass her pretty little baby. So enthralled was she by the advent of a female babe, for she had been sure the baby would be a boy and the image of his father, that she paid no attention to anything else that was taking place in the room.

After washing herself down in a pail of water just warm from its position adjacent to the fire, Maura started to tidy up the tiny dishevelled room, removing all the evidence of the upheaval of childbirth. Wrapping the afterbirth in a piece of sacking that she had used to clean up the blood and detritus of the birth and depositing it near the door for future burial, she then gathered Ellen's discarded garments from the floor where they had fallen in the throes of labour and noticed a discrepancy in the weight of her shift. Glancing at mother and daughter, oblivious to all activity outside their own private kingdom, Maura discovered the purse tied to the shift and peered inside. Her eyes opened wide in amazement and she gasped loud enough to drag Ellen's gaze towards her. She took in Maura's shocked expression and realised that the other woman had found the ruby ring so long hidden in her clothes.

"I imagine you didn't steal this or you wouldn't have been here having your baba. This is what made you so sure that Bill will come back to you?"

"Yes. This is the inheritance for his sons and for their sons and their sons. Bill told me it brings luck to the Campbells so I cannot use it to keep the babe or me. I know that keeping it safe will keep Bill safe wherever he is and whatever he is doing."

Maura was a bit disgruntled that Ellen had kept this secret from her. "Did she think I would steal it from her?" she thought before saying out loud, "Or we could just sell it and live happily for the rest of our lives."

The colour drained from Ellen's already pale cheeks as she looked at her friend, not knowing how or what to say to make her understand that the ring could not be sold.

However, Maura's good nature soon reasserted itself and she handed the ruby back to Ellen saying in a gruff voice, "Here, put it away…" The rest of her sentence was lost as Ellen gave an almighty groan, almost doubling over in agony. Maura was immediately alert.

"Oh my God, it hurts so much," breathed Ellen, looking much shocked by the resumption of the pain she had so recently been delivered from.

"Here, take the babe. I must get up or I will mess the bed," but before she could get herself into an upright position she was again seized by the dreadful pain.

For a moment Maura stood motionless as her thoughts flew in every direction to find a reason for this unusual pattern. The answer burst upon her and she laughed out loud. Ellen glared at her from the bed.

"It's no laughing matter. I need to shit, quickly!" she squealed holding her stomach.

"No, you don't. How could I have missed it? I don't know, but I reckon you are having another baba.

"Twins!" she exclaimed as Maura nodded at her before setting about the whole process of childbirth once more. This time the actual birthing was much easier as the earlier baby had opened the passage for the subsequent child to slip through. Again Ellen squatted on her, by now much weakened legs, but with Maura's support and encouragement it was not long before she was able to see her second child. There was little to choose between them in looks. Each had a tuft of auburn red hair on their little round heads and, when they were settled each side of their mother, it could be seen they shared a strong chin that augured ill for peace in future years. The little creatures enchanted both women.

"Not a third one I hope?" joked Maura as Ellen winced as she tried to shift position without letting go of her precious bundles.

"No, my perfect children." Ellen looked from one to the other with pride shining on her face. "Sarah and John. How I wish their father was here beside me at this moment." She sighed sadly.

"Bill said the ruby ring brought luck to the Campbells, and he left it here with you to bring luck to your twins. He'll be back to claim you; all three of you," prophesied Maura.

Chapter Nineteen

"Peggy, will you stop moping about the kitchen? You only have yourself to blame that you are not sitting at your own fireside watching your bairns play at your feet."

Peggy gritted her teeth for this was not the first time her mother had chastised her for not going out with her sister.

"It's not even the first time today," thought Peggy morosely. She agreed she could have been courting or indeed, as her mother suggested, married and settled with her own babies, but Peggy could not forget her first love and deep inside her no one compared to Alec Irvine. It made it hard to explain why she rejected every man who came to court her, for neither of her parents had known about her romance with Alec and did not connect her rebuff of all suitors to his prolonged absence.

"And I have no intention of telling Ma for she plagues me enough without knowing why I don't entertain any of the local lads. I'll just hold ma wheest." She smiled to herself as she thought how her mother used her favourite phrase when she was not getting her own way. "She's a grandmother, but she surely can nag!"

It had long been known in the community that Alec and her brother Bill had been seized by the press gang some seven years earlier. The family had been expecting the boys' return for over a year, but, since it was believed they were now on a man o' war, it was unlikely they would return until the war with France was ended. It had been in progress now for about eight years and although Peggy's love for Alec had not waned with the passage of time, she was beginning to believe he had either been killed or had decided not to come back to her. Both families had been devastated when the news of the young men having been impressed broke but, as time had gone on, they had accepted the loss and got on with their lives, however Peggy had not been able to reconcile herself to the absence of her beloved. At first her parents had put her lethargy down to missing her elder sibling, for they had been very close all her life, but seven years on she showed no more sign of getting her life together than she had at the time. Her mother, who liked to believe she knew what her children were thinking and could solve all their problems, if only they would tell them to her, had become really concerned for her daughter.

"It's true I can see no physical problem for she works harder than ever, taking on many of Amy's chores while she goes of gallivanting around the countryside like she is today." Sarah took a moment from worrying about Peggy to review her concerns on the score of her younger daughter. She often commented that Amy was a flighty piece, but Peggy always reassured her that Amy had a wise head on her shoulders and was simply enjoying being young.

"Let her have her fun while she can. Time enough for her to become responsible when she marries and has her own home to see to. It's good to be young and carefree," she sighed, reminiscently.

"Humph!" her mother replied. "There's no need for you to talk as if your young days were well in the past. You're not an old maid yet but you will be if you don't watch out; there will be no young men asking you to walk out on a Sunday afternoon." She turned away realising she had said too much. Again.

"I know I shouldn't nag her but she fair gets on ma goat when she answers a nice lad's offer of an outing with a 'No, thank you very much' just as if he had asked her if she wanted milk in her tea."

While Sarah continued to consider the different personalities of her daughters a rare spark of amusement came over her face. "Here I am worried that one won't go out and the other won't stay in!" she laughed at the incongruity as she appreciated the worry over the girls was nothing compared to the very grave concern she felt for her oldest son and the guilt that plagued her every waking moment for having turned Ellen Irvine from her door with bitter words.

"If only I knew where she is now," she thought for the umpteenth time since that fatal day when Ellen had revealed her condition. "And a Campbell grandbaby too. I'm that ashamed of myself."

Just as she tried to chivvy Peggy into encouraging a beau, so George tried to encourage his wife to forgive herself for her harsh words and actions.

"You were so upset by Bill's disappearance that you did not know what you were saying. You cannot blame yourself forever, Sarah, my darling. Have you not tried to find her? How many times have you been to Meadow Farm to be turned away by Andy Irvine?" were the arguments George used in an attempt to alleviate his wife's guilt. He, himself, had been hard pushed not to take his fist to the stubborn smuggler who had cast off his own flesh and blood and no matter what arguments George put forward, Andy had stood firm. "If he knows where that lass is he's not saying for I'm sure he knows if I had an inkling where she is I would go and fetch her back and that would not suit Mr High and Mighty Irvine's dignity," he thought with anger. "God forbid it should happen to my lass, but as sure as eggs is eggs she would not be abandoned just because of a few titters in the Kirk."

But Sarah could not be made to absolve herself and kept her guilt warm by constantly recalling her disgust, "And disgust is not too strong a word for my behaviour to that young lass." And as each day followed day, her spirits got lower and lower until she was as she was today, terrified that when her son returned he would spurn her.

"For how can I ever face my son again when I have all but called his child a bastard and neglected to show compassion to his sweetheart?"

Her thoughts had now run along their normal path and she returned to reality, bringing her gaze back to Peggy who had been washing up at the pump and looking out over the lane as she dreamed her dreams. When Sarah looked in her direction she was stunned. The daughter who had been standing in the kitchen a moment ago was gone and in her place was a different woman. A woman with a glowing countenance as if illuminated from the inside. Her normal 'couldn't care less' posture gone, to be replaced by a straight-backed, shoulders-set alert body, but the greatest change Sarah noticed was that where there had been downcast features there now was a look of pure joy and a huge grinning smile. Sarah stood gob smacked for a minute quite taken aback by the sudden change.

"What...?" she began, but, before she could get her sentence out, Peggy was off out the door with apron flying and drying cloth discarded she was running across the stockyard and down the lane as if the hounds of Hell were chasing her.

As she followed more slowly into the stockyard she could just make out Peggy throwing herself into the arms of a broad dark-haired man but at that distance Sarah could not make out his features. She tutted to herself at the wayward conduct of her normally sedate daughter, quite forgetting that only a few minutes ago she had been castigating Peggy for not walking out with any of the local youths.

"But who can it be?" she mused. "I don't recognise him."

Suddenly, as the two men came closer and her eyesight was not so strained, her heart thumped in her throat. She could swear it had stopped for a beat; she identified the other man, who was now being hugged and kissed by Peggy. The excited girl placed herself between the two men and holding an arm of each as if to ensure they didn't escape she skipped with exuberance back into the stockyard, turning every now and then as if to satisfy herself that she was not dreaming and gave each arm a squeeze to establish they were flesh and blood and not figments of her imagination.

All colour had fled from Sarah's cheeks as her legs wobbled and she landed in a heap by the kitchen door from where Bill picked her up and, enclosing her in his strong arms, hugged his mother until she protested.

"Oh my Billy, my Billy," sobbed Sarah as she cradled his tousled head in the crook of her arm just as she had done when he was her first born, new born son. "I'm so sorry Billy! Forgive me! I've tried to find them, honestly I have. Your father will tell you! I didn't mean to be unkind! Oh Billy, is it really you?"

Sarah had no idea what the words were that were flying from her brain to her mouth, but Bill, listening to her staccato sentences was able to get the gist of her meaning. Quickly understanding that his long-held hope of finding Ellen and his child safely ensconced in the heart of his family was unfounded he tried to hide his disappointment, realising that the competent healthy-looking mother he had joked with on his way out of the kitchen on that fateful night seven years ago had been replaced with a grey-haired, sallow-skinned old woman whose dark rimmed eyes explained more than any words how much anguish she had been undergone in the intervening years.

"Ma," he whispered quietly to her, both of them ignoring the delight of the reunited lovers who were so engrossed in each other that they paid no attention to what was going on around them. "It's good to be home, Ma."

He helped his mother rise to her feet but her legs would not hold her. Bill took her weight in his immense arms and gently placed her in a seat by the hearth.

"But you've been unwell?" he questioned "You look ill and you barely weigh as much as a fairy child." His concern for the health of his parent made him blind to the further anguish that passed over Sarah's face before she took control of herself and, grasping his cheeks in her red work roughened hands, pulled his face towards her own, surprising him with a smacking kiss.

"I'm glad to see you home as well, Billy. Just let me look at you for a minute, because when you know what I've done, what a disservice I've done you, you won't want to own me for a mother. I'm that ashamed of myself."

"Leave it, Ma!" came a sharp voice from the doorway where Peggy was standing encircled by Alec Irvine's brawny arms. "Just let's be glad these boys are here and alive. Recriminations can wait till later!"

Bill looked up at the sharp tone of his sister's voice and was astounded to realise she was sending warning glances at him.

"Aren't I the hero of the hour?" he thought, a bit disgruntled, but continued out loud, "I expect the fatted calf. You know that's what greets the prodigal son." He laughed into his mother's face.

Catching his sister's eye, the siblings recaptured the intimacy of their youth and a crooked half smile quirked the corner of Bill's mouth as he acknowledged his sensible sister's desire to keep the homecoming on a light note for the time being.

"Later," mouthed Peg and just as they had when they were children they combined their efforts into changing the atmosphere by taking their conversation in another direction.

From her place by the fire Sarah was able to take in the scene and for the first time since seeing Peggy gallop off out of the kitchen she was aware that here was the reason for Peggy's disdain of all social functions and invitations from men. In the space of ten minutes her dour, spinster daughter appeared to have lost years of her age. It wasn't just the physical difference that made the transformation but it seemed to Sarah that Peggy had become a woman, a woman confident in her love for her man and his for her.

As she took in the radiant vision before her she stuttered, "Peggy, why? You never said. I would have understood."

"Would you, Ma? Alec and I didn't tell you years ago of our love for each other because you know you never had a good word to say for any of the Irvines. But I'm telling you now, and I've no wish to hurt you for I love you dearly, I will not be parted again from this darling man."

As she finished her defiant speech she felt Alec's arm tighten around her waist and, twisting her neck up to take in his beloved face, she beamed at him.

"And so I warn you too, Alec Irvine," she laughed.

Having successfully diverted her mother's attention from her guilt at Bill not finding Ellen and his child at the farmhouse, Peggy drew Alec into the kitchen, pulled out a chair at the table and invited him to take a seat with a gesture of her hand and nodded to her brother saying, "You'll still know how to find your place at this table, long time though it be you've been missing from it. Now tell us where you have been and what you have been up to while we have been pining away with worry for you both."

Peggy wanted to give her mother some time just to wallow in the return of her darling boy before they got onto the more painful subject of Ellen.

"We have been fighting for King and country, but since we were sailors we had a wife in every port. I'm not sure I will want to settle down with just one woman," teased Alec, but hurriedly changed the subject as he saw Peggy's face cloud over.

"Honestly it wasn't much fun. We were pressed as you know so we had no clothes but those we stood up in, but after lots of hard work and many battles at sea we have both come home with enough money to set us up. So I'll be able to keep you in new frocks, never fear."

"The worst bit was at Trafalgar, when the ship was being fired on from all angles and we were firing from both sides of the ship. The noise was awful and the blood just washed everywhere with every roll of the ship. I spent hours spreading sand on the floor so that we didn't slip on the blood while we were priming the guns."

"I can't imagine what it must have been like. The broadsheets are full of Nelson's praise but such a lot of men died. It was agony not knowing if you were dead or alive," said Peggy.

"Aye, and all good brave men who died, both at sea and on land. This has been a bloody war. In one day we lost all our other messmates when a shot hit the hull and splinters flew everywhere. I'm not talking about wee slithers that we would get in our fingers chopping logs but pointed missiles two or three feet long," said Bill quietly, thinking back to his friends Mac and Dingo who had died in this way.

"With all the noise from the cannon and the smoke from the guns and men running here and there in the dark. Oh, that blasted hellhole of a gun deck where you think the hosts of Hell are chasing you; you can't see where you are, where your friends are, worst of all where the shot that will kill you is coming from," reminisced Bill

"But there were better times. We played with the enemy fleet in Cadiz, holding them in place so they could not get out to regroup and there was a lot of prize money to be gained from capturing their ships. The Spanish merchant fleet were the best, for they carried lots of goods and gold."

"I'll say this for the Navy. They may have forced us on board and worked us like slaves with no redress against ill treatment, but every man Jack of us was paid our wages and our prize money and shipmate looked after shipmate," continued Alec, slanting a glance at Bill who answered the unspoken question with a slight shake of his head.

The kitchen door opened and Peter and his father came in, not at first recognising the men seated at the table.

"Fine thing when a father doesn't recognise his son when he's only been away for a few years," laughed Bill, getting up to embrace his father.

"Oh, what a surprise, but lad it's great to see your face." He scanned his son from head to toe, noting that he still had all his limbs, then once more encompassed him in his arms as the tears trickled down his cheeks. Bill noticed that, like his mother, his father had aged since he had seen him last. In the seven years since he had been away his parents seemed to have become old.

"And this must be Peter," said Bill turning to his brother with his hand out to shake the other's. "I don't think I would have known you if you hadn't been standing in this kitchen. Are you the farmer now?"

Peter blushed but answered, "You've been away a long time and Faither needed me, but you needn't worry; there's plenty room for all of us," he added quickly, not wanting his big brother, whom he had idolised as a child, to think he wasn't welcome back on the farm.

George had quietly placed himself behind Sarah's chair and gently touched her shoulders. She raised one hand and grasped that of her husband's and felt a new surge take over her body. She spoke for the first time since the men had started to tell the story of their travels.

"I think we need to have some supper. Georgie, have you got a wee drop of something ben the house?"

"No need to worry about that, Pa. Me and Alec have brought a drop of the hard stuff in our sea bags and with Ma's cooking, which I have to say I've been dreaming of since we were paid off, we will have something of a celebration."

As the family gathered round the table Bill looked at the happy faces of his parents and brothers and sisters, especially Peggy as she held hands with Alec, his heart lurched in his chest for his Ellen was missing.

"But I'll find her if it takes me till the end of my days."

****

The Reunion.

"Just one more push and you'll be holding the wee darling in your arms," encouraged Ellen from her cramped position between the legs of the crouching woman.

"Take my hand and squeeze tight," added the soothing voice of the girl sitting at the opposite end to where her mother was busy carrying out her duties to the labouring woman. She took a cloth and, rinsing it out in a basin of cold water, wiped tenderly at the woman's sweating face and neck. "Not be long now," she glanced at her mother for confirmation and received a bright smile from her in return.

As the woman put all her effort into the next push Ellen was soon holding the tiny infant up for the other two to see. "A fine wee lad, Mary. Just a quick cuddle then Sarah will wrap him up while I see to the afterbirth." She handed the new babe to his mother and felt the lump in her throat as she always did when she witnessed the coming of a new life.

Mary, the wife of a ploughman on the estate, was delighted with her son and kissed and stroked his tiny fingers before grudgingly handing him over to the midwife's daughter but, as Ellen went about the business of cleaning up the exhausted woman, she noticed that Mary did not take her eyes off her newborn son. Sarah carefully cleaned the remnants of the birth from the babe's tiny body and cooed at him as she gently wrapped him up in the cosy shawl that had been warming by the fire for his triumphant arrival and laid him in the cradle, lovingly carved by his father, standing, just for a minute, hovering over it as if she were the mother herself.

Although not quite seven years old, Sarah was a great help to her mother and Ellen was justifiably proud of the calm way she had about her that, despite both her young age and diminutive build, somehow inveigled mothers into feeling confident in her presence. She sat back on her heels and watched Sarah swing the kettle off the whirlie and pour the contents into a teapot, which she then sat on the hearth to brew while she gathered cups from the huge oak sideboard that took up the whole of one wall of the cottage.

"By she's a bonny bairn," she thought to herself as she took in the almost invisible eyebrows above the shining green eyes with the pert nose and beautifully shaped lips, all set in the translucent skin that often accompanies the deep red hair that framed her face. She was skinny but remarkably strong and wiry. "She'll break hearts will my Sarah," she thought as she rose to her feet, and helping Mary sit up in bed, handed her a cup of restorative tea before accepting one for herself from Sarah.

The three sat sipping at the tea while the babe recovered from his ordeal by falling instantly and deeply asleep.

Ellen laughed, saying, "Take it while it is going, for when that lad realises he has a doting Mam, who will answer his every squawk, there will not be much rest for you. Have you and Col got a name for him?"

"I think we will call him William for his grandfather, Col's father you know. My da will be disappointed he's not called for him as is the way but it's not likely Wull will live long enough to see a second child called for him and he has been such a help to us."

Ellen nodded, remembering that Wull McCormick was one of the few people Maura supplied with her special mixture of herbs and roots to keep away the pains that attacked his whole body from the wasting disease it was unlikely he would recover from.

"He'll be mad keen to see this wee man though and so will Col. What a surprise when he gets back from market to see you have gone ahead and had the wean on your own." She cast a glance over the babe in the cradle and estimated that he had not been born too early despite both Maura and her predicting he would not arrive for another six weeks. "You never can tell with babies especially the lads, they come when they're ready," she thought, remembering another market day when Sarah and her twin had been born unexpectedly.

There had not been any conscious decision that Sarah would become her mother's helper, indeed, Ellen often felt that she had stolen the girl's childhood by allowing her to accompany her on her midwifery visits. It came about quite accidentally when Sarah had just had her fifth birthday and had been enjoying a rare quiet few hours alone with Ellen, since John had gone off with Maura while she gathered her herbs.

Sarah was the quieter of the twins, never making any attempt to outshine her brother who was always striving to get and keep his mother's attention so that Ellen was happy when John, as usual full of energy, elected to accompany 'Auntie Maura' on a foraging expedition. Mother and daughter had been engaged in household chores, chatting back and forward, Ellen listening to her daughter ramble on as she did not do when John and Maura were present. Ellen loved these times when they were together because she was more able to see the personality of her quiet child.

"Never were twins so different," she had mused. "John, a rapscallion bundle of energy, sturdy and strong, he could be taken for Sarah's older brother. Every bit of them opposite to the other; John's nature demanding and loud, full of laughter, with little care for anything other than his stomach; where Sarah with her quieter more thoughtful demeanour is always the peacemaker. Even in looks, although, obviously siblings, their individual features are at variance; Sarah, fair-skinned and ginger-haired, John's darker auburn hair matching his more bronzed skin tone. The only feature they have in common is their eyes; both have those lovely mossy green eyes, but where Sarah's are light and sparkling, John's are a deeper more hazel colour. But always my darling children," thought Ellen, giving herself a shake.

Whenever Ellen compared the children in looks her heart was broken, for despite the individual features being so grossly dissimilar, they both resembled their father, whom Ellen, despite the intervening years, was convinced would turn up one day to claim his family.

While mother and daughter were spending the afternoon together a frantic knocking had been heard on the door. Answering it, Ellen realised that she must hurry to the aid of one of the estate worker's daughters who, whilst visiting her father, had started with her baby several weeks before it was due. The agitated father told Ellen to bring Sarah with her since she could not be left alone in the cottage. The girl, Pearl by name, was panicking and as she rushed upstairs to tend to her she had assumed Sarah would stay in the kitchen with Pearl's father, but some time into the labour Ellen noticed that Pearl had become much calmer. When she looked up from her task, she felt shocked to see her daughter holding Pearl's hand while she supported the girl on her shoulder, talking ten to the dozen of what it would be like to see the baby and how all Pearl had to think of was to follow her Ma's directions, for wasn't she the best person ever at delivering babies?

Whatever might have been the outcome if Pearl had continued to behave irrationally and ignored the instructions of the midwife could only be guessed at, but the quiet belief in her mother's ability that Sarah exuded had won the day and the delivery of the tiny baby girl soon took place. Pearl was delighted with her child, anxious to have her in her arms as Ellen tidied up the evidence of the birth, settled the new mother and handed her the precious bundle. Just as the two were taking stock of each other for the first time the door had opened and in came Sarah, carefully carrying a cup of tea. Ellen could not help laughing at the concentration on her child's face; the tip of her tongue sticking out the corner of her mouth as she endeavoured not to spill the liquid. Handing over the welcome cup of tea she had asked shyly to look at the baby and when Pearl pulled away the shawl from the newborn's face Sarah stood transfixed in wonder at the miracle her mother had performed.

Ellen was shortly able to leave Pearl in the kind hands of a neighbour and walk slowly back home with her own daughter. Sarah's eyes gleamed as she spoke of the recent experience. She bombarded her mother with questions on childbirth. "Does it hurt a lot? Why does the baby need help? What do you do to make the baby come?

Can I do that?" The questions left her mouth as fast as they could get from her brain to her lips. Sometimes Ellen took a breath to answer a question, but Sarah's rapid thought process had produced yet another question.

No one brought up in the country could be unaware of the miracle of nature, but it appeared to Ellen that in that mean cottage on the side of the loch Sarah had found her vocation and, from that day to this, she had been unable to deny her daughter's wish to accompany her on her visits to labouring women. She had so much belief that all would be well that Ellen began to believe that Sarah's intuition was infallible and, if her daughter was with her, she was relaxed and better able to help with the births.

When Mary's husband returned and was in control of mother and baby, and having agreed to call in on his mother and deliver the news about the new babe on the way home, Ellen and Sarah left the cottage hoping to arrive home in time to prepare the main meal for Maura and John when they also arrived back from their expedition. After the arrival of the twins Ellen was afraid she would soon outstay her welcome in Maura's home. The shack, for really that was all it could have been called, was not big enough for the two women never mind the addition of two babies and Ellen was conscious that her children were not quiet. Surprisingly it had been Sarah who had been the more demanding baby as she cried constantly if not in her mother's arms. John was a more placid babe requiring only to be clean, warm and with a full tummy to make him a contented child, and so he naturally became more attached to Maura, who loved him every bit as much as did his mother, while Ellen nurtured the more fractious child. Ellen wondered if that was why John craved her attention now. "Is there some part of his being that feels he was deprived early on? Without realising it did he feel deprived in some way? Is that what caused him to change his nature? It's as if as they grew up they had swapped personality, John, the more demanding and Sarah, my quiet angel."

Since moving into Maura's tiny hut and, after the birth of John and Sarah showed the women the necessity, they had enlarged their living space. Looking at the cottage from the outside it still resembled a sheep pen with a roof, but with both of them making and selling simples and sharing the work of laying out the dead and delivering the babies in the area over the years, they had been able to gather stone and pay a little money to some of the men on the estate to build two more rooms onto the hut. They now had a room devoted to the herbs and plants that Maura used for her potions and tonics, with a tall cabinet to store her medicaments. The original room became the kitchen and the other a bedroom for the children. When more funds were available they planned to build on another bedroom but, with two growing children to feed and clothe, Ellen wondered when this might be. Despite constant assurance from Maura that she was happy to share in the family atmosphere, something she had not experienced as a child, Ellen still felt she was taking advantage of Maura's good nature.

"She has given me so much. She works so hard and helps so much with the children. All I've given her is a share of raising my monsters." She worried about the situation from time to time but as a general rule, even as the children were less dependent, she did not have time for much soul searching. Even when lying alone in her bed she had time for little else but planning the next day's chores. However, just occasionally her thoughts would turn to her darling Bill and what he would think of his children. Being a pretty woman she had had many admirers and she was touched by offers she had received from a few men over the years to marry her and bring up her children as their own. There had naturally been offers of a very different type and both Maura and she had to steer clear of those who tried to take advantage of two pretty women living as they did. She admitted to herself that she did miss the physical side of love, but could not bring herself to cast Bill from her heart.

"Oh, how I miss you Bill," she whispered to the sky.

****

"Johnny, Johnny, hey! Over here!" yelled Jack Brown as he waved his arms vigorously in the air to attract the attention of his friend. "Come and join us. Have you got your marbles?"

John looked over to where his friend was standing with a number of other boys on a piece of scrubby land off the side of the market square. He waved and smiled before turning to his companion and saying in a wheedling voice, "Can I go, Auntie Maura?"

Maura smiled down and, looking into his imploring eyes, tousled his hair, saying, "Go on, then. I'll be around the market if you need me, or," she said trying to keep a straight face, "or if you get hungry." She gave him a playful push in the direction of his friends knowing that his voracious appetite would guide him back to her in good time for their departure home. In actual fact she was pleased to see that John had friends and made them easily. It never failed to amaze her that these children of Ellen's were not shunned by the villagers as she had been as a child. They lived in the same house she had done and were supported only by women as she had with her grandmother, she and Ellen carried out the same profession as her granny but no careful mother ever pulled her child close and told them to keep away from the twins.

"Is it that they are twins? Is it that they are pretty and friendly? Have people finally decided I'm not a witch?" She had no idea what the reason but she was delighted that as soon as John put his nose into the town the boys wanted to play with him. "And it's good for him to have friends his own age. They both spend too much time with Ellen and I." She sighed and, with only one backward glance to see John was settled at his game, went off to her preferred spot to do business.

"Your Mama is gone off. Get your marbles out," Jack called. He had seven round clay balls in his filthy hand. He had dug the hole in the ground that was to be the target for the marbles with his fingers and would later get a slap on the ear from his mother for getting dirty, but just now that punishment was far from his thoughts.

John dug deep in his pocket and brought out a rag. It was supposed to do duty as a handkerchief but John found it more useful to tie his treasures in it. He had one beautiful marble that he had won from one of the sons of the estate owner and he was very proud of this. Most of the other boys had roughly made balls of clay that had been baked by the fire, and he had a few of those himself made from the red clay on the banks of the castle loch, but his favourite was about twice the size and made of glass. Bruce, from whom he had won it, told him it was made by the glassblower in Newcastle who had used up the spare coloured glass left at the end of the day to make paperweights and marbles. When John held it up to the light it sparkled like a diamond and the twists of coloured glass inside it looked like multicoloured tadpoles swimming in clear water. This marble and the other boys' desire to win it from him was what was making him such a popular opponent today, but John was not about to risk his treasure and wrapped it back up in his rag and played with the same marbles as everyone else. He was very good at the game, often managing to throw his marble right into the target and winning his opponent's marble, but they had decided not to play 'keepsie' so when the game ended they would all keep their marbles... unless... anyone could persuade John to a match with his glass bool. That was worth risking a keepsie game!

The boys soon tired of playing their game and wandered off to see if there was any chance of earning a farthing or an apple or even a drink of milk. These boys whose parents had fed and dressed them in warm clothing that morning had no idea how these same boys could portray themselves as starving urchins to any farmer's wife who might look at the woebegone faces of the lads and feel sorry for their starvation.

As the boys skipped from stall to stall, often running an errand here or packing eggs for a farm maid in boxes with straw to keep them safe or any other chore that seemed likely to produce sustenance, they had been spotted by a man walking through the market. For some reason his eyes landed on John and he felt a strange jolt of recognition at the sight of him.

Bill had been scouring the country for months now, asking at every farmhouse or alehouse but had not found Ellen. At first he had gone to Hill End and spoken to Andy Irvine but got no clue to her whereabouts from her father.

"If you find that whore of a daughter of mine, you can tell her from me that she had better not show her face anywhere near Powfoot for I'll not have her shaming me with her bastard."

"As soon as I find Ellen we will be married, as we would have if I had not been pressed. I knew she was having a baby and I am sorely sorry that she was left to bear the pain herself, but I will make it up to her, sir."

"Sir, sir is it?" Andy sneered at Bill. "Don't come crawling around my farm thinking you can sweet talk me with your nonsense."

"I am sorry to have called you such, for while I was serving in the Navy I learned to call my betters 'sir', and you're right, it was wrong of me to give you that title. Good day to you." Bill turned and stormed off out of the stack yard and over the field gate in the direction of home. As he was striding through the copse he heard his name being called and he turned to find Ellen's sister, Christina, puffing towards him with a red hue to her cheeks.

"My Teen, you have grown up since I saw you last," smiled Bill his heart beginning to beat a tattoo in his chest. "Surely she wouldn't have followed me if she didn't know where Ellen is," he thought.

Teen bent forward with her hands on her knees to get her breath back before explaining, "I had to run all the way round so that Faither didn't see me come after you. Ma said to tell you that she had heard from someone at Church that Ellen had been seen in the markets around the county. The thing is she has been looking herself as often as she can get away but, you see, she can only go when Faither is away, for he will not have Ellen's name mentioned."

"What market was she seen at?" asked Bill quickly.

"That's just it. We don't know. The woman who told Ma had heard it from someone who had heard it from someone else who had heard it from someone else again. Over the last few years Ma has been round every market from here to Gretna but she could be anywhere." She went on, "Ma says if you find her you are to tell her to wait till Faither is off on a trip to the Isle of Mann then come to her and to bring the bairn."

Bill answered, "I'll find her, never fear. I have a lot to make up to her. I just hope she is well for I'll never forgive myself if any harm has come to her."

"Bill?" Teen said quietly, obviously discomfited by what she was about to say, "Ma said you should bear in mind that she might have married in all the time you have been away and she hopes you won't blame her if she has."

Bill looked through Teen as if she didn't exist and whispered, "Married? I never thought. Of course, any man would jump at marrying Ellen. Oh, my God, what have I done?" He stood transfixed for some moments as his muddled brain tried to assimilate this new and tragic notion, then as if realising that Teen had put herself in some jeopardy by coming after him, he thanked her and told her to hurry home before her father missed her.

As she turned to retrace her steps, Teen stopped for a moment further to give Bill encouragement. "Ma said to warn you, and I have but…" Her apparent distress found its way through Bill's discordant thoughts as she paused before continuing, "She won't have married anyone else, Bill, for she loved you truly."

Embarrassed to have given this hero of her childhood her opinion, she reddened, then took off for all the world as if she were a deer startled by a stalker.

Tears filled Bill's eyes as he renewed his vow to find Ellen.

Today, Bill had walked round the market stalls laid out under the tower in the centre of Lochmaben village on the lookout for Ellen. He had been visiting the weekly markets in the county but he knew it was only luck that would find him in the right place at the right time.

"If only I still had the lucky ruby," he thought, "but it's better with Ellen if it really does carry the luck of the Campbells." He was standing leaning against a wall idly scanning the movement of the market and smoking a cheroot. It was nothing compared to the perique from his navy days but, although an expensive extravagance, one he was unable to stop, he felt it kept him calm. His eyes rested on a group of tykes rushing from stall to stall and something about the look of one of the boys made him straighten up and pay attention.

"He looks just like Peter did when he was a wee lad," he thought, screwing up his eyes the better to focus on the boy's features. "Same hair, same build and a very crooked smile. I wonder." He started to walk toward the boys but suddenly, for no reason Bill could see, the boys all shot off in different directions. Jack came bowling towards him and Bill moved directly into his path so that the boy stopped short, right in front of him.

"Hello," said Bill

Jack made no answer but hung his head. This was his default position, always assuming if an adult wanted to speak to him it was because he had done something he shouldn't have. He peeped up at the hulk of a man in front of him.

"What's your name, lad? I'm Bill and I want some information from you."

"I don't know nuffing," said a sullen Jack.

"Those boys you were with. Do you know their names?"

"Some."

"Go on then."

"Pete, Jimmy, Johnny, Pat, Freddy. We didn't do anything wrong, mister."

"Do they come with their fathers to the market? Are they farm boys?"

"Naw, none of them are from farms. Freddy's da is the butcher, Jimmy's a roadman, Pete hasn't got a da and neither does Johnny."

"Where do Pete and Johnny come from?"

"Pete's ma lives up at the cemetery with her da. Pete's da died last year. He was buried in the cemetery. Imagine living with your da buried in the garden. Spooky."

"And Johnny?"

"His ma comes to the market. I see'd her often with her baskets of lotions and stuff. Ma buys ointment for our chilblains from her. In the winter that is."

"Do you know where he lives? Is it in the village?"

Jack shrugged his shoulders. "They came in by the Church this morning but I don't know where he lives. We play together when he comes with his ma." He thought for a moment taking in Bill's height and tanned skin. "He looks a bit like you, mister. Are you his da?"

"I don't know, Jack. How old is he?"

Again Jack shrugged his shoulders. "'Bout my age, I think."

Bill laughed asking, "And how old is that?"

"I'm seven."

Bill's stomach turned over with the thought that this Johnny could be his son. And what a son! A lad to be proud of.

"Where do you think he will be just now?"

"He went off to find his ma and get ready to go home. He said he didn't want to miss his dinner. And mister? I don't want to miss mine."

Pulling a penny out of his pocket, Bill tossed it to the boy, saying, "You are one smart lad. Work hard and you will be rich one day."

Jack could hardly believe his luck but grabbing the penny and stowing it in his pocket he rushed off to see what his mother was putting on the plate for his dinner.

Bill hurriedly walked around the market again looking for the lad. He had seen one woman selling ointments and herbs but it certainly wasn't Ellen. Would there be enough business for two such women in the market?

He was disappointed for it seemed that wherever the food was to be delivered to Johnny, it was not at the market. Farmers were collecting their carts and their wives and if Bill didn't make a move soon there would be no one to ask about the simples seller. He looked around him and selected a pleasant-faced middle-aged woman and approached her.

"Excuse me, ma'am. I wonder if you could tell me where to find the woman who sells the ointment for chilblains. I seem to have missed her," he asked politely. Like all handsome men, he knew how to get to the heart of the ladies.

"You're never needing chilblain ointment at this time of year." She laughed at him, much taken with his good looks and courteous manners.

"My nana likes to be in front of herself and she'll send me off with a ringing ear if I don't bring her what she asks for," he answered, sacrificing his grandmother in his cause.

The woman looked around her and said that he had just missed her for she had been here not ten minutes since. "But she will be back next week for sure."

"Do you know where I might find her, to save my ears from ringing?" He gave his crooked grin.

"I don't know exactly where her house is but it's close to the castle loch on the Bruce estate. If you're set on finding her I would cut down the left-hand side of the church and follow that road until you see the entrance to the castle. I don't know her name but any of the estate workers will tell you where to find her. She is quite famous for her treatments. She's not a witch, mind," she finished.

Bill thanked her and with a smile went off as she had directed. He was breathless with excitement. "Will I find my Ellen today? Is Johnny my son?" Then, more despondently; "Is Ellen married?"

"No, if it is her, my friend Jake said Johnny had no da."

"Sarah, can you put the plates on the table? I'm going to dish up the dinner. No, John. Wash your hands. No buts, wash," instructed Ellen as John, as usual, tried to sit at the table without washing his muddy hands.

"Maura, come and eat while it's hot," called Ellen through to Maura who was in the herb room. She came into the kitchen sniffing the aroma from the stewpot.

"Mmm, smells good. Your mother may not be much use at mixing herbs for physics but she surely knows how to use them in the kitchen," she teased the children who already had plates of the thick meat and vegetables in front of them. They all bowed their heads and thanked the Lord for providing them with their dinner and, just as Sarah had lifted her spoon to her mouth, they heard a knock at the door. It was common for people to come looking for the women. Maura was often called on to relieve the suffering of the sick and, as time had gone on, Ellen had taken on more of the midwifery of the area so they were not surprised.

"Always at meal times," said Maura, rolling her eyes in her head. "See who it is, will you Sarah, while I grab a quick bite?"

Sarah slipped off her stool and went to the door where she saw a tall man standing in front of her.

"Peg?" he gasped before recollecting himself. "I'm sorry to disturb you but is your mother at home?"

"Ma," she called over her shoulder. "There's a man looking for you."

Ellen rose from the table and came to the door with a smile on her face expecting it to be an anxious father wanting her to tend to his wife, but she went white when she looked at the tall man standing there with the sun shining behind him, dazzling her so that she did not believe what she was seeing.

"Hello, Ellen. It's taken me a long time to find you."

"Bill! Oh Bill, is it really you?"

They stood staring at each other for a few seconds, each taking in the other until they were interrupted by John asking belligerently, "Who is it, Ma? What does he want?"

"Bill, this is John, your son." She pulled John into the crook of her arm.

"But the wee lass called you Ma! Have you married and had another bairn?" His voice quavered with emotion. Had he found her only to lose her again?

Ellen took in his disappointed face and said laughing. "No, Bill, Sarah is my eldest child and your daughter and this scamp," she again cuddled John into her side with a quick squeeze, "is her twin, John."

"Twins?"

"Twins."

Chapter Twenty

Back to the Studio

"You see Bill had handed on the ruby before the children were even born and it lay quietly in the pouch for over sixty years keeping the family from calamity. No one gave it more than a passing thought except, of course, whenever a disaster had been averted this shining bauble took the credit. As you have heard, despite the horrendous conditions and all the perils of the sea Bill came home not much scarred by his time away. Perhaps he was a better man because of it."

Mark, much to his relief, had thought of a question.

"Are you a supporter of the National Service then? Would you be for the amendment if it was brought to the vote, now that you are in the House of Lords?" he queried

Lord John Campbell kept a serious and thoughtful expression on his face as he weighed up the words he was about to voice. It was a habit that had stood him in good stead. He wondered if he might have been foolish to have shared so much of his family history but, in the words of Magnus Magnusson, "I've started, so I'll finish."

"I will say here that I am not in favour of any forced labour, like with the sex slaves imported and bound to an avaricious man; it was called pimping in my day, and illegal, but that's for another day. I am in favour of everybody working and contributing to the wealth of the country, not to an elite class."

"Lord Campbell, is that a roundabout way of saying that you, the great socialist, would scrap our benefits system and encourage free enterprise?" Even to Mark this seemed a ridiculous question to ask of the former reformer.

"Read your Bible Mark. The man who spent his gold had none, the man who buried his gold only had what he had saved, but the man who spread his bread upon the water, metaphorically you understand, had it returned threefold. In simple terms:

1.   "You have to spend money to make money and
2.   "If you shared the World's wealth equally amongst the population tomorrow, by Friday most of the money would be in the hands of only a few people.

"What I am in favour of is full employment for all because I believe that idleness is what creates dissent. It gives people time to ponder on life and naturally as human beings we want what others have. Humans are greedy and single-minded. 'I'll take what I want and if it hurts you, so what.' *That* I think is what causes war. Oh, we call them Holy Wars or Righteous Wars, have done for hundreds of years, but is that just an excuse to take what another has?

"That is the attitude of today's generation right enough, but I wonder if you have any thoughts of that approach being the fault of the last generation for spoiling their children because they have lived through the austerity of World War II?" was Mark's next query.

"At this late stage in my life I doubt there is anything new either in life or in politics. I've said before, I'm sure I have, that everything has a fashion. If you look at the miniskirt in the 1960s; that was a reaction to the more straight-laced era that predated it and the after effects of war. If you look at the furore that my noble friends across the House make about immigration in the twenty-first century from Europe and the Dominions and how it equates to unrest among Britons born in this country, which too has been 'in' before."

"So you won't be standing up in the House and asking for our borders to be closed and all our unemployed sent into the forces?" was Mark's follow-on question.

"Not this year at any rate, but if there were to be a war I would certainly be in favour of conscription; there you see, that is another fashion that comes and goes. If you look at the lives of my ancestors in the turbulent borders, in times of national need they rallied to the banner but when the country, and therefore the Borders, were at peace much industry took place because men, and women too, for I'm no sexist, need a purpose."

He grinned at Mark, who responded, "That just might be the only thing you've not been accused of over your long career."

Smiling, Big Jock went on, "Men and women need to be active so in times of peace, when they are not thinking of weapons of mass destruction, they are creating new technology. So it was when young Victoria was on the throne and again by coincidence, or fashion, when we had her, however many times great, granddaughter Elizabeth II ruling our fair land."

"So far you have told us a gory tale of your ancestors and I don't know if the audience agree," he waited for the reaction which didn't come, since all the watchers wanted was to listen to the remainder of Lord John's fascinating tale, "but it seems to me to be the women who have been the backbone of the family caring for the farms and the children while their husbands went off on wild, dangerous exploits of their own."

"The Borders were a wild and dangerous place to be at certain times in its history but when there was no war or cattle rustling to contend with they applied their brains in other directions. When Bill came back from the navy a few years after Trafalgar, he came home to a country very different to the one he had left. The people had had their fill of war and the useless destruction of life that it carried with it. Men, certainly the men in my family, took back control of everyday life and, with no vicious intent, tried to force their womenfolk back into their inferior role, but – and there is always a but – women were not content to be pushed into a shape they had broken out of. They were beginning to rebel against society's treatment of them as mere chattels, so they were ready to break the chains that bound them and had kept them as much enslaved as any negro dragged across the Atlantic. When a pretty young queen came to the throne obliging all the great statesmen to bow to her bidding, women were ripe for emancipation; to put it in today's vernacular, the young women in the eighteen fifties said 'I'll have some of that'."

This last drew a ripple of laughter over the studio and Mark was a bit annoyed, since the reaction to Lord John's jest was better than his. He tried to hide his frustration but he realised that he was well out of his depth; he had no prior knowledge from which he could frame questions. Actually, he admitted, his presence in the studio was unnecessary and he reluctantly tipped his hat to the master orator.

"Where does your story go from here or have we heard the life and times of the ruby ring?

"As I was saying, there was peace in the Borders, the reivers and the smugglers had almost completely lost their trade with the advent of new tax laws. It just wasn't viable to import on the sly, so the versatile Borderers turned their minds to invention. In the 1800s, there were great strides in invention. To be fair the whole country was rife with new ideas. Lister had discovered antiseptics, Dunlop rubber, Fleming anaesthetics, Watt the steam engine; but we Scots take much more pride in the achievements of our own local heroes. In Lowland Scotland, Kirkpatrick McMillan had invented a bicycle, the ports at Annan and Newbie were heavily involved in the building of tea clippers and since they were bringing a bit of money to the ordinary man the Reverend Henry Duncan from Ruthwell had started a savings bank. There were many more inventions but not all were to the good of the general workforce," started Lord John.

However, as he took a breath, Mark chipped in with, "Invention of machines could only be good for the working class surely, for it would decrease the hard labour in many industries."

"In a way that's correct," responded Big Jock, "and some did increase the job market in the early years; the railway, for instance, was hard manual labour and there was plenty of it about to build the tracks and the engines, but when they were built it only took a fraction of these men to maintain and drive the steam engines. Lots of men learnt lots of skills when building the ships and clippers but, if no one wanted to buy a ship, they too were surplus to requirement,"

"But surely there would still be work in the Borders where it is predominantly agricultural based?" frowned Mark.

"Yes, there was some mechanisation on the farm, but for the most part farming was pretty immune to change; it is seasonal work and for many years depended on migrant labour, usually from Ireland or Romany Gypsies both happy to work, when the harvest was due, for lesser pay than the now redundant Scots, so tempers run high."

"So that was the political climate of the time, but what has it do with your story? Where does the lucky ruby surface next?" Mark tried to jolly Big Jock along and get him back on track, but he would only get to the end of his saga at his own pace.

"Times were changing." Big Jock stopped and thought about what he had said. "I've said that a few times now and I begin to think it is a sign because the next recipient was a woman. Gasp. Horror." He grinned out into the audience and exchanged a wink with his wife, still sitting passively just out of Mark's eyeline.

"Now you've really got me going. Lord Campbell, the clue is in the name. If the ruby started to go down the female line how does it still sit on the finger of a Campbell?"

"Ah well, times they are a-changing," sang Big Jock out of tune. "It was like this…"

Chapter Twenty-One

Sal

"Ma, I'm off to Aunt Sarah's," came the breathless shout from Sal as she careered down the farmhouse stairs, and before her mother could form a word of protest the door had slammed behind her flying heels.

"That girl will be the death of me," said Liza with a grim smile. "She spends more time with your sister than she does at home."

John lifted his eyes to look at his pretty buxom wife and answered in his usual fashion, "Leave the lass be. She'll come to no harm with Sarah. She loves our Sally as if she were her own."

"That's not the point, Jake. You know I want her to settle down here, perhaps marry a nice lad and give us grandbairns but the ideas your Sarah puts into her head makes her think she is too good to be a farmer's wife." She argued for perhaps the hundredth time but, even as she said the words, she knew she would get no support from her husband, for in his eyes his twin could do no wrong.

Realising that he had upset his wife by his words he laid down his paper and, removing his small round eyeglasses, tried to placate her with his words. "She's just young, Liz, let her explore a bit. No good will come of pushing her in the direction she doesn't want to go. Not everyone meets their Prince when they are bairns at the Sunday school like you did." He finished with his fascinating grin, knowing that despite their years together Liza was still susceptible to his charm.

They had been married for over twenty years. They had been peaceful years and they had both grown a bit complacent. Liza's once jet-black hair that John had revelled in as it hung straight and glossy down her back had turned to grey and she had lost her trim figure to childbirth, but she was still his pretty sweetheart. "Even if her tongue has gained a hint of vinegar over the years," he smiled to himself, then grinned as his thought expanded. "I'm not the handsome lad she married either; her hair might be grey but at least she has some, unlike me." It was true that the years had not been kind to John Campbell. The inclement weather of the Borders was unrelenting and, since his work involved being out of doors no matter what the weather (sheep and cows needed to be fed and cared for, no matter if the sun was bursting out of the sky or the snow six feet deep in drifts), he had aged much more than his wife. He often joked, as his hairline receded in proportion to the broadening of his girth, that it was either worrying about 'his girls' or the wearing of his 'bunnet' that had made him an old man before his time.

He may have joked about living with so many women being the cause of his aging but his health was not good either. His constantly pale, translucent skin, a result of succumbing to frequent bouts of the new disease, bronchitis the doctor called it, but what his knowledgeable sister called phthisis, made him appear ready to meet his maker; and there was no doubt that John spent a lot of his time worrying what would happen to 'his girls' when a bout eventually carried him away.

"There's not a lad to carry on with the farm and how will they keep themselves without it?" he often pondered this issue, always coming up with the same answer. "I'll just have to make sure I live until they are all grown up and able to care for their mother."

He smiled his winning smile at Liza who, unable to resist, smiled back. She would not allow him to know how much she worried about his health.

Liz heaved a sigh, knowing there was no use trying to persuade him to ask his sister to spend less time with her eldest niece for, although Sal went to visit her aunt in her cottage on the edge of Rammerscales Estate, she also naturally gravitated to her grandparents' farmhouse at nearby Hightae, where Sarah was more often than not found when not engaged on a case for Dr Wilson.

"Maybe John's right and I should just let her get this nursing thing out of her system, but what will happen to the farm if my girls don't marry?"

Liza looked slowly round her warm kitchen and realised how much she would miss this cosy, homely farmhouse if she had to leave it. When she and John had moved in, the place had been uninhabited for several years and in a state of decay but, as young newlyweds, she and John had worked all the hours they could spare away from their acres in rebuilding and modernising the farmhouse. She was particularly pleased with her kitchen sink which John and his father had installed and she remembered how she had been so proud of her running water that she had stood for an hour just turning the flow on and off. They had various conveniences now in their house, many the result of John's smuggling exploits which he had carried out clandestinely with his Uncle Alec. She again cast her eyes round the room taking in the horsehair sofa, the table with its seven high-backed wooden chairs set around it; the range with its ovens and hot plates; the cabinet against the wall where she displayed her delft plates and cups; her pride and joy, the timepiece ticking softly on the mantelpiece, the only audible sound at this moment in the peaceful room. Her eye lastly landed on her husband who was sitting near the stove with his stockinged feet stretched out to the heat, enjoying a well-earned rest after his week's exertions.

Her face softened momentarily until she realised that he was engaged in filling his clay pipe with his stinking tobacco mix. She had watched this ritual often. John took his worn leather pouch from his waistcoat pocket and, cutting off a piece of his stick of black tarry tobacco, began to chop it up in the palm of his left hand with his penknife. This process could take some minutes, for John had explained to her that for the pipe to give the utmost pleasure preparation of the tobacco was the key. When the tobacco had been shredded to the correct consistency John packed it into the bowl of his clay pipe, took it out and repacked it until he was satisfied with the distribution, took a few exploratory drags on the stem end and then, when satisfied all was as it should be, he took a long spill of tightly rolled-up newspaper from the pot in the hearth and with it lit the tobacco. The consistency of the substance made it hard to light and many attempts were made before the pipe began to billow smoke from its bowl. Cupping his right hand over the smouldering substance he began to draw the smoke into his lungs and blow it out again through the side of his mouth. As Liza watched her husband's shoulders relax in front of her she refrained from nagging at him about his unsavoury habit.

"What good would it do to stop the wee bit of pleasure he has? Sarah is always telling him to stop it because it is not good for him, but he thinks it makes his chest better and I think maybe he is right." She glanced over at her husband as he took a long suck of the smoke into his lungs and began to cough. He became quite blue in the face and Liza had to stop herself from grabbing the pipe away from him but, having seen this often, she simply handed him a piece of newspaper into which he spat trails of stringy mucous, rolled up the paper and threw it through the open range door into the fire where she could hear it sizzle with the heat.

"Ah, that's better," John rested his head on the embroidered antimacassar on the back of his chair, stretched his feet out on the rag rug, crossed his ankles, shut his eyes and looked the picture of contentment with the cloud of smoke hovering above his head. A contented man.

****

"Has it come, Aunt Sarah?" were the first words out of Sal's mouth as she knocked and entered her aunt's cottage.

"Hello to you too," laughed Sarah Campbell, giving a little jump at the precipitous entry of her niece. "Can't a woman get a minute's peace to rest her weary legs?" she scolded, looking over her half spectacles at her visitor.

Sal came over to her aunt's chair bending down to kiss her affectionately on the cheek. Her aunt responded with a loving pat on her rear end followed by a quick squeeze at her waist. Sal's visits were the highlight of her life because, in Sal, Sarah saw herself as a young woman; identifying in her niece the nearest thing she would ever have to a daughter and a heartfelt belief that the compassionate youngster had the nature to follow in her footsteps. At the very least she hoped she would care for those less well off than herself, for despite her eagerness to learn of disease and nursing, Sarah knew that Liza had earmarked her daughter for marriage and the saving of the farm. Liza's fear of destitution if her husband's illness led to his premature death appeared to Sarah, his loving sister, to be mercenary while at the same time she acknowledged that Liza had her family to think of as well as her husband. This thought naturally raised the image of her twin to her mind allowing a sad look to overtake her features, which Sal interpreted as her aunt being annoyed at her boisterous entrance.

"Sorry, Aunt Sarah. I ran all the way hoping you had received the book. I'm that excited!"

Sarah pushed herself up from her chair and leaned over to place the kettle over the fire which burned brightly in the hearth. She walked over to the corner cupboard from which she took a small wooden tea caddy and a biscuit tin. Placing these on the table she opened the door into her pantry bringing out a can full of milk. She dipped a small ladle into the can and put the milk into a jug which she immediately covered with a crocheted cover to stop any dirt getting into the milk. Sal watched, realising she would get nothing out of her aunt until the niceties of tea making had been concluded. Making tea in Sarah's cottage was very different from that in the farmhouse for Sarah believed that the cause of illness could be transmitted in food even if you could not see what was causing it.

When Sal had explained her aunt's theory to her mother she had been angry, turning on her daughter and exclaiming, "Is Sarah Campbell telling me my kitchen isn't clean? The cheek of her! Who does she think she is? The madam!"

"No, no, Ma. She has spent a long time with Dr Jardine and he believes that the things that cause disease are living things, so small we can't see them, that live on or eat food and that if we keep food clean it will stop disease," her flustered daughter tried to placate her.

"So now it's my food that isn't clean?" she continued, getting more upset by the minute.

Sal wished that she had kept Sarah's preventive methods to herself. On her way home, she had been visualising the changes that could be made in the kitchen at home, so that, by the time that she burst in through the door, her words just bubbled out without thought as to how her mother would take them. She chastised herself: "I should have known better than talk to Ma about anything Aunt Sarah says for she really has a bee in her bonnet about her. I will be careful in future."

So Sal had said no more on Sarah's theories and kept any description of her visits to the tidy cottage to mundane matters that did not upset her mother. As she sat at the table waiting impatiently for her aunt to prepare the tea and get to the object of her visit she took in the appearance of her father's twin. "She doesn't look nearly as old as Pa and her hair still has only the odd streak of grey, like silver threads scattered among the gold, although scraped back and pinned off her face as it is you would think it would make her look older," she mused. "I don't think I've ever seen Aunt Sarah dressed in anything but her striped print dresses and button boots. I suppose that's because she has to always be ready to go to a 'case' at short notice." Just for a moment she let her thoughts wander to what it must be like to nurse the ill gentlemen and women in the big houses round about, for Sarah was much in demand and recommended by Drs Jardine and Wilson whenever careful nursing was required. Her reputation as a midwife gave her a standing in the community, those in the village and cottages around placing her on a level with the doctors who frequently asked her advice on matters to do with childbirth.

Sal was brought out of her reverie by a thump on the table which made her jump. She looked up to see her aunt smiling genially at her and catching her eye, nodded at the tome she had deposited on the table by her niece's place.

"You'll need to stop that daydreaming if you are going to be a nurse," she grinned. "First rule of the job is to be alert at all times for changes in your patient's condition." She pulled out a chair at the opposite side of the table and watched as Sal pulled the book towards her reverently. "*Buchanan's Domestic Medicine*," she breathed, lifting the book and sniffing the new smell of paper and print before gently opening it randomly at a page with gruesome pictures. "Oh!" she ejaculated slamming the book shut and pushing it away from her. "Oh, that's horrible, Aunt Sarah."

Sarah laughed, taking the book and leafing through it herself. "I admit there are some pretty graphic pictures in this but they look even worse in the flesh. You have to become immune to the sight of festering sores *and* the smell of putrid wounds. If you can't look at them in the book how will you be able to deal with them in real life?" she cautioned Sal. "There is no glamour in nursing the sick. The jobs you get are much worse than those of a scullery maid or even a day labourer."

"But you work in all the gentlemen's houses, birthing their bairns, caring for their children when they have a fever, tending them when they are dying. Surely you don't have to deal with sights such as these?" she wondered aloud.

"Illness does not just touch the rich, Sal. The poor in our area fare much worse for they have no money to make illness more comfortable, although, to be fair, the rich men have their trails too. Many have stinking, festering ulcers, or overburdened hearts from carrying too much weight; granted these conditions are usually from too rich food and an excess of brandy, but nevertheless, their pain and suffering is no less severe. Money does not buy them a cure any more than it does a poor man. It's true I have worked in all the big houses round about and I am paid well, but when a poor man comes to my door to ask for aid for his wife or his bairns I cannot refuse to help because they cannot pay. You must recognise the need to give comfort to whoever may be in need of it. Nurses in this country are not thought well off, many think of our sisterhood as little better than harlots."

Sal was shocked by this revelation and wondered if Sarah was making it up to turn her against her chosen vocation. Her mother had a very low opinion of Sarah's work. In fact, she had a low opinion of anything about Sarah. Sal had often heard her mother rage at her father.

"She's unnatural. What kind of woman spends her time cleaning up the shit and piss of a man she's not married to? What type of creature is she to prefer to tend the lousy and scabbed Irish immigrant bairns rather than marry a man and have his children like any sane woman? Mark my words, John Campbell, that sister of yours will be living in that new looney bin up the Bankend Road before she's done. It's not normal and I don't want Sal to turn out like her."

"Is that how others think about Aunt Sarah?" she thought as she idly stretched out her hand and retrieved the book which she once more began to flick through.

"Aunt Sarah?"

"Yes pet."

"Did you never want to get married? I mean, are you not lonely living here all by yourself?"

"Since I was hardly able to toddle I've wanted to help those suffering in any way I could. I suppose if you and your sisters weren't around I might have missed having children, but I have the best of both worlds. I wouldn't be able to take off to a case at any hour I'm needed if I had a man and bairns to care for. A working man would consider himself neglected if his dinner wasn't on the table or his wife left their bed in the night to aid an anguished soul. But…" she smiled across the table cheekily, "If I had found a man I cared for more than the freedom to tend my patients, I would have married him; I just never have. Sometimes I am enraged at the lot of the women I treat. They accept their husband's word as law, continuing to struggle through their chores close to death, while their menfolk rest themselves waiting to be served. I may be unnatural but I could not bow to that sort of treatment, so I've never married. Things are changing though, since we have a new young queen on the throne, and men are beginning to see women more as equal, well some men, anyway." She laughed and, looking slyly at Sal, continued, "Even women, like your mother, who want nothing more than a man to work for and a babe in the cradle every year, are starting to think that life could be a bit fairer."

Sal sat still for a few moments as she rifled the pages of the book, stopping occasionally to look at the pictures and screwing up her face.

"What kind of nurse will I make if I feel sick at the sight of illness in a book? Do you think I'm wrong to go against Ma?"

"I can't tell if you have what it takes to nurse a sick person, but I will say that when you are dealing with a particularly gruesome injury or a swollen sore oozing pus you don't really see the horrendous sight; you just feel compassion for the person who can't walk away from the stench of a gangrenous foot or must bear the pain of a chancroid eating into his flesh. I think you have what it takes but only when you have to deal with the situation do you know if you can cope. I will say, if you want to train as a nurse you will have to fight your ma and you need to know it will be worth the battle before you start the war." She smiled to lighten the mood, opened the biscuit tin and offered Sal one of her mouth-watering homemade potato farls.

"May I take this book home with me?"

"Of course you can. Have a read and then if you still think it is what you want I will come with you and talk to your ma and pa. I have a plan that I think may just work."

****

Sarah and Liz sat hunched over their cups of tea in Hartwood Farm kitchen. It had been a long night as the women had taken it in turns to sit with Bill Campbell while he struggled to fight the fever that had eventually, as the dawn was breaking on a new day, taken his life. The good sisters were, for once, of the same opinion that it had been a blessing for Bill to go to his meet his maker for he had long suffered prolonged pain from a growth in his bowels and had wasted away.

A tall young man entered the kitchen and came forward to give each woman a hug and a kiss on the cheek. "I'm really sorry about Uncle Bill. How is Aunt Ellen taking it?"

Sarah caught his arm and gave it a squeeze before answering, "We have put her to bed for a sleep. I gave her some herbal tea that will let her drift off. Thanks, Jim." She again gave his arm a quick squeeze. "You'll need to keep an eye on her after we go, if that's all right."

"Aye, fine. Aunt Ellen has always been good to me and Uncle Bill too," he added quickly, lest they think he was not sorry to see the old man die. "I'll just go and pay my respects."

As he left the kitchen, intent on his sad duty, Liz harrumphed. "Makes out he is sorry but who'll inherit the farm, I ask you? Him, no doubt. Always running about, doing every blessed thing Bill asked. Had an eye to an inheritance, if you ask me."

"He wouldn't be here if you had agreed to move into Hartwood when you got married, but oh no, not Elizabeth Dixon. You plagued Johnny into having a place of his own so that you could swan about telling all your friends in the village how much better than them you were. So don't sneer at the man who has loved Bill as if he was his own father!" snapped Sarah then burst into tears, covering her eyes with her hands and sobbing fit to burst.

She felt a hand on her arm that alerted her to her brother's presence and turned to seek comfort in his arms. "Shush, shush, you're just tired. It has been a long night and you've not slept now for weeks. Go and crawl in beside Ma and have a nap," he said gently as he stroked her hair and, lifting her head from his shoulder where it was buried, handed her his handkerchief.

Sarah, much calmer for the presence of her twin, sniffed and turned to her sister-in-law and apologized.

"Johnny's right. I'm tired and I didn't mean to snap at you. You have been good to Ma and Pa. Do you want to help me with the laying out or will I get Sal to help?"

Liza lifted her head and Sarah was truly sorry she had been short with her. Liza was a good wife to her brother and they only fought because each was jealous of how close the other was to John.

"Let Sal do it. You're right too, Sarah; I need to let her go her own way." And she smiled at her husband's twin, knowing she really had no axe to grind against her. "Maybe the laying out will change her mind".

Sarah called her niece and together they collected the requirements for the laying out before mounting the stairs to the bedroom where the soulless body of Bill Campbell lay awaiting their ministrations. Sal immediately went to close the window saying, "Brr, it's cold in here."

"Yes, close the window. I must have been too upset to do it earlier when I opened it to let his soul escape. I really should have fastened it immediately to prevent it flying back in," said Sarah as she approached her father and started to remove the top covers from his still warm body. "Are you ready to see what a body looks like? Take your time. I can wait for you for a moment or so. Just remember this is the last service you can give. This was your grandfather but you must give the same care and respect to any body, for each one is someone's dear relative."

Sal looked around herself and whispered, "It looks so spooky in here with the cold and the closed curtains and the mirrors covered. Why do we do these things? Papa loved the light and the open air."

"Custom, superstition, who knows?" shrugged Sarah, completely functioning on a professional level. "The curtains are closed as a mark of respect and will remain so until after the funeral, the mirrors are covered to prevent the soul from becoming confused and taking the wrong direction to heaven, as is the stopping of the clocks. I suppose we just keep doing it because our parents did it before us."

Sal nodded that she was ready and Sarah lowered the sheet covering the dead man's face guiding Sal through the laying-out process. First they carefully washed his body and Sal was able to see how gently her aunt dealt with her grandfather. She had one dreadful moment when the body was rolled towards her and it let out a sigh. "Aunt Sarah, he's breathing!" she squeaked in fright and stepped hurriedly away from the bed, leaving her aunt to react quickly to prevent the body from landing face first on the floor.

"Sorry, Sal," she said. "I should have warned you that moving him would release any air that was in his lungs. Are you all right or will you go and ask your ma to help me?"

"No, I'm fine. I just didn't expect it." Sal gritted her teeth, determined not to give her mother any more reason to veto her desire to be a nurse.

Sarah ran her eyes over the young girl who was chalk white and shaking. "There's no need to worry, you know; your papa wouldn't have hurt you in life, so why would he do so in death? Do we get on?"

Nodding Sal once more approached the bedside and followed Sarah's instructions. Soon they had the mortal remains shrouded in a winding sheet with his arms crossed across his body ready to be kisted when the coffin was ready. As Sarah tidied up the room she watched Sal bend over and kiss her grandfather on the cheek. "Goodbye, Papa. God rest your soul," she whispered before giving herself a shake and looking at her aunt through tear-drenched eyes.

"I'll miss him but doing this last task for him has made me even more determined to follow in your footsteps. Papa was so proud of the work you did. He always said you were a born nurse and, just maybe, it's in my blood too."

Sarah did not reply but took the girl in her arms and they clung together for several moments, each with their own thoughts of the man they had both loved. They knew that once they left this room all signs of emotion would have to be covered up as it was frowned upon to cry for the dead in public.

Over the next few days the formalities of death took over. John was reminded by the minister that because of the new law, he must go into Lockerbie and register the passing of his father, officially, at the town hall. He did this while Liza and Sarah ordered the funeral meats from the butcher and grocer. The funeral itself had been set for six days later to allow everyone in the community time to pay their respects. The women had no time to mourn, for the lykewake was a busy time for them ensuring that everyone who visited was supplied with a dram and a bit of food, but eventually the day of the burial dawned and everyone watched as the coffin was screwed down and lifted from the two chairs that had been supporting it. As the young women of the family raised the coffin for the first time, Ellen and Sarah turned the chairs upside down to make sure Bill's ghost would not be able to sit on the chair and thus miss out on his opportunity to reach heaven, then the men took over and carried the casket feet first over the threshold and off to the cemetery.

Ellen appeared to shrink before Sal's eyes as her husband's body left the farmhouse and the frail little woman watched the procession as it made its first stop to change bearers. She smiled bleakly as the men all threw a stone into the roadside as a mark of respect and she knew this would happen at every stop on the way to the churchyard.

Sal read the funeral service from the Bible and they prayed for the soul of the departed, but each knew that life had to go on and as soon as the proprieties had been observed they set about preparing the funeral feast. Sal found herself cutting boiled tongue for her grandmother, who seemed to have shrugged off her burdens as the last amen of the prayer sounded, and was now regaling Sal with tales of funeral feasts of the past as she appeared to find some relief in talking.

"When your Papa's great-grandfather died we had a seven-course meal for the whole village and surrounding areas. We cooked for a week, roasting pigs, boiling mutton, baking bread. Everyone came for a dram and a meal to celebrate him going to Heaven and I remember my nana complaining then because there was no dance after the meal." She gave a smothered giggle as she thought of her long-dead relative and her disgust that 'the auld ways' were dying out. She squinted across the table at her oldest granddaughter.

"You might not think this is the time or the place to talk about your future but I want to tell you that you should follow your heart and do what makes you happy. This is not for others to hear Sally, just between you and me, and certainly not for your mother's ears, all right?"

Sal nodded, wondering what could be so serious. Her grandmother continued with a faraway look in her eye.

"My mother and father threw me out when I was younger than you because I followed my heart and fell in love with your papa. I had no choice but to find a way to feed and rear my bairns when he was caught by the press gang and I made a living delivering other women's babies for food for mine. Your Aunt Sarah helped me from the time she was five and I see the same caring look on your face. It may not be your destiny, but, if it is, then don't let anyone stop you from following your dream." She came round the table and hugged her granddaughter before chiding her in a louder voice that indicated that intimate confessions were at an end. "Get those lazy sisters of yours in here to help butter the bread. Do they think they are ladies to sit waiting to be served?"

After the men returned from the graveyard and everyone had been fed and had toasted the life of Bill Campbell, Ellen graciously accepted the sincere condolences of her husband's contemporaries. The women had cleared up the remnants of the meal as the men has adjourned to the barn with the whisky bottles and the youngest members of the family had gone for a walk to get away from their older relatives and their reminiscences, as was natural when all were recalling the life of a much-loved patriarch; but to the youngsters the time for mourning was past and life went on as usual. The four women of the family found themselves alone in Ellen's homely kitchen, each nursing a small glass of whisky much diluted with water. Ellen was relishing her portion for she had defied custom and had her share served with hot water and sugar, which she found very much to her taste. She laughed at her daughter-in-law's face as she had watched her make this beverage and smiled across at her.

"Once a smuggler, always a smuggler. This is how the men of my family drank their whisky, as a toddy, and to be honest, how Bill and I had it after a cold night in the field at the lambing. Warms the cockles of your heart."

"What will you do now?" asked Liza.

"What do you mean?" she replied.

"Well, you won't be keeping on the farm, will you? Not with Bill gone and my John has enough to do without caring for Hartwood as well. You'll have to sell up and live with Sarah," answered Liza, ignoring the anguished look from her daughter.

"Things will go on here as they did when Bill was alive. He spoke to John about moving here years ago and he didn't want to and Sarah is content doing what she does, so I will continue to run the farm with Jim in charge and when I die, it will be his."

"But what about us? We should get half the farm. It's our right," spluttered Liza, too upset to mind her words.

"I don't see my son starving or leaving you destitute for he is a shrewd man but... No, never mind." She broke off.

"What? What were you going to say?"

"It was just a thought and I'm sure it wouldn't suit you so I'll say no more." Ellen closed her lips tightly as if to keep the words from jumping out without her permission.

"Come on, Ma," wheedled Liza. "Tell us what you are thinking about the farm."

"It was just a thought, Liz. If Sal came to live here and help me with the chores the farm could be left to her when I go, but I'm not planning on leaving for a long while yet and maybe she could help Sarah out as well when there's not much work for her here. I know you wouldn't wish to lose your eldest daughter though and none of the rest are old enough, so it wouldn't work," she said innocently.

Liza, unable to believe that she was not going to have to fight to keep the farm in the family, grasped at the opportunity. "You'll have it all settled legally, like?"

"Of course I would."

Liza looked complacently around the women, her eyes darting from one to the other to gauge their reaction to the proposition. A twinge of conscience smote her, for this was neither the time nor the place to plan the future, but she thrust these pangs aside, telling herself she must think of her family before any other consideration; if she didn't strike now Ellen may change her mind. This would be her security. It would make Sal a prize to be sought after by the young men; a farm as a dowry was not to be sneezed at. She knew she could convince John to accept the deal, even though it meant his sister was cut out of the succession, especially as Sarah showed no desire to argue her rights.

"Then I accept. Once you get things settled Sal will move over here," she stated smugly.

Ellen held up her hand. "Just a minute. Let's hear what Sal has to say. She may not want the responsibility of living here with an old woman." She turned to look at Sal who was deep in her own thoughts.

"Nana told me to follow my heart and she knows I want to nurse. Is she making it easy for me by taking me away from Ma or is this her way of thwarting my ambition? It would certainly be easier to spend time with Aunt Sarah while I'm living here." Her thoughts flew round her head until she became aware of her grandmother's gentle, kindly smile upon her and, seeing the raised eyebrow, she immediately knew that her soft, malleable granny was handling her daughter-in-law so cleverly Liza had no idea she was being manipulated by the older woman. "Clever Nana!" she thought, then, speaking out loud went on reluctantly, "I don't know Nana. I'm not much good with a butter churn and I've never used a poss tub. I might be more hindrance than help."

"You'll do exactly as your grandmother wants and that's the end of the matter. It's settled. You move in with Nana and she leaves you Hartwood."

Seeing the smile on her mother's face and realising she felt she had outwitted everyone, Sal found it difficult to keep the smile from her lips so she bent her head and murmured, "Yes, Ma."

****

"Mistress. Mammy says can you send the doctor wumman? Mammy is real sick and so are two o' the babbies. Pleeease mistress," pleaded the ragamuffin standing on the doorstep of Harwood farmhouse with dirty tracks on his cheeks where his tears had overflowed.

"Sarah isn't here and won't be today for she is up at the big house where Mrs Bell has had her bairn early and she'll bide until the wet nurse arrives tomorrow. What ails your mother?"

"She's no weel."

Sal made a quick decision and turned to tell her nana where she was off to. "I'll go and see what ails them and if I can't help I'll go for Aunt Sarah and stay with the baby so that she might help." Without waiting to hear what her grandmother though of this idea she grabbed her jacket, slipped on her boots and, taking the small boy by the hand, instructed him to lead the way.

Paulie, for that was what he called himself, told her all about his family as they trekked across the fields: he was the fourth of seven children and they lived with his father, mother, grandmother and aunt in one of the cottages down by the Annan while his father looked for work. Roger, his oldest brother who was eleven, had been taken on as a ploughboy on one of the farms, but he was the only one to be in regular work. He had been left to look after his mother and the little ones while his gran and Mary Ann had taken the other two off on the tramp to try for odd jobs in the surrounding villages and towns.

As they walked along Sal wracked her brain to think where they were staying. There were no cottages down by the river and, except for an old bothy, no buildings at all. Surely so many of them couldn't be living in the bothy but as they approached the river that is exactly where Paulie took her. Before she even entered the house, if such it could be called, she could detect the smell of human waste and damp. As she entered the building she had to wait until her eyes adjusted to the gloom, but then she was horrified by what was displayed in front of her. There were no windows or doors; a couple of pieces of old sacking had been tied together to cover the entry into the house, but it also kept in the unbearable stench. Sal gagged as the reek hit her nose; the floor was beaten earth and there were puddles of muddy water where the ground was uneven; one child was guddling in the murky water and, from the mud spattered all around his mouth and emaciated naked little body, it was clear he had been treating himself to a meal of filth. He at first seemed to be the only other human being in the place but, as Sal became a bit more used to the smell and stepped further in, she was able to make out a heap of rags lying beside a tiny fire over which hung a smoke-blackened pot. This turned out to be Paulie's mother, cuddled round her sick children.

"Hello," said Sal. "I've come to see if I can help you." She knelt down on the cold floor and felt the woman's head, which was burning hot. Her eyes were red-rimmed and Sal did not know if this was the sickness or the smoke from the fire.

She turned to Paulie saying, "You be a good lad and see if you can find me some dry sticks along the bank." Then, thinking quickly, changed her mind and said, "You are a big boy and I need you to help me to help your mammy, so you run back to the farmhouse and ask my nana for some logs from the shed and some candles and blankets and a can of milk. Can you remember that?"

"I can. I'm good at minding. But will yer nanny let me have them? Folk don't like us Irish. They chase us away from their doors."

"My nana will give you what I say if you tell her I sent you."

"Will my mammy get better?"

"I'll look after her till you come back. You've been a brave boy."

Paulie sped off to do his task while Sal turned back towards the young woman. She didn't know what to do to make her better but she surmised that she could at least make her more comfortable, so she moved the rags and gasped in disbelief as she uncovered the skeletal figure of a woman, a child of about two and a tiny baby who looked newborn. The woman's eyes appeared huge and worried and Sal touched her gently, trying to show that she meant no harm to the little family. She tenderly removed the baby from its place by its mother's side and, cradling it in the crook of her arm, peered at its fragile body in the flickering light of the fire. The baby's face looked like the porcelain doll her Uncle Alec had brought her back from one of his smuggling trips, and it was just as still. Sal realised that whatever help she might be to the mother and child, the baby had gone from this world. She looked round for somewhere to place the child but there was no furniture in the hovel, so she wrapped the mite up in a cardigan she took from the straw pallet and laid him down, away from his mother.

"Well wee one; let's have a look at you," she said as she picked up the older child who was wearing what was probably one of the older boys' shirt, for it was too big. Examining the body beneath Sal noticed many red spots covering her face and neck. The child just lay in her arms and Sal was hard put not to burst into tears. The baby was very hot and even to the untutored Sal it was obvious she had a fever. She looked around the room trying to find some basin or pot to bring water from the river, but it appeared there was only the pot over the fire that contained some kind of herbs boiling in water. So, quietly laying the tot down next to her mother she took another piece of material from the makeshift bed and, wetting it in the river, returned to sponge the child down. Having done her best, she laid her down and turned her attention to her mother.

"How much use will I be? How I wish I knew what to do to make them better. What would Aunt Sarah do?" she muttered to herself as she repeated her trip to the river and began to tend to the woman as tenderly as she had handled her child. The woman was so thin she appeared to be bones barely covered with skin; her huge red-rimmed and swollen eyes staring from a gaunt expressionless face, her lips cracked and dry. She looked up at Sal and mouthed, "The we'ans, take care o' ma babas."

Sal stretched out her hand to stroke the woman's hair away from her face and reassured her that she would do her best for the children.

"Paulie has gone off to get firewood and some milk for the babies and as soon as he is back we will get you all sorted out," she consoled, praying that she would be able to deliver what she was promising. She thought back to her book *Domestic Medicine* and thought she recognised that the family were suffering from measles. "If this is measles I can do what Ma did for me when I had measles, but how do I even give her a drink? How can we let people live like this?" she thought, but, just as she was trying to formulate, a plan the light from the doorway was blocked by a shadow that she soon realised was a man.

"Hello?" he whispered quietly. "Are you in here, Sal?" Like Sal before him, he could not believe that Paulie had brought him to the right place. This derelict bothy was not fit to keep pigs in, but it seemed that recently served as home to a family of eleven.

"Jim! How glad I am to see you, but where are the things I asked for? And I need a lot more stuff for there is nothing here to drink from or eat or sleep or anything!" She threw her arms out wide to encompass the bare room in her frustration.

"Your nana said no human should sleep in this bothy when they were well never mind when they were ill, so I've been sent to fetch you and the poor, ailing creatures up to the farmstead. By the time we get there Aunt Ellen will have worked something out. That is what I am to tell you and I don't defy her so you better do as you're told." He grinned at her and, despite her concern for the mother and child lying behind her, she smiled back.

"How will we get them to the farm though?" she lowered her voice. "The little baby is dead and the mother is not fit to sit up, never mind walk over the rough field."

"All under control. I will carry the mistress to the cart on the track and you can follow with the sick child and the mud pie over there." He nodded in the direction of the infant staring up at them from the floor. "Then I will come back for the poor dead bairn."

This plan was carried out and soon they were all being rocked from side to side down the rutted track in a high-sided cart her grandfather had used to take animals to market. The young woman looked fearful at being taken away and tried to speak to Sal, but her mouth was too sore and she so weak she could only just mutter, "Michael, tell Michael."

"Don't you worry, once we have you settled and on the mend Jim here will go and bring your husband to you. Have no fear; we will help you. Rest now and save your strength."

When they arrived at the farm Ellen had the bothy set up for the arrivals. The only resemblance to the hovel they had come from was its name. although the room was small, it was designed for three farm lads to sleep in, only it had a window and a fireplace where one of the ploughmen's wives was hurriedly setting the fire by the simple act of carrying a smoking, red-hot shovel of coals snatched from the ever-burning kitchen fire and placing it ready burning into the cold hearth.

"I've had the fire lit under the boiler too so that you will have hot water to bathe them and I'm going to bring over a pot of my potato soup and some milk for the baby but, Sal, you'll have to care for them yourself for I don't think I'm fit for it anymore," Ellen instructed.

"You've done enough Nana, but can you just say if you think they have measles? I think that is what it is but I'm not sure."

"Looks like it, and if they have all been sleeping together in that ruin they will all take it, but see to these ones now." She bustled off to find what she could to relieve the distressed family.

Sal set to with a will and in a short time she had bathed both the mother and baby and had them tucked up on a palate close to the fire. The young woman was now resplendent in a flannel nightie with the baby wrapped in a shawl left over from her father's time as a baby. When she had combed the woman's hair to tie it back off her neck Sal was horrified to find the lank hair was full of lice and nits, but she decided that was something that could wait to be tackled. She had fed the woman sips of cold water and was gratified that she could swallow despite her dry and crusted lips, for try as she would the water just trickled in and out of the baby's mouth. Sal sat by the fire for some time trying to wet the babe's mouth with a rag dipped in water and at the same time sponging its tiny body to cool the vicious rash, but eventually as the baby slept she laid her down beside her mother and turned her attention to the other two children.

"Paulie, bring your brother and follow me." With a quick glance round the room to see all was as good as it could be with her patients, she marched the boys to the granary shed where Jim had put a tin bath and, on Sal's instructions, half-filled it with warm water. Picking up the younger boy, allowing the huge threadbare garment he was wearing to fall off, she plonked him in the bath and, before he had opened his mouth to protest, was lavishly covering him in soapy bubbles while she rubbed and scrubbed to clean the engrained dirt of months without washing.

"What's his name?" she asked of Paulie as she investigated if he too was infested by lice. He was, so Sal gave his head another dosing of carbolic soap and scrubbed harder. She knew how to deal with these little beasties but also that it was a long and painstaking business to comb out every last egg. As she brought her soapy hand from the water with a louse lying on it, she caught it between two fingernails and was gratified with a click that told her she had at least one less to worry about.

"He's Paddy," came a small voice. "Miss, you won't put me in that water, will you? I'm feared." He eyed his brother's predicament with awe, being quite determined that he would fight any such an assault on his person. The fever hadn't killed him but he was sure that being plunged naked into water and scrubbed from head to foot would. He feared not only for his life, but for that of his younger sibling.

Sal did not answer him directly but turned her attention to the lad in the water, where he was becoming aware that it was a warm and comfortable place to be despite being attacked by Sal's rough cloth. "Well Paddy, I hope you are hungry for it looks like you will need to eat Paulie's share of my nana's tattie soup. You know my nana makes the best tattie soup in the county. When my sisters and I were small like you we always liked to get up here for a bowl of soup." She glanced over at Paulie to see if he was taking in the implication of not having a bath, and was delighted to see a worried look on his face. She hoisted Paddy out of the bath, wrapped him round in a huge towel and began to rub his arms and legs vigorously. Keeping him wrapped up warmly she combed his hair off his face and was surprised to see that the dirty tyke had been transformed by soap and water into a cherub. There were no clothes small enough for the lad so, soon he was dressed in an old petticoat and wrapped up in a blanket with his feet encased in some of Bill Campbell's socks sticking out below, Sal thought he would melt the heart of Scrooge.

"You next, Paulie?" she indicated the bath now considerably less clean.

"No, no, not me. I've never had all my clothes off at once. It's not right, miss," he pleaded.

"As you wish Paulie. I'll just go and get Paddy his soup." She rose and went from the granary across to the washhouse where she filled a large ewer from the water tank, under which the fire was now dying, and carried it back to where the two boys hadn't moved since she left.

"Paulie, I've brought some clean hot water and if you want to be fed, you have to get your clothes off and get into that bath. Now!" she finished sternly. Paulie was used to being shouted at and he was no stranger to a clout on the ear or any part of his body his angered father could reach, so he recognised when he was beaten and slowly began to take off his dirty rags.

"Will it hurt much?" he asked timidly.

Sal laughed and with a quick dive lifted him off his feet and deposited him in the bath, sitting him down before he had time to protest. "Does it hurt, then?" she smiled, rubbing vast quantities of soap onto a rag. "Now shut your eyes and don't open them until I tell you, for if the soap gets in your eyes it will sting. Think of the soup."

Even although Paulie shivered and shook it took Sal no time at all to have him as clean as possible and once he was dried and dressed in some clean and warm, if big, clothes she stood back and looked at the results of her effort.

"Don't move," she ordered and with a swirl of her skirt was off out the door. The boys looked at each other in dismay, not knowing what to make of the treatment they had just received. Sal did not frighten them and for some unknown reason they trusted she would do no harm to them or the rest of the family, but never in all of Paulie's life had he met anyone who had been kind to his itinerant Irish family.

Sal returned with a tray from which Paulie could detect the most wonderful smell that set his mouth watering. A large bowl of soup was handed to him and a chunk of soft bread and butter. Paulie's eyes were out on stalks as he hesitated to take the proffered basin from Sal.

"Go on," she encouraged. "I'm not going to worry about your table manners tonight."

Not understanding what her words meant, but deciding that she meant him to have the bowl of thick fragrant soup, he put it to his lips and savoured the taste of the hot liquid. Meanwhile Sal picked up his little brother and smiled kindly at him, correctly surmising that he would not be able to feed himself.

"I'll help you, shall I?" She broke off fragments of bread and, after dipping them in the soup offered the delicious morsel to Paddy, who after the initial one opened his mouth like a gosling every time a scrap came near. In no time at all the bowls were empty and the boys had each finished off their meal with a drink of frothy milk. Their eyes were beginning to close so Sal lifted Paddy and, indicating to Paulie that he should follow, carried him back to the bothy where his mother and sibling were still asleep. Sal carefully laid the little boy down on a bunk bed and lifted Paulie in beside him saying, "We'll leave the other bunk for your da and Roger. You get some sleep now."

She turned to the fire and put a few more logs on before checking on the mother and child. The little girl seemed to be much less flushed but when Sal laid her hand on her brow her skin was hot and dry, so she once more stripped her and swabbed her down with lukewarm water, covered her up and turned to her mother who was roiling restlessly on the bed, sweating profusely. In the short space of time while Sal was dealing with the boys a rash had appeared on the woman's face and, now that Sal was sure that she was dealing with measles, she was confident she could cope with the needs of the little family.

She left them all while she went over to the farmhouse to see if Jim had been able to find the rest of the family, but when he had waited at the riverside bothy he had not seen either the son, Roger or the father. He said he would visit again before he went to bed and if he had any news he would come immediately to let Sal know.

"You are a kind lass. Just like your Aunt Sarah," he commented as he laid a hand on her shoulder as he passed her place at the table on his way out the door.

That evening and night was a torment for Sal. She wanted her aunt very badly, for however much she tried she could not ease the suffering of the young woman as she tossed and turned mumbling incoherently in her distress. Sal mopped her hot sweat-drenched skin, paying particular attention to her eyes which were tending to crust and looked really painful. She had fed her some tea that her nana had suggested and tried to get her to drink as much water as she could, but in the dark hours of the night Sal was frightened that the woman would die. Towards morning the little girl began to cry as she woke up and Sal did not know whether to be glad or if this was a bad sign. At least she was rousing which must be better than lying like the dead. She picked the child up and carried her to the chair by the fire where she cuddled and shushed her;

she could have cried with delight when the child took some water and then, a little later, a few drops of milk.

"Maybe she's on the mend. Praise be to God," she murmured to herself.

As dawn broke the two boys began to stir and Sal suggested that Paulie should run over to see if his father or brother were to be found at the bothy. However, when he returned a short time later, it was to report that there was no sign of them even having spent the night there. Sal sighed, for she had a suspicion that the rest of the family had gone off leaving the most vulnerable members of the family to the care of a six-year-old boy.

As the day progressed it became apparent that the mother and child were indeed improving. By dinnertime the little girl, whom Paulie informed her was called Angela, was sitting up taking notice and Sal was pleased to see that she managed to take quite a few mouthfuls of the sops she made from bread, hot milk and sugar. She was still lethargic and when not being nursed by Sal lay languidly on the bunk, staring into space. Her mother however was approaching the crisis. Not, of course, that Sal knew this; it took all her time to keep the demented woman on the bed for she tossed this way and that, shouting and flailing her skinny arms. Sal consulted her book and determined that she had just to keep her calm and cool, so to this end she spent her afternoon sponging the woman's body and trying to get her to drink both herbal tea and water until, towards evening, when Sal could hear the lowing of the cows coming in to be milked, she suddenly noticed that her patient had become still. Sal felt the colour drain out of her body as she approached the pallet, worried that the fever had taken the poor soul to another world, but was gratified to see that the woman was sleeping peacefully. The crisis was over.

Overcome with tiredness now that the emergency had passed, Sal sat down in the chair by the fire and slept for a few hours, only wakening when the older boys came in through the door ready to go to bed; for Sarah had arrived back while she had been asleep. When peeping in and seeing all was well in the bothy she had fed the boys, disgusted them by insisting they have another wash, before sending them off to their beds. Sal spent that night dosing and dealing with her two patients but it was now clear that both would recover if given sufficient food and rest. In her waking moments Sal wondered how it was possible for people to live as this little family had, and became furious when she realised how the ill mother had been abandoned by those who should have cared for her.

Sal was relieved when her aunt came in to check on the patients the next morning, beaming with pleasure when her aunt said, "I would have done nothing different. You kept calm and used your common sense which is the best commodity a nurse can bring to her care. The baby was past saving and we will need to tell his mother that he has died, but you have to accept that you cannot work miracles."

Sal spent many hours in the bothy as her first patients recovered. She discovered that the woman was Roseanne Quinn and that she had been married to Michael Quinn, a crofter from County Sligo who, until their potato crop got blight two years running, had been a good provider. With no hope of reversing the death of his crop Michael had decided to move permanently to Scotland where he had been coming every year to work during the harvest for as long as they had been married. They had left Ireland with very little money, a big family to feed and high hopes of a new life, but times had changed in Scotland, as they had all over the mainland, with the mechanism of the mills and machines being invented in every industry that had made men redundant. Where they had thought Michael would get a tied job on one of the farms he had come to before, they found only hostility from the Scots who saw them as a threat to the few jobs available, as the starving Irish peasants would work for much less than a Scotsman simply because his family were starving.

Roseanne told how they had been working their way from Girvan where they had landed, for the Ayrshire farms had always provided Michael with work before. They were turned away time and again, or chased out of a village as soon as they entered. When they were brought to the realisation that the dream of a new life would not become a reality in Ayrshire they began their soul-destroying trek around the coastal farms into Dumfriesshire, where most of the family had succumbed to 'the fever'. It became apparent to Sal, horrified at the idea, that the weakest of the family had been abandoned to perish, if not from the fever, then from starvation.

"When you have been beaten with sticks and pelted with sods, not to mention the names they call us, you begin to lose hope," she went on sadly. "I don't blame Michael for leaving me when he thought we were dying for he had the other bairns and his ma and sister to think of too. I would have died along with the babbies if you hadn't come along. What I blame them for is not taking Paulie and Paddy, for they had gotten better from the fever, but then I suppose they were too wee to work." She sighed, then, catching Sal's hand, blushed and continued, "I can't thank you enough for what you did for me and my weans and your grandmother for letting us stay till we are fit to go on the tramp again."

Sal squeezed her hand and replied, "Don't think about going off until you are fit and well, and it might be a good idea to look for work first and a place to call your own. The lads here are fine, sleeping like puppies by the kitchen fire," she laughed, "In fact I think they like it better than this old bothy."

Later that day Sal wandered off by herself to the riverbank where she had first come across the family. She sat idly listening to the purr of the river as it flowed through the lush green field that she had always known as home, where it had a tranquilising effect on her senses. She was deep in thought when she was disturbed by footsteps coming towards her through the long grass. She turned and smiled as she recognised Jim. He plonked himself down beside her, not speaking at first as he too looked at the flow of the river, but eventually smiled that crooked Campbell smile and said, "Penny for your thoughts, Sal?"

"I don't know if they are worth that. I was just putting myself in Roseanne's place. She trusted her man to care for her and her bairns and came all the way over to Scotland, away from her own family, only to be cast off when caring for them became too hard, yet she doesn't blame him for what he did. She thinks it was his right to make the decision to let her die in that shed over there." She nodded her head in the direction of the bothy. "How can a man have the right to do that? Is it not time that women had a right to be a person without deferring to a man, be it her husband or her father?"

"You'll be joining those women demanding rights for women if you're not careful," he answered, smiling at her vehemence, but it went down the wrong way and Sal's eyes flashed at him.

"What's wrong with women having rights? We work and we slave just like men do. Why should we not be allowed to make our own decisions? Just because you are a man it gives you the right to think you know better than me just because I'm a woman. Do you think that's fair?" she demanded.

"Whoa Sal, I don't think I'm better than you and if you think about it neither have any of the men of this family. Each of them chose wives who complemented them and worked with them, not for them. Our grandfathers were what they were through their mother, not their father: they never knew their father for he was dead before he was twenty-one. Aunt Ellen always had a say in what Uncle Bill decided and your own mother won't even let your father think without consulting her," he finished, trying to lighten the atmosphere. It worked for thinking of her dominant mother made her smile.

"Maybe you're right and... Yes, you are; for I have not given women's rights a thought before seeing Roseanne's situation because I looked at the examples near home and we have more than equal rights, if you take my mother into consideration." She nudged him, keen to let him know she wasn't taking offence at the dig about her mother.

"Well, I may not go to meetings and flaunt myself about the streets, but I am even more determined to be a nurse and earn my own living so that I run no risk of being deserted by a man when he thinks I'm not worth his care."

Jim knew then that this was not the time to tell Sal how he felt about her, how he had always felt about her. It was difficult enough when everyone in the family would be thinking he wanted to court Sal for the farm he had failed to inherit from Ellen, but he would gladly give up the farm and go to work as a ploughman elsewhere if Sal was his. He held out his hand to pull her to her feet.

"Come on, Rebel. I'll walk you back."

Chapter Twenty-Two

"Sal, can you come in for a bit?" called Ellen from the kitchen door across the yard to the byre where Sal was busy washing the cows' udders before milking. Jim had expanded the byre to take the bigger herd so that they now had eight stalls purpose built to house the dairy cows in winter. Sal was fascinated that each cow knew exactly which stall to go to. She had joked with Jim when he had chalked the name of each cow on the wall behind the stall that he had educated the cows better than the dominii had taught her sisters.

On hearing her grandmother's voice, she called back, "Be there in a minute, Nana: I'm just about finished here." She patted the rump of the last cow and, setting free her tail from where she had it pinioned over the beast's flank, was just in time to jump clear as Maggie showed what she thought of the enterprise by emptying her bowels in a splatter only inches from Sal's booted feet.

"Missed!" she laughed, giving the cow another flap on the rump. She caught up the animal's tail again and once more washed the teats on the sagging udder just for good measure. "There you go, my lady, you're clean as a whistle." She quickly caught up a byre brush and, throwing a bucket of water over the excrement, swiftly brushed it along the drain that ran the full length of the byre ending in the midden, where it joined many others to rot and ferment until, in the spring, the resultant fertiliser would be spread on the ploughed field to nurture the next year's crop.

As she made her way along the farmyard she ducked her head into the barn and told Jim where she was going. "I'll be back soon to help with the milking. The girls like my soft fingers better than your old gnarled ones."

"Get away with you, you cheeky madam. One of these days you'll get your comeuppance and I'll be there to see it." He chuckled and stood still as he watched Sal's womanly behind sway as she hurried towards the house.

"Only Sal could look enticing in her workaday clothes, smelling of dung and wearing wellies." But nevertheless he felt his temperature rising just at the sight of her. "Who would have believed these new rubber boots (invented by those ingenious men Hutchinson and Dunlop, so much better than clogs for keeping the feet dry) could make a maid look so desirable?" As Sal disappeared through the back door he sighed and turned back to his monotonous job, his mood improved just by a glimpse of his vision. He grinned as a fleeting thought tickled his fancy, "I bet the old Iron Duke didn't look so well in his boots as my Sal does in hers!"

"I'm here, Nana!"

"In the parlour Sal, come on through." Sal slipped off her wellington boots and walked in her stocking feet through the kitchen, up the dark passageway beside the looming stairs and into the parlour. In all her eighteen years Sal had only been in here twice so she became a bit concerned that something was amiss and she felt herself become flustered. She hesitantly pushed open the door to see her ma and nana seated on the horsehair settle with Dr Jardine in one high-backed oak chair and Lady Johnstone perched on the edge of the other.

"Whatever this is about, Ma is mighty pleased at the idea of it," thought Sal and she came further into the room and realised that her aunt was standing by the tea table playing with the good tea set, another product of her father's secret life. She hurriedly tried to tidy her hair and ran her hands down over her skirt in order not to come under her mother's censure, for being neat and tidy in company was one of Liza's idiosyncrasies. The sight of Lady Johnstone in her nana's home was not unusual nor did the presence of the doctor cause her any concern, for they were both good friends of Ellen, but that her presence was required at this august gathering did unsettle her. However, Sal's manners were perfect and checking to see there were no lingering remnants of the byre on her hand, she stepped forward with it extended and greeted Lady Johnstone with a smile which the petite little lady returned in full. Sal then, half curtseying to the doctor with whom she was on easy terms and this their common greeting, asked what was wanted off her. Before anyone else could speak her mother started to explain, "Lady Johnstone is here today, along with Dr Jardine, to offer you a great opportunity which not many girls your age are fortunate enough to receive," she simpered in the direction of Lady Johnstone.

Sal, who knew her better than anyone, was aware that there was little her mother would not do to please the little lady because, if truth be known, she was jealous of Ellen's relationship with her, since the mistress of Lochwood Tower was nearer Liza's age than Ellen's. This knowledge of her mother led her to read between the lines of her parent's words and interpret the sentence to be 'You will say Yes to whatever Lady Johnstone wants or you will answer to me.' So she answered brightly and contritely, "Yes, Ma," and waited to hear what it was she had agreed to. She was not by any stretch of the imagination a docile daughter, but as she entered the room she had been aware that her nana and aunt were not in the least upset, leading her to believe they agreed with what was about to be offered.

Dr Jardine took over. "I have heard of your actions with the poor family left to their own devices in the bothy and I have to say I was impressed that you could diagnose their condition and treat it properly, although maybe I shouldn't be, given that your grandma saved many a bairn when I was a raw young doctor." He grinned in Ellen's direction as they both reflected how times had changed.

Sal saw the skin tighten on her mother's face and, not wanting her to get upset, smiled up at the doctor and said, "Ma always taught me to be kind to those less fortunate so I was just doing what she brought me up to do."

Liza sent her a grateful look that made Sal want to hoot with laughter, "It's like being in a play where everyone tries to keep everyone else happy for their own ends."

Dr Jardine went on. "Lady Johnstone, as you know, has been very much involved with setting up the new mill following on from the ideas of the Cadbury and Owen enterprises and she is keen to find some enthusiastic people with compassion and flair to undertake a similar project here. If you are willing, we will need you to move into the infirmary wing being built at the mill and work under my instructions. You will be paid, of course, not a lot at first, as you will have much to learn, but as your experience grows I will want you to pass your knowledge on to others." He smiled encouragingly at her. "What do you say?"

Sal stood stock still for a few moments before hearing her mother answer for her.

"She will be delighted to do anything to help yourself and my lady. She is overcome with gratitude."

Although the words sounded polite to the others, Sal recognised the underlying threat in the tone of her mother's voice. Nevertheless she remained still, passing the proffered position through her befuddled brain, where question tumbled over question in rapid succession before she voiced her worry to the couple sitting patiently waiting for her response.

"I don't know enough. I was lucky to have had measles and could use my experience of what Ma did for me. I might make a mistake. Do you think I could do it?" This last directed at her aunt as she hurriedly twisted round to face her, for a second forgetting the presence of her mother and how it would anger her not to be the one consulted about her future. But Sal knew that her mother would walk barefoot over broken glass, never mind send her daughter off to dance to Lady Johnstone's tune, if she thought there was a chance of inveigling her way into Lady Johnstone's circle.

Ignoring Liza's annoyance, Sarah spoke quietly to her pretty niece. "I think you will deal very well with Dr Jardine and your ma or even nana will be around if you need help."

Although Sarah had not said in so many words that she would also be around, Sal knew this would be the case and that her aunt was being politic in naming her mother as a mentor, allowing Liza to save face and make life easier for her niece.

Sal cast her eyes around the watching adults, taking in the various expressions on their faces. Four out of five of them smiled encouragingly in her direction while her mother sat with straight back and shoulders and her mouth in a straight line, her eyes shafting threatening arrows at Sal, daring her to disgrace her by repudiating her previous agreement.

"We-ee-ll, if you think I would be any good, I would love to give it a go," she said her eyes alight at the thought of working with the good doctor whom she had known all her life.

"That's settled then," sighed Liza in relief at so easily cowing her independent daughter. "You run along and get on with your work and I will discuss the arrangements with my Lady here." She flapped her hand in the direction of the door paying little heed to her headstrong daughter now that she had prevailed upon her to do her bidding.

Sal closed the parlour door behind her and, covering her mouth with her hands to hold in her mirth lest her mother hear and realise how she had been manipulated by the others, sped back the way she had come until she was once more in the granary with Jim, where she gave full rein to her emotions and danced a jig around the bemused young man.

"What's put you in such a humour?" he grinned at her obvious pleasure.

"Nana and Aunt Sarah," was all she could splutter between gales of laughter.

"What have they done that is so funny?" Jim asked, trying to restrain the laugh that Sal's infectious giggle had provoked.

Sal held her arms tight over her stomach as she bent over with another burst of laughter. "Oh, it hurts to laugh but you should have seen Ma's face. They rolled her up and stuffed her... and she is so pleased with herself... She thinks it's all her idea... Aunt Sarah looking innocent... Lady Johnstone deferring to Ma... Oh, Jim... So fu... un... ny." She stopped trying to explain as she once more burst out laughing and tears trickled down her cheeks.

Jim gave her a few minutes to compose herself before he tried again, "What has put you into such whoops, Sal?"

Sal swallowed and pulled herself together, telling Jim the gist of the conversation in the parlour with only the occasional chuckle escaping while she explained how her dream was about to come true, and with her mother's blessing. Jim's heart sank deeper with every sentence as he realised that *his* dream would move further away as hers drew closer, but he summoned up a smile and congratulated her on her luck.

"I'll miss you. The cows will miss you. You said yourself they like the feel of your gentle fingers. Don't you get too grand to speak to the likes of me and Maggie and Lizzie, now," he finished.

"As if I could ever forget you, Jim. And you will be so involved with your agricultural improvements you won't remember who I am when I come home to visit."

"I'll not forget you, Sal," he said seriously out loud, but continued the thought to himself, "No, I'll not forget you. I could never forget you, for you are what makes me work hard and improve the farm; every ditch I dig, every field I plough, every hedge I plant, I do to make you proud. Now you won't be here to see my improvements."

****

Jim stopped the horse and looked back over the field he had just finished spreading with the sweet-smelling dung from the midden behind the stackyard. All winter he had tended the waste from the byres, the cow shit mixed in with the straw from the bedding that, with the help of the worms, had been turned into fertiliser to spread on his increased acres. Over the last two years he had become used to being solely responsible for Hartwood Farm as Ellen deferred more and more to his ideas. Yes, Liza made periodic appearances to remind him that the farm would belong to her daughter when Ellen passed away, but she knew little about the new methods that he employed, so, despite throwing her weight around, made little difference to the day-to-day running of the farm.

"It's a good job Aunt Ellen is still in charge, for she gives me free rein to try my new ideas. And I've increased the income this year despite spending money on draining the fields and employing extra men to lay the tiled drains. I really believe that we will have a bigger yield on the oats and corn with the water running off the field rather than rotting the roots from the crops."

He looked back at the barren field behind him but he did not see the brown earth newly ploughed and fertilised, both with manure and lime, but the sea of golden corn he imagined being cut with the McCormick reaper when he could persuade Ellen it was better to spend the money on the new machine than on employing more men with sickles and scythes. He smiled to himself, for he knew he would be able to make her see the benefits of the machine age and then he might be able to afford the thresher he had set his heart on, *then* the money would really come in, for he could charge all the farmers around to thrash their corn and the machine would soon pay for itself. Not a day went by but Jim thanked his lucky stars that Bill Campbell had given him the opportunity to come to Hartwood.

"Uncle Bill was always forward thinking and looking at what was to come rather than what had been in the past. He taught me not to be afraid of progress and what a lesson that has turned out to be," he thought to himself as he recalled many days out in the fields with his uncle, who had treated him just like a son.

The farm was booming. He had introduced a small herd of beef cattle and tried his hand at breeding, crossing the delightful red and white Ayrshire cows with a shorthorn bull, and the results had been good, increasing quality as well as quantity.

Milk and beef production were both on the up and, with the increase in the families coming into the valley to work in the cotton mill and in the shipbuilding in Annan, demand for both commodities were at their height. His own father has scoffed at his ideas when he had talked of them when his Uncle Bill had died, but even he was convinced and did not hesitate to ask an opinion of his youngest son.

"But none of the improvements or the money that comes into the farm is mine to do with as I like. It all belongs to Hartwood and Aunt Ellen and when she goes, to Sal. What will there be for me then?" he wondered.

As if the thought of Sal had conjured her out of thin air he spied her making her way around the edges of the field in his direction. Even with her being so far away he recognised her distinctive way of moving. "Sal is always in a hurry; never enough hours in the day for her to do all she has set her mind to." Pushing his own reflections to the back of his mind, he wondered what had brought her out to the fields. His heart jumped into his throat as he realised that something must be amiss, so leaving his precious horses to fend for themselves he ran to meet her.

"Hello there. What's ado?" he said as soon as he was within shouting distance.

"Nothing new; but Pa has been coughing up blood again and this time Ma is in a panic. She sent for me to come home to see to him but you know Pa, he won't have any fuss. He likes to pretend to Ma and Nana that he is fit when a blind man can see he is anything but."

Jim put his arm round Sal's shoulders and felt her relax against him. "Thank goodness for you, Jim. I don't know what I would do without you." She sighed as she let the security of his arms comfort her.

It took all of Jim's willpower not to bend his head and kiss her, but he knew she did not think of him in a romantic way. It was hard for him to hold her so close, smelling the fresh lemony tang of soap that always sent his senses reeling, without making any romantic overtures. She had no brothers, and he believed that she saw him only in that light, so he overcame his impulse, satisfying himself by giving her a quick hug before asking,

"How bad is it this time?"

"I honestly don't think he is any worse than he was last Sunday but it is hard for Ma. She doesn't know what to do for him." She looked up into Jim's face, then went on, "I know you all think Ma is heartless but she adores Da and she is frightened, and jealous of her rights too. I have been sent off with a flea in my ear for suggesting that she let Aunt Sarah help with him. She won't leave them alone together but I think Aunt Sarah could ease his mind." She gave a deep sigh of frustration.

"Families, eh? Is there anything I can do to help? You know you only have to ask."

"Yes, I do, Jim. I'm grateful to you just for being here and I know I can call on you to help out if Da isn't fit. His ploughmen are all young lads and the dairyman knows nothing but his cows. None of them can work without Da telling them what needs doing and when."

"Are you staying on at Annanbank or are you off back to the Infirmary tonight?" asked Bill quietly, hoping Sal would remain in the circle of his arms for a few minutes longer.

"I am staying just for tonight; to give Ma a bit of space. Da is no worse as I said before but every time she sends a message to me I fear the worst. Unless he becomes worse I will need to return, for the place is full of workmen with influenza and they need careful nursing. I came to see you to ask a favour of you." She smiled up at him.

"Whatever you want, you only need to ask," Jim volunteered.

"You are so good to me, Jim. What I want to ask of you is to try to keep an eye on the farm. I know you are up to your eyes in it here but with Da in bed and Ma not a bit of use with beasts or crops and none of the girls capable of taking charge, I need to be sure the men get the work done. Da will get up too soon if I can't reassure him his acres are in good hands. And you're to pay no heed to Ma, for it is Da who is asking this favour of you." She finished in a rush, knowing it was asking a great deal of their friendship for him to face her mother's need to prove herself better than everyone else.

"Just let me get the cart and horses then I'll walk back with you and reassure John I'll keep the farm turning over until he is fit again." Seeing the bleak look come over Sal's eyes he joked to try to lighten the mood, "I'd offer you a lift in my carriage but it's been muckspreading and would dirty your dainty dress."

"Dainty? Are you blind? I ran straight home without changing. I look like a scarecrow and certainly not a dainty one," she responded but laughed nevertheless. She became serious again quickly as she recalled why she was dressed as she was. Influenza was rife in Mill village; she and every one of the other girls were working day and night, sponging down the sweating bodies when needed, heaping blankets on when the next minute the patients were shivering, keeping watch to ensure no harm came to those who were out of their mind with fever, and encourage the sick to drink water, to say nothing of the mundane and distasteful tasks of changing the bed linen and cleaning up the excrement from the weakened invalids.

"Is it very bad at the Infirmary?" asked Jim, noticing the furrows on her normally smooth brow.

"It is bad; but at least my patients have a chance of recovering. Dr Jardine told me that as yet no one has survived in Moorheads Hospital in Dumfries. It might be that they have to be on their last legs to commit themselves to the Paupers, but I think the people from Mill village are so much better fed and have better living conditions that means they have the stamina to fight the illness. Evans at the village shop has done away with truck. Well, if I'm honest, Lord Johnstone had to go to Wales to find an honest grocer for the village; most of the ones who applied wanted to continue to charge unrealistic prices for poor quality food, and with rent reasonable and the only deduction a pittance to pay for medical care, the standards in the mill workers' houses are envied by everyone."

"Aye. We are lucky on the farm too, for we always have food and warmth; even the poor cotters round about manage to keep warm by living in one room and bringing their animals into the other. They produce heat, and cow dung may not smell good but it keeps the fire going."

Sal burst out laughing and clasped onto Jim's arm. "That reminds me of something." She chuckled again before saying. "That's one use of the cow that the schoolmaster hasn't thought of." Sal noticed Jim was not following her, so she began to explain.

"You know that Lady Mary Johnstone is keen to follow the example of Robert Owen, albeit on a much smaller scale?"

Jim nodded and Sal carried on, "Well she has all the bairns under nine in the schoolroom next to the infirmary every morning and has employed a schoolmaster to teach them to read, write and count. Lady Mary wanted a woman but she was outvoted by the other directors because they thought a woman wasn't educated enough or wouldn't be able to discipline the unruly boys, some such excuse." She flapped her hand to show how much truth there was in the edict. "Even some of the men who are really keen on the Mill Village system still don't think the working class need to be educated and believe the apprentices would be better off in the Mill making a wage to increase the family's standard of living: and unfortunately some of their fathers agree, but that's by the by.

"The thing is that Lady Mary isn't in favour of harsh discipline. Do you remember being struck with the 'taws' when you were at school? I was often and not for any major crime. I remember once forgetting to bring my bucket of coal; you had to in those days, to keep the stove alight."

"Yes. In your young days, many years ago," laughed Jim. "But aye, I know what you mean. They didn't spare the rod. I remember being slapped on the head with a ruler time after time to make me learn my twelve times table. Mind you, I can't say if it was wrong for I haven't forgotten how many twelve twelves are." He rubbed his head as if he could still feel the sting of the ruler now.

"You know we were lucky; my sisters and I, I mean, for you were a boy and a superior being so you would always have had some schooling, but if Ma had been in charge she would not have 'wasted' the money on educating girls, who were only going to marry and have babies, but Da is so forward thinking he insisted we could be pretty and smart."

Sal blushed as she realised what she had said, but Jim just nodded and agreed that her father was indeed a man before his time. Sal hurried on.

"Anyway, as I was saying Lady Mary would have preferred a woman to nurture the children, however, she interviewed a good number of strict disciplinarians who were put forward for the job but she eventually chose Mr Hamilton. She employed a man." Sal's giggle alerted Jim that she found this amusing.

"Are men so funny?" he asked.

"Well, not normally, but to look at Mr Hamilton you would think the children, not only the boys, mind, wouldn't listen to him for he is such a small, frail-looking creature, much more feminine-looking than me; he has long lashes and black eyes that I want to claw out of his head, I'm that jealous of them; but the thing is he is a fabulous teacher. The children love him and he is kind; no belting in his class."

"Quite a paragon," said Jim in a voice that made Sal look at him sharply.

"Well, yes he is. The children adore him and hang on his every word," she answered innocently. "And that's what I was saying. He makes up poems to show them how much use animals and plants are. Not long dirges like I learnt at school but lighter stuff, and he has one about a cow. I fell about laughing when I heard the children reciting it. It was so funny, but true too."

"Let's hear it then," said Jim, trying hard to remove the image of an educated man romancing Sal and her laughing in response.

Sal stopped, faced Jim with a stern expression and, hands clasped in front of her just as the little children did at school, she began:

"*The Cow*
Come children listen to me now
And you shall hear about the cow.
You'll find her useful live or dead
Whether she's black, white or red.
When milkmaids milk her morn and night
She gives us milk so fresh and white
And this we little children think
Is very nice for us to drink.
The milk we skim and shake in churns
And then it into butter turns.
The curdled milk we press and squeeze
And so we make it into cheese.
The skin, with lime and bark together
The tanner tans and makes it leather;
And without this what would we do

For soles for every boot and shoe?
This is not all as you will see
Her flesh is food for you and me.
Her fat provides us glue and oil,
Her bones tend to improve the soil.
And last of all if taken with care
Her horns make combs to comb our hair,
And so we learn, thanks to our teachers,
That cows are very useful creatures.
The End."

Sal finished with a deep curtsey. Jim was delighted with the poem, laughing out loud both at the words and at Sal's prim delivery.

"Very good, that," he snorted, almost choking on the words, but soon became serious again. "What type of man is this Mr Hamilton?"

Sal, who admired Mr Hamilton's skill with children indifferent to the classroom, began to sing his praises, not realising that with every word of tribute that left her mouth, Jim sunk into a deeper chasm of disappointment. Not a man to preen himself, he saw in this paragon, working in such close proximity to Sal, a rival for her affections. He noticed her flushed cheeks and shining eyes as she related the man's goods points with illustrations, giving Jim the impression that Sal was already half in love with the schoolmaster.

"She would never look at a plain old cowman when she can have a man of equal standing and education," he thought to himself as they once more continued their walk towards Annanbank and Sal's more immediate problems.

In fact, Sal had not given any more thought to Mr Hamilton, or Paul, as he had asked her to call him when they met at staff meals or for meetings about the health of the children. She was deeply involved with Lady Mary's plans and had no time to waste on a love interest despite the hints from her mother that it was high time she was thinking of getting herself a husband and forgetting this 'independent nonsense'. Sal knew that one day, sooner or later, her mother would lose patience with her and demand she leave the care of the sick to others and set about the vital purpose of producing an heir for the farm. The only thing holding her back at present was the influence of Lady Johnstone and her desire to please her ladyship was, for the moment, allowing her daughter to follow her own path. Sal sighed, for she knew her mother was worried what would happen to her and her other daughters if there was no master at Annanbank.

"It would never cross her mind to go out into the stackyard and take charge of the men herself," she thought. "It just wasn't done in her day but she has Nana's example to follow. If Da had taken a leaf out of Papa's book and brought in a manager when he first became sick, they would not be dependent on me to marry a farmer to keep them safe. I know Ma isn't even fussy who it is, just so long as I bring a man home to keep the farm."

As Jim walked along beside her, pretending not to see her faraway look, he made up his mind that her distraction was caused by the mention of the schoolmaster. He took this as a sign that she was sweet on him and it was enough to solidify his own resolve to save up his wages in order to buy a threshing mill with which he could earn his living when Sal married her schoolmaster, thus making him master of Hartwood, "And when that day dawns I'll be long gone, for I couldn't bear to see her happy with another man."

****

"Oh, what a relief," breathed Sal as she smiled across the table at Roseanne Quinn who had just placed a mug of strong hot tea in front of her. Sal bent down and unbuttoning her boots kicked them off, giving her toes a pleasurable wiggle to ease them.

"It has been such a day. Twenty-six more cases of typhoid! They are dropping like flies! So many to tend and not enough to do the nursing. Dr Wilson is going to see if he can recruit some of the ploughmen's wives but I don't hold out much hope for that. They have families to care for and don't want to risk carrying the infection home."

"Maybe I could be more use to you in the sickrooms than in the kitchen?" replied Roseanne, who was devoted to Sal, not only for saving the lives of her and her children but for ensuring her this job that allowed her to keep the remnants of her family together. She never forgot that Sal had saved her from the workhouse, or the Paupers as it was called locally, by insisting that Lady Johnstone employ her as cook in her new manufactory.

"No," said Sal quickly. "I have more need of you in the kitchen making all the necessary soups and puddings to build up my patients when they start to improve. And what would I do without you to make sure I get my mug of tea every time I get too tired to keep my eyes open?" She grimaced again as she tried to ease the stiffness from her shoulders. She was bone tired. Every muscle ached. There were times when she just knew her legs would no longer support her; at these times she broke her own rules and sat on the edge of the bed while she completed her ministrations.

"Why don't you have a wee nap in the chair by the stove, Sal? You are dead beat. I won't let you sleep for more than a couple of hours. You haven't closed your eyes in three days now and I don't want to have to be nursing you, what with all the work you give me," she finished, trying to bring a smile to Sal's pale lips.

"I don't think I could sleep but I will stretch out in the chair, but don't let me miss Dr Wilson for he is coming to tell me what outcome he has had with finding the source of the outbreak. He said he'd find time to call in today."

While speaking these words she had risen from the table and hobbled over to the chair by the stove like a woman three times her age. She now stretched herself to her full height while the muscles in her back complained; she raised her arms above her head and once more tried to ease the ache in her shoulders and arms before settling herself on the comfy chair with a little sigh of relief. She closed her eyes, rested her head on the back of the chair, shuffled the cushion into a more comfortable position in the small of her back and, before Roseanne could say another word, was off into another world where mopping brows and emptying bedpans was unheard of.

Roseanne took in the appearance of the young woman. There were great dark circles under her eyes, testifying to the nights of disturbed rest and the hollows of her cheeks made her look gaunt and malnourished.

Roseanne thought to herself, "She needs someone to take care of her, bless her. Up all hours of the day and night, nursing the sick and attending to all the jobs those flighty maids leave, knowing she will pick them up with never a word of condemnation. I'd soon have them dancing to a different tune, the brazen hussies!"

Despite her words, Roseanne knew that all the girls were busy with the outbreak, even the housemaids had been commandeered into the Infirmary, but they went off to bed after a hard shift leaving much undone that Sal stayed awake to take care off.

Sal slept like the dead for around two hours until Roseanne woke her when she saw Dr Wilson's carriage approaching. Before he had alighted and knocked on the door, Sal was up and, having splashed her face in cold water and tidied her hair, was opening the door and asking the doctor to come in. He removed his hat and shook hands with Sal. She had had less to do with Dr Wilson than with Dr Jardine, as he had been responsible for training her into the excellent and knowledgeable nurse she now was, but was not on such friendly terms with the middle-aged clinician whom she rarely saw.

"Have you any news about where this infection is coming from?" Sal asked as soon as the formalities had been got out of the way.

"It looks like it has come from the water from the stream that feeds the Annan. There is a family all found nearly dead upstream and they had been emptying their chamber pots into the burn. It has washed down into the river and the hot weather has allowed the germs to multiply and infect all those who take their water from the river... and, of course, the animals who drink it and pass their milk on to us humans."

"Do we have to stop drinking the water and the milk then?" asked Roseanne, who had been listening carefully to the doctor. He turned round and gave her a look that would have soured milk, for he held himself in high esteem and did not feel the cook/

maid of the house had any right to question him; his was the power to dictate what should or should not be done in this crisis. His look left neither woman in any doubt how he felt about interference from females who did not know their place.

He went on in a pompous and pedantic manner, "All water or milk drunk must be boiled. You cannot see the germs that are causing the disease but you will take my word for it that they are there. Great men have invented ways to see the beasts but you women must accept that men know better and remember to follow my instructions to the letter. You must not question those whom the good Lord have put on this earth to make decisions for those less able by gender to make for themselves."

It was fortunate for Dr Wilson that as the two women blinked at the obvious dislike shown by his words that the door into the kitchen from the infirmary opened to disclose Dr Jardine. If he had heard his colleague's disparaging remark he gave no sign but greeted him good-humouredly, holding out his hand and smiling beneficently.

"What news, dear fellow?" he asked.

Shaking hands, Dr Wilson again repeated his tale to Dr Jardine who, with such innocence on his face no one would ever accuse him of making mock of the other man, answered beaming at Sal and Roseanne where they stood frozen to the spot.

"Roseanne was only just last night telling me that she had taken orders from Sal to boil all the water and milk before using it for the invalids. They will both be glad to hear that their caution has been justified by your findings." He ushered his companion through the door from which he had himself emerged while continuing to update him on the state of his patients, "We are lucky here not to have lost anyone to the vile disease, but our patients have had the luxury of being tended by well instructed nurses. In other places…"

As the doctor's voice faded from the listening women's ears they grinned at each other, then giggled at the scene they had just witnessed. Before they could revive themselves to discuss the doctor's words a knock was heard at the door and Sal crossed the kitchen to answer it, where she found one of her nurses, Janie Anderson, barely able to stand.

"I'm so sorry to bother you but I feel so bad. I can't even get up the front steps to get into the Infirmary."

Taking in the young girl's appearance she quickly ushered her through the kitchen and out the way the doctors had gone just moments earlier.

"Come into this room here and let me have a look at you. Have you been sleeping?"

"I have been going to bed directly I have finished my chores and slept off and on, but I have such a headache that it wakes me and I feel sick when I move. Even after a night's sleep I am languid and tired all day. I have no energy. I've felt badly for a few days now but with so many invalids to care for, I just thought I was tired from the long hours and hard work. This morning though I have been running to the privy and that has exhausted me." She flopped onto the chair like a puppet with the strings cut.

Sal stood over her taking in all aspects of her condition and her heart sank as she recognised the symptoms of typhoid fever; her face was white with heavy, expressionless eyes staring at nothing; her skin felt hot and clammy and emitted a rank smell, typical of the disease. On ordering the girl to open her mouth she saw that her tongue was swollen with a moist dirty coating and when she felt the lumps in her neck and saw the rose-coloured spots on her chest, she knew that her worst fear was confirmed.

"I'm afraid you have caught the fever," she said gently, taking the woman in her arms to console her. "We must get you into bed. Not in your dormitory for if we can avoid the others catching it, so much the better."

She spoke in a matter-of-fact voice but inside her stomach was churning with the fear that, since the girls lived in such close proximity, it would take a miracle to save the spread. Janie had been infected for at least a few days, living and working with her fellow nurses and in such conditions that bred infection. Nevertheless, her priority was to get Jane into bed and see what she could do to comfort her. For the next twenty-four hours Sal stayed with Janie as much as possible but she, of necessity, had to make rounds of the infirmary to give orders about the other patients' care. On one of these spells out of the sickroom she wrote a note to her Aunt Sarah begging her to find her some helpers, since she now had three more of her nurses down with the fever and sharing Janie's sickroom. As always when a crisis arose she had no fear that her strong and able family would come to her aid. She stipulated what she needed, never doubting that Sarah would find some way to come up with what was wanted.

"They need not be trained, for wiping a brow and emptying foul pans does not need much training, but my patients who are recovering need to be fed and tended carefully. Please tell any who would come that the invalids they will be asked to care for are on the mend and not thought to be infectious."

This note brought, not only her aunt and grandmother with three women Sal recognised as being the wives of men employed on Hartwood, but also her mother, bristling with displeasure at her daughter's involvement with the sick.

"You are to come home at once, at once, you understand. I will not have you putting yourself in danger to save some useless weaver!" she almost screamed, quite beside herself with fear for her daughter's health.

Sal placed her hands on her mother's shoulders and tried to calm her down. She could have done without this distraction but in order for her to continue to do her work she needed to get her mother on her side, if only temporarily.

"Ma," she smiled up at her while with her most winning tone she continued. "I am so glad to see you. Roseanne cannot make such good broth as you and that is what my patients need to bring them back to health. There are only a few cases still in the early stages when they eat very little, but as they improve so does their appetite to make up for weeks of not eating properly. Will you be my angel Ma, and make some soup before you go back to Da? You know I would love to keep you here to care for me, but Da really needs you more."

"Now, Sal, you will stop this nonsense immediately and get into that trap and come home with me. I should never have agreed for you to come here in the first place. No decent man will want you after you have seen and done all these disgusting things to men. They will think you a brazen hussy!"

Sarah, ignoring her sister-in-law's outburst, indicated the women who had volunteered to help the ailing workers and quietly asked Sal where she should put them to work. She explained that Ellen had offered to feed their husbands and children while they were employed in nursing the sick.

"None of us can stay indefinitely, Ma has promised to care for the children," she stifled a laugh, "Jim is keeping them in check today until their fathers finish their tasks but he cannot be left for long. He is very willing but having no bairns of his own is quite at a loss as to how to cope with the little beggars." She smothered her chuckles, but just to hear her aunt's quiet humour was enough to lift Sal's spirits, for if Sarah was able to laugh in the face of the situation, perhaps it was not as dire as she had first thought.

Sarah continued, rolling up her sleeves, "You, my dear, will go to bed. No argument!" she started pushing Sal into her mother's arms. "See she does Liza. I said no argument." She held up her hand to stop the protests of both women. "Liza, your daughter is sleeping on her feet; if you don't want her to be the next victim get her into bed and let her sleep before you harangue her. Sal, I cannot stay, for I have patients of my own to tend to but I will take over these girls," she indicated the sweating bodies on the straw mattresses, "for the time being, so there is no need to worry. Your Ma, I'm sure, will make some soup and milk puddings to help Roseanne and you may argue whether to stay or go when you have rested. Go."

Ellen stood with a half-smile on her face as she listened to her daughter give her orders and was much struck that even Liza obeyed. It was obvious to everyone in the room that Sarah had taken control and was not to be thwarted. Ellen's heart swelled with pride as, just for a minute, she wished Bill was here to share her pride in their eldest child who had always been one to go her own way no matter what anyone else thought.

While Sal slept and before Sarah began her vigil over the sick nurses, she walked around the overcrowded infirmary with its beds supplemented by pallets on the floor and assessed where the extra hands would be best used. The women she had brought had all either nursed a family member without succumbing to the disease or recovered from the fever themselves, so she had little fear that they would contract the illness. Even although the patients they were to care for were on the mend, Sarah had explained that when they volunteered they would need to remain in the infirmary until the epidemic passed and she was grateful that they had agreed to help out, for many feared the sickness and sometimes abandoned even close family to die in discomfort, as Roseanne could surely testify to.

Once she had seen the women settled to their work she poked her head into the kitchen where Roseanne and Liza were deep in conversation, deciding what would be best to tempt the appetites of the invalids. As she hesitated on the threshold she heard Roseanne speak about how wonderful Sal was and how she had kept everyone together and been on top of things until her nurses themselves fell victim to the indiscriminating disease. Sarah noticed that Roseanne's words were having more effect on Liza than anything she could say, so she quietly backed away without being seen and returned to the sickroom to relieve Ellen, who despite her wish to be helpful, was feeling her age and her arthritic joints and was glad that her portion of the work was to feed and care for the families on Hartwood, while the younger women did the soul-destroying and backbreaking work of nursing.

By the time Sal re-entered the kitchen some six hours later she was shocked to see her mother in charge and Mr Hamilton sitting addressing a cup of tea and a newly baked scone. There was no sign of Roseanne but it appeared that her mother and the schoolmaster were getting on well together. Catching sight of her daughter, she ushered her in and indicated she should take a place opposite Mr Hamilton, where she deposited a cup of tea and a warm, well-buttered scone in front of her. Sal flashed a grateful grin at her mother and sank her teeth into the soft freshness of her mother's baking.

"Oh, Ma, this is heaven. You have no idea how much I yearn for your baking. No one makes scones like my ma, Mr Hamilton," she finished noticing that he had helped himself to another one.

"No indeed, Miss Campbell. I was just telling your charming mother I have not tasted anything so delightful before." He threw Liza a conspiratorial glance that was totally missed by Sal. "You have indeed been lucky to learn from such a wonderful cook. If I were you I would not have left the farmhouse." He laughed to show he was making a joke.

"Give me no credit for learning from Ma, Mr Hamilton, for unlike my other sisters I spent my youth out in the fields trailing my father or off tagging behind my aunt while she went about her business. I have no domestic talent," she chuckled back at him, "and if my ma told you I could bake she is perhaps remembering that as a little girl my da pretended to like my hard, flat, grey scones."

"Sal, you will have Mr Hamilton believing you have been badly brought up," remonstrated her mother, trying to hide her displeasure.

"Better that than believe I have a skill I do not," she retorted, then rose from the table shaking the crumbs from her scone onto the table and draining her tea cup. "Besides, I must go and relieve Aunt Sarah. Excuse me, Mr Hamilton."

"Now, Miss Campbell, did we not agree you would call me Paul? Won't you stay for a few minutes more and give us the pleasure of your company? I've seen very little of you lately," he cajoled.

Although his tone made Sal wonder if his intentions were romantic, an idea that had not occurred to her before, she remained adamant and left the kitchen, dropping a kiss on her mother's cheek in passing as she said, "Thank you Ma. That was just what I needed to remind me how lucky I am to have you. You're always there when any of us girls are in trouble." And, giving her mother's arm a quick squeeze, she was gone.

After getting an update from her aunt and grandmother on the condition of her patients and on receiving Sarah's confirmation that the disease appeared to be on the wane, as well as a few congratulatory words on her handling of the sick workers, Sarah made ready to leave.

Putting on her coat and hat, she said, "Oh Ma, I'll be a few minutes more. I promised Roseanne I would look at little Paddy for he has a cough again. I won't be more than ten minutes, I promise."

"Take your time. Sarah, Sal and I haven't had a chat together for a long time. It's well overdue. Come and spare me a few minutes, my Sally." She smiled at her granddaughter.

Sal, who loved and respected her grandmother, felt she must make time to talk to her despite all the work she knew was waiting for her when her rescuers left, sat down beside Ellen and gave her a hug.

"Nana, I know I've been neglecting you lately but I promise when this influx is over I will get over to see you every week. I've just been so busy."

"I know how busy you have been and it is right that you should make your own way. I'm getting old, and forgetful too, so I took the chance to come over with Sarah today in the hope of seeing you for a few minutes alone. I'm sorry for the timing, with you having so much worry on your plate, but it has been tormenting me for some time now. I have something for you." She fumbled in her bag and produced a purse, a small, much worn leather purse, which she handed to Sal and for an instant they both held the purse between their hands.

Noticing Sal's surprised look, she started to explain. "Your papa gave me this the first time we were together as man and wife, although we were not at that time married." She saw the shocked look on Sal's face and gave a little giggle, allowing

Sal a glimpse of the young Ellen Irvine. "In my day we fell in love, just like young people do today, and we are not always sensible where we love, but in our case, and Sal, I truly believe it was because of the contents of that purse, despite his horror-filled time in the navy he came home and found me and Sarah and John and we have had a good life. Your papa said this was the luck of the Campbells and until today has been handed down to a Campbell man for generations. I suppose, if I'm truthful, the charm was given to your father before he was born but as either way it would come to you, I want you to take it now and treasure it and when the time comes, pass it on once more."

"Can I open the purse?"

"Yes. See the beauty that has kept our family safe and prosperous for two hundred years."

Sal, with some trepidations, pulled the worn leather string that held the mouth of the purse closed, putting her hand into the space to remove the ruby ring which she held up to the light and gazed at in fascination.

"This holds the luck of the Campbells?" she whispered to her grandmother.

"Yes. That is the lucky ruby."

Chapter Twenty-Three

The Studio

"So you see, we Campbells were into women's lib long before Emmaline Pankhurst and her kind. I'm proud that my ancestors were so unbigoted."

"From your tale, correct me, if I'm wrong, Sal's mother was pretty keen for her to follow the traditional path and marry and have children like all her friend's children, though wasn't she?"

"That's true and I admit the fact that Sal was allowed her head was, certainly in part, due to John's influence over his wife. He would not have been able to influence her if she had not been ruled by her hidebound ideas that women should know their place and obey their husbands. Presumably she was brainwashed by her parents into thinking that was her place in society, so she feared her strong-willed daughter would not find a man, since she believed men wanted women who did as they were told. Smart men of the past had that written into the wedding vows."

He once more slanted a look at his wife before continuing in obvious amusement, "But *really* smart men know where the power lies and accept their lot gracefully. Smart men *know* that they need to marry a strong woman to get on in life. Ever heard the saying, 'Behind every successful man is a successful woman?' Well it's true and if it wasn't for the nagging and dominating woman I married I'd still be threshing corn like my father. You should see her wield her rolling pin."

Mark laughed as did the audience for Lady Marion Campbell was often photographed at her husband's side but rarely spoke in public, and never to the media, so the thought of the diminutive lady dictating to her giant husband appeared ridiculous to contemplate. She seemed to have no opinions other than those voiced by her husband and throughout Lord John's long career as a politician, both at local level, then later as leader of his country, her only concern was to allow her children to grow up in anonymity.

"My children have been lucky to have been allowed to find their own path in this world unfettered by the expectations of the previous generations. I will say that their success is laid totally at the feet of my wife. She was the driving force that endorsed their belief in their ambitions. If I had been given any input, I would have pushed for them to reach for the sky and be dammed to the consequences but my wife nurtured each child with skill and tact. Despite the media circus that raises up us poor individuals in the public eye to unsustainable pinnacles of perfection with the only purpose to find ways to bring us back down to earth by showing our feet of clay, there has been no scandal published about my family. My wife would tell you that many times I wanted to be the heavy handed parent, vetoing fashions... Oh yes particularly fashions," he rolled his eyes and every father in the audience knew exactly what he meant and gave a sympathetic titter.

"But the quiet belief of Marion made me realise her parenting skills were well beyond mine when she so frequently said, 'If we don't give them anything to rebel against, we won't get a rebellion.' Smart woman I married, huh?" he asked Mark

"Lord Campbell, you are digressing again. We are all agog to know what happened to the ruby when John had only daughters. Not," he continued hurriedly, "that there is anything wrong with having daughters, but what happened next?" was Mark's frustrated question. He had always prided himself on being able to handle politicians, but Lord John had never been one to give a straight answer.

"Yes, well, society's attitude does play a part in this story and you know how much I pander to society's attitude." He sent Mark a cheeky grin.

Mark sighed and admitted defeat. He would get the story but only in Lord John's own time. He decided not to force the issue so he just said, "How?"

"You might say that the lack of war early in Victoria's reign began the change we now call socialism. It wasn't just the Borders that thrived in the early to mid nineteenth century. The Quaker Cadbury family had followed the same kind of plan at Bourneville as Robert Owen in Scotland and many philanthropic men and women, such as Lady Johnstone, designed villages where their workforce were treated as human beings and with the successful outcome, which to ordinary businessmen was profit, many began to realise the way to productivity was a happy workforce. Perhaps today's multinational conglomerates should look carefully at the model and adopt the slogan, 'People, Quality, Profit'," he said in an aside. "What you may not realise is that Owenism failed eventually as did most of the Victorian 'isms' played with by the reformers. I have no wish to bore you with politics tonight but new labourism is not a new idea. In Victorian times there was new conservatism, new liberalism, new trade unionism, anarchism, social Darwinism, secularism and spiritualism to name but a few however unlike almost all of Europe, there was no Marxism to speak of in Britain of the eighteen fifties. Was the little woman on the throne responsible for the rise in women's lib? Who knows? Nonetheless the fact is that women were beginning to think for themselves and we men did not like it."

"You say women were coming into their own, but surely Sal was being pressurized by her mother to conform to the norm?"

"Yes, that's true, Elizabeth Campbell was between a rock and a hard place, because she wanted to conform to peer pressure and marry her daughter young to show her friends what a good match she could make and, of course, to get security for herself and her children. You have to remember that the only way of life for most women was marriage; to have a man to work and support them was the aim of every woman of the time. Although Ellen broke the mould by keeping Hartwood on Bill's death and Sarah had never married, these examples meant nothing to Liza. She felt inferior to a man and believed a man, any man, was necessary for a woman's security. Nevertheless, she admired the pluck of Lady Johnstone and did not want to be diminished in her eyes by demanding her daughter marry instead of having a career. We find that strange today when women happily juggle home, husband, children and career, and not always in that order. Incidentally, Liza seems to have been much more lenient with her younger daughters. From the stories told in the family it was only the eldest daughter she plagued to marry. You might think she was selfish to sacrifice her daughter's happiness for her own safety but that is how she had been raised and she expected obedience from her daughter. You have to remember that society changes slowly and Elizabeth Campbell was in the middle of societal change."

Mark had another attempt to get Lord John back to his subject.

"Much though I could listen to you all night, and I am an admirer of your thoughts about socialism, we are all spellbound and hanging by a thread desperate to hear what happened to Sal."

Lord John appeared to realise that he had been rambling so moved his position, gave his faraway look and went on.

"Jim had bought the much desired threshing mill and started to contract around the other farms and was making a good living in his own right, incidentally the very same threshing mill my father used in my youth. They knew how to build to last in those days," he grinned around before sighing and continuing. "He still stayed at Hartwood and ran the farm for the increasingly frail Ellen, but he planned to move into a cottage of his own when Sal brought her educated husband to farming. Sal pleased her mother by walking out with Paul Hamilton with a plan to marry when Sal could train another to take over her position in the Infirmary, but she was in no hurry to speed up the wedding."

"But she did have the lucky ruby ring though, so presumably her luck continued?" queried Mark.

"Life, as we all know, has a way of surprising us," smiled Big Jock as he once more leaned back in his chair and held forth to his audience.

Chapter Twenty-Four

"Can't you stand still?" asked Paul of his betrothed as they stood on the platform waiting for their first journey by train. "It really is unseemly for you to be running up and down like a child. Why don't we sit quietly on the bench and await the engine's approach?" he finished. It was apparent that he was annoyed by Sal's exuberant behaviour.

"Oh, Paul. Are you not excited by the prospect of this new steam engine? It is said that we will take only an hour to reach Dumfries instead of half a day as Jim has to with his pigs in the cart," she answered, looking up at him with her face shining with anticipation.

Over the last eighteen months Sal had found Paul a comfortable companion able to speak to her about her concerns for the workers of Mill village and the prospects for his pupils, but having promised to marry him she was now finding him reticent about sharing her ideas and schemes. He frequently dismissed her notions when they did not coincide with his thoughts on the matters they discussed. She frowned as she realised this was the first time they had been out alone together since they had met, as their courtship, such as it was, had taken place either on evening strolls along the riverbank or on sedate walks to church where they were surrounded by others from the village.

"My dear Sarah," he started, for he alone called her this having a dislike of pet names, "running along the platform to peer along the empty tracks will not make the train appear any sooner. I am naturally happy to experience the novelty of rail travel but I am a respected member of the community and cannot be seem cavorting around on a wooden platform and you, my dear, as my future wife, should be aware of how your actions reflect on me," was his pedantic statement, quite taking the edge off Sal's enjoyment.

"I'm sorry, Paul. I wasn't thinking about how others might view us," she answered, much cowed, sitting herself down primly by his side. He smiled at her submissive expression as he took in her graceful look. She was dressed in her very best clothes, a lilac tweed suit with a white, lace-collared blouse, neat woollen stockings and black button boots that showed beneath the shorter length of her fashionable skirt. She had twisted her hair up into a chignon at the nape of her neck and crowned it with a bonnet that matched her suit; even her mother had approved the sight of her daughter as she left Annanbank that morning. As Sal sat by his side, back straight and holding her handbag clutched in her black leather-gloved hands, properly on her knees, Paul surveyed her from head to foot finding little to fault in the appearance of his promised wife.

"Her manner needs to be a bit more sober but when she finds herself in more sophisticated company she will not embarrass me," he thought, congratulating himself on acquiring such a good-looking bride. His brow creased just for a moment while he thought of the one disadvantage of Sal; her work as a nurse in the Infirmary. It was not remotely respectable, in his view, for an unmarried girl to attend, intimately, to any man other than her husband; if it had not been that Lord and Lady Johnstone were on friendly terms with the family, and his high hopes that these connections would further his ambition to be a person of standing in the community, Sal would not have been his choice. His tastes ran to more sedate and malleable women. "But once we are married she will cease her independent ways and accept my judgements are superior to hers."

"I can hear the chunter of the wheels on the track," said Sal jumping to her feet once more to strain her neck for the first glimpse of the engine. Indeed, it was approaching the little station where it stopped in a cloud of steam to allow the passengers to ascend. Paul held open the door to allow Sal to climb in before him. She sat down on one of the wooden benches and was lucky enough to obtain a seat next to the window. On seating himself beside her Paul removed his bowler hat, unbuttoned his gloves and drawing them from his fingers placed them in the hat, laying them together with his horn-headed walking cane on the seat beside him. He was very careful to ensure that the seat he sat on was not dusty, for he had heard that the passenger carriage could be full of smuts from the coal burned in the firebox of the engine to produce the steam that ran the machinery to pull the train along the rails.

Sal gave a little smile to herself as she noticed him fussing with his trousers and taking a handkerchief from his inside pocket gave his highly polished shoes a few flicks to remove some specks of dust he imagined he saw. He also was dressed in his best, with his linen immaculately starched and the neck cloth a masterpiece any dandy would have been proud of. Sal wondered if, when she was responsible for his linen, she would be able to compete with the weaver's wife who currently washed his clothes.

"For I don't think he believes I have no domestic talent. I wish Ma would not praise me so extravagantly when they meet." She gave herself a shake. "I'm not going to think of mundane daily tasks today. I am having a holiday."

She turned and beamed one of her dazzling smiles on Paul, catching his coat sleeve in her excitement as she spoke, "Let's enjoy today and buy each other a fairing."

"We'll see," came the not so enthusiastic answer. Paul Hamilton definitely thought he was allowing his companion to indulge in an activity far beneath him.

Paul suffered Sal's exclamations of delight as they rushed through the green countryside, over bridges built to allow the railway passage over streams. He ignored her squeals of delight at the sharp blowing of the whistle as the train drew into and out of the small stations along the way. He sat looking straight ahead as she was fascinated by the clouds of steam that floated past the windows. He did remonstrate once or twice when Sal's enthusiasm led her to jump up and put her head out of the window to feel the hot air blowing back from the smoking engine. She was as excited as any of his pupils would have been. It wasn't that Sal had never been to Dumfries, but today was special because of the railway trip and the greatly anticipated visit to the town's Rood Fair where she had big plans to spend her wages if she could find some bargains.

They detrained at the busy station and both stood in awe for some moments as they viewed the hustle and bustle on the platform as people ran hither and thither; errand boys bringing packages to be taken to stations further along the line; families meeting friends who had, like Paul and Sal, made the journey to visit the town's fair; relatives fussing as they waved farewell to excited family members making a journey. There were even a few sheep being driven into a luggage van attached to the passenger carriage by a harassed railway porter.

"This is the future, Paul. Think how quickly coal and meat and even animals can be transported about the country," indicating, with her head, the sheep trying desperately to avoid the prods forcing them into the dark van. "Nothing will ever be the same now travel is so easy."

"I disagree. Only the poor will use the train. Gentlemen will continue to travel in their own chaises with changes of horses posted at inns along the way. I think you are right too though," he continued so condescendingly that Sal had to bite her lip not to make a sharp reply. "Provender will be moved more quickly. You must get Jim to increase the number of pigs on the farm. I hear they love the green pork from Dumfriesshire pigs in London and it can command as fine a price as Westphalian Ham. Indeed, I heard it said that some smart businessman bought all the bacon he could at one market and transported it to be sold in the smart part of London as just that, thus making his fortune."

"I have no say in what happens on either farm," she laughed. "Can you imagine me telling Da or Jim how to run their stock? I may be a farm girl but my ability does not run to husbandry."

"Naturally while your father is alive you will need to heed his words, but someday both of these farms will be yours and it will be necessary for them to provide us with an income suitable to our status."

Sal squinted a puzzled look at her fiancé. Unaware of his recent flights of fancy to have a prominent place in local society, she found his comment perplexing, but she answered brightly, "You will endow me with all your worldly goods, Paul. That will be enough for me. We will do very well on your salary. I am not such an extravagant person as to spend all your income on a pretty bonnet, I promise you." She smiled coyly at him.

Paul felt this was not the right time to advise Sal how he planned them to live after their marriage, so he just smiled at her, offering his arm for her to take as he escorted her away from the train station and into the town.

As they sauntered down the narrow streets into the centre of the town they could hear the furore of the many traders and performers who visited the Rood Fair. This was the last fair of the year and was always held on the last Wednesday in September, meaning if it was at all possible to attend local people would not miss this last chance to buy necessities for the coming winter.

The main business of the fair took place on the Whitesands, or as some still called it the lower sand beds, for it lay so low and flat that it flooded with any abnormal tide, causing much hardship to traders and those who dwelt in the nearby 'stinking vennel'. The buying and selling of horses took place here. It was also the meeting place for farm workers who were looking for a new position for the winter months. Sal knew how difficult it was for these families to find work and shelter since winter was a slow time on the farms around, leading many farmers to dispense with their workers at this season. Paul was careful to keep Sal away from the horse sales since he knew the men bartering their beasts were prone to use profanity not fit for a lady's ears. In fact, Paul was not at all pleased to have been inveigled into accompanying Sal to the busy, noisy and crowded town, but she had a list of commodities that could only be found when the travelling traders called 'dusty feet' were allowed to sell their wares.

"We need to go up High Street and down Buccleugh Street as far as the new bridge, or maybe even onto the Green Sands to find some of the spices Nana has asked for. She likes to have some for the Christmas festivities." She waved a long list at Paul who sighed, realising that it would not be easy to detach Sal from the fair and interest her in taking tea in a tea room as a more refined alternative to walking through the smelly crowd. Paul was very fastidious and scorned those who were less so. He crinkled up his nose as he heard the traders call out their wares, each trying to out shout his neighbour.

"This may be the town with a reputation of 'guid neebors' but today it's all about the trade," giggled Sal as she listened in delight to the calls around her, turning her head this way and that as each stallholder called his wares. Her eyes shining and her colour heightened with the excitement of the day, she presented a bonny picture.

"Come buy your cames here. Horn cames of the finest quality!"

"All kinds of leddir, pointis, beltis shin, bits, straight from my tannery o'er the brig."

"Best chine cups in the toon. Cam awa ledies. Crystal bowels fur yir table."

"Bacon and chops, sausage an' puddin, Houston's the best!"

"Ploumedames, aipels, peers. Ripe fur yer jam and sweet to eat."

All the traders shouted at the crowd to come a see their wares and a holiday atmosphere pervaded the town. Much banter could be heard between the 'dusty feet' and the townsfolk as gossip was exchanged and goods bartered for. Many had come out just to hear the stories of the recently landed travelling pedlars and to soak up the atmosphere rather than to trade.

"My, the street is so busy. I don't know how I'll get to meet Jim, for I'm sure I'll not find him in this chaos. I'll need to hurry and get my messages before we meet him for I've no desire to carry all my packages back on the train."

"I thought we were to meet him at the Mid Steeple when all your purchases were made and his business done?" queried Paul, who hadn't paid much notice to what Jim and Sal had arranged. "You don't want to be carting stinking spices around in your handbag," he laughed, but it was obvious to Sal that as yet Paul was not enjoying his day and if she was honest he was making, what she had hoped to be a fun day, much less of a pleasure for her with his habit of throwing a wet blanket over everything with his desire to be 'genteel'.

"Yes and I must meet him there, then we can walk around and see all the entertainments. There are jugglers and acrobats and I saw a picture of a dancing bear at the top of High Street. There are so many things to see and do I don't think we will have half enough time to enjoy ourselves. Perhaps we can buy tickets to watch the players in their makeshift theatre?"

As she finished this sentence she was distracted by a stallholder calling out his wares which she had on her list, thereby missing the look of disgust on Paul's face as he heard her plan to roam around the fair. She hurried over to the stall, made her purchases, turned around and was soon in deep discussion with a woman who had many hues of tweed lengths on her stall while Paul turned away, ostensively to look at long under drawers, but actually to plan how to prise Sal away from the raucous entertainments she was planning.

"I don't know which one I like best," she told the stallholder as she lifted one length of material after another. "I'm so confused with all your lovely colours. I work in a cotton weaving village but we don't have different colours, only plain natural colour cloth because it goes elsewhere to be dyed."

"Aye, we do some of the dying on cottons too but our tweeds show the beauty of the countryside. I always think of the heather clad glens when I look at my material," answered the friendly woman. "You already have a wee heather-coloured suit on so perhaps you might like to take some of these soft blues or greens? The green would bring out the colour of your eyes and draw you a fine beau," encouraged the woman as she produced length after length for her customer's appraisal.

Sal held up first a length of material that had every shade of blue from navy to the colour of the sky on a sunny day, then a green piece that looked like the various colours of the rolling sea when she visited Powfoot. However, she was then struck by a glimpse of a burgundy red lying under a pile of other lengths and she went to dig it out to inspect it.

"This is it!" she exclaimed as she wound the length off worsted around her waist, looking down to see how it would look as a skirt. "I'll take it. And that nice deep red wool too. Do you have two skeins of that for I think it will suit my ma too?"

The small woman grinned up at her as she collected what Sal required and parcelled it up into a bundle. "You'll look grand in that, lass," and she patted Sal's hand as she gave her back some pence in change.

Turning to see Paul was busy at a stall opposite that was selling men's unmentionables Sal decided he would not want her to be present at his intimate shopping, so she continued to wander two stalls down where she purchased some pepper and ginger. The man at the stall told her he had come into the port at the Kingholm Quay that morning from Ireland. This was his first of the autumn markets he would be attending with his spices as fresh from the East as they could be. Sal pretended to be taken in by his sales pitch and bought a bag of his ginger rock, which she intended to keep in her infirmary for when she had sick children. When normal food did not tempt their poor appetite a sweetie always could. She thought back to her own childhood when her mother would always pop a bit of sugar candy in her mouth if she had to take a nasty-tasting medicine. With these thoughts in her head she thanked the merchant and heedlessly wandered on.

She stopped to buy some pins and a packet of needles and cotton from an old woman cooried into a shawl. Sal noticed the old woman's eyes were red-rimmed; she looked flushed and hot. She leaned towards her and asked if she was feeling ill.

"Aye, I've no been weel these three nichts. I'm warm then cauld an ma heid hurts most awfa."

Sal felt her head and counted her pulse to find it was racing. She had seen Dr Jardine use willow bark ground down and taken with water clear up these symptoms in no time, so was sure she could cure the woman. Just then Paul caught up with her and she smiled in relief at his presence.

"Thank goodness you are here. This poor woman is ill; in need of some of the salacin that Dr Jardine uses. Will you purchase some for me from the apothecary Mr Fingland while I get this poor creature a hot drink?"

"You will come away immediately and leave that flea-ridden woman to her own kind," Paul demanded in a tight voice, holding in his desire to chastise her more thoroughly. Only the proximity of others stopped him from dragging her forcefully away from the old crone.

"I'll do no such thing," answered an indignant Sal. "The poor soul is sick. I can't turn my back on her. If you will not help, then I will go myself and you can go and find Jim and ask him to collect my purchases." She turned to the woman saying, "I'll go to the apothecary and be right back. Stay where you are, my dear."

"All right, all right. I will go this time but only because I won't have you making a scene," agreed a disgruntled Paul as he turned on his heel and vanished into the pressing crowd, wishing fervently that Sal would obey him. Through gritted teeth he made a resolution that she would not be allowed to repudiate him again. Nevertheless, he found the apothecary and making the required purchase returned to the scene of his embarrassment. By this time, he had convinced himself that the whole street of stallholders were laughing at his inability to control his woman. He felt let down.

Sal meanwhile had managed to find a tea shop nearby and was able to persuade the owner to trust her with a cup of the beverage on her faithful promise to return the cup when the tea had been drunk. Sal hurried back to the old woman whom she helped to sit on the stool at the back of her stall, herself taking over serving customers while the grateful woman sipped the hot tea and, when Paul returned, coaxed her to take half of the medicine he had purchased on her behalf.

"Now you try to keep warm; take the other half of the powder tonight and if you still don't feel any better you really must take yourself to Moorfields Hospital. Anyone will show you where to go." Sal cast her professional eye over the woman, unhappy to be leaving her to her own devices because she was sure the woman would not heed her advice. She laid her hand on the older woman's arm saying softly, "It would be better to go now, out of this cold air, and rest until the medicine takes effect."

Looking round she caught the sour expression on Paul's face; quickly finishing her conversation in order not to antagonise him further, she said, "I must go now, but if I can I will look for you later and see how you go on."

After returning the cup to the tearoom Sal and Paul continued with her shopping in angry silence. Each was disappointed with the conduct of the other; perhaps they were both aware they had glimpsed traits of personality that they did not like that boded ill for their future life together. All Sal's earlier delight in the fair had been marred by Paul's behaviour and she wanted nothing more than to deliver her purchases to Jim and go home.

"For two pins I'd leave the man here and ask Jim for a ride in the farm cart but I suppose we should make up our argument," she sighed. "I'll not apologise for caring for that poor woman, no matter what he says," she thought defiantly.

The two were early at the courthouse where they had agreed to meet Jim; neither wanted to discuss the incident in the market so they both looked around the town square watching the comings and goings of those enjoying a better day than they. Sal was especially drawn to a young couple, arm in arm, chuckling at each other's words as they joyously made their way up the cobbled street oblivious to any outside activity. The young woman looked lovingly at her partner who appeared to be just as smitten with her; their obvious love for each other caught Sal by surprise. No such radiant glow emanated from Paul and her, which gave her much food for thought as they awaited the arrival of Jim.

Making an assignation in front of the Mid Steeple was a good plan as it could be seen from all over the town. Sal looked up at the spire high above the building and thought how impressive the court house and prison looked.

In an attempt to lighten the mood of her companion, she said, "Papa told me that he came here to pay his respects to Rabbie Burns when he lay kisted here from his death until his funeral. He was a poet I admired since his poems were about the everyday folks and farmers like us. Do you teach the bairns Burns's poems?"

Deciding he had better make an effort now that Sal was showing some remorse at flaunting his wishes, he answered, "I've not much use for him, myself. He wasn't an educated man and from what I have heard he was a ladies' man and not true to his wife. Some of his work is passable, for children, I suppose."

"I love his songs. They are so romantic. 'I'll love you till the seas run dry' don't you think that is romantic? Imagine being loved so much."

"I think he could have been a bit more restrained with his ideas and emotions. Ladies don't like too much emotion in their husbands," he laughed, but it was a very self-conscious laugh and, while Sal was thinking of something further to say to stop another long silence developing, she was pleased to notice Jim loping along towards them.

"Hullo, Sal, Paul," he greeted them, holding out his hand to the other man and grinning broadly at Sal. "Have you spent all your wages on fripperies and furbelows or is that a secret you'll keep to yourself?"

"You can safely look in all my packages, for there is nothing but household wares. I have bought you a wee sweetie, for being a wee sweetie, you understand," Sal replied as she handed over a small bag of the cinder toffee she knew was his favourite. "Now don't steal the rock I've bought for the Infirmary," she commanded

Jim quickly popped a piece of the toffee in his mouth and began to suck it, making exaggerated slurping sounds. Sal laughed but Paul remained po-faced as he watched the two jealously. Although he did not think Sal realised it, he could see that Jim was sweet on her and Paul was not going to give him a chance to woo her away from him. He wrinkled his nose in revulsion at the smell that rose from the workaday clothes

Jim was wearing, conveniently forgetting that today was a work day for Jim, who had spent the last few hours among the animals for sale in the market and preened himself with the fact that Sal could never prefer the rough manners of the farmer to his own refined etiquette.

"What do you want to do now that you have unburdened yourself and we have a few hours before our train back?" he asked trying to distract Sal's thoughts from their quarrel.

"What are you going to do, Jim? Is it straight home or are you off to have a glass at the inn?" Sal asked curiously.

"I'm going off on veerrry important business," he announced, throwing out his chest. "I am instructed by Lydia to purchase her some pretty material to make herself a dress, for I believe she has a sweetheart. It is urgent, she informed me; but Ma is not to know; it's our secret." He held his finger to his lips. "She is to make it on her new sewing machine," he finished.

"And you are to buy it for her?" She flung her arms round Jim's neck as she smiled in delight. "You are a veeerrry good brother but have you the least idea what a young girl will think pretty?" she mimicked. "She plagued you for a sewing machine and now you have to buy the material as well. Your poor wife will never have a penny to call her own the way you spoil that lass."

"Ach well, she's young and I can afford it." Jim blushed, whether at this praise or at the hug from Sal was left open to debate, but Sal quickly had another idea.

"Since you are going in the direction of the material stall would you look for an old woman selling pins and needles?" She dug into her handbag and drew out some coins which she pressed into Jim's hand, asking, "Could you buy her a hot drink or some soup for she is quite unwell? Tell her to go down the Green Sands to the bathhouse and ask if they will let her sit in the warmth for a bit. I know the warden there has a good heart."

"Keep your pennies. Lydia has not spent so much of my money that I can't help someone in need. I'll look out for her, Sal."

"You'd do better to avoid her altogether for she hasn't seen soap and water for many a year and I expect she is crawling with beasts," said Paul, trying desperately to remove Sal from her cousin. He turned towards her.

"Shall we have afternoon tea at the County Hotel and see a play at the Theatre Royal, or do you want to have a walk along the river towards the port? I am at your command."

Sal screwed up her eyes, wondering how Paul could change from a cold heartless man one minute to the perfect gentleman the next. She grinned at Jim and asked, "What would you suggest would be most ladylike?"

"Tea at the County, definitely; then you can tell your Ma and score points for she will be over the moon at her daughter rubbing shoulders with the rich and titled ladies of the town." Then, turning his grin upon Paul, he said in a loud whisper, "You'd better watch her. Give her a taste of the fare at the County and she'll have all your copper spent before you can earn it."

Sal punched him on the arm. "Watch your cheek, you. I'll have you know I've always been a lady to Paul and he knows just where to take me to tea and won't worry about his groats either." She stuck her tongue out and flounced over to take Paul's crooked arm.

"Lead on my good man. Pay no heed to this serf. Leave us now." This last was addressed to Jim and intended as a jest. He took it as just that and bowed in Sal's direction with a flourish and a leg that would not have been out of place at Queen Victoria's court.

The couple did indeed have afternoon tea at the County Hotel and Sal chose a walk along the river instead of the stuffy little theatre. As they strolled beside the River Nith she heard Paul's quiet voice apologising for his earlier behaviour, but since he laboured each point and used the phrase, 'in my position' so often she stopped listening and tuned into her own reeling thoughts to what life would be like as Mrs Paul Hamilton. The prospect did not please her, although she carried on with their programme for the rest of the day. If Paul had cared to pay attention to her, he might have seen a frown on her pretty brow that augured ill for their future.

****

"Da? Are you awake?" asked Sal as she poked her head round the bedroom door where her father was lying in bed recovering from another bout of his distressing cough and wheeze. Sal had asked Dr Jardine what she could do to help him but he had shaken his head sadly, saying, "I'm sorry, Sal but there is no more treatment to improve his condition. I have seen it before in farmers and also in weavers. I think it is caused by the dust and damp conditions, but then again I have seen it in young lasses who have neither worked nor lacked care, coming from the gentry. The disease will take its course and all you can do for your father is keep him out of the fields when it is wet and close to home when he is at his worst. He is lucky to have such a good family."

Sal sighed but continued with her questions. "I mean no disrespect, Dr Jardine, and we are all grateful to you for your care of Da, but Dr Wilson has sent Mrs Henderson from Lockerbie to a seaside spa town saying that the fresh air and sea breeze will improve her health. Would that be a benefit to Da?"

"I really don't think so but if you want to try it do by all means. Nothing would make me happier than to be proved wrong. Dr Wilson has been exchanging letters with Dr Brehmer at his clinic in Switzerland and he has attended many talks by Dr John Davy, who advocates that long periods of rest in clean air and nutritious food will always cure this disease they are now calling tuberculosis." He put his arm around her shoulders. "But, Sal, even if this proves to be the case, and there is some evidence that the Swiss Alps clinics have success, your father's condition has gone beyond cure. He has nothing left to fight with." Seeing the look of abject horror come over Sal's face he hurried on, "I don't mean he is close to death, my dear, only that his illness is too well established to benefit from the Spartan treatment advocated by these learned doctors. Besides, many of their cures advocate sleeping with cows and drinking their milk and although your father doesn't exactly sleep with the cows, he has spent his whole life amongst them."

As Sal stood in the doorway of the bedroom this last conversation passed through her mind. "Da doesn't look so uncomfortable today," she thought as she took in his breathing, which was slow and rhythmic and he was not fighting for each breath.

"Da?" she almost whispered.

"Aye lass, come you in." He opened his eyes to smile at his eldest daughter. "Who would complain about not having a son to carry on if they were blessed with a daughter like my Sal?" he thought, beckoning her to come further into the room. "What has taken the lovely smile off your face?" He stretched out to touch her cheek and she blushed to think she might upset him with her words.

"Come on then. Spit it out and shame the Devil. Something has been bothering you for a while now. Tell your old da and he will fix it." He smiled that crooked grin that was so characteristically him.

Sal stood by the bed biting her lip. Now that she had plucked up the courage to talk to her father she wondered if that had been the right choice. John patted the patchwork quilt that was the work of all the family and the pride and joy of her ma. "Just tell me, Sal. Nothing is so bad that we can't talk it better."

She slowly sat down on the side of her father's bed and immediately felt the comfort of his arm as it snaked around her waist. "Da's right. I have to get it off my chest and if he can make me see I'm being silly, so much the better," she thought, lifting her eyes to meet her father's where she saw his love for her shining out.

"I don't think I want to get married to Paul," she said quickly before she lost her courage.

"Why not?" was the quiet reply.

"There's nothing *wrong* with him. He is everything Ma could want in a son-in-law; he's polite, educated, handsome, caring in his way, but Da, it's not my way. I don't know how to explain it. He is kind and respectful to me but it's as if he is a far better person than me. He is, of course, but when I marry him I get the feeling that my opinions won't matter and I'll become just Paul Hamilton's wife, a chattel, not a partner like you and Ma or Papa and Nana."

She stood up and paced around the room in her frustration as John watched the turmoil in his daughter's expression. She clasped herself with both arms as she continued to try to explain her feelings to her father,

"I feel as if I will no longer be me. Paul cares very much for society and its opinions. He tries to hide it but he doesn't think nursing is respectable and he can't wait for me to leave Mill village and become a housewife. Oh Da," she knelt down by the side of the bed. "Can you imagine me a housewife, spending all my time talking to other wives about how to whiten the doorstoop or how to dolly his shirts and starch his cuffs? Even if I wanted to spend my life like that I have no domestic talent and I'm very sure that I will disappoint him with my lack of wifely attributes."

She buried her head in the quilt and allowed her father to stroke her hair as he had done when she was a child and pleading for his support when her mother wanted her to do something alien to her nature. John's hand stilled for a moment before he gave his advice.

"It is possible that with the wedding only two weeks away you are having cold feet. Believe me I was so nervous when I thought about how to keep a wife and family when I wed your Ma that I nearly joined the Navy. No wait, not yet!" He held up his hand to stop Sal's protests, "But if, now that you have told me your fears you go off and think better of the decision, there is nothing to do. I want you to think about it today and if by tomorrow your instinct is still the same, and you feel you can't marry Paul, then all you have to do is tell him. It won't be pleasant for he is an arrogant young man and will take being jilted badly, but in fairness to him you must tell him how you feel. Your ma and I will support you."

Sal's expression said all she was thinking and John laughed so hard it brought on his cough and for the next few moments the tension in the room was relaxed as Sal tended her father, patting his back as he strained to move the thick mucous from the very depths of his lungs, then gently wiping his sweating brow and settling him back on his pillows when his breathing returned to normal. Silently, while her father laid his head back on the snow-white pillow, a pristine whiteness Sal had no idea how to achieve, she surreptitiously glanced at the phlegm her father had caught in a piece of newspaper and was relieved that, although the substance was thick and plentiful, there was no blood in the sputum. She hastily rewrapped it and threw it into the heart of the fire. She turned and offered her father a drink, taking in his pale thin body, and sending a prayer arrowing to God to keep her father comfortable.

"Your ma will support your decision, you know," came the quiet voice of her father. "She wants to see you wed, it's true, but above all else she wants to see you happy and if you can't be happy with Paul, then that's that." He shrugged his shoulders as if it was the easiest thing in the world to break an engagement of which her mother had so publically bragged.

"Now, I want to sleep before your ma comes to make my life miserable; she doesn't, you know, that's just her way. She is the best wife a man could wish for because, even after all these years, my hair going, my lungs breaking up and my good looks passed on to my girls." He smiled at his own jest. "She is a faithful and caring darling who has been the rock I cling to in times of trouble. We are two halves of the same person; we make each other whole."

Sal gave her father a long hug, cuddling into him and revelling in the feeling of peace and security that the smell of him gave her. She drew back and kissed him on the top of his bald head. "You are the best father a girl could have. I need to marry someone like you who cares for me more than for themselves," she whispered.

"Aye, you do that, my lass," he whispered in return, bringing the tears to Sal's eyes.

She spent a restless night thinking about their conversation and about what her life would be like married to Paul, also what her life would be like not married to Paul, and finally what her life would be like unmarried. As she lay awake tortured by the machinations of her busy brain she began a list in her head. Children featured heavily on this list.

"What if I don't marry Paul and have no children? Will I regret not marrying him even if we have children? Is it the desire to have bairns that drives me to marry at all? Is it Ma's desire for grandbairns that makes me want them badly too?" The thoughts chased each other round and round in her head as night became day. Although it was barely light Sal felt there was nothing to be gained by lying sleepless in the ravaged bed so got herself up, gave her sister Jess a shake awake to tell her she need not get up yet as she, Sal, was off to bring the cows in and help out in the dairy.

As she passed the chain around the first cow's neck and felt the warmth of her large body close to her own, Sal knew milking had been the right decision this morning. She continued with her chore of preparing the cow for milking, then settled herself on a stool with her head pressed to the round protuberance of the cow's belly and immediately felt at peace. She was in a world of her own, where she belonged, alone to do as she pleased. She sat where she was long after her nimble fingers had extracted all the milk from the udder, unaware of the everyday life of the farm passing her by. Peter, the dairyman, had quietly finished milking the other beasts and it was the swoosh of his byre brush cleaning up after the animals that brought Sal back to the real world. Her real world. It was not as wife to a schoolmaster, however good he was. Her life was caring, for her patients or for the farm stock, not worrying about keeping up appearances and pretending to ape her betters. Her mind was made up. She would not marry Paul. All she had to do now was tell him!

But first she had to tell her ma!

Sal wandered tentatively into the warm kitchen, immediately struck by the homely smell of the place. The bright flames of the fire, the smell of bacon frying in the pan mixed with the warm delicious smell of newly baked bread cooling on the windowsill. It was a myriad of memories rolled up to encapsulate her life. This morning and after her decision she felt all her senses renewed as she herself felt reborn and light. Casting her eyes over the kitchen it seemed unchanged since her childhood. In her imagination she saw herself with her younger sisters, laughing around this same table as Liza tried to teach them to bake scones; the same grey, flat hard ones her father had pretended were delicious. The smoked bacon hanging on hooks from the ceiling, that caused such hilarity when as a child she had been determined to bring down the ham to cook breakfast when her fourth sister had just been born and her Ma was not in the kitchen as usual. The scrubbed oak table with the bevel in the middle from years of pounding bread dough; the dresser against the wall that her mother loved and with its china cups and plates that had been gathered over the years, the rag rugs on the floor that were made up of scraps from garments worn by her parents and sisters reminded her how, as a family, they had squabbled over the mixing of colours and patterns; how her father had allowed each of his girls to climb on his knee after a long hard day in the fields. The memories of happy times in this kitchen gave her the necessary fillip she needed to talk to her mother. She took two cups down from where they hung on the dresser and, carrying them over to the well-loved table, filled them with strong black tea from the pot left warming on the whirlie by the fire.

Offering one to her mother, she said, "Sit down, Ma. I have something to tell you."

"By the look on your physiog it's not good news." Her mother squinted at her as she drew out a chair and sat down. "What is it, then? Don't let me think the worst."

"Ma. I have been awake all night and I have come to a decision that I can't marry Paul. It would be wrong to get wed feeling as I do about him."

"How *do* you feel about him?" Liza asked quietly

Surprised that her mother had not hit the roof or screamed at her not to be stupid, Sal realised that her da was, as usual, right in his surmise that her mother wanted only what was best for her daughter. She smiled into her mother's face and stretched out her hand to grip the other woman's wrist before saying, "Can I tell you what my thoughts have been overnight?"

"Go on," said Liza, trying to regain the harsh manner she normally portrayed.

"He is a gentleman. A kind, clever, well-dressed man. He is a great teacher in the classroom and the children adore him."

"So what's the problem for you?" Liza interrupted. "You are telling me he is an admirable man. I know that from talking to him."

"Yes, but he is also very sure he always knows best. My opinion counts for nothing. *He* will make the decisions in our marriage; they won't be up for discussion. He doesn't think I am respectable because I work in the Infirmary at the village and I'm afraid he wants me to conform to his idea of a wife. One who will obey his orders implicitly. Oh, Ma, he wants so many things from me that are just not in my power to give. I love being independent and making my own money to say nothing of the pride I take in my job. He wants me to cook and clean, have babies and… Oh, suffocate… I can't do it, Ma."

"If he was the right man for you, you would not be having these worries. When you love a man better than yourself that is when you know it is right. Paul is not for you then; but he will not be happy. To be a jilted man is hard on a proud man and Paul *is* a proud man."

"I know, but I cannot marry him just to save his pride."

"What about you? Do you realise you will be the talk of the town and, as he is so well-liked, you will receive hard criticism from those in the village? Are you prepared for the tales and gossip that will follow?" asked her mother.

"I can't marry him to save my face any more than to save his. Anyway, those I care about know me and will not pay attention to any mention of a slur on my reputation."

"Then tell him and tell him soon for the banns have been called once and much embarrassment will ensue for you both. If Paul is not right, you should not marry him. I'm glad you realised it before the wedding, but I could wish you had discovered your error sooner." Liza got up from her place opposite and, coming round the table, clasped her eldest daughter to her chest allowing her to lay her head on her bosom as the two swayed together, comforter and comforted. Just as her father had predicted, her mother would be her support.

****

"There you go Mr Jones, that's you nice and comfy for your wife coming in to visit," smiled Sal as she collected her trolley complete with all the necessities she had used for her patient's ablutions. He had been caught in a spinning machine and the resultant injury had become infected, initiating his admittance to Sal's care. Although he had been in a bad way when he had been brought into her Infirmary, fevered and barely lucid, the drugs prescribed by Dr Jardine and Sal's nursing care now had him on the mend. She looked over at the small, cowed man who was still fighting against the stigma of his early life in the workhouse in Manchester, despite having become a man to be depended upon, both by his workmates and his employers. The harsh treatment meted out by the keepers of the workhouse had left him feeling inferior and undeserving. Even the fact that he now held a vital role in the day-to-day running of the mill could not take away his dread of being put out of work because of his injury.

"Aye, she'll be glad to see me back at work and earning," he answered but Sal could tell he was not happy with his situation. He feared he would not be able to return to work and then how would he feed his family?

"Lord Johnstone has guaranteed your wage while you are in hospital and will find you something suitable when you are fit to go back to work." She smiled at him, then glanced behind her to see his wife glowering at them. "Now here's your wife to make you feel better." She smiled and beckoned the woman to come forward saying, "I'm just finished shaving him so that he looks young and handsome for you."

Mrs Jones, the Irish lilt still apparent in her voice despite her never having set foot in that country, pursed her lips and gripping her handbag tightly in both hands in front of her, pushing her large bosom up to make her look like an angry banty cock, looked Sal directly in the eye and warned, "I'll thank you to keep your hands off my husband. He's a respectable man and wants nothing to do with the likes of you. You're nothing but a hussy and not fit to be near decent women."

"Well, Mr Jones is so much better I think Dr Jardine will be sending him home to you soon and he'll just need the wounds redressed when they seep though." Sal smiled at the woman as if she had not heard the disparaging words. "I'll leave you to your visit." And she departed pulling open the screens that had surrounded the bed, which allowed the other men in the ward to see how uncomfortable her patient was with his wife's comments.

"Damn!" she said under her breath as she pushed her trolley away to be disinfected and the contents destroyed. "I should not have exposed him to the ridicule of his mates. It was badly done of me. Whoever would have thought Paul could be so vindictive?"

After telling Paul of her decision she had been originally gratified that he had behaved in a very gentlemanly way, saying that of course he realised that if she was not happy to marry him she must not do so. He would release her from her promise. He had wanted no explanation of her reasons and calmly bade her 'good day', turned and was gone, leaving her relieved but slightly guilty for not being able to love him enough to marry him.

Over the last two months since that fateful day Sal had found it trying to be shunned by people she had formally called neighbours and friends. When she entered the Mill village shop silence fell until she was served and had left, then the buzz of whispered gossip could be heard continuing before the bell had stopped jangling and the door closed against her back. She walked from the Infirmary to her own lodgings and heard the muffled shouts of 'hussy' and 'whore' behind her. She tried hard to ignore them or, like today with Mrs Jones, hold onto her professional manner. She knew that Mrs Jones had fought hard to keep her husband at home in order to keep him away from the influence of such a 'bad woman' but had been forced to submit to his admission when Dr Jardine had, in plain words, told her the only nurse who might save her husband was Sal. Now of course, since he was recovering, she heaped even more scorn on Sal since she had been able to help her husband where his respectable, decent wife couldn't.

Paul meantime had revelled in the ease with which he had been able to denigrate his former fiancée. A word here and look there when talking to the mothers of his pupils had been all that it took to place him securely in the victim corner, a role he delighted in playing. He never openly miscalled her, but jubilant at the fact that the women of the village shunned her. However, having the ignorant mill workers ignoring her wasn't enough to placate his desire to humiliate her. The minister of Ruthwell Church where they had planned to get married had heard Sal's side of the story and while he privately condemned her, it was not for reneging on her promise to marry but for making the promise in the first place without taking advice from God and his minion on earth. He had explained to Paul that as Sal was such a young woman, only just at her majority, it was not unusual for her not to know her own mind and that he should show her compassion. The last thing Paul wanted was to show Sal compassion. Lord Johnstone had visited him to convey his sorrow for the anguish of his schoolmaster but as he made it clear that he had done so at his wife's behest to assure Sal, who was worried about the distress she had caused him, it gave him no pleasure to be assured by him that he was bearing up manfully.

Dr Jardine also agreed that Sal had been sensible not to marry when she was unsure of her feelings and continued to be partisan of her case, but Dr Wilson had wrung his hands, saying how sorry he was that the betrothal had come to nothing.

"Especially as she will come into her grandmother's property when she goes. It must be a great loss to lose both the estate and the wife in one swoop. After all, a contract is a contract, whether it is to buy a horse or a wife," he chuckled,

It was these words of balm from Dr Wilson that led him to his next move. He wanted her to be humbled and disgraced wherever she went, and by the very people who now supported her, so he had devised a plan that not only would demean Sal so that she wanted to hide her face forever but would bring him some financial gain.

****

"Dr Jardine. Could you spare me a few minutes when you are finished with your surgery?"

"Of course, Sal. I'll only be a short time."

"I'll be in the Infirmary whenever you have the time. There is no hurry." She smiled at her mentor and hurried out of the room to allow him to finish his consultation.

Sal continued with her rounds, checking her orders were being carried out as she had instructed. She had spent a lot of her sleepless hours working out her rules for the Infirmary and was now engaged in ensuring that they were carried out properly. There would be no necessity now for her to find a successor. She sighed sadly as she felt the long anticipated letter crackle in her apron pocket. This was what she wanted to discuss with Dr Jardine.

"Hello, Sal," came the cheery voice of the doctor as he entered her room, immediately going over to the fire and rubbing his hands in front of the blazing flames. "It's mighty chilly coming over from the surgery. What can I do for you?"

Sal pulled the letter from her pocket and silently handed it to the doctor. He glanced at her sombre face and surmised there was no good news within the missive. He removed his spectacles from his waistcoat pocket and, opening the sheet of paper, began to read the words that had been addressed to his protégée.

My Dear Miss Campbell,

Miss Nightingale has advised me to write to you to indicate that she rejects your request to accompany her and her band of _trained_ nurses to the Crimea. She wishes to make it plain that only ladies of a certain level in society are fit to deal with the injuries and conditions of the male sex without succumbing to the blandishments of soldiers and becoming a burden on her resources.

She believes that the condition of these men, rife with diseases such as cholera and typhus, would be far beyond your rustic training and begs that you confine yourself to your own stratum.

She does feel however that you may make a valuable contribution to the care of our soldiers by getting together with your friends and making warm clothing and blankets for our poor soldiers. These may be remitted to the address below or to the London Times who are raising funds on her behalf.

Yours Faithfully
William Nightingale

"What do you think of that?" asked Sal as she paced around the room, red in the face with embarrassment at being spoken of in such an insulting manner. "Not of a fit mentality to nurse her precious soldiers but, oh yes, I can send her some money. Not fit to work with her lady nurses but to look after the inferior class to which I belong! The cheek of the woman! I would bet I have nursed more cases of typhoid and cholera than she has! Does she intend to sit up all night bathing a fevered patient or feeding them gruel every hour to build them up? I bet she doesn't!"

"No, Sal, calm yourself. You and I both know you are a wonderful nurse and I can't help being glad that you are not off to Constantinople with the nursing ladies. You are not the only one who has fallen short of Miss Nightingale's standards. My friend Seacole's daughter has been rejected simply for being black. Mary is half Scottish, half Jamaican and has been 'doctoring' for years but she is not fit to join the illustrious band either. Miss Nightingale may say as she likes that only women of her own class are immune to the sight of naked male bodies, but I believe her frequent rejections of well-practised nurses is to ensure no one disputes her superiority." He came across the room, threw the disparaging letter on the desk and clasped Sal in a great bear hug.

For a second, Sal let go of her anger and accepted the comfort of the doctor's arms before saying sadly, "I so wanted to go with the band and be useful, and if I'm honest to get away from the backstabbing and gossip about my jilting Paul. I will never live that down. I will always be the woman who was courted for what she might bring to her husband; a husband who was willing to take me on despite being employed in a demeaning capacity. Can you believe it?" She strode across the room, grabbing the infamous letter from the desk, took hold of the paper as she would have liked to have taken the haughty Miss Nightingale's neck and wrung it between her fingers until it was shredded, but this action did little to assuage the feeling of revulsion engendered by the insulting missive.

She continued to rant. "Am I really at such a low level of society that... that... *woman* dare put her darling soldiers' recovery at risk simply because I'm not a lady? How many of the men her group of *ladies* will be confronted with are gentlemen or does she intend *only* to offer succour to the officers? Will she let the ordinary soldier lie in his filth with his wounds bleeding and festering because he is not of sufficient rank to warrant the attention of her nice clean nurses?"

She blew out her frustrations and as the doctor listened patiently to her tirade while she paced the room, he noticed that her heightened colour made her prettier than ever, making him wonder how anyone, even Paul Hamilton, would prefer a docile subservient wife rather than this termagant before him.

Sal once more took herself off around the room, striding out in her frustration and disappointment. She took some pleasure in punching a cushion and kicking a waste paper basket that got under her feet until her temper calmed. She grinned sheepishly at the doctor, apologising profusely for her behaviour. He waved away her apology, but enquired what had caused her to lose control of her patience so badly.

"It appears Miss Nightingale is of the same opinion as Paul, so maybe I'm as well off with neither of them. I'll stay where I'm appreciated and, like my Aunt Sarah, dedicate my life to helping others. That's if *you'll* still want me now that I am a jilt."

Doctor Jardine grasped both of her hands in his feeling the delicate bones of her fingers and wrists under his touch, realising that the real cause of Sal's outburst was not the rude letter from the Nightingales but a symptom of the stress she had been under since the termination of her betrothal. She had tried to ignore the taunts and whisperings but they had taken their toll on her normally resilient nerves.

"No one really believes the only attraction Paul Hamilton saw in you was your nana's farm but everyone likes a gossip; life is very dull in the villages around here, you know." The doctor laughed. "For me this letter from Miss Nightingale is a boon, for I can't tell you how much of a miss you would be to the Infirmary and to the whole Mill village. Who would care for my patients as you do? Miss Nightingale is not a trained nurse, and indeed does not wish to take part in any of the actual care of the poor soldiers she professes to think might seduce a maid, when they are lying trying to hold onto their lives in poor conditions, little wholesome food and sanitary conditions that invite all manner of rodents and pests that carry disease. A scratch wound from a musket ball can be fatal simply because the overcrowded, cramped and dirty hospital is the only place to send our soldiers. She should perhaps look at the environment you have created with your 'Cleanliness next to Godliness' attitude. If she manages to clean up the abominable conditions at Scutari then she will be proclaimed a national heroine. Don't be disappointed, Sal." He produced another of his fatherly hugs and grinned down at her.

She had changed over the last few months. Her normally cheery personality had taken a severe knock with the notoriety of the court case. As he held her for a moment against his broad chest he could feel the frailty of her bones and a glimpse at her face showed the signs of many sleepless nights, her eyes being dull and lacklustre. The only time he saw her smile these days was when she had a patient in her care or when Jim came to meet her, as he did every night, to ensure she was not harangued on her way home. He knew that it would take many a day before Sal regained her self-belief after the ignominious case of breach of promise she had just been through. It too had begun with a less than polite letter. It had been Jim who had brought it to his attention, asking for advice on how to proceed. He thought back to the day the harassed young man had visited him in his surgery.

"I wonder if you could give me some guidance about this letter Sal has received today. My instinct is to rout the bugger out and knock him into next week, but John has asked me to bring it to you."

He handed the letter to the doctor and watched his expression as he perused the damming epistle.

McJerrow, McJerrow & Stevenson
Lockerbie

Dear Miss Campbell,
I am instructed by my client, Paul Hamilton, to inform you of his intention to sue you in a court of law for damages brought about by your breach of contract to marry on 21ˢᵗ day of November of this year of Our Lord Eighteen Hundred and Fifty-Three.
In order for this case not to be brought before the magistrates at the next assizes I advise you that a sum of One Thousand Pounds Sterling (£1,000) would satisfy my client.

Yours Faithfully

James McJerrow

That had been the start of the worst time of Sal's young life. Her father, Jim and Dr Jardine had colluded to keep as much of the nastiness of the case away from Sal but inevitably the news leaked out in their community and Sal was extremely self-conscious of the taunts and smirks that followed her wherever she went. Paul Hamilton was a very charismatic man and many of the villagers, and especially the parents of his pupils, were decidedly on his side even without knowing the ins and outs of the situation. The women followed the accounts of the court action that were printed in the *Dumfries Standard* avidly and were quick to take sides, their husbands were less inclined to sympathise with a man who had taken the step of going to law against his fiancée.

Dr Jardine had not given his advice immediately but had taken the letter with him to visit a university friend, James Gordon, who had qualified in law and practised as a writer in Dumfries. After an excellent dinner and while their wives adjourned to the salon the two men drew their chairs closer and began to discuss the case in hand.

"What can he believe warrants him one thousand pounds, for goodness sake?" asked Gordon

Dr Jardine shrugged. "The banns had been proclaimed once from the pulpit and I admit it would have been better if she had changed her mind sooner, but he prides himself on being a gentleman and surely the gentlemanly thing to do would be to accept her decision calmly."

"I could write to Robert McJerrow and request some enlightenment. That much I can do for you, but if it must be brought before the court I will need to be instructed by the young lady herself. It might be a protracted and expensive business but if he feels a thousand pounds is reasonable she must be well endowed for a farmer's daughter?"

"That is just the point I can't figure. She has no money; she is my trainee, or rather she was; she is an excellent nurse both in Lady Johnstone's village infirmary and in the farm cottages around where she tends the sick, no matter if they do not pay, which is more than can be said for many."

James Gordon poured his friend another glass of port and looked thoughtfully into his own glass before stating. "The best thing to do is find out why he is claiming this money and how he thinks she can pay him, then take it from there." He raised his glass to his lips and the men changed the subject and soon joined their spouses for a convivial evening.

It was several days later that the doctor received a communication from his friend which he took immediately to Annanbank to share with John Campbell. It was one of John's good days and he was ensconced by the fireside in his favourite chair. It was obvious to Dr Jardine that his patient had been indulging himself with a pipe of tobacco as the offending instrument was still in the frail hand that lay along the leg of his corduroy breeches. Dr Jardine had long since given up pressurizing him to give up the evil weed, but he let his gaze rest on the incriminating pipe for a moment without saying a word.

"Hello, Doctor, are you well? We were not expecting you, were we?" asked John with a chuckle.

"Obviously not."

"Och, I'm a dying man; what harm can a wee draw do me now?"

"I've not come to talk about your health, although I'm glad to see you are not so wheezy today. It must be this sharp cold air that is to thank for that," came the professional answer. "I've brought you news from James Gordon; here, read this," and he handed over the letter to be shared.

Messrs. Gordon, Primrose and Gordon
Bank Street
Dumfries
Dr Graham Jardine
Ruthwell

Dear Graham,

As per our conversation on Saturday last I have instigated inquiries from Messrs McJerrow and Stevenson and I enclose their reply for your perusal.

I would be glad to take on the case for Miss Campbell at a minimal rate as I believe this case will be easily defended.

My advice therefore, is not to accede to the terms advocated in their initial letter but rather to have Miss Campbell take counsel from myself at her earliest convenience.

I remain your friend

James Gordon.

John read the letter handed to him then held his hand out for the enclosure

McJerrow, McJerrow & Stevenson
Townhead Street
Lockerbie

James Gordon
Bank Street
Dumfries.

Dear Mr Gordon,

It appears that you are acting for Miss Sarah Campbell in the matter of a case of breach of promise on behalf of my client, Mr Paul Hamilton.

Mr Hamilton is suing for recompense for loss of property he would have gained had the marriage gone ahead as planned sic: as 'feme covert', putting her under the protection and influence of her husband, the said Paul Hamilton. Upon the contracted marriage, the husband and wife becoming one person under the law, as the property of the wife would be surrendered to her husband, and her legal identity cease to exist.

As Miss Campbell, a woman of low profession, is expected to inherit a substantial amount in the form of the farm known as Hartwood on the death of her paternal grandmother and is in possession of various jewels of great value it is my client's contention that with the breach of her promise to marry she has deprived him of the sums he could count as his own as the contract had been agreed between the parties.

Mr Hamilton further attests that as the profession of his former betrothed is inferior to his situation he is entitled to damages against his personal esteem.

I repeat the offer of settlement of One Thousand Pounds Sterling (£1000) and await your further correspondence.

John sat in amazed silence for some considerable time then reread both letters before bursting into great roars of laughter which, of course, started a coughing bout. When he had recovered his brimming eyes caught Dr Jardine's and he continued a silent chuckle.

"It's all very well for you to laugh, John, but if a lawyer is willing to take it to court it would appear there is a case to answer. What will become of Sal? How will she stand up to the notoriety?"

John's face took on a serious expression as he replied, "Sal is a Campbell. She will weather any storm; Mr Paul Hamilton has come to the wrong trough. He might believe we will roll over and pay him compensation but he has baited the wrong hook; he'll have his day in court if that is what he wants but he will rue the day he challenged my family honour."

"Do you want me to make arrangements for Sal to see Gordon?"

"Aye, you do that and if you could go out of your way a bit and go to my mother's and ask Jim to come visit me, I will be much obliged. I'm not fit to escort her to a court hearing but Jim will more than adequately take my place. He is a good loyal man."

The doctor was as good as his word and before very long Jim Campbell came riding into the stackyard on his rattling velocipede. He was met by Jess and Liz who were alerted to his presence by the noise of his bicycle. They both looked at the fine-looking man; Jess was a little bit in love with him but, young as she was, her woman's intuition told her that Jim was not for her, but how she wished she could find a beau as handsome as he. With his 'Black Campbell' looks he was a contrast to her father and grandfather. It was said that he took his colouring from his French ancestors, but whatever the way of it he was well set up, tall and dark with laughing features and a very complaisant temperament. She sighed.

"What on earth is that contraption? You'll scare the cows into going dry," laughed Jess as she walked around the strange machine. "Look. Liz, Jim has a…" She stopped, not knowing what to make of the strange machine. "What is it, Jim?"

"Where on earth did you come across that monstrosity and what does it do?" asked Liz, also walking around the cycle and taking in the unusual nature of the apparatus.

Jim grinned as he once more mounted the bicycle and demonstrated how he could propel himself forward by working the pedals that hung on either side of the front wheel to turn both wheels. He was a bit wobbly on the uneven ground but the girls were enthralled by his skill.

"I have a loan of it from James Johnston. The blacksmith from Keir, Kilpatrick Macmillan, invented it and made James one too. It is not too comfortable but it saves me miles of walking when I go to see Sal home from the Infirmary. It's the metal rims that make the noise, not the cycle falling apart."

"You never put her on that, do you?" giggled Liz as she imagined her big sister sitting crouched on the machine. "It's not dignified!" She examined the wooden frame and wheels; a small wheel at the front that was attached to the pedals and could be steered in the right direction by a pair of handles and the large wheel at the back that had an uncomfortable seat slung by leather straps above it for the cyclist to sit.

"No, you daftie, I cycle to the village and walk Sal through it to her room then I cycle back home and jump into bed." He tickled Liz under the chin.

"Jump up and I'll hold you while you take a ride."

Liz wasted no time in accepting this offer and was soon perched on the seat being wheeled around the stackyard. She squealed as they went over bumps but was delighted with the whole idea, but when her sister was offered a turn, she flushed red and rejected the offer.

"It's not dignified. Ma would have a fit if she saw you cavorting on that thing and showing off your drawers."

"Oh Jess, you are such a snob. Jim isn't interested in my drawers or yours either for that matter. Why are you here?" Liz turned to ask Jim.

"Don't be nosy, miss," came the voice of their mother. "He might have come to take me for a ride on his contraption." She laughed, then said, "Come you in, Jim, John is waiting for you and has a favour to ask of you."

While Liza made tea and scones for the two men they discussed the letters John had already read and John explained what he wanted Jim to do.

"I'm not fit to go gallivanting to Dumfries and I can't face the idea of Sal having to go on her own, so I wanted to ask you to accompany her to the lawyer's office. I am already indebted to you for escorting her home each evening. I know we can't protect her all the time and there will be those who take any opportunity to demean her, but you are certainly keeping the pack at bay. I never could understand why women take such delight in the sorrows of other women but I suppose, since I'm just a humble male, I never will."

"What I don't understand, John, is why they blame her for breaking the engagement. Surely another woman should understand what it takes to make such a decision?"

"Maybe it's plain jealousy. There were girls who were jealous when she began to walk out with Paul; others who are married to men who treat them badly and can't get out of a bad marriage, who perhaps wish they could. Paul looked like a good catch, a man who had a clean job; a man to be respected; an educated man; a man who could provide a wife with enough of a wage not to worry about how to feed their children. Or it could just be that, nature being nature, they revel in the distresses of others. Who can tell what happens in a woman's mind? Not me."

"You'll feel what happens to a daft man, if you're not careful, John Campbell; I hope you're not tarring me with that brush," interrupted Liza, who entered the parlour and brought with her the smell of freshly baked scones. She grimaced as she remembered the first time she had met Paul and how struck she had been by the fastidious way he had eaten his scone, and how in some part she was responsible for the courtship and, although she would never admit it to John, how she had encouraged him to see the benefits of marriage to Sal by complaining to him of Sal's desire to nurse, despite being her grandmother's heir and having no need to earn her living.

****

"You don't need to come with me, you know; I'm sure you have better things to do than accompany me to town." Sal looked over at Jim as they both sat waiting for the train that would take her to Dumfries and the court where, today, it would be decided whether she must pay Paul for breaking her contract. She was nervous and glad that Jim was beside her. What a blessing he had been during the weeks they had waited for the case to be brought before the court at the Midsteeple in Dumfries. They had been trying weeks, since it was impossible to avoid Paul as they went about their daily business. If at all possible Sal tried to be at work on the ward before there was any chance of meeting him on his way to school, but he appeared to have a second sight when it came to 'accidentally' encountering her. If she arrived early one day, the next he too would be about the village long before there was any need for the schoolmaster to be out of bed. It had appeared that he watched for her leaving in the evening before he too left the schoolroom. To some extent the advent of Jim with his bizarre bicycle had put a stop to that, but when there was no Paul there were all his supporters, mainly the women of the weaving village, to cause her heartache. The wives of the mill workers had mostly arrived from the cities south of the Border, with high moral codes for others, if not for themselves. Some of them had got together and approached Dr Jardine to request that he ask Lady Johnstone to remove her from the Infirmary, giving their reason that she should not be in a position to seduce their husbands or besmirch their children. Lady Johnstone, God bless her, had sent back a message that in the meantime she would not take sides and if they wanted Sal dismissed then Paul must go too. The women resented the fact that Lady Johnstone was in a position to dispose of both Sal and Paul and in order that they retain their schoolmaster they accepted

Sal's continuation in the village, but they missed no chance to let Sal know how they felt about such a brazen hussy being in charge of the Infirmary.

Sal's thoughts moved on to the few stalwarts who supported her. Roseanne Quinn had been very verbal when she came across any gossip and, combined with a few of the village women she had nursed or whose family she had cared for, they managed to keep the worst of the insults from reaching Sal.

"And Jim, of course; he has been such a comfort. Always giving up his time to see me home; missing days of profitable work to take me to Dumfries and sitting like a sentinel in the court while my life has been ripped apart and scrutinized. I don't know how he can have borne it," she thought, taking in Jim's gentle profile as he sat beside her, quite at his ease, long legs stretched out before him and hands stuffed in his jacket pockets away from the frosty early morning air. "He looks so solid and dependable," she mused but then her thoughts were disturbed by the blaring of the train whistle and Jim grabbing her hand and giving it a squeeze of support. She smiled up at him, once more realizing what a blessing he was, never thinking of himself; prepared to sit quietly when she was too deeply disturbed to talk and making her laugh despite the seriousness of her situation.

The train journey to Dumfries had lost its novelty over the course of the weeks she had travelled back and forth, initially to confer with Mr Gordon and then to attend the court proceedings. They had been hard enough but the reaction of the public had been hardest to bear. People, women particularly, had made judgement from what they had read in the paper and crowded outside the court to see the woman who had broken her word for no reason other than she found she did not love the man she had agreed to marry. It was an unhappy realization to Sal that women felt a jilt, as she was frequently called, was only one step away from a whore and a person that no decent woman would have any dealings with.

Jim took her elbow as they left the station at Dumfries and they strolled through the town towards the court. In this fashion few people recognized her: It was a part of her day when she could breathe easily. Over the weeks she had wondered if she would be forced to move to the town or even further afield to find the anonymity she craved.

She stopped just short of the town centre, and addressed Jim. "I need to thank you for being so kind to me while this case has been going on. You have no idea how much I appreciate what you have put yourself through to be by my side. It was unjust of Da to ask it of you, but I don't think I could have made it this far without you sitting quietly beside me giving me strength to carry on."

"Whatever the outcome today, you will still be Sal, a good person. I have nothing but disgust for any man who attempts to take away the character of a woman for his own ends, but even if the court rules in his favour, for those who know and love you, yours will be the moral victory." He paused.

"Since we are unsure of what might happen today I want to tell you now that I love you, Sal, I always have; since you were a little scrap visiting with your parents. I didn't speak before you went to the Infirmary because people would think *I* was after the farm when Aunt Ellen made that deal with your Ma. Then you became engaged to Paul and I decided to keep quiet. I wish I hadn't and I'm not asking you to make any promise now. I just want you to know that this case means nothing to me, however it turns out, and I will continue to be your friend forever."

Sal stood very still for a moment looking into that dear face that had been part of her life for as long as she could remember and suddenly realized that she could not imagine life without Jim in it. She gave him a hug and whispered, "Thank you for saying that now. It gives me courage to face the mob."

They walked on together to the courthouse where already a crowd was gathered to hear the denouement. Sal climbed the steps up to the entrance and felt a surge of confidence flow through her. She gripped the old leather purse that contained the lucky ruby and swore that, whatever damages she had to pay Paul, the ruby would be staying firmly in her pocket.

She was not an inferior being. She was a woman who was loved.

****

"All stand for the Procurator!" called the court usher. The jury and all the attendant officers of the court stood to attention as Lord William Maxwell, resplendent in wig and gown, disposed himself on the throne-like seat above the court.

Sal caught the gleam in Paul's eye and recognized it as complacency.; He was very sure that he was going to leave the court the winner, having degraded Sal as much as it was possible to do.

She turned away and took in the jury of twelve men sitting to the side of the court. They looked very serious and their grim faces did nothing to soothe Sal's trepidations. She sat shaking on her bench, gripping her lips hard between her teeth to prevent them jittering. She had been careful at every session to be neatly and plainly dressed from head to foot but today, in need of having her spirits lifted, she had donned a frivolous bonnet tied under her chin with a blue ribbon. Now she worried this had been a mistake that would sway the jury in Paul's favour, making it appear she scorned their decision.

"Mr McJerrow, would you make your address to the jury?" intoned the procurator.

McJerrow rose, bowed to the bench and addressed the jury.

"I act for this spurned young man in this action," he indicated Paul with a smile in his direction. "A man who has been sadly let down by the woman he loved and thought to make his companion for the rest of his life. You have heard in evidence how the two met and made their contract to marry and how only two weeks, yes, two weeks, gentlemen," he held up two stubby fingers in emphasis, "from the marriage Miss Campbell decided to renege on her vow. Miss Campbell had not entered precipitously into this contract but had been on friendly terms with the petitioner for more than two years before a contract of marriage was entered into and the agreement to marry was set before the minister of Ruthwell Church. My client was willing to overlook Miss Campbell's rather suspect vocation and honour his part of the bargain. There is no doubt in my mind that that Miss Campbell would have benefitted morally from this marriage.

"It is the contention of the prosecution that for *no good reason* Miss Campbell changed her mind thus depriving Mr Hamilton of property that would have come to his wife in the fullness of time and that he had relied upon for their livelihood and manner of living and had made certain purchases on the understanding that this income would be forthcoming and is now substantially in debt, a debt which I suggest Miss Campbell is in duty bound to repay.

"I ask you to award my client £3,500 damages for the loss of the income he was entitled to expect, for amounts paid out in expectation of the nuptials and for his considerable personal distress. I thank you, gentlemen."

He again bowed gravely and with a flourish of his cloak seated himself beside Paul, who sat looking the epitome of a successful gentleman in his spotless linen and well cut coat. Even in these dreadful circumstances Sal was relieved that the laundering of Paul's linen would now never be her remit.

Sal could discern nothing from the immobile faces of the jury but she held her head high and continued to sit as still as possible. It had been hard to sit silent while Mr McJerrow was making his speech, but the worst was over and it was time for Mr Gordon to do his bit.

Mr Gordon rose slowly and paced across the floor to stand in front of Sal. He looked at her keenly, then smiled as he turned to the jury.

"Gentlemen, I represent Sarah Campbell in this insidious case. I use the word advisedly for who would imagine a man being so motivated by revenge as to put the woman, the woman he professed to love, through such a torturous experience? You have heard the evidence of several well-known and respected members of the community, that far from being a pariah of society, Miss Campbell is a hardworking and conscientious member of her locality where she, and indeed her entire family, have been upstanding members of the community for generations. I put it to you that Miss Campbell could not remain in her position in the Infirmary at Mill village, sponsored by both Dr Jardine and my Lady Johnstone if she were indeed, as indicated by the prosecution, a woman of loose morals. My learned friend," he bowed low to Mr McJerrow, "has been unable to bring any *proof* of misdemeanor, only hearsay and gossip which must be abhorrent to any man of intelligence. If indeed Mr Hamilton was reviled by Miss Campbell's employment, one wonders at him courting her and subsequently proposing to her. Her work was no secret from him as they were both employed by the board of Mill village.

"Mr McJerrow has been at some pains throughout this case to emphasize that his client is a gentleman, but gentlemen, members of the jury, do not, to use a modern euphemism, air their dirty laundry in public. My client has maintained throughout this case that she only discovered the error of her heart two weeks before the marriage and, after taking much advice, apologized to Mr Hamilton and broke her engagement. She has resolutely refused to cast aspersions on Mr Hamilton's manner or behavior for which, in justice, you must admire her. As a father of daughters, how many of you would advise a much loved daughter to go forward with a marriage when her emotions are no longer engaged?

"My client is employed as a nurse/doctor's assistant at the Mill Village Infirmary and this is her only means of support. I say to you that since Miss Campbell has not actually come into any inheritance that *may* be forthcoming, her failure to marry Mr Hamilton has in fact lost him nothing. I remind you of the adage that it is a woman's prerogative to change her mind. I ask you to find for the defendant in this case. Thank you gentlemen, my lord."

Mr Gordon gathered up Sal and Jim as if they were his stray lambs and escorted them to a small room set aside for their convenience while the jury made their deliberations. Very little was said during the thirty or so minutes it took the jury to come to its verdict, but, as the clerk of the court came to direct them back into the courtroom, Mr Gordon took her hand and bowing over it addressed her with old fashioned chivalry.

"It has been a quick decision which might well mean it has not gone our way. May I take this opportunity of telling you how I have admired your stoicism throughout. It must have been difficult to maintain your position not to reveal your reasons for breaking your betrothal and, for what it is worth Miss Campbell, I fully concur with your decision. It would have been a great error to have married the man." He blushed right up to his ears and became confused by his deviation from his professional manner. They hurried back into court.

Lord William Maxwell as the presiding procurator addressed the jury asking if they had selected a spokesman and whether they had come to a conclusion from the evidence before them.

Mr George Payne had been elected foreman and agreed that they had arrived at a verdict.

Paul and Sal were asked to stand and face the jury which they did. Sal didn't know how she managed to keep upright since her knees were so wobbly she was sure they would not support her for long, but she had not long to wait.

"How do you find? For the petitioner or the defendant?"

"Sir, we find that Miss Campbell did breach a contract to marry and as such we find for the petitioner."

Paul grasped Mr McJerrow's hand and, grinning wildly, threw a gloating look in Sal's direction, but she was not looking his way. Rather, her attention was upon the jury, for Mr Payne was indicating to Lord Maxwell that he had more to say. The procurator called for quiet and indicated that the foreman should continue.

"Thank you, my Lord. We as jurymen believe that Mr Hamilton is a fortune hunter and as such should not profit at the expense of the unfortunate young woman. We have been told that she has no property and would have had no property at the date of the proposed marriage as her grandmother whose heir she is, is very much alive and in charge of her own affairs and we respectfully request that the award of this court be of the smallest coin of the realm."

"Thank you, Mr Payne, members of the jury. You are excused."

The judge waited patiently while the jurymen filed out of the jury box and seated themselves in the body of the court to listen to the pronouncing of the award before he continued.

"Men are entitled to claim damages from an inconstant woman, although most gentlemen accept such blows magnanimously. It appears that Miss Campbell became unsure in her mind and, as stated, it is a woman's right to change her mind.

"I find that Miss Campbell acted honourably in immediately breaking off her engagement; but the fact remains that she *did* breach her contract to marry and as such Mr Hamilton is entitled to damages. I concur with the jurors that Mr Hamilton, who describes himself as a gentleman, should not profit by his obvious desire for revenge and set the damages at one shilling Scots and order that each party should be responsible for their own representatives' fees. Good morning."

He rose and left the bench while Sal stood with her mouth half open, not knowing whether to laugh or cry. It was over: so many months of stress and worry for a shilling: poor Paul!

She grasped the ruby in its casing and vowed that she would keep it safe to bring luck to another generation.

As she left the courtroom she was stopped by an unknown young woman who immediately hugged her and asked for a few words in private. Sal was reluctant, but the woman was so insistent that Mr Gordon escorted both ladies to the little holding room where they had awaited the verdict.

"I know the last thing you want is to be accosted by an unknown female but I represent a group of local women trying to gain women the same rights as men and we would like to pay your legal costs in exchange for your speaking to our group. We would hope you would join us, but the offer stands as long as you tell your story to our organization. What do you say?"

Sal laughed joyously.

Chapter Twenty-Five

"More than any other member of my family, past or present, I attribute the desire to better the conditions of the working class to Sal, a woman before her time. If Sal had been born in my lifetime, she would have been sitting here in my place; and I fully admit she would have done a better job than I have done, for her vision was so much clearer."

"That is a bold statement, Lord John. Can you give us your reasons for your belief?" asked Mark.

"Well yes, I have just told you about her brush with the unfair laws that allowed her intended husband to sue her for breach of promise. So, embarrassed by this demeaning slur to her womanhood she became an advocate for rights for women and became a suffragist, using her not inconsiderable power gained by the backfiring of Paul Hamilton's plan."

"Surely, though, the court ruled in her favour and he went off with his tail between his legs?"

"Paul's sole aim was to cause Sal as much distress as possible. I'm going to acquit him of avarice as his main objective in wooing Sal. She was a pretty, clever woman; a Campbell woman. A bit of a catch for a poor schoolmaster." He smiled, cranking up his own personality. "He was angry and saw a loophole where he could embarrass his erstwhile fiancée; no one wants to be flung over at the last minute; who would believe she had changed her mind without him falling short of her expectations?"

"But how did that backfire? He had his day in court," wondered Mark, confused, not for the first time, by Lord John's convoluted story telling.

"The press in the days before the paparazzi were gentlemen, yes go on quote me," he paused with a grin. "They reported the case in the refined manner of the day, for the most part taking the lady's side, and showing Sal as an innocent victim and Paul as the villain of the piece. Today that would have made sensational headlines and she would have been demonised, as indeed she was by the local women. You see how quickly they turned on her? She dared go against convention and in no time at all she was pilloried by the women; accused of every immoral act they could visualise. Victorian men had emancipated slaves, improved the conditions in our hospitals and prisons but they kept their womenfolk the property of men; even Queen Victoria was against women having a voice; she famously said, 'Women should stay at home and do what women do'. Fine words from a woman who ruled not only the country but her husband. But I digress." He winked at Mark in a conspiratorial manner, understanding exactly why Mark was not keeping him to the point. He carried on.

"Suffragists were just beginning to appear with bills going before Parliament which were being laughed out of both Houses, but there was unrest in the female community and with her high profile Sal was invited by the suffragists to join them and their cause."

"You call them 'suffragists', not suffragettes as I have always thought of these valiant ladies."

"Well spotted, Mark," said Big Jock, leaning forward with a broad grin on his face to pat Mark on the leg. "The suffragists were non militant, unlike their later sisters the suffragettes; they believed that men would be able to see the sense in making women equal if their inequality were only brought to their attention. Might have worked too, if men had not made a career of marrying to increase their estates and finances and married for love instead. These were the men with the vote. I know you know your history, Mark, so you will know that until 1868 only landed gentry were enfranchised. If they held off the vote for the working class men, how likely were they to give it to women?"

He gave a thoughtful look up into the higher reaches of the studio where the sound boom and the rolling cameras were working out of sight of the audience.

"Young men today are making a life choice more and more to be kept by women. The boy who won't leave home because his mother has pandered to him all his life and thinks him 'a puir wee soul' who can't live without her support; or the young man who finds himself a wife who will work, not necessarily at a better paid job than him either, while he spends his days very much like the man about town in Victorian times; he went to 'his club' while today's species goes to the gym or the pool hall. No, no, don't mistake what I'm saying as tarring all young men with the same brush or, as some of my constituents believe, being anti-youth. I admit that is a fault I have striven to avoid but I am passionate about giving our young people, men, particularly, opportunities to change their lifestyle. Maybe because women had to fight so hard to get a say in what they do and to think for themselves they have emasculated their menfolk."

Mark was astounded at these revelations by Lord John and felt he had to take full advantage of his unprecedented luck in catching him on an evening where he was being less than his normal circumspect self, but all he could come up with on the spur of the moment was, "You think today's young men prey on women?"

"Perhaps the women prey on the men?" shrugged Big Jock. "Such as it has always been; my own life with Lady Marion is an example of how women manipulate their men to where they want them."

The audience laughed with him.

"But let me be serious for a moment. Whatever the reason, be it that men are no longer needed in the matriarchal society where even fertilisation is possible without all the posing and fluttering that took place in Victorian times, or, and I like this theory, that men have used their brains to allow themselves a life of ease; men have been demotivated. The man was the breadwinner, the hero, the conqueror, the star of our society and his place has been usurped by women. Is that because the pre-Victorian men knew if you gave a woman her head she would use it and show up our imperfections? Look at the queen bee in the hive with her male workers or the ancient society of the Amazon women. Yes, if Sal had been born later she would have had it all. Sadly, the glory of women in politics had to wait for Lady Thatcher and it took Sal's great-grandson to keep Ms Sturgeon out of my office."

Big Jock glanced at Mark's nonplussed expression and gave a great guffaw before continuing with a, not quite innocent expression.

"Maybe, now that I am a free man, able to be outspoken and stir things up I might make male emancipation my goal." Although there was a mischievous look on Big Jock's face it was clear that this was a serious subject to the retired politician.

"You think men need to be freed from women?" asked the incredulous Mark.

"I think rather, that men have to stand up and be counted. Don't get me wrong; there are some sterling men in all walks of life and for each loser I can quote you, you will be able to quote me a winner, but what we need in society is equality, men with women, fifty-fifty partnerships. In the Victorian era women were not respected and their opinions negated; today we have come almost full circle with the power in the country being held predominately by women. Women are visible in every walk of life doing what men used to believe was 'man's work' and doing it as well and often better than men." His face took on a thoughtful expression as he went on. "Maybe the luck of the Campbells is not bound up in this bauble," he said, flasheing the enormous stone towards the camera, "but in the ability of our family to marry equal partners and share responsibility. Who knows?"

"You have left me speechless," said the normally verbose interviewer. "My brain is in such turmoil that all I can come up with is 'Who? Why? When?'"

"I can be even more controversial," went on Big Jock jocularly, by now having lost all signs of the discreet politician. "By the time the Second World War broke out in 1939, in my family it was the women who were the heroines. OK, they played no part in the actual fighting but, and I imagine like every other family in the country, the women took on all the dangerous jobs; some were in munitions; some in the armed forces, although not as soldiers, they had to be where the soldiers were in order to carry out their duties; some as support for the army in the role of doctors and nurses. Women worked where men worked so, while I take nothing away from the brave men who fought for, and many gave their lives for, our country and gritted their teeth in horrendous circumstances to keep us free from the dictator, we need to remember the quiet and unobtrusive contribution these women made to our success."

Lord John leaned back in his chair, well aware of the conflict he had caused in Mark's head, surveying the audience. He could not make out specific faces but he knew the studio was full and, as his story had developed, news of his interview had spread until now there were more bodies squashed into the space behind the seated spectators than there were in the seating area. He appeared to be at his ease as his long legs stretched out in front of him crossed casually at the ankles and his face showed a Puck-like expression of amusement. It had not been his intention to tell the story of his family tonight but he certainly was enjoying the experience of speaking without first scrutinising his words and their effect. As his eyes wandered over to Mark Henderson he noticed that the interviewer had gathered himself together and was preparing his next question. Big Jock sat up in his chair and awaited events.

"After telling us this remarkable story and giving the credit for the success of your family to the ruby on your finger, are you telling us now that you have no belief in it?" was his question.

Lord John considered for a moment or two while the audience held its breath in order not to miss a word. Lord John held them in the thrall of his magnetic personality.

He leaned forward once more and continued, "No, I would not deny the ruby ring its part in our history. I believe that the power of the ring lies in its ability to make us feel protected. From the Bible to the fairy tale we have relied on the legend of Good overcoming Evil and I think what the luck invested in the ruby by tradition gives us is a feeling that if we fight for right, we will be invincible." He shrugged himself into a more comfortable position before adding, "That sounds smug and pretentious but I'm not willing to refute the mysticism of the ruby. As a mascot it has done its duty and perhaps the belief in it is what helped our family to come through the next century when the world was torn apart by war."

"Where does the ruby take us from here? Does the ruby have more adventures or are we at the end of the tale?" interrupted Mark.

"Well, as I'm sure you have guessed by now, Sal and Jim eventually married; not immediately, but several years later and settled down at Hartwood to a happy married life. Jim allowed Sal to be herself; she continued to run Dr Jardine's hospital and became an advocate for the local women's group with support from Jim until they began to have children. After the turmoil of her youth it seemed only just that there was no more trauma in their lives. The only fly in the ointment, and not such a big fly at that, was that it took twenty years and a family of eight girls before Peter arrived to complete their family and become the next recipient of the ruby.

"Sal and Jim ended their days in the bosom of their family where, as far as we know, there was no need for the ruby's magic powers."

"You mentioned the world wars and, given that the Campbell men have a propensity to go to war, I presume they too took some part in hostilities?"

"Not as much as their more ferocious ancestors. Land management or, as I still call it, farming, was made a protected occupation and since Peter was an only son he was obliged to stay on the family acres. Whether this was to his taste, I can't tell you but while his contemporaries were off fighting the mud in the trenches at Mons, Ypres and Passchendaele, Peter was fighting the mud in his fields in an effort to keep the troops, and the country, fed. He married late in life and whether it was the influence of the ruby or just pure genetics he and his wife produced only one son, Wull Campbell, to carry on the name.

"In the next war the ruby must have been stretched to capacity, for there was a lot of danger for the members of the family to be protected from. Mr Chamberlain had confirmed that Britain was once again at war with Germany and that everyone would need to pull together to stop the German tanks rolling over our lands; the Campbell family was patriotic to the last man... and woman."

Chapter Twenty-Six

"I'm going to volunteer for the munitions, then I can stay at home still. Lots of my friends are going too. It will be killing two birds with one stone. We will have a laugh and make ammo for the boys in the army," exclaimed Ruby, sticking out her defiant chin at her parent.

The whole family were gathered round the kitchen table at Hartwood discussing the news of another war. At first they had been lulled into a false sense of security as life had continued as normal on the farm since the declaration several months ago, but now there was a tense excitement in the youngsters as they debated the advertisement that had appeared in yesterday's paper urging everyone to volunteer for war work. Peter sat quietly in his chair by the fire looking at the empty rocking chair opposite him where, when the last war had been declared, his wife Mabel had been sitting; how he missed that little woman's smiling face and fun-filled laughter. Who would have believed that despite never having a sick day in her life she should just keel over while making the porridge and be dead before she hit the floor? At least, that is what Dr McLean had told him and he had no reason to doubt his word, for he was a family friend as well as being their medical advisor. He remembered how as a young doctor he had bullied them into having the children vaccinated and attended when they had suffered measles and scarlet fever, stitched up the wounds from farm accidents and sat on the edge of the very kitchen table the children were crowded around now, swinging his long leg nonchalantly while looking down his elongated nose as he made his pronouncement of how to treat the many childhood illnesses that his family had come through.

He called his family children but they were all grown up now; Wull, a carbon copy of himself in his young days, another Black Campbell with all the characteristics inherited from ancestors in their distant past. His young wife settling into the farmhouse ready to take over the reins of the farm when he, Peter, was ready to retire, whenever that might be; Mame promised to the fine young man who worked in the savings bank and rapidly collecting her trousseau in her bottom drawer; Helen home for a break from her nurse training, despite her dazzling good looks and ample figure, dedicating her life to nursing the sick. So independent, she had vowed never to marry since taking that step would mean the end of her career. As his eyes took in her determined mouth and bold demeanour he felt sorry that no man would have the pleasure of calling her his own. He smiled reflectively, but as his thoughts turned back to the threat of war his brow wrinkled as he thought, "She might be the one in most danger from this dratted war." Peg and Ruby had just left school and were working in the dairy, Peg here on the farm and Ruby in the bottling plant in nearby Lochmaben; as for Jen, well, the very thought of Jen brought a smile to his lips. Jen the middle child; the daddy's girl; the joy of his heart. Oh, he loved them all dearly, but there was just something about Jen that tugged at his heartstrings. Maybe it was that, of all his children, Jen had inherited her mother's petite frame and delicate features, or that she was always full of fun and ready for any prank but for whatever the reason, no matter how bad the scrape she had got herself into, he only had to look at the tiny frail girl to feel a lump in his throat. He was glad that she was his.

Peter had heard the chatter while his thoughts were twisting here and there; he was used to hearing his family prattle and usually he listened but did not take part in it; it was really just background noise, no different than when, as youngsters, they had fought their sibling squabbles. His recollections of his family were interrupted as he realised that the conversation had stopped and all the children were looking at him for a response to something that had been said.

"I'm going to volunteer for the munitions, Dad," Ruby repeated, defiance still in her voice.

"Well, I expect you will need to do your bit if we are to keep the enemy across the water," he replied mildly to the amazement of his family. "We'll all have to tighten our belts and pull together."

Suddenly realising that she was not going to have to fight her father over her decision, Ruby hung over the back of his chair and planted a kiss on top of his balding head. "Do you mean it? I can go? It won't make any difference to the farm as Peg takes care of that," said a jubilant Ruby, dancing around the room in her delight. She had been dreading telling her father of her ambition.

"What if I want to go to the munitions as well?" piped up Peg. She was not going to let her sister off the hook that easily. "I'm older than you, so you should stay at home and let me go to the factory."

"Pooh!" Ruby shrugged off Peg's words with a wave of her hand. "You know you wouldn't want to leave the farm. You won't even go to the dance in the church hall. Don't try to tell me you are brave enough to go among other girls, for I won't believe you, and besides Nellie will be here," replied Ruby as if playing her trump card.

"Don't upset your sister, Rube, she is every bit as brave as you," her father said sharply. "She has a point, and we will need to discuss it if she desires to go away from the farm. You may talk as you like but if this war is anything like the last one none of you will have any say in where you go, for the jumped-up officials will make all your decisions for you."

"That's why I want to volunteer now; before it gets to be that I have to go into WAC. You wouldn't like me to mix with the rough soldiers, would you Dad?" Ruby wheedled. "Everyone says that the army is no place for women."

"War is no place for a woman or a man for that matter. I hope that, if that is what is required of you, you would do it with grace and not *dis*grace me," Peter replied. "But if to work in a dangerous, noisy, smelly factory at a soulless and backbreaking job is what you choose then I have no objections, only that you behave as befits my daughter. Don't think you can volunteer for a few weeks until you get bored and tired; if you take on this task you will be obligated to see it through to the bitter end."

"Oh, yes, I will. I've heard how hard the work is from some of my friend's mothers who were in munitions in the last war. I'm not making a romantic gesture Dad, I promise."

Peter caught at her hand where it rested on his shoulder and said, "Then go with my blessing, Ruby. And," turning to smile at Peg he continued, "if you want to go to the munitions or indeed volunteer for any other war work I will support you too. There is no need for the two of you to fight over it."

"What about the rest of you? Will you be able to enlist, Wull, or will you need to stay on the farm as Dad did in the last war?" Peg asked quickly, uncomfortably aware that she was blushing at her father's words and anxious to remove the attention from herself.

"I'm not sure," Wull said slowly, keeping his eye on Nellie, his wife. They had talked about the possibility of him being conscripted but, although his feet itched to be away with the other young men of his acquaintance, he knew that Nellie was worried about him leaving. "It may be that I will be exempt, like Dad, but I have registered with the Home Guard in Lockerbie so my fate will be in the hands of officialdom."

"If I were a man, I should like to join the Navy." This quiet statement from Jen surprised the group, "But they don't let women go to sea and with my luck I would be seasick anyway," she laughed, then went on quite seriously, "You'd think after the last war the generals and admirals would have lost their blinkers and realised that women were capable of any job the men can do and sometimes better!"

"Why does everyone keep harking back to the last war? Things will be very different this time. War won't change the opinions of men, only time will change that. One day men will accept a woman as an equal. When I'm out on the wards it makes my blood boil to see how every nurse in the place panders to the most junior doctor even when they *know* he is ordering treatment that will harm their patient," Helen exclaimed, showing her frustration by raising her voice. "I think when I have finished my training I might apply for the QAIMNS."

"The QAIMNS?" queried Peg.

"Queen Alexandra's Imperial Military Nursing Service. That's their official title but the girls always call them the QA.

"They go out to all the arenas of war and deal with all kinds of cases, from a cold to bullet wounds and shrapnel burns. I've been thinking about what area to specialise in. I like the buzz of casualty when you have to make quick decisions and think for yourself and I think that might be useful in the theatres of war," Helen explained.

"There have always been unconventional women in this family," laughed Peter, turning to look at his second daughter. "Your granny would have liked to have gone to the Crimea, she told me often enough how she was turned down by Florence Nightingale; believe me, I'm glad they never met for the wonderful Miss Nightingale would not have survived the scorn my mother would have heaped on her. If it is your wish to nurse the soldiers, you won't find any opposition in this house. Her ghost would come back to haunt me"

"What about you, Peg? *Do* you want to come to the munitions with me?" enquired Ruby, keen to know, now that she had achieved her own goal, what the rest of the family were planning.

"If I'm not allowed to stay at home," she smiled around the company. "That's what I *want* to do, but if I'm not I will apply for the land army. I am used to the comings and goings on a farm and you know I'm not much of a one for change," said timid Peg.

Unlike the rest of his boisterous children Peg had been the quietest of his brood. None had seen their peaceable sister lose her temper. Even when very young with elder siblings teasing her and stealing her toys she had shrugged and smiled, turned around finding something else to distract her. She was serene, working quietly at her chores, helping everyone whenever she could, taking on her more volatile sisters' tasks when they forgot them with never a word of complaint. She looked nothing like her mother, being tall and having inherited very strong Campbell features, the hazel eyes and black hair emphasising the translucent skin that covered her face and long neck. The pronounced quirk in her lips as she smiled were at odds with her pleasant temperament which showed that at the core Peg was her mother's child.

Wull hugged his sister in a warm embrace. "We could manage fine without these layabouts but this farm would fall to bits if you weren't here to keep us all up to the mark. Dad will just have to request that you stay here or hide you in the hayshed. What possible good could it do the war effort to move you to another farm? Don't you fret. Dad and I will see you're all right. If I have to go away to the forces, Dad will need you as his right-hand man."

So intent had Wull been to reassure his sister he had not noticed Nellie turn pale at the thought of losing her husband so soon after they had settled down at the farm. They had been married only a few weeks before the outbreak of war and her biggest nightmare was that her darling Wull would be eaten up by the vicious war machine. Nellie had not been brought up on a farm and found the work hard and often distasteful, but she was trying hard to fill the place vacated by Wull's mother. This was not difficult in the house for she was a very good housekeeper and, since none of the girls were domestically minded, there had been no battle for power in the kitchen. The girls had been happy to hand over the cleaning and cooking to Nellie who had eagerly accepted the charge. Only when Peter had put his foot down, chiding his children for putting their everyday jobs onto Nellie, did the sisters again share the household tasks. If truth be known Nellie would rather have kept doing all the inside duties to be exempt from feeding the calves and chickens or working in the dairy. Although they sold most of the milk to the local dairyman where Ruby worked there was always a certain amount held back to make their very profitable butter and cheese. Nellie had had more than a few disasters and was worried that she would never learn to be a farmer's wife, but when they were cuddled up in their bed in the roof at night, Wull told her how proud he was of her, often quoting his father, who said, "She's doing fine. Give the lass time. Could you make butter the first time you tried?" but Nellie still felt she was letting him down. She knew there had been plenty of farm girls after her handsome boy and her greatest fear was that he would regret marrying her. Despite having been married to Wull for some months she still could not quite believe that he had chosen to marry her rather than any of her prettier and more outgoing contemporaries. Wull always reassured her that she was beautiful in his eyes.

"I like tall women with gorgeous long legs and dark, sweet-smelling hair that I can bury my face in; I like your blue eyes that shine a bit brighter when I appear unexpectedly; your soft shapely body measuring its length against mine in the cold winter nights is what I fantasise about when I'm out in the fields. I like all those parts of you, but it's being close to you as we dream of the future that makes me love you, makes you my special Nellie," he had assured her one precious night as he cradled her in his arms before showing her just how much he loved her.

Mame had seen the colour leave her sister-in-law's cheeks and recognised the emotions that went with it. She felt exactly the same about her Ronald. "At least Nellie has a fair chance of keeping her husband at home since farming is a reserved occupation, but Ronald works in the bank and I can hope for no such reprieve. He is already talking about going into the RAF before he is conscripted and has no choice."

She and Ronald had talked endlessly about the topic of war and how it would change their plans. Since they had not set a date for the wedding they argued about when it should be. Mame thought that if he was going to volunteer then they should marry before he went off to do his basic training, but Ronald wanted to wait until the war was over. However they resolved it she would not be even considering volunteering until she knew what the future held for Ronald. Her job as cook at the flying school, where every day they had new volunteers, would come under the heading of 'war work' so there was no need for her to worry about enlisting in the forces. She knew Ronald had asked to talk to her father this evening, so she was impatient for their meeting.

"It seems strange to have our lives decided for us by someone in the War Office. I don't feel as if my life is my own. I wake up every morning wondering if this will be the day the War will end and we can all get back to normal. I don't understand how what Adolf Hitler does in Germany can affect the little life I enjoy here in our quiet little backwater and, if I'm honest, I'm more concerned about those close to me here than an unknown Jew in Europe. It seems so unfair," Nellie pouted.

Peter looked grave as he spoke seriously for once. "We cannot give in to dictators, lass. We must at all costs emancipate these beleaguered countries from the terror of anti-Semitism. To have a free world we must fight when necessary and sacrifices have to be made by everybody. Just at present, the Government are working out how to own your bodies, but, before this war is over, you won't own your soul, mark my words."

Chapter Twenty-Seven

"Come on, Ruby! We will miss the bus if you don't get a hurry on!" called Gina over her shoulder. Ruby was struggling up the hill on her bicycle which had caught a puncture somewhere along the journey. In frustration she jumped off the offending machine and flung it from her into the roadside before running to catch up with her friend. It would not do to miss the bus for there was no other until the next shift were collected at midday, and Ruby particularly did not want to work a backshift on this of all days. She pounded after her friend, and since she was a fit country girl, used to tramping around the fields, she reached the bus stop only minutes after her cycling friend.

"You might have given me a seatie," she laughed at her friend while she bent over with hands on her knees to catch her breath.

"What? Up that hill? You are joking. I can barely get myself up the hill, never mind a lump like you, but at least it is all downhill home," answered Gina, grinning at her disordered friend. "Here's the bus. We've just made it."

The two girls clambered onto the rickety bus that was sent from the Royal Ordinance Factory at Powfoot to pick up the workers from all the outlying villages and towns. The girls often joked that what it needed was some of the gunpowder they dealt with every day to get its struggling engine to pull it up the hills. The bus was pretty full by the time the girls boarded, so they had to part company to get seated on the long wooden seats. Not that it mattered where you sat on this bus for everyone knew everyone else and chat was general. Of course some of the girls had particular friendships but as a group they got on well, realising that they had to work together whether they had similar personalities or not. They, at least, were not far from their families, not living in a hostel hundreds of miles from home with few luxuries, such as privacy, the comfort of their own folks, as some of their friends were. Neither Ruby or Gina would have liked hostel life.

As the bus drew up to the gates of the factory they could smell the cordite hanging on the air and were glad that the Luftwaffe, who so far, thank God, had not found them, had no way of detecting the smell that came from the release of chemicals into the air.

The chat was jovial, mostly about the latest Lucille Ball film that they had seen in the canteen yesterday, then the conversation broadened to their favourite screen heart-throbs. Lucille Ball's new husband, Desi Arnez was discussed first, with the general consensus being that she was to be envied her handsome boy with the 'come to bed eyes'. Some of the girls swooned over pictures of Clark Gable or Cary Grant, others wishing Fred Astaire or Mickey Rooney would attend the dances they did. It was all light-hearted and passed the time as they stood in the queue to be searched as they entered the factory. This was the least pleasant time of the day as, no matter what the weather, they were not permitted to enter the factory until they had been searched and all contraband confiscated.

"I don't know what he thinks we are bringing in," said one of the newer recruits petulantly. "I mean, I can see the force of searching us on the way out for who knows, we *might* have a six-pound bomb under our coat," she chuckled looking around to see if her wit was appreciated, "but what can we bring in, I ask you?"

Janie Anderson, an older married woman, tacitly agreed to be the leader of the shift, answered quite sharply, "The first thing you need to know, and you should have been told on your first day, is that the materials you work with are extremely dangerous; the least little spark and you will be meeting St Peter at the Pearly Gates. You must have nothing metal on you. Hairgrips or wedding rings are easily forgotten about when you come to work, but one lapse of memory and we will all be singing hymns in the heavens. So just shut up and let the men get about their business; the sooner they get us frisked the sooner we get into the warmth."

The younger girl hung her head and mumbled, "I didn't mean anything. I know not to put grips in my hair and all that. I'm just cold standing out here in this freezing wind."

"Well, you'll not be cold for long. Once you're inside you will soon be wishing yourself back outside, for there is more musty fog in there than there ever was smog over London."

"Gie the lassie a brek why don't ye?" broke in another woman. "We're aw here fur the same joab. Ye're aye moitherin aboot summat. "

Gina turned to Ruby and commented, "Isn't it funny how all the easy jobs go to the men. The supervisors are men, the managers are men, even the security guards are men when the workforce here are almost all women?"

"Now Gina, you know that we are replaceable and many more of our kind are easily accessible, but these men are precious and it is our duty to protect their poor wee backsides," joked Ruby, tongue in cheek. "Just see how old McQuirter with his gammy leg 'a product of the last war' as he is at great pains to tell us, can fairly skip to the shelter before the siren has properly started."

The girls giggled and others nearby joined in with them, for Mr McQuirter was not a popular manager as he cared only for his own skin. He might have been more respected if he hadn't been so full of himself and his position. He was a short, tubby man, resembling nothing so much as the *Daily Express*'s cartoon of Colonel Blimp, showing all the characteristics of that irascible gentleman when peering with a sour expression at the work being undertaken in the factory.

Eventually the girls got to their stations and took over from the night shift. This was a long shift and manned often by married women who shared the job in order that they could care for one another's children while both earned a much needed wage. With their husbands and support enlisted in the army, purse strings were tight and working part time eased the strain of feeding the family, as pay in the munitions was often better than the pre-war wages of their husbands.

"Hello, Moira," said Ruby jovially before realising her mistake. "Sorry, Morag. You can't tell one of us from the other with this shapeless outfit on. I don't expect it will catch on in the high fashion magazines." She smiled, holding out her baggy overall and twirling around on one plimsolled foot. This made Morag smile, a very tired smile.

"You look exhausted, Mo. Is this your last shift? I thought it would be Moira I was taking over from."

"Should have been," was the slow answer from Morag as she went on to explain, "because Moira's youngest boy has the chickenpox she wasn't able to work last night so I'm doing her shifts too to ensure we don't lose the wages. She will make it up to me when he is better, but I'll be glad of a few hours' sleep while my bairns are at school. The trouble is with us sharing our children if one gets something, the next you know the rest of the brood have it too; there's no saying when things will get back to normal. Hmph! What's normal? There's a war on," she finished as she tiredly dragged herself off to get changed and home to bed.

Ruby thought about the older woman as she checked she had enough material to be going on with. She knew that in a short time the young lad who portered the compounds around the factory would reach her before she ran out. Pushing a stray hair into her all-encompassing turban she began her day's work of putting the cotton in to soak in the vast vat and stirring it with her wooden tongs. She was careful not to stir too vigorously as splashes of the acid mix burnt anything it came in contact with, including skin. She had been on this detail since she had started in the factory and was now able to attend to her work with only half a mind. She hummed along to the music that was being piped into the factory in an effort to ease the tedium of the backbreaking, leg-trembling work.

"Dad was right with all he said about this job but I feel that I am helping the war effort and having some fun as well," she thought as her eyes lit up at the thought of what was planned for the coming evening. She daydreamed her way through her shift, dunking cotton fibre into her vat and stirring it until it was well impregnated before passing it through to its next stage of its journey to the front line.

The hooter screeched at ten o'clock and the workers made their way to the canteen for their well-deserved break. The food was plain but wholesome and, although not what Ruby was used to, some of the girls on her shift said they had never had such good food; even the poor fare served up in the hostels was better than many had been used to in their life so far. As Ruby ate a slice of toast, washing it down with a big mug of tea, she kept her eyes open for her special group of friends. They did not all work in the same parts of the factory and, as visiting each other was strictly forbidden, Ruby was anxious to hear how the others were preparing for the evening ahead. She caught sight of Gina entering the huge canteen with Milly and Hannah on either side of her. She felt a momentary pang that she was not working in the same section as the other girls but quickly quelled her feeling, remembering that she was paid extra for working in the more dangerous area. She waved to attract their attention and, when they had helped themselves from the buffet laid out in front of the cookhouse, they joined her at the table.

"What are you going to wear tonight, Milly?" asked Ruby, keen to talk about the outing that had taken up so much of her mind for the last few days.

"I'm borrowing a dress from my sister. She can't wear it meantime since she is due to give birth any minute now," Milly explained. "It's brown and cream with a pleated skirt that flares out when you turn and I plan to do lots of birling tonight. What about you lot?"

"I've got the frock I wore last summer holidays. It's a wee bit short since I've grown an inch or so but it looks all right when I'm sitting down. I do have a pair of silk stockings though," bragged Hannah, pleased to get one over on the other three, for none of them had stockings and would either go bare legged or wear ankle socks just as they had done at school.

"You haven't!"

"You lucky thing!" There was no doubt that Hannah had scored with her admission of having the most desired of all accoutrements.

"Give with the info, Hannah. What did you have to do to get those?" asked Ruby with a jealous gleam in her eye.

"Not what you're thinking, anyway," chided Hannah "I was asking Dad if I could go to the dance and that started him remembering how Mum and him would go dancing in the village hall when they were courting, eons ago."

"What has that to do with you having silk stockings?" asked impatient Milly.

"Well as he was reminiscing he talked about how he had got a glimpse of her calf when she was waltzing and how nice a silk-covered leg was and its effect on a young man. You know, the usual claptrap they feed you; how to make sure no boy gets to see your legs or you will be a fallen woman," she sneered

"And!" the girls chorused.

"And he said he'd never been able to part with her stockings even although she has been dead for such a long time. They remind him of the good times. So I asked him, quietly like, if he had more than one pair and he said there were lots of them, for you know my mother was in service to the Maxwells, and it seems that she was often given pairs of stockings by the young ladies to throw away when one was snagged or holed and Mum, being smart, had kept the unladdered one and matched it up over time. She had lots of mended pairs too that she wore all her life. She kept them all and so did my sentimental old dad!" she finished in triumph.

"Whoof, you'll be the belle of the ball," remarked Gina, not quite sincerely. "I'm wearing a skirt and blouse that I made myself. I got a pattern from the draper and Mum helped. I'm pleased with it. I only wish I could have a pair of court shoes but I haven't saved enough for them yet."

"It won't take long with the pocket money you get," came the slightly nasty comment from Milly, who was the breadwinner in her house and had to hand over her wages to her mother to keep the house, while Gina, whose parents didn't really need her money, gave her back more than half her wages to do with as she pleased. Ruby made no comment about the savings for she too was allowed a much bigger allotment from her wages than either of the other girls, so she rapidly changed the subject.

"My sister-in-law has given me the end of her lipstick and we can all share it. I'm not letting Dad see me with it on so I will need to apply it on the bus." She pouted her lips and made such ridiculous faces that their little jealousies were soon forgotten in their laughter.

"Come, come, girls. You should be finished by now and back in line to start work, not sitting here gossiping," the harsh voice of Mr McQuirter broke into their laughter.

Ruby, never afraid to speak her mind, answered immediately. "We are not late; the hooter hasn't gone yet."

"You know you should be back at your posts ready to start when the hooter goes, not sitting here shirking. If you're still here when the hooter goes I will dock your wages." He turned and strutted off to the next table. Ruby opened her mouth to challenge this order but she was hastily silenced by Gina, who was used to calming her more volatile friend's temper.

"Leave it, Rube. The squirt's not worth getting docked for."

She gave a puzzled look around as her pals burst out laughing as did those at the nearest tables.

"What?"

"You've just given that man a nickname that I'm sure is going to stick. The Squirt. Perfect."

The girls all got up from the table and hurried out of the canteen, but as they went back to their labours they chatted to others and before the day was out no one was referring to the manager as anything other than Squirt.

****

The girls huddled together to listen to one another's chatter as they waited for yet another bus, but this was a special one as it had been hired by the factory manager to transport the girls from Powfoot to RAF Dumfries for a dance organised by the officers there. It was the first time any of the girls Ruby was friendly with had been asked to attend and as such a general feeling of excitement was felt among the munitions workers crammed into the bus. They had had to listen to a lecture from Mr McQuirter on how they represented the munitions works and that they were allowed to dance with the fliers but not to make a spectacle of themselves. The girls had listened with one ear, as nothing the Squirt could say had not been already engraved in their minds by their parents. None of the girls, who were word perfect on what not to do, were sure what it was they *were* allowed to do. Some thought kissing was how you made babies while others thought holding hands was going astray; so since they had little idea what they were being warned against they just dismissed the warnings and got on with enjoying their first big dance to a real professional band.

"What a place. Look at all the pictures on the wall."

The girls looked around what, by day, did service as a canteen but for this evening had been transformed into a ballroom by simply dimming the lights and tacking up film posters and pin-ups of Hollywood stars on the bare metal walls. There was a small platform at one end of the hall where a four-piece band provided the dance music that set the girls' feet tapping as soon as they entered.

"That's Betty Grable and next to her is Rita Heyworth. Hasn't she got fabulous legs?"

"I wonder if she has silk stockings to wear on them?" teased Ruby.

"Oh you, I bet your legs are as good as hers," Hannah countered

"Perhaps, but even with silk stockings on my dad would kill me if I showed as much leg as that," said Ruby as she took in the long bare legs, high-heeled shoes and red-painted toenails of the glamorous movie stars in swimsuits that decorated the walls while she considered what her father would think of these decadent females.

"Especially in silk stockings," came a rejoinder from behind.

Ruby swung round to confront her sister. "What on earth are you doing here? Are you working? You poor thing."

"No. I'm having an evening off. Ronald has been sent here to learn to fly and I, as a 'wife or fiancée', had an invitation so here I am. You needn't worry, Ruby; I'm not out to spoil your fun. I'm just Ronald's girlfriend tonight so no big sister lectures." She hurriedly added this last as she took in the less than happy expression on her little sister's face. Ronald came up to them at that moment and put his arms round Mame's waist, pulling him to her in a possessive manner Ruby had not so far seen. There was no jealousy between the sisters but Ruby acknowledged that Ronald was a very handsome man and part of her hoped that, one day, she would meet and fall in love with someone equally handsome. She wondered fleetingly if she and Mame had the same 'type' as she took in the pleasant dark features of her sister's boyfriend and recognised them as very pleasing to her eye.

"Come and dance with me," Ronald whispered in Mame's ear. As she turned her head to smile at him their lips almost met. Ruby was stunned into motionless awe by the daring of her sister and the obvious emotion that added a luminous glow to her skin and a sparkle to her eyes as she looked up into Ronald's face, where her happy smile was reflected in his. Ronald winked over at the girls before saying, "I'm going to take this mother hen off to dance and be frivolous so you chicks can go on and enjoy yourselves without her. I see too little of her to share her with her friends." He drew Mame away and soon they were to be seen foxtrotting round the floor.

"Well!" exclaimed Ruby, "I never did: was that my perfect sister behaving like a, a, a, oh, I don't know what! But did you ever imagine *Mame* to behave in that lovesick manner?"

"Come on, Rube, never mind your sister; let's get ourselves a drink and find a seat," urged Hannah, pulling on Ruby's arm. "What will there be to drink, do you think?"

"Won't matter what there is to drink. I only want lemonade. That's one bit of my dad's advice I have taken to heart. He thinks strong drink should only be used in an emergency."

"Well, it's an emergency now for I'm parched," said Milly, trying to hurry her companions towards the bar where they were served by a handsome boy with hair slicked back with brylcreem and sporting a white jacket and black bow tie. The girls sniggered at first, but as they looked around the hall most of the young men had at least the same hairstyle. There were a few other young men in white jackets, but most of the company were wearing the khaki blue uniform of the air force.

"There you are, ladies, four lemonades. Will that be all, no port to go with them?"

"No thank you," answered Gina lifting one of the glasses and taking a sip. "We will be quite happy with these." They turned away and each carrying her glass carefully in one hand with the other over the top to prevent the liquid spilling on the dance floor they made their way to an empty table near the band. The music was loud and they could barely hear one another but the excitement of the occasion was not marred by this tiny detail. The band played all the tunes they knew and soon they were singing quietly along with the singer when they knew the words of the song. Since conversation was difficult the girls talked very little but sat taking in the ambiance of the hall. The dancers swayed to the music; skirts whirled by in a myriad of colours; girls laughed in high-pitched voices that were drowned out by the deeper ones of the men. The girls sat mesmerised taking in the scene. The dancers stopped and the couples on the floor stood clapping for a moment before their partners escorted them back to their seats, but when the music restarted the floor was quickly filled up again.

"May I have this dance?" brought Ruby out of her daydream as she took in the tall, young airmen standing in front of them. One held his hand out to her with his head at a questioning angle and, glancing at her friends, she smiled an acceptance and swung out onto the floor in the arms of the flier. The dance band were good and the young man was a practised dancer so although to Ruby it felt strange to be in a man's arms, it was a pleasant experience.

"Have you just come back from overseas?" asked Mike, for that was his name. Ruby gave him a puzzled look and he went on, "You look very brown; all of you girls look well tanned for this time of year."

The penny dropped. Ruby realised that in the dimmed artificial light of the NAAFI the tainted dye that stained her skin as a result of her occupation, which in the light of day made her look sallow or even yellow and jaundiced-looking, enhanced her appearance in the gloom.

She laughed. "No such luck." But that was all she was allowed to say. It was forbidden to discuss where she worked and at what because of the risk of traitors and third columnists, so she just smiled her pretty smile and continued with the dance. When the music finished he said, "Will you stay up?" and she agreed to one more dance, then another, and another.

Finally, she grinned at him and said, "I must sit down, I'm exhausted, but it was fun, wasn't it?"

"Yes, I really enjoyed dancing with you. You are light on your feet for..." He stopped what he was saying and blushed violently but Ruby just chuckled and finished his sentence.

"For a big girl?"

"No, oh no, I wasn't going to say that. I wasn't. Honest," he stammered, but Ruby laughed.

"It's all right, you know; I am big; big hands big feet."

"Your feet didn't tramp on me once," he came back at her, trying desperately to wriggle out of his faux pas. "Can I get you a drink?"

"No thanks, Mike. I've only had a sip or two from the one I've got."

As he accompanied her back to her seat she noticed that all her friends were still on the dance floor with their respective partners, so when Mike asked if he could join her she consented. She really was warm and wanted more than anything to visit the cloakroom and cool her damp cheeks, but she thought it would be rude to tell him so. However, before many minutes of trying to hear each other over the sound of the band he invited her to accompany him outside. Ignoring all the warnings, both from her father and from the Squirt, she agreed and soon they were outside in the cool evening air.

Ruby breathed a sigh of relief and watched as her partner dug a packet of cigarettes out of his pocket and offered her one. She refused with a shake of her head and he lit his own, taking in a huge drag of the smoke before leaning his shoulder on the wall and turning towards her.

"This is better," he said. "I can hear what you are saying and it is mighty warm in there with all the bodies writhing about. I'm not much of a one for dancing though; my mother forced me to lessons when I was too young to appreciate holding a girl in my arms." He looked admiringly at Ruby but, noticing her unease at the compliment, he continued quickly, "I only came to stop the boys ragging me."

"What is it you do here?" Ruby was disappointed that he wasn't keen on dancing but she was quite happy to pass the time chatting while she cooled off. She could feel the perspiration cooling on her skin and she wondered if the goose bumps she was beginning to feel were caused by the air on her hot skin or by the presence of her companion.

"I'm what they call a grease monkey at present." He laughed at the look on Ruby's face. "I keep the moving parts of the planes moving, usually with grease," he explained but, and his expression changed on the instant as he continued, "I have applied to be trained as a pilot and my CO thinks I have a good chance, so maybe soon I'll be depending on someone else to be the monkey," he finished.

Ruby could feel the excitement radiating from him as she took in his appearance. He was fairly tall, not as tall as her brother, but then the Campbell men were extraordinarily tall; his uniform fitted him perfectly and showed a well-built physique to its best advantage. Like all the other men she had seen this evening he wore his hair slicked back from his forehead, making it difficult to decide if it was fair or dark, his features were not perfectly symmetrical but he had a glint in his grey eyes which was enhanced by the uniform he wore. As they stood in the moonlight, he looked remarkably handsome to Ruby.

"Seen enough?" he enquired with an enigmatic grin.

Ruby blushed. "Was I staring? I'm sorry."

"No need to be sorry. I like it when a girl looks at me as if I was something special."

Ruby's blush deepened at these words, for it was as if he had read her mind. He was good-looking and pleasant and Ruby hoped that when they went back into the dance he would once more ask her to dance with him. They stood and chatted for some time, mostly about his work, as she was restricted to what she could tell him about her war work, but she did manage to tell him about the farm and her family in exchange for his funny stories about living on the aerodrome. Suddenly Ruby shivered and putting his arm round her shoulders, he began to guide her back to the dance.

Just before they entered the noisy room he held her back to ask, "Can I see you again, Ruby?"

"That might not be easy with the lack of buses since I'm a country girl but yes, I would like to see you again."

"Maybe we could work out a way. Perhaps we could go to the cinema or there will likely be more dances here when we could meet. The officers are mighty keen on keeping up the spirits of the men and there is nothing better for doing that than meeting pretty girls. Please give me your address and if I can get a loan of a jeep I will come visit, if that's all right."

Ruby was delighted with this invitation and when he produced a battered notebook from his tunic pocket, she gladly wrote down her address.

"I'll drop you a card when I've got something worked out," he said happily. "Meantime, let's go join the throng." He took her by the elbow and guided her back to her table where her friends were also entertaining young flying officers.

The two joined up with the others and there was no more time for private talk as the airmen danced with each girl in turn, bought them glasses of lemonade and kept up a running banter, little of which could be understood as they were competing with the band. At half-time though, when the band took their break, the girls were able to hear some of the amusing incidents that had happened on the airfield. Ruby noticed that the boys often had a sad look when a fellow flier's name was mentioned and realised that these young men were daily living with death. It had not really entered her consciousness that boys her own age would be dying horrifically; until now she had seen the war only as an opportunity to escape from the farm. However, seeing the sadness come over the face of these airmen, she realised that she was doing a vital job that was helping to protect these young heroes and, perhaps for the first time, she was proud to be doing the job she did.

Near the end of the dance the lights flashed on and off signalling the band were about to play the last tune of the night. It was a slow waltz and Mike drew Ruby onto the floor to dance it with him. Nobody knew, or at least nobody owned up to, who had found the main light switch, but for several moments the hall was in total darkness and none of the young men who were dancing were slow to take advantage of the dark. Ruby found herself being kissed on the lips; at first she was shocked, not having had any idea that such a thing would happen, but, when the lights came back on and everyone hurriedly adjusted their distance, she had a feeling of loss. She had enjoyed her first kiss.

When the lights were turned on full there was their driver ready to escort the ladies through the blackout to their bus so that it was impossible for the girls to make further arrangements. Ruby was glad that she had already given Mike the means to contact her again if he so wished, and she hoped he would.

On the bus home the girls giggled and compared their individual experiences. Occasionally a small group at the back of the bus urged everyone to sing, but Ruby and her pals were huddled together talking about the boys they had met. Ruby had told them about giving Mike her address and was rueing the fact that she hadn't had the presence of mind to give him the phone number of the farm.

"Oh you lucky thing. Was that what you were doing when you were outside? Don't think we didn't see you," ragged Milly who was disappointed that her partner, despite dancing with her all night, had not asked to see her again.

"I was outside because it was too warm inside," explained Ruby.

Her heightened colour led to more teasing by the others. They pretended to be shocked by her behaviour, to believe that she had been up to no good in the flier's arms. The attention of the group made her blush even more, but she felt a bubble of happiness filling her insides as she recalled the kisses that she had experienced on the dance floor. No matter how she tried to hide her pleasure, her friends could see that dancing with Mike had somehow changed Ruby. "Peter and Joe are going to be at the next dance if they can but I don't know how that helps us," Gina moped. "It's not likely they will ferry us over to the airfield for every dance. There are plenty of local girls for the men to invite."

"Don't be such worrywarts," started Hannah. "There are always ways to get us invited. It's called keeping up the morale; do you think the Squirt would have sent us tonight if he had any say in the matter? Mark my words, we will be asked back and, if the boys you danced with tonight aren't there, you can bet there will be more just as eager to dance with us. After all, in the dim light we look very exotic," she finished on a laugh.

The conversation turned to how they had each been asked about their lovely tans.

It was all light-hearted until Madge Peacock interrupted their conversation with, "Preen yourselves now, for when the same lads who thought you pretty tonight see you in the cold light of day, you won't see them for dust. Yellow skin and green hair doesn't become anyone."

On this sour note the girls' gossip faltered; no more was said about the boys they had danced with and soon they were stopping at the hostel where those who were not living out left the bus. Gina and Ruby found themselves alone as the bus made stop after stop on its slow progress and, although Ruby hugged her moments of bliss to herself, the girls talked about their next shift rather than the night's dancing. When they were dropped off the bus, Wull was waiting to guide them home in the blackout, not that country girls such as those needed guiding for they had managed all their lives with the light of the moon.

****

Ruby was on tenterhooks. Today was the day Mike was coming to meet the family. Ruby wondered if he would be disappointed by her home. Mike came from a very different background, having been brought up on his parent's estate in Surrey and been educated privately; he was more used to visiting farms as a landlord rather than a visitor. Dad had been privy to her fears consoling her slightly by saying, "If we're not good enough for him, he is not good enough for you."

Although the couple had been meeting now for six months this did not represent as many meetings as they would have liked since transport was difficult, not to mention that Mike had been accepted for pilot training and spent many hours at his books desperate to be posted to a 'live' station where he would fly a bomber over Germany.

"I would like to ask your father's permission for us to marry," had come out of the blue on their last date after they had been to the cinema. Mike was fired up by watching the Pathe News which showed action over enemy territory; if he could have got into a cockpit there and then he would have left Ruby sitting and gone to join these brave lads. He was straining at the leash to 'do his bit' but he wanted to have the matter of their life together settled before he was posted. He did not want to run the risk of losing Ruby to another.

Ruby was sitting in the window seat of the kitchen so that she could see him as soon as he came into view. In her anxiety she tried to see the kitchen through Mike's eyes. She was used to the clutter and noise therefore she paid little attention to her surroundings. The range took up most of one wall with its many ovens and hotplates. It was the heart of the kitchen. There was no washing on the pulley above today but on wet days, when there was no chance of the laundry drying outside, the kitchen resembled a steamie. As her eyes roamed around the room she noted that everything was very clean and tidy. "Nellie's work," she smiled to herself, for Nellie much preferred the confines of the house to the caring of even the smallest of animals. Ruby recalled a time when, newly married, Nellie had gone off to collect eggs with instructions from Wull but no sooner was she out the door than she flew back in with an angry hen chasing her with flapping wings. Nellie was not to know the hen was just as frightened of her as she was of it. Feeding the pigs or the calves too was a trial for her since these nosy beasts made a beeline for her whenever she approached. Nellie could not be made to believe they wished her no harm but were keen to see her because she brought the food. These reflections passed through Ruby's brain and she laughed, but she was very fond of Nellie; knowing her big brother was besotted with her, all of his sisters tried to make life easier for her where they could.

"But Nellie doesn't need any help indoors. She is a better housekeeper than any of us. There's no 'lick and a promise' from Nellie," she thought. With one eye watching the farm track for any sign of life she continued to look at the kitchen with an impartial eye. Every surface gleamed with many hours of polishing, the wooden table and stone floor flags had been freshly scrubbed that morning and everything was neat and tidy. There would be no cause to blush for her home. She caught a glimpse of movement out of the corner of her eye and in seconds had recognised this as the approaching Mike. Taking a quick glance in the mirror to see she looked her best, she flew out of the door and raced to meet him. They embraced briefly and, holding hands, walked slowly back to the farmhouse where every one of her family had been stationed at a window to catch sight of the boy who had won Ruby's heart. By the time they reached the house the family were all gathered in the kitchen to greet their guest.

Peter rose from his chair and held out his hand, introducing himself and his family. Each in turn shook hands with the young man and welcomed him to their home.

"We don't stand on ceremony here, Mike. Sit you down here and Ruby will fetch the tea," said Peter.

Mike felt such a lump in his throat that he was sure he would be unable to swallow water. His mouth was dry and his palms sweaty, but, after several attempts to moisten his lips, he answered, "Could I possibly have a word with you alone first, sir?"

The kitchen echoed with the sound of laughter at his use of the word 'sir'. Peg was in stitches, covering her mouth with a tea cloth to smother her shriek of amusement. Ruby was mortified by her sister's reaction and pinched her on the arm in an effort to curb her mirth. Meanwhile, straight faced and serious, Peter invited Mike to accompany him to the parlour where he carefully closed the door tightly against the prying of his daughters. They were in the room so long that Ruby began to worry that her father was not going to give his consent to their marriage. She began to pace up and down the floor giving quick glances at the parlour door. She would have given much to be able to hear what was taking place behind it.

"Calm down, Ruby," soothed Nellie. "Your father is no ogre to deny you what you want. He will just be making sure he can support you and care for you when you marry. My dad was just the same when Wull asked me to marry him. It's a father's duty to make sure you will be well cared for when you leave the shelter of his home."

"I know. Dad told me unless he was Bluebeard, ready to sweep me off to his dark and dingy castle on the edge of a cliff, he would not deny him when he asked." She smiled a very pained smile. "But they have been in there for a long time. What on earth can they be talking about?"

Just at that moment the door opened and the men returned to the kitchen. Ruby scanned both faces but could detect nothing from either expression.

Peter rubbed his palms together, asking, "Where's that tea then?"

Nellie hurried to pour the boiling water from the kettle into the big teapot that had been the succour of the family through good times and bad. While the tea was brewing she brought plates of sandwiches and a fruitcake to the already laid table. Soon they were all sitting round drinking the tea and chatting about the war, the lack of petrol and other topics of general conversation. Ruby could not join in. She was anxious to know what the outcome of the interview had been. She was pretty sure it had gone well just from the ease with which the two men addressed each other, but wondered why she was to be left in the dark.

"Do you fancy a little stroll up the lane, Ruby?" the voice interjected her thoughts and she gave a little jump, so deep had been her consideration.

"What? Oh, sorry, I was miles away. Yes, yes, of course," she hurriedly replied, rising from the table and making her way to the door which Mike opened for her, ushering her out before him. The two walked in silence out of the stackyard and had begun the walk up the lane when Mike asked if they might go down to the river that he could hear bubbling in the distance. They climbed the five-bar gate at the entrance to the field through which the Annan flowed and sauntered through the long grass to the riverbank, where Mike caught her up in his arms and kissed her lips while cuddling her to him.

"Whew," he breathed as he flung himself down on the grassy bank above the tumbling river. He loosened his tie and grinned up at the exasperated Ruby.

"Mike Gardiner, if you don't tell me what you and Dad talked about I'll... I'll explode!" she told him as she punched him on the arm that was stretched out to invite her to sit with him. She threw herself down beside him. He looked at her for a moment, taking in the rosy cheeks and the flashing eyes that indicated she was nearly at bursting point, and he decided to put her out of her misery.

"Ruby, I know we haven't had much time to get to know each other but there's a war on and, as my training as a pilot is nearly over, I will be sent to a live squadron flying bombers over Germany, so, and with your father's permission, I want us to become engaged. What do you say?"

"I say yes," answered Ruby eagerly. There was nothing coy about Ruby. She would not play games with him such as he and her father had played on her. "Yes, yes, yes." In her excitement she flung her arms around his neck and kissed him.

"Here hold on, you brazen hussy. I'm supposed to do the kissing," and he did. It was some minutes before conversation was recommenced, by which time they were both breathless. They sat staring at the river as it flowed by, singing its own merry tune for the sweethearts to listen to.

"I'll never forget this moment, sitting here with your arms around me listening to the songs of the river and the birds. I'm sure they know how happy I am at this moment."

"You know I could be posted any day now so when next you have a day off, I think we should go into town and buy you a ring to seal the deal."

"I don't need a ring. I have you," said the straight-talking Ruby.

"Nevertheless, I want my ring on your finger before I go off to my next assignment, then no Johnny-come-lately will run away with you. I want there to be no doubt in anybody's mind that you are spoken for."

"Will you tell your parents? Will they be cross that you're not marrying a girl out of the top drawer?" she asked quietly, for there was no doubt that Mike came from very different circumstances and she could just imagine his father looking down his nose at her.

"My parents certainly had ambitions of me marrying someone from their own sphere, but they will love you as much as I do when they meet you. I will write tonight to let them know we are to be married."

"When are we to be married?"

"Well, not right away since your father is concerned about you marrying too young. At least that is what he says, but I really think he is worried because I am going to be a pilot. He tells me that your older sister is being sensible and not getting married until her Ronald comes home when the war is over."

"Yes, that's true but I don't want to be left here unhappy worrying about you as Mame is about Ronald. She would have married him without a second thought if he hadn't been so sensible. I don't think getting married is a time to be sensible." She became coy. "Unless you don't want us to get married?"

"There isn't anything I want more but your father is right. We haven't spent too much time together and either of us may change our minds." Seeing the fierce expression on her face he went on quickly, "Your father hasn't forbidden the banns; he just wants us to be engaged for a time to be sure that we're sure," he finished.

"I'm sure now," came her defiant answer. "But I'll work on Dad and we'll show him we are serious, then we can be married."

They lay back on the grass staring up at the cloudless blue sky each thinking their own thoughts until, unable to restrain himself any longer, Mike rolled onto his side to face her and gathered her up in his arms with their bodies pressed together. They lay so for some time. Ruby could feel the hard muscular thighs that were hidden by his uniform and the comforting circle of his arms made her relax into his embrace. They kissed and talked, then kissed some more until it was time for them to return to the house and announce their news to the family.

As soon as the door opened Ruby could see her family were expecting the announcement since silence fell when the couple appeared. So, nudging Mike, she kept a deadpan face and said nothing of their engagement.

She and Mike sat down on chairs opposite each other and Ruby asked, "Is there any tea left in the pot? I'm parched after our walk."

Nellie hurried to find cups which she filled with strong tea that had been stewing on the hob since tea time. It was rare for there not to be pot of tea ready when anyone called but, since the beginning of the war, they tried to preserve their tiny amount of tea leaves by using them over and over. When the leaves were left in the pot over time the resultant brew became dark and strong. Ruby accepted a cup and, since on the farm there was no shortage of milk, she added a drop to her cup and sipped the contents.

Mike looked at his wristwatch. He jumped up declaring he must hurry or he would miss the only bus back to the airfield. He said hurried goodbyes and in minutes he and Ruby were hurrying up the track to the main road leaving all on the farm in ignorance of the change in their situation. Since they had jogged up the road they were a few minutes early for the bus, so they used their time to organise a meeting in Dumfries two days later to shop for the proposed ring. Just as they could hear the bus chugging up the hill they had a final kiss, which was so filled with emotion that it left Ruby tingling. They pulled apart just as the bus came over the hill, braked and stopped to let Mike board. She watched until the rickety old bus was lost from her sight before turning around to make her way home. She was so excited that she skipped along the road unable to hold in her delight at being engaged to her handsome boy. The future looked bright for Ruby.

Chapter Twenty-Eight

As Ruby entered the kitchen, Wull was just getting ready to go out on parade with his platoon. He looked very dapper in his new uniform. When he had first joined up he had been issued with an LDV armband as a uniform but as time had gone on more fragments had appeared. It was hit and miss as the outfitters did not seem to be at all organised about where and what they sent out.

"It's to be hoped the boys out in the trenches will be better kitted out than we are. Fifteen thousand rounds of bullets they sent us but no guns to shoot them with, twenty pairs of bootlaces but no boots. That will be some conchie in stores protecting his backside with no thought for those who are fighting to save his paltry life."

The four women listening were surprised to hear Wull rage about the conscientious objectors, those who could not right it with their conscience to kill, but Wull's normally placid nature had been cracked by those whom he saw evading the war on principle. He was very much against the war himself, but knew that it was the duty of every self-respecting man to fight against the atrocities that were being dealt out by the Nazi warlords. He, who would much have preferred to be in the army fighting for right, had a sinecure of a job simply because he was a producer of food.

He left the farmhouse and made off through the fields to his platoon in Lockerbie where he felt they were wasting their time drilling, for with only ammunition and no weapons how could they be expected to hold off an invasion? As he walked he became aware of a droning in the sky above and, within a few seconds of him looking up, he recognised it as a German plane. He hurriedly got out his airplane recognition pamphlet and, leafing through it, identified it as a Fieseler Fi 156, an aircraft much used for reconnaissance. He watched it for a few moments as it soared through the sky in ever-increasing circles taking in the area he knew to be the munitions factory where Ruby worked. He was wishing he had the means to bring it down when it suddenly changed tack and disappeared into a bank of cloud. Within seconds the sounds of its engines could no longer be heard. Wull stood for a time straining his ears and eyes in case the plane reappeared, but it seemed it had got what it wanted and was heading home. He shrugged, made a mental note to inform Captain Jessop of the incident and thought no more of it until he suddenly wondered if the aeroplane he had sighted had identified the munitions factory and marked it as a target for the bombers who flew overhead most nights now.

"If it hits anywhere in that factory no one will get out," he thought as he tried to remember what shift Ruby was on that week. Having five sisters he spent a lot of time worrying about them, particularly Ruby who was still very young and naive. He smiled to think of her being married; when compared to his Nellie, Ruby was just a bairn. He was surprised that his father had given consent to the marriage. "Or at least I think he must have, not that Rube was going to give anything away when she knew we were all waiting with our tongues hanging out for her to announce her engagement."

He arrived at the church hall where he met with the other Home Guard soldiers. They were mostly much older than he was, some had seen service in the First World War and the captain of the platoon, at seventy, had seen all the atrocities of war before he retired from the army.

"It's like playing at soldiers when I was a bit of a lad," sneered Wull to one of the older men. "Here I am presenting arms with a brush shank and pretending to kill you with it when we are on exercise. What good does it do? If Gerry lands on our coast, he will die laughing at the barrier we can put up. Do you think he is going to lie down dead when I point my brush handle at him and shout 'Bang'!"

"Drilling is necessary so that we obey our commands instantly in a battle. If you stop to think about the probabilities and possibilities, you will either not act at all or be too late. As a soldier in the army you have no free will; you have signed it over to your commander. Men have been shot for failing to obey a simple command. The officers may make wrong decisions but your role is to get on with doing exactly what you are told," he chided the younger man.

"In battle! Don't be daft. What makes you think the enemy army will land all this way up the coast. They have their sights set on the south of England," mocked Wull, although his recollection of the enemy plane flying over jumped into his head. He drew breath to continue with his spiel, but was interrupted by his commanding officer.

"A moment, Campbell," he said sharply, holding the door open to let Wull go before him out of the hall.

Wull saluted and stood to attention until the captain told him to stand easy before continuing with what he wanted to say. "I know you are frustrated and I fully understand that what we are doing is like being toy soldiers; I am, myself, frustrated that when I put in a requisition for rifles or handguns I get no more response than 'not available'. We are in this position because so many men, just like yourself have volunteered for the Local Defence that the country just doesn't have the weaponry to arm every local branch. It is only the ingenuity of some of these old soldiers in there," he inclined his head in the direction of the Hall they had so recently quit, "that we have any weapons at all. Binding spikes onto metal poles might not be your idea of a weapon but if we come across a landing of the enemy force it is *something* to fight back with. If the plane you spotted had been dropping parachutists, we would be required to capture them at all costs before they were able to do any damage or set lights to guide the bombers."

"Sir, I mean no disrespect. I suppose I'm just disappointed not to be on the front line. No. It is more than that; I feel belittled, as if while other able-bodied men are giving their lives I am sitting on my arse allowing them to fight my battles. Two of our cowmen have enlisted. I would have given anything to go in their place. I feel guilty to be sitting at home in comparative ease while they are suffering overseas. Yes, it is guilt I feel welling up inside me ready to burst out."

"I understand very well where you are coming from, but you must remember that without you and the other farmers of this country we would be unable to sustain the war in Europe because the nation would starve. With German U-boats scuppering many of the flotillas coming across the ocean there would be a dearth of food. You are doing sterling work even although you, and I imagine many young farmers in your position, yearn for a more heroic role. We are at war, a vile war, a disgrace to humanity and every man must do what is asked of him and be content to give of his best in whatever route he is destined to follow. I too would rather be on the front line, but since my metier is to train men to defend our country should the enemy invade, I must grin and bear it. So remember when you are craving to be in the line of fire in Europe you have a much bigger role to fulfil feeding the troops and defending our freedom."

After the drilling and some lessons in map reading Wull made his way home. He was in no particular hurry so as he walked slowly he thought over the comments of Captain Jessop and, although these could not reconcile him to being part of the Home Guard rather than enlisting in the prestigious Borders Regiment, he had more of an understanding why he and his, not inconsiderable knowledge of agriculture, was needed on the home front. He vowed to wring every last grain of corn out of their fertile acres.

On reaching the farmhouse he surprised Nellie, who was sitting at the kitchen table frowning over the multitude of papers and demands that were sent by the Ministry of Food Control, by catching her round the waist and nuzzling her neck. She let out a squeal of surprise, then responded by squirming round into his arms and planting a kiss on his lips.

"Here is my hero, home to his wife," she grinned up at her tall handsome man. Ever since the first day he had shyly asked her out and she started courting Wull Campbell, she had always felt a buzz in her head and a tingle in her belly when he appeared after they had been apart, even for a few hours. The months of living with him had not dulled her love for Wull and she fully admitted she had no greater ambition than to be with him for the rest of her life.

"What are you up to? It's not often I come in and find you sitting idle," Wull asked.

"It's these quotas that have just arrived. I have no idea how we can meet them. It is all very well to tell us the farm has to produce thirty percent more to be patriotic and help the war effort, but I wish one of those paper shufflers would come and tell the chickens they have to lay thirty percent more eggs. We cannot give them what we haven't got. I've a good mind to take one of the hens to the town hall and ask the bods there to tell it to lay more." Her frustration with the paper work was obvious and made Wull realise just how much the war was affecting them all. When he and Nellie had married she had not expected to have to take on the task of keeping the government officials who hounded them at bay.

"The trouble is those pen pushers sit in their offices calculating what each farm must supply without the first idea of how crops are grown or animals reared. If they want us to produce thirty percent more eggs we need thirty percent more hens. Leave that for now and come for a wander down the river. I hardly ever see you alone these days and I don't like a wife with a wrinkly brow meeting me at the door," he finished, soothing her brow with his rough, work-scarred hands.

"I must make some sense out of all these forms." She looked in disgust at the pile of pamphlets and instruction leaflets spread out on the table. "I don't even know where to start, but Peter couldn't understand them either, so I said I would help; but I don't understand half the words. It's gobbledegook to me." She picked up a sheaf of the offending forms and waved them under her husband's nose. Wull quietly removed them, placed them on the table and ushered her out of the door by force. She cast a backward glance at the pile of papers she knew had to be dealt with, but the soft evening sun and the promise of some undisturbed time with her husband won in the end.

She laughed at his boyish antics, allowing him to catch her hand and pull her, protesting weakly, behind him as they both ran out of the door, like children escaping their chores. However, after their initial wild flight, she stayed his exuberance, took his arm, hugging it close, enjoying the closeness of their bodies as, with matching strides, they sauntered out of the farmyard, over the stile and onto the banks of the River Annan where it bubbled and rumbled its way to the sea. They separated as the terrain became rougher, going hand in hand giggling and laughing like bairns as they jumped over burns and squelched through mossy pools along the length of the meandering river bank. They stopped occasionally to kiss or to hold buttercups under each other's chins or to gather forget-me-nots to give to each other before they wended their way into the wood.

They had been wandering aimlessly for some time in the cool cover of the trees when Nellie clutched at Wull, saying, "You do know how to get us out of this wood, don't you? It's like another world; this calm peaceful haven far away from the war and all our worries. All I can hear is the wind in the trees and the happy birdsong with the tune of the river accompanying them. Perhaps we could build a gingerbread house and live here until all the wars have passed by."

"It would be wonderful, right enough: you could collect berries and mushrooms while I'm out catching a salmon or trapping a rabbit for our dinner. We could roam the woods through the daytime and cuddle up together at night with nothing and no one to disturb our peace. If only life were that simple." Wull once more cuddled his wife and as their embrace became more urgent. They sank down to the warm leaf strewn earth with their bodies so close together they could hear each other's heartbeat.

As they moved to stretch out on the ground, Nellie gave a sharp cry, "Ouch! Something stabbed into me."

The mood was lost as the pair sat up to see what had caused her discomfort. When they had been squirming around on the ground they had uncovered a package carefully buried in the pile of leaves they had thought to use as a bed.

"What on earth is that?" asked Nellie, tentatively kicking it with the toe of her wellie. Wull looked serious for a moment or two then got up and walked about their arbour, peering into the depths of the trees. He broke off a low branch and began poking it into the undergrowth as if it was a sword. Nellie was in stitches laughing at his antics.

"You look so silly doing that. What are you after digging around in the bushes?" Wull did not answer but held up his finger to his mouth to indicate that she should be quiet. Nellie was just about to make another remark when he abandoned his search and returned to kneel down beside the large parcel. Giving one last glance behind him, he tentatively opened the parcel to expose some silk material tied up with rope.

"What is it?" asked Nellie creeping closer to peer over his shoulder.

"I think it's a parachute. Look, here is a radio tucked into its folds. It must have been the corner of it that stabbed you," he began, then started to think out loud, "I saw a German plane flying overhead when I was going to the LDV. They must have been dropping a spy. You know, they know there are munitions factories on this coast and I bet they are trying to pinpoint them. I reported it to Captain Jessop but we'll need to get back to the farm so that I can phone HQ with this information."

Nellie could see that Wull was excited about the prospect of foiling an enemy plan so she argued that he should go ahead to the farmhouse since she, with her shorter legs, would hold him back, but Wull was having none of it.

"We don't know how many of them there are or where they are. I don't expect they flew all the way from Germany to drop off one spy. We will go back together," he concluded.

After he had made the call to HQ he was told to await the arrival of his platoon. While he was waiting he ran his immediate assumptions through his mind, noting the discrepancies in his conclusions. His brow furrowed and a cold shiver of fear ran down his spine.

"Would they would have risked dropping spies in broad daylight? I don't think so. Maybe the plane I saw yesterday was responding to a message sent from someone who was here already." He wracked his brain to recall if he had heard engine noises during any of the preceding nights, but, with the loss of two farmhands to the forces, by the time he reached his bed at night he slept like the dead, often needing Nellie to awaken him for the milking. He spoke of his ruminations to the platoon commander when he arrived. He agreed that he was probably correct, however; they now knew there were enemy agents in the vicinity and their remit was to capture them. The Home Guard, with their pitiful weapons but defiant courage, were to spread out in the woods and lay low until evening in the hopes that whoever had used the parachute would return to use the radio to communicate with their command.

Wull gathered the family together to tell them of the danger, making it plain that his wife and sisters were to stay indoors. It was arranged that Peter would walk up to the end of the road to collect Ruby and Gina to walk them home. Peter spun on his heel with a grim look on his face, entering the farm office from where he reappeared a few moments later with an ancient gun and a canvas bag. It was a short, long-bored gun and the bag held the ball and shot it required.

"This was my great grandfather's. I've not had occasion to fire it before but as a lad my papa showed me how to keep it clean and oiled so I think it should be handy if you get into a sticky situation."

He then gave Wull a quick demonstration on how to use the gun, warning him that the kick from the firing of the powder was likely to unbalance him. When he and Wull left the house on their separate missions he instructed Peg, Mame and Nellie to lock all the doors and keep out of sight.

"I don't think a wee farm will be their target, but I want you girls to be as careful as possible, so try to keep away from the windows and, if you do spy someone in the yard, don't try any heroics. All right?"

The girls agreed to do exactly as he asked and the men left. Soon Peter was back with Ruby, who was flushed with excitement.

"Fancy there being spies in our quiet little backwater," she enthused. "Wull and his pals will be heroes saving us from a fate worse than death."

"Now, see here Ruby, this is no laughing matter. If these are enemy spies, landing here is a serious business, what with all the different munitions in the area to say nothing of RAF Dumfries and the aerodrome at Annan. If they succeed in sending the coordinates back to their squadron thousands of deaths may result. Even worse, if they succeed in blowing up the factories it will take months to set up similar plants and our boys on the front line will have no ammunition."

A cowed Ruby replied, "Sorry Dad. I'm not really making light of the seriousness of the situation. It's just how we girls in the factories deal with desperate circumstances. Every day we go to work with the most volatile materials and hope against hope that no one makes a mistake or takes their mind off the job for a few seconds and we are all blown to kingdom come. You have to joke about the job or we would never go near the place again. Most of the time we are light-hearted, joshing with each other, but at the back of our minds we all realise the danger we are in."

The patrol searched the woods and lay hidden in the undergrowth until morning without any signs of the men belonging to the parachutes. They had found two more of them hidden at intervals; one stuffed into the root system of an ancient oak, another pushed deep within a prickly gorse bush. Once they were aware what they were looking for it was easy to find them. It appeared as if the spies were sure they would not be detected. The only hope that kept the watchers going was that they did not believe the secret agents would have abandoned the radio as it was a vital part of their equipment. All other Home Guard units were on the alert for any stranger appearing in their midst so it was to be hoped that it would not be long before the enemy were captured. Despite all their vigilance, as weeks passed and no sign of further enemy activity was observed, Captain Jessop collected the radio and reduced the watch being kept to two men on three shifts, but still the parachutists did not return. When three months had passed with never an indication of the men in the district the watch was a called off altogether and life returned to normal.

As summer came and the work on the farm began to be too much for the two men, Peter made an application to the prisoner-of-war camp at Halmuir Farm with the result that two prisoners became a fixture on the farm. In the beginning different prisoners came on each occasion but Peter and Wull became friendly with Jan and Adam and requested that they should be a permanent allocation. Before very long the two men had integrated into the family and it is doubtful whether anyone remembered they were, in fact, enemy aliens. They worked hard and were polite to everyone; the only difference between them and the men who had worked on the land before the war was that they had to return to their camp in the evening and that they were paid by the Department of Agriculture rather than by Peter. Both the men on the farm realised that what Jan and Adam were being paid was a pittance and, since food was neither plentiful nor tasty in the POW camp, Nellie saw to it that the hardworking men were fed at the same time as her husband and father-in-law. Although food was rationed for everyone those on the farm fared better than most since they had the ability to stretch unrationed food further. Turnips that had previously been fed to sheep now made their way into most of the dishes on the menu while carrots, with their sweeter taste, made an adequate substitute for sugar when baking. Between them Nellie and the resourceful Mame managed to invent strange combinations of ingredients to make tasteful and filling plates of food. Mame, particularly, experimented with plants that grew in the woods and hedgerows; the successful became part of the menu in the NAAFI, where the always hungry young men devoured all of her offerings with relish. They suffered from lack of sugar, as did everyone in the country since the merchant navy ships were targets for both the Luftwaffe and the U-boats, but by saving up their ration they were able to make jam from the fruits of the hedgerows.

Nellie too was a dab hand at anything to do with baking or cooking and amazing results came from her mixing of odd ingredients. She was friendly with an old man who lived in a tiny cottage just at the edge of the Rammerscales estate. He knew what was edible, where it grew and when the time was right to harvest berries and fruit. He kept Nellie well supplied with brambles, rosehips, crab apples and sloes and she in turn fed him whenever he came to the kitchen and often visited him with a rabbit stew or a pot of soup. There was always fish in the river and rabbit and hare made their appearance on the dinner table more often than beef or pork, so all in all those who worked on the farm were fed.

"I'm just off up to the cottage with a few pancakes and an egg for Tommy," she told Mame as she slipped on her wellies and departed. "I'll not be long."

"All right," agreed Mame without lifting her eyes from her magazine and barely taking in what her sister-in-law had said. It was several hours later before she realised that Nellie had not returned, but since she wasn't sure how long she had been away, she thought no more about it. It was only when the men came in for their dinner and still Nellie was absent that alarm bells began to ring.

"What a lazy bugger you are. Sitting there reading when we hungry men are needing fed," chided her father as he noticed dinner was not on the table as it usually was when Nellie was around.

"Where is Nellie?" asked Wull as he took off his boots and wandered over to the stove, lifting the lid on the pot where the raw potatoes were waiting to be boiled. Wull swung round, asking sharply again, "Where is Nellie?"

"She went out a while ago to see Tommy. She said she wouldn't be long but I'm afraid she might have been gone longer than I thought because it's not like her to forget about the dinner," she finished, but by the time the words had left her lips Wull was across the kitchen, slipped his boots back on and was halfway across the farmyard. He had a horrible feeling that something was amiss with his Nellie. He ran off in the direction of the adjacent estate with his heart in his mouth as he prayed, "Dear Lord, let no harm have come to Nellie."

As he approached Tommy's cottage he saw no evidence that anyone was there so he slowed down and inspected the area around the isolated hut. It was unnaturally quiet: in all the years that Tommy had lived here Wull never remembered the door of his cottage being closed during the day. Tommy had spent most of his life as a shepherd on the nearby Eskdalemuir hills and did not like to be shut in, but today the door was shut, alerting Wull to the possibility that something untoward was taking place. He stealthily approached the tiny house and surreptitiously raised his head until he could look in the window. His blood ran cold as he saw Nellie standing by the fireside while Tommy held her at gunpoint. The old man held a rifle in his hands, poised to shoot if Nellie made any movement. He could see that the old shepherd was talking continuously and that Nellie was wildly looking around herself as if for some escape. That she was afraid to move was obvious to Wull. He just hoped she would not notice him peering in at the window and call out, for he realised that the thing to do would be to surprise Tommy by suddenly appearing beside his wife. He quickly circled the cottage, hoping against hope that the back door would not be locked, and his prayers were answered as, when he tried the handle, it turned in his grasp. Inch by quiet inch he opened the door, then, calculating how long it would take him to reach his wife and push her to safety, he entered the kitchen. From his vantage point he could see the scene taking place in the main room. He heard Tommy talking but felt sure the words were not directed at Nellie. He was cursing and swearing, threatening to teach someone a lesson for invading his space and stealing his chickens and digging up his garden.

"Bloody hell!" thought Wull, "The old man is off his trolley. How on earth am I to get Nellie out of there without her being hurt or, worse, killed?"

The old man continued to rant; the same speech going on and on as if recorded. "I'll teach ye to interfere with my belongings. You needny think I won't use this gun. One move from ye and ye'll be a deed man. Ma chickens, ma vegetables, ma breeks."

This last almost undid Wull for, in spite of the seriousness of the situation, it was funny. Someone had been stealing from Tommy; the impact of that action was to tip him over the edge into insanity. Wull made a desperate plan and before he could think over the implications, he was through the door and greeting Tommy as if nothing odd was happening.

"Hello, Tom, how are you today? I see Nellie's here. I hope she is going to make me a cuppa; I'm that parched." With two strides he was beside Nellie. He caught hold of her and shoved her into the kitchen while he continued to talk to the old man. He took in his appearance. There was no physical evidence that the shepherd had lost his mind. He was a man of medium height, a sparse man. The years of tending to the sheep on the hill could be seen written on his hands and skinny wrists that poked out from the frayed cuffs of his coarse linen shirt. The long, thin, blue-veined fingers extended from the remarkably silk-soft hands, the result of many years of handling fleeces greasy with lanolin. In years gone by he might have been handsome, but the man standing in front of Wull was in his eighty-fourth year with features that showed his age; his hair and moustache were gunmetal grey and hung in shaggy untended profusion over his eyes and lips. Normally a very dapper man, today Wull noticed that he was wearing a pyjama jacket under a woollen waistcoat that was inside out, while his trousers were not fastened with the ballop unbuttoned and his drawers protruding through the space.

Wull took this in at a glance, but continued talking. "Have you been cleaning your rifle? It looks in good trim. I could be doing with a loan of that to take to the Home Guard. We are drilling with shovels and hoes at the minute," he babbled on, hoping to distract Tommy's attention.

The old man ceased his rambling and smiled at Wull, who breathed a great sigh of relief, for it was obvious that Tommy had recognised him for who he was and not the intruder he had been raving at, but Wull was still wary and kept his gaze on Tommy since he was still holding the rifle poised to shoot.

"Away there, Wullie. It's a long time since I seen ye or yon bonny wee lassie o yourn. Are ye fairing weel?"

"Och, Nellie's busy on the farm, what with the war and all. She'll be up to see you soon, never fear." Wull carried on talking, never taking his eyes of the old man. "That's a good rifle you've got there. Is it loaded?"

An angry look came over Tommy's face as he began to tell Wull about his recent experience.

"There was a couple o' tramps came in the garden. It was the racket the hens put up that alerted me to them for I was out front smoking ma pipe in the sun. When I went round the back they had already helped themselves to some potatoes and a bunch of carrots, but they were trying to catch one of the hens. Well I turned back and collected auld faithful here. I caught one of them and had him here at gunpoint, until ye came in an' he escaped," he said sorrowfully.

It was apparent that Tommy had imagined Nellie to be one of the culprits that he believed he had taken prisoner.

"Maybe you should put that rifle away; you wouldn't want anyone to get hurt," coaxed Wull.

"I damned well would want to hurt the bugger that stole ma breeks. Ma geed breeks made out o' yon thick cordy roy," he answered, becoming angry once more at the thought of losing his almost new trousers to a tramp. Nevertheless, he did lay his gun up against the wall and came towards where Wull was standing at the kitchen door, but he posed no threat as he sat himself down on his hard, black, horsehair settle, that was many years older than he was himself, and invited Wull to sit down too. Wull complied and they chatted amicably for several minutes. By now Tommy was showing no signs that he knew what he had been doing and was happily chatting about local affairs and the shortages caused by the war. As Wull stood up to go using his dinner as an excuse, Tommy also rose and lifted the rifle from where he had placed it earlier.

Wull stood, still worried that Tommy now thought he was the intruder, but Tommy handed the gun to Wull, saying, "If this is ony use to you tae fight against the enemy, ye mun huv it."

Since Wull had been wondering how he could manage to remove the weapon from the older man without causing him any more anguish he gladly accepted it, vowing to return it when the war had been won and Tommy could once more go out to shoot a rabbit for his supper. He left the cottage carrying the gun, now broken and emptied of cartridges. Walking back towards the farm he came upon Nellie sitting on the unearthed root of a huge horse chestnut tree. She smiled weakly as Wull came up to her.

"Oh, Wull, my darling Wull. He hasn't harmed you. I was terrified he'd shoot you. My legs wouldn't carry me any further. I tried to get back to the farm but I just froze and had to sit down for a while. What if he had shot and killed you while I'm swooning here like a loony?" she said from the shelter of his arms where she had flung herself at the sight of her husband's uninjured body.

"Wheest lass. I'm grand. I think he just had a wee episode where he forgot himself but man, my heart nearly stopped when I saw him holding you up and blethering about you being a tramp after his veg," came a muffled response from Wull, whose face was buried in Nellie's sweet smelling hair.

"But I don't think that was imagination, Wull," responded Nellie seriously. "When I came up to the cottage all the hens were out in the front garden and there is no doubt that someone has been digging in the garden. Just when I was about to walk in the door, Tommy came breenging out with the rifle at his shoulder. That was when he took me for the thief. I don't think he meant to shoot anybody really and I was just in the wrong place at the wrong time. I think there might well have been someone there before me who had skedaddled while Tommy was off getting his rifle."

"Never mind that just now. He is safe enough; I have his rifle which he handed over like a lamb. Let's get back to the farm and get some dinner or I'll need to be looking for another wife; one that will feed me," he finished with a grin.

"That's typical. We are both nearly shot and all you can think of is your stomach," said an indignant Nellie. "There's me worrying myself sick, wondering if you'll come out of that cottage alive and all you can think of is your mince and tatties."

"I only hope that no-use sister of mine has thought to put the tatties on to boil or it'll be my supper I'll be needing. That lass may be a grand cook but she has no idea about housekeeping. Woe betide Ronald when he takes her to wife. I hope he can wield a broom or they will be living up to their eyeballs in dust," he joked, trying to take Nellie's mind off her recent experience.

In the event there was no need to worry about their dinner for Mame had the meal ready by the time they arrived. Perhaps Wull was right in thinking Mame had no housewifely talents, but as a cook there was none better. Although he would never think of saying so to his wife, Mame seemed to possess magic in her fingers making everything she cooked taste better than anyone else's food. However bad she may have been at keeping house she was a compassionate soul and it was no time at all before she was sympathising with Nellie over a cup of tea, strongly laced with some of the precious sugar ration. Mame petted and reassured her sister-in-law, telling her to tell the story again and again in an attempt to make her see her life-threatening ordeal in a less frightening light.

Nellie was grateful and felt herself recovered but, as she went to rise from the chair, her head became dizzy and she was forced to sit back down in a hurry. Mame had noticed this and quickly called her brother instructing him to take his wife up to her bed and make her stay there for the rest of the afternoon. Nellie knew she should refuse since she had all manner of unfinished chores to do but, since Peter and Wull joined their voices to Mame's, she was soon tucked up in bed with the quilt pulled up to her chin. Just as Wull was leaving there was a knock at the bedroom door and Mame entered bringing a hot water bottle for Nellie to cuddle.

"For the shock," said Mame, leaving immediately, happy that she had thought of all she could do to counter the effect of being held at gunpoint. She reflected on Nellie's situation, realising just how much Nellie meant to them all. Although not much older than any of the girls, in the year or so she had been married she had taken on the position of mother in the family. Mame realised that she was very fond of Nellie.

Meanwhile Wull had been relating the incident to Peter and the others around the table. He asked his father if he thought Tommy had imagined the tramps or, remembering the parachutes they had found in the wood a few months ago, if he thought these men might have had reason to come back and it was they who had raided Tommy's garden.

Peter gave the idea some thought before answering, "If it wasn't for the trousers, I would be likely to think as you do, but stealing washing off the line is a more tramp action, don't you think? But I'll tell you what you should do; take Jan and Adam back to Halmuir and drop in at the police station and tell them the whole story. You might as well wait at the station and bring Jen and Peg back when their train comes in from Carlisle." He sighed, "This war! It's making an old man of me. How can I protect my girls when they are never in the same place two minutes running? If Peg got on all right today, I might just be able to keep her here on the farm, but there is no doubt about it Jen will be in uniform before we know what has hit us, and God knows where she will end up."

While Peter went back to work and Nellie slept fitfully in their bed, Wull, Jan and Adam piled into the old pickup and sped off down the road. After dropping the men off at the camp and explaining why they were back early, Wull went to the police station and reported the incident. Since he was able to assure the constable that he had removed the gun from Tommy's vicinity and that they would ensure a doctor took a look at him, PC Carruthers decided all he need do was call Captain Jessop to make him aware of the situation in case this was an indication that the parachutists had returned.

Still not quite satisfied with the way the police had shrugged off his concern Wull passed the incident through his mind as he waited outside the station for his sisters' train to arrive. He had just formatted a plan in his head when he heard the sound of the approaching train. With the arrival of the girls he had no more time to contemplate his actions for the girls were in good form, having achieved what they had set out to gain from their visit to the various recruitment offices in Carlisle. Peg's face was shining since she had been allocated a 'peach of a job'. Because there was no aspect of farming she was not expert in she had been allocated to be an instructor for the land girls who were being sent to rural Dumfriesshire to take up the jobs left empty by the men who had enlisted.

"I'm to be based in Lockerbie but to go around making sure the girls are taught how to milk or harvest or, oh, anything I think they need to know!" she exclaimed, running out of words in her excitement. "But best of all I am going to be able to stay at home and help out there, although the supervisor thinks I might have to move if we get Land Girls. It wouldn't do for them to be living in the same place as me," she concluded a bit less happily.

Wull, extremely fond of his younger sister, leaned over to the passenger seat patting her thigh. "We won't be having land girls because we have Jan and Adam from the POW camp and I know Dad wants to keep them because they are such hard workers, despite neither of them having done any farm work before."

"I know yummy Jan was a lawyer in the Ukraine before he was conscripted," began Jen, "and Adam was a shop assistant. You couldn't find two more opposite jobs than they have but they are making the best of their situation." She was sitting in the back seat of the truck and, from her vantage point behind Peg, could see the colour rise on her neck and cheeks at the mention of the men. "I wonder," she mused. "Yes, I wonder if Peg is sweet on one of the men? Mmm..."

Deciding to keep an eye on her little sister, Jen said nothing about her idea but pushed the notion to the back of her mind while she described to her brother how her interview had gone at the WAAF recruiting office. "I waited with lots of other girls my age in a drab cold room, maybe that was to make us realise conditions in the WAAF would not be like living at home. But anyway, after nearly an hour a smartly dressed WAAF came into the room and took all our names. She was a bit snooty but I didn't mind that so much as she made us all feel as if we had arrived for our interviews in our granny's cast-offs. You should have seen her make-up, powder and bright red lipstick. I was about fourth to go in. I was told by the WAAF to stand up straight in front of the desk where an old man with lots of medals on his chest asked me all sorts of questions about what I had done so far in my life. Could I drive? Had I even been away from home? What would I have done if war hadn't been declared? I didn't know what the right answers were but I must have done all right because Miss Snooty Pants took me to wait with three others in a cold little cell. After a time, when four more girls had joined us and we were chatting happily, the WAAF returned and took us into what looked like a school room where we were told to sit at the desks and do the tests set out there. The tests were easy, just general knowledge. When we were finished the old soldier came in and we were given a spelling test and some mental arithmetic. There was even more waiting around while he took all the test papers away to look at. When the WAAF came back into the room she told three of the girls they would need to go to another recruitment office, then one by one we were taken back to see the big cheese who told us we were privileged to be accepted for the Women's Auxiliary Air Force and would be sent our postings and travel warrants within the week. I'm going to be a WAAF! I'm so excited!" she finished. Wull was silent for a moment or two before congratulating his sister. It was ironic that it was the women of the family who were to go to war while the men stayed home and looked after the farm. He was pleased for his sister, but was still aware of a pang of jealousy at her good fortune.

"So we are to lose you to the big wide world are we?" he eventually grinned round at Jen, who was far too intent on telling her story to notice his despondency. She hurriedly replied, "You won't miss me and Peg is the one who really understands the farm. She'll be a Land Army colonel before the war ends," she laughed, saluting her sister as if she was already in that position.

Wull then told the story of Nellie's ordeal and, by the time they reached the farm, there was no more time for him to fret about his place in the war effort being usurped by his sisters.

Chapter Twenty-Nine

Ruby was on the dreaded night shift. It was unusual for a single girl to be given the more antisocial shift as there were plenty of women like Moira and Morag who were happy to leave their sleeping children with a friend while they went to work. They knew that they would need to return the favour when their friend was on duty. These women were luckier than most as being in an area where munitions were made allowed them not only to subsidize their soldier husband's wage, but to combat the loneliness of caring for their children singlehanded. Morag and Moira did not just share a job but also the soul-destroying stand in the queue whenever luxury items such as meat or sugar were in the shops. Ruby listened to the women talk about their lives outside of work and realised why these women looked so tired. The war was hard on women too; although the whole country praised the male population for answering the call to arms, no one thought about the women who were struggling with rations and work, to say nothing of the danger they were in from possible attack from the Luftwaffe who knew the factories were in the area, but had as yet not pinpointed them.

As the women worked away, Ruby became aware of a disruption at the other end of the long room she worked in, and peered over her tub of acids and cotton to see what the kerfuffle was all about. She recognised a girl called Doris, whom she knew only slightly, being carried off to sick bay. The Squirt, who was on night shift in order to goad the women into producing more, scurried out after the little procession just as the hooter went to indicate the shift could take a break.

Ruby accompanied some of the older women to the canteen where they were fed their meal. The talk was all about the girl who had folded in the factory.

"She'll be for it," said one and others nodded.

"It's not as if she was new to munitions. She came here from the Longtown factory because her husband was posted to the flying school in Dumfries."

"Aye," agreed a third. "She might just have gotten away with it if the Squirt hadn't been on, but you know how he hates to see anyone getting the better of him."

"But what did she do? The woman fainted. Why will the Squirt think she is trying to pull the wool over his eyes?" asked Ruby, quite at sea to understand what the women were talking about.

"You've not been on the night shift before, have you?" questioned Grace Irving, the oldest of the women round the table.

"No," answered Ruby, "this is the first time. The Squirt put me on nights because I missed the bus twice last week. He said if I couldn't get up in the morning I could come on night shift. He said I wouldn't be late for the night shift, but really it is because I laughed at him and the little tyrant doesn't like anyone to flout his authority. Honest, Hitler has nothing on auld McQuirter," she finished, but wrinkled her nose and went back to the subject they had been discussing. "Why will Doris fainting get on his goat?"

"The Gerrys are shooting down so many of our bombers that they are recalling some of the older fliers to take up the slack. Since her husband is a distinguished pilot he is required to return to a live station. He is on embarkation leave and has to get his train tomorrow dinnertime. This is Doris's last chance to spend the night with him for who knows how long, so she stuck her head over the tub deliberately in order to faint and be sent home. It's a trick many women use to get off, but I think the Squirt was watching her just at the moment she did it. She was careful to be in a position where she would slide to the floor without hurting herself, so I reckon he's off to read her the riot act."

"I didn't know the mixture could make you faint. It makes me sick to my stomach but I've never as much as felt woozy when I'm at work," said Ruby. "Even if she did do it on purpose what can he do about it? We need every hand we can get to keep these tubs going to make the arms for our soldiers. He can't sack her. He won't be allowed to."

"That's just the point. *He* knows that *we* know he is a toothless tiger with no real power. Everyone here is employed at the bequest of the War Office officials which means he can threaten the loss of your job till the cows come home but he can't, in fact, give you your cards."

"No, but he can make life hard if you don't fall in with his ways, if you know what I mean," another woman chimed in, but hurriedly got a nudge from Grace who said sharply, "That's enough of that, Pat. Ruby is just a young girl. No need to tell her what the old bugger gets up to."

An unrepentant Pat answered indignantly, "Well, if she is going to be on this shift, it's as well she should know what the sod gets up to on *his* night shifts. Keep out of dark corners when he's around, Ruby, that's all I'm saying. We even go to the lavvy—"

Her speech was broken into by the strident ringing of the air raid warning. No one had any time now to dawdle and exchange gossip. They rose as one from the table and made for the canteen door and into the passage which led down to the air raid shelter built into the cliff nearby. Just as they were making their way in a snake-like procession, the lights went out and they were plunged into darkness.

"That old bastard!" came Grace's voice. "As soon as he has himself into the bunker he switches off the lights and we have to feel our way down the tunnels to the shelter. And don't think when you get there he'll be a gentlemen and give up the bunk for us to sit on. Selfish old bugger!"

Ruby had never known anything as frightening as that dark crawl along the corridor. It seemed to go on for ever and with the warning siren still ringing in her ears, she felt like she was making a descent into Hell. As she came to a part where there was no wall to follow, she stopped short, not knowing what to do or where to go.

Pat, however, who had just bumped into her from behind, grabbed her hand and whispered, "It's all right, lass. We have just come to a corner. I'll go past you and lead you on to the shelter. Keep hold of my hand; we are nearly there."

Despite these encouraging words and the firm grip of Pat's fingers, Ruby felt she had been in the black dark for a very long time with visions of bombers gleefully dropping bombs above her dancing before her eyes. With each tentative step she took she wondered if she would ever see her father and sisters again. After what seemed to her to be an hour but was in fact only about five minutes, they arrived at the shelter where, as predicted by her co-workers, Mr McQuirter was ensconced on the bunk, leaving all the workers to find themselves places on the cold rock floor. The Squirt made himself comfortable, lying back on the pillows of the bunk, crossed his ankles and placed his arms behind his head, for all the world as if he was lying on a golden beach soaking up the sun.

Several of the women went to the back of the bunker and before long blankets were being handed back to the other occupants, music was playing tunes of the day piped down from the factory. Soon the women were singing along to the Andrews Sisters, Peggy Lee and Vera Lynn and humming to the melodies played by Benny Goodman and his orchestra and Ruby was joining in with the others. They sang favourites like *Don't Sit Under the Apple Tree*, *Down at the Old Bull and Bush*, *Bill Bailey* and *Bless 'Em All* and there was a convivial atmosphere in the shelter. Once the siren had stopped there was a deathly silence in which Ruby was sure she could hear planes overhead. She wondered what had happened to Doris. Was she sheltering somewhere outside, her route home perhaps that of the bombers? She could not have been far away when the warning went but since she was not in the shelter she must have left the factory just before the warning sounded. How dreadful to have managed to get sent home to her husband only to be killed on her way there. Suddenly the war seemed very real to Ruby.

Chatter continued with no one taking any notice of their supervisor, although he was constantly looking at his watch and calculating each minute of lost productivity.

"Ho Ruby. Tell us about your young man," asked Pat, "It's so long since I was courting I wouldn't know how to go about it these days," she laughed, nudging Ruby. "C'mon, out with the dirty details."

Ruby smiled at the teasing and complied. "Well, he's handsome, of course, he's going to be a flier; leaves for his unit in a few weeks if he passes his flying exam. He wants us to get married before he goes, just in case... you know?" explained Ruby, becoming coy.

"We don't want to know that kind of thing about him. How are his kisses? Do you go weak at the knees? What kind of lover is he?" asked Pat.

Ruby blushed red as she realised that what she had meant as, 'in case he doesn't come back' the women had interpreted as 'in case I'm up the spout.' She tried to rectify the impression she had given but the women were having none of it and continued to send sly digs at her until the all clear sounded. As they were hurrying back to their posts Ruby made one last attempt to put the record straight when she spoke to Grace about how she had not meant she had gone to bed with him. "We haven't been alone long enough to snatch a couple of kisses, never mind *that*," she stuttered, her cheeks glowing.

Grace reassured her. "The women know fine what you meant. They are only teasing. Don't give it another thought." But her words came back to haunt her the very next night.

****

"I wonder why the boss is in again tonight," commented Pat as she and Ruby shuffled their way through the security barrier and into the factory. "It's not like him to be in two nights together. Too fond of his warm bed, if you ask me."

Ruby shrugged in response. She was not enjoying her stint on nights. Oh, the girls were all right and the banter fun, but she had no time to make arrangements to see Mike and he was coming close to the end of his training and could be assigned to a bomber unit any day now. As her father had said when she complained 'there's a war on'.

"I hate this war," Ruby spoke out loud.

"You and everyone else in the country," laughed Pat while placing a sympathetic arm around Ruby's shoulders. "Our lives are not our own. In times of peace we kid ourselves that we have free will but as soon as the country is threatened, we realise we are just as much slaves as those poor buggers who were shipped out of Africa. What's got into you tonight?"

"I suppose I just don't like working in the night time."

"And maybe that you can't see your young man when he works through the day and you through the night," consoled Pat, showing she completely understood where the younger girl was coming from. "There's nothing more depressing than working while the rest of the country sleep, but..."

"There's a war on," finished Ruby suddenly laughing at herself. She said no more about her feelings as they came to the top of the queue and, after being searched, filed into the factory to take up their positions for the shift ahead. As Ruby automatically checked the tubs under her care, time passed and before she knew where she was the hooter had sounded for the break. She had almost left the factory floor when she heard her name called.

It was the Squirt.

"Just a moment, Ruby, I want to see you in the office!" he called, turning on his heel and heading back in that direction.

"What have I done now?" thought Ruby as she retraced her steps and followed the man up to the supervisor's office, which was situated directly above the factory floor in order that anyone in the office could have a bird's eye view of what was taking place beneath them. She passed the last few days through her mind in an attempt to discover what particular fault Mr McQuirter could have found. She knew the man to be petty and shrewdly judged it to be because, despite being in charge of the factory, he had no real power to hire and fire since all hands were needed on the production lines and were appointed by the command of the War Office.

"Shut the door," came the clipped tone of the Squirt's voice as she entered his domain. Here, with his view over all he surveyed, he felt like a king, a king who should not be disobeyed. Ruby obediently closed the door, but, as she heard the click, she began to feel uneasy. However, she turned to face the Squirt with a smile pinned to her lips.

"Come and sit down, Ruby. I have been watching you and I am agreeably surprised by how well you do the job." He peered at her from behind his desk where he had strategically placed himself in order to intimidate the young woman.

Ruby was so surprised at this unusual praise that for a time she could not take in what the man was saying. Thoughts ran through her mind as she tried to figure out what had prompted him to compliment her. So deep was she in contemplation she did not hear when he started to speak once more. She rapidly brought herself back to reality when she realised his tone had become sharp.

"Sorry," she smiled, "I was miles away for a moment. What was it you wanted me for?"

Rather disgruntled that he had to repeat his words he held in his anger and reiterated his words.

"I need a supervisor on this shift and I think you would be best for the position." He smirked at Ruby who was totally aghast at being offered this position. Up until this very minute she would have sworn that the Squirt hated her.

Since she was not a stupid girl she was sceptical about his offer and asked, "Why me? There are women on this shift who are better workers, better managers, need the money. Why me?" she asked again.

"You can be much use to me. Reporting back to me all those who slack, like the woman who deliberately used the fumes coming off the vat to allow her to go home. You would report to me every morning to give me an update on what had happened on the night shift. You would be able to leave the factory floor and sit comfortably in this office, mistress of the workforce. What do you say?"

"I say," commenced Ruby slowly as she ran the scenario in her head, "what's in it for you?"

Angry now because Ruby had seen through his ploy, but nevertheless not willing to give up his plan so readily, he managed to swallow his sarcastic words and once more smiled his leering grin at Ruby before coming to the point.

"All you need to do is be nice to me." He lifted an eyebrow and squinted at her to see if she had got the point, but, innocent of all knowledge of the world, Ruby did not cotton on to his meaning so he went on. "I am a lonely man who is in need of some companionship and if you agree to be that companion I am in the position to make your life easy. It's not as if you are a stranger to the needs of a man. I heard you bragging in the shelter last night. I could have had you removed for being of such low morals, but I choose to forgive you for a small concession from you." While he was speaking, he had risen and come round the desk to put his arms around Ruby, kneading her buttocks with his small podgy hands while trying to aim a kiss on her lips. Ruby stood like a statue, completely flummoxed by the actions of the little man. The Squirt took her inaction for compliance and he moved his hand to cover her overall-encased breast while the other hand tried to climb up her leg. The feel of his clammy fingers on her bare skin brought Ruby out of her brown study and her right hand curled into a fist to fly into contact with her supervisor's chin. Such a force was there behind her punch, the Squirt lost his balance and landed on the floor on his well-padded bottom. Ruby had no sympathy for his predicament; there was already a bruise, that he would need to explain to his wife, forming on his cheek; but her anger was apparent to the supervisor who was now worried that having picked the wrong girl to proposition his own position would be in jeopardy.

Never had Ruby been so angry. She ranted at him as she towered over him where he sat dumbfounded on the floor, and with no thought now of appeasing the man she called him all the nasty names she could think of. "Pervert!" she almost screamed at him. "I've a good mind to go to the authorities and let you explain to them why you think it is in order for you to blackmail women into playing your little game," she finished.

Realising if Ruby did indeed contact his superiors his goose would be well and truly cooked, he tried to make light of the situation, attempting to explain to Ruby that she had made an error and all he had been offering was fatherly advice.

"My father has given me that kind of advice for all my life but he never once thought it appropriate to feel my bum or my bosom. He also gave me advice about what to do if I was accosted by a sleekit get trying to have his way with me. My *father* knew what kind of animals I might encounter and warned me what to do, so *Mr McQuirter* thank your lucky stars you still have your balls!" she growled at him. If the daggers flying from her eyes had been real there is no doubt that the man would have been lying dead at her feet. She turned on her heel and made to leave the small office. With her hand on the handle she turned once more holding him with her infuriated stare and said, "I will be telling my father what has occurred here tonight and if I am ill-treated in any way or hear so much as a rumour that you are using others as you would have me, I will not stop him from teaching you a lesson." She whirled round and in a moment her feet could be heard on the metal treads of the stair case as she returned to her work.

After her week on night shift Ruby was relieved to meet Gina to catch their bus the next Monday morning. She had lain awake worrying about what would happen when she once more had to work on shift with the supervisor in charge. She had confided, not in her father, as she had told the Squirt she would, but in her brother and his wife. Nellie had laughed till she cried when she heard how Ruby had dealt with the over-amorous advances and praised Ruby's presence of mind, but Wull was more perturbed.

"All right, he didn't get you in his net but what of other women who are not in the position you are, who are not as well educated as you, who don't realise his job is a sinecure with no real power, who may give him what he wants because he threatens to sack them? There are many women working today who never would have done if there had not been a war on. Women who do not have their husbands and natural protectors to act for them. What then? Do you think he should go unpunished?"

"Well put like that I suppose you are right. I did tell him if I heard any talk that he was still perpetrating his nasty little scheme I would tell the powers that be, but really I think I gave him a big enough fright." But still on her first morning shift after the incident she had been loath to face the little martinet.

"What's up with you? I thought you would have been over the moon with being back on the day shift. Come on, buck up or we will miss that bus and we'll *both* be on night shift for the duration." They caught the bus and with all the gossip to be caught up on Ruby had no more time to think about how she might be received by Mr

McQuirter. In the event all the sleepless hours had been in vain, for the supervisor did not come near her, neither in the factory or when with her chums in the canteen and as the one day bled into another, she began to forget about the incident.

Chapter Thirty

Nellie and Peg were taking the men their food out to the field where all the men and girls were working to get the harvest in while the weather remained clement. Nellie had insisted on carrying one of the baskets although Peg had tried to carry, both hoping to relieve her sister-in-law of the burden since she was by now carrying 'the heir' as the family joking called it. When Peg had come in from the field to collect the dinner time 'piece' for all the workers, Nellie had the baskets ready and was preparing to make the walk back with Peg.

"I can carry the empty baskets back when everyone has been fed. It was a great idea of yours to get a gang together and go from farm to farm reaping and stooking. This way everyone gets their harvest in quickly." Nellie was beginning to understand the workings of the farm year.

"Well yes, as long as it stays dry. It might not be so popular if one crop is wasted by the wind and rain while they have been off helping their neighbour get his under cover but fortunately, fingers crossed, we have been lucky in not having two crops ripe at exactly the same time. It helps that Wull is the only one around here with a threshing machine and every farm has to wait for him to have their threshing done," explained Peg. She had fairly come out of her shell since she had been working with the Land Army girls. The whole family were surprised how well she had taken to the job of teaching the raw recruits, many from cities in the south of England who didn't know one end of a cow from the other or what was wheat and what was grass, and binding them into a battalion of capable agricultural workers. It seemed Peg, the shy home loving girl was no more and in her place was the competent, organised woman capable of making any decisions required. She loved her job as superintendent of the Land Army and many a farmer in the Borders was beholden to her for moulding their helpers. She had a quiet way of dealing with people, not only the Land Girls, but she had developed the ability to argue for what was right. Much to everyone's surprise she was even able to stand up to gnarly old farmers who tried to take advantage of the Land Girls by working them too hard or asking them to tackle jobs that were not within their remit. This ability was brought to the attention of her family one night in particular when Peg was asking her father's advice about some simple treatment for soothing the cows' teats while they were suckling their calves, when her father had commented that it was strange to see the roles reversed and women doing the tough heavy jobs on the farm, when in his day women took pride in their home and were only required to tend to the less strenuous jobs on the farm. This random statement had made Peg lose her temper saying, "You are the last person I would have believed would want to put a girl in her place; in the kitchen and the house! I spend all day trying to make bigoted old men, and some arrogant young ones too, see that the Land Girls are NOT on their farms to cook and clean when their day's work is done. Farm work is ALL they are required to do. Yes, they are expected to work hard and they sometimes have to work long hours in the fields when there are crops to harvest, but they are not there to be playmates or servants to lecherous farmers. They should be grateful to have them when their ploughman and dairymen are off to the forces." Peg stammered to a halt and apologised to her father, but this outburst had been enough for Peter to realise that Peg, the little homebody, was a force to be reckoned with when she got her dander up. This opinion was solidified a few weeks later when a fellow farmer told Peter how his daughter had scolded a notorious miserly farmer for not feeding the Land Girls on his farm properly. "It was a sight to behold. I've known your Peg since she was knee high to a grasshopper and a quieter wee lass I've never come across, but there she was standing toe to toe with old Baxter telling him if he continued to ill use the girls they would be taken away leaving him to manage the farm by himself. I tell you, boy, I laughed for a week and it still makes me chuckle; but, you know what? Those Land Girls are being fed at his table. I do believe he would go without to feed them now if he thought it would keep your Peg from haranguing him."

As Peg and Nellie approached the field with its stacks of sheaves and bare-looking ground they saw the workers break off from their toil to settle under the hedge in the shadow of the trees to eat their hard-earned piece. The girls handed out the cups before pouring tea from a thermos flask for everyone. The workers helped themselves to the sandwiches and spread out to eat their meal. Nellie and Wull moved a bit away from the others while he chided her for walking so far in the heat but, as he took in the healthy shine on her face and her radiant smile, he was only half hearted in his attempt to make her stay in the farmhouse resting. It was a pleasant diversion to be siting sharing his dinner with her. While the harvest was in full swing he was barely at home. He and the others worked from sunup till dark and with his commitment to the Home Guard he spent very little time with his wife. He crept out of bed before dawn in order to do the routine chores of the farm before it was time to make his way to whatever farm was being harvested, and he came to bed hours after Nellie had fallen asleep. It was pleasant to crawl into bed with his wife, but they rarely talked and planned as they had done in the early months of their marriage.

"It will be better after the harvest and when the babe is born it will be in winter and I'll have plenty of time to help," he consoled himself, but days like today were to be cherished and Wull took full advantage of his wife's presence. They chatted idly about nothing in particular until Nellie gave him a nudge and indicted with her head that there was something he should see happening behind him. He turned round, but could not at once identify what Nellie was talking about.

She whispered to him, "Look at Peg with Jan."

"What about them? They are talking and eating."

Nellie huffed, "Men, you are all the same. Can't see what's happening right under your nose? Look at Peg's face. Jan can't keep his eyes off it." She laughed. "No, Wull," she said, pulling him back round to face her, "Don't let them see you have seen them. Peg is like a nervous colt; if she imagines you notice she is paying attention to Jan, that will be the end of it."

"What on earth are you talking about?" asked Wull, not in the least understanding what Nellie meant.

"They make a lovely couple, don't you think?" continued Nellie, forcing Wull to take another surreptitious glance at the pair who were laughing about something one of them had said.

"Don't be daft. Peg's not one for the boys. She's too young," he expostulated.

"Not as young as Ruby and she is engaged to be married. Not as young as I was when we got together. She's not young, Wull. And she has become much more confident since she took on the Land Army girls. She might be learning as much from them as they are from her, but in quite a different manner."

"Our Peg courting? You must be mistaken."

"Well if I am we will see. I beg you Wull, don't tease her. Let her enjoy her romance. If it comes to anything, well, you don't dislike Jan and he is a prisoner only because he was brave and fought for his country; that doesn't make him a bad man."

"Of course it doesn't," said Wull quickly. "If he made Peg happy I would not worry about her being with him. It's just... just..."

"Just that she's your little sister and you can't imagine anyone being good enough for her," finished Nellie.

Wull placed his strong brown hands over the bump of their baby and sighed, "I hope this one is a boy, for girls bring you nothing but worry."

"You cheeky sod," remonstrated Nellie, giving him a sound whack on the leg. "I'll teach you to be cheeky about us girls." But Wull would not take back his words.

"I mean it. Dad and I are constantly on the watch to make sure no harm comes to the girls. What with that bugger in munitions, and that is not settled yet, by any means," he glowered as he thought what could so easily have happened to Ruby. "And Jen off to her WAAF training in God knows where, Helen out in Egypt with her nursing corps, and barely a word from her because of the disruption of mail boats, you and the heir." The smile broke out on his face, making him look as young as he had before the war had blighted their life, and he leaned over to give Nellie a kiss before continuing with his list of worries. "Well obviously you are my prime concern, but I had thought Peg to be the least of them. If you think she is sweet on Jan they will need to have an eye kept on them, and what with Mame moping around as if she had lost a shilling and found sixpence it's no wonder my hair is going grey."

"Your hair is not going grey, and even if it was it would just be distinguished." Nellie ran her finger over his hair, lifting a few tendrils, pulling his head down until she could smell the sun on his hair. "It's just as black as it has always been and it smells like new mown hay, well maybe since your cutting corn it smells of that," she corrected herself, but still drawing in the smell of her husband. She too was missing the times they spent cuddled in bed, this was their intimate time; the time they planned their family; what they would do once the war was over, when they could joke and laugh with each other without worry about the day-to-day struggles they faced to produce enough food for not only their own needs, but for the needs of the country.

After her moment of absorption in her husband she picked up on something he had said earlier. "Do you think Mame is unhappy?"

"I do," he said thoughtfully. "Mame has always been so composed and sure of herself. I suppose being the oldest she felt a bit superior to us and, if I'm honest, I don't know how to approach her. She is so self-contained; but something is bothering her."

"Do you want me to have a chat with her and see if I can find out what it is?"

"Have a chat by all means, but for goodness sake don't let her think we're prying. Maybe it is just not being part of the war effort that is upsetting her. Every time she comes home she seems a bit sadder. I'm sure if she wanted to she could move from her positon to the Land Army or the munitions, although," a mischievous grin came over his face "the thought of Mame encountering that supervisor at Powfoot would be enough to keep us laughing till the war ends. He wouldn't know what had hit him if he had to manage our Mame."

"I hope he is not bullying any other of the girls. Ruby said one of the older women had been moved onto the night shift permanently to be the supervisor, but whether her promotion was prompted by her agreeing terms with him she doesn't know. She thinks, and I do too, that it's none of her business and anyway, Ruby will be able to hold her own with the Squirt, as she calls him."

"Aye, Ruby won't let anyone force her into doing anything against her conscience," agreed Wull as he rose to his feet. It was time for him to get the workers back to the harvest. He leaned down to give Nellie a long kiss on the lips before he turned back to his task.

On her way back to the farm Nellie played over how she would bring up Mame's unhappiness in conversation. The two did not have a close bond but she knew that

Wull was very close to his sister and if she could help Mame, it would be one less worry for Wull.

As luck would have it she found the opportunity the next day when Mame came home from her work as cook in the NAAFI at the aerodrome canteen. Mame was not one to offer help on her days off, but her father had asked her to help Nellie with the heavy work in the dairy and because she saw Nellie was getting bigger every day, Mame agreed, so the two women found themselves working side by side. They were not in the habit of making small talk but they chatted about what they were doing, about Wull and Ronald and about the coming baby. Nellie became aware of a change in Mame's attitude when she talked of the family they were planning to have. Mame got very quiet and the conversation dried up. Mame turned away from Nellie, but not quickly enough to disguise the tears trickling down her face. Nellie, a most compassionate woman, took the girl in her arms and held her there while Mame sobbed her sorrow into her shoulder.

Some minutes later, with the tears spent, Mame drew herself away from Nellie, saying, "I'm so sorry. I don't know what can have come over me. I didn't mean to upset you."

"I understand perfectly. Seeing me with this little blighter," she cradled the bump of her belly, "must be awful for you when you would have expected to be in this situation yourself by now."

Mame nodded, not trusting herself to speak yet. Nellie once more gathered her sister-in-law into her embrace to comfort her. Suddenly Mame started to talk. The words flew from her mouth as if of their own volition. It seemed once the tap had opened, it was not going to be closed until every last word had tumbled one over the other into Nellie's ears.

"Ronald said he wouldn't let us get married until after the war. He said it was only delaying our wedding by a few months but the war has dragged on and he is off being a fighter pilot and having a great time in the mess after every sortie. I know he is just doing his duty and he is in such danger on a daily basis that he needs to let off steam, but I can't help myself from thinking he is having such a good time, he has forgotten me and all our plans for the future. A few weeks ago a new instructor came to the airbase and when I heard him telling others he had come from RAF Felixstowe, I made a point of asking him if he knew of Ronald. He presumed I was his sister and told me how he and his squadron were all flying missions and having a rare old time when they were on the base, 'You know, wine women and song,' he said. That was bad enough but when he asked innocently if we had met his fiancé, still under the impression that I was his sister, I laughed at him and said I had more than met her, I was her. He clammed up immediately and hasn't spoken to me since. So it seems I have been passed over for a better model. I wrote to Ronald two weeks ago. I haven't had an answer. Oh, I tell myself there hasn't been enough time but I think inside here," she indicated the area over her heart, "that he just doesn't want to tell me he's found someone else."

Nellie was at a standstill. There was nothing she could say that would comfort the miserable girl. Only Ronald could do that, but she tried to console Mame.

"You don't know for sure that he has another girlfriend. The instructor could have been getting him mixed up with someone else. He won't be the only Scottish man in the air force," she said, but really she had little belief in her statement, and Mame had even less.

"If only he would write, even if it was to tell me we are finished and he had found someone better, I would know where I stand."

"Believe me, he won't have found someone better, perhaps he did mistake his feelings for you and has fallen in love with someone he has met in England, but it won't be someone better. And if he has gotten himself engaged to another woman you are better off without such a louse, for any decent man would have broken off with one girl before promising to marry another." Nellie tried to comfort Mame but, even as she said the words, she knew they would be no consolation to the unhappy Mame.

****

Ruby stood looking at herself in the mirror. She could not quite believe her eyes. The image in the mirror bore no resemblance to the Ruby she was in the habit of seeing reflected there. She had stood still allowing her sisters to push her this way and that as they strove to make the borrowed wedding dress look its best. They had done a sterling job; she looked like a fairy tale princess; not many brides during this time of war were able to be married in a dress as beautiful as this. Nellie had come up trumps. She had insisted on loaning her pre-war wedding dress and gossamer veil for the occasion and Ruby was grateful for her generosity. One of the women in the munitions had told her about the scheme locally where you could borrow a wedding dress for the day, but when she had been shown these dresses hanging limply in a council office her heart had sank. There and then she had decided not to borrow a dress but to buy some material with her clothing coupons and inveigle her sisters into helping her make a simple dress for the wedding, but when she had broached this idea Nellie had vetoed it, saying shyly that she would be proud to lend her wedding dress to Ruby if she didn't mind wearing second hand. "For it too has been worn before."

Ruby had speedily accepted, informing her sister-in-law that nothing could please her more than to wear the dress on her happy day. "Your dress is beautiful but are you sure you are all right with lending it for it will need to be lengthened to fit me, then you won't be able to get into it on your twentieth anniversary," asked Ruby seriously.

Now that the offer had been made she would have been devastated if Nellie had had second thoughts.

"No. I would like you to wear it and I can always take the hem up again or have it shortened if I want to wear it again. Ruby was grateful for the generosity of her sister in law, for the dress, surely, but also for the unexpected present she had received that morning. Before she had even thought of getting out of bed there had been a knock at the door, followed immediately by Nellie's head peering round it.

"I brought you some tea and toast to start off your day," she started, placing the tray on Ruby's knees, "and these," she finished shyly.

"What?" asked Ruby as she held up Nellie's offering, then quickly ridding herself of the tea tray she jumped out of bed and hugged the other woman.

"Nellie. How did you know? Oh, nothing could have been better." Hugging Nellie once more in her enthusiasm she again cast her eyes over the two pairs of silk camiknickers lying on her bed unable to believe their presence. She picked them up, enjoying the feel of the silk and admiring the little bows and fragments of lace that adorned them before laughing into Nellie's face. "Thank you, thank you. How could you afford such luxury?"

Nellie, quite red with delight at Ruby's reaction, anxiously explained. "They are new. No one wore them before but I didn't buy them. I made them. I thought what I could get you for a wedding present, how I would feel if it was me being with Wull for the first time and it came to me that I wouldn't like him to see me in any of the awful underwear we are all forced to wear, so I came up with these. The silk is from the parachute Wull found in the wood, no elastic I'm afraid but I think Mike might quite like untying the ribbons." She flushed red at talking so to the unmarried girl, then hurried on to explain that the lace was from an old collar she had bought at a rags sale so that they met two criteria of the brides' rhyme. Something old, the lace; something new, the knickers; something borrowed, the wedding dress. There was only 'something blue' missing.

So now Ruby was standing alone regarding herself critically in the full-length mirror gazing in disbelief at the pretty picture she made. She was not a vain girl, having spent little energy on dolling herself up as some of the women in the factory did when they went out to dance, some of them even daring to go to a bar for a drink. Ruby was not fond of alcohol so she had not been tempted to accompany any of her colleagues, but she knew that Gina had once gone out with a boy who had taken her to a pub, coming home with stories about how some women were dressed to the nines and accepting drinks from any man who would buy them one. Both Gina and Ruby had decided that was not for them and, in any case, Gina was now courting a young man in the munitions office who had bad lungs and had been denied the dubious pleasure of dying for his country.

As she stood there gazing at the vision of herself in all her finery she could not keep a pang of sympathy out of her mind, for the next bride in her family had been expected to be Mame. Ruby realised just how generous-spirited her sister was by being her maid of honour today, for she must be sad that Ronald had been so unfaithful. Ruby remembered how thin and wan Mame had become after Ronald had not answered her letter asking if it was true he was engaged to another girl. She put on a brave face but there could be no doubt that Mame was suffering. Ruby hoped that, unlike most of the girls they knew, with Mame working in the NAAFI and meeting all sorts of young men she might meet someone who would care for her as she deserved. As if her thoughts had conjured her up Mame came in the door, stopping to gaze in wonder at her little sister, the baby of the family, all grown up and looking like a film star. She came over to Ruby stretching her fingers to tweak her veil into a better fold.

There were tears in her eyes as she told Ruby, "Ma would have been so proud of you today. She would have wanted you to wear this on your special day." So saying she placed a fine silver chain round her neck and, turning her round, burrowed under the veil to fasten it at the back. Ruby looked down to see the forget-me-not pendant that her father always said was like the colour of their mother's eyes, hanging just above the sweetheart neck of her dress. You are very beautiful. Mike is a lucky man." She smiled at Ruby's reflection in the mirror.

"I can't really believe it's true. I thought I might have to elope to get married, but Dad giving me his blessing and even if I'm not getting married in Ruthwell, I will have all the ones I love dearly with me."

Mame replied, "I admit I thought you were flying against the wind when you spoke to Dad, but I'm glad what happened with Ronald hasn't biased him against Mike."

Ruby thought back to the arguments she had used with Peter and felt a little guilty.

"I really must get married before Mike goes off to his new base," she had said. "We want to grab what happiness we can. I hate to say this, Dad, but if you don't agree I will leave and go wherever Mike is sent and live with him." Ruby's chin stuck out as it always did when she was determined to get her own way. Her father looked at her sadly.

"You know it would make more sense for you to wait until the war is over and you have something to start off with. You are both very young; you have your whole life ahead of you." He stopped her argument by holding up his hand. "I just want you to be sure before you go rushing into things. I understand you feel you can't live without him. Give it some thought, and I mean real thought; you will be parted almost at once, you might not know where Mike is for weeks or even months because he won't be at Dumfries, you know. Then, if you come to me having seriously considered all it will mean to be married, I will be happy to give my permission. I like Mike and I don't think you will come to any harm married to him, but please remember what happened with Ronald when he left here and found himself in a different environment." He scowled as he thought of how badly Ronald had let his daughter down. He most decidedly did not want the same thing to happen to his youngest daughter.

Ruby flung her arms round her father's neck and kissed him soundly on the cheek. "You are the best father in the entire world," she said happily as she sped out of the parlour with pictures of her wedding flowing through her head.

She and Mike had managed to make a date with the padre who served the airfield and they had sat in his office listening to him repeat all that Peter had said before. They exchanged a look of glee which Ruby quickly smothered in case the padre thought she wasn't taking him seriously. The date had been set and Ruby was glowing when they left the little chapel next to the NAAFI. Mike had to go back to work so Ruby took her enthusiasm into the NAAFI and spilled it over her sister without thinking how much her happiness was hurting Mame. Now here was Mame giving her blessing on what must be a painful occasion for her. Mame, as well as providing the 'something blue', was ready to keep Ruby right with the other old traditions also produced a silver sixpence to place in her shoe and made her promise to leave the house with her right foot in front, so that she started married life on the right footing.

When she entered the kitchen, Wull gave a wolf whistle, "You scrub up well. Who would think you were my baby sister who preferred to roll in the mud rather than play prettily with her doll?"

If Wull had been surprised, her father was speechless. He took in the glowing features of his daughter and thought she had never looked better than she did today. It seemed only yesterday he and Mabel had placed her in a cradle before the fire. Although Ruby favoured the Campbell side of the family, at this moment he believed he caught a glimpse of his wife in her features. Maybe it was the happiness that was radiating from her or it may have been the way she held her head but, whatever it was, Ruby looked a picture. He felt tears fill his throat as he looked at his girls standing together, all dressed up for the wedding. Only Helen was missing as Jen had been able to get leave, but since Helen's nursing corps was still in Egypt there had been no chance of her being allowed leave to come home. He wondered how long it would be before he saw her again. He sent a silent prayer to keep her from harm.

The car arrived to take him and Ruby to the airfield. Mike's commanding officer had arranged for petrol for this occasion, so they went in style. Alone in the back of the car Peter spoke of the years when she had been growing up. How proud her mother would have been today to see her get married. "I expect she is looking down on us shaking her head because my tie isn't straight or my hair not well enough cut for the occasion. We had a grand marriage, a partnership. I loved her as much on the day she died as I did the day I married her. We argued, of course we did, but we never went to bed on an argument. If there is one piece of advice I can offer you on married life it is that it's a compromise. There is always a middle way no matter how hard you to have to dig to find it." He turned the ring on his finger and held it up for Ruby to see. The ruby ring, the one they all laughed about being the 'Luck of the Campbells' was having an outing in the hope that the blessing it was deemed to carry would be sufficient to keep his family safe through this war.

When they arrived at the airfield they were waved through security and the car drew up at the pretty little chapel where a host of friends were waiting to greet the bride. Since it was wartime and rations were not enough to feed the number of guests they would have liked, many of Ruby's fellow munitions workers and a good number of Mike's colleagues, those who could be freed from their duties, had gathered outside the chapel. Of course there were the inevitable children who had a nose for a wedding. In wartime the youngsters made their pocket money by attending as many 'scrammels' as possible. It was traditional to have the wedding scramble at the bride's house but, since they lived in the middle of nowhere, Peter had held over the throwing of pennies and halfpennies until they were at the door of the church.

Gina came to the car as soon as it drew up and offered Ruby a lovely bouquet of greenery with a few flowers added. Ruby was very touched by this since there was very little space to grow flowers in wartime when every inch of fertile soil had been commandeered to grow food. "I've tucked a wee sprig of white heather into it for good luck. Not that you'll need it," she added quickly in case Ruby should get the wrong idea.

Smiling her thanks to her friend who was invited to the wedding, they having been chums all their lives, she exited the car, took her father's arm and made her way to the chapel where Mike stood nervously waiting at the altar with his best man. He turned as she entered the chapel and the look on his face as he caught his first glimpse of his wife to be in all her fine clothes made Peter happy, for the expression on his face indicated to him that his daughter had made a good choice. The service was short and before many minutes passed the beaming bride and groom were standing on the chapel steps being cheered by their friends.

The wedding reception was to be held in the NAAFI canteen. Mike's co-workers had decorated the room giving it a very festive look; some of the decorations were meant to be for Christmas but no one minded. They lent a feeling of frivolity to the event. On a table in the corner stood a three-tier wedding cake that quite took Ruby by surprise, for she knew that there had not been enough coupons to spare for a cake after they had scrimped and scraped to find enough to feed those they had invited to celebrate with them. Mame had been in charge of the food, saying there was no point in having a cook in the family if she wasn't to be allowed to showcase her skill. Ruby worried that Mame had skimped on the food in order to have the big cake but her worry was short lived as when, after greeting her guests as the new Mrs Gardiner she was led over to the table that held the cake, Mame whispered to her, "Just pretend to cut the cake. This is a cardboard one, just for the pictures. I have a loan of a camera from one of Mike's friend to take a few photographs so that you will have something to remember today by."

Ruby clutched at Mike's arm, indeed she had held tight to it ever since the padre had announced, "I now proclaim you husband and wife" and they had had their first kiss as a married couple. "I'll have this big lad here to remind me of today," she said happily thrusting the thought of Mike's coming posting out of her head. She would not think of that today. Today was for celebrations.

Mame had excelled herself. She had bartered some of her coupons, raided her father's henhouse for eggs, begged favours of neighbours and sweet-talked her boss until she had enough provisions to provide a two-course sit down meal. Everyone was astounded that she had done so much with so little. The chicken casserole was more vegetable than chicken but tasted delicious, as did the hearty soup she served before it. Instead of the pound of cooked ham she had been allowed for a wedding meal she had bargained with the butcher to provide her with his sugar ration and some dried fruit which she had used to make a small cake. When it was cut up and served no one would realise it was not the cake they believed they had witnessed the bride and groom cutting.

After the meal was cleared away the band Mike had hired tuned up and began to play dance music that got the feet tapping. "I hope we don't have a raid tonight," said one of the guests to another, "for this is the best day out I've had for many a day."

Ruby smiled as Mike led her onto the floor to dance the first dance with him. They waltzed twice round the floor then signalled that the others should join them. By this time most of the couples' friends had arrived for the dance and the dance floor was soon crowded. Congestion occurred as Ruby and Mike were constantly being stopped and congratulated by other dancers. After the first dance, the new couple parted and danced with as many of their guests as possible until Ruby finally threw herself down on a chair beside Peg.

"Oh my poor feet!" she complained. "They are almost worn through." She slipped off her shoes and rubbed her aching feet, stretching her toes out and sighing with relief. When she had dealt with her tender members she sat up to look around herself and found that Peg was in conversation with Jan. He and Adam had been given permission to be absent from the POW camp for the night and were to stay at the farmhouse after the wedding reception. She did not quite know what made her think this was strange for she had often seen Peg and Jan talking, but tonight for some reason there was something she just could not put her finger on. Without being aware of it her unconscious mind had taken in the glow that emanated from Peg and the animated way she addressed Jan.

Suddenly, the thought jumped into her mind: "Peg is sweet on Jan and what's more Jan is sweet on Peg."

She stared at the couple for a full minute while this idea penetrated her mind and came up with the conclusion she was in favour of a romance between her sister and the Ukrainian.

"The war gives us all strange bedfellows," she mused. "I would not have met Mike if it had not been for the war. Mame would have been happily married with her own little family, Helen would have been nursing in a hospital near home rather than in far off Egypt at risk of being bombed or shot by the enemy so who knows, maybe the war will bring Peg the happiness she deserves."

As she contemplated the war and its disruption of their lives she was interrupted by her husband. He wanted to take her away from the party in order that they could make the best of what time they had left before he was posted to risk his life flying bombers.

She allowed him to pull her up into an embrace and, with arms twined, they slipped away leaving their guests to entertain themselves.

The party continued with much dancing and changing of partners. It had been some time since Wull had seen his wife and, anxious for her well-being, he walked round the hall until he noticed her sitting alone at a table well back from the dance floor. He pushed through the dancers to stand at his wife's side with a crooked grin on his face, intending to take Nellie in his arms and dance her round the floor. As he came up beside her he immediately saw that something was amiss. Nellie was ghostly white and there was a worried expression on her face that seemed to have aged her. She tried to smile up at him but only managed a grimace. At once Wull was on his knees in front of her asking what was wrong and what he could do to fix it.

"I think the baby is not too happy that I have been dancing so I've decided to sit here for a while and rest. Don't worry. The baby is not due for two months yet. I've just got a stitch." She tried to make light of the situation by joking, "This must be the heir right enough for only a man could complain about nothing." She looked into Wull's eyes where her own worry was reflected and said, "Maybe we should go to the new baby hospital since we are so close. Do you think there is anyone here who could drive us there?"

"I'll find someone." Wull got to his feet and, ignoring his wife's plea not to cause a fuss, he hurried across the floor to find his father to whom he delegated the task of finding transport to take them to Cresswell Counties Maternity Hospital at the other end of the town. Peter went off to find one of the RAF officers who in turn ordered a staff car to be at their disposal to take them where they needed to go. Within a short time, Nellie was ensconced in the car and soon they were arriving at the maternity home where she was quickly reassured by a specialist doctor. Peter had no experience of childbirth in hospital as the women he knew had all handled their births at home. It was a new idea to bring women to hospital to give birth in stark and sterile conditions. There had been much opposition to the cost of building this single-purpose hospital, with people, many of them women, scoffing and assuring each other that women had dealt with their business privately and behind closed doors for centuries, so there was no need to interfere with nature's way. Peter had no strong feelings either way. "But at least we will know that Nellie is all right." He had planned to wait until she had been checked up by the doctor and then to ask the driver to take them home to allow Nellie to rest, since he knew she was not due to give birth for some weeks yet. However, when a shaken Wull returned to the waiting room, he was very worried.

"It seems that Nellie is in labour and it is too early. The doctor and the midwife have chased me off from under their feet so that they can deal with her. Oh Da, she is so terrified; I wanted to stay. I begged them to let me stay, just to keep her company but they shooed me out as if I was a recalcitrant child; that's what I feel like anyhow." Peter could see the frustration on Wull's face and rose to take his son in his arms.

"Now stop fretting. If Nellie had been at home the midwife would have got rid of you too when her time came. The women are all the same. They like to believe that we men have no part in the process. Did they tell you how long you would have to be waiting or did they not know?"

"I don't know what they said. I was too worried about Nellie; she looked awful, lying there almost as white as the pillowcase her head was leaning on."

"Let's go outside and get some air. It will do you good to get out of this depressing sterility," Peter suggested, but Wull could not be persuaded to leave the waiting room.

"What if she needs me and they come to find me and I'm not here? No, I'll stay here. You go back to the wedding though. I'll find my own way home. They are going to keep Nellie and the baby for a few days anyway."

Peter made no answer but Wull knew that his father had decided to remain with him until the birth was over. The minutes passed and turned into hours as Wull bit his fingers in his distress. At first Peter had tried to distract him by talking about the chores needing done on the farm, but Wull's brain could think of nothing but the distress he had witnessed on his wife's face. He jumped every time anyone walked past the waiting room, running out into the corridor at every click of a door, at the sound of feet echoing along the corridor in his direction, but it was never for him. The clock on the wall slowly moved as minute followed minute, then hour followed hour until in the early hours of the morning, when both men were exhausted and silent a midwife came to collect Wull to escort him through the corridors to a small room where his wife was lying, pale and sad. There were tear streaks down her cheeks and Wull hurried to her side to take her wracked body in his arms.

"That's enough, Mother. You will upset your husband if you carry on as if the world has ended," snapped Sister Hannah. Wull was surprised, but his interest was focused on his distraught wife.

"Thank God, thank God you are all right. You are all right, aren't you?" he leaned back so as to be take in her tear-stained features and repeated, "You are all right?"

"I'm all right. It's the baby," she whispered as Sister Hannah made her departure.

"What about the baby? Is it a girl or a boy?" he belatedly asked. He had been so concerned about Nellie's frail look that he had completely forgotten that there should be a baby in the bassinette beside her bed.

"The baby has been removed to the nursery. I'm so sorry Wull; she was too early and the doctors said she wasn't ready to be born. I'm sorry, Wull. I know how much you wanted an heir." Nellie once more burst into tears and nothing he could say could staunch their flow.

"Nellie, Nellie. I don't mind at all that she is a girl." He leaned forward and clumsily took her in his arms, frightened that he would hurt her by giving her a much-needed cuddle. "She will grow up to be just as beautiful as her mother and make all the boys hearts thumps just as you make mine." He drew away from her to look at her face. There were signs of her recent ordeal patent on her face and Wull could detect sorrow in her clouded eyes and downturned mouth. For the moment all he wanted was to cheer up his wife. He only gave a thought to his tiny daughter when the nurse reappeared to ask if he did not want to see the addition to his family.

Loath to leave Nellie, he kissed her quickly on the brow telling her he would be back soon. He followed the midwife, so different from those he knew in his locality. This woman, a girl really, was businesslike and supercilious making him feel he was lucky that she had condescended to take some time out of her busy day to deal with a father; after all they caused the problems her mothers faced. As they approached the nursery she spoke for the first time since leaving the ward.

"Stand at that window and I will show you baby Campbell."

She wasted no more words on Wull but entered the nursery with a brisk step. She lifted a bundle from a tiny bed and, pulling the blanket off her face, held his petite, doll-like daughter up for inspection. Wull felt such a rush of emotion he was hard put to blink back the tears. He wanted to hold the precious bundle, but already Sister Hannah had spirited her away from his gaze and had settled her back in her bed. She quickly left the nursery after a fleeting glance around the room to ensure there was nothing out of place.

"Doctor Driscoll will come and see you in the waiting room if you can make your way there."

"I must see Nellie again. I need to tell her how beautiful our daughter is. She is convinced she has failed me by having a girl."

Sister Hannah forgot her professional demeanour for a moment and Wull was able to detect a softening in her manner as she answered, "Only a few minutes then, but your wife is extremely tired and needs to rest."

"I promise not to upset her." He grinned for the first time since entering the hospital. There was no responsive smile on Sister Hannah's face, but Wull was too intent on relieving his wife's sorrow to notice.

He was back in the waiting room within minutes and with no delay told his father all that had taken place. Peter wiped a relieved tear from his eye as he stuck his hand out to shake that of his son. "Congratulations, a daughter. Only a real man gets daughters," he laughed. It was not many minutes until Sister Hannah returned to ask them to follow her as the doctor wanted a word with them. On squeezing into a stuffy little room that housed an inordinately large desk and chair Wull had a feeling he was in the schoolmaster's office to be punished for some misdemeanour. The serious-faced doctor shook hands and introduced himself to the two men before getting quickly to the point of the interview.

"I'm sorry to tell you that your daughter was born too early. Her lungs and heart are not strong and I believe nothing can be done for her. I am very sorry."

Wull looked at Peter in disbelief, then at the doctor where he sat behind his desk as if to keep himself apart from the news he had just conveyed. Dr Driscoll wondered if perhaps Wull had not understood what he said. Although he looked intelligent it was possible that he had misunderstood his meaning.

He was about to explain further when Wull asked, "How long? Have you told my wife?"

Dr Driscoll shrugged his shoulders. "I can't tell. Hours, maybe days. Certainly no more than a few days. We think it's best not to tell your wife until she is more recovered from the birth. It is best if she does not see the child," he finished, relieved to have the ordeal over.

"No," said Wull, just as his father was about to say the same word. "She must see our baby and be told how things stand."

The doctor once more shrugged his thin shoulders, "If that is what you wish we will see to it."

"No," said Wull once more. "I want to tell her and take her to see our baby."

"It is not wise. I have to tell you that it against hospital policy. We do know best, you know," he said condescendingly.

"Nevertheless, I will take full responsibility," said Wull quietly.

Wull escorted Nellie to the nursery where he used his personality to persuade the little nurse in charge to allow them to hold their tiny daughter. He could see that the girl was uneasy as she was afraid of being caught disobeying hospital rules, but her heart went out to the sad woman who was about to lose her baby. She allowed them both a cuddle and kiss with the infant before shoo-ing them out of the room, but she placed the cot bed right next to the window where they could look at her. Nellie leaned into Wull's shoulder as they watched the baby struggle to breathe. Wull found himself willing the child to take another breath, but their vigil was short-lived; after only seven hours of life, her breathing stopped. Nellie turned her face into Wull's chest and he could feel her silent tears soaking into his shirt. He swallowed hard to prevent his own tears as he slowly walked his sad little wife back to her bed.

"Come on now. That is quite enough. You are a young woman with many more years left to you to have more children; boys to grow up as useless as your husband," Sister Hannah commented snidely. "There is no use upsetting yourself about something you can do nothing about. It was God's will that your baby didn't survive. It is best to forget all about it and get on with your life. You should never have been allowed to see the baby. It does not do!" As she made these brisk statements she rushed around the bed tucking Nellie in so tight she felt she could not breathe, but Wull noticed she did not make eye contact with Nellie throughout this scolding. He wondered if perhaps Sister Hannah was not as hard as she made herself out to be.

The doctor had advised that they let the hospital take care of disposing of the tiny corpse and that they should go home and try again, but neither Nellie or Wull could leave their grief so soon. Nellie had cried herself to sleep and spent her waking hours thinking of the little inert body she had held to her breast, until Wull had gently removed it from her and handed it over to the nurse. It was ironic that she had been allowed to cuddle her dead baby, albeit against the doctor's advice, but while she was a living breathing infant this succour had been denied her. Nellie, usually the most amenable of people, ignored the midwife as she continued to cry for her baby, upsetting Sister Hannah who liked a regimented ward where everyone obeyed her orders.

"If you don't stop that snivelling right now I will send your husband home and get doctor to give you a sedative," she said briskly.

Wull didn't know what shocked him most. The harsh way the midwife spoke to his wife or the sudden birth and death of his babe. While he tried to make sense of the situation there was one thought clear in his mind. He had to get Nellie out of this hospital. It may have all the specialist equipment and well-trained nurses and doctors, but Nellie needed nurturing, not haranguing. He wanted desperately to have her home where he could comfort her. He was worried that to remove her from the hospital might harm her but, as he listened to Sister Hannah, he formulated a plan of escape.

"Thank God Nellie is all right. She must be all right. That harridan would not be scolding her like that if she was in danger."

Wull turned his considerable charm on the midwifery sister in an attempt to save Nellie from her bitter tongue.

"I must thank you, Sister Hannah, for caring so well for Nellie. We are a little upset by the happenings tonight. After Nellie has had a sleep she will be able to see things more clearly. The main thing is that she is well or will be after she has rested from her ordeal."

Nellie saw Wull wink at her as he praised the nurse and realised that she could, as always, leave everything to Wull. She settled herself back on her pillow and prepared to sleep.

Yes, she could always depend on Wull. He would not let her down.

Chapter Thirty-One

It was companionably quiet in the kitchen. Peter didn't often have time to think about his boisterous family and the danger the girls could be in; Helen, perhaps under enemy fire trying her best to patch up soldiers only to send them back to the front line; Jen, the frail child of his heart, in his opinion the one least able to care for herself, somewhere deep in the English countryside in some secret bunker unable to give him any comfort with her sparse letters. "It's all very well for the rest of them to tell me she will be all right but they know as much as I do about her whereabouts." He sighed. He was very much a family man and while he was proud of his family for the parts they had chosen to play in this dreadful war he was much of the opinion that women should be kept at home and cherished, not sent out into the war zones endangering their safety, to say nothing of his peace of mind. Although having been exempt from the forces in the last war, the war to end wars, as he had thought at the time, he had heard many of the tales brought back by the few men he knew who *had* come back. Many didn't survive the horrendous conditions in the trenches and those who did returned with something missing; some innate part of them, perhaps the part that made them human, having been dead and buried in the mud of France. Maybe the ones who died were the lucky ones, not having to live with the atrocities they had witnessed. "Please God my girls come back in one piece."

Having thought about his chicks who were well away from the nest he then turned his thoughts to the rest of his brood. Ruby: well she was settled with her Mike and likely to remain in the ordinance factory for the duration of the war. Dangerous? Yes, but it was necessary to make the ammunition the army needed so desperately. Just at the moment there was no need for Peter to worry about Ruby. Mame was another matter! Of course she had not been called up as she already worked on the airfield. Peter did not understand how she had gone from one day being a cook/maid in the airfield kitchens to be a flight lieutenant in the air force. Mame had tried to explain that it was just an exercise on paper: she continued to deal with the cooking and serving of the airmen just as before, but now she was being paid by the War Office instead of the airfield officials. Peter recalled how she had swung on the arm of his chair after displaying herself in her official uniform and, planting a kiss on his cheek, said playfully, "You'll all have to address me as Ma'am, now that I'm the ranking officer in this family." He smiled as he recalled how this statement had resulted in a barrage of insults being thrown back and forwards between the siblings; there was no animosity between them really and Mame took the ribbing just as she always had when her younger siblings had taunted her; she smiled that superior smile that she knew annoyed her family. "If only Mame could lose that sad look that has been in her eyes since that dammed no-user swanned off to pastures greener." His brows wrinkled as he once more wished he had Ronald within his reach. He'd teach him to play fast and loose with his daughter.

He leaned forward to encourage more heat from the fire with his handy poker but, when he had increased the blaze satisfactorily, he still kept his position allowing his thoughts free range as they passed through the years he had spent in this chair with the children squabbling at his feet and the doting face of his wife looking down on them all as she baked or cooked at the table. Her hands were rarely ever still; she had been a grand hand at the baking and even Mame, who had learnt the art from her mother, did not make such a delicious rabbit stew as his Mabel did. As he came out of this reverie he could almost see Mabel standing there now but as the mists of the past rolled away, he realised that it was Peg who was standing at the table shuffling through a huge mound of clothes. Surely this little family could not make so much washing?

"What are you up to, lass? What is making your pretty face frown?" he asked, now totally back in the kitchen and life in the moment.

"Not anything really. I have these uniforms for the Land Army, lots of them." She lifted a few garments to let him see what she had. "The powers that be seem to think all the girls in the Land Army are six foot two and fifteen stone, while in reality most of them are five foot two and seven stone. Nothing fits! Those poor girls! What with being despised by farmers' wives and the villagers I don't want them to go around like tramps, hitching up their breeches and tying their jackets with bits of binder twine."

Peter took in Peg's frustration, thinking for a moment before passing judgement on the piles of garments littered all over the kitchen. His eyes slid over Peg in her Land Army uniform of perfectly fitting shirt and jumper worn over knee breeches and long woollen socks, with her feet encased in tough brogues, and thought how much the war had brought her out of her shell. No need to worry about this daughter's war.

Grimacing at the pile of clothing gathered on the table, he, always willing to help any of his children out of a predicament and remembering how Peg had altered her uniform to fit, said thoughtfully, "What bits of the uniform can be used as they are? Maybe we could sort out what must be altered from what is usable, then we can think of a strategy for the rest." He picked up a heavy beige overcoat with a sheepskin lining, running his fingers over it. "This is good quality." His lopsided grin appeared on his face as he tried on the three quarter length jacket. "Good grief, Peg, I'm a mountain and it is big for me. Come on, I'll give you a hand to whale the uniforms."

The two worked side by side making piles of things like long woollen socks, hats, belts, shoes with wellies, oilskins and aprons among the items that could be worn without alteration. This made large piles on the kitchen floor but there was still a mound of cream shirts, green jumpers and sheepskin jackets on the table. They had only found four that could be worn by the girls Peg was in charge of. As Peg folded up her stock into hessian bags Peter made a move to put the kettle on the stove. His brow was puckered since he had the seed of an idea turning over in his head. He motioned Peg to sit in the chair opposite him while he put his idea to her.

"Do you have any funds you could use to have these items altered?"

"I have a bit of money to pay for petrol, but since I only use my wee van when I need to meet a train I have quite a lot of that spare. Why?"

"I wonder if the women of the rural or the guild would undertake to alter these garments for your girls? They would need to buy sewing things." He blushed, worried that he was showing his daughter how little he knew about dressmaking. "Years ago my aunt had a machine for sewing but I don't know if many women have them still or really how they would go about it but I think it's worth a try don't you?" he finished, taking in the beaming smile that bloomed on Peg's face.

She leaned forward, catching both sides of his face with her rough red hands and kissed his bald head before exclaiming, "You are a genius, Dad. That is just what the doctor ordered. I will wander down to the church hall next time there is a SWRI meeting. The same women are usually in both the rural and the church guild and I'm sure the girls will be delighted to meet other people in the villages." She frowned for a moment before continuing, "Most of the girls are really keen to learn the work, but since they come from towns they have little idea of what is expected of them and sometimes the farmers don't adjust to having a 'wee lassie' rather than the strong country lads they are used to. One man, I'm not telling you who, but you might hear about the flea I put in his ear at the market," she giggled up at her father allowing him to realise just what a pretty girl Peg was when she was animated. She choked on the recollection, "told me he would keep the 'lass' to warm his bed but he was 'putting in' for a couple of evacuated lads to do the farm work."

"Aye, it's hard for they wee lassies right enough, and I have a good idea who you are talking about, but they just need to be patient with them. Neither Adam or Jan had any experience of agriculture but look how they have taken to it since they have been here. That Jan, particularly, is as good as any dairyman I've known. Unlike the stories I've heard about your girls who think milk only comes in a bottle!"

Ignoring her father's jibe and in an effort to avoid letting him see her reaction to his praising Jan, she hurriedly collected the bags of clothes and made to the door intending to store the uniforms in her Land Army pickup. She was just catching the bags under her chin to leave her hands free to lift the sneck on the door when it burst open, pushing her back against the table forcing the breath out of her lungs. Peter had his back to the door having realised Peg wanted to keep her feelings about Jan to herself, but Peter wasn't blind and had noticed the growing relationship between his daughter and the prisoner of war. It was a pity there was a war on for that was one enemy he would gladly accept into his family.

He turned quickly but not in time to prevent the two tough men entering his kitchen, which they made appear cramped by their presence. The men were both over six foot tall with burly chests swamped in heavy overcoats and knee-high, much-scuffed leather boots. The coats looked like they had been being used as blankets since they were crushed and bespattered with leaves and twigs. Neither showed a pleasant expression on their unshaven faces and, with their greasy overlong hair, presented a frightening aspect to Peg and her father. Peter stepped forward but immediately the leader of the pair brandished a handgun in his direction.

"Stay! We will not kill you if you do as you are told!" he barked, swinging his weapon from Peter to Peg, "You," he pointed in Peg's direction. "How many of you are here?"

"Just us two," answered Peg serenely, for all the world as if armed gunmen entering the farm kitchen was an everyday event. "What is it you want that you have to ask for it at gunpoint?" she asked blandly with an inane smile dawning on her face, making Peter very proud of her as he realised she had rapidly taken in the threat and intended to play the bucolic idiot. "We have no money or valuables to steal." She bit on her lip to stop herself from antagonising the men with further words. The years of ignoring her siblings' taunts and torments were now standing her in good stead. While her face showed no expression her quick brain had worked out that these must be two of the spies whom Wull and his Home Guard had been unsuccessfully hunting all over the county for months now. She hoped that if she could get them to believe there was no one else expected at the farm, they might be taken off their guard believing all they had to deal with was an idiotic girl and an old man. She wondered if they had left one, or more, of their number outside on guard. After all, there had been three parachutes. If so, was he in hiding, ready to pounce on anyone who approached the farm house? It was just possible she could manipulate the men by offering food. Surely, if their appearance was anything to go by, they must be hungry and if a meal was served they would at the very least take some out to their compatriot.

She nonchalantly lifted the rest of the clothing off the table and suggested the gunman should put away his weapon while she found something for them to eat. Peter sat himself down on the chair giving the impression that he held no threat, but his brain was rapidly running through ploys to capture the men. If Peg could distract them with food, perhaps he could find a way to raise an alarm; get to the office and alert the police by phone, perhaps.

"How I wish I hadn't made Wull store Tommy's gun in the bothy," he thought, but there was no use in worrying about what couldn't be helped.

Peg, ignoring the threat of the gun, managed to make it appear that there was nothing she liked better than feeding strays who barged into the kitchen without an invitation, and set about laying a meal on the table. She carefully kept all expression from her face in the hope that the men facing her would not pay any particular attention to her but, like her father, the wheels were turning in her head. She tried to remember where the rest of her family were and when they would be home. She was unsure if the men from the POW camp were still outside. They normally went into Lockerbie with Wull but, since it had been unseasonably warm, he and Nellie had taken the opportunity to walk Ruby to the bus and spend some quality time with each other on the way back, for Nellie was still grieving for her lost baby and Wull took every chance he could to reassure her that its loss was no one's fault. No matter that the doctor advised they should go home and put their minds to trying for another Nellie was still distraught, depending heavily on Wull's willingness to talk about their dual loss. So Jan and Adam may still be around the farm buildings. They would not come to the kitchen but would wait in the bothy for Wull to return. "But what if they saw these men arrive and recognised them as fellow soldiers? Both Adam and Jan had been fighting for our enemy. No, they couldn't harm us. No. Not Jan?"

While these thoughts were whirling round her active brain she had laid the table with a loaf of fresh aromatic bread and a dish of butter. She turned to the stove to ladle some soup into two delft bowls and sneaked a look at her father, who gave her an infinitesimal nod without making any eye contact. They understood each other and would make an opportunity to outwit the men. They looked tired and hungry, so perhaps if they ate, and with the warmth of the kitchen, they might be lulled to sleep. Whatever the chance both Peg and Peter were prepared to try their luck.

With head down she placed the bowls on the table and indicated the men should draw up chairs and eat. She saw a look of consternation on their faces at being treated so well. This gave Peg an idea.

"Are you on the tramp?" she asked in as emotionless a voice as she could manage. "You're the first we've had this year. You haven't been here before else you wouldn't use a gun to get us to provide you with food. There is always a place at this table for a hungry Irishman looking for work." As she turned back to the stove to lift the teapot she slanted a look at the men who, after a quick glance at each other registering that Peg thought they were Irish migrants, they rapidly emptied the bowls in front of them. Peg had not put any knives on the table but the men did not seem to be worried as they pulled off chunks of the tasty bread, stuffing it into their mouth without bothering with butter. They then lifted the mugs of tea and sipped at the scalding liquid.

"I haven't put milk in it for I know you Irish don't like anything but whisky in your tea and we have none of that since the war started."

Peg wondered if she had gone too far but, whether the men understood her or not, they made no reply. Instead, they just leaned back on their chairs and savoured the tea as it settled into their full bellies.

Twice during the next hour either Peg or her father attempted to leave the kitchen. Neither tried to go out the back door because that meant passing close to the soldiers who, despite their weary look, showed no signs of sleeping; even though the gun now lay on the table beside the first man he was quick to grab it at the least movement of his hostages. It was a mystery to both of them what the men were waiting for, but it appeared they were expecting something to happen and Peter and Peg were to stay under their eye until that event took place.

Peg hummed as she washed up the dishes and chided her father for not eating his portion of the soup that she had handed him as he sat in his fireside chair. Anyone watching would have surmised she was a bit lacking in her top storey and she hoped the men were taken in by her act. She stretched up to place some clean crockery on a shelf by the fireside, took down a pile of towels and made for the door that led into the passage that connected the rest of the house to the kitchen. She had taken two steps along the passage when she was grabbed from behind by one of the men. Her nostrils were assailed by the sweaty rancid smell of him and she unwittingly wrinkled her nose. The man noticed her reaction and leered at her.

"You don't like the smell of Franz, eh?"

Thinking quickly Peg replied, "No, no, it's your coat. It smells musty and wet. Do you want to take it off and dry it at the fire?"

"I will take all my clothes off and Benj will too and you will too if you want the old man to live. We have an hour yet to wait and we shall spend it having some fun." His strong thin fingers painfully grasped her chin, turning her face towards him as he leaned in for a kiss.

Try as she might Peg could not hide her revulsion. The best she could manage was to pretend to be frightened of her father. "Faither wouldn't like me to be kissing a man. He will take his belt to me." She managed a tremulous voice to support her words, but they backfired on her.

The man called Benj called from the kitchen in German that Peg did not understand. "Wir können den alten Mann schießen."

The sound of his voice sent a cold shiver down her spine even without the reaction of her captor, who shrugged and looked her in the eye. "Benj will shoot your father, then you need not worry about him." He laughed to see the fear in her eyes.

"No, don't hurt my father. I will do as you ask."

Hoping her father would get the chance to escape to bring help she reconciled herself to the forthcoming ordeal. The men smirked and joked together in their own tongue. "Sie macht einen gutes Bett-Begleiter. Ja?"

"Vor dem Vater."

"In der Küche mit dem Feuer auf den Rücken, Himmel."

They became excited with their idea of having their way with her in the kitchen in front of her father. The tone of their voices brought a reaction from Peter who sprang out of his seat, lunging towards Peg, but Benj was quick to restrain him, pushing him roughly onto his chair. He leered at Peter, then laughed in delight as his companion hustled Peg back into the kitchen.

****

Nellie and Wull sauntered down the lane towards the farm. Wull was reluctant to return Nellie to the farmhouse for this afternoon, she had appeared to find some pleasure in their being alone together by the river; the place where they had dreamed their dreams of the forthcoming dynasty that they were in the process of founding. Today they had sat and talked about their frail little daughter, cried for her passing, but most pleasing of all for Wull was his belief that at long last he had persuaded his wife that she had not been at fault. He knew Nellie spent many wakeful nights flaying herself with 'what ifs'. Should she not have gone to the wedding? Should she have rested more? But today Wull was confident that Nellie had turned the corner and, with his love and care, she would recover from this heartbreaking loss. He tried hard to be a support to Nellie for he knew how much he was hurting over the baby's death; how much more pain was Nellie feeling, having carried the baby for so many months? He slanted a glance at her face and for the first time since the baby's loss, Nellie appeared to be at peace with herself. Wull took a deep breath and hoped this short time together away from the everyday chores would prove to have righted their universe. He knew what they really needed was time alone together, however, neither of them could ignore their commitments, both to the farm and the war effort, making these few stolen minutes precious. No sooner had he congratulated himself on his wife's imminent recovery than another cloud rose on his horizon. Adam was flying towards him on Peg's bike, shirt tail flying out behind him as he strove to get the best speed from the ramshackle boneshaker. His face was beetroot red from his exertions and it was obvious to Wull that there was some emergency in the offing.

"Woah there, Adam. What's ado? Could you not wait for me to take you back to the camp?" he laughed a bit warily, but whatever was the matter he did not want to upset Nellie.

Adam jumped off the bike and dropped it on the grass verge without paying any attention to it while he caught his breath to explain his actions to Wull.

"Niemieccy szpiedzy są gospodarstwa więzień w gospodarstwie," panted Adam, quite breathless from his exertions.

"Speak English, man. I don't understand." Nellie glanced up at her husband's sharp tone. This conveyed to her how anxious he had been made by the distress of the young Pole.

"The German spies!" he puffed out. "At the farmhouse." He held up two fingers to indicate how many. "They wait. No know what for. Jan, he watches. I go for soldiers. Yes?"

Wull ran the words through his brain relegating each new idea to the trash as he figured how best to deal with the situation. It did not take long for him to formulate a plan. Even in this dire situation his first thought was to protect his wife.

"You go to Tommy's cottage. You will be safe there even if he doesn't recognise you today for his gun is in the bothy at home. Stay till one of us comes for you and keep the door locked."

As Nellie ran back the way she had come, Wull turned to watch her progress towards the shepherd's cottage where he could see Tommy sitting in the doorway puffing away at his pipe. No one had disturbed him today.

"Adam, I think I should go for the Home Guard and the police because they will act quickly if I go. There will be all sorts of questioning and such if you turn up at the police station by yourself. You run over to Rammerscales and get them to phone the commandant at the airfield. They will believe you because they know how much we trust you and Jan. See if you can find a few men to come back and keep watch for others arriving. We know there were three parachutes." He stuck out his hand to give Adam's a quick shake saying, "Good man," before throwing his leg over the bicycle and pedalling off in the direction of the police station. In the event when he arrived at the police station everything was in a furore with constables from the police house next door getting dressed as they listened to the orders from their sergeant.

"Wull! Glad you got here!" shouted Captain Jessop. "That POW of yours is a smart lad. He did what you told him but also got them to phone through here so we are all on the alert. Won't be long before the rest of the lads are here and we can be off." Just at that moment they heard the squeal of worn tyres as a truck drew up outside the police station. Those who had arrived were soon clambering into the back of the lorry. There was an assortment of police, most dressed in uniform, a goodly number of the Home Guard in all types of apparel, having run out without waiting to don uniform. The squad were armed with everything from a rounders bat to a WWI bayonet hastily grabbed off the wall by a Great War veteran. Wull was a bit taken aback at the attitude of the men. They appeared to Wull as if they were off on a jaunt to the nearby beach for a picnic rather than on a life or death mission. The mood was cheery with the young men, boys mostly, discussing what they would do to 'Fritz' when they caught 'the blighter'. Wull recognised this as the type of dialogue the boys could see at the pictures where the storylines were mostly directed at keeping up the morale, but no matter if his squad were mimicking the propaganda from the big screen Wull became irritated by their gung-ho attitude. This was his family that were in danger!

He pursed his lips to prevent him retaliating and was staring over the edge of the truck, watching the fields pass by, when he felt a hand descend to his shoulder and grasp it firmly.

"Don't worry, young Campell. They are only letting off steam. If truth be known, they are terrified and this lot is just bravado to stop them shitting their breeches. It's all very well to talk of being a daredevil when there is no call for you to be one, but each of these brave lads have turned out to do their duty and they will do it too. Don't think badly of them. Look at them; what are they really but schoolboys? But I'm proud of every man jack of them who threw down what they were doing to answer the call."

Wull looked around the grinning boys realising that his superior officer was right. At first glance the lads looked to be enjoying a spree but, on closer inspection, he could see the strained expressions beneath the boasting and understood why Captain Jessop was so proud of them. His thoughts were interrupted by the sudden braking of the truck; it was a simple method of transport with no unnecessary items such as a roof or seats, so as it came to an abrupt standstill the men were thrown into an undignified pile behind the driver's cabin. Those who had not been lucky enough to have a grip of the sides were all but decanted onto the rough track in front of the truck, being saved from this by the smart thinking of their comrades who grabbed any body part they could to anchor their pals. Much hilarity was found in this situation until the troops were silenced as two very formidable women, dressed smartly in Home Guard uniforms, approached and saluted Captain Jessop, who quickly stood to attention while trying to fix his disordered uniform.

"Captain Jessop, Ma'am," he introduced himself. He knew of the lady officers but as yet had not come across them in the line of business despite having been privy to many conversations at HQ where the topic had been 'those darned women' playing at soldiers. However, the top brass had been forced to accept them into their number as they were both wife and daughter respectively of a colonel and a brigadier so it was with considerable trepidation they had been allocated their own branches of the Home Guard. Contrary to everyone's expectations Lady Jane Johnstone and Margaret Buchanan each headed up a squad of volunteers who jumped at their every command and with no prompting, happily accepted their fair management, indeed they were among the best platoons in Dumfriesshire.

Lady Jane, who had known the Campbells all her life, hurried round the jeep to commiserate with Wull about the situation explaining that Adam had been so worried about the farmer and his daughter that he had alerted everyone he could think of who might be able to help. She had brought six men from the Lochmaben branch; all she could raise at such short notice, but others may well arrive as news spread and Margaret's Castlemilk crew had arrived to swell the ranks.

"We'll soon have your Dad and Peg out of there, don't fret. They are both smart enough not to antagonise a desperate alien. You had best go tend to your wife."

"Thanks, Lady Jane, but if it's all the same to you I'd rather help with capturing the spies. I know the ways into the house and I promise to follow orders. I just couldn't bear not to take part since this is our land. I know every hiding place, every tree on the farm." He looked pleadingly at the diminutive women who had gained so much respect from her troop of men made up, for the most part, of farm workers.

"Well, so long as you follow orders and don't go off bald headed with ideas of your own." She squinted up into his face to detect his reaction to this diktat. Satisfied with what she saw she again joined her opposite numbers to hash out a plan. They speculated on what the two men were waiting for. Was it simply for night time to cover their exodus? Were they awaiting further members of their band? How many were expected to arrive?

They speedily concocted a plan to lay low until they had sussed out why the men had burst into the house instead of quietly going on their way; after all, if it were to be the men who had hidden their parachutes in the woods here so many months ago there had been three of them, so it was likely the farmhouse was their designated meeting place. The plan was rapidly put into action. The truck was hidden behind the derelict cottage and the men hastily took up position among the trees and the crops blowing gently in the breeze. All was surreally silent, even the birds seemed to have been cowed by the hiding men who lay on their bellies with the late afternoon sun beating down on their backs making them uncomfortably hot. Wull, with his knowledge of the farm, had been taken into conference with the officers; he had been given charge of a few men in order to lead them to surround the house, but no sooner were they in position than Nellie could be seen flying across the field with her hair streaming behind her as she ran towards the group commanding the sortie.

"Oh, thank goodness you are here!" she panted. "Adam and Tommy are trying to hold an intruder. I think he was making for the farmhouse with Adam trailing him; as he passed the cottage Adam waved Tommy to join him and they are both lying on top of him at this minute. Come quickly before he has the chance to raise the alarm." She pulled Captain Jessop's sleeve in her haste to make him follow her. He was taken aback at this assault on his person, for he was used to being treated with awe, but Margaret Buchanan took charge just as if the platoon were her servants and in no time six of the biggest boys were following her as she strode mannishly over the cornfield towards the shepherd's hut. She had chosen her men well; young they might be, but they had righteousness on their side and with the glee that can only be experienced by boys about to get into a tussle and freed from any fear of repercussions they were ready for the fight. As they approached the cottage garden they came upon the struggling pair. Grins split the men's faces; even their commander gave a wry grin at the spectacle before her. Adam had the large man spread-eagled face down on the vegetable plot while Tommy stood guard with a fierce-looking grape in his hand sporadically poking Adam's prisoner every time he managed to free one of his limbs. He was a fine specimen of a man; it was obvious wherever the men had been hiding for the months since they landed they had not been starved of food. Adam by himself was no match for the muscle power of the taller man, so he was glad to see help bounding towards him. His attention diverted for a moment his prisoner sensed his opportunity and, with a heave, managed to divest himself of Adam's weight, quickly jumping up to make his escape, running to the garden gate with Tommy chasing him with his fork. He turned to confront the old man, estimating one punch would free him from the nuisance of the painful jabs but, as he raised his fist to deliver the blow, he was surprised to feel himself falling under the weight of six fervent youths. Margaret Buchanan turned her back on the melee while she checked that Tommy and Adam, the heroes of the hour, were for the most part uninjured. She quietly removed the hey grape from Tommy's grasp and, with some force, stuck it into what an hour ago had been Tommy's vegetable garden but now showed evidence of the recent struggle. "These cabbages and leeks won't survive," she said sadly, but Tommy surprised her by his rejoinder.

"I'd give a great deal more than a few veggies to have had the chance to stick that Gerry with my grape," he enthused, red in the face from the unexpected exertion but with cheeks glowing and eyes shining as he remembered his part in the foray. He turned round breathless and laughing to Adam, sticking out his hand to shake that of the younger man, just rising from the ground where he had lain for a moment getting his breath back. Taking Tommy's hand, he pulled himself upright, eying the old man suspiciously, but Tommy had no axe to grind with Adam. Yes, he was a POW, but he had tried his best to save the family Tommy cared for, so in his book that negated his enemy status.

Margaret thought her lads had been allowed free rein for long enough so she left the two men grinning at each other as they recalled their part in the incident and rapped out orders to her boys to tie up their prisoner and march him back to the lorry. She followed behind, pleased with how the arrest had gone. "No doubt those lads will have enjoyed the exercise," she thought to herself as she watched them bouncing over the now downtrodden crop.

"Hey!" shouted Adam at her retreating back as he raced towards her. "He dropped his bag!" He gestured with the shabby rucksack. "Maybe you will find what he was doing in there."

He swiped a hand over his brow, flicking his ruffled hair out of his eyes and continued, stopping frequently to find the right English word to express his emotions. "I went to war because I had no option; just like the men here, I was called up to do my patriotic duty but I am not a partisan of war. Your prisoner despised me and spat at me for being a traitor, but these people have treated me well so I could not stand by and watch them be injured." He shrugged. "He was doing his duty too, as we are bound to. He is a brave man."

"I understand what you say," Margaret answered brusquely, touched that a prisoner being held in pretty cramped and unsanitary conditions should fight to save his captors rather than aid his comrade.

Adam accepted her handshake before remarking, "I had better get back to my chores." He turned abruptly and marched back to where Tommy was trying to salvage his plants.

Jan had sat as quiet as a mouse in the bothy, straining his ears to hear what was happening in the kitchen. He could hear the murmur of Peg's voice and the occasional rumble of Peter's, but the two interlopers said very little. He was frustrated for he had no idea if the men who had invaded the kitchen were robbers or if they were some of his own army. There had been much talk a while ago about Germans having landed near here. "But that was months ago. Surely they will be long gone by now?"

He was in a dilemma. He had been a part of the forces of the Third Reich and as such bound to aid any of that army in any way he could, but these people on this farm were his friends. He hoped, one day, when this dreadful war was over, that they would become family, but he must not think of that while he had nothing to offer, not even a roof for his own head. However, if only Peg would see him as a man she could spend her life with, he would not ask for anything else.

These thoughts cascaded through his mind as he listened to the hum of voices until he heard a harsh voice laughing cruelly. This voice was raised to a level that he could decipher the words and his blood ran cold. It was not the recognition that the men were German that caused this reaction, but that the man was planning to shoot Peter. Unfortunately, the voice became quieter, as if it had moved out of the kitchen, so he was unable to hear the following conversation. That did not matter, however, for he had heard enough to realise that Peter was in danger and that he must do his best to help his kind benefactor. His mind raced as he thought of and discarded several ideas before his eyes lighted on the shotgun, half hidden in the cupboard whose door was ajar. Cautiously he removed the weapon; realising there was no cartridges in the barrels he rummaged in the cupboard as quietly as he could. He did not know how well the sound of his movements might be heard on the other side of the wall but, no matter where he looked, there was no ammunition to be found.

While he was still scanning the room to see if he had perhaps missed a hiding place, he once more was brought to a standstill as he heard the words that took all sense from him. As he propelled himself out of the bothy, diving for the kitchen door, he cared not a jot that there was no ammunition in the rifle. Indeed, it was debateable if he even remembered he was still holding the useless firearm. The only thought in his head was to get to his love before anything happened to her. He catapulted himself through the door, momentarily stunning all the occupants of the room, which gave a slight advantage. Quickly realising that the stunned soldiers were unaware that the gun was not loaded he brandished it in front of them and, speaking in German, barked an order at the astonished men.

Benj was first to come out of his brown study and smiled at Jan. "Nun traf meinen Freund. Gekommen Sie sind, um uns zu helfen?"

Jan stood for a moment with his eyes fixed on Benj before slanting a glance at Franz. When this war had started he had been on the same side as these men facing him. He should side with them but the leering expression on Franz's face made any patriotic move his conscience might have demanded of him immaterial. His loyalty, and his heart, were Peg's.

"Nein." He raised the rifle to his shoulder and, hoping his fear was not visible, he pointed the gun at Benj, who was nearest to Peg. "Laß sie zu mir kommen."

Benj laughed. Looking at Peg, he sneered at her. "He is a traitor to the Fürher. How would you like to see him die before we deal with you?"

"She comes to me NOW or you die." Jan pointed the rifle at Franz, who had recovered enough to raise his Mauser pistol in his direction, but Jan ignored the threat, indicating to Peg that she should move carefully round the table. As she started to move, Franz took aim and, just as he had pressed the trigger and Peg was sure Jan was going to be killed, she screamed, "No!" The kitchen was filled with noise as the gun exploded and Jan felt himself being knocked back against the open doorpost.

"Run, Peg!" he shouted and she flew out the door, straight into the arms of her brother who was heading the posse surging towards the farmhouse. In no time at all the men were restrained by the Home Guard and being marched off to meet up with their erstwhile companion.

Peg rushed to crouch beside Jan as he bled onto the stone floor where there was a pool of blood rapidly forming. "Oh no, Jan, my darling Jan. Don't die. Don't die," she pleaded as she forced a towel against his bleeding face while she cradled his head in her lap. He had shut his eyes since he could not see, as much from shock as because the blood dripping into them, but, at hearing her voice, he opened them, staring up into her concerned face and hurried to reassure her.

"It is only a scratch. Your father kicked his gun arm just at the right moment. The bullet only grazed me but I'm afraid your father overbalanced and knocked his head on the edge of the fireplace. I am good. Tend to the brave man who saved my life."

As Peg attempted to go to her father's aid she saw that Wull was gently clasping her father's wrist. He had a frown on his face for a few seconds but, as he found the pulse beating beneath his fingers, he turned and smiled at his little sister. "I think he has given himself a bad bang but his heart is beating strongly. Can you take over here while I find someone to go for the doctor?"

Peg, reassured that since wiping the blood from Jan's forehead that he was only suffering from a skin wound that was already beginning to clot, transferred herself to care for her unconscious father. Like her brother, she felt for his pulse and was reassured that it was slow and steady, she then pinched his earlobe in an attempt to rouse him. Although he did not open his eyes it was obvious to Peg that he was reacting to her stimulus since he groaned and moved at her touch. She noted that he was a bit pale but there was some colour in his cheeks, so that she was not surprised when within minutes of these ministrations he had come back to them. She breathed a sigh of relief.

"Lie still just for a bit. You have knocked your head and Wull has gone for the doctor, but I'm pretty sure you will live to tell the tale of your heroism," she babbled in her delight that he was not seriously hurt. "You saved Jan's life," she explained, holding him down as he attempted to rise from the uncomfortable position he was in.

"Don't fuss, Peg. I'm grand. I'm glad Jan isn't hurt too badly, but if my aim had been truer he wouldn't have been hurt at all. It's Jan we have to thank for saving US. Oi, Wull!" he cried as his son once more entered the kitchen, "give me a hand up and tell this daft sister of yours I'm fine." Wull duly helped his father into the chair, satisfied that he would do no harm by allowing him to move to his seat.

He grinned at his father and his sister, then deliberately walked across the kitchen to slap Jan on the shoulder and declare, "Well, how's that for romance? I could have wished you had chosen a less dramatic way to announce your desire to join the family, but I for one have no objection." He nodded in Peg's direction before continuing, "You'll have to have her now that she has declared her feelings for you, the brazen hussy."

The four occupants of the kitchen laughed, allowing any embarrassment Peg or Jan had felt at showing their true feelings in the heat of the moment to be glossed over. Leaving Peg to deal with the invalids and the forthcoming visit from the doctor, Wull ran out to bring his wife up to speed with events and ask her to take her time going back to the house.

"I have to go back with the lads to have a debrief and find out what is to be done with our prisoners." He frowned. "They can't be held in the POW camp here since

Jan and Adam instigated their capture but…" He grinned. "We can leave the lady officers to work out a plan. They haven't done too badly today. For women, that is."

"Wull Campbell, you are a chauvinistic pig!" declared his wife aiming a blow at her husband's broad chest before she realised he was only teasing her.

He continued, "Aye, women have played the biggest part in this war and, if they are all like my darling wife," he caught her in a bear hug, "the war will soon be over."

Chapter Thirty-Two

Helen gave a last look round her ward making sure that everything was neat and tidy with all her patients settled and as comfortable as she could make them in this hot, clammy, humid hellhole. Helen had been getting repeated whiffs of her own sweat almost since she had started her shift but there was no help for it. The ablutions available in the nurses' quarters left much to be desired and even if she managed to get a shower before coming on duty, it was only a matter of minutes before the summer temperatures had her body's cooling mechanism sent into overdrive. As she dreamed of sliding into a hot foaming bath where she could soak for hours she began to count her blessings. This had become her way to combat the horrendous conditions in which her patients arrived at her makeshift ward.

"At least things are better than they were now that the soldiers are issued with Sulfa powder." She cast her mind back to the days before this innovation when her patients had arrived with stinking, festering wounds that caused the men excruciating pain and fever almost robbing them of their wits. These had been trying times but with the wounds being sprinkled with the antibacterial powder by any ambulance driver, or indeed any comrade, they arrived in much better condition than previously. Helen was very proud of her countryman, Alexander Fleming who had discovered the 'magic drug' penicillin that was responsible for so many of these poor men's lives. Her searching gaze found nothing out of place so she hurried off towards her barracks, clutching the long awaited letters from home.

"Oh, how I long for a sight of the family," she sighed. Despite having been away from home long before the war; she had thought Glasgow a long way from home in those days; there had always been the assurance that she could visit whenever she wanted. She loved her job, was dedicated to her career and could think of nothing better than to watch her well-honed skills have the desired effect on her patients.

"But we patch them up, sort them out, then sent then back out to face the enemy tanks. If only this dreadful war would end!"

Cherishing the thought of her letters she was determined to make the best of them, so after taking off her uniform, managing a quick wash and making herself a drink, she sauntered out to a rare shaded area under the few sparse bushes and prepared herself for an orgy of news.

Firstly, she relaxed her tired shoulders and neck, pulling open the collar of her thin blouse and wafting it to catch any air that was circulating, then she took out each envelope, trying to decide which was from whom and in what order they had been written. Letters were like gold to the girls and were shared communally, as any news from home helped the, often homesick, girls to imagine they were not so far away from their homeland.

Selecting the fat, official-looking brown envelope, she saw that it had come from the QA training hospital in Surrey. Helen had never visited the hospital having already qualified as a Registered General Nurse before the war. There was a lot of joking and rivalry among her colleagues, who were mostly English and called State Registered Nurses, about who had the better training but it was all light-hearted, with all in the contingent supporting one another. By now they were experienced in all manner of nursing procedures that they invented as the occasion warranted. No hospital training could have prepared them for the horrors they faced daily. The letter had taken several months to arrive but, when she opened it, she discovered it was many communications, one inside the other. "This is like Christmas!" She laughed in joy as she poured the letters into her lap, neatly documenting them into date order. The first she picked up told her that the nursing corps had been assigned military ranks and that enclosed she would find her captain's epaulettes which were to be worn at all times when in uniform. There was a long list of protocols, who she should salute, who she should command, and no fraternising with soldiers below her rank, to name but a few. Helen scanned these quickly, paying little attention, feeling pretty confident in her belief that none of her colleagues would take this seriously. She wondered if the other girls had received this communication as well. It would be an excellent excuse for a party if they ever had time or clothes to party. She choked on a laugh as she recalled the many attempts her group had made to make clothes other than their uniform. "No, no party in the foreseeable future."

Having extracted as much enjoyment out of this letter as possible she selected the next one. After slitting it open she became quite ashen as she read the contents.

By the King's Order the name of Senior Sister Helen Campbell,
Queen Alexandra's Imperial Military Nursing Service,
was published in the London Gazette on 19 July, 1944,
as mentioned in a Despatch for distinguished service.
I am charged to record His Majesty's high appreciation.
Secretary of State for War

Helen's shaking hands flew to her mouth as she gasped for air. "How the hell did that come about?" she swore out loud. She turned the letter over and over feeling sure this was a joke. She looked around her half expecting to see some of her friends having played a prank on her. She looked once more at the name on the citation and felt her eyes fill with tears. "How proud Dad would be of me. He had not tried to stop me following my heart and joining up; here was his reward." After several minutes had passed she unfolded the second piece of paper that had been contained in the envelope. This described the reason for the citation. Several months previously she had been delegated to the front line emergency theatre where she and her surgeon had been caught under fire while performing a life-saving operation on a young man, with another writhing in agony as he waited his turn. Chris, the doctor, had wanted to send her to safety but she had thrown him a tin hat, placing a second on her head at a jaunty angle and joked with him. "Come on, Doc Chris, if the poor old Tommies have to put up with being bombed, the least we can do is defy the buggers to sort them out." With no more words spoken between them, and by using tent poles for drip stands, Helen acted as junior doctor, scrub nurse and porter so that they could finish both operations and make sure the patients were as comfortable as possible until the raid was over. Then they were on their way to a safer environment, before falling into each other's arms and exclaiming how terrified they had been every time the tent was shaken by the crump of an exploding bomb, followed by the strafing of gunfire. Both of them had survived as had their patients; neither of them thought of themselves as having been particularly brave since in order to stop themselves shaking they had raided the officer's mess for a bottle of 'medicinal' brandy, which left them waking next morning snuggled together with the empty bottle between them and a hangover that would have disgraced many a hoary old salt.

Helen sat in a rare period of peace and quiet letting the images of her war glide over her consciousness until she remembered that she had only opened one of her letters. There were a few official letters in her package, directing her to remember etiquette, to wear her uniform proudly and other such minutiae that the pen-pushers in England spent their days imagining.

"I'm sure they think we are off on holiday. Do they really think we have time to 'consort with lower ranks?" She threw these communications aside in order to tackle her letters from home.

The next she opened was from Mame and fairly long with much news of the family. Helen half closed her eyes and was instantly back in the room they had shared as children listening to Mame breathlessly 'dish the dirt'. It told her that Mame had also been given an air force rank and how 'her' pilots laughed at having to salute the dinner lady. She was pleased to see that this letter had no mention of Ronald but included many funny anecdotes about her dancing with the American fliers.

"Nothing serious, Helen; they are good fun and are only here a short time while they are instructed how to fly our bombers but good fun never the less. I've done more dancing since they arrived because the local boys who would usually decorate the wall have been prodded into asking you up because if they don't 'the bloody Yanks will'. So you can imagine I am well entertained as is our little sister Ruby, sad though

she is not to have had more than one quick leave with Mike since they married. He is still flying bombers over Germany which causes Ruby to worry a lot. The big news is that Dad and Peg are heroes. Yes! I can see your look of disbelief. They were involved in capturing three German spies who were caught with the locations of all our munitions factories and airfields ready to be transported back to Germany. I was on duty when the plane sent to pick them up entered out airspace and was shot down by our gallant fliers.

"I haven't told you the best part yet though. Peg is in love. She really is and you'll never guess who with. Well you won't so I'll tell you. It's Jan. One of the POWs that Dad took on. He has to stay in the camp but he has already decided he wants to stay here when the war is over and marry Peg. What do you think of that? Seriously, you would not recognise Peg these days since she became 'high up' in the Land Army. Every one sits up and listens when she speaks. Imagine shy Peg?

"Dad misses you all but he and Nellie are the powers to be obeyed about the house forming an alliance to make us all do as we are told, so Nellie has taken over my 'big sister' role and we all love her dearly.

"I think that is all our news so I will sign off reminding you that we are all praying you come home safely.

Much Love from your big sister Mame. Xx"

Helen sat smiling down on this letter as she tried to imagine Mame, with her straight-laced and serious outlook on life, dancing and sharing jokes with the fliers where she worked. "Well, good for her," she finally decided. "At least someone is getting some good from this terrible war. She moved her position to crane her neck towards her dormitory window as she heard the tuneless singing of the nurses' anthem, sung when they needed to cheer themselves up.

"There's a home for tired nurses,
above the bright blue sky,
where Matrons never grumble
and Colonels never pry.
And all the little sorrows
are drowned in cups of tea,
and all the bloody bedpans...
rest eternally!"

This indicated to Helen that her peaceful time was almost at an end but since she surmised that at least some of her fellow nurses would have received letters in the bumper crop that had just arrived from their World travels she still had a few minutes left. She had two letters remaining. It was difficult to decide which to open first but she plumped for what she thought must be Nellie's, which she slit open eagerly pulling out the thin sheets of paper. The writing was very cramped indicting that Nellie had much to say and very little space to say it in. This made the letter difficult to read until her eyes became accustomed to following the line of writing from left to right. Unfortunately, the first two pages of the letter reiterated the news she had read in Mame's before it went on about more local news. She laughed as Nellie described her father's plan to 'smarten up the Land Girls'. It appeared he had taken Peg's charges under his wing becoming their advocate and knight errant, taking on farmers who did not treat the girls as if they were his daughters.

"It started when some of the rural women sniffed at being asked to help alter the uniforms sent to Peg. When he heard how they belittled the girls who were only trying to do their bit for the war effort, despite their ignorance of country ways, he got on his high horse; you know how he does. He invited the rural women to use his kitchen as a workroom and Lady Jane to chair the initial meeting. Boy does he know how to manipulate women! Wull says it comes from years living in a house of women and jokes Dad has handed down his knowledge to him. You know how Wull just needs to look soppy and smile at us to get his own way. Anyway, now when any of them have a problem, or are just homesick, they turn up to visit with Dad and he sorts them out. Wull says he treats them just as he did you all when you were younger. There is much laughter in our kitchen despite the war.

"Life goes on much as usual here with Jan and Adam joining Peg's Land Girls to form a 'Mill Party' as they traipse from farm to farm with the old threshing mill. Since I am in a delicate condition again; yes. I'm expecting again; I am only allowed to make the pieces and keep house so although I am secretly happy not to be out in the fields, I feel I am the only one not doing my bit. Wull and Dad treat me like precious china. Oh, I do love these Campbell men!

"We are all very proud of your being mentioned in dispatches. You have become a heroine to the little girls who were in your Sunday school class, so expect a HUGE party when you come home."

Having tried to write as much as possible Nellie had left no space to even sign this record of daily life on the farm, but Helen was grateful to her for this blast of normality when everything around her was so far from normal.

The last envelope felt thin, almost as if the writer had forgotten to enclose the letter but as she opened it, out fluttered two sheets of wafer-thin paper blotted and almost illegible. "Must be from Jen," she smiled as she screwed up her eyes in order to decipher the words. Jen had used both sides of the paper and the ink had bled from one side to the other. "So like my little sister," she thought while realising that Jen would have little news of the family or even much about her wartime job since she was in the WAAF and unable to divulge 'sensitive information' in case the mail was intercepted by the enemy. Helen managed to make out that Jen was well and enjoying her work, no mention of the type of work or where it was at. If Helen didn't know her sister had enlisted in the WAAF the letter could be read that Jen was a lady of leisure, spending time being taken out by decadent young men who had avoided the draft. The only indication that Jen was attached to an aerodrome was that she sometimes mentioned American men as contributing to her entertainment. Helen expected Jen would have loved writing this letter, leaving much to Helen's imagination, for the sisters, although close in age, had been very different in personality as children; Helen being quite serious and responsible while Jen was the risk taker that Helen often had to save from the consequences of her actions. Helen recognised the tongue-in-cheek references about her social life as Jen's need to make her sister concerned for her.

"And it works every time. The sly minx. My head will spin with all the things that could happen to Jen when I'm not there to hold her back." However just as she began to worry about her devil-may-care sister she read the post script below Jen's scrawled signature.

"PS. Have been spending much time with a handsome young man who is caring for me like a brother. *His name is Mike Gardiner. He keeps his eye on me."*

Helen let out a deep sigh of relief as this seemingly throwaway remark told her, not only that Jen wouldn't get into too much trouble, but almost exactly where she was since Ruby had known where Mike was posted before Helen had embarked at Greenock with her fellow band of QAs being posted overseas. "I'll smack that besom's face when I see her," thought Helen, while all the time acknowledging that she was only glad Jen was safe.

Her last thought as she watched the chattering nurses running across the garden towards her was, "How I wish this dreadful war was over!"

As the girls came within earshot she heard their words:

"Victory in Europe!"

Chapter Thirty-Three

It would have been possible to cut the atmosphere of anticipation in the audience with a knife so intent were they on Lord John's story, which was nearing its end. For the last few hours, since this rendition of Big Jock's ancestry had commenced, the crowd had been held almost hypnotised by the deeds carried out as described in explicit detail by Big Jock himself. This was no media fabrication but as the former prime minister himself would have said, 'straight from the horse's mouth.' Mark, just as mesmerised as everyone else in the studio, struggled to bring himself back to the present.

Playing for time, he asked, "Did all the members of your family come safely through the war?" He had hoped it would take Lord John a few minutes to answer this question, giving him time to focus on where he wanted to take this interview next.

However, there were no flies on Big Jock; smirking like a schoolboy, he answered shortly, "Yes," while he leaned back, quite at his ease. Rotating the ruby ring, the innocent instigator of this prolonged interview, around his finger, he noticed how the bright studio lights hit its many facets, sending beams of harlequin colour dashing all over the set.

Grasping at straws Mark came up with the only question he could manufacture in his confusion. "Were you the baby Nellie was expecting at the end of the war?"

Taking pity on the interviewer, Lord John relieved Mark's stress by giving a more detailed answer, allowing Mark to gain control of his wits.

"No." Glancing impishly at Mark, whose considerable colour drained from his face as he groped for a follow up question, he carried on as if unaware of his interrogator's unease. "That was my sister Mary, Mamy for short. The war was long over before I made my appearance when Mamy was, maybe three?" he looked up to the ceiling as if the beams festooned with lights and cameras would deliver him the right answer.

"Once Nellie and Wull, my ma and pa, got started they managed to increase the family fairly quickly. There was Mamy, then Sarah, our Sal, the next year before I entered the stakes, quickly followed by my brother Bill or William, to give him his Sunday name." Big Jock was counting on his fingers making an aside to the audience. "Never was much good at counting but I know there were seven of us," he laughed at his own joke. The audience was totally enamoured with him; that conspiratorial manner of his with his constituents, the main reason for his longevity in the cut-throat world of politics. Continuing to count off his siblings on his chubby fingers, he rushed through the family: "Mary, Sarah, yours truly, William, Janet, Helen and Margaret. All conforming to the conventions of the time to carry on the Christian names from previous generations." He sat back beaming smugly before leaning forward to make the audience think he was taking them into their confidence, he finished, "Please don't ask me to name the next generation for John and Mary have gone out of fashion." Pretending to count once more on his overworked fingers he screwed his face into a caricature of Les Dawson, saying, "Britney, Madonna, Romeo," a pause before, "that shed behind the cinema."

This elicited the reaction Big Jock had been aiming for; the audience roared with laughter, making the pause that his interrogator sorely needed. By the time they had settled once more Mark was back in charge of proceedings.

"You attribute the survival of all your family members serving during the war to the luck carried by the ruby?" Mark could not help but sound sceptical but there was no avoiding the truth of the fact that, when almost every family in the country had lost close family members, with almost all of the Campbell family in places of violent enemy action, they had all returned to serve useful and profitable lives, post-war.

"Maybe the Ruby kept them safe. My grandfather certainly gave it credit for bringing his lambs back to the fold. Was it the ruby that made my parents, aunts and uncles pillars of society or was it, which I suggest is nearer the truth, the war?"

Mark gave a half laugh. He had never been able to establish when Lord Campbell was winding him up but, taking the bull by the horns, he boldly asked his next question.

"Lord John, are you seriously suggesting that war was a good thing? Surely not? You are on record as saying the world would be a better place if countries stopped trying to be top dog. I think you are pulling my leg," he finished lamely.

"By no means do I mean that war is a good thing." Big Jock leaned forward to stress his denial of this conclusion. "I abhor the senseless taking of life no matter in what manner. I suggest to you, and it should be no surprise to you, for I have advocated this policy during my entire political career, that the adverse situation people found themselves in during World War Two took people out of the comfort zone and forced them to think about others. If you take my family for an example; my grandfather would not have, in the normal way of life, taken up arms in support of young women. I would go so far as to say that he would have tutted and huffed about the 'youth of today'. Listening to his wartime tales was part of my childhood and I don't ignore the possibility that these stories were part of what lured me into politics. It was the attitude of 'doing it together' that brought that generation so close that they fought as one. Take Adam and my uncle Jan, forced by the invaders to fight for a cause they did not believe in. See how quickly the humane way they were treated as POWs changed their outlook on the war. Others were not so lucky," he finished disconsolately, lifting his glass to take a sip of water, but it was apparent to every member of the audience that the crack in Big Jock's voice and the tear in his eye were brought about by his overflowing emotions. Perhaps it was having so recently related the saga of his family that brought these feeling to the surface; whatever the reason, the audience were left in no doubt that Big Jock's feelings were real. Everyone, cameramen, make-up operatives, sound men as well as the audience were stunned at his next statement, delivered in an emotional tone not natural to Lord John Campbell.

"I am proud of every man, women or child who lived through the last world war, and please God it *is* the last, no matter how important or lowly the position they filled for they allowed me and mine to grow up in a tolerant world. Personally I fear that this tolerance is being eroded by bigotry and narrow mindedness. If I had a say in world politics, I would urge every country, every religion and every ethnic group to work together towards a united peace."

Silence reigned.

Big Jock, feeling he had revealed too much of himself in his heartfelt declaration and, true to his politician's roots, he quickly changed the mood by grimacing at Mark saying, "Like all true Miss World contestants, I will use my prize money toward world peace."

Mark marvelled at the ease with which Lord John had swung the audience from serious to frivolous with only a few words, quietly wishing that he had this same ability. What an asset Big Jock would be as an interviewer. No sooner had the idea entered his head than he had framed a question to put to the master orator.

"Now that you are a free man, so to speak, do you have any ideas about your future? A career as an interviewer, perhaps?"

"You're quite safe, Mark. I have no aspirations to winkle information out of unwilling guests." Once more that famous crooked smile made an appearance on Big Jock's face.

"Actually, until tonight, I hadn't really given much thought to what comes next, other than taking Lady Marion..." he broke off, shaking his head, with an amused look on his face. "That still tickles me, for Little John and Maid Marion read Big Jock and Lady Mairn."

The grin still on his face, he commented to Mark as if he was letting him into a state secret, "I'll get my head and my hands to play with when that little woman gets me home tonight."

He mimicked such a terrified face that the audience burst out laughing; Big Jock could even detect a quirk on his wife's lips. She was well used to being his stooge.

"So there is no chance of you following some of your contemporaries into the media? Some notable names spring to mind: Jeffrey Archer, Kilroy-Silk, Michael Portillo, just off the top of my head."

Appearing to give the idea some thought Big Jock was quiet for such a long time Mark began to worry he had gone too far, but as he prompted the politician with "Lord

John?" Big Jock appeared to come out of his stupor, catching his wife's eye where she sat sedately watching his every move. He became serious once more.

"You have listened all evening to the tale of my family in Lockerbie. It is the tale of an ordinary Lowland family developing through the ages but also the story of romance. The ruby has been given the credit for our family's luck, but was it the power of the ruby that kept my ancestors safe? You might say in justification of the Ruby's power that, when Watt was not in possession of the talisman, he came to a sticky end and it is true that he, to date, has been the only one of our clan who has died in battle since Geordie's brother way back before the branch made its home in Lockerbie, and even he didn't die by the sword.

"Early on in our history it was the men doing what was necessary in times of hardship and war. Dreadful deeds committed by hard men, in some cases, in the name of God. You would be hard pushed to find many families in the Border counties without connections to the reivers or the smugglers, because poor men had to make a living and they owed fealty to the landowners. Women, who were little more than possessions of men who saw more worth in the crops they grew or the animals they reared than in the women they chose to make their helpmeets, were more or less disregarded. What makes the stoic women of our clan, and my story, unique is that they, almost without exception, were regarded by their husbands as equals, sharing all the decisions as an entity.

"As generation followed generation the rest of the world caught up until today women have turned a whole three sixty degrees and, as I said earlier, are the ones in control. I am proud to say that Sarah, Sal and my ma were women before their time, or maybe it was the canny nature of the Campbell men in choosing women to be partners rather than chattels that has resulted in our luck not running out.

"As you know my family have had a generations long association with the former lords of Annandale and as a young man I was fortunate enough to marry the Honourable Marion Johnstone, a jewel beyond price. Yesterday, after all her years of marriage with me, I was able to put her back in her rightful place; in the peerage. She would tell you, if she ever did an interview, that she has no need of a title and was happy to be plain Mrs Marion Campbell, but out of all the things I have done in my life, making Marion, Lady Marion Campbell was the proudest moment of my life."

He stopped suddenly, standing up and waving into the back of the audience. As one person, those watching turned round to see who was being singled out by the great man. As no one moved at the back of the room and unseen by the rest of the congregation, Lady Marion silently slipped out of her seat, leaving, unseen, by a door at the side of the studio to return several minutes later leading an obviously pregnant woman towards the stage. A murmur whispered though the crowd as people asked each other who this was, but no one could identify the woman. Silence followed as attention once more focused on the party on the stage. By this time Mark had ceded his position as master of ceremonies to Lord Campbell and had no idea what was coming next. He exited into the wings, bringing back a stool which he kept to himself while offering his seat to the expectant mother. Having seated the newcomer, Big Jock looked in Mark's direction to let him know he was ready to continue with this special interview.

Mark turned to the audience shrugging his shoulders as he said, "Ladies and Gentlemen. I am a redundant interviewer. I now hand you over to my Lord John Campbell of Lockerbie."

Big Jock stood up once more, going to stand behind the young woman placing his hands on her shoulders. The audience were aware that she was embarrassed by her position in the spotlight. Patting her shoulder and bending down to whisper something in her ear, he straightened up and addressed the audience.

"I am humbled by your attention to my tale tonight so I feel you need to be allowed to hear the fate of the lucky ruby." He looked towards the young woman, giving her a look of encouragement.

"This is my eldest granddaughter, Ruby, and as you have no doubt deduced for yourselves she is about to make me a great-grandfather." He smiled down on the discomfited girl with what was intended to be a supportive nod, but the audience could see that she was not a woman who liked to appear in the limelight. "Since Ruby has no aspirations for her fifteen minutes of fame I will make this short. By the wonders of science, we know that this great-grandchild of mine is to be a girl. I think it fitting that the tradition started by Geordie Campbell should continue but be updated. If King Charles and the Parliament of the seventeenth century could enact a policy to keep the succession in the male line and King Charles and Parliament of the twenty-first rescind that law; taking into account, the part small but prominent part the King Charleses of this country have played in our history…" He drew the massive ruby ring, that had been his trademark all the while he had been in office, from his finger, he presented it to his granddaughter, who showed her genetic connection to the long dead Geordie Campbell in her charismatic crooked grin.

He kissed her on the cheek, saying, "Let the lucky ruby take care of my descendants for the next four hundred years."

"Na obliviscaris."